KALEIDOSCOPE

KALEIDOSCOPE

PAUL GEHRMAN

New Intellectual Press, LLC
Mill Valley, California

Cover design, interior design and illustrations by Kevin Barnard
Editing by Anila Manning

First printing.
ISBN-13: 978-0-9823664-0-0
ISBN-10: 0-982-3664-0-X
Library of Congress Control Number: 2009903534

Printed in the United States of America.

Reprint permissions provided by:

Estate of Ayn Rand: Introduction to the 25th Anniversary of *The Fountainhead* by Ayn Rand

W.W. Norton and Company: *The End of Faith* (2004) by Sam Harris

Oxford University Press: *The Selfish Gene* (1989) by Richard Dawkins

Basic Books, a member of Perseus Books Group: *Thomas Paine Apostle of Freedom* (1994) by Jack Fruchtman, Jr., and *Religion Explained* (2002) by Pascal Boyer

American Humanist Association: *Humanist Manifesto II* (1973)

HarperCollins Publishers: *The True Believer* (1951) by Eric Hoffer

Random House (Bantam): *The Six Pillars of Self-Esteem* (1994) by Nathaniel Branden

Prometheus Books: *Holy Horrors* (1999) by James A. Haught

Alfred Publishing Co., Inc.: *Skin*, words and music by Danny Elfman. © 1989 FSMGI (IMRO). All rights administered by State One Music America (BMI). All rights reserved.

To Juliet Nelson and Elizabeth Ludington
in loving memory

CHAPTER 1

One is based on deference to primitive texts and mystical revelation, while the other rigorously challenges existing beliefs in a never-ending search for the truth. Even on questions of moral philosophy, it is hard to imagine how a closed thought system based on faith could answer difficult questions with the same degree of utility as one that is open and primarily concerned with humanity's welfare. It is further hard to fathom how these thought systems could ever achieve a peaceful coexistence.

—David Chambers

The sun shone brightly on a warm spring day in the Rose Garden of the White House. Two military officers saluted the President as he walked toward the podium where a small crowd had gathered for a presentation of the Presidential Medal of Freedom.

"Good afternoon. I'd like to welcome everyone here today—members of the public, Congress, the press, and of course, David Chambers." The President put his hand behind Chambers' back and held it there momentarily while Chambers took a slow breath, drawing in the light fragrance of flowers and freshly cut grass. He wanted to capture every detail of the moment and etch it into his memory. He had never felt more proud.

"Today, we've come together to honor David Chambers with our nation's highest civilian award, the Presidential Medal of Freedom. This award is a fitting tribute to David's distinguished service to the nation. Although most people receive the award at the end of their careers, David is still a young man. I've chosen to recognize him now because he's already achieved more than what most people even dream about. His example should inspire everyone to pursue their dreams without limits.

"Over the years, I've been honored to have David as a frequent guest at the White House. I'm grateful that he's come here one last time before I leave office. It's a privilege to finally recognize him for all that he's done for our nation. But let me start by acknowledging our personal relationship. We've been good friends for many years and he's served as a trusted confidant during my presidency. Although I expect to lose a lot of friends when I'm just an ordinary citizen again, I hope that we'll remain close."

The audience chuckled. Chambers smiled and nodded politely.

"Of course, David's path hasn't always been easy. He has overcome many obstacles. In spite of a serious leg injury, he became one of the top flight testers for the Air Force after graduating summa cum laude from Caltech with a degree in aerospace engineering. This is truly a remarkable feat. Not to make light of his disability, but I still don't understand how he became a flight tester without meeting the strict physical requirements; we're investigating that." The President smiled. "Actually, I know that David can be very persuasive and charismatic, so I'm not surprised that he talked his way onto a flight squadron. Nothing he does surprises me. He simply never takes no for an answer.

"David possesses the rare combination of engineering genius and entrepreneurial vision. He holds over forty patents for innovations in his field. After his service in the Air Force, he founded Chambers Aerospace, which has propelled the industry forward with unprecedented breakthroughs, including combat planes better equipped to deal with complex and ever-changing threats. I point specifically to the company's development of unmanned aerial vehicles and reconnaissance aircraft, both of which have saved countless American lives. Our nation continues to face threats to its peace, prosperity, and freedom. David's efforts have been crucial in meeting these challenges and in keeping America's military strong.

"Perhaps David's most significant contribution though is through his philanthropy. He has devoted himself to making a difference in the lives of children. Several years ago, he established the Kaleidoscope Foundation whose mission is to provide educational opportunities and support to underprivileged kids, enabling them to develop their unique talents and potential. The Kaleidoscope Foundation has also been a tireless advocate for science education, awarding hundreds of scholarships each year to students pursuing technical careers. This is especially vital so that America will continue to lead the world in technology and innovation. More importantly, these efforts have opened young minds to the wonders of science and inspired our youth to make a lifelong commitment to learning.

"America owes a special debt to David Chambers and we recognize him today for his dedication to the highest ideals of the American spirit. It is with great honor that I present him with the Presidential Medal of Freedom."

The crowd applauded while the President handed Chambers a dark walnut case lined with silver-gray velvet and white satin. Inside was a five-pointed white star set on a red pentagon, with gold eagles engraved between each of the star's points. A certificate signed by the President formally detailed Chambers' achievements.

Chambers shook the President's hand and hugged him before he stepped to the podium and waved at the audience. He was a tall, forty-four-year-old man with long, thin limbs, and light brown hair that hung comfortably just above his shoulders. His features weren't striking, though they suggested a focused congruity even when he was relaxed. Some described him as an overgrown boy because of his youthful enthusiasm, but he was universally admired as one of the greatest success stories in the United States. His notoriety was due in no small part to the President, who had used his influence to promote Chambers and his endeavors.

"Mr. President, friends, I'm honored and grateful to receive this Medal of Freedom. I know how rare and important it is, so I fully appreciate the tribute you're paying me today. This is a great award from the greatest country on Earth. Mr. President, I sincerely thank you. But as you honor me today, I must recognize those who stood with me through the toughest challenges. First, my partner Ernesto

Sosa. We met in the Air Force over twenty years ago and we've been partners ever since. No one has worked harder to achieve our goals." Chambers motioned to Ernesto who was sitting in the front row. "I love you, buddy. Come on up here."

Ernesto stepped to the podium and shook the President's hand before embracing Chambers. "Congratulations, David. You deserve this."

"Thanks for this moment, Ernesto," Chambers whispered.

Ernesto bowed politely to the crowd as he returned to his seat.

"I'd also like to recognize my friends and colleagues at Chambers Aerospace and the Kaleidoscope Foundation. These extraordinary men and women have dedicated themselves to excellence. They are the heroes who continually inspire me and they certainly deserve their share of today's award. I'd like to express my deepest appreciation to them for making this possible."

Chambers waved toward a group of his employees. "Thank you. Thank you. I love you. Thank you.

"Finally, I want to thank my grandparents for their love and support, and for raising me after the death of my parents. My grandfather, who passed away several years ago, was a World War II vet who taught me never to take freedom for granted, and to fight for it if it's ever threatened. He experienced firsthand the great cooperative effort and sacrifice made by Americans to win that war. Through his example and my own life experience, I've learned that success is always based on cooperation with others. Everyone has a role to play and no person is unimportant. That's why I'm so grateful. I'm grateful because we can all work together to make a difference."

Chambers paused as the audience clapped.

"People look up to me because I've achieved a lot in my life, and I'm often asked what I do differently. You know, the truth is I've always had trouble answering that question because I'm not really any different. I don't have any secret strategies or unique insights. I've always just trusted my own mind and followed my conscience. This simple philosophy has given me clarity and allowed me to find meaning and purpose in life."

The President suppressed a smile. He quietly reflected on all the conversations he'd had with Chambers about man's search for meaning. Then he wondered what Chambers really thought of him. In order to get elected, the President had trumpeted his religious faith, even though he didn't believe any of the tired dogma speechwriters liberally injected into his communications. He had simply accepted that telling people what they wanted to hear was an absolute in politics. That was probably the main thing that separated him from Chambers, and he knew that Chambers didn't fully respect him because of it. Nevertheless, the President took great satisfaction in awarding Chambers the Presidential

Medal of Freedom because it brought him closer to the man and the ideals he embodied.

"Mr. President, the United States of America is the world's greatest defender of freedom, democracy, and the rule of law. I commend you for standing firm whenever our liberty is threatened, and for championing freedom and democracy abroad. Throughout your life in public service, you've never wavered in that commitment. Let me conclude by expressing my gratitude and the gratitude of all Americans. Thank you." Chambers embraced the President again.

CHAPTER 2

People whose lives are barren and insecure seem to show a greater willingness to obey than people who are self-sufficient and self-confident. To the frustrated, freedom from responsibility is more attractive than freedom from constraint. They are eager to barter their independence for relief from the burdens of willing, deciding and being responsible for inevitable failure. They willingly abdicate the directing of their lives to those who want to plan, command and shoulder all responsibility.

—ERIC HOFFER, *THE TRUE BELIEVER*

The stage was invisible, blanketed in darkness awaiting the arrival of Reverend Robert Newhall. Hundreds of lilies lined the front of the stage, while a plush, red-velvet curtain shrouded the rest of the extravagant props. A woman in a long white dress sat quietly behind an ornate pipe organ, her fingers trembling in anticipation of the Reverend's entrance.

The last of the Infinity followers filed in as the house lights dimmed, shadowing two gun-toting, gorilla-faced guards who stood on either side of the stage. Each guard stood taut, trying to look alert and important, with his hand in his pocket clutching a semi-automatic pistol. Reverend Newhall never went anywhere without his armed bodyguards.

The Infinity Christian Network owned the venue, Revival Hall, a restored theater in Nashville, Tennessee. Although decorated like a church, the hall was not solely a place of worship, but a magnificent multi-purpose event center seating over four thousand people. Newhall had spoken in much larger venues, selling out stadiums holding a hundred thousand people, but his sermons from Revival Hall were televised, so he figured he could reach just as many people, and more importantly, bring in just as much money. The typical show ran like a telethon, with a battery of dedicated volunteers staffing the phones and agreeing enthusiastically with callers that Newhall was indeed the closest thing to God currently on Earth.

A low hum vibrated across the auditorium as the deep tones of the organ rose out of the darkness. Light fell slowly from the ceiling as the curtain opened, revealing an elevated altar encircled by exquisitely crafted stained glass and a ninety-person choir that burst into song as Newhall emerged.

Save us, thou Almighty King,
We rejoice at the power of your universe displayed;
The awesome wonder of your world divine,
We surrender to thee, our obedient embrace;
We kneel down, our souls in your hands;
Our souls we give to thee;
Our souls we give to thee!

Newhall strode gracefully to the pulpit while audience members rejoiced. Some sang joyfully along with the choir. Others quietly recited Scripture or held the hand of a loved one. Some wept, unable to contain their emotions. But when Newhall stood before them and opened his arms in invitation, the house drew silent as they surrendered themselves completely to his divine presence.

"Welcome my friends, welcome," Newhall began. "I am delighted to be with you this evening as we worship the Lord in these troubled times. I'd like to begin tonight by discussing something that is very important to all of us as citizens of this great country. We are all aware of the threat that terrorists and rogue foreign nations pose to our well-being; people who don't share our values and who resent our Christian way of life. Of course, these people are dangerous, but I believe we face an even greater threat here at home. There are people within our own country who refuse God and His plan for salvation. They reject the teachings in the Bible and instead live sinfully, driving our society further into decay.

"The great tragedy is that some of these people believe that they don't need God. They think they can decide for themselves how to live a moral life. They believe they're smarter than God; that their feeble minds can match our Almighty Creator. I know it sounds absurd when you consider it. And it is absurd. Unfortunately, they won't realize their error until they die. But then it's too late.

"Now you may be asking yourself whether this matters to you. You accept God's word in the Bible and you obey. You've got nothing to worry about, right? Let the unrepentant sinners go to Hell; that's no concern of mine." Newhall paused. "If you think that way, you're wrong. Dead wrong. Even if we obey God's word ourselves that is no longer enough. We must demand that everyone live in accordance with God's laws, and we cannot tolerate those who put their own selfish needs ahead of God. God expects us to fight. Indeed, he commands us to restore the world He created for us."

Newhall spoke evenly, his voice resonating like a finely-tuned instrument. He held the audience spellbound with his quiet passion, but then quickly shifted to a state of moral indignation, raising his voice while his face became swollen with fury. "What kind of world do we live in now? A world where our children cannot pray at school and liberal judges threaten to strip the words 'under God' from our Pledge of Allegiance. A world where secularists want to remove the cross from all public places. But it gets worse. They support same-sex marriages and promiscuous homosexual lifestyles. Deathstyles, I call them. They urge us to be tolerant while this gay plague, AIDS, spreads across the country, even claiming the lives of some of our Christian brothers and sisters. Abortion clinics have sprouted up like weeds while the most helpless among us, our unborn children, are slaughtered. We must put a stop to this! We must put a stop to this by standing up for God; by sacrificing our lives to Him!" Newhall pounded the altar.

"What have you done today? Have you done anything to further God's laws on Earth? Or have you been selfish, thinking only of your next meal or the vacation you'd like to take? How many times a day do you stand up for your Lord and Savior?"

Newhall paused, scanning the glazed expressions of his flock.

"You think you're a good person? Do you? You think you've lived a moral life?" Newhall's face hardened. "Well, you couldn't be more wrong. In God's eyes, man will always be a sinful creature no matter how many good things we do. That will never change. So what can we do? How can we achieve salvation? It is not enough just to think about God or pray; we must commit ourselves to bringing God's laws down to Earth. We must prepare for the Day of Judgment."

Newhall lowered his voice as the lights dimmed. "Let us pray for forgiveness, and for the strength to do battle as soldiers in the army of Christ. Almighty God…"

Newhall's personal assistant watched the show from backstage and marveled at the effect of his performance on the audience. The hypnotic quality of his voice, the magnetism of his personality, and the raw energy of his fiery brand of Christianity drew them into a world where they felt special; a world where their lives were infused with purpose. Without Newhall, they were ordinary middle-class folks drifting aimlessly. With him, they were warriors in a cosmic battle of good versus evil. They no longer had to worry whether they were "good" people; being part of Newhall's flock was proof positive of their piety—an ecclesiastical version of owning a Mercedes.

Newhall could move an audience to tears, fill them with joy, or summon their innermost anger. People experienced rapturous highs during his orations, but afterwards remembered almost nothing of what he actually said. But they did remember the extraordinary impression of power—the intense hatred, fury, and passion emanating from his voice.

Newhall possessed an instinctive sensitivity to the mood of an audience; a knack for divining the hidden desires, resentments, and longings in their minds. He diagnosed the ills from which they were suffering and his words pierced each person's private wounds, liberating their unconscious and exposing its innermost fears. Infinity followers finally had a justification for their own hatred, and an outlet for their frustrations; they regressed to an emotional state where they could be incited to action.

Although Newhall's physical appearance was unimpressive and his face undistinguished, he could express rapidly changing moods—one moment smiling and charming, the next cold and imperious. His eyes would fill with tears, then blaze with contempt, but his favorite expressions were the faraway look of a visionary and the bold confidence of a prophet. He was a consummate actor who absorbed himself in a role and convinced his audience of whatever he needed them to believe. In the early years, he was occasionally awkward and unconvincing, but with practice, all the roles he needed to play became second nature and he fine-tuned them with the detail and precision of a craftsman.

Newhall finished the prayer with an earnest "Amen" while an army of black-suited men appeared holding shiny, gold collection plates. They moved methodically from pew to pew like a well-trained battalion, passing the plates down the aisles while emotionally charged audience members reached into their purses and wallets, happily filling Newhall's coffers. Although most of the congregation could scarcely afford a large donation to the church, they felt compelled to give because Newhall convinced them that they were selfless patriots of freedom and morality; the men and women with reserved seats at God's table. He perfected an evangelical version of good cop/bad cop, chastising people harshly for not devoting their lives fully to God, but offering heavenly rewards for unquestioning obedience. Newhall's goal was to inject doubt into each person's psyche, leading them to question whether they could be a good person without his spiritual guidance.

One man in the audience told his eight-year old daughter that he couldn't afford to buy her a bicycle, yet he didn't hesitate to drop five crisp twenty-dollar bills onto the offering plate. He forgot completely about his young child until he heard her crying softly when he returned home. He loved his daughter and wanted to give her everything she desired, but he believed that putting the needs of his family before God was selfish. The man felt a nagging sense of guilt that he couldn't seem to shake. Giving to Newhall was the only way he knew to dull his pain.

Another man told his family that they couldn't afford a vacation because money was tight. Nevertheless, he felt an urgent drive, and then a calm feeling of relief, as he parted with a check for one hundred and fifty dollars. He figured that everyone had to make sacrifices just as Christ had made the ultimate sacrifice to cleanse man of his sins. Besides, he reasoned, his family didn't really need a vacation. The kids could play in the back yard and Disneyland wasn't that great anyway.

A young woman, working as a waitress and trying to raise a son on her own, pulled a wad of ones and a handful of change from her purse and deposited them onto the plate. Her son spent his life in a day care facility that she cursed, yet she refused to save enough money to give him something better. She loved her son and he was the most important person in her life, but she believed that nobody was more important than God—or Newhall, his representative on Earth.

People who gave to Newhall were not unlike the general populace as a whole. They lived, more or less, on the same continuum of fear and pride. With the cancerous spread of fear throughout their souls came the reciprocal decimation of their pride. As they ceded more and more control over their thinking to Newhall, they preserved less and less of their self-worth and identity outside the church. Instead, they accepted the neatly-packaged, God-fearing identity provided to them by Infinity. Practically speaking, more fear meant larger donations to the Network, and Newhall's speechwriters gave this careful consideration before any of his sermons were prepared. Before he went on stage, his press secretary reminded him with a simple phrase: "Fear first." Newhall always came through.

As the ushers retreated backstage, their collection plates overflowing with spoils, Newhall delivered his final remarks. "Please remember this, my friends. If we don't stand up for God, we are destined to perish in eternal darkness. But if we sacrifice, we will be rewarded with eternal life. God bless you, and God bless America."

Newhall gave a triumphant wave to the audience as he stepped backstage.

"Terrific sermon, Reverend," Newhall's assistant greeted.

"How much did we take in tonight?" Newhall responded brusquely.

"I don't know yet, sir. We're still counting it."

"I'm going back to the hotel. Call me with the numbers." Newhall disappeared out the back door into his waiting limousine.

CHAPTER 3

Journalist: Mr. Lassater, many people are angered by your crusade against the Catholic Church; they say you've gone too far. How do you respond to those people?

Ray Lassater: First of all, I object to the term "crusade." That word comes from the Crusades of the Middle Ages when Christians mindlessly slaughtered Jews and Muslims in the name of their superstition. It's true that I'm in a fight, but I'm not on the side of the Crusaders. I stand against their deification of ignorance, and in the case of the Catholic Church, their rape of children.

Journalist: You've been quoted as saying that not only should the Church be held responsible for the sexual abuse, but that parents of the victims should be sent to prison as well.

Lassater: Parents who taught their children that the conduct of priests is divinely inspired and beyond question are at least partially responsible. Almost all of the victims told us they knew the abuse was wrong when it was happening, but that it must be okay because of what their parents had taught them about the Church. This is another case of the Church creating moral ambiguity. Since the molested children had been indoctrinated with an irrational belief system, they accepted the abuse in spite of having strong moral impulses telling them it was wrong.

Journalist: But jail for parents; isn't that a little extreme? Aren't our prisons crowded enough?

Lassater: The men of religion tell us that we're all guilty because Eve ate the apple. Luckily, this concept was rejected in our system of jurisprudence. Otherwise, our prisons would really be overcrowded. But the idea of original sin and the guilt that flows from that is what creates the real prison—the prison up here.

Journalist: The prison of the mind?

Lassater: Precisely.

Ray Lassater, age eight, found himself alone at the front of the school bus with a backpack resting comfortably on his lap. He looked outside the window, but it was too dark to see. He turned around and scanned the back of the bus. There weren't any other people, just empty seats. He wondered vaguely what was in the backpack so he opened it and pulled out a small plastic bag. The bag contained a roast beef sandwich, but it smelled like aftershave lotion. Ray hesitated for a moment as a tingle of fear raced down his spine. He took the sandwich carefully out of the bag and cupped it in his hands. As he turned the bread over, maggots engulfed his hands and cockroaches scrambled up his arms. Ray tried frantically to slap the insects off his body, but they suddenly disappeared. Ray tried to run toward the door, but he couldn't move. He felt cold until a blast of warm air spread down his back. He turned around, but all he could see was a distorted face with a sinister smile. Then an arm appeared. It didn't have a hand, only a long metal hook. The hook moved closer and Ray tried to back away, but it slashed through the front of his pants, ripping into his crotch. "Ahhhhhh!" Ray woke up with a start and then grabbed a glass off his nightstand, throwing it against the wall. "I can't stand this anymore! I can't!"

After catching his breath and wiping the sweat off his face, Ray lay back down and tried to relax, but he could only weep, surrendering to the exquisite torture that ravaged his psyche.

* * *

Martin Dushane quickly gulped down his third cup of coffee and stared at himself in the bathroom mirror at the District Attorney's office in Boston. His face was pleasantly masculine with dark brown skin, heavy cheekbones, and a slightly hooked nose, but his broad lips were his most distinguishing feature, dominating his face whenever he smiled.

This is going to be difficult, Dushane thought as he walked from the bathroom towards Lassater's office. Lassater was the District Attorney of Suffolk County and Dushane worked under him as an Assistant DA. Lassater's agenda was to prosecute the Catholic Church for decades of sexual abuse. Unfortunately, Dushane needed to tell him there were major problems with the cases against the Church. And now his head hurt from too much caffeine.

Despite Dushane's current state of apprehension, he loved Ray Lassater and they usually spoke easily. They had worked together for over a year, pursuing unprecedented cases against the Catholic Church and its leadership for thousands of sexual assaults against children. The opportunity to try cases had initially attracted Dushane to the DA's office, but what he found even more compelling was how Lassater had spoken to him at their first meeting. Whenever Dushane reflected on the encounter, he always conjured up an image of a general in a great war, inspiring his troops to crush its enemies without mercy.

Above all though, the thing Dushane loved most about Lassater was that he refused to speak to him differently because he was black. All his life whites had patronized him, carefully avoiding any disagreements even when he was talking nonsense. They had always tried to appear politically correct and not prejudiced, causing them to get all constricted and formal trying not to offend him. It was impossible to have a decent human conversation. Ray Lassater, on the other hand, spoke freely and didn't care who he offended.

Lassater had assured Dushane that he had been hired because he was the most qualified person for the job. This was important because Dushane had dealt with accusations of being a racial preference token his entire life. He wanted nothing to do with a thought system that implicitly classified him as a second-class citizen.

Dushane's palms were wet with perspiration so he wiped them quickly on the back of his pants. When he got to Lassater's office, he knocked and then peered in sheepishly. Lassater looked up from behind several towers of paper. Dushane tried to force a normal tone, but all he could manage was a whisper. "Ray…uh…Ray, could I speak with you for a moment?"

Ray Lassater was short and solid. He had a thick neck and a protruding face with eyes that bugged out when he spoke. He had large hands, which he spread wide when he gestured. Good hands to choke somebody with, Dushane thought. His smile was bright and inviting, but his frown was devastating—like a death sentence. Dushane likened his boss' temperament to a stick of dynamite, just waiting for someone to light the fuse. He hoped that what he had to say wouldn't trigger an explosion.

"Certainly Martin, what's on your mind?" Lassater's eyes looked tired, but he stood up enthusiastically and extended his hand. "Have a seat."

Dushane remained standing and stared down at the floor. "Uh… well…uh…I'm a little concerned about these new cases." His face felt hot, but he continued slowly. "I've been reviewing the facts and the law, and…well…I'm not so sure we'll be able to make a case against the bishops or the Cardinal. The criminal statutes in Massachusetts don't seem to support a prosecution for covering up sexual abuse or for shifting abusive priests around. We've also got a potential statute of limitations problem."

Lassater stared hard at Dushane.

"And our biggest problem is that the department is running out of money," Dushane continued. "We'll need to hire at least two more attorneys to help prosecute these cases. We're overwhelmed right now." Dushane looked up cautiously. Lassater's mouth was calm, but his brow was furrowed, like a father about to discipline his son.

"What are you trying to tell me, Martin?" Lassater responded coldly.

Dushane's fingers began to tremble as he struggled to get the words out. "I…I think…I think we should consider dropping some of these cases. I don't know if we can make a case against all these guys. Even if we could, we can't win them all with the resources we've got. They're going all out on the defense side. You know the Church; they've got practically unlimited funds. I mean, I don't think we should spread ourselves too thin." Dushane wiped a bead of sweat off his forehead.

Lassater placed his hands calmly on the arms of his chair and sprang up in a quick motion as if he had just pushed the ejection button in a fighter plane. A dark purple vein popped out of his neck.

"If you think I give a shit about the statute of limitations or the goddamn budget, I suggest you get the fuck out of my office." Lassater stepped out from behind his desk and lurched toward Dushane, coming so close that Dushane had to stiffen his lower back muscles to avoid falling.

"Your job is to make a case against all the defendants. The rapist priests as well as the bishops and the Cardinal who covered it up. Can you do that, Martin? Can you please do that? That's your goddamn job. If you can't handle it, I'll find somebody who can."

"Well…I…"

"I'm only going to say this one time," Lassater interrupted. "Those bastards stole my childhood. They stole it. So I don't give a damn what anyone else does, I'm going to make them pay. If you don't want to help me, then get out of here. But I'm not going to let this stand. This will not stand!"

Dushane took two steps back towards the door. He tried to think of something weighty to say, but couldn't. "I'm on your side, Ray; I'm with you," he said feebly. "Believe me, I want to get those bastards too, but we have a budget."

"Get out of here!"

Lassater sat back down as his intercom buzzed. "Ray, David Chambers on two."

Lassater quickly erased the unpleasant meeting with Dushane and picked up the phone. "How are you, David?" he said cheerfully.

"Great. How's the dark side?"

Lassater laughed. "We're working against it. Of course, we could really use your help."

"Well, you know me, I'm always looking for a good fight. What do you need?"

"The budget's tight around here; we need money to hire some additional attorneys. Another million and we can vigorously prosecute every case."

"Sounds like a worthwhile investment to me. Same delivery?"

"Yeah, that would be great. I really appreciate this, David."

"So do I, Ray. Take care of yourself."

Ray Lassater and David Chambers had become friends almost a year before the first cases were filed against the Catholic Church. Chambers heard of Lassater's intent to bring the Church to justice and he immediately offered to help. The two men instantly hit it off.

Although it was illegal to accept donations from private parties to fund a criminal prosecution, Lassater happily accepted Chambers' offer to help with the initial investigative work, which consisted of locating witnesses, interviewing victims, and hiring private investigators. The Church was a wealthy, powerful, and highly secretive organization and Lassater knew that he would need every weapon at his disposal to bring it down.

Dushane had an important role in the investigation as the liaison between the DA's office and the Boston Archdiocese. He informed the Archdiocese that his office planned to prosecute sexually abusive priests and he urged cooperation. He requested copies of all personnel files of any priest who had ever been accused of abuse. Church officials balked at turning over the records, arguing that the statute of limitations had expired with respect to most of the alleged abusers and, in any case, it was up to the Church to decide what documents, if any, they would release. While Dushane was initially startled by the display of arrogance, he quickly learned that Church officials were used to living in a culture of deference that included law enforcement officials and judges. Because of the predominance of Catholics in Massachusetts, there had been little appetite to prosecute priests or to embarrass the Church. The First Amendment had also served to deter secular officials from probing too deeply into Church affairs, and it was considered taboo for anyone in power to throw their weight around with the Church. When Dushane reported the Church's stonewalling to Lassater, Lassater called the Cardinal's mansion directly. He was directed to the Cardinal's personal assistant, Jack O'Shea.

"Jack, this is Ray Lassater from the Suffolk County District Attorney's office. It's very important that I speak with McManus."

"First of all, Mr. Lassater, the Cardinal is properly addressed as 'Your Eminence,'" O'Shea responded.

Lassater chuckled. "Are you joking?"

"No. The Cardinal insists on being addressed with respect." O'Shea wasn't kidding. The Cardinal required that everyone address him as "Your Eminence." He also demanded that people refer to the Pope as "His Holiness."

"Well, I don't respect him so I'll just have to keep calling him McManus," Lassater shot back.

O'Shea didn't respond.

"You still there, O'Shea? As much as I'm enjoying this conversation, I'm still waiting to talk to McManus. Please put me through."

"I don't know who you think you are…"

"I'm the District Attorney for Suffolk County," Lassater interrupted. "I prosecute criminals, including those who obstruct my investigations. I suggest you connect me to McManus. Now!"

Lassater heard a short click and then a gruff voice, "This is Cardinal McManus."

"Good afternoon, Cardinal. This is Ray Lassater from the Suffolk County District Attorney's office. Apparently there's been a misunderstanding between your Archdiocese and my assistant, Martin Dushane. Martin tells me that the Archdiocese is refusing to cooperate with our criminal investigation of sexually abusive priests. Is that correct?"

"I'm not aware of that," the Cardinal replied tersely.

"Well, then your underlings aren't keeping you informed. I suggest you speak with them about that. This is a very serious matter. Nobody in the Archdiocese has been cooperating with our investigation, and frankly, their conduct is an obstruction of justice. We need cooperation now. I won't tolerate any further delay."

"I have no comment," the Cardinal barked before quickly hanging up.

Lassater held the phone in silence for a few seconds and then exploded into a fit of blinding anger. *That filthy son of a bitch! Filthy… bastard! The evil…the evil!* He resolved to get the Cardinal and the rest of the criminals if it was the absolute last thing he did on Earth. He slammed the phone down and then quickly picked it up again and dialed Dushane.

"Hello."

"Martin, when are you going to file the charges against Cardinal McManus?"

"Friday."

"Good. We're going to do it, Martin. The Cardinal will answer for what he's done."

"Okay, Ray. I'll let you know when it's done."

"Good."

Dushane hung up and felt uneasy. He worried about the repercussions of challenging a major figure in one of the world's wealthiest and most powerful organizations. But he knew that Lassater would push him to do whatever it took. Dushane had already subpoenaed thousands of Church records, but Lassater demanded every piece of information about any priest who had ever been accused of inappropriate sexual conduct. In the Boston Archdiocese alone, over seventy priests had been accused of sexual abuse—most of them repeatedly.

Dushane took a deep breath and tried to psych himself up. He thought more about a battle with the Cardinal and his uneasiness was soon replaced by rage as he realized just how much he hated the man. Dushane had interviewed many victims and their families and he had heard the same stories over and over. But a few stuck in his memory. One girl who was fondled over the course of two years was so traumatized that she couldn't bear to be touched, even by her father, fifteen years later. A young boy who was raped developed violent tendencies that brought him into frequent conflict with law enforcement authorities. Other victims expressed profound distrust of others and an inability to establish intimate and meaningful relationships. But the most devastating cases involved people who turned to alcohol or drugs, or who spent their lives under a dark cloud of depression, which in at least three cases had resulted in suicide.

CHAPTER 4

How so many absurd rules of conduct, as well as so many absurd religious beliefs, have originated, we do not know; nor how it is that they have become, in all quarters of the world, so deeply impressed on the minds of men; but it is worthy of remark that a belief constantly inculcated during the early years of life, while the brain is impressionable, appears to acquire almost the nature of an instinct; and the very essence of an instinct is that it is followed independently of reason.

—CHARLES DARWIN, *THE DESCENT OF MAN*

Dushane sat quietly at the prosecution's table and smiled as he looked into the eyes of Ray Lassater. He knew his boss was about to set off some fireworks.

"The prosecution calls Patrick Dunphy," Lassater announced to the judge.

The judge motioned to a stout, middle-aged Irishman sitting in the front row. "Mr. Dunphy, please take the stand."

Lassater's presentation of the case against Cardinal McManus was nearing its end and Lassater had saved Dunphy for a devastating finale. Dunphy had been one of Cardinal McManus' bishops, but he had turned state's evidence in exchange for immunity. Catholics in Massachusetts and across the country had vilified him for standing up against the Cardinal, and a few high-ranking Church officials had urged him to reconsider, promising that the Pope would personally reverse his excommunication and all charges of heresy would be dropped. But Dunphy had decided to follow his conscience and then move across the country and start over under a witness protection program.

Although Lassater felt confident that he would secure a conviction, the trial had not been easy. McManus employed a powerful team of attorneys and Church supporters had threatened him throughout the case. It didn't help that the Cardinal was a popular figure in Boston, which was home to the third-largest archdiocese in the United States. As well as enjoying the perks of his office, which included a large mansion and several servants, McManus had developed a reputation for reaching out to people in the community, particularly the Jewish population who distrusted the Church. The idea that the Jews murdered Jesus Christ had been passed down by Catholics for generations leading to an instinctive hatred and numerous instances of verbal and physical harassment. One of the Cardinal's goals was to repair some of this damage. Unfortunately, atoning for years of anti-Semitism was not the Cardinal's biggest challenge. He had been protecting priests accused of sexual abuse for almost three decades.

As Dunphy took his place on the witness stand and was sworn in, Lassater strode casually past the jury, making quick eye contact with each person on the panel. He had salivated for years over prosecuting McManus because the Cardinal was not only actively involved in covering up the sexual abuse; he was the one man who could have prevented much of it. But he had done nothing.

Lassater took a deep breath and gauged his readiness. He held a short list of notes in his hand, but imagined that the small sheet of paper contained a nuclear warhead. He was about to vaporize the Cardinal and blast shockwaves through the man's entire medieval organization.

"Good morning, Mr. Dunphy," Lassater began. "Can you please

state your full name for the record?"

"Good morning. Patrick Aidan Dunphy."

"Mr. Dunphy, what is your relationship to the defendant?"

"I was one of his bishops. I worked closely with him for over ten years."

"Did you deal with the sexual abuse scandal?"

"Yes; not alone, but with other members of the Church."

"Did you arrange monetary compensation for any of the victims?"

"Yes."

"Did the Church have a monetary fund set up for this purpose?"

"Yes."

"Is that what the Boston Daily News refers to as the 'peddy cash' fund?"

"I believe so, yes."

"And did any of the other bishops know about this fund?"

"Yes, they all did; all the local bishops at least. We discussed it openly at our meetings."

"Can you tell me specifically what was discussed at these meetings?"

"Well, after the fund was set up, we discussed how we were going to get enough money. We also discussed the best strategy for dealing with parishioners who reported abuse. If there was any chance they were planning to go to the authorities, a payoff was made. Other times, we persuaded them not to report anything. We convinced a lot of parishioners that it would irreparably damage the Church and their faith if they went to the authorities. This worked in many cases."

"Did anyone object to these procedures?"

"No, not to my knowledge. I never heard any objection."

"To your knowledge, did you or anyone else in the Church report any sexual abuse allegations to law enforcement authorities?"

"No."

"Why not?"

"The Cardinal called a meeting of all the bishops and he told us that allegations of sexual abuse needed to be handled within the Church and that nothing should be reported to secular authorities."

"Did anyone object to that policy?"

"No. There was no objection by anyone, at least not to my knowledge."

"Why not? Why didn't you object?"

"Well, frankly, I was afraid to lose my position in the Church. I worked hard to get there and I figured that a scandal of that magnitude had the potential to bring us all down."

"Did you do anything?"

"Yeah, I mean if a priest had molested multiple times, we would typically recommend their transfer to another diocese."

21

"A transfer. Okay. Did you at least warn the other diocese that you were sending them a pervert?"

"Objection!" McManus' attorney leapt out of his chair. "Your Honor, we object to the use of the term 'pervert.' It's clearly designed to inflame the jury."

Before the judge could rule on the objection, Lassater lunged toward the defendant's table and stood toe to toe with McManus' attorney. "You object to the term 'pervert?' Is that a joke? How about 'pathetic excuse for a human being!' You like that better?"

"Mr. Lassater!" the judge yelled from the bench.

Lassater turned to the judge. "They're worried about the jury being inflamed? Of course they're inflamed. Everyone in this courtroom is inflamed except for the defendant and his mindless cronies."

"Mr. Lassater, you will control yourself in my courtroom. Sit down!"

"Your Honor, this is outrageous behavior. I move for a new trial," McManus' attorney pleaded.

"Your motion is denied," the judge responded without hesitation. "Counsel, approach the bench."

The judge glared sternly at Lassater. "You control yourself, Mr. Lassater, or I will order a new trial. Do you understand me?"

"Yes, your Honor."

The judge turned to the jury. "The objection is sustained. The jury is instructed to disregard the prosecutor's outburst. Let's take a twenty-minute recess."

Lassater spoke briefly with his assistant and then a guard escorted him to his office. Lassater had twenty-four-hour armed protection. He sat down behind his desk and sighed. Although he felt increasingly confident that the Cardinal would go down, he couldn't shake the traumatic memories from his past.

* * *

"Hi, Ray. How are you?" Father Monahan greeted as he entered eight-year old Ray Lassater's bedroom.

Ray put his book down. "Hi Father, I…I'm fine. I wasn't expecting you."

"I thought you might like to go out for some ice cream."

Ray didn't answer. He had nothing against the priest, who had always been friendly, but he felt uneasy. Although he couldn't articulate it, there was something odd about the man—an incongruity that was difficult to pinpoint. But Ray's instinctive warning was outweighed by what he had been taught from birth—priests were men of God who had chosen life's highest calling. They were to be revered and obeyed.

"Your mom told me that strawberry is your favorite flavor. Come on, it'll be fun."

"Okay, Father."

Ray Lassater was raised in a devout Catholic family in Lynn, Massachusetts, a suburb north of Boston. His father died of pneumonia when he was seven. His mother, Michelle, hadn't worked outside the home since Ray was born, but she was forced to go back to work to support Ray and his younger sister. She found it difficult to find a job on her own, but the Church helped her locate work at a seafood processing plant owned by another parishioner.

Father Monahan stopped by the Lassater house frequently after the death of Ray's father and Michelle was glad to have a positive male role model around. At first, he took Ray out for walks down to the park to play catch or to get some ice cream at the corner soda fountain. When they returned to the house, he would tuck Ray into bed and they would say a prayer together. The first sexual assault occurred during a prayer when the priest slid his hand underneath Ray's pajama bottoms and lightly fondled his penis. This happened a couple more times with Monahan fondling him a little bit longer each time. Ray closed his eyes tightly during these episodes and didn't move. Although it felt wrong, he trusted the man and it was unthinkable to question a priest's actions.

Monahan's next move was to invite Ray to the rectory for milk and cookies after Sunday school. During these encounters, they would sit so close to each other on the couch that Father Monahan's aftershave made Ray sneeze. Monahan's typical routine was to put his hand on Ray's leg and then gradually slide it up over his penis, rubbing softly back and forth. Monahan explained that it was part of God's plan for priests to show their love in special ways. Ray told the Father that he didn't like it, but the priest told him that if he loved God, he would love his priest, too.

One day after Sunday school, Monahan took Ray back to the rectory and told him that they needed to shower together to cleanse themselves. Monahan began disrobing while Ray watched nervously. After he was naked, he told Ray to get undressed. Ray hesitated, but did as he was told. Father Monahan sat down and motioned for Ray to sit on his lap. He took Ray's hand and guided it to his erect penis, moving it up and down. "That's it, Ray. Keep going, up and down, up and down…"

Ray kept jerking until Monahan ejaculated, but then recoiled as the hot, sticky substance spilled onto his hands. Monahan told him to go into the bathroom and wash up.

As they got dressed, Monahan counseled Ray that their relationship was special and that God wanted them to keep it a secret. Ray felt awkward about the episode, but he agreed not to tell anyone. But the next time Father Monahan came by the house, Ray told his mother that he didn't want to see him. His mother asked why, but Ray refused to explain. She went back into the living room and told Father Monahan that Ray was feeling ill and wanted to go to bed early. After Father Monahan left, she went back into Ray's room and put her hand on his stomach.

"Ahhhhhh!"

"Ray! What's wrong?"

"I don't like being touched!" Ray screamed as he burst into tears. "I…I…don't like being naked or…or being touched by…by…Father Monahan!"

"What are you saying? Ray! Tell me!"

"Fa…Fa…Father Monahan," Ray stuttered between sobs.

"Did Father Monahan touch you? Did he touch you, Ray?"

"Yes!"

"Where did he touch you, honey? Show me where he touched you."

"He…he…" Ray put his hand on his crotch.

"He touched your penis? Did Father Monahan touch your penis?"

"Ya…ya…"

"When did this happen?"

"After…after Sunday school."

"I need you to tell me everything that happened, honey."

"I…I…I…" Ray tried to get the words out, but he couldn't stop crying.

Michelle held her son tightly until he calmed down. "It's okay, honey. Ray, honey, it's okay. Tell mommy what happened."

"He touched me and…and…we got naked after…after Sunday school and he made…he made me touch him."

Michelle couldn't believe what she was hearing, but she knew her son was telling the truth. "It's okay, honey, it's okay," she whispered, pulling him close and stroking his hair.

The next morning, Michelle went to the office of the local bishop. As she told her story, the Bishop remained expressionless until Michelle finally erupted. "Aren't you shocked by what I'm telling you? My son was molested!"

"Yes, I'm concerned, very concerned," the bishop replied calmly.

Michelle didn't know that the bishop had heard similar stories from three other mothers.

"You need to keep this quiet, Michelle," the bishop continued. "We have to do everything we can to prevent scandal. That would only hurt the Church."

"I don't want to start a scandal. I just want to make sure that Father Monahan doesn't touch my son," Michelle retorted.

"I understand your concern. I will speak with Father Monahan about

24

this personally. But again, for the sake of the Church, this must remain a private matter."

"Okay," Michelle agreed. She wasn't entirely satisfied with the bishop's response, but she decided she would just keep her son away from the man.

The next time Father Monahan called on the family, Michelle told him that Ray didn't want to spend time with him anymore. She didn't give any reasons, but the priest expressed no surprise and left without an argument. Ray prayed and prayed that he would never have to spend time with the priest again.

Father Monahan never came by the house again, but a few months later, he walked into Ray's Sunday school class and told Ray that he needed to speak with him in the rectory. Ray felt frightened and confused, but he couldn't say no to the priest in front of everybody. Ray went with the Father into the rectory where they were alone.

"I've missed seeing you, Ray," Monahan began. "Have some cookies."

Ray looked down at the lacquered hardwood floor and prayed silently that the priest would leave him alone.

"Come on, Ray. You know how much I care about you; I just want you to get closer to God. Let's sit down and pray."

They sat down on the couch and Father Monahan moved in close. The smell of the priest's aftershave was stronger than he remembered. "O Almighty Father…" Monahan began as he ran his hand up Ray's thigh. Ray tried to jump off the couch, but Monahan held him down. "Let me go!" Ray screamed.

"Hold still, Ray. This is our own special way of praying to our Heavenly Father."

Ray struggled to get free, but Monahan pushed him off the couch onto the cold rectory floor and grabbed the back of his head. Monahan held it firmly while he pulled the back of Ray's pants down. Monahan threw his robe over his shoulder and then pulled down his own underwear while Ray cried hysterically on the floor. With one violent thrust, he slammed his erect penis into Ray's anus, ripping the delicate tissue. Ray gasped in pain. Monahan grabbed Ray's hips with both hands and guided his body up and down on his penis until he ejaculated twenty seconds later. After the priest pulled out, Ray collapsed onto the floor, gasping in pain.

Monahan went into the other room and came back with a towel that he used to mop up the mess. "Ray, my son, we need to shower now." Monahan picked him up and took him into the bathroom. He wiped Ray's body with a sponge.

"It…it hurts. It really hurts," Ray whimpered.

"It's okay, Ray. Sometimes we must suffer for God. It brings us closer to Christ who suffered for us."

Before Ray left, Father Monahan reminded him, "Ray, we are both sworn to secrecy about our relationship. God gets angry when we talk about things like this. People who don't obey go to Hell. Do you understand?"

Ray nodded solemnly and limped home, every step aggravating his injury. When he got to his house, he heard his mother in the kitchen so he tried to scamper quickly into his bedroom.

"Ray? Ray, is that you?" his mother called.

"Yeah, mom," Ray answered quietly and continued towards his room.

"Come in here; I've got an egg salad sandwich for you."

"I'm not hungry right now."

"What's wrong? Come in here, I want to talk to you."

Ray walked into the kitchen.

"Since when do you turn down an egg salad sandwich?"

"Just not hungry right now," Ray said quietly, his eyes glued to the floor.

"Look at me, Ray." Michelle put her hand under his chin and lifted his head up. "Are you feeling okay?"

"I'm okay, mom. I'm just tired."

"All right. Why don't you go take a short nap? You can eat your lunch later."

Ray turned around and started to walk out of the kitchen. There was a huge stain on the back of his pants.

"Ray! What's that on your Sunday pants?"

Ray kept going towards the stairs.

"Hey! Stop! I'm talking to you. What happened to your pants?"

"I…I…"

"I hope they're not ruined. Take them off so I can clean them."

Ray didn't move.

"I'm talking to you, young man. Take off your pants right now."

"I don't want to take my pants off!" Ray exploded, bursting into tears.

"Oh my God! What is it?"

"Mom! Don't make me take my pants off! Don't make me! I don't want to!"

"Ray…Ray…it's okay." Michelle held him while he wept. Then she carried him into the living room and held him in her lap on the couch.

"What's going on, honey? Please tell me. How did you get your pants dirty?"

"I don't want to go to Hell!"

"What are you talking about? You're not going to Hell. Did somebody say something to you at church today?"

"I...I..."

"Please tell me."

"I...I...saw Father Monahan today."

"What! What happened?"

"I went...I went with him to the rectory..."

"He took you to the rectory? Oh no...oh no...what happened? Oh no...your pants. Ray, take off your pants."

"Mom...I..."

"Ray, take off your pants, now!"

"I can't! I can't!"

Michelle reached over and unbuttoned Ray's pants and then pulled them down over his shoes. She looked carefully at the stain. "This is blood. Oh my god, this is blood...Ray, no..."

"Mom, I don't want to go to Hell!" Ray screamed. "I don't want to go to Hell!"

"I need to see what happened, honey. Take your underwear off. I need to see."

Ray stood up, revealing a dark red splotch of blood on the back of his underpants.

Michelle put her hand over her mouth. "Oh my god..." She pulled his underwear down slowly. His anus was bright red and some of the rips had already started to scab. She carried him into the bedroom and helped him put on some new clothes and then drove him to the emergency room. The ER doctor said there was nothing that could be done, but she prescribed some antibiotics to kill any potential infection.

Michelle dropped Ray off at her mother's house and went to the rectory, but Father Monahan was nowhere to be found. The next day, she confronted the local bishop. Again, he recommended that she keep quiet so that the Church would be spared from scandal. Michelle threatened to go to the police.

The bishop called the Archdiocese's attorney and explained the situation. The attorney called Michelle the next morning.

"Michelle, this is Rod McConkey. Bishop Lawton asked me to give you a call. I'm sorry to hear about the incident regarding your son."

"You're sorry? My son was attacked."

"Well, we care about your son, but we're concerned that it would hurt the Church if allegations of this nature were publicly released. Can you appreciate that?"

"My son was anally raped!"

"I know you're upset and I understand, but for the sake of your son and your faith, we need to keep this incident inside the Church."

"I don't know what Bishop Lawton told you, but this is the second time! Something needs to be done or I'm calling the police!"

McConkey was an experienced attorney who had negotiated with the parents of several abuse victims. He had a number of proven strategies at his disposal. The first was to accuse the child of lying. The Church handled a significant number of cases this way, although McConkey decided not to try it here. Monahan had been accused by several other children and it was too risky to call all of his victims liars.

The second strategy was to convince the parent that the Church would deal with the situation, and that reporting the abuse would hurt the victim's faith. McConkey figured this strategy wouldn't work either because it was the second time Michelle had complained to the bishop. The next strategy was to offer a monetary settlement.

"Michelle, the Church wants to make sure that you have adequate medical care for your son and we want to put this episode behind us. We'd like to offer $40,000 to help you."

"You want to pay me to be quiet? That's outrageous! Money isn't going to make this go away!"

McConkey realized that he needed to employ his final strategy—threats. "Michelle, please understand that if you report this, other parishioners in the Archdiocese will be upset. I'd hate to see this incident affect your job."

"What are you talking about?" Michelle cried incredulously. She had been a devout member of the Church her entire life and she couldn't believe that anybody would threaten her job.

"Your boss, Jack Flaherty, he's a loyal member of our parish. He'd be very disappointed to hear that you betrayed your faith."

"I…I don't know what to say…"

"Why don't you think it over? I'll call you again tomorrow morning."

When McConkey called back the next day, Michelle accepted the payoff and agreed to sign a confidentiality agreement. She couldn't afford to lose her job. But she never set foot in a Catholic Church again.

* * *

"Please continue your questioning of the witness, Mr. Lassater," the judge directed as the trial continued.

"Thank you, your Honor. Mr. Dunphy, did you warn the new diocese that you were sending them a priest who had been accused of sexual abuse?"

"No. Never."

"Why not?"

"All I cared about was getting the problem out of our diocese. That way, I figured I had a better chance of protecting myself."

"Protecting yourself? What do you mean by that?"

"That I would be able to maintain my standing in the community."

"So you're telling this jury that your sole motivation was to stay in power regardless of the consequences? Is that correct?"

"Well, I hate to think of it that way, but I suppose that's correct."

"What about helping the victims? Did you ever discuss that in your meetings?"

"No, we never did."

"Well, did you feel any moral responsibility for what was happening to the victims?"

"I'm ashamed to admit it, but at the time I didn't give it much thought. I feel terrible now."

"Can you explain to this jury how you could feel no moral responsibility for the repeated and systematic sexual abuse of children?"

"I guess I just figured that I was part of the Church and I didn't have to take personal responsibility for what others in the Church did."

"What about your conscience? Weren't you bothered by what was happening?"

"Again, I'd have to say that I never thought about it that way. I was part of the Church so I never thought about my individual actions being moral or immoral. I believed that the Church was pursuing a higher good and it was my obligation to protect the Church and my fellow priests."

Lassater faced the jury and gave them a long look.

"What about Cardinal McManus? Did he have any knowledge of the 'pedophile' fund?"

"Yes."

"How do you know that he had this knowledge?"

"I told him myself."

"And what did you tell him exactly?"

"I told him that we had a fund set up and that we had approximately four million dollars, which we were using, as needed, to pay off families that were reporting sexual abuse."

"Did you tell him how 'peddy cash' was being funded?"

"Yeah, I told him it was funded mostly from donations by parishioners. You know, at Mass, we would collect money and then put it in there."

"And what did he say when you revealed this to him?"

"He asked me if we had enough money to keep everyone quiet."

"What did you tell him?"

"I told him that at the rate claims were coming in, we wouldn't have enough. I also told him that the claims were putting a serious strain on the Archdiocese's finances."

"What did the Cardinal say to that?"

"He told me to compile a current list of the one hundred largest donors to the Archdiocese."

"Do you know why he made this request?"

"He told me that he wanted to appeal to them personally to help us through this crisis."

"Did you ever discuss the welfare of the victims with Cardinal McManus?"

"Well, like I said before, the victims were almost never discussed and no discussion ever took place in my presence. I only remember the subject coming up once. I told the Cardinal that maybe we should consider providing some help to the victims; maybe some counseling or some type of support. I mean, after a while there were literally hundreds of victims and I figured it made sense to do something for them."

"How did the Cardinal respond to your proposal?"

"It's hard to describe his response. He looked at me with this blank stare like he had no idea what I was talking about. And then—I'll never forget it—he said, 'We've got other priorities.' And then he turned and left the room."

Cardinal McManus sat in stony silence at the defendant's table, gray and drained. Lassater cringed every time he looked at the pathetic sight, but his compassion was snuffed out by murderous rage. He had to consciously resist the temptation to pounce on the man and rip his throat out.

"Thank you, Mr. Dunphy. I have no further questions." Lassater walked past the defense table. "Your witness."

"Your Honor, I'd like to request a short recess so that I can confer with my client," McManus' attorney said.

The judge nodded. "We'll reconvene in fifteen minutes."

Dushane patted Lassater on the back as he sat down.

"That was masterful."

Lassater heaved a sigh.

"I'm going outside to get some fresh air," Dushane said.

"Okay."

Dushane walked out of the courtroom, followed closely by the bodyguard assigned to protect him. He stepped into the lobby and then moved towards the outer door.

"Martin, you're not supposed to…" the bodyguard started.

"I just need some fresh air," Dushane interrupted. "Don't worry." Although he had been warned not to go outside because angry protesters had been staging demonstrations throughout the trial, Dushane had promised himself that he would not be intimated. He walked out onto the courthouse steps and surveyed the scene. A police barrier had been set up and at least a hundred protesters were corralled on the street. There was a man selling concessions from a small stand at the bottom of the steps.

"I'm going to get a pretzel," Dushane said.

The bodyguard grabbed Dushane's shoulder. "Don't do that."

Dushane kept going. "I'll just be a second."

As Dushane got closer to the crowd, several protesters started screaming as they recognized him. Dushane ignored them. "I'd like a pretzel, please."

"Yes, sir. Salt or no salt?"

"No."

The man reached into his cart and pulled out a hot doughy pretzel. He handed it to Dushane.

"Thanks."

Dushane scanned the crowd again and made eye contact with a heavy-set white man leaning against the police barrier. The man's head shot forward as he spat, "Nigger!"

CHAPTER 5

It is thought virtuous to have Faith—that is to say, to have a conviction which cannot be shaken by contrary evidence. Or, if contrary evidence might induce doubt, it is held that contrary evidence must be suppressed.

—BERTRAND RUSSELL

Dushane dug his cleats into the turf in right field as an oversized ten-year-old stepped into the batter's box. Dushane knew the hitter well because they had played on the same team the previous season. Although they weren't close friends, they had gotten along well as teammates.

Dushane took a few steps backward. He punched his fist into the heel of his mitt as the pitcher wound up and dealt the first pitch. The batter swung hard and hit the ball squarely, knocking it high in the air towards the gap between Dushane and the center fielder. Dushane took off, trying to follow the flight of the ball as he sprinted across the field. He ran until the last possible second and then dove at the base of the wall, his elongated frame flying sideways through space and then sliding across the grass. He extended his arm as far as he could and opened his mitt. The ball hit the web of his glove as thin blades of grass sheared off the ground into his mouth. Dushane rolled over onto his back and lifted up his glove, proudly displaying the ball.

"Nice catch, Martin," the center fielder congratulated.

"Thanks."

Dushane jogged in, smiling. He rarely made good plays in the field and he basked in the pride of his accomplishment. As he made his way to the dugout, he ran past the boy who had hit the ball. "Great hit, Joe. I made a lucky catch."

The boy looked up and sneered. "You...nigger!"

Dushane froze, the words tearing a corrosive gash. Although he had heard the word before, the indignity had never been uttered so unexpectedly. He wondered if anyone else had heard it. He looked around, but everything was hazy. He spun around, but then felt lightheaded. He stumbled around the infield.

"Martin!" The coach grabbed his shoulder. "What are you doing? The inning's over. Are you okay?"

Dushane's senses suddenly jolted back to reality. "Yeah, yeah. I..."

"Well, let's go. Come on."

Dushane trotted back to the dugout with his head down. A few days later, a scab developed, but the wound festered bitterly under the surface, never fully healing.

* * *

Dushane dropped his pretzel and leapt over the police barrier, jumping straight into the man's torso, knocking him backwards onto the pavement. Dushane pinned the man's arms and grabbed his throat, holding him down while unloading his fist on the man's face. The man tried to wriggle free, but Dushane wrapped both hands around his neck and slammed his head on the cement until four police officers intervened. They pulled Dushane off and restrained him while the man lay moaning softly, his face bloody and disfigured. An officer cuffed Dushane and escorted him back into the courthouse. The other officers tried to subdue the excited crowd.

* * *

"You broke that gentleman's nose," Lassater said sternly as he walked into the police holding room.

Dushane dropped his head. "I'm sorry, Ray, I just…lost it."

"I posted bail for you."

"Thanks."

"The trial's in recess until tomorrow. This hurts our case; you know that."

"I know."

"We've got to restrain ourselves. Do you know how many times I've wanted to slap McManus and those other monsters? We can't sink to that level. We've got a job to do and we can't let anything stand in our way. I won't let anything stand in our way."

"You're right," Dushane said softly. "I wish I could take it back."

"As your boss, I'm not happy about this." Lassater sat down and put his hand on Dushane's shoulder. "But as your friend, I couldn't be more proud. It takes courage to stand up to that. I wish I could've been there to see it."

Dushane smiled. "Thanks, Ray."

* * *

As the trial of Cardinal McManus continued, Lassater introduced thousands of once-secret Church documents confirming that the Church's modus operandi was to reassign a molesting priest to a new parish without disclosing that the priest was a pedophile. The evidence also showed that the Church's leadership, including several bishops and the Cardinal, had specifically authorized this practice. But perhaps the most damning documents revealed that one priest in the Boston Archdiocese, who had been accused of sexual abuse by twenty-two different boys, had openly advocated sex between men and boys as an acceptable and healthy practice. Lassater conclusively established that Cardinal McManus had been informed on at least ten separate occasions that this particular priest had been accused of sexual abuse. The Cardinal had also received a copy of the document in which the priest had advocated man-boy love. The last piece of evidence Lassater introduced was a letter Cardinal McManus had written to the priest upon his retirement.

> This letter provides me with an opportunity to thank you personally and in the name of the people of the Archdiocese for the special ministry you have provided over the years. For thirty years, you brought God's word and His love to the

people. You have an impressive record and all of us are truly grateful for your priestly care and for all the lives and hearts that have been touched by your sharing of the Lord's Spirit. You are truly appreciated for all that you have done.

With grateful remembrance and with my blessing and promise of prayer, I remain,

Sincerely yours in Christ,

Reverend Cardinal Sean C. McManus, Archbishop of Boston

The first time Lassater read the letter, he held his breath and clenched his fists in a fit of suffocating rage until he exploded, throwing his desk lamp against the wall. But he maintained his composure in court, imploring the jury to make sure that the Cardinal spent the rest of his days in a jail cell.

Cardinal McManus refused to testify, taking the Fifth Amendment; however, he had given an interview the previous year. He admitted that there was a problem with sexual molestation by priests, but that "sexual abuse was not on my radar screen." He also tried to shift the blame for the scandal, arguing that the abused children's parents were at least partially responsible for "not providing adequate supervision."

Lassater couldn't understand how any human being could ignore a problem that was destroying people's lives, but he did what he could to make sure that it would never happen again. McManus was convicted and sentenced to ten years in prison.

The Suffolk County DA's office prosecuted twenty-three cases against sexually abusive priests and the Church leaders who ignored it and tried to cover it up. Twenty of the cases resulted in a conviction or plea agreement with sixteen members of the Church ordered to serve time in prison. More importantly to Lassater, the truth about the Catholic Church came out. The Church had known for years about the abuse, but had done virtually nothing to stop it.

Cardinal McManus was the last defendant prosecuted by the DA's office, but the legal proceedings didn't end there. Hundreds of victims filed civil suits and Lassater shared all of the information from his criminal investigation. The onslaught of civil cases was so great that the Boston Archdiocese, even with its vast wealth, had to call on the Vatican for an emergency infusion of cash.

* * *

"Good afternoon, my dear," Lassater said cheerfully to his secretary.
"Hi, Ray. David Chambers called."
"Excellent. Thank you." Lassater sat behind his desk and dialed Chambers' number.

"This is David."

"David. Ray."

"Ray! Congratulations!"

"Thanks."

"It's hard to believe it's finally over."

"It'll never be over, but we stopped a few of them."

"You prevented new ones."

"Maybe. I haven't had any more nightmares."

"You're kidding?"

"No. It's been two months. I've never gone that long."

"That's the best news I've heard all year. Next time you're in California, let's celebrate."

"Sure."

"What do you plan to do next?"

"I'm going after Infinity."

"Infinity?" Chambers knew a little about Infinity, but he didn't think much of it. He figured the organization would eventually implode. "I thought you were leaving the DA's office."

"I am."

"Then how…?"

"An independent investigation; I'll have more leeway."

"Why Infinity?"

"The breach…the denial…it's such an all-encompassing betrayal. Infinity's got the potential to be more destructive than the Catholic Church."

"I know they've been growing…"

"They're a cancer; just wait."

"Well, if you think that's the right path for you."

Lassater chuckled. "There's only one path. You know that better than I do."

"Yeah, I just…I hope you can take some time off," Chambers said, changing the subject.

"Yeah, I plan to. I may be out your way soon."

"Good. Bring your golf clubs; we'll play Pebble."

"How's the leg?"

"I can still hobble through eighteen."

"Then I suppose I can still take your money."

Chambers laughed. "See you soon, Ray."

CHAPTER 6

Most people are bothered by those passages of Scripture they do not understand, but the passages that bother me are those I do understand.

—MARK TWAIN

Robert Newhall stepped over the threshold of his new home and drew in a deep breath. Construction workers had just finished preparing the house for his arrival and he could smell the satisfying aroma of fresh paint. Newhall had purchased the house for eleven million dollars and his wife planned to spend an additional five million renovating it to her tastes. The luxurious estate had twenty-seven rooms and was situated on a stretch of private beach in Southern California.

Newhall walked across the foyer to the floor-to-ceiling living room windows and admired the breathtaking view of the ocean. He stood quietly and felt at peace until he suddenly remembered a video he had seen earlier in the week about starving children in Africa. He pictured the sharp, bony appendages; bloated bellies; ribs pushing against paper-thin layers of flesh; and sallow, emaciated faces with flies buzzing overhead awaiting a drawn-out death. Newhall quickly dismissed the unwelcome intrusion, but he couldn't help wondering why God had blessed him so richly.

* * *

Had he been a businessman instead of a religious leader, the story of Robert Newhall would have been legendary rags-to-riches, but men of the church weren't supposed to get rich doing God's work. Then again, Robert Newhall was no ordinary man of God. He was born and raised a devout Southern Baptist in Greenville, South Carolina, the oldest of three children. His family lived in a modest home and like most people in town, they were deeply religious. They believed that the Bible was infallible and the only authority on moral or spiritual questions.

Robert's father, Jeb, had grown up in the Appalachian mountains of North Carolina, the youngest child in a poor farming family. He took up carpentry and moved to Greenville in his early twenties to escape the white-trash environment he came from, but he still had an unmistakable hillbilly drawl. Robert's mother, Tammy, was a quiet, subservient homemaker who had lived Greenville her entire life. She had grown up in the Methodist Church, but had converted to her husband's religion upon their marriage. Although she didn't know exactly what the Southern Baptists believed, she hadn't given it much thought. It was customary for women to change their religious affiliation upon marriage and she figured the only thing that mattered was a strong belief in the Bible. She also wanted to be part of an active social circle and the Southern Baptists appeared to have a strong sense of community. The only catch was that they looked upon women differently than the way she was accustomed. The Church's mission statement provided that "A wife must submit herself graciously to the servant leadership of her husband," and Baptists cited Chapter 5, verse 24 of Apostle Paul's letter to the Ephesian Christians for support:

You married women, obey your husbands as you obey the Lord, because a husband is the head of his wife as Christ is the Head of the Church.

Tammy Newhall was further reassured when the leader of the Baptist Church explained why women should be treated as inferior.

We believe that the Scriptures are the inspired word of God. It is easy for those who don't believe to scoff at such "out of date" ideas, but for those of us who accept the Bible as God's word, it is our duty to first accept what is written there. We can discuss interpretations to our heart's content, but in the end we must accept the words that are written whether or not they conform to the "wisdom" of our generation.

The Southern Baptist Convention was an old and powerful force, established in 1845 explicitly to support slavery, which had caused the break from Baptists in the North. Although they had been criticized for racist tendencies for over a hundred years, the Southern Baptists didn't apologize until 1995 for supporting slavery and opposing the civil rights initiatives of the 1950s and '60s.

Consistent with Baptist teachings, Tammy Newhall devoted herself to managing the family home and raising Robert and his two sisters, although she did have an active social life. In addition to the pedestrian calendar of a suburban housewife, including Tupperware parties, bridge, and church events, she was a psychic junkie who threw fortune-telling parties once a month. Tammy knew that the Church frowned on this activity, so she advertised the gatherings as Bible studies. Nevertheless, meetings quickly degenerated into discussions of Biblical prophecy, Nostradamus, communicating with spirits, and the latest predictions of tabloid psychics.

As a teenager, Robert observed these gatherings and was impressed by the credulous nature of the people in attendance. They wanted more than anything to believe. He thought the whole thing was a colossal display of ignorance until one of his mother's friends had a vision of him becoming one of the most powerful and influential men in the country.

Newhall's parents were uneducated, simple people, but they loved their son and raised him as best they could. They tried to give him a happy childhood and encouraged him to play with other boys in the neighborhood. Unfortunately, Robert was a small child, not well coordinated, and possessed little athletic skill. The other boys his age liked to play sports, but they hated playing with Newhall because he was usually the worst player. When they chose teams, they always picked him last and laughed at the way he played. Newhall frequently lashed out at anyone who criticized him and he got into several fights, which he almost always lost. But he never backed down. Eventually, he made some friends who respected his toughness and willingness to stand up for himself. But this didn't resolve the inner conflict that had begun to take root. He started feeling guilty because he wanted to beat up the boys who were mean to him, despite being taught in church that he was supposed to love his enemies. On the other hand, he had learned that he would always be a sinner, so maybe he should just give in to his anger and violent thoughts. In any case, every church member was expected to live in accordance with the Ten Commandments. The church prohibited gambling, for example, based on its interpretation of the Tenth Commandment: "Thou shalt not covet thy neighbor's house, thou shalt not covet thy neighbor's wife, nor his manservant, nor his maidservant, nor his ox, nor his ass, nor any thing that is thy neighbor's." Although Newhall and his high school friends never coveted each other's asses, they did get together for a poker game once a month. It was usually the same five guys, but on one occasion a boy named Rick Reeves joined the game. Reeves was tall and muscular with blond hair and blue eyes. He played on the football team, earned National Merit Scholar honors, and volunteered as an acolyte at the church.

Although Newhall usually beat his friends handily at poker, he was no match for Reeves, who was as adept at poker as he was at everything else. He quickly cleaned Newhall out and then chuckled to Newhall's best friend, Mike Watson, "Like taking candy from a baby. I thought you said this guy knew how to play poker." With extraordinary effort, Newhall silently repressed his rage, but the next day he called Jerry Reeves, Rick's father, and confessed to the poker game. Jerry Reeves confronted his son with the charges, calling him a "disgraceful sinner." Rick countered that a poker game wasn't any different from "playing the market," which Jerry Reeves frequently bragged about. "How dare you disrespect me!" his father thundered, backhanding his son so hard that it left a bloody gash on his left cheek. He grounded Rick for two months and made him quit the football team. He also forced his son to attend several prayer meetings with the church pastor.

Jeb Newhall also found out about the poker game and was equally upset. He attacked Robert as a worthless good-for-nothing who would never amount to anything. Although the criticism stung, Newhall savored his revenge against Rick Reeves. He also promised himself that he would do whatever it took to prove his father wrong. Indeed, he was going to prove to everyone that he was a force to be reckoned with.

Realizing that power resided in the church, Newhall spent all of his spare time volunteering and developing relationships with people in the congregation. Although he had conflicting beliefs and impulses, he found himself thinking less and less about the truth of Christian doctrine, instead focusing on how that doctrine could be used to control others.

Newhall quickly began to understand the dynamics of the church's ability to control people by strictly regulating values and beliefs. He concluded that in order to manipulate others in such an environment, he had to control his own personal behavior, so he lived according to a strict set of rules—no drinking, smoking, gambling, dancing, cussing, or sex.

As a result of his involvement in the church and the moral standards he set for himself, church leaders gave him the opportunity to address the full congregation when he was just seventeen years old. Newhall didn't disappoint, wowing the hometown crowd with his fire-and-brimstone style.

"Jesus said, 'Thou shalt not commit adultery, but I say unto you, that whoever looks upon a woman to lust after her, has committed adultery with her in his heart.' Jesus said that if we so much as get angry without cause, we are in danger of Judgment, and that 'every idle word a man speaks, he will give account thereof on the Day of Judgment.' Jesus taught that each of has broken God's law. We are all guilty! Every single one of us!

"The Bible says that if we hate someone, we have committed murder in our heart. If we have told one lie, or stolen one thing, then we are lying thieves! So what can we do to avoid being found guilty on Judgment Day? How can we escape the damnation of Hell? Should we live good lives? Should we love our fellow man? That won't help! If we sin on Monday and then live a good life for the rest of the week, we are still sinners! A man is forever in debt to justice and must be punished according to God's law! Each of us has sinned against God and no amount of righteous living, prayer, or good works can wash away the stain of our guilt! The law calls for our blood and the penalty is death and eternal damnation!"

Newhall pounded his fist on the lectern and then lowered his voice, continuing in a soft, even tone. "But there is hope. The Savior Jesus Christ paid the fine for us. He died for our sins and then rose from the dead, defeating death itself. Now all who repent and trust in Him receive remission of sins. There is no other way. Jesus said, 'I am the way, the truth, and the life. No man comes to the Father but through me.' There is only one Savior. We must accept Him and obey in order to secure our eternal salvation."

After he spoke, Newhall felt invincible, like he could conquer anything or anybody—as if God had infused him with Almighty strength. Church members greeted him warmly after the service and praised him for his forceful words. Newhall was immediately addicted to the new power at his command. He had found his calling.

The church elders, figuring that Newhall was destined to be a future leader, gave him many more opportunities to speak and two things became immediately apparent. First, he spoke with limitless energy and charisma. Second, offerings were twenty-five to fifty percent higher on the days that he spoke. Church leaders experimented with collection times, trying to determine when the congregation was likely to give the most. They concluded that it was right after Newhall had finished speaking.

In addition to his oratory skills, Newhall developed a repertoire of moves that he used when he met people. He might put his hand on a person's elbow or shoulder indicating his affection and interest in the person. For people he knew well, he wouldn't hesitate to give them a warm hug. But his favorite technique was sharing a light secret; flattering his acquaintance and making them feel as if they were part of his inner circle.

After graduating from high school, Newhall attended Bob Jones University in his hometown of Greenville. Critics denounced the university for its long-standing ban on interracial dating as well as its bigotry and intolerance of other faiths, but his father encouraged him to attend. Jeb Newhall knew his son would receive a strong Christian education and he told Robert that "the races should just associate with their own kind."

Newhall thrived at BJU. He was elected class president and led two popular Bible study groups. He read and studied the Bible fanatically, hoping to be recognized as one of the foremost experts on the Holy Book. Although he felt a little guilty, he found himself especially excited by the stories of genocide, slavery, and rape. One of his favorite verses was from Deuteronomy:

> When you draw near to a city to fight against it, offer terms of peace to it. And if its answer to you is peace and it opens to you, then all the people who are found in it shall do forced labor for you and shall serve you. But if it makes no peace with you, but makes war against you, then you shall besiege it; and when the LORD your God gives it into your hand you shall put all its males to the sword, but the women and the little ones, the cattle, and everything else in the city, all its spoil, you shall take as booty for yourselves; and you shall enjoy the spoil of your enemies, which the LORD your God has given you. Thus you shall do to all the cities which are very far from you, which are not cities of the nations here. But in the cities of these peoples that the LORD your God gives you for an inheritance, you shall save alive nothing that breathes, but you shall utterly destroy them.

Newhall identified with God's power and angry wrath. He found justification for his own anger and started to believe that God had chosen him to lead the faithful. He fantasized about becoming a great historical figure like Christ, Paul, or Martin Luther.

The final thing Newhall needed was a supportive woman by his side. He met his future wife, Patricia Altman, during his junior year and was immediately attracted to her soft features, shoulder-length blond hair, and large, shapely breasts. He also figured that she was the richest coed on campus. Her family owned a ten-thousand-acre orange grove in Florida as well as extensive real estate in Tampa, Orlando, and St. Petersburg. Newhall courted her for two years and then proposed shortly after graduation. Although Patricia's parents didn't care for Jeb Newhall's hillbilly origins, they were thrilled that their daughter was marrying a man of God who appeared destined for stardom.

Newhall began his career immediately after he finished his studies. He started as an assistant pastor at his boyhood church in Greenville, but he had grand ambitions, recognizing the potential power of uniting all Christians into one organization. With the financial backing of his wife's parents, he began a search for the perfect location to realize his vision—the Infinity Christian Network.

After considering several locations, Newhall decided to establish Infinity Headquarters in Orange County, California, a good location for two reasons. First, it was densely populated with conservative Christians, many of them wealthy. Second, there were more media professionals in Southern California than in any other place in the world. Newhall dreamt of building a Christian media empire that spanned the globe.

While the headquarters was under construction, Newhall traveled across the country talking to prominent Christians about his vision. When he traveled, a flock of yes-men and women buzzed about him—secretaries, bodyguards, a chauffeur, and several advisors. Newhall barked orders at them and they happily obeyed, their souls wriggling in delight that he allowed them a role in his world. But none of them understood the motivations of the man they revered.

Mike Watson, Newhall's best friend, had been working as a CPA when Newhall called to share his vision of the Network and invite him to be a partner. Newhall needed someone he could trust to set up and manage the Network's finances and organizational structure. Watson believed strongly in the Christian cause and was thrilled at the chance to spread God's word. The two men started by purchasing a small radio station and producing a show for cable television. They also recruited several pastors from churches throughout Southern California to help them build membership. Watson took charge of Infinity's finances and worked with attorneys and bankers to set up the fledgling empire.

Within a decade, Newhall had amassed a large fortune and built Infinity into a media powerhouse. Infinity's most valuable asset was the Infinity Media Network, which aired programs over three thousand television stations and twenty-one satellites worldwide. Infinity's television programs included speeches by Newhall and other Infinity officials as well as programs on health and nutrition, childrearing, political action, and fundraising. It also created children's programs on how to be a good Christian.

The Infinity Network owned a separate publishing company, which produced all of its written literature, including Christian books, Bibles, and a bi-weekly magazine called *New Hope*. Newhall used *New Hope* to prescribe the behavioral requirements dictated by Scripture, including the appropriate amount of money to donate. He also advised followers on what they should think about specific television shows, movies, and music.

Infinity's publishing arm translated its material into twenty-three different languages and then distributed and sold its wares at independent bookstores and on the Internet. Infinity also owned and operated a chain of almost three hundred bookstores devoted exclusively to Infinity materials and other "approved" literature. Infinity produced books for every age group with a special emphasis on children's books. The bestseller was called *Life Lessons for Children*. It included images and memory games that children could use to help them memorize the Ten Commandments and learn how to pray correctly.

While Infinity evangelists preached that donated funds would be used for church and charitable purposes, much of the money went into bank accounts and corporations controlled by Newhall. But this could never be proven. Besides Newhall and a handful of lawyers who were prohibited from revealing their client's activities by the attorney-client privilege, Watson was the only man who knew all the details about Newhall's secretive financial dealings. Watson set it up so that Newhall's name didn't appear on any documents; instead, Infinity attorneys created a complicated network of holding companies and shell corporations.

* * *

Newhall walked out to the deck where a gentle ocean breeze whisked across his face. He sniffed the salt air as he pulled out his cell phone. He dialed his wife's personal assistant.

"Hello."

"Jane, it's Reverend Newhall."

"Good morning, Reverend."

"Have you seen Patricia?"

"She left a couple hours ago."

"Where did she go?"

"Shopping."

"Again?"

"She hired a new wardrobe consultant."

Newhall shook his head. His wife had gone through four consultants over the past year. "Do you know when she's coming back?"

"I don't know, sir. She has a nail appointment at 2:30."

"Well, I need you to call her. Tell her to meet me at John Wayne Airport, hangar 12, at three. Her driver knows how to get there."

"Can I tell her what this is about? She might get upset if…"

"Don't worry," Newhall interrupted. "Tell her it's important. Tell her it's an emergency if you have to."

"Yes, sir."

CHAPTER 7

When it comes to bullshit, big-time, major league bullshit, you have to stand in awe of the all-time champion of false promises and exaggerated claims: religion. No contest.

Think about it. Religion has actually convinced people that there's an invisible man—living in the sky—who watches everything you do, every minute of every day. And the invisible man has a special list of ten things he does not want you to do. And if you do any of these ten things, he has a special place, full of fire and smoke and burning and torture and anguish, where he will send you to live and suffer and burn and choke and scream and cry forever and ever 'til the end of time! But He loves you. He loves you, and He needs money! He always needs money! He's all-powerful, all-perfect, all-knowing, and all-wise, somehow just can't handle money! Religion takes in billions of dollars, they pay no taxes, and they always need a little more.

—George Carlin

"How wonderful to see you, honey," Newhall greeted as his wife stepped out of the limousine. "You look lovely. Is that a new dress?"

"No," Patricia Newhall replied tersely. "I bought this three weeks ago. Don't you remember? I wore it to the prayer breakfast in Anaheim."

"Ah, yes, of course; it's beautiful on you." Newhall didn't understand his wife's obsession with clothes and jewelry, but he couldn't complain; she was always impeccably dressed in the most stylish fashions.

"I missed my nail appointment," Patricia added crossly. "I hope this isn't another one of your surprise trips."

"No, no, I've got a much better surprise for you. Come with me."

As Newhall escorted his wife into the spacious hangar, he told himself that he loved her. Besides being an exquisite trophy that other men envied, she was an articulate spokesperson for Infinity. Most of all though, he felt eternally grateful because Patricia's family had gotten him started in the business and they had important connections to wealthy, powerful people. He had become rich beyond his wildest dreams.

The hangar was empty except for a large tarp hanging down from the ceiling. Newhall motioned to a young man standing on a catwalk in the rafters. "Lift it up."

The young man cranked a winch, slowly raising the cloth and revealing a shiny, fourteen-seat passenger jet. The plane came equipped with a gourmet kitchen and bar, and all of the seats folded into beds. In the rear of the aircraft, there was an expansive lounge with three leather couches. The plane had two full bathrooms, each with a separate tub and shower. Newhall's newest toy carried a price tag of nine million dollars.

"What is this?"

Newhall smiled broadly and held out his arms. "My gift to you."

"Oh my gosh…Robert…this is for me?"

"All for you."

Although the jet was an extravagant purchase, Newhall had several reasons for buying it. In the past, he and his wife and other senior Infinity officials had either flown first class or chartered a plane. Patricia objected to both. She hated flying commercial because it tied her to an inflexible schedule and she found the service unacceptable. Flight attendants quickly tired of her excessive requests and often treated her coldly. Chartering a private jet was an improvement, but Patricia wanted to employ her own staff, including a chef and a personal attendant that would cheerfully cater to her needs. She also wanted to decorate the plane to her own tastes. She detested the stark interiors of most charter aircraft, which weren't even color coordinated.

Patricia walked around the plane and gently fingered the fuselage.

"This is…this is beautiful."

"Take a look at the tail," Newhall pointed. "Custom designed for Patricia Newhall" was painted in bright red letters.

"I…I don't know what to say." Patricia wrapped her arms around her husband's neck and kissed him lightly on the cheek. "Honey, thank you. Thank you."

"Only the best for you, my dear."

Newhall didn't often receive affection from his wife, but whenever he did it reminded him of how their relationship used to be. Before they had achieved spectacular wealth and fame through the Infinity Network, they had been much closer. On the other hand, even then, Newhall reflected, they had never shared their innermost thoughts. Indeed, he had no idea what made his wife tick. Newhall often longed for closer relationships, not only with his wife, but with anyone.

"Why don't we take a look inside?" Newhall offered. "I spared no expense on the interior and I retained a decorator to assist you with any modifications you'd like to make."

"Yes, I can't wait to see it."

Newhall wheeled a set of portable stairs against the side of the plane. He climbed the steps and pulled open the heavy steel door. He was about to enter the aircraft when a small gold plaque above the door caught his eye. It read: "Chambers Aerospace."

* * *

"Did you think I wouldn't find about this?" Mike Watson seethed as he burst into Newhall's office.

"It's polite to knock."

"Are you out of your mind? Are you completely out of your mind?"

"Calm down. What are you talking about?"

"The jet! What do you think I'm talking about!"

"What about it?"

"What about it! Since when do you make a decision like that without consulting me! You spent nine million dollars without consulting me!"

"I made a decision. I'm the CEO and I made a decision. Besides, it'll only take a half million a year out of our cash flow."

"This is insane!"

"I don't know why you're so upset; you'll get to use it as much as anyone."

"Buying a jet is totally frivolous!"

Newhall shrugged. "It is what it is."

Watson clenched his jaw as blood bubbled into his face. He turned and stormed out, slamming the door behind him. He went back to his office and simmered quietly, trying desperately to control his emotions.

Although Watson had occasional disagreements with Newhall, he believed strongly in Infinity's mission. He also figured that they had both worked hard and deserved to be rewarded for their efforts. Like Newhall, Watson drew a generous salary with perks, including a six-thousand-square-foot beachfront house, a convertible Jaguar, and two live-in servants. But as time went on, Watson had become increasingly uncomfortable as Newhall funneled larger and larger sums of money to personal bank accounts in the Caymans. Watson had raised the issue several times, but Newhall had always refused to discuss it. The jet was the last straw.

After stewing for almost an hour, Watson went back to Newhall's office. "We need to talk."

"So talk."

"I'm worried about your spending habits; not just with the plane, but with everything. And your wife…she's way out of control."

"Since when have you have been concerned about my spending habits?" Newhall retorted sharply. "Who just built a new swimming pool?"

"My old pool had a leak."

Newhall rolled his eyes. "What's your point?"

"Do you have any idea how hard it is to handle the finances around here? Right now, I can't account for almost two million dollars? It just disappeared. Gone. Did your wife spend that, too? If we get audited…"

"Let me worry about that; that's my business. And leave my wife out of this."

"It's just as much my business," Watson shot back. "And I can't let you worry about it. You're the problem."

"What are you trying to say?"

"People give us money to do Christ's work. Pandering to your wife's vanity is contrary to everything we stand for. Do you understand that we receive donations through a tax-exempt organization? That means we have a legal responsibility."

"Don't you dare lecture me," Newhall warned.

"We also have a moral responsibility," Watson continued angrily. "I've been trying to tell you this for over a year now, but you don't listen. I don't know if you're in this for the right reasons anymore."

"You're way out of line!" Newhall erupted, jumping out of his chair. "How dare you talk to me that way!"

"Then start listening! Wake up and start listening!"

"You…two-bit…you'd still be rotting away at some accounting firm if it weren't for me! You're nothing without me! You get it? Nothing!"

Watson suddenly fell backwards as if he'd been pushed. He quickly steadied himself and tried to speak, but he couldn't get any words out.

"If you don't like the way I do things, then get out! Quit! I don't need you!"

Watson stared hard at Newhall, but didn't speak.

"Now get out of my office! Get out before I throw you out!"

Watson had worked tirelessly for Infinity and Newhall's words deeply offended him. He stumbled back to his desk and immediately drafted an angry letter of resignation. When he got home, he debated whether he could leave the organization he had spent so many years building. He stayed up all night praying and knew by morning that he had no choice. He went to the office early and spent the day copying his files. Then he quietly placed his resignation letter on Newhall's desk

CHAPTER 8

A man is flying in a hot air balloon and realizes that he's lost. He spots a man down below and lowers the balloon so that he can yell down:

"Hey, can you help me? I'm lost! Can you tell me where I am?"

The man on the ground shouts back, "You're fifty feet off the ground in a hot air balloon!"

"You must be a lawyer," the balloonist says.

"I am," the man replied. "How did you know?"

"Because what you just told me was one hundred percent accurate and totally useless."

The phone rang. Chambers put his coffee cup down and pressed Speaker. "This is David."

"David. Tom Jeffries. I've got bad news."

"What is it?"

"A six hundred million dollar lawsuit has been filed against Chambers Aerospace."

"What?"

"A strike suit. For securities fraud."

"That's crazy."

"And we're up against the worst law firm."

"This is absurd. Meet me in my office. I want to see this."

For most of its history, Chambers Aerospace had avoided any significant legal disputes. Other than a few routine contractual disagreements with suppliers, all of which were settled amicably out of court, the company had never been involved in a large lawsuit or any action alleging illegal activity.

Tom Jeffries served as the company's general counsel. He was a competent and experienced attorney, but Chambers always laughed whenever he received a memo from him because Jeffries always put the abbreviation "Esq." after his name. Although Chambers knew that this was an ancient custom in the legal profession, it still struck him as oddly and pathetically pompous.

Chambers rarely spoke with Jeffries because most of the company's legal issues didn't require his involvement. But a strike suit threatened to cripple the company. Indeed, the strike suit was perhaps the most powerful weapon held by the Bar, and its beauty was in its simplicity. After a company's stock price went down, an attorney would file a suit on behalf of the shareholders alleging securities fraud—but without any regard to the underlying facts. Companies could either defend themselves and pay a multi-million-dollar legal bill from their defense counsel, or simply settle the case for roughly the same sum, but without the hassle or risk of completely destroying the company. It was an insidious form of extortion, but extremely profitable.

Since Chambers Aerospace was a relatively new company in the aerospace industry, its stock was particularly volatile. The company had recently bid on a large contract to design and manufacture avionics components for one of the Army's transport aircraft, and the stock shot up after rumors spread that it was favored to get the work. Unfortunately, the contract was awarded to another firm and the stock came crashing down, losing twenty percent of its value in one day. Less than twenty-four hours later, Don Leachman, the undisputed kingpin of the strike suit enterprise, filed a class action lawsuit alleging securities fraud.

Jeffries worried because Leachman was legendary in his ability to plunder giant settlements from frightened companies, despite the legal validity of his claims. Chambers Aerospace was now in his crosshairs.

After a brief meeting with Chambers, Jeffries reviewed the suit and quickly determined that it had no merit. He called Don Leachman, hoping that he could deal with his adversary in a collegial manner.

"Look Don, from one attorney to another, you're barking up the wrong tree here. The case you filed has no merit. I guarantee you there's no basis for recovery here."

Leachman chuckled condescendingly. "What the hell are you talking about? I don't give a shit about the merits. This is business."

Jeffries was taken aback by Leachman's forceful manner. Usually, other attorneys showed deference, or at the least the appropriate amount of respect. He was, after all, the general counsel for Chambers Aerospace. "You can't recover on a fraud suit with no evidence," Jeffries countered.

"Man, you *are* fucking clueless. I don't need a shred of evidence. You're going to have to hire an outside firm to defend yourself and they're going to bleed you. Let me give you a piece of advice. Talk to the attorneys from other companies I've sued. They'll teach you the drill and prevent you from making a fool of yourself in front of your board."

Jeffries felt foolish already. He had no idea what he was dealing with. He called a meeting with Chambers and his legal team to discuss the suit.

"Good afternoon everyone," Jeffries began. "As everyone here already knows, we've been served with a six hundred million dollar strike suit. We need to deal with this quickly. The stock price has already taken a huge hit and it's only going to get worse the longer this thing drags out. I think we should settle and move on. I don't want this thing dogging us for two or three years down the road."

A few others at the table nodded silently in agreement, but everyone looked at Chambers for his reaction.

"The suit alleges fraud," Chambers said evenly. "Is that right, Tom?"

"That's right, but let's not get sidetracked here. The issue is not whether there was any fraud; clearly, there wasn't. We need to decide how to deal with this from a business perspective. It's probably cheaper in the long run to settle the case rather than trying to fight it. I don't like that any more than you do, but it just isn't worth the cost, or risk, of defending."

"If we settle this, then we're admitting we did something wrong," Chambers said.

"No, I don't think that's true," Jeffries insisted. "Companies settle these cases all the time and everyone knows they didn't do anything wrong—it's just a cost of doing business. Besides, we can put language in the settlement agreement that says we admit no liability."

"If we settle this case, could these shysters sue us again?" Chambers asked. He rarely used the term "shyster" except when he was pissed off.

"Yeah, they could," Jeffries conceded.

"Then it seems to me that in the long run we're better off not settling. If they know we're willing to crumble, they'll attack again. The way I see it, if we settle, we're either admitting that we did something wrong or that we're too chickenshit to stand up for ourselves. Now, we all know that we didn't do anything wrong, and *I* know we don't have any chickenshits in this room." Chambers made eye contact with each person at the table. "As far as the stock price is concerned, I'm by far the biggest shareholder so I've got the most to lose if it continues going down. But I don't give a damn about that if it means selling my integrity. If the other shareholders expect me to do that, then they've invested in the wrong company."

Jeffries sighed and slumped in his chair. "All right, David. It's obviously your call, but the plaintiff's attorneys have scheduled a settlement meeting that I've agreed to attend. I think you should come with me. It'll give you an idea of the kind of people we're dealing with."

Chambers nodded. "Okay."

* * *

Chambers Aerospace was a public company with a market capitalization of almost fifteen billion dollars. It produced civilian and military aircraft as well as avionics and other components. Although it wasn't the biggest aerospace company in the world, it consistently created the most innovations and secured more patents every year than any other company. Even its rivals conceded that Chambers Aerospace employed the most talented engineers in the business.

The company was the first to develop an unmanned aerial vehicle, also known as a UAV—a drone plane that flies remotely without a pilot. Development of this aircraft had catapulted the company into a leadership position in the aerospace industry and the U.S. military saw great promise in the hardware. Privately, many of the military's top brass figured that UAVs would be used almost exclusively in future wars, drastically reducing the number of U.S. casualties. The planes could travel at much greater speeds and maneuver at radically steeper angles than manned planes, which were subject to the limitations of the human body. Consequently, UAV's were much harder to shoot down or even track on a radar screen.

David Chambers served as the chief executive officer, chairman of the board, and the largest single shareholder. Ernesto Sosa held the title of chief operating officer, and had responsibility for running the company's day-to-day operations. The company's headquarters were in Novato, California, twenty miles north of San Francisco, with additional manufacturing and design facilities in San Diego and Wichita, Kansas.

Unlike other firms, Chambers Aerospace was not unionized, despite continuous pressure and badgering by union bosses. The company paid its employees a competitive wage plus what their union dues would've been, so they were effectively higher-paid than their unionized counterparts.

The unions accused Chambers of being anti-labor. Chambers accused the union of being irrelevant and corrupt. "We have an anti-parasite policy," Chambers would say whenever he was asked about his refusal to deal with the unions. The employees agreed, consistently rebuffing overtures from national union officials attempting to expand their franchise. Naturally, the power elites in the union considered Chambers a bitter enemy, and they urged the politicians they owned to pressure him. But Chambers never backed down.

* * *

Chambers and Jeffries walked into the well-appointed offices of Millard, Grunfeld & Leachman, which occupied the top five floors of the tallest building in San Francisco's financial district. The lobby was draped in imported marble with handcrafted designer furniture on either side of the reception area, staffed by three attractive female receptionists.

"Please have a seat, gentlemen," one of the women said. "Can I offer you something to drink?"

"No thanks," Jeffries said.

Chambers sat down and picked up a notebook that said, "Millard, Grunfeld & Leachman: Press Mentions." It contained newspaper clippings and magazine articles about the firm, although most of the articles were about Don Leachman, the firm's unquestioned leader, or in legal parlance, the person who brought in the most money. Chambers flipped through the notebook; there were several pictures of Leachman posing with top-shelf politicians, including the President. Leachman was a large donor to both major political parties and he always got the favors he paid for.

Chambers stopped when he came to an article entitled "Leachman Blazes the Trail for a New Breed of Legal Entrepreneurs." *Entrepreneur!* Chambers silently fumed. He fought the urge to rip the article out of the notebook and tear it to shreds. *Entrepreneurs are creators. Leachman is a destroyer.* Chambers was already angry about wasting his time at Leachman's office and the article made his blood pressure shoot up even higher.

A few minutes later, an attractive, dark-haired woman escorted them to a conference room with a long, deeply burnished mahogany table and an unobstructed view of the Golden Gate Bridge. They waited for a few more minutes while the woman took the elevator up to the top floor to retrieve Leachman. She heard him on the phone as she got closer to his office.

"I'll haul his ass into court and smack him!" Leachman bellowed. "Yeah. If they don't put up a shitload of money, the nukes are gonna launch! You tell that son of a bitch if he doesn't cough up ten million, I'm gonna take his fucking condo in Aspen!" Leachman slammed the phone down.

The dark-haired woman walked into Leachman's eight-hundred-square-foot office, appointed with floor to ceiling windows offering panoramic views of San Francisco Bay. One corner of the office featured a slate-topped bar with a selection of some of the most expensive cognacs in the world. Another corner boasted a twenty-foot-long table, which displayed several rows of alabaster "tombstones." Each tombstone memorialized one of Leachman's huge out-of-court settlements. To be tombstone-worthy, the settlement had to be at least twenty million dollars.

To Leachman's credit, he had developed the ultimate business model—or anti-business model. He filed an astronomical number of lawsuits and rounding up plaintiffs was never a problem. In addition to stockbrokers and other lawyers who brought him clients, Leachman had a roster of shareholders who owned stakes in hundreds of companies and allowed him to attach their names to his suits. These professional plaintiffs turned up repeatedly in suit after suit, with one man racking up forty-two appearances, including two appearances over a year after he had died. Luckily for Leachman, despite their willingness to participate in his lawsuits, his plaintiffs always stayed out of his way, leading him to boast, "I have the greatest practice in the world. I can ignore my clients." Leachman also employed an army of attorneys whose only job was to draft complaints and monitor the financial wires, looking for new companies to sue.

Millard, Grunfeld & Leachman almost always served as lead plaintiff's counsel in any large class action, and this allowed them to control the case and the other law firms involved. If any of the attorneys at the other firms crossed him, Leachman would do whatever he could to make their lives miserable, including cutting them out of future cases. Since Leachman controlled most of the big money strike suit litigation, no one challenged his tactics.

"Don, your two o'clock settlement meeting is ready for you," the woman said.

Leachman looked up and smiled. "Thanks, babe."

The woman's face hardened and she walked out.

Leachman was shaped like a pear with a fiery red face and an unkempt mop of brown hair. As a youngster, other kids teased him with the nickname "doughboy." But nobody made fun of him now—he was a ruthless assassin who showed no mercy to his enemies. Today, he was wearing a ten-thousand-dollar, charcoal gray Armani suit with a tie the color of a well-aged Cabernet Sauvignon. He had been wearing the tie lately for good luck whenever he had a settlement meeting with the potential for a big payoff—a payoff big enough so that he could buy a winery in Napa Valley, the next item on his wish list.

When Leachman came down to the conference room, two other men joined him—Clive Harrison, the firm's damages expert, and a young associate named Adam Sharf. Harrison's specialty was calculating how much a company's "fraud" damaged the shareholders. Leachman could always count on Harrison to come up with a huge number. Privately, Harrison joked that his damage calculations were based on the philosophy of "If you can't dazzle them with brilliance, baffle them with bullshit." To the eyes of most people, it was impossible to tell whether his calculations were bullshit or brilliance because they were excruciatingly complicated. But it usually wasn't necessary for anyone to understand them because most of the cases settled before trial. Harrison's calculations just provided the big stick, which Leachman trotted out in settlement meetings to scare his victims.

Sharf was just learning the trade and was impressed by the minimal amount of work required to plunder a huge settlement. He was also impressed by Leachman's ten-million-dollar hilltop estate in Marin and his seven-thousand-square-foot vacation home on Lake Tahoe. Nothing wrong with wanting a piece of the good life, he figured.

The men exchanged introductions and Leachman passed control of the meeting over to Harrison.

"We have some numbers here that I think are reasonable in light of the damages suffered," Harrison began as he passed copies of a document to Chambers and Jeffries. Jeffries scanned it quickly while Chambers stared at Leachman's triple chin. *I wonder what makes a man like this possible?* Chambers reflected that he knew the answer but couldn't bear to dwell on it.

Jeffries looked up from the document. "Well, first of all, I..."

"Tom," Chambers interrupted. "Sorry to cut you off, but I can save us some time here. I don't know what this document says and I don't care. The settlement terms are as follows." Chambers paused and then looked directly at Leachman, holding up a clenched fist. "You can have every dime that you're able to pry from this hand."

Sharf's eyes widened. He had never seen anybody stand up to Leachman.

Leachman didn't flinch, but he quickly flew into attack mode. "Oh no! No! No! No! We will bury you! Destroy you! You've got no fucking idea who you're dealing with!"

"Who I'm dealing with!" Chambers jumped out of his chair. "How about bloodsucking parasites! You will not extort money from me! Not while I have breath in this body!"

Leachman smirked. He had seen defiant attitudes before, only to wear his opponent down with a blitzkrieg of expensive and exhaustive legal maneuvering. "That's it then, this meeting is over. Please get the fuck out of my office."

Chambers walked past Leachman, glaring through seething teeth, "If you slander my name again…"

Adam Sharf watched Chambers walk out and he felt an unexpected shot of adrenaline rush through his veins. He couldn't articulate the cause of the feeling, nor could he explain the dream he had that night of Chambers crushing him like an insect.

CHAPTER 9

I have examined all the known superstitions of the world, and I do not find in our particular superstition of Christianity one redeeming feature. They are all alike founded on fables and mythology. Millions of innocent men, women and children, since the introduction of Christianity, have been burnt, tortured, fined and imprisoned. What has been the effect of this coercion? To make one half the world fools and the other half hypocrites; to support roguery and error all over the earth.

—THOMAS JEFFERSON, LETTER TO WILLIAM SHORT

Newhall walked from his office into the expansive lobby of Infinity Headquarters. He admired the cool, polished sheets of granite covering the floor, and the Italian Renaissance furniture that his wife had recently picked up on a trip to Europe. He couldn't help but smile. She had impeccable taste.

John Heilbrenner had been waiting for a few minutes, lounging casually on a leather couch.

"Good afternoon, Mr. Heilbrenner," Newhall greeted amiably. "I'm Robert Newhall."

Heilbrenner stood up. "Nice to meet you." The men shook hands and quickly sized each other up.

The guy's not much to look at, Newhall thought. Heilbrenner's eyes flittered nervously when he spoke and his pale skin had a sickly, wax paper quality. When he smiled, he revealed cigarette-colored teeth, although he didn't smoke.

"Let's go back to my office and we can talk."

"This is quite a building," Heilbrenner offered as the men strode down a long hallway.

"Yes. Thank you. God inspires us here."

"People usually aren't as impressive as the buildings they create for themselves."

What the hell's that supposed to mean? Newhall wondered. He glanced at Heilbrenner and made eye contact, but quickly looked away. He suddenly felt naked. Neither man spoke again until they reached Newhall's office.

"Have a seat," Newhall said gruffly, motioning to a chair on the other side of his desk.

"Thanks." Heilbrenner took off his jacket and placed it on a coat rack next to the door, and then sat down.

Well, let's see what this guy's got. Newhall wasn't entirely sure what he wanted out of a second-in-command, but he kept imagining a gritty street fighter or a barroom brawler who would intimidate and crush his rivals. "You've got quite a reputation, Mr. Heilbrenner. What interests you about the Infinity Network?"

Heilbrenner sat back comfortably in his chair and crossed his legs. "You're a charismatic leader and you appear to have at least some understanding of what motivates people. You've had some success so far, but I can help you serve "God" more efficiently." Heilbrenner paused on the word "God," moving the first two fingers of each hand to indicate quotation marks around it.

"What is that?" Newhall squinted. He had expected Heilbrenner to say something about how he wanted to serve the Lord, or at least do something for the public good.

"I'm not a true believer either," Heilbrenner said matter-of-factly. "But I do believe in what you're doing."

"What is this?" Newhall reacted. He was caught off-guard, but slipped quickly into the role of morally indignant preacher. "I'm not sure what you mean by that, but I can assure you that it isn't funny!"

"It's not supposed to be funny," Heilbrenner responded casually.

Newhall stared hard at Heilbrenner and wondered whether the man really had the ability to read him so accurately. *No, he's bluffing. Put him in his place.* "I don't know where you get off..." Newhall scowled.

"Are you always this obvious?" Heilbrenner retorted incredulously.

Newhall suddenly felt paralyzed by an uncomfortable jolt of adrenaline. He thought of being caught cheating in school. There was no escape, only surrender.

"This was a waste of time." Heilbrenner stood up, grabbed his coat, and started toward the door. "Good luck."

"Wait, wait, wait," Newhall pleaded.

Heilbrenner stopped and turned back around.

"Have a seat. Please. Let's start again."

"Okay." Heilbrenner hung his coat back on the rack, but remained standing. "Are we done playing games?"

"Yes, yes, you were saying...what...something about belief?"

"I believe in the same things you do," Heilbrenner said. "We can help these people and they need our help, but in order to do that, you need my help."

"What can you do?"

"When I was in advertising, I designed ad campaigns that generated billions of dollars in sales and made thousands of people rich. You're trying to sell religion. I can sell that as easily as I've sold everything else."

Newhall couldn't believe what he was hearing. He studied the man standing before him intently; he wasn't used to the forcefully direct manner in which Heilbrenner spoke, but he was equally taken aback by how right it felt, as if Heilbrenner had completely figured him out and knew exactly how to entice him. "Go on," Newhall said.

"When I was in politics, I ran campaigns that raised millions of dollars and catapulted candidates into power. Do you really want to succeed? I mean really succeed by fulfilling your destiny and seizing the power God has offered you."

Newhall nodded, but didn't smile. He didn't want to reveal that the thought of great power intoxicated him.

"I'm not talking about leading a few congregations," Heilbrenner continued. "That's a waste of time. I'm talking about being the most powerful religious leader in the United States. If that's what you're after, I can take you there."

"How?" Newhall challenged.

Heilbrenner smiled confidently. "Let's just say that I do whatever it takes to get the job done—without any limitations."

Newhall's face lit up and a warm, relaxed feeling flowed over his body. "You're an interesting man, Mr. Heilbrenner. I'd like to discuss your role in the Network. Do you mind if I call you John?"

* * *

John Heilbrenner, age seven, screamed as his stepfather slid the thick black belt through the loops of his pants. He tried to run, but the large man grabbed him by the neck and threw him down onto the couch, holding the belt in one hand and pulling Heilbrenner's pants down with the other. The beating started slowly at first, but the force and tempo increased with each blow, digger deeper and deeper into the tender skin of Heilbrenner's buttocks. But after every strike, John Heilbrenner's resolve hardened.

The identity of Heilbrenner's biological father was unknown. He had been conceived after a one-night stand between his mother and a man she had met at a bar. Although his mother never saw the man again and Heilbrenner had never met him, Heilbrenner had inherited the DNA of a genius.

Heilbrenner never got along with his stepfather who was a bitter, mediocre man. He fought with and physically abused Heilbrenner's mother, and then blamed the young boy for the couple's fights. Although Heilbrenner recognized his stepfather as a pitiful man, he had nevertheless learned many self-destructive behaviors. In school, he berated his teachers when they made a mistake or couldn't answer his questions. He did the same thing with other kids who couldn't match his intellectual prowess. But perhaps his worst trait was dishonesty. He lied constantly and learned to make up convincing stories—stories so detailed and realistic that no one figured he could have made them up.

He both loved and hated his mother. He hated her for relying on her husband or God to make things right. But his mother's life taught him one of his most important early lessons—people were easily dominated and controlled, especially if they had low self-esteem.

In high school, Heilbrenner wasn't popular because he had no patience for people who lacked his mental gifts. Most of the boys he gravitated to were tougher kids from similarly abusive backgrounds. His classes generally bored him, but he took an interest in journalism because he recognized the power of the written word. He tried to join the school newspaper, which was run by a popular clique of students, but they convinced the faculty advisor to exclude him. Heilbrenner ignored the rebuff. He started his own newspaper in his basement with old equipment that he had salvaged from a printing factory. He wrote few articles, instead employing friends to dig up embarrassing gossip about his rivals at the school's official paper. Then he devoted most of his copy to attacking them.

Despite his deviousness, Heilbrenner achieved good grades and scored in the top one percentile of his college entrance exams. During his senior year, he accepted a scholarship to a state university. Before he moved away to school, he helped his mother find an attorney and file for a divorce. Then he threw all of his stepfather's clothes onto the driveway and doused them with lighter fluid. When his stepfather discovered what he had done, he charged into Heilbrenner's bedroom, but Heilbrenner was ready. He jumped out from behind the door and swung a lead pipe into the side of his stepfather's face, shattering his jaw and crushing the orbital bone below his eye. Then he kicked the man in the ribs for several minutes, only stopping because his leg got tired. The beating fractured most of his stepfather's ribs and collapsed one of his lungs. When he was sure that his stepfather wouldn't be getting up, Heilbrenner went outside and enjoyed a warm bonfire.

Heilbrenner received probation for the attack, but never saw his stepfather again. After spending two months in the hospital, his stepfather moved into a trailer, but it burned into charred rubble shortly after he bought it. The police never determined the cause of the fire.

In college, Heilbrenner earned the nickname "Spock," after the character in the TV show *Star Trek*. One of his fraternity brothers described him as "cold and calculating with a brilliant mind that'll rip you apart." He graduated first in his class with a double major in psychology and political science and landed a job with an advertising agency in New York. He carried the title of Creative Analyst, but his coworkers referred to him informally as the "manipulation specialist." Heilbrenner designed ad campaigns that were devastatingly effective— selling laundry detergent, beer, deodorant, and a host of other consumer products to people across the demographic spectrum.

Although he didn't have a charismatic personality, often remaining silent with a dull look on his face, his demeanor belied the intricate workings of his mind. When he did speak, it was clear that he had taken detailed mental notes of everyone and everything around him, and had drawn the appropriate conclusions. Heilbrenner was especially adept at quickly sizing people up and determining their weaknesses. Nobody had greater skill in understanding the essence of human motivation and behavior, and then exploiting that knowledge for advantage.

Because of his legendary success in the advertising business, other opportunities followed. A virtually unknown candidate running for governor of New York tapped him at the age of twenty-eight to work on his political campaign. Although a political neophyte, Heilbrenner learned the ropes of the campaign process quickly, adding to his already formidable Machiavellian instincts. He learned one of the most important principles of right-wing politics—people are more motivated by what they hate than by what they love, and that trying to inspire voters was much less effective than spreading negative rumors.

During the course of his career, Heilbrenner piloted two successful campaigns for governor and three for the United States Senate. At the time of his job interview with Newhall, Heilbrenner, age forty-one, was considered the top political strategist in the country.

Newhall hired Heilbrenner officially as the Network's chief operations officer with responsibility for running its day-to-day operations, but he became much more, assuming the additional roles of speechwriter, press agent, economic adviser, and strategist. People who wanted something to happen in the Infinity Network called John Heilbrenner; he was the only man in the entire organization whom Newhall spoke with consistently, and the only person whom Newhall trusted.

Heilbrenner began his tenure at Infinity by familiarizing himself with its financial operations. He was impressed by what Newhall's former second-in-command Mike Watson had set up, although he immediately recognized that much of it was illegal. He reviewed all of the documentation carefully with Infinity's attorneys and concluded that the chances of getting caught were small. The government simply never challenged religious organizations, especially Christian ones.

Heilbrenner's biggest initial challenge was consolidating Newhall's power base. Other men of God, also intent on leading the faithful, presented a threat to Newhall's position as the undisputed leader of the nation's new religious awakening. Heilbrenner advised Newhall not to attack his rivals, but to invite them to become part of the morally pure society that he envisioned. Newhall succeeded where others failed because he presented a grand and intense vision of a new world order based strictly on God's law with no room for compromise. Followers couldn't resist the fanatical passion of his ideology, which freed them from making difficult moral choices and focused the full power of their frustration on people who were "destroying the fabric of the nation." Eventually, few challenged Newhall's status as the country's most prominent Christian, and most enthusiastically joined the Network, content to ride Newhall's star to heavenly greatness.

But there was one prominent preacher who refused to follow. Eddie Bidwell, a middle-aged, down-home pastor from Mississippi had been preaching across the Bible Belt for over thirty years. Bidwell was a formidable opponent because he had a large and loyal following, and was well-funded. Newhall invited him to join the Network, but Bidwell refused, preferring to lead his own ministry. Three months later, a supermarket tabloid published photos of Bidwell in the company of a prostitute. Although he denied having sex with the woman, Bidwell admitted kissing her, explaining that she had come on to him aggressively. He asked for forgiveness.

Newhall denounced Bidwell in a television interview that was broadcast across the South. "God shows no mercy for a man weak in the face of worldly temptations. We can pray for our Christian brother, but we can no longer follow any man who has let Satan get the better of him."

Heilbrenner quickly dispatched a team of Infinity evangelists to aggressively recruit members formerly loyal to Bidwell. Newhall didn't know who had taken the photos of Bidwell or why the prostitute had preyed on him. But John Heilbrenner knew.

Heilbrenner felt confident that all of Newhall's rivals were either on board or out of the way. It was time to expand the operation.

CHAPTER 10

Let no man deceive himself. If any man among you seemeth to be wise in this world, let him become a fool, that he may be wise. For the wisdom of this world is foolishness with God.

—BIBLE, 1 CORINTHIANS 3:18-19

Wayne Richardson, the Dean of Harvard Law School, knew that Martin Dushane's appointment to the faculty would be controversial, and he needed to appease several different constituencies. Catholics hated Dushane for humiliating the Church, as did affirmative action advocates who resented his stance against racial preferences. On the other hand, many in the Harvard community liked him for the same reasons and admired his academic and professional records. A few others, although unhappy with his views on affirmative action, nonetheless supported him because he was black and would increase the percentage of minorities on the Harvard faculty.

In order to defuse some of the opposition to Dushane's appointment, the Dean scheduled a press conference to introduce him. Prior to the press conference, Dushane met with the Dean, a man he didn't know much about, but couldn't help suspecting that there wasn't much to know. Although he came across as a little slow, Richardson had tremendous political skills—an ability to schmooze his friends and enemies alike. He had been elevated to Dean as a result of a compromise at Harvard between conservatives and liberals. Richardson was a safe choice because he stood for nothing, and thus wouldn't offend either group.

"Martin, all you have to do is say a few words about yourself; you know, about how you respect people of all religions, you're not anti-Catholic, etcetera. Just try to smooth things over with the Catholic community here. And don't talk about affirmative action; that's a divisive issue. Try to keep your remarks brief."

Dushane paid little attention.

On the day of the press conference, Dushane and Dean Richardson walked on to the stage of a large lecture hall. The Dean looked weedy, with thick, soda-bottle glasses and a suit that hung awkwardly from his gawky frame. He gave Dushane a knowing look as he adjusted the microphone. The room was overflowing with people—in the seats, in the aisles, and standing in the back.

"I've called you all here this afternoon to introduce the latest addition to the faculty at Harvard Law School. Most of you already know who Martin Dushane is so I'll keep my introductory remarks brief. For those of you who don't watch the news or read the papers, Mr. Dushane comes to us from the Suffolk County District Attorney's office here in Boston, where he spent the last four years as a prosecutor. He's also published several articles and I expect him to contribute greatly to the scholarship here as well. Please help me welcome Martin Dushane." The Dean stepped aside and started clapping. Most of the audience joined him, although there were a few loud boos.

Dushane stepped up to the podium and smiled at the audience. He was in a good mood and felt remarkably at ease. "Thank you very much,

Dean Richardson. I was hoping to get a few more boos, but I guess this is a quiet audience." A chorus of laughter mixed with boos erupted. Dushane waited until the noise died down and then continued. "It's a pleasure to be here with you today. I'm excited about joining the faculty here at Harvard. It's always been a dream of mine to be a law school professor and I'd like to thank Dean Richardson and others here at Harvard for making this dream come true.

"I realize that there's been some controversy regarding my appointment, particularly among the Catholic population and among proponents of racial preferences. While I don't have much to say about either religion or affirmative action above and beyond what I've already said, this is probably an opportune time for me to restate my basic philosophy since it's been badly misrepresented. Contrary to what's been said, I'm not anti-Catholic; I'm anti-criminal. When I was at the District Attorney's office, we prosecuted crimes—vicious crimes committed by vicious people. I won't make any apology for that. There's no doubt in my mind that we took appropriate and necessary action, both morally and legally. Beyond that, many people have expressed concern about my comments regarding the priesthood and religion in general. During the course of my work at the DA's office, I discovered that many deeply immoral people were in the priesthood or in the upper echelons of power in the Catholic Church. I'm talking about people with no regard for the welfare of others; people more concerned with their own power than helping their fellow man; people who looked the other way as lives were destroyed; people without a conscience."

The audience was quiet, shocked by the directness of Dushane's remarks.

"I don't know what's wrong with these people, but I can tell you what I saw. As we prepared the sexual abuse cases, we sought assistance from several prominent psychologists regarding the motivations of the priests, the bishops, and the Cardinal. We often sought this type of advice whenever we dealt with complex questions of motivation because we wanted to understand the psyche of each defendant. This would help us predict and deal with their behavior throughout the course of the trial. In these cases, we received numerous opinions about why a man would supposedly devote himself to good, yet consistently act in an evil way. We concluded that these people believed that the priesthood would provide them with a convenient social mask; a mask of respectability that they could hide behind. They deluded themselves into believing that they were moral because society anointed them with a badge of morality on the basis of their position in the Church."

A few loud boos rose from the audience. Dushane didn't attempt to speak over the noise. He scanned the audience of over five hundred people. In the back, some students were holding up a sign that said:

"No Hate at Harvard" in bright red letters. Another student was bobbing up and down with a sign that said, "Uncle Tom." Dushane chuckled lightly to himself. *Not too original*, he thought. He looked down toward the front of the room and a woman in the second row caught his attention. She was wearing a conservative gray suit with a high collar that wrapped around her delicate neck. She had lavish dark brown hair that cascaded down her shoulders, and large, deeply set blue eyes that lit up her soft, feminine face. She made eye contact with him and smiled suggestively. Dushane tried to smile back, but he stood there, unable to move. *That woman is absolutely gorgeous. My God!*

Dushane hesitated for a moment, and then quickly remembered that he wanted to talk about Ray Lassater. "I'd also like to comment briefly on Ray Lassater, my friend and mentor at the DA's office. Ray has been vilified in the press on several fronts, the most notable being that he had a conflict of interest in light of his personal history of being sexually abused. I worked side-by-side with Ray for four years and I can say without reservation that he is a man of tremendous integrity. He was the ideal person to prosecute the cases against the Church because he knew first-hand how the Church could shatter a person's life. Believe me, even though Ray is the toughest person I've ever met, I saw the anguish and pain he experienced.

"In the course of our criminal investigation, I spoke with many officials at the Boston Archdiocese, including Cardinal McManus and several of his bishops, and they never, not a single time, showed concern for their victims. In fact, they never even asked about the victims. They weren't sorry for what happened. They were sorry they got caught."

The Dean stepped up next to Dushane, gently tapped his back, and gave him a look that said, "Stop talking." Dushane ignored him and continued.

"My views of religion changed as a result of working with Ray. It's true, as I've been accused, that I am now a strong opponent of organized religion, but I'm nonetheless committed to respecting people of all beliefs." *Wow, that's a giant lie*, Dushane thought. *But whatever. Isn't that what religion is—socially acceptable lying?*

"I've written a few articles about the separation of church and state, and my view is that the government shouldn't take any action that even remotely endorses religion because with endorsement comes exclusion. Whenever the government takes any action that has even the slightest appearance of endorsing a specific religious sect, or religion generally, this can only result in people of different religions, or no religion, feeling excluded."

Dushane paused. The beautiful woman in the second row smiled at him again. He held her gaze until she looked away.

"Let me conclude my remarks by discussing racial preferences. I was lucky to grow up poor because I learned to enjoy life without material things, and I had to earn everything I got. I also got a taste of the values that keep people helpless and poverty-stricken. Poor people, and particularly poor blacks, are told that it's all right, and indeed a badge of honor, to be a victim. They're taught that society owes them something. And the thing that people don't realize is that this same brainwashing takes place constantly behind closed doors in black churches, black schools, black community organizations, and in black families. And then it gets reinforced by whites who treat us like invalids. I was lucky. In my family, relying on someone else for what I wanted out of life was totally unacceptable. But I see the attitude of dependence everywhere. From what I've observed as a black man who grew up in the ghetto, it's clear to me that most of the affirmative action proposals consist of a bait-and-switch game. The black, inner-city poor furnish the statistical evidence for the proposals, but the benefits go primarily to the people who don't need really need them. Most of the black youth where I grew up in New Orleans are totally ignored by the government; at least until it's time to compile those statistics and exploit white guilt.

"Many people have criticized me because they say that I wouldn't be here today if it wasn't for affirmative action. Let me state unequivocally…" Dushane paused. A young man was running down the steps toward the front of the room, his arms flailing, and yelling, "You! You're dead! You're dead!" The kid pulled out a handgun from the front of his pants as he barreled toward the podium. Dushane was so surprised that he didn't attempt to move until he heard the first shot blast out of the gun. The bullet missed him, careening off the back wall of the stage. Dushane tried to jump away from the podium, but the second shot hit him in the chest, knocking him down. Pain shot through his upper body as he fought to breathe, and blood oozed through his shirt, curdling in a thick, circular puddle around him. The shooter put the gun in his mouth and pulled the trigger, blowing his brains out the back of his head.

Dushane twitched in pain while the Dean hovered over him. He felt a dream-like sensation—things were either moving in slow motion or his thoughts were moving fast. Dushane had heard that your whole life flashes before your eyes when you think you're about to die. He was surprised to discover the truth of that statement.

* * *

Martin Dushane, age six, walked with his mother Vicky up the sidewalk to a large house in the Garden District of New Orleans. He grasped her hand tightly. Vicky knocked on the door and an attractive, smartly dressed, middle-aged woman greeted them.

"Hello Vicky, nice to see you," Janet Geautreaux said. "Please come in." Then she bent down to address the young Dushane. "And hello to you, Martin. How are you today?"

"I'm fine ma'am."

"So have you started school yet?"

"No ma'am. We start next week."

"Well, that's great. Why don't you come with me to the playroom? We have some new toys you might like."

Dushane took Janet's hand and followed her into the playroom while Vicky went into the kitchen and got the cleaning supplies from under the sink. Vicky cleaned two large houses a day, six days a week, and she couldn't afford day care. Luckily, most of her clients didn't mind that she brought her son along with her.

Dushane sat quietly in the playroom and stared blankly at the toys strewn across the thick plush-carpeted floor—blocks, coloring books, a fire truck, and a few stuffed animals. He didn't have much interest in any of them. He walked out of the room and went into the study, a warm, expansive space with dark wood paneling and a stately oak desk and black leather chair against the back wall. There were also two bookcases that entirely covered each of the room's side walls. Dushane stood in front of one of the bookcases and looked up at them. They stretched from the floor to the ceiling and seemed as wide as his Uncle Nat's pickup truck. Dushane liked all the different colors and shapes and the way some of the books were old and worn while others were shiny and new. He had never seen so many books in one room. None of the people in his neighborhood had books like that. Although he wasn't sure why, he wanted to know everything in every single one of the books.

Dushane came with his mother to the Geautreaux house twice a week and normally he wasn't left by himself. Janet Geautreaux had a son named Charlie who was the same age as Dushane and the boys took an immediate liking to each other despite their very different backgrounds.

Dushane and his mother lived in a crumbling section of New Orleans, a few blocks from the French Quarter. The neighborhood was dirty and run-down, but it was an improvement from the housing project where they had started. Vicky Dushane hated the projects and she didn't want her son exposed to a life teeming with bottom-dwellers who inhaled the sickness of victimhood and despair like toxic waste. With the help of her brother Nathaniel, she had rented a small house in a better neighborhood with many colorful old homes, although few of the houses were well maintained. Dushane had to avoid walking too close to the house next door because dead animal smells wafted from the open windows and the back yard. Despite the condition of the neighborhood, Dushane grew up in a relatively stable environment. He never knew his father, who took off shortly after he was born, but his Uncle Nat largely assumed that role and made sure that Dushane never succumbed to the seduction of underclass values.

Dushane began working shortly after his eleventh birthday. His first job was a paper route that required him to get up at five o'clock every morning and deliver papers on his bike. He took the job seriously, never missing a day for three years and saving almost fifteen hundred dollars. When he was fourteen, he started working for a builder named James Mitchell. Mitchell constructed residential housing around the New Orleans area and he appreciated Dushane's work ethic and reliability. Mitchell had also hired his uncle on several occasions to do custom carpentry and cabinetry work, and the two men counted each other as friends.

After two summers of hot, humid construction work, and shortly after his sixteenth birthday, Mitchell gave Dushane a 1976 cherry-red Pontiac Grand Prix with a four-hundred-cubic-inch engine. Dushane figured that it went from sixty to one-twenty faster than any other car on the road. The only problem was keeping it on the road; the car needed engine work. Luckily, his friend Charlie Geautreaux knew a lot about cars.

Charlie Geautreaux was an anomaly in his family, which had been in New Orleans for almost two hundred years and was well established in New Orleans society. Charlie hated the formality of his parents—the fancy clothes, stiff manners, and social pretensions. But despite his disdain for the trappings of wealth, his tall, lean body and sharp, angular features gave him the appearance of being well-bred and refined.

One evening at the dinner table, Charlie's father, who was influential in city politics, described the city's current black mayor as a nigger who belonged in a cotton field. Charlie got up from the table and told his dad that he would never eat with family again if he had to listen to his dad's racist rhetoric. Charlie's dad told him to sit down. Charlie told his dad to go to hell and stormed out of the room.

Charlie's father was silent for a week and then finally apologized when it was clear that his son wasn't going to back down. Charlie did back down on one issue, though. He was not a good student. He would get F's in school and proclaim proudly to Dushane, "F is for freedom baby. F is for freedom." He didn't want anyone to hold a grade over his head. His parents protested, threatening to take his car away, so he finally relented and pulled his grades up—almost effortlessly.

Charlie Geautreaux knew more about cars than most mechanics so he kept Dushane's car running smoothly. The body was still a piece of junk, with chipped, faded paint, dented doors, and a trunk that wouldn't open, but Dushane didn't care. He figured that if he ever decided to get rid of it, he would enter it in a demolition derby.

The car had an old cassette deck and Geautreaux helped Dushane install a new set of speakers. Unfortunately, Geautreaux didn't know nearly as much about stereos as he did about engines. Sometimes the sound would cut out and one of the boys would have to bang on the dash to get it going again. They drove around listening to music as loud as the speakers would go and belt out the words to their favorite songs.

Dushane loved the car because of the feeling of freedom that you can only get with a beater; being able to trash it without caring. In a way, Dushane felt like he was cheating because he did not care about material possessions like society, through its vapid culture of advertising and television sitcoms, told him he was supposed to. Sometimes, Dushane and Geautreaux would drive by the local mall and watch people walking out with arms full of plastic. "What a waste," Geautreaux would say. Dushane agreed, thinking of one of his Uncle Nat's favorite sayings: "You don't own your possessions. Your possessions own you."

Dushane lived with his mother, but was raised to a large extent by his uncle—born Nathaniel, but known by everyone as Nat. Nat was thick and muscular, with broad shoulders and powerful hands, built for a life of hard, physical labor. He worked almost every day of his life since leaving school in the ninth grade. He worked in construction mostly, and did some carpentry. He had a large, clapboard workshop behind his house where he built shelves and bookcases, most of which he sold to retail furniture stores. He also built custom cabinetry for many of the most expensive homes in New Orleans.

While he was out in the workshop, Nat usually listened to Miles Davis or Duke Ellington—Davis when he felt energetic and upbeat and the Duke when he wanted to relax. Dushane liked the music too, and he spent many hours enjoying the warm sound flowing out of Nat's old phonograph, a vintage 1957 RCA with a solid oak case. It was one of the few possessions Nat treasured.

Nat was generally a quiet and reserved man who kept his thoughts to himself. He didn't like to talk about his past, but he spoke often of his nephew's future. "Martin," he would say, and then lean forward, close to the young boy's face, "In my day, we didn't have the kind of opportunities you have. Appreciate your opportunities and take advantage of them. And don't ever let the white man—or any man—tell you that you ain't good enough. Believe in yourself—always."

Dushane had heard this several times, but he had also heard his uncle talk disparagingly about white people; calling them white trash or racists. When Dushane was seventeen, he finally asked his uncle why he talked about white people that way.

Nat sat silent for a minute with a frown on his face. He looked at his nephew with heavy eyes and then looked away. "I've never told anyone this story, not even your mother."

Dushane waited expectantly for his uncle to tell the story, but he just sat there muttering to himself.

"Uncle Nat?"

"Ah…well…maybe it'll be good for you to know about it," Nat said in a low voice, his tough exterior suddenly melting away.

"I was with a good friend of mine out in Metairie, many years ago. His name was Marvin, but everyone called him Red because he had a temper on him, and he didn't take crap from no one. We were working construction on some houses out there. It was tough to get work like that in white neighborhoods back in those days, but the owner of the construction company was a good man and he didn't care what color we were as long as we did a good job. One night we were coming back from work. I had this old, beat-up truck. It wasn't much of a truck, but we carried our tools and such in the bed. Anyway, we were driving back and somehow we got a flat tire. I pulled over, took out the spare and started jacking it up. Next thing I know, these two drunken white boys, probably not much older than twenty, stopped their truck on the other side of the street. I'll never forget that faded black truck. It had these big tires and a shiny metal grill, but the main thing I remember about it was this Confederate flag they had pasted on the window.

"Red was leaning against the back of my truck smoking a cigarette, when one of the boys yelled over to him, 'Whacha doin' boy?' Whites usually wouldn't call you a nigger to your face, but they'd still try to put you down by calling you boy. Red just stood there, puffing on that cigarette, not saying anything. Then, the kid said again, 'I'm talking to you boy. Whacha doin'?'

"Now, I was surprised that Red didn't jump all over those guys when they called him boy. At the construction site, when any white guy called him boy, Red got up in their face. He'd even get in their face if they called me boy. Those guys would back down every time. Red was one of the few guys who stood up to them and you could tell from the look on his face that you didn't want to mess with him; he had fire in his eyes. But on this particular night, I think he was tired from a long day of work because he just said quietly, 'What the hell do you want?'"

"'I wanna know why they's two niggas in my neighborhood,' the kid said."

"Red dropped his cigarette and walked toward their truck. 'What did you call me?'"

"'Nigga,' the kid says again and then he drives the truck a little further up the street so Red can't get near him. I'm still kneeling down, jacking up the truck so I can change the tire, and I says to Red, 'Forget about those boys, we need to change this tire and get on back home.' Red looked back it me with those wild eyes of his, made him look crazy, and he said, 'They can't talk like that. I ain't going to let them boys talk like that.' Now, I didn't like hearing the word nigger either, but I didn't see no point to staying around there and arguin.' You ain't gonna solve nothin' that way. Anyway, they drove the truck a little bit further down the road and then turned it around. Red was standing in the middle of the road, waiting for them to come back. They start driving back, honking the horn and yelling, coming closer and closer to us. Red was still standing out there waitin,' and then the truck sped up, comin' straight for Red. I think he must've been caught off-guard, expectin' them to stop, but then he realized that he needed to get out of the way. But when he tried to move, he slipped on somethin' and fell to his knees. The kid driving the truck tried to swerve out of the way at the last second, but he hit Red square with one side of the truck. It threw him a good ten feet or so off the road and he landed on his head. I jumped from where I was sittin' and ran over to him. His body was all contorted and I could tell that one of his legs was broken because the bone was popped right out through his skin. I was so scared. I leaned down, but Red was barely breathin' and them kids took off. I picked Red up and put him in the bed of the truck. I drove as fast as I could to the emergency room in Metairie. I ran in there and told them my friend was hurt real bad and we needed help, but they told me to wait; sit down and wait. Can you believe that? My friend is dyin' and they're telling me to wait. I ran back outside to Red, but there was nothin' I could do; he was unconscious, still barely breathing. I didn't want to move him because I was afraid I would hurt him worse. I was just holding his hand, telling him to breathe; just breathe I kept sayin'. Finally, someone came out to the truck and put Red on a stretcher, but it was too late. After an hour or so, the doctor came out and told me Red was dead."

Uncle Nat paused and took a handkerchief out of his shirt pocket. A small tear dribbled down his cheek; he wiped it away quickly.

"The next day, I went over to the police station in Metairie and these white cops start givin' me this attitude like 'What the hell are you doing here?' I said, 'My friend was murdered last night and we need to find out who did it.' I gave them as much description of the truck and the boys as I could, but I didn't see the license plate or nothin'. I figured they could at least look for that Confederate flag on the window, but the police told me they didn't have enough description. Then, they asked me what we were doing in Metairie. They said it like they were accusing me of somethin.' I got real mad and I said, 'We got as much right to be in Metairie as anyone else, and my friend was murdered by a couple of white boys, and the police...the police, they better do somethin' about it!' I stormed out of there; I wanted to kill someone I was so mad. Then I checked back at the police station a few times, but they never did nothin' about it. My friend died for nothin.'"

Nat drew in a deep breath and exhaled a long sigh, as though his memory had been eased of a long burden. Then the tears began streaming down his face as he let his head sink into his hands. It was the first time Dushane had ever seen his uncle cry and he didn't know what to say. "I'm sorry Uncle Nat," he said finally and put his hand on his uncle's knee. He decided that he wouldn't ever let his uncle down.

Dushane and his mother lived comfortably on her earnings as a house cleaner and Dushane's contributions from his construction job, but two of Vicky's best clients moved away during the same summer and her income decreased substantially. When school started again, Dushane had to quit his construction job, so the only money coming in was Vicky's depleted house cleaning earnings. She had very little savings, making it a struggle to pay for basic necessities. One day when Dushane came home from school, she told him that the only solution was for them to apply for public assistance. Dushane protested that they shouldn't accept handouts, but his mother said that there was no alternative. "Let's talk to Uncle Nat about this," Dushane pleaded, but his mother already felt too indebted to Uncle Nat and she didn't want to burden him further.

Dushane and his mother took the bus down to the government office to fill out a formal application for welfare. On the ride, Dushane kept his head down and averted his eyes from people getting on and off the bus, fearful that they would see dependency written all over his face. When they got to the office, they waited in line for an hour, and then filled out the paperwork on a wobbly metal desk. Dushane thought he might suffocate.

The first check arrived a month later and the money continued coming for the following three months, along with a visit from a caseworker who interviewed Dushane and his mother to evaluate how they were spending the money. Dushane squirmed throughout the interview and had trouble keeping his eyes from the floor. He couldn't imagine what Uncle Nat would say if he saw the scene and he still felt conflicted over accepting public assistance. The money obviously helped and Dushane had no interest in doing without. On the other hand, he always felt sick and shameful whenever he thought that he and his mother were relying on strangers to take care of them. Finally, after listening to several minutes of the case worker's bureaucratic drone and watching the submissive look on his mother's face, Dushane snapped.

"I can't do this! I can't take another check! Never! No more of this!"

The caseworker looked at him incredulously.

"Quiet down, Martin," his mother ordered.

"No! I can't live this way!"

"Sit down, Martin!" his mother yelled.

Dushane stormed out the front door and ran over to Uncle Nat's place.

"Uncle Nat! Uncle Nat!"

"What the hell's wrong, boy?"

"Mom and I...we...we went on welfare, and the caseworker came over and...and I told her I couldn't take any more handouts, and then mom yelled at me, and...and then I ran over here," Dushane rambled, trying to catch his breath.

"Slow down, boy. Calm down. You're saying you and Vicky went on welfare? When did this happen? Why didn't either of you tell me about it? We need to straighten this whole thing out."

Dushane and Uncle Nat marched back to Vicky's house. Nat barreled through the doorway with Dushane following close behind. The caseworker was still sitting in the living room.

"We can take care of this situation," Uncle Nat said to the caseworker. "There's been a misunderstanding here."

"Nat, no..." Vicky started, but Nat cut her off.

"There's not going to be any discussion about this," he said as he moved his hands out and down, in a gesture of finality. "My family ain't going to take no handouts."

The caseworker mumbled something, picked up her papers, and walked out. The Dushane family sat down to talk.

"Listen here," Nat said. "Martin, are you ready to start working again to help out your mom?"

"Of course, but I can't work construction any more because of school."

"I know that. I don't want to disrupt your schoolwork, but let me give James Mitchell a call. He might be able to help us."

Nat called Mitchell and explained the situation. Luckily, Mitchell knew a number of businessmen who owned retail establishments in the downtown area and he was able to arrange an interview at one of them for Dushane. Dushane caught the bus downtown to meet Jerry Klein, the owner of a five and dime. Based on the recommendation from Mitchell, Klein hired Dushane on the spot as a stock boy at a salary of $3.35 an hour for twenty hours a week after school and on the weekends. Dushane made about $275 dollars a month, which was $25 dollars more than they received from public assistance. But to Dushane it seemed like much more. The family never took another government handout.

Dushane attended high school a few blocks from his house at an institution best known for its football program, which usually produced one of the best teams in the city. The school didn't have a reputation as an academic powerhouse, with less than ten percent of its graduating class going on to college. In spite of that, Dushane's mother and Uncle Nat encouraged his studies.

At the beginning of his senior year, Dushane was near the top of his class and he had scored in the top ten percent nationally on his SAT so he was virtually guaranteed admission to a good university, with a chance for an academic scholarship. His guidance counselor, Francie Gibbons, helped him obtain applications to several universities and he spent several hours with his mother filling them out. All that was left to do was review the applications with Ms. Gibbons and then send them off. On the appointed day, Dushane strode confidently into Ms. Gibbon's office, a cramped but homey space with numerous pictures of her family displayed liberally on her desk.

"Hi, Ms. Gibbons. How are you today?" Dushane said.

"I'm great, Martin," she said enthusiastically and motioned to a chair on the opposite side of her desk. Gibbons was white and had spent the first fifteen years of her career at one of the best private high schools in the city. But she had eventually lost interest in helping rich kids who, for the most part, didn't need her help. She decided that she wanted to have a bigger impact and her primary goal was to increase the percentage of students who went to college, a challenging task that kept her motivated.

Gibbons was in her late forties, with short, spiky blond hair. Her face was youthful, with soft skin and lips, and she had cheerful blue eyes. She was wearing her usual guidance counselor garb—a conservative suit with a colorful scarf slung carefully around her neck to give the outfit just a touch of pizzazz.

"I appreciate your help with my applications," Dushane said. "Have you had a chance to review them?"

"Yes I have," she said. "I'm very excited for you. You have an incredible record. I think you can attend college wherever you want." She paused and then put her hand gently on top of the applications. "I would like to go through your applications, though; I think we should make a few small changes."

"Okay," Dushane nodded.

Gibbons' voice took on a more serious tone. "I noticed on your applications that you didn't check any of the boxes regarding your race." She pointed to the section on one of the applications where there were several checkboxes: Hispanic, Pacific Islander, Eskimo/ Alaska Native, Chinese, Japanese, Southeast Asian, African-American,

Persian, Turkish, Arab, White, Native American, Afghani, and Indian/ Pakistani. "You need to mark this box," she continued, pointing to African-American. "Schools do take that into account and they won't accept your application if it isn't complete."

Dushane had figured that this issue would come up, so he was prepared. "Oh, well, the reason I didn't do that was because I was concerned they might not really look at my record. I mean I've worked hard. I want to make sure that they look at my record." Every time Dushane saw or thought of those little boxes, he thought of the day he saw his Uncle Nat's birth certificate, which described him as "colored." He also remembered what Uncle Nat had said about it. *Can you believe that? Colored. And now we're not even real Americans, we're African-Americans. They want us to pretend like we have some allegiance to Africa. I don't live in Africa. I'm an American. I'm sick of those damn sons of bitches treating us like second-class citizens.*

"Oh Martin, of course they will," Gibbons said in her most soothing and motherly voice. "Your record is exceptional. We're all very proud of you. But, you know, my job is to make sure you maximize your opportunities. I know how these universities work, what criteria are important. I want to give you the best possible chance."

"What do you think we should do then?" Dushane said softly.

"Well, first of all, we need to designate your race as African-American here. A lot of colleges have policies in place to help disadvantaged groups. African-Americans have great opportunities to be accepted at some of the best universities these days."

Dushane began to feel uncomfortable. *I know African-Americans get better treatment*, he thought, *but I don't want that. I can't do that.* He heard Uncle Nat's voice again. *"Don't you ever let the white man tell you that they's better than you. And don't ever take no handouts. Men don't take handouts."*

"I understand what you're saying, but I don't want special treatment. I just want what's fair."

"Of course. Of course," Gibbons said, trying to reassure him. "I just want to make sure that you have the best chance, you understand. Affirmative action programs are designed for your benefit. Why not take advantage of them?"

"Well, I just don't like being classified by the color of my skin. I mean I'm not from Africa; my mom and my uncle were born in Louisiana. We have a good family. I don't want special treatment."

"Well, don't worry about that Martin, you need to do what's best for you. You need to think about yourself. Don't concern yourself with all that other stuff."

"Don't concern myself?" Dushane felt the heat creep up the back of his neck. "I don't like being treated…I just want to be like everyone else." Dushane stood up and then sat back down and grabbed a pen off the desk. "Here, can I see those applications?" he said sharply.

Gibbons picked up the stack and passed it across the desk. Dushane rifled through the applications quickly and checked the box that said "White" on every document that asked for a racial classification. He passed the applications back across the desk to Ms. Gibbons. She thumbed though them slowly. "You can't do this," she pleaded. "This is dishonest."

Dushane stood up again. "So is all this box-checking!" He was angry, but checked himself. "I'm sorry, Ms. Gibbons. I know you're trying to help, but I can't. I'll send these applications in myself." Dushane grabbed the applications and walked out.

Dushane lied about his race on every single one of his applications, but he was accepted to a state college and received a partial scholarship that covered seventy-five percent of his expenses. The remainder he paid himself, with a little help from his Uncle Nat who had been saving for his nephew's college education for several years. Dushane tried to refuse the gift, but Uncle Nat insisted. "I'm gonna make damn sure you get the education I never got."

A few weeks before his college classes were scheduled to start, Dushane went on a road trip to Florida with Charlie Geautreaux. Geautreaux took his father's Ferrari, which he was expressly forbidden to drive. Geautreaux had made a copy of the key and prayed that his father hadn't written down the mileage before he left.

On a highway just outside of Tallahassee, they hit 130 miles per hour. Dushane was scared, but when he turned to his friend to tell him to slow down, he saw Dean Richardson. "Martin, can you hear me? Martin…"

When the paramedics arrived, Dushane was still conscious, focusing all of his mental energy on taking short, steady breaths. The emergency crew applied a pressure dressing to the wound to control the bloodletting and then started an IV. Then they put an oxygen mask on his face and hooked him up to an EKG monitor. Dushane passed out as they loaded him into the ambulance and rushed him to the hospital.

CHAPTER 11

[W]e all know that religious institutions provide particular services and receive specific benefits in exchange—but we generally tend to think of these economic aspects as consequences of religious organizations rather than its source. That is, we assume that doctrine comes first, and its implementation leads to particular economic and political behavior. This assumption may be misguided. Indeed, some crucial aspects of religious institutions make sense only if we understand what the market for religious services is like, what kind of commodity religious knowledge and ritual constitute.

One might think that the services provided by religious scholars—for example, ritual performance and scriptural knowledge—are essentially different from making shoes or tanning leather…[R]eligious goods and services are indeed different, but in a way that makes the priests' position much more fragile than that of other groups. Specialized craftsmen often have no difficulty maintaining exclusive supply, either because other people do not want to perform their…tasks, or because these tasks require technical knowledge and a long apprenticeship. In contrast, religious specialists supply something—rituals, a guarantee that they are efficient in dealing with supernatural agents—that could very easily be provided by outsiders.

Given the elusive nature of the services they provide, literate groups of religious specialists always remain in a precarious position…One solution is to turn the guild's ministration into a brand, that is, a service that is (1) distinct from what others could provide, (2) similar regardless of which member of the guild provides it, (3) easily recognizable by its particular features and (4) exclusively provided by one particular organization…Now the creation of recognizable brands of religious services has important consequences on the kinds of concepts put forward by religious institutions.

—PASCAL BOYER, *RELIGION EXPLAINED*

Robert Newhall pounded his fist on the table, startling Heilbrenner. "We've got to increase our revenues!"

"Well, to do that we've got to increase our membership," Heilbrenner responded.

"That's what I hired you to do—increase membership. How are you going to do that?"

"Trust me. I know what we need to do and I'm already on top of it, but we're going to need some help. I've hired a consulting firm with expertise in public relations and advertising. They're old friends of mine and they're ruthless. They've suggested an aggressive marketing campaign on all available media; increasing our advertising budget to twenty million dollars a year."

"Twenty million!" Newhall bellowed. "What are they going to do with twenty million?"

"They're going to increase our exposure; make Infinity a household name. Make us the name people turn to when they need spiritual direction. It's all in the marketing."

Newhall rubbed his chin and thought quietly. *Infinity as a household name. That's good. That means I'll be a household name.* "All right. Set up a meeting. What else?"

"We need to be smarter about our public speaking. You have a unique gift for communication, but instead of long sermons or TV programs, we should focus on short sound bites. We're never going to appeal to intellectuals or the upper class; our audience is the common man—the masses. To that man, fear is supreme."

Newhall nodded in understanding.

"We need to hammer home short, easy-to-understand ideas over and over. People don't want to hear an argument or a program; they want an emotional experience, the more intense the better."

Heilbrenner had torn this idea straight out of Adolph Hitler's playbook, but he didn't stop there. He compiled a list of trigger words; words designed to cut through a person's capacity to reason and appeal directly to prejudice. The list included terms proven to summon hate: "homosexual," "feminist," "atheist," "liberal," "secular humanist," "agnostic," "Darwinist." Heilbrenner urged every person in the organization to include a healthy dose of those words in their evangelism.

"All right, I like that idea, let's move on it," Newhall said. "What else?"

"You're addressing the evangelists in two days. I've prepared your speech." Heilbrenner slid a ten-page document across the table.

"Okay. I'll review this tonight."

* * *

Heilbrenner had organized a gathering of over two thousand Network evangelists for a three-day training seminar. He had designed the seminar to fulfill two primary goals—to train followers how to evangelize effectively, and to pump them up. In order to raise the greatest amount of money, he needed to keep morale and enthusiasm up for Infinity's cause. Newhall gave the keynote address to kick off the event.

It is truly a wondrous day when God brings so many men and women of the faith together; men and women called by God and inspired by Him to spread the word. Thank you all for being here. I look forward to fellowship with you over the next few days.

We can start with some congratulations for our hard work. By the grace of our Lord, the last few years have been a time of joy and celebration as we've shown the light and the power of our faith to millions of people across the globe. But our work has just begun, and not all the news is good. Many of you probably don't know that we lose over eighty percent of our conversions; people who say they've made a decision for Christ, yet within a year are nowhere to be found in the church. Why is that? Why is it that with the power of God at our disposal, people backslide from the faith? Fortunately, God provides us with a clear answer; it's based entirely on our methods of evangelism.

The great tragedy of modern evangelism is that we sell God as some sort of life improvement strategy, and the Bible as a self-help book. We tell people that they'll get peace, love, happiness, and fulfillment by making a decision for Christ. Since people desperately want these things, they enthusiastically agree to accept the faith. But then what happens? Their lives don't change. They don't get the peace, love, happiness, and fulfillment they were promised and they become disillusioned. They abandon the faith because it didn't live up to their expectations. Now, here's the problem. Any person whose motivation to accept Jesus Christ is to improve his life has the completely wrong motivation. This person will always be disappointed because their heart is in the wrong place to start with. The first thing a person must do is recognize that they're a sinner who has broken God's laws. The second thing they must do is sincerely repent. As evangelists, our job is to point out to people how they have sinned, and then explain to them why they must repent. Above all, we must stress to sinners that God will judge them harshly if they don't repent. They must understand the eternal pain and suffering that awaits them if they fail to confess their sins and accept Jesus Christ as their Savior. Only after a person has sufficiently repented will their heart be right and their motivations pure. Remember that showing repentance and accepting Christ is not about getting something, it's about accepting that we have all broken God's laws, and that we will be judged and punished unless we surrender.

After Newhall concluded his remarks, ushers handed out a booklet instructing Infinity evangelists on specific techniques to win over new followers. The booklet directed evangelists to focus on people's bad thoughts because that applied to everyone, even people with the highest moral standards who would never act on them. The booklet also instructed evangelists to exploit guilt because of its debilitating effect on the potential convert's self-esteem. Infinity even provided specific phrases that evangelists could use to evoke fear and guilt.

> God has given you life, what have you done for Him? You will never be able to repay Him. Have you even tried? Have you done everything you can? Have you devoted your life fully to God? If you haven't, are you willing to risk Hell? Doesn't it make sense to do everything you possibly can to ensure your eternal salvation?

Heilbrenner also directed evangelists to pepper recruits with questions that would force them to accept their inherently sinful nature.

> Have you ever told a lie—even one lie? Have you ever taken something that didn't belong to you no matter how small? Have you ever coveted anything owned by someone else? You've broken God's law and it doesn't matter what you've done to redeem yourself. It doesn't matter if you think you've lived a good life. You've broken the law and you will be judged.

Besides evangelizing, Heilbrenner's other strategy was to forge alliances with certain religious groups while demonizing others. Infinity needed a devil like Hitler needed the Jews, but unlike Hitler, Infinity courted the Jews because they were one of the most powerful groups in the country. Jews couldn't join the Network because they weren't Christians, but Heilbrenner devised a strategy to rally their support. He directed Infinity officials to stress the Network's support for Israel against its Islamic enemies, consistent with the Christian belief that the triumph of Israel was God's will. The Jews' return to their homeland and sole ownership of territories that Arabs and Israelis both lay claim to was a precondition for the second coming of Christ, according to many evangelical Christians' interpretation of the Book of Revelations.

Many Jews appreciated Infinity's support for Israel, but others argued that its Biblical scenario was not a savory one. The rest of the story that Infinity didn't publicize was that there would be a Battle of Armageddon in the Middle East in which Christ would triumph and begin ruling the earth. At this point, good Christians (including Jews who accepted Jesus as the Messiah and converted to Christianity) would be saved, but any remaining Jews would be destroyed along with everyone else who refused to accept Christian superstition.

Heilbrenner courted Catholics by proclaiming that the Pope was a great religious leader. He also disciplined Infinity evangelists who criticized the Pope or the Catholic Church, and he stated that the Catholic Apocrypha, though not having the same force as accepted Protestant gospels, was nonetheless important. Finally, Heilbrenner offered revenue sharing to Catholic dioceses. Catholic authorities found this offer enticing because several dioceses teetered on the verge of bankruptcy as a result of legal claims from the sexual abuse scandal.

The final piece of the Infinity membership puzzle involved the Mormons. Heilbrenner wanted them in the Network, or at least as supporters of Infinity's objectives. Traditionally, Mormons had isolationist tendencies and many mainline Christians despised Mormon theology. Indeed, many Protestants questioned whether Mormons were even Christians. Mormons, on the other hand, claimed that they were the only true Christians.

According to Mormon theology, after the resurrection of Jesus, the Christian Church fell into what Mormons called the "Great Apostasy." Mormons believed that there was no "real" church for some 1,700 years until Joseph Smith received his divine revelations in the nineteenth century and reestablished a "true" church. Thus, Mormons believed that Catholic and Protestant churches were all apostate organizations that had perpetuated false claims to be Christian.

Other battle lines had been drawn around the issue of baptism. Mormon leaders, beginning with Joseph Smith, refused to recognize the baptisms of Protestant denominations, calling the Protestant tradition of infant baptisms a "mockery before God," and charging that those who practiced it were "in danger of death, hell and endless torment." Mormons also believed that God was a flesh-and-bones man and was married. Similarly, they believed that angels were human beings at another level of exaltation, serving as messengers sent from God. Evangelical Christians believed that angels were another order of being, separate from humans. Mormons also rejected the doctrine of original sin, and had different interpretations of the nature and meaning of Christ's atonement.

Perhaps the biggest issue for non-Mormons, though, was the Mormon idea that Joseph Smith and his successors were prophets who received divine revelations. This was an extremely dangerous idea because it opened the door to other non-Biblical characters making prophetic claims. This had the potential to open the floodgates as people could conceivably act as their own prophet and therefore have no need for a church. Thus, according to Protestants, no one (including the Mormon Seer) was allowed to make prophetic claims or receive any special revelations until Jesus came back to Earth.

But since Mormonism was one of the fastest growing Christian sects with a net worth in the billions, Heilbrenner coveted them—and he had something to offer. The current Mormon Prophet, Seer, and Revelator desperately wanted mainstream respectability for its university, BYU, which had been heavily criticized by academics because of its hostility to academic freedom. For years, BYU had allowed church dogma to trump conflicting factual evidence, and one of the most frustrating and embarrassing issues dogging the current Mormon Prophet was Phi Beta Kappa's rejection of BYU's application for a chapter. Phi Beta Kappa's denial stung because it implied that the university had willfully compromised its intellectual integrity. In a private meeting with the Prophet, Heilbrenner proposed that he would use his connections to pressure Phi Beta Kappa to reconsider BYU's application if the Mormons would throw their support behind the Network. The Prophet readily agreed to the quid pro quo.

Heilbrenner's other big idea involved staging huge rallies to unite the faithful and to show everyone in the country that Infinity was a commanding force to be reckoned with. The Infinity Awakening Rally was held twice a year and attracted over three hundred thousand people to a stadium in Southern California, the biggest stadium in the nation. The rallies pulsed with the energy and excitement of a rock concert, and Christian musicians fired up the audience with songs about the power of God and sacrifice to the holy cause.

The sense of power, force, and unity was irresistible, and it peaked at the supreme moment when Newhall made his entry, striding like a conquering emperor through the center of the crowd. People in the audience swayed in mystical ecstasy, but the man most affected by the spectacle was Newhall himself, ascending to a state of powerful self-intoxication from the overflowing adoration of his followers. As he spoke, he animated his face with conviction and punctuated his words with powerful gestures. His voice rose and fell hypnotically, melting the audience into an unthinking mass. It was an impressive event that few could resist. Even Newhall's critics had to concede that it was brilliantly staged.

In addition to the Awakening Rallies, Heilbrenner staged smaller gatherings across the country that featured local Infinity evangelists. Heilbrenner had learned how to organize events with great skill from his days as a political operative, and he built the largest grassroots organization in the country. He kept followers continuously motivated and enthusiastic about the cause.

In order to keep Infinity youth excited, Heilbrenner created a symbol they could wear as a reminder of their faith. The Mormons had sacred underwear, but Heilbrenner wanted something youth could proudly flaunt. He hired a jewelry design firm to create a thin metal bracelet, engraved with the words "Faith in the Lord through Infinity," and surrounded by a circle of small crosses. Heilbrenner ordered five hundred thousand bracelets and directed officials at local churches to distribute them to junior high and high school Sunday school classes. Youth were told that they should wear the bracelet at all times because it represented their total devotion and sacrifice to God. The bracelets soon became a hot fashion item, worn by children as proof of their piety and self-worth. Kids without bracelets wanted to join Infinity so they could get a bracelet and join the in-crowd.

Heilbrenner also commissioned the creation of small pewter crucifixion nails. He wanted followers to display them as a reminder of Christ's sacrifice. Unfortunately, in an effort to get closer to their Savior, some people used the nails as the Romans had against Jesus. Two people bled to death and three others died from infection. Heilbrenner immediately halted production of the dangerous implements, but he praised the dead as courageous martyrs.

The final piece in Heilbrenner's master plan was the Packer campaign for the Presidency. Howard Packer, an ambitious, God-fearing governor from Alabama had secured the Republican nomination and enthusiastically supported Infinity's efforts to unite all Christians. His campaign manager, Al Rogers, had crafted a strategy already proven effective in presidential politics—court evangelical Christians, exploit racial fears in the South, and viciously attack your opponent with negative campaigning. Rogers and Heilbrenner met to discuss Infinity's role in the campaign and the two men immediately recognized their common outlook. Neither man was a true believer, but they both understood the intricacies of manipulation. Consequently, the alliance was tenuous because neither man trusted the other. But Heilbrenner nevertheless agreed to work for Packer in an unofficial capacity, promising to secure the Infinity vote.

Heilbrenner set up a volunteer network of twelve thousand operatives who campaigned door-to-door and staged demonstrations against the opposing candidate. He also dispatched volunteers to member churches and directed them to set up voter registration booths. Volunteers urged followers to vote for Packer and to contribute to his campaign. Campaign officials from Packer's opponent complained bitterly and filed several lawsuits, but Rogers and Heilbrenner responded by branding them as anti-religious, striking a chord with the electorate. Polls indicated that voters were concerned about a candidate's moral fiber, which they equated with membership in an established church and frequent invocation of "faith" in speeches. Packer's opponent was forced to backpedal and proclaim that his piety was equal to Packer's and that he believed just as strongly in the same Almighty God.

Infinity spent fifty million dollars on the effort to elect Packer and, as promised, it delivered the Network. Packer swept the South and the lower Midwest, including over eighty percent of the vote in rural areas. He won the election by thirty-six electoral votes.

CHAPTER 12

We [Mormons] consider it [slavery] to be of divine institution, and not to be abolished until the curse pronounced on Ham shall have been removed from his descendants.

Ham will continue to be the servant of servants, as the Lord has decreed, until the curse is removed. Will the present struggle free the slave? No…Can you destroy the decrees of the Almighty? You cannot.

—Brigham Young

Dushane woke up to the sterile walls and light ammonia fragrance of his hospital room. His arm was tied down and hooked up to an IV, which dripped morphine and antibiotics to dull the pain and prevent infection. The room was quiet except for an EKG machine that whirred softly next to him.

The gunshot had damaged Dushane's shoulder and left lung. Surgery repaired the vascular damage in his shoulder, but he still had a torn lung, which required a chest tube to help reinflate it. Dushane tried to remember what had happened, but the memory was fuzzy. He knew that he had been giving a speech, but he didn't remember anything about being shot. He tried to sit up, but a sharp pain shot through his chest and shoulder. He fell back and closed his eyes for a few minutes until he heard someone walk into the room.

"Hi Martin. How are you feeling?" a young doctor asked as she hovered over the bed.

Dushane opened his eyes slowly, pleased to see a smiling face. "Uh… tired…hungry," he said in a scratchy voice.

"Good. You're getting your appetite back. You'll need to build up your strength." She paused and then bent down closer. "You're a lucky man. A very lucky man. You lost a lot of blood, but the bullet didn't hit any major organs. Missed your heart by three inches." The doctor grinned cheerfully and spread her fingers apart to indicate the distance. "Very lucky."

Dushane put his hand underneath his hospital gown and felt the bandages just below his left shoulder.

"You were in surgery last night to remove the bullet," the doctor continued. "Everything went well, but you'll probably have a good scar. And you'll have some physical rehab to do. Otherwise, I expect a full recovery." The doctor looked at the EKG machine and jotted a few notes on Dushane's chart.

"You've had several visitors the past couple of days. We couldn't let them see you because of your condition, but you're much better now. I think your family went back to their hotel to get some sleep, but there's one visitor here now. Would you like to see her?"

"Her? Who is it?"

"I don't know the woman's name, but she's attractive." The doctor winked. "You have a girlfriend?"

"No."

"Shall I go get her?"

"Sure."

Josephine Holladay walked quietly into the room and stood motionless at the end of the bed. Dushane didn't recognize her at first because his senses weren't operating at their normal capacity, but after a few seconds, it hit him. It was the beautiful woman sitting in the second row at his press conference.

"Hello, Martin," Josephine said softly.

Dushane wondered if he was dreaming until he tried to sit up again. A sharp pain shot through his chest and shoulder, assuring him that he was awake. "Ahhhh…" he grimaced as Josephine hurried to the side of the bed.

"Don't move, Martin. Stay still." She placed her hand gently on top of his. Dushane's entire body tingled.

"I don't know you, do I?" Dushane asked.

"No, but I wanted to make sure you were all right. My name's Josephine Holladay. I'm a professor at the law school."

"Oh…nice to meet you."

"I liked what you said at the press conference. I've never seen anyone make the Dean squirm so much."

Dushane started to chuckle, but he hacked instead.

"Here, have some water." Josephine picked up a glass from the table next to the bed.

Dushane took a sip. "Thanks. Do you think the Dean was offended?"

Josephine laughed enthusiastically. "No, no, the Dean has no principles to offend. But he doesn't want anyone else to be offended. He sweats anytime he hears something controversial—or original."

Dushane smiled. He felt a powerful connection to Josephine and he wondered what she thought of him. He tried to think of something intelligent to say, but he drew a blank so he just stared at her and nodded.

"I met your parents," Josephine said after a few moments of silence. "They're nice people. They love you."

"I know. If it wasn't for their love and support, my life probably would've turned out a lot differently."

I don't know where I'd be without my parents either, Josephine thought. She hadn't seen her parents in several years, although she wondered about them often. *I can't fathom how different my life would be if I'd followed the path they'd chosen for me.*

* * *

"Josephine, it's time to practice your testimony."

"Okay, daddy." Two-year-old Josephine jumped onto her father's lap.

"Repeat after me. My name is Josephine Holladay."

"My name is Josephine Holladay."

"I know how to obey the scriptures."

91

"I know how to obey the striptures."

"No, honey. Try again. I know how to obey the scriptures. Scriptures. That's a very important word. Okay?"

"I know how to obey the scriptures."

"Good. Now. I bear testimony that the Church and the Book of Mormon are true."

"I bear testimony that the Church is true."

"Almost, honey. Let's try it again. I bear testimony."

"I bear testimony."

"That the Church."

"That the Church."

"And the Book of Mormon."

"And the Book of Mormon."

"Are true."

"Are true."

"Very good, sweetie. Now, can you say the whole sentence? I bear testimony that the Church and the Book of Mormon are true."

"I bear testimony that the Church and the Book of Mormon…"

"Are true."

"Oh yeah. Are true."

"Good. In the name of Jesus Christ, Amen."

"In the name of Jesus Christ, Amen."

"Great, honey!" Gordon Holladay hugged his daughter. "I knew you could do it."

Josephine grinned happily and wrapped her arms around her father's neck.

* * *

Josephine Holladay was born in Salt Lake City to Gordon and Emma Holladay, two devout young members of the Church of Jesus Christ of Latter-day Saints. Gordon worked as a regional manager for a large department store chain while Emma took care of the family home. The Holladays lived in a modest three-bedroom house that was like many in suburbia except for a couple of uniquely Mormon features. A large, framed picture of the Church's leadership hung prominently on the living room wall. The picture included the President of the Church (formally referred to as the Church's Prophet, Seer, and Revelator) and his two counselors. Below them, were the Twelve Apostles. Pictures of the Church's leadership, known collectively as the General Authorities, were common in Mormon homes, meetinghouses, and in *Ensign*, the monthly Mormon magazine.

The Holladay house also had a basement full of food and supplies—a year's worth by Gordon Holladay's calculation—consisting of canned food, dried fruit and milk, fifty-gallon barrels of water, forty-pound bags of grain, candles, and seeds. *Ensign* frequently published advisories on food storage, a practice considered critically important in light of Biblical warnings about famine, pestilence, and flood.

Although Josephine experienced a relatively normal childhood, her unique mental gifts became evident at an early age. She started speaking in complete sentences at eight months, and after her first birthday, her parents reckoned that her vocabulary doubled every week. By her second birthday, she was speaking in complex sentences with precise terminology. Since Josephine was Gordon and Emma's first child, they didn't fully appreciate her advanced intellectual ability, and they found her other advanced traits such as high levels of energy and little need for sleep to be annoying.

Gordon Holladay served as a bishop in his ward. Ward members typically met every Sunday morning at the local meetinghouse for sacrament and Sunday school, with the first Sunday of every month being set aside for testimony. On testimony Sunday, people in the ward would stand in front of the group and say something about their gratitude to be part of the Church, or their conviction that the Church and its gospel were true. In Gordon Holladay's ward, no child had ever given testimony before the age of four, but he was determined that his daughter would be the first. Shortly after her second birthday and every evening for several weeks, Gordon taught his daughter how to recite a proper Mormon testimony.

When Josephine could recite the entire testimony on her own, Gordon became increasingly excited as the day of her performance neared. He had told several of his fellow Saints that his daughter would be the youngest ever to testify in the ward, and perhaps the youngest in Church history. The Saturday evening before the testimony meeting, he drilled his daughter a final time.

"Tomorrow's your big day, sweetie. Can you recite your testimony for daddy, please?"

"I don't feel like it right now, daddy," Josephine said, her drowsy eyes half open.

Gordon furrowed his brow. His daughter had never said no to him before. "Honey, we need to practice so that we'll be ready for tomorrow. Please say your testimony for me."

"No, daddy," Josephine said flatly.

"Listen honey, I'm your father and I'm asking you to recite your testimony right now."

"I don't want to."

Heat began to rise in Gordon's face. "Josephine. You obey me. I'm telling you to recite your testimony! Now!"

"No."

Gordon grabbed her firmly by the shoulders. "Josephine! Obey me!"

Josephine started crying and Emma quickly rushed in from the kitchen. "What's going on, Gordon?"

Gordon looked up furiously. "She won't recite her testimony."

Emma didn't agree with her husband pushing Josephine, but she never challenged any of his decisions or his authority over their daughter. She had been conditioned from an early age to believe that a good Mormon wife always supported her husband and let him make all important family decisions. Nevertheless, she instinctively reacted to protect her daughter. "Leave her alone, Gordon," she snapped. She picked Josephine up and held her. "It's okay, baby. You don't have to say anything right now. It's okay."

The next day, Gordon Holladay felt tiny beads of sweat trickle down his chest, dampening the thin cloth of his shirt as he walked into the ward meetinghouse. He walked past pictures of every Church Seer since Joseph Smith and he wondered vaguely what they would do in his situation. Everyone was expecting Josephine to give her testimony. Gordon opened the meeting without mentioning his daughter, and then quickly passed control to others in the ward scheduled to testify.

Emma Holladay sat quietly in the back of the room with Josephine. Gordon weaved his way toward them and sat next to Josephine. He scowled at his daughter, but she smiled back. As he pondered whether he should keep quiet or make up an excuse to explain his daughter's failure to testify, Josephine interrupted his thoughts. "I want to say my testimony," she said softly.

"What, honey?"

"I want to say my testimony," she repeated.

"Gordon..." Emma jumped in.

"I want to say my testimony," Josephine insisted.

"I think it's okay, Emma," Gordon said as he put his arm around Josephine.

After all the other Saints had finished speaking, Josephine walked hand-in-hand with her father to the front of the room. She stood patiently while her father set up his video camera. "Okay, honey. Go ahead."

"My name is Josephine Holladay. I know how to obey the scriptures. I bear testimony that the Church and the Book of Mormon are true. In the name of Jesus Christ, Amen."

The Saints clapped enthusiastically while Gordon Holladay let out a sigh of relief.

* * *

Despite Gordon Holladay's aggressive indoctrination of his daughter, he was a loving man and Josephine appeared well adjusted. She had friends, she obeyed her parents, and she did what was expected of her in the Church. She especially loved stories and Gordon read to her often. Shortly after her third birthday, Gordon began reading a story that he had read to her six months previously. He asked her if she remembered it. Josephine proceeded to recite the entire twenty-five-page story from start to finish in almost verbatim detail. Gordon didn't know what to do with his young child prodigy. Emma decided to teach Josephine to read while her husband was at work. Three months later, Josephine didn't need her father to read to her anymore.

Josephine rarely questioned her father about the tenets of the Mormon faith; she simply accepted them like all children did. She had heard over and over again that the Mormons were special, and that their church was the only true one. But then one of the family's close friends got into a terrible car accident. Josephine prayed day and night for God to heal him, but the man died after a week in the hospital, leaving a wife and two young children behind. Josephine asked her father why God, who was all-powerful, didn't help.

"God has a plan, honey," Gordon Holladay answered matter-of-factly.

Josephine didn't understand, and the first doubt registered in her psyche.

Josephine preferred playing with boys and engaging in traditionally male activities such as science fiction and fantasy games. She had a vivid imagination and had no interest in playing with dolls or pretending that she was a housewife. Her parents were initially encouraged when she met a girl down the street named Holly Matson. Holly was much like the other girls in the neighborhood except that her parents were not members of the Church. Nevertheless, Josephine's parents liked Holly and they allowed the girls to play together. But then a troubling incident occurred. Two young Mormon missionaries called on Bob Matson, Holly's father, and tried to convert him. Matson explained to the boys that he had been raised in the Church, but didn't agree with its rigid dogma. He told them he didn't believe that the Mormon Church, or any church, was based on facts. He also counseled the boys to think for themselves, investigate the Church's teachings critically, and question the Church's leadership if something didn't make sense.

The missionaries had been trained to report any unusual visits to their supervisor so they immediately informed him about their conversation with Bob Matson. After hearing the story, the supervisor called Gordon Holladay for further instructions. Gordon was furious. *What a nerve, telling our missionaries to question the Church!* The General Authorities had taught him that people like Matson, who sought to discredit the church, were directly influenced by Satan. And being so well conditioned, the thought of questioning Church leadership had never entered his mind. In any case, he couldn't tolerate anyone in his family keeping company with dangerous apostates. As a ward bishop, he had to set an example.

Josephine's sixth birthday party was coming up and the invitations had been prepared, but not yet sent out. Gordon instructed his wife not to send an invitation to Holly Matson. Emma Holladay didn't agree with her husband, but she quietly capitulated. For good measure, Gordon called Bob Matson.

"I don't think our daughters should remain friends," Gordon snapped testily. "I'm not comfortable with that kind of negative influence."

"What negative influence?"

"On our faith."

Bob Matson's blood pressure shot up, but he kept his composure. "If that's how you feel, that's fine, but I don't agree with letting your bigotry affect the friendship of two innocent girls."

"Bigotry?" Gordon erupted. "You're out of line, Bob. I'm just not going to let our faith be challenged."

"Our?"

"Yes. My family."

Matson wondered how anyone could believe that a six-year-old freely chose a religious belief. But perhaps that was the whole point. Matson reckoned that choice, and specifically a choice based on rational thought, had no relevance to life in the Church.

"Okay," Matson said and hung up the phone. He felt sad for his daughter because it was difficult for her to make friends. Most of the activities in the community revolved around the Church and non-members were not welcome.

On the day of the party Josephine cried because Holly wasn't there. Gordon and Emma had to send the other kids home early. Gordon initially scolded his daughter for making a fool out of him, but he also realized that he had hurt her. He tried to console her by explaining that Holly's father was a bad influence. Josephine was confused because Bob Matson had always been nice to her, often taking the girls to the park or out for ice cream. Josephine didn't know what to believe, but she trusted her father. She never asked to play with Holly Matson again.

Josephine coasted through elementary school, her biggest challenge fighting boredom. She usually finished her schoolwork in half the time it took her classmates and her teachers weren't sure what to do with her. Some of them gave her additional work to do. Others let her read the books she always brought to class.

Josephine read voraciously. By the age of seven, she had read the biographies of several famous women including Amelia Earhart, Eleanor Roosevelt, and Georgia O'Keefe. She told her father that she wanted to be a famous inventor or a great artist. Gordon Holladay never encouraged those dreams, nor did he encourage her reading. He knew that his main responsibility as a parent was to teach her appropriate values such as tithing. At the end of every week, he gave Josephine an allowance of one dollar, always consisting of ten dimes. He would start by giving her all ten and then she would give one back, which was then earmarked for the Church. Another value that Gordon Holladay stressed was that Sunday was the Sabbath and people shouldn't work on that day. This meant that you shouldn't cause other people to work either. The Holladays never went to the store or filled the car with gas on Sunday and Josephine was cautioned to use electricity sparingly because it wasn't right to cause people at the electric company to work on Sunday either. Josephine never thought much about the rule until later when she discovered an exception for Mormon NFL players who were given "special permission" to work on Sundays.

By the time she was eight, no one doubted that Josephine had advanced way beyond anyone in her peer group. She was able to solve math problems at a high-school level and she seemed to remember everything she read or heard. She stayed in her room for hours at a time reading, not even noticing when one of her parents walked into her room.

But it wasn't until she took the standardized IQ tests required by the State of Utah that her intelligence was objectively quantifiable. Josephine achieved the highest test scores in state history. Unfortunately, this posed a dilemma for school authorities. A few of them argued that they needed to design a special academic program to maximize her potential. One woman was especially vocal, "This girl has the potential for greatness. She needs individualized instruction and someone to mentor her. If we squander her potential, we're guilty of murder."

Others argued that it would be unfair to give her special treatment. They decided to call Gordon Holladay. Although he loved his daughter and wanted her to be happy, he told them flatly that he didn't want any special treatment for her because it would interfere with her commitment to the Church. He didn't want her spiritual education threatened, or her place in the Church hierarchy questioned. Since Gordon Holladay was the bishop in the local ward, school officials deferred to his wishes.

Despite the lack of challenge at school, Josephine excelled in all of her classes. At first, her father praised her effusively, but as she reached her teenage years, he suddenly became strangely silent about her academic success. Instead, he encouraged her to be more social and try to get along better with other girls. Josephine preferred spending time alone reading and thinking, and most of the other girls thought she was weird because she always asked strange questions. Why is there a universe? How come women don't get revelations from God? Why do people believe that prayer works?

Josephine had no patience for the ordinary or the mediocre, and her impatience left her with few friends. Behind her back, the other girls gossiped that they didn't like her, although they were all secretly intimidated by her intelligence and her looks. They also resented that all the boys liked her best.

Josephine had a particular gift for creative writing. She frequently wrote moralistic tales with strong themes of heroism and justice, usually involving ordinary people overcoming obstacles. But Gordon worried because Josephine's thoughts were independent and original, and she had a strong sense of right and wrong based her own observations and conclusions—not on Church teachings or Scripture. Her father counseled her that she didn't need arguments to justify morality and insisted that she need only read the Scriptures and follow the guidance of Church prophets. Josephine didn't understand.

Josephine's teachers admonished her frequently for asking too many questions in class and for having "crazy ideas." But at least her teachers tried to answer her. Sunday school was worse. Josephine asked how anybody knew that the Bible was true. The teacher replied that the Bible was true because it said so right in the Bible. It was Josephine's first taste of circular logic. After Sunday school, her teacher warned her not to ask questions like that in front of the other kids. If she had questions in the future, she was told to ask them privately.

At age fourteen, Josephine joined the Mormon young women's program. The first meeting was a special reception in a room decorated with glowing candles and white roses. The leader of the program told the girls that one of their most important responsibilities was to preserve their chastity. She took a rose out of one of the vases and remarked how beautiful and pure and clean it was. Then she started crumpling the petals. She told the girls that they were pure like the rose, but if they allowed boys to touch them, or do things that were reserved for marriage, they would end up like the disfigured rose and no one would want them.

The regimen for becoming a good Mormon also included classes where girls were given rules for dating, such as a prohibition until age sixteen, and a strong recommendation to double-date until age eighteen. There were also rules against parking with a boy, lying on top of each other, petting, and praying together ("Something inappropriate might happen while you're down on your knees"). In addition, Church members organized classes to teach girls how to cook, can food, sew, and raise children. The goal of these activities was to prepare women to assume their proper role as good mothers and housewives. This was extremely important, Josephine was taught, because the only way for a woman to achieve celestial glory and reach the highest level of Heaven was through a man. Thus, women needed to do whatever they could to be attractive to men.

The other activity Josephine regularly participated in was baptism for the dead. Mormons believed that baptizing the deceased was an early Christian practice that had been lost with the early apostasy of the Christian church, but then restored by Joseph Smith. The aim was to allow everyone who had ever lived to choose Christ in the afterlife and enter his kingdom. Mormons baptized dead U.S. presidents, signers of the Declaration of Independence, as well as dead Catholics and Jews. But not every dead person was baptized. Prior to 1974, baptisms could not be performed "for people who had any Negro blood in their veins." The General Authorities changed this policy in 1974 after learning of a potential NAACP lawsuit and a congressional investigation of using census records for racially discriminatory purposes.

In addition to high school, Josephine attended classes in the Church Educational System, which offered religious instruction. The required course sequence covered the Bible, the Mormon scriptures, and selected Church history. Church authorities carefully standardized the curriculum and they urged seminary teachers to stress the uniqueness and exclusiveness of the Mormon version of the gospels, forbidding discussions of controversial issues such as polygamy. The authorities also discouraged exploration of other spiritual practices, or intellectual or scientific investigations into any subject.

Josephine's seminary experience started while the priesthood was still denied to males of African descent. For well over a century, Mormon prophets had taught that God didn't allow a person with any black African blood to be admitted to the priesthood. This was significant for several reasons. In the Mormon Church, priesthood was critical because it was a necessary condition for receiving temple endowments and eternal sealings of marriage that admitted its holders to the highest tier in heaven. Thus, racial bigotry and segregation would continue in the afterlife with blacks relegated to Heaven's second tier.

Josephine asked questions about the racial ban on several occasions and was told that it was not an appropriate question to ask. By her junior year of high school, however, she had a new seminary teacher who was willing to entertain the question. He told the class that racial discrimination was based on the Scriptures and commanded by God. According to the sacred texts and revelations received by the prophets, dark skin was a curse from God for sinfulness. The seeds of Cain were black and black people had descended through the loins of Cain. The fact that blacks descended from Cain (and Ham, another wicked Biblical figure) was significant because Mormons believed that they perpetuated a priesthood line that went all the way back to Adam, a man with light skin. Those cursed with black skin wouldn't be eligible to receive their priesthood until all others (whites) received theirs. This was mandated by the words of Brigham Young himself, who also had strong opinions on miscegenation.

> Shall I tell you the law of God in regard to the African race? If the white man who belongs to the chosen seed mixes his blood with the seed of Cain, the penalty, under the law of God, is death on the spot. This will always be so.

While there were no reported incidents of anyone dying on the spot, Mormons nonetheless diligently obeyed Young's commands. Despite the eventual removal of the ban against blacks in the priesthood, the Church still counseled strongly against interracial dating.

Josephine wondered why an accident of birth condemned people to a life of inferiority. Her seminary teacher had an answer for this as well. According to Mormon doctrine, spirits existed in Heaven before they were put into a body and their conduct there determined the conditions in which they took on human form. Thus, God had cursed blacks on Earth for "spiritual inadequacy in preexistence."

In 1978, the Church's Seer, Prophet, and Revelator received a revelation from God to lift the racist priesthood ban. This coincided with vigorous efforts by the Church to recruit new followers in countries like Brazil where racial classifications were hopelessly complex. The Church was also under pressure from civil rights groups and ordinary citizens who criticized the Church's overt racism as barbaric.

Despite the command from God, Mormon leaders instructed seminary teachers not to discuss the long-standing ban. Josephine thought the policy change was odd given the Church's insistence that Mormon prophets and scripture were never wrong. Josephine didn't know what to believe. *Did God change his mind? I thought he had perfect knowledge of everything.* She had a burning desire to find answers.

Over the next year, Josephine spent all her spare time at the Salt Lake City Public Library reading every book she could find about the Mormon Church. Over the course of six months, she read thirty books about the Church, as well as the Book of Mormon, but she wasn't satisfied. Everything she read portrayed the Church in a favorable light and didn't discuss controversial issues such as racial discrimination or polygamy. She asked to speak with the librarian in charge of obtaining new books and was introduced to Katherine McKay, a middle-aged woman with light streaks of gray running through her sandy brown hair. Her eyes were bright and alive, but she moved with hesitation.

"Hi. I'm looking for some additional books on the history of the Church," Josephine said. "I've read just about everything you have on the shelf."

"That's all we've got," Katherine replied automatically.

"Are you sure?"

"Yes."

"Well, it's just seems like your selection is limited. Do you expect to get any new books in soon?"

Katherine sighed impatiently. "If any new books come in, I can hold them for you. What's your name?"

"Josephine Holladay."

"Josephine Holladay!" Katherine exclaimed, and then lurched forward as if someone had pushed her.

Josephine jumped back. "What?"

"Oh, I'm sorry. I didn't mean to startle you. I just remember reading about you. You're gifted."

"Yeah, I guess so," Josephine said softly. She didn't often hear the word "gifted"; her parents discouraged it, and they told her to be humble and not publicize the intelligence that God had blessed her with. She was also surprised because her intellectual endowments were not well known. She wondered how Katherine knew about it, especially since nothing had been mentioned in the news for several years.

Katherine's body straightened as if she had just been infused with a jolt of energy. "I'm Katherine McKay. It's so good to meet you."

"Nice to meet you, too, Mrs. McKay."

"Call me Katherine."

"Okay. Are you any relation to Boyd McKay?" Boyd was a member of the General Authorities and he had a reputation as an uncompromising Church conservative.

"Yes," Katherine said and looked down, suddenly deflated again.

"Really? I was just kidding."

"He's my husband," she said in a low voice.

"Oh."

Katherine looked away. "It was nice to meet you, Josephine. I'll let you know if any books come in."

After Josephine left, Katherine sat down and slumped in her chair. She felt the familiar pain of trying to reconcile conflicting feelings. On one hand, she was a practical woman with a good family, many friends, and a comfortable lifestyle. On the other hand, she didn't love her husband because he treated her dismissively and didn't allow her to meaningfully participate in family decisions. She also cursed herself for intellectual dishonesty and her failure to stand up to the Church's false claims. She recognized her own repressed spirit in Josephine.

Katherine kept her eye out for Josephine, who returned to the library a week after their first encounter. Katherine scribbled a quick note and placed it carefully in the middle of a book. She walked over to Josephine and placed the book on the desk where she was reading. "Hi, Josephine. Here's a book I thought you might be interested in."

"Hi, Katherine. Thanks." Josephine noticed the piece of paper sticking out of the book and pulled it out: *Meet me outside by the back door thirty minutes after closing.* Josephine ripped up the note and threw it into a nearby trashcan.

At exactly 8:30 pm, Katherine opened the back door of the library and motioned for Josephine to come in. Josephine followed her down into the basement and then into a small storage room. Katherine pointed to a large file cabinet. "We need to move this out of the way. Take that side."

The women pulled the cabinet out from the wall, revealing a padlocked door. Katherine took a small key out of her jacket pocket and opened the lock. The door creaked as Katherine swung it open, and it was impossible to see anything inside. Katherine pulled a flashlight out of her purse and shined it into the dark space. "We need to go back in here," she said.

They walked down a short corridor, which was cold and empty except for several pipes that ran across the wall. Small beads of water dripped from one of the pipes and fell gently to the floor. There were three large wooden trunks at the end of the corridor, each secured with a heavy padlock. Katherine opened them one after another, and they all contained books, about twenty in each trunk.

"What is all this is?" Josephine asked.

"These are the books you're looking for."

"What do you mean?

"These are books about the history of the Church."

"Why are they down here?"

Katherine hesitated and looked away. "I'm…I'm sorry. I'm a little nervous about this."

Josephine didn't say anything, but smiled hopefully.

"Well…it's just…"

"Look, Mrs. McKay, I promise I won't tell anyone. You can trust me."

Katherine looked into Josephine's eyes. "Okay. Let's sit down." The women closed the trunks and sat down across from each other. Katherine recounted her story. She had married when she was seventeen to Boyd McKay, a twenty-eight-year-old rising star in both the business world and the Church. Although she was young, her parents had encouraged her to marry because it was a great opportunity to join a successful man, and it was not uncommon for Mormon girls to marry in their teenage years. Katherine wasn't sure whether she was in love with him, but it seemed like the right thing to do.

She started having children immediately and had a total of seven, all of whom were now adults. She had never worked outside the home, but with her children out of the house, her husband had permitted her to take a job at the library. The previous librarian had allowed books that were either critical of the Church, or differed from the Church's position on certain issues, to remain on the shelves despite repeated warnings by the General Authorities to remove the scandalous literature. Eventually, the woman was dismissed from her job and excommunicated for her failure to obey. Katherine McKay had been a faithful Mormon all of her life and her record was perfect, making her a safe replacement.

Like her predecessor, Katherine had been counseled explicitly to keep anti-Mormon books off the shelves. If she wasn't sure whether a particular book was heretical, she was directed to bring the book to her husband's attention and he would submit it to the General Authorities for their recommendation. As she soon discovered, she had help in this enterprise of censorship. Any books critical of the Church were often stolen or defaced. Occasionally, the General Authorities sent her a list of books not to order, or if they were already on the shelves, to remove.

Josephine sat quietly, shocked by what she was hearing.

"I was ordered to remove these books from the shelves and destroy them, but I couldn't," Katherine said quietly. "And any book on the General Authorities' list that I didn't have, I secretly ordered."

"I'm glad you didn't destroy these, Mrs. McKay. You did the right thing." Josephine put her hand on top of Katherine's.

Katherine nodded. "Let me show you what I've got."

For the next hour, Katherine chronicled books on a broad array of subjects about the Church—polygamy, the "gold Bible," racism, revisions of embarrassing or inconvenient scripture, and the accuracy of the Book of Mormon. Josephine began to get excited. She was finally going to uncover the truth.

"These books aren't marked with the library's stamp. Don't tell anyone where you got them."

"I won't," Josephine promised.

"Take as many books as you can read in two weeks; then you can exchange them for more."

Over the next three months, Josephine read twenty-five books, most of which contradicted what she had been learning in her seminary classes and in Sunday school. For the first time in her life, she felt a seething rage that quickly transformed into a burning and passionate rebellion. Her schoolwork began to suffer and she complained bitterly to her parents about having to go to Church functions.

Gordon Holladay noticed the change in Josephine's disposition and behavior, but every time he asked her what was wrong, she replied with a terse "Nothing." Her father's concern culminated in an explosive episode at the ward meetinghouse. Josephine rarely spoke at the meetinghouse, but she stood up one Sunday and offered testimony.

> My name is Josephine Holladay. I know the Church and the scriptures are true. I'm so happy that everyone in the ward is white because I don't want to be around any people who are cursed by God and aren't white and delightsome. I'm also happy that women can't join the priesthood because God said that it wasn't our proper role. I just want to grow up, have lots of children, and obey my husband. I'm also happy that this is the only true church and all the other churches are wrong. I feel so lucky that we're the only people on Earth who know the truth.

It was a sarcastic slap to the ward, but only a few people got the joke. Gordon had to resist the urge to jump out of his chair and tackle her. Josephine trotted out of the meetinghouse and Gordon ran after her, grabbing her by the arm and spinning her around vigorously. "How dare you disrespect me like that!" he thundered.

"Get your hands off me!" Josephine jerked away.

"I won't tolerate your disrespect!"

"You disrespect yourself!" Josephine shot back. "You and everyone else in that room! I'm sick of all the lies! This church is a lie!"

Gordon grabbed her shoulders. "Don't you ever talk about the Church that way! You hear me!"

"Let me go!"

Gordon didn't know the reason for the change in his daughter and he worried that she might be experimenting with drugs or alcohol. He thoroughly searched her room while she was at school, but the only contraband he found was books hidden under a pile of blankets in her closet. He leafed through a few of them and then checked the list of dangerous literature compiled by the General Authorities. Several of the books were on the list. When Josephine came home from school, he confronted her.

"Where did you get these books?" he bristled angrily.

"Where did you find those?"

"They were in your room."

"What were you doing in my room? You have no right to be in my room!"

"You listen to me, young lady. As long as you live under this roof, I have every right to make sure you behave appropriately. These books are unacceptable and I won't tolerate them in this house. Do you understand me? Now where did you get them?"

"Don't you ever go into my room again!" Josephine screamed and stormed out.

Josephine lay in the grass at a nearby park for several hours while her parents frantically called everyone they knew in an effort to locate her. Although Josephine was extremely angry with her father, it hurt to be away from her family because she still loved them. When she finally returned home, her father insisted that she speak with a Church counselor.

The Church had trained several special counselors whose job was to deal with teenagers questioning the Church. Josephine agreed to go see the counselor because she was curious what the person would say to convince her that the Church had any value.

Mormon authorities directed counselors to base their advice on a directive issued by the Seer, Prophet, and Revelator. The counselor read it aloud to Josephine.

> Remember that faith and doubt cannot exist in the same mind at the same time, for one will dispel the other. Should doubt knock at your doorway, just say to those skeptical, disturbing, rebellious thoughts: "I propose to stay with my faith, with the faith of my people. I know that happiness and contentment are there, and I forbid you, agnostic, doubting thoughts, to destroy the house of my faith. I acknowledge that I do not understand the process of creation, but I accept the fact of it. I grant that I cannot explain the miracles of the Bible, and I do not attempt to do so, but I accept God's word. I wasn't with Joseph, but I believe him. My faith did not come to me through science, and I will not permit so-called science to destroy it."

"You see, Josephine. The key is to rid your mind of doubting thoughts. You can't let them affect your faith. I think you should memorize the words of our prophet."

Although she tried as hard as she could to control herself, the corners of Josephine's mouth began to curl upward and she burst into a fit of laughter. The counselor sat stone-faced on the other side of the desk, fidgeting uncomfortably until Josephine regained her composure.

"I don't know what you find so funny here!" the counselor lashed out.

"So-called science? That's just too much—even for the Church."

The counselor quickly shifted to an alternative strategy. "We're talking about your faith. Your parents and everyone else in the Church cares about you. We want you to be happy. If you don't care about that, I hope you at least care about your parents who've sacrificed for you. Your behavior has hurt them deeply."

It was a classic play on guilt, but Josephine never played that game. "They sacrifice for themselves," she replied calmly.

"That's quite an attitude to take. You're being pretty selfish right now."

Josephine had known for a long time that the Church was misguided, but she hadn't fully appreciated what drove it. Now, she totally understood. "Ignorance is bliss," she said.

"What?"

"Ignorance is bliss."

"What are you trying to say?"

Josephine looked at the woman carefully. *She has absolutely no clue what's going on*, Josephine thought. "I'm not trying to say anything," Josephine said finally, and then walked out.

At the end of her junior year in high school, Mary Robinson, the school's guidance counselor met individually with students to discuss their future plans. The school didn't often send students to elite universities and Robinson normally recommended that good Mormon students apply to BYU. But Josephine's case was different. While she had a strong Mormon lineage and BYU had respectable programs in many areas, Robinson knew that her talents would be completely wasted at BYU, which still had a reputation as "the best place for a Mormon girl to find a husband."

Robinson was prepared to persuade Josephine of the merits of an Ivy League school, but persuasion wasn't necessary because Josephine had already decided that she wanted to leave Utah and study somewhere with a strong humanities department. After discussing several options, Robinson recommended that Josephine apply to Yale, and she promised to obtain an application and help her with the admissions process.

When the subject of college came up at home, Josephine told her father that she was going to apply to Yale. Gordon expressed shock. Since both he and his wife had graduated from BYU, he expected his daughter to carry on the family tradition. They discussed it briefly, but Josephine had made up her mind.

Gordon knew that he would lose his daughter if she was introduced to new ideas outside of the insular Utah community, and his concerns were well founded. The Church had compiled statistics that showed a strong correlation between those students who left Utah to study and those who subsequently left the Church. An even more disturbing statistic showed that even those students who remained in the Church after leaving Utah for college were less likely to satisfy their full tithing requirement. Church leaders recognized that it was impossible to prevent students who left from being exposed to new ideas and to people from different backgrounds. The other problem was that it was much harder to monitor their behavior. At BYU, other students operated as a moral police force providing the heavy weight of peer pressure, disapproval, and even spying to keep other students in line. The other advantage at BYU was the requirement of religious study, providing additional indoctrination at a time when many students were searching for answers and were prone to freethinking. The next day, Gordon Holladay called Mary Robinson.

"Mary, this is Gordon Holladay."

"Hi, Gordon. How are you?" Robinson said cheerfully.

"Well, frankly I'm a little concerned," Gordon replied sharply. "Josephine told us last night that she wants to go away to school. I understand you've talked her into Yale."

"Well…I….I…I didn't talk her into anything," Robinson stuttered. Gordon's tone had caught her off guard. "She told me that she wanted to study at a university with a strong reputation in the humanities. I recommended Yale because I think it's a perfect fit for her. With her record, she'll definitely get in."

"Listen Mary, I realize you're trying to help my daughter and I appreciate that. I suppose I should have spoken with you earlier, but I feel that Josephine should stay close to home and attend BYU."

"With all due respect to BYU, I think that would be a disservice to your daughter; she's brilliant. Of course, you already know that. She needs to be challenged. I don't think BYU can offer that."

Gordon couldn't believe that a woman was challenging him. "This isn't an issue we can discuss in terms of reasons. This is about our family and our faith. Josephine's faith has already been shaken and I can't let it erode further."

Robinson sighed. "Okay, Gordon. You're her father. What do you want me to do?"

"I suggest you stop putting these ideas into Josephine's head. I won't tolerate it."

"I can't lie to her."

"Lie?" Gordon raised his voice. "You need to do what you're supposed to do. You know how we've had to deal with people who don't follow our decisions. I'd hate to see you jeopardize your future."

Robinson was angered by the unstated, but unmistakable threat of excommunication, but she kept her composure. She figured it wasn't worth jeopardizing her Church membership, which made up a huge part of her identity and provided her entire social network. "I understand," she said softly.

At a follow-up meeting with Josephine, Robinson told her that perhaps BYU would be a good choice after all. She explained that the university had upgraded its faculty in recent years and had a fine tradition in the humanities. Josephine didn't know much about BYU, but she felt uncomfortable because Robinson avoided eye contact with her.

"I appreciate your advice, but I've decided on Yale," Josephine said. "When will we get the application?"

Robinson let out an agonizing sigh. "I'm sorry, Josephine. I can't help you."

Josephine went home and appealed to her father for help, but he told her flatly that there would be no discussion. "I'm your father and you'll attend BYU."

Josephine cried, but she didn't have enough strength to resist her father. She still needed his support and blessing so she enrolled at BYU.

BYU was the largest religiously sponsored university in the United States with over half of its budget coming from Church tithes, and its board consisting entirely of Church officials. The faculty was also made up mostly of temple-worthy Mormons and BYU had a requirement that faculty obtain a temple recommend from their bishop every year. This process involved the bishop making sure that the faculty member was active in their ward and had paid their full ten percent tithe. He also tested their loyalty to Church leaders and asked them if they had faithfully upheld Church teachings, lived a morally clean life, obeyed the Words of Wisdom, and wore their sacred underclothes.

BYU required students to take several religion courses, including classes on the Book of Mormon and the Doctrine and Covenants. BYU also offered courses in Church history, although professors were cautioned to teach only "Church-approved accounts of history." This meant that all the embarrassing facts in the Church's history could not be discussed. The president of the university compiled a list of topics, including polygamy, racism, the Mountain Meadows massacre, changes to Mormon scripture, blood atonement, Joseph Smith's money-digging and interest in the occult, the influence of Masonry on Mormon rituals, Adam as God, and any criticism of the actions or decisions of any past or present Church leaders. The last prohibition was a catchall and included anything that the current Church leadership found objectionable. As the president of the university explained, "It is intolerable to criticize a person who has been called to the performance of their office by God. It doesn't matter if the criticism is true."

After several years of active recruiting, BYU had attracted many faculty members with strong academic credentials, although this was a mixed blessing. The school experienced great difficulty trying to balance the needs of the Mormon faith with academic freedom. Many of the new scholars, particularly in the humanities, felt a stronger desire to pursue honest scholarship than to compromise their integrity. This created a powder keg as academic freedom and Church orthodoxy struggled to coexist. Recognizing the growing controversy, the university drafted guidelines providing that academic freedom would be supported except in cases of "any activity or expression that seriously and adversely affects the mission of BYU or the Church of Jesus Christ of Latter-day Saints." Faculty members soon discovered that this policy restricted whatever the General Authorities didn't like.

The first crackdown by university officials involved pressuring faculty members to suppress scholarship that disproved or shed doubt on Church claims or scripture. When this didn't work, they denied tenure or threatened termination. This led to Phi Beta Kappa consistently rejecting BYU's application for a chapter on the grounds that its mission was incompatible with academic freedom. Similarly, the American Association of University Professors censured the university for promoting censorship and discouraging academic freedom. Church leadership was undeterred, although they changed their future hiring criteria, asking prospective faculty members during the interview process whether they would be willing, if asked, to suppress potentially troubling research. If the candidate answered no, then an offer of employment would not be extended. The school also adopted a written hiring policy which stated that "any person who is a threat to the religious faith of the students or faculty at the university, or a critic of the Church or its leaders, will not be hired."

Based on her extensive reading in high school, Josephine knew as much about the history of the Church as her professors, and she knew a substantial amount more on the embarrassing subjects. She frequently challenged her professors on Church history and asked questions which implicitly challenged Church teachings. On several occasions, other students reported her behavior to university authorities and they warned her not to challenge her professors on issues involving Church doctrine. Josephine ignored the warnings and was eventually put on probation for "insubordination." University officials contacted her father who was furious and threatened to pull her out of school. Josephine replied that she would be happy to leave because it was impossible to learn in a place where the truth wasn't valued.

After Josephine's fifth episode of challenging the Church in the classroom, university officials expelled her. After the initial shock wore off, the first thing she did was load everything she owned into her car. Then she drove to the bank and withdrew all of her money. For the next three days, she drove east. She still dreamt of going to Yale and she knew the only way she was going to get there was through her own efforts.

On the drive, Josephine's mind swung like a pendulum from one extreme to another. Breaking from her parents scared her. On the other hand, there was no doubt in her mind that intellectual dishonesty was a cancer. She also felt occasional pangs of worry that other universities would ostracize her, although she soon discovered that being kicked out of BYU, particularly for challenging its repression of academic freedom, was a badge of honor. Many people in academia thought that a religious university was an oxymoron and would eventually either self-destruct or choose one mission over the other. BYU had chosen religion, losing the respect of institutions whose mission was the exact opposite—discovering the truth through facts and honest inquiry.

Josephine eventually got into and graduated from Yale. She went on to Harvard Law School, where she was hired as a professor upon her graduation. She had only spoken to her parents once since she had left Utah. She had asked them to forgive her, but her father wouldn't speak with her. Josephine's mother cried often and urged her husband to reconcile, but he steadfastly refused. When people asked him what had happened to his daughter, he replied simply: "She was taken by Satan."

* * *

"Josephine? Josephine?"

"I'm sorry. Did you say something, Martin?"

"You look troubled."

"No. I was just…thinking. I need to leave now. I hope you feel better. I'll visit again soon."

"Thanks for coming. I really appreciate the visit." Dushane smiled. He hoped he had made a good impression.

Josephine leaned over and kissed him on the cheek. "Goodbye, Martin."

CHAPTER 13

Integrity is one of several paths. It distinguishes itself from the others because it is the right path, and the only one upon which you will never get lost.

—M.H. McKee

"David! David!" Tom Jeffries banged excitedly on Chambers' office door, but no one answered. "David? Are in you in there?" Jeffries knocked firmly a few more times and tried to wait patiently, but he couldn't control his excitement, finally bursting in. "David!"

Chambers was sitting on the floor with his back to the door. He didn't turn around.

"David! I've got great news!"

Chambers stayed perfectly still.

"David?" Jeffries knelt down and gently shook Chambers' shoulder. "David?"

Chambers looked up, but Jeffries' presence didn't immediately register in his consciousness. He was still trying to return from a state of deep meditation.

"Hey, sorry to interrupt you, but I've got great news. Are you okay?"

Chambers meditated every morning at six, a routine he had maintained for almost twenty years. The practice helped him clear his mind and reconnect to his highest values, eliminating inner conflict. It also allowed him to act decisively, and he knew of no better way to prepare himself for the challenges of the day. "What is it, Tom?" he said softly.

"We won the strike suit. The judge dismissed the strike suit."

Chambers stood up. "That's…that's wonderful; that's absolutely wonderful." He wrapped his arms around Jeffries and pulled him close. "Thank you. Thanks for all your hard work."

"Of course, I…you were right along. Settling with those thieves would've been disastrous."

Chambers released his grip and smiled.

"Hey, I'm going to go spread the news to the rest of the team," Jeffries said. "I can't wait to tell everybody."

"We need to celebrate. Tell everyone we're all going away for a week of vacation; families included. Anywhere they want to go."

"Anywhere?"

"Yeah. In the meantime, I want to get everyone together for lunch this Friday."

* * *

After the judgment became final, Chambers framed it and hung it prominently on his office wall. Unfortunately, the victory hadn't come cheap. During the course of the suit, the company had been forced to produce over seven hundred boxes of documents in response to Leachman's discovery requests, and the bill from the company's outside law firm was over a million dollars. But it wasn't a bad investment. After the strike suit was dismissed, Jeffries filed an action against Millard,

Grunfeld & Leachman for abuse of process. After a three-week trial, the jury slapped the law firm with punitive damages of forty million dollars, which they reluctantly paid after a failed appeal and a scathing opinion by the appellate court accusing Leachman of using the legal system as a tool for blackmail and extortion.

Shortly after the legal proceedings ended, Chambers organized a group of CEOs from companies across the country to unite and defend themselves against strike suits. "It's NATO for business," he said at a meeting attended by representatives from over two hundred leading companies. Chambers proposed that the group adopt a provision similar to Article 5 of the actual North Atlantic Treaty:

> The Parties agree that a strike suit attack against one or more of them shall be considered an attack against them all and consequently they agree that if such an attack occurs, each of them, in exercise of the right of individual and collective self-defense, will assist the Party or Parties so attacked by taking, individually and in concert with the other Parties, such action as it deems necessary.

The purpose of the group was to vigorously defend its members against frivolous lawsuits and under no circumstances offer a settlement to the attacker. Chambers recommended that the companies set up a law firm solely devoted to serving the new entity, which he called the "Frivolous Lawsuit Defense Organization," or FIDO for short. Although the acronym didn't quite fit, Chambers wanted to convey the image of a junkyard dog that would rip its enemies apart.

Business leaders and entrepreneurs praised FIDO as long overdue, but trial lawyer's groups criticized it. Of course, this wasn't surprising since they opposed anything that decreased the amount of loot available to their practitioners. Several Bar associations also publicly opposed FIDO for the stated reason that its "no settlement under any circumstances" policy would inhibit the attorney's independent judgment, thus violating the Bar's code of ethics. The real reason behind the opposition, though, was that the Bar had no interest in slowing down the flood of legal jobs created by Leachman's strike suit machine. He had single-handedly pumped up the net worths of hundreds of influential attorneys who had mimicked his strategies. Indeed, few members of the Bar spoke out against strike suits. Besides plaintiffs' attorneys who gouged astronomical sums, defense attorneys also devoured a large slice of the pie. Every time a strike suit was filed, a company had no choice but to hire a high-priced lawyer to negotiate the intricate complexities of the action. The only people who weren't getting rich were the "defrauded" shareholders. Studies showed that after the lawyers grabbed the lion's share of any settlement, shareholders only recovered, on average, ten percent of their losses.

Leachman notwithstanding, the partners at Millard, Grunfeld & Leachman recognized the futility of challenging FIDO, so they adopted a firm-wide policy against taking any case involving a FIDO member company. Leachman went ballistic, threatening to leave the firm. Although he recognized the risk and difficulty of challenging FIDO, he didn't care. He wanted to destroy Chambers no matter what the obstacles.

Leachman finally calmed down after one of his partners reminded him that he would still rake in a healthy eight-figure salary even without the FIDO suits. Although his blood still boiled, Leachman was a practical man. He wanted to add another wing to his Marin estate and the purchase of a winery was still a twinkle in his eye. But he didn't forget about Chambers. He decided to prepare for the next battle. He called his associate, Adam Sharf.

"Adam, I've got some more work for you on the Chambers case."

"What Chambers case?"

"Chambers Aerospace."

"Isn't that case over?"

"It's never over. I want you to make sure we get everyone on our plaintiffs roster in Chambers Aerospace—ASAP."

"Why? I thought we adopted a policy and…"

"Just do it," Leachman interrupted.

"All right, but that's over four hundred plaintiffs."

"I don't care how many it is; I want them all in. And if they don't have the money, you let me know. I'll buy the shares for them if I have to."

"Uh….okay."

"One other thing; I want you to call all of our litigation partners—every single one of them. I want an agreement that they won't touch Chambers unless they get permission from me. If they give you any guff, you tell them that they're off the gravy train—permanently."

"Okay," Sharf replied somberly. He couldn't help thinking about the contrast between Leachman's vindictive nihilism and Chambers' powerful, creative energy, which he had studied during the course of the strike suit. Indeed, he had become almost obsessed with Chambers, a man with a wholeness of purpose that he lacked—that all attorneys he dealt with lacked. Sharf suddenly felt a painful crack in the mask he had worn his entire adult life. He silently prayed that the feeling would go away.

* * *

Ray Lassater carefully explained his plan to take Infinity down and then studied the faces of the three investigators he had hired to help

114

him execute it. He tried to gauge each man's reaction to his aggressive strategy. "Any thoughts?" he asked.

The three men silently eyed each other, each waiting for the others to speak.

"Somebody must have an opinion," Lassater said.

"Well, I think your plan is solid," one of the men remarked finally. "I just don't know…well, I just don't know if it's legal. Some of the…"

"Legal?" Lassater interrupted angrily. "What the hell are you talking about?"

"What you're proposing; I'm not sure…"

Lassater waved his hand dismissively and pounded his fist on the table. "Is it legal for those manipulators to steal money from their followers? Is it legal to make false promises?"

"Well, let's…"

"Don't interrupt me!" Lassater boomed. "I'm not finished! These people lie to satisfy their sick vanity and ego gratification. If that's legal, then I'll commit suicide right now. As long as I'm on this planet, I won't stand for it."

Lassater looked around the table and made eye contact with each man. "In or out?" he said firmly. "It's a simple decision. You're either all in or all out; there's no room for compromise."

"In," one of the men said without hesitation.

The next man nodded. "I'm in, too."

Lassater stared hard at the final man.

"Yeah, I'm with you, Ray. Count me in."

CHAPTER 14

Hell is the impossibility of reason.

—FROM OLIVER STONE'S *PLATOON*

The inauguration of Howard Packer as the President of the United States was a jubilant affair. Infinity followers packed the capital and looked enthusiastically to the future. No longer would they be relegated to the sidelines while secular intellectuals ran the country into Godless oblivion. It was time to reestablish the moral fiber of the nation.

The faithful crowd brimmed with confidence as Packer addressed the nation.

> My fellow Americans, these are critical times. We find ourselves at a crossroads, as a people and as a nation. We are faced with the most important choice any society can ever face—a choice involving nothing less than the soul of this nation. A choice between living in accordance with God's laws or ignoring those laws. I believe that the very existence of our republic rests on that choice.
>
> We've been led for too long by politicians who have refused to take a courageous stand against the evils in our society—greed, drug use, sexual perversion, and abortion. Our leaders have been silent while the traditional family, and the values upon which this country was founded are attacked. But now, at the beginning of a new era in this country's history, we have an opportunity for rebirth; an opportunity to cleanse and purify our souls. I call on all citizens of this great nation to join me in celebration as we begin a journey into a glorious future with the Almighty God at our side.
>
> At no other time in our history has our faith been more important. And it is only through faith that we can return this country to greatness. As your President, I will pursue honor and justice for America and I will use all the resources at my disposal. I call on all Americans to join me in this struggle to defeat evil and to protect the heart of America. But let's make no mistake about it; our task will not be easy. America has enemies, both at home and abroad. They challenge our faith and our core beliefs. As your President, I will stand up to our enemies and I will demand that our allies around the world decide: You are either with us or you are against us.
>
> We will win this struggle. God bless you, and God bless America.

* * *

As a reward for his efforts in the campaign, Packer appointed Al Rogers as his Chief of Staff. Heilbrenner spent the next two months working with Rogers and the President to build the new Administration, and Heilbrenner knew the most important rule of politics—get your own people in positions of power. He succeeded in getting Infinity members installed in high positions in every department of the new Administration, including the Attorney General. Packer also agreed to nominate Infinity members for federal judgeships and Supreme Court vacancies.

Like Infinity, he was anxious to destroy the most important cornerstone of Western democracy—the separation of church and state.

After the successful infiltration into the federal government, Heilbrenner focused on Infinity's youth programs. He started by establishing the Infinity Scouts, an organization similar to the Boy Scouts, except more explicitly religious. Heilbrenner had decided that a separate scouting program was necessary to train and educate youth in the Network because the Boy Scouts were in jeopardy of losing their right to enforce moral standards. They had come under increasing attacks for their exclusion of homosexuals, and for requiring scouts to sign a "Declaration of Religious Principles" requiring "duty" and "reverence" to God, and the faithful carrying out of "religious duties." According to a Scout official, "In order to become good citizens, scouts must believe in God."

Although the Boy Scouts had been successful in fighting off legal challenges to their exclusionary practices, Heilbrenner worried that they were vulnerable to attack because of their extensive ties to the government. The U.S. Congress had chartered the Scouts in 1916 and since that time they had become heavily intertwined with public institutions, the most notable being public schools where they often received free room rental. Public school teachers were also their most active and successful recruiters.

The Boy Scouts prohibited adult homosexuals from being leaders because homosexuality was an abomination against God's law. Thus, those who "chose" the homosexual path were deemed immoral and unfit.

Heilbrenner envisioned the Infinity Scouts as a religiously centered organization, funded by Infinity, that wouldn't accept any government money, thus reducing its likelihood of being sued. Every boy who joined Infinity Scouts was required to accept Infinity's Statement of Faith and pledge their loyalty to God and Infinity. They were also required to attend a local Christian church of their choosing.

Heilbrenner also stepped up Infinity's publishing efforts targeted at young adults, and he prepared recommended book lists. When kids reached their high school and college years and naturally began to question, he recommended *God Doesn't Believe in Doubters*, which counseled young men and women:

> If you feel intimidated by non-believers—if you think they are "intellectuals," understand that they are just the opposite. Their minds are closed to the reality of God. To reject God is to reject everything. God's existence can be proven regardless of the fantasy world of science relied upon by atheists.

Let doubters believe what they wish. They end up with nothing. And what does the believer have? Everything. With belief, all questions are answered, anything is possible, and all things can come true. Think.

Heilbrenner directed adult members of the Network to read *The End Time Believer's Evidence Bible*. Here, a person could learn about the absurdity of evolution; prove the authenticity of the Bible through prophecy; and read the terrified last words of famous people who died without accepting Christ as their Savior. Another section of the book instructed members how to speak with a Buddhist, Hindu, Muslim, Jew, or anyone else who rejected Christ as the Messiah or any other tenet of Christian superstition. On several occasions, Newhall touted the book as "the ultimate resource for Christians in their moral struggle against scientists and other nonbelievers."

Under Heilbrenner's leadership, Infinity published over five thousand books and other materials on Christian subjects. Heilbrenner's favorites were books about health and nutrition, including *What Would Jesus Eat?*, which recommended a diet based on Biblical principles. Although the book consisted of inane drivel, Heilbrenner loved it; its utter absurdity always brought a smile to his face.

But Heilbrenner's real interest was in publishing political materials. He dreamed of building a national political machine where he could pull all the strings. Since Infinity already had a strong foothold in the federal government, Heilbrenner focused on local politics. He created and distributed political literature nationwide through a network of satellite offices in 320 cities across the country. The chief function of the volunteers who staffed these offices was to print position papers on local issues, as well as lists of candidates—always including specific directions on how to vote. Officials at Infinity Headquarters in Southern California dictated positions and acceptable candidates, and it maintained a staff of forty people devoted solely to this purpose.

Heilbrenner also exploited his followers' fascination with celebrities by recruiting several country music stars and establishing the Infinity Music Center in Nashville. The Music Center consisted of a recording studio and a concert hall. Both were open to "approved" musicians whose music was deemed—by a panel of Infinity experts—to be Christian, or at least morally appropriate. Infinity also recorded radio programs at the Music Center and broadcast them across the 215 radio stations it controlled.

The Network was interdenominational and ecumenical, but at the same time adhered to a strict set of beliefs. Heilbrenner concluded that it was important to allow as many people as possible to join the Network because there was greater strength—and money—in numbers.

At the same time, he recognized the importance of enforcing a rigid set of beliefs because it made people feel special. He also knew that the acts of self-denial required by strict belief, whether they made sense or not, gave people a sense of power and therefore an emotional connection to the movement.

The only requirement for membership in the Network was acceptance of Infinity's Statement of Faith.

> We believe that the Holy Bible is the inspired, infallible word of God, and the authoritative source of Christian doctrine.
>
> We believe that man was created in the image of God, but as a result of sin is lost and powerless to save himself.
>
> We believe that there is one God, eternally existent in three persons: Father, Son, and Holy Spirit.
>
> We believe that the only hope for man is to believe in Jesus Christ, the virgin-born Son of God, who died and took upon Himself the punishment for the sins of mankind, and who rose from the dead. By receiving Him as Savior and Lord, man is redeemed by His blood.

While all of the beliefs were important, Newhall and Heilbrenner stressed the first two. Infallibility of the Bible was critical because if any of its claims were subjected to the scientific process and doubt was shed, doubt would immediately be shed on the Holy Book (and Infinity) in its entirety. More importantly, Infinity could require any behavior it wanted from its members because the Bible was ultimately subject to Infinity's interpretation.

The second belief in Infinity's Statement of Faith was just original sin stated another way—humans as filthy, depraved, contemptible creatures. Anyone who believed in his own innocence or the sacredness of his own life was dangerous because such a person would naturally reject a thought system based on blind obedience.

Finally, Heilbrenner had to make a critical decision about whether Christians should try to prove any of their claims through factual evidence. The Mormons had tried this and the results had been disastrous. Heilbrenner figured that trying to prove that Jesus rose from the grave, or that there was a worldwide flood was impossible. Indeed, all the previous attempts to hijack science in order to prove Biblical claims had resulted in the movement looking foolish. Thus, Infinity issued a directive that no member should cite any scientific evidence for proof of any Christian or Biblical claim.

After only two years under Heilbrenner's stewardship, the Network had grown to forty million members, but Heilbrenner's recruitment efforts didn't stop there. He also called on religious leaders from across the Christian spectrum to join the Network. Many did, particularly those in smaller towns, because Infinity promised to publish their sermons, thus giving them a national audience. These were men of God who, like Newhall, wanted to control the hearts and minds of their followers and relieve them of their worldly sorrows. At the same time, they recognized the virtue of suffering and promoted it, feeding a consistent foe they could heroically conquer, providing a reason for their continued existence.

Heilbrenner kept in close contact with many of these pastors in order to determine what ideas and phrases were keeping people motivated in the movement. To what extent could they demonize Muslims? Could they aggressively denounce all intellectuals and other nonbelievers? Was it too politically risky to criticize Jews? Heilbrenner's primary goal was gaining access to the part of each member's brain that didn't think, but just reacted emotionally. And Heilbrenner knew from his experience in politics that religion was no different than negative campaigning; it was much easier to motivate people by what they hated than by what they loved.

The greatest advantage from recruiting additional men of God into the Network was that these men were required to give a percentage of their revenues to Infinity. This was highly lucrative, generating an additional seventy-five million dollars a year into Infinity's coffers. Newhall referred to these additional men of God as his "special assistants." Heilbrenner just called them "useful idiots."

Infinity rarely excommunicated its members, but Heilbrenner occasionally had to remove pastors whose ideas didn't conform to the Infinity line. The most publicized case involved a group of pastors in Vermont who proclaimed that the Christian religion should have only one commandment: love thy fellow man. They argued for no churches, no scriptures, no theology, and no need for worship—only love, expressed by each person being true to his or her own individual conscience. Newhall was outraged, as were many other conservative Christians. They insisted that faith and infallible doctrine were crucial to Christianity, and Infinity reaffirmed that its Statement of Faith must be accepted in its entirety. Anyone who expressed doubt about the actual bodily resurrection of Christ were reminded of Paul's admonition that if the resurrection story was not literally true, then the Christian faith was in vain.

Infinity brought in more money per member than any religious organization in the world and its secret was pursuing every possible source and method of donation. In addition to soliciting funds during church services, on television, over the radio, and on the Internet, Infinity retained a small army of estate-planning attorneys who offered members numerous options to support the Network upon their death. Heilbrenner also employed a team of expert "collection efficiency consultants," whose job was to determine the most effective fundraising techniques and then share those techniques with Infinity-affiliated congregations across the country. Infinity then took a cut of all funds collected.

Despite Infinity's pervasive influence and power, its evangelists did not escape negative press. Critics denounced them for demanding cash in return for prayers to God, which they did on both their television programs and on their web site. But they never stopped the practice, raking in over a hundred thousand dollars a day. Nobody at Infinity ever made any actual prayers, although Heilbrenner rationalized his actions every time he reviewed the revenue numbers. *They're getting exactly what they pay for. Nothing more, nothing less.* He knew it wasn't about prayer; the donations alleviated followers' feelings of guilt and inadequacy, which Infinity provided with or without prayers.

Occasionally, Infinity was criticized for its religious doctrine. On one of their television programs, an evangelist predicted the date God would destroy all homosexuals. This was inflammatory rhetoric in the gay community, but it was a clever political calculation. Infinity leaders knew that the bulk of their support came from people who believed that the Bible condemned homosexuality. More importantly, Heilbrenner knew that Infinity's followers always needed a devil, or better yet, several devils. Homosexuals were devils guaranteed to spark the hate of the Christian faithful. As for the predicted date for homosexual destruction, it was conveniently thirty years in the future.

Newhall took the criticism of Infinity in stride, rarely defending its specific practices, but instead simply saying that his detractors were spiritually misguided and hadn't found God. Most of the time, criticism faded quietly with little effect. Heilbrenner's only real worry was that questions would be raised about Infinity's financial dealings and organizational structure.

As a vehicle for its fundraising efforts, Infinity's attorneys had set up several corporations that were exempt from taxation under federal and state tax codes. According to the law, only corporations that did not seek to make a profit, did not sell business services, and had a clear educational, charitable, or religious purpose could claim the tax exemption. In addition, tax-exempt organizations were prohibited from partisan political activities and could only use a small portion of their revenues for lobbying. Violations of any of these conditions could lead the IRS to revoke a corporation's tax-exempt status and levy stiff penalties. This was a problem for Infinity because it continuously and openly engaged in political activities, and highly partisan ones. Because of this, Infinity attorneys set up some for-profit corporations to provide cover for Infinity's extensive political work.

Although Heilbrenner and Infinity attorneys warned Newhall repeatedly not to commingle funds between the non-profit and political entities, Newhall treated all of Infinity's assets as his personal checkbook, frequently using non-profit funds for his own purposes, including extensive travel and improvements to his mansion. He also controlled several holding companies and offshore accounts, the primary purpose of which was to evade income taxes—but the IRS left him alone. After Packer's election, IRS agents were discouraged from auditing any religious organization, and Infinity was specifically off limits.

Heilbrenner exercised more caution than Newhall, although he also enjoyed a large mansion and other trappings of wealth. But Heilbrenner didn't really care about money. He started purchasing rare Ferraris and accumulated an impressive collection. He didn't particularly like the cars, but he took delight in the power to throw money away indiscriminately.

Like the vast majority of religious organizations, Infinity's leadership structure was patriarchal and authoritarian. Heilbrenner admired both the Catholic and Mormon models, which prohibited women from holding the highest positions of authority, but he figured that women could be enthusiastic and persuasive evangelists for Infinity's cause. Women were allowed to assume evangelist roles as well as administrative functions, but they were not permitted in upper leadership, which consisted of Newhall and Heilbrenner, as well as several hundred regional and local operatives.

Although a few civil rights groups protested Infinity's leadership policies, keeping women down was an easy Biblical sell to the rank and file. First, all of Christ's original Apostles were male. Second, the Bible contained several explicit commands regarding the role of women. In the book of Genesis, after Eve ate the forbidden fruit, God said to her, "I will greatly multiply thy sorrow and thy conception; in sorrow thou shalt bring forth children; and thy desire shall be to thy husband, and he shall rule over thee." Biblical scholars interpreted this to mean that when Eve ate the apple and enticed Adam to sin with her, one of the consequences for women was loss of equality with men, which allowed men to rule over women. But Newhall's favorite statements about women were from the New Testament.

> Let your women keep silence in the churches: for it is not permitted unto them to speak; but they are commanded to be under obedience, as also saith the law. (1 Corinthians 14:34).

> Let the woman learn in silence with all subjection. But I suffer not a woman to teach, nor to usurp authority over the man, but to be in silence. (1 Timothy 2:11-12).

Keeping women in line was easy; recruiting people to manage the Network wasn't. Newhall and Heilbrenner both recognized the danger of hiring men who could think and act independently so they focused their recruitment efforts on men who had achieved little success in previous endeavors—men who would be uncritical and unthinking recipients of orders. Even with these precautions, however, some underlings didn't always agree with edicts issued from above. To prevent challenges to their power, Newhall and Heilbrenner always met with their lieutenants in small groups, making it more difficult for them to combine and revolt. At the slightest hint of dissent, Heilbrenner moved rapidly to purge the offender.

Infinity had achieved enormous success by any measure of a mass movement, but Heilbrenner wasn't satisfied. He wanted people to think of Infinity every time they thought of the Almighty. Ultimately, he wanted the two concepts to be interchangeable.

CHAPTER 15

Tell a devout Christian that his wife is cheating on him, or that frozen yogurt can make a man invisible, and he is likely to require as much evidence as anyone else, and to be persuaded to the extent that you give it. Tell him that the book he keeps by his bed was written by an invisible deity who will punish him with fire for eternity if he fails to accept its every incredible claim about the universe, and he seems to require no evidence whatsoever.

—SAM HARRIS, *THE END OF FAITH*

The phone rang, stirring Chambers from a catnap at his desk. "Hello."

"You're still at the office?" Ernesto Sosa said. "It's 6:15 in the morning."

Chambers yawned. "Shareholder's meeting next week."

"We need to hire you some more help. You're going to burn yourself out."

"This company's my baby. Our baby."

"Well, I'm flying us up. You need to get some sleep."

"Yeah. Maybe I can catch a nap on the way."

"I'll be there in half an hour."

"Okay." Chambers hung up the phone and walked over to the employee lounge. He grabbed an orange juice out of the refrigerator and sat down on a couch. He turned on the television with the remote control. Although he rarely watched television, the shows never failed to surprise him. He channel surfed for a few minutes, and then stopped when he got to Infinity TV. The Network was airing a show called *Communicating with the Spirits*. It featured an Infinity spiritual medium who communicated with the dead relatives of audience members.

Chambers had heard of the show; it was a huge hit after initially generating controversy because the Bible appeared to prohibit the show's "channeling" and necromancy. Deuteronomy 18:10-11 provided:

> There shall not be found among you any one that maketh his son or his daughter to pass through the fire, or that useth divination, or an observer of times, or an enchanter, or a witch. Or a charmer, or a consulter with familiar spirits, or a wizard, or a necromancer.

Like so many passages in the Bible, the verse was poorly written, incomprehensible, and subject to interpretation—Infinity's interpretation. Infinity officials defended the show, arguing that it was consistent with Biblical commands because, unlike the thousands of swindlers throughout history who pretended to communicate with the "beyond," Infinity mediums had a direct, verifiable connection to Heavenly spirits. Infinity also stressed the vital importance of the show because it gave people a preview of Heaven if they sacrificed their lives to God. For Heilbrenner, the show was critical because it established that Infinity had unique spiritual knowledge unavailable to the rest of humanity and, more importantly, that such knowledge didn't require any scientific proof.

The actual content of the show didn't fuel much controversy because the medium always pursued a line of spiritual communication consistent with established Christian depictions of Heaven and the afterlife.

The show was highly popular and generated handsome advertising revenues and attendance fees. People happily paid fifty dollars to be in the audience and the show always sold out.

At the beginning of the show, the medium asked audience members who wanted to communicate with a dead relative to raise their hands.

The medium pointed to an elderly woman. "Good evening, ma'am. What's your name?"

"Ruth."

The medium went into the audience and put one hand on the woman's shoulder. He put his other hand on his temple to symbolize making a connection with her.

"I'm seeing…I'm seeing a man. Could it be your husband?"

"Yes," the woman answered enthusiastically. "My husband passed away last year."

"Yes, that's right. Now…did your husband linger on in the hospital or did he pass quickly?"

"Oh, he died almost immediately!"

"Yes, because he's saying to me, 'I didn't suffer. I was spared any pain.' Now…I'm seeing something in the chest area. Is that related to his death?"

"Yes, yes, he died of a heart attack," the woman replied excitedly.

"Yes, I see that. Now, I'm seeing an M sounding name. Or maybe a J." The woman shook her head.

"Or perhaps a C…or something with a D…does that make sense to you?"

"No."

"I'm seeing that your husband had a hobby. Is that right?"

"Yes, he liked to garden."

"Yes, he liked being outdoors. And I'm seeing something yellow… yellow and purple. Did your husband like flowers?"

"Yes, he planted flowers in the garden."

"I'm making a connection to him. Yes…I can hear him. He's speaking to me very clearly and he has a message for you."

The woman's eyes widened.

"He says that he's at peace in Heaven, but he misses you. I'm also seeing that he misses some others. He was close to others. Is that right?"

"We had two sons."

"Yes, I'm seeing two men. Does the M or J sounding name apply to either of them?"

"No."

"Or maybe a Charlie."

"Charlie was the name of my dog," a woman sitting three rows back blurted out.

The medium shifted his attention to this new woman, who appeared to be in her late fifties. "Yes! I'm seeing that this dog had a relationship with someone who's passed on. The dog had a close relationship with its owner."

"Yes."

"Was it with your father?"

"No, my father didn't like the dog."

"Well...I'm seeing your father here. I think your father is trying to communicate with us. I'm seeing something red. What is this please?"

"Hmmm...well, my dad had a red car many years ago."

"Yes, a wonderful red car that he loved. And he liked to travel. Is that right?"

"Yes, occasionally."

"I'm seeing a beach. A beautiful beach with clear blue water. Your father liked beach vacations."

"No. He had fair skin so he couldn't stay out in the sun too long."

"Well, this beach is significant. I'm getting a strong connection here. What's the connection here, please?"

The woman shrugged. "I'm not sure."

"Please think about this when you go home tonight," the medium scolded. "I'm sure you'll see a connection." He walked to the other side of the room.

"Now, I'm hearing a J sound like Jane, or maybe Jennifer."

A man raised his hand.

"Yes, sir."

"My wife Genevieve passed away recently."

"Yes, yes, your wife. I believe she's trying to communicate with us."

Chambers thought the show was somewhat amusing, but what he really wanted to see was a medium who told an audience member, "I'm so sorry, your mother went to Hell and I can't reach her." He'd pay fifty bucks to see that.

Chambers turned off the television and sprawled across the couch, dozing for a few minutes until Ernesto shook him.

"Wake up, sleeping beauty, your prince charming is here."

"Ahhhh...." Chambers spread his arms above his head and rubbed his eyes. "I think you're right; I could use a little more sleep."

"You ready to roll?"

"Yeah, let me grab my notebook."

* * *

Ernesto whistled his favorite part from Beethoven's Ninth Symphony as he guided the helicopter up the California coast toward Oregon. Chambers felt groggy, but he couldn't sleep.

"Ernesto, have you ever seen Infinity TV?"

"Shocking, isn't it?"

"Yeah."

"Get used to it. Now that Packer's been inaugurated, it's only going to get worse."

"You think Packer eats his own dog food?"

"What?"

"Do you think he really believes all that religious crap he spouts?"

Ernesto chuckled. "Doesn't matter what he believes. That's his meal ticket. There are Bible slappers running all over the White House now. Haven't you been watching the news?"

"No, the company's got me so busy lately, I've barely seen a newspaper." Chambers yawned.

"Look, why don't you take a nap; I may need you to help me fly back. I'll wake you up when we get there."

"Okay."

Two hours later, the chopper hovered over the property that Chambers and Sosa had recently purchased on the California-Oregon border—30,000 acres of wilderness where Chambers planned to build his dream.

"Hey, David. Wake up, buddy. We're here."

"What? Ahhh…." Chambers opened his eyes and yawned.

"Our very own middle of nowhere paradise."

Chambers looked out the window. The rolling hills were covered in redwood trees, without a trace of civilization in sight. "Man, I'd forgotten how perfect this place is."

Chambers had always been interested in what made the economy go and the people who drove it. He'd previously written a book about his own business success, but he was much more interested in what made the U.S. economy successful. He hoped to write about that. His master plan was to build a policy research center and retreat, and he planned to assemble a team of analysts who would write books and articles promoting ideas that would help people succeed. He had received donations from several philanthropists, including the former President.

Although Chambers realized that governmental policies were important, he planned to focus his research on the values and beliefs of the entrepreneurs who created the wealth. To his surprise, he'd discovered that many business leaders didn't fully understand or embrace the ideas and values that made a free society and a robust economy possible.

Chambers also wanted to establish camps and educational programs for children. He loved kids and had been a major supporter of children's charities throughout his life. He wanted to give children the benefit of his experience, helping to build their pride and self-esteem, indispensable components of a healthy, productive life.

"Looks like they've got most of the road in," Ernesto said.

"Yeah. And we're supposed to have sewer and electric by next month. Then we can start construction."

Ernesto shook his head. "This is quite an undertaking. I'm still not sure I should've agreed to this."

"Come on. It's going to be great. This ranch will be the greatest adventure of your life." Chambers paused. "The Kaleidoscope Ranch; that's what we'll call it."

"The what?"

"The Kaleidoscope Ranch. That's what we're going to call it."

* * *

David Chambers took a deep breath and then blew out all eleven candles on his birthday cake.

"Yay! Happy birthday!" his grandmother exclaimed.

"Thanks for the cake, grandma," Chambers said. He sat back in his chair and waited in anticipation for his birthday gift.

"Happy birthday, David," his grandfather said, handing him a small, brightly wrapped package.

Chambers' grandparents Hank and Loretta had raised him since his parents died in an automobile accident when he was four years old.

Chambers removed the wrapping paper quickly and uncovered a small cylinder, eight inches long and an inch and a half in diameter. It was made of brass, which was dull from age, but had recently been polished. "What is this, grandpa?"

"It's a kaleidoscope. Here, let me show you how it works."

David handed the kaleidoscope to his grandfather. "You look into this end and then turn the dial on this other end. Here, you try it."

Chambers looked into the kaleidoscope while turning the dial slowly. He marveled at the intricate images and exquisite colors. "Wow! This is neat! Thanks, grandpa!"

"You're welcome, David, but there's something you need to know about this kaleidoscope. It comes with a story."

"Uh oh. I'll leave you two alone to talk about guy stories," Loretta Chambers said as she went back into the kitchen.

"Let's go sit on the couch, David."

"Okay."

Hank Chambers had a gentle demeanor, but he was a tough World War II veteran who had served in the Navy. He had a thin frame, with gangly arms and legs, and his Navy buddies had nicknamed him "Spider." Although he was in his mid-seventies, he still had a full head of silver hair that he combed straight back off of his forehead.

David didn't know much about his grandfather's past because Hank Chambers was a quiet man who spent most of his time reading and gardening. But Chambers did know that his grandfather had a collection of books about World War II, which he kept in a special room with his other war memorabilia—his medals, uniform, and several pictures with his Navy buddies. David had never been in the room.

"David, you know that I served in World War II," Hank Chambers said quietly.

"Yeah. Grandma told me you don't like to talk about it."

"I don't, but I think it's important for you to hear this story now that you're in charge of the kaleidoscope."

"Okay, grandpa."

"I fought in the Pacific against the Japanese for two years, and I had a good buddy named Fred Carson who fought alongside me. We were both in New Guinea serving on a PT boat and we got into a lot of skirmishes out there."

"What's a PT boat, grandpa?"

"It stands for Patrol Torpedo. It was a small wood boat that carried enough firepower to sink a battleship; more firepower per pound that any other craft in the Navy. It was also faster than anything on the water."

"Wow…"

"Near the end of 1944, the skipper of our boat called the crew together for a briefing. He said he didn't want to scare us, but he told us to write our last letters home for a while. He said we were going to be involved in something really big, and we'd be told about the mission while we were underway. Now I don't know about the rest of the guys, but I was scared. I didn't know if I'd ever see my family again, and I worried about your grandmother especially."

"I'm glad you made it home okay."

Hank Chambers smiled. "Me, too. So we left New Guinea and headed out to open sea. It took six days and nights until we finally reached our destination. Then we found out that our mission was to invade the Philippines. A couple of years before, the Japs had kicked us out of there. Now, it was time to take it back. Our troops were preparing to land on the island while battleships, cruisers, and other ships were shelling the shores to make a beachhead. All kinds of planes were in the air; our planes and Japanese, and shrapnel was falling from the sky all over the place. There were kamikazes there too and they took out one of our battleships."

"What's a kamikaze?"

"That's when a pilot flies his plane into the side of a boat, trying to damage it or sink it. It's an act of suicide, but the Japs trained their pilots to do it. Anyway, it's hard to explain everything that was happening out

131

there, but there was no time to eat. Somebody would hand me a piece of beef jerky at my gunnery station, and I'd eat in a hurry, bursting blasts of machine-gun fire between bites. I was manning one of the machine guns. Fred Carson was next to me, firing the cannon."

"Did you think you were going to die, grandpa?"

Hank Chambers chuckled lightly. "No David, I never thought that. There wasn't any time to think about that. I wasn't scared anymore either. Once you start fighting for your life, the only thing you focus on is getting the job done and trying to survive. I figured the only way I was going to stay alive was to destroy as many Japanese ships and planes as I could.

"We did pretty well in the initial battle, but later on, we had to go to this place called the Surigao Strait to guard against Japanese reinforcements. Our intelligence people told us they might try sailing through there. And they came through all right—we spotted nine Japanese warships on our radar. Fred was yelling 'The Japs are coming! The Japs are coming!' We all manned our battle stations and I said a quick prayer and prepared to fight.

"All the PT boats we had out there went to intercept the Japanese destroyers, but our boat took the lead. Unfortunately, the Japs spotted us right away and blew us out of the water. Other PT boats came and picked up our dead and wounded and then put us on a cruiser. I wasn't hurt too bad, but Fred had gotten burned pretty badly, and he had some internal injuries." Hank Chambers stroked his forearm, which was covered with reddish scar tissue.

"What about your arm, grandpa?"

"I got lucky. This is nothing, especially compared to Fred. When we got inside the cruiser, the docs tried to fix him up, but he was hurt bad. When I went in to see him, he could barely speak, but he told me to get his pants next to the bed. They were bloody and all ripped up, but he told me to reach into one of the side pockets. I put my hand in there and pulled out the kaleidoscope, which I'd never seen before. I looked through it like you just did and I couldn't believe how beautiful it was. I said to Fred, 'This is so beautiful, but why do you carry it around with you?' He told me that the kaleidoscope reminded him why we were fighting the war; the colors and images represented all the people in the world and the beautiful combinations that were possible when people came together."

"Is Fred…?"

"No, Fred died a few days later. You know, I still think about him almost every day. Sometimes it hurts because I miss him, but I feel blessed to have been his friend, and I'm glad that I can share his story with you." Hank Chambers turned away and rubbed his eyes.

"That's a sad story, grandpa. Is that why you never talk about the war?"

"That's one of the reasons, but the main reason is that war is horrible. It's not exciting, it's not glamorous, it's just bad; people getting killed, being away from your family. I hope you never have to go to war, but don't take your freedom for granted either. You have to fight if anyone ever tries to take your freedom away."

CHAPTER 16

If a man also lie with mankind, as he lieth with a woman,
both of them have committed an abomination:
they shall surely be put to death;
their blood shall be upon them.

—BIBLE, LEVITICUS 20:13

Nathan Robb crouched in the back of his van, barely able to control his anger. *Fuckin' faggot lover!* He waited patiently until Darren Barnett parked his car in the driveway and went inside his small suburban home near Minneapolis. Robb bowed his head and said a quick prayer.

Almighty God, I am your faithful servant and I obey your commands.
Give me the courage and the strength to carry out your will.

Robb climbed out of the van and strapped a fully loaded assault rifle across his chest. He walked quickly up the steps to the Barnett residence and then steadied the rifle on his shoulder. *Sinnerrrrrrr!* He pulled the trigger and held it down, blasting the ammunition out of the gun and shattering the living room window into thousands of tiny shards. Robb jumped through the opening, landing in front of the terrified family.

"You mock the Lord!" Robb yelled, pointing his gun at Barnett.

"Don't shoot! Don't shoot!" Barnett jumped up and held his arms high in surrender.

"The Lord must strike you down!" Robb unleashed a stream of bullets that tore into Barnett's neck and shoulders, turning his upper body into a shredded mass of bloody pulp, nearly severing his head. As Barnett fell lifeless on the carpet in a pool of blood, Robb fired one last time, lodging several bullets comfortably into Barnett's brain. When he was sure that Barnett was dead, Robb ran out to his van and peeled off while Barnett's wife and three kids shrieked in terror and disbelief.

* * *

Barnett had been a junior high school principal, a devoted father, and a tireless volunteer at his local Episcopal Church. He was also an important lay leader in the House of Deputies, which consisted of priests and lay leaders from every Episcopal diocese in the United States.

Barnett was well known for his outspoken arguments criticizing the Church's stance against same-sex marriages. He also condemned the Church's prohibition against openly gay men serving as bishops. At the last Episcopalian General Convention, Barnett had made news when he argued strenuously that scripture was unnecessary, irrelevant, and sometimes even harmful when people faced difficult moral choices. He insisted that people needed to trust their own God-given judgment, and that God would not stand for the hatred shown toward gays by refusing to accept them just as God had created them. Although Barnett's opinions had generated controversy and contributed to the already deep divisions in the Church, his supporters knew him as a man committed to Christ's way of love and inclusion. His detractors branded him a dangerous heretic.

The murder of Barnett was one of a rash of attacks against homosexuals

135

and their supporters. Since President Packer had assumed office, he had thrown his weight behind a Constitutional amendment stating that marriage could only be between a man and a woman. Although the President urged tolerance of homosexuals, he declared that homosexual behavior was sinful and therefore should not be legally or morally sanctioned in American society.

* * *

John Heilbrenner sat quietly in the back of the room hoping that no one would recognize him. He was waiting for the arrival of the first speaker at Christian Brotherhood, an annual gathering of Christians at a sprawling 2,000-acre compound in Clarksville, Idaho. Marvin Butler owned the property and had hosted the event for the past four years. The land included a spacious meeting hall, a large nondenominational Christian church, several smaller chapels, and a paramilitary and survivalist training center. Three thousand believers lived at the compound full time.

Butler advertised the compound as a place where God-fearing Christians could escape when the Tribulation occurred. According to several prominent theologians, most of the world's population would die within the first hour of the Apocalypse, leaving a select group of people to rebuild society and usher in the millennial rule of Christ. Butler excited his followers by telling them that God had promised to give him advance warning of the end so that they would be well-prepared, and be the first to meet the Almighty and eternally unite with Christ.

Butler and his lieutenants employed many of the historically proven techniques used by religious leaders to control followers. This included requiring members to share property and sign it over to the group upon admission, limiting interactions with the outside world, restricting certain reading material, communal work efforts, constant meetings and Bible studies, mortification procedures such as confession, mutual surveillance and denunciation, and billing Butler as a living prophet who had a direct connection to God.

Butler's Christians built their own houses, which were modest, ranging in size from twelve to fifteen hundred square feet. They were also required to help build Butler's house, which was an eight-thousand-square-foot, sprawling ranch-style home that sat on ten fenced-off acres. It included private stables, a fitness center, a swimming pool, and a hot tub.

New initiates always started their service to God by working directly for Butler, who would properly condition them. He would make them build a fence and then without explanation, order them tear it down. He would tell them to move boulders from one side of the compound to the other, and then order them to move the boulders back to their original location. Occasionally, a new recruit asked why. "There is no why here!" Butler would rage. His strategy was to destroy his followers' inclinations to reason by subjecting them to absurdities that had no logical reason. If people became convinced that they weren't equipped to understand the world around them, this created a need for a "higher power." Butler was a master at creating and manipulating this need.

The compound also housed a large weapons cache, including two thousand hand grenades, five hundred assault rifles, thirty machine guns, three antitank rockets, twenty-five anti-aircraft missiles with launchers, forty pounds of plastic explosives, and a large drum of cyanide. Inhabitants also laid land mines around the periphery of the property and stockpiled three years worth of food.

During the day, group members worked at various tasks required to sustain the compound, as well as engaging in military drills. In the evenings, the group held Bible studies or other fellowship meetings where they discussed Christian martyrs and the importance of personal sacrifice. Leaders encouraged members to bring up any behavioral indiscretions that they had witnessed from other members. And this included the worse indiscretion of all—personal pride. When this happened, the person guilty of pride would sit in a special chair while the others would lay their hands on him and speak in tongues to cure him. After the others had confronted and humiliated the person, he or she would pray for forgiveness. Occasionally, Butler directed group leaders to unfairly accuse someone of sinful behavior. This would cause both the accuser and the follower's inherent sense of fairness to be shaken and keep them in fear.

Consistent with Biblical teachings regarding the proper role of women, group leaders required women to remain silent unless spoken to by a man. Women also called their husbands "lord" as a sign of respect, in imitation of the way the Biblical character Sarah referred to her husband, Abraham.

Although Butler generally had a good relationship with officials in the Packer Administration, government officials worried for two reasons: Butler was a loose cannon and his followers were mentally unstable. Nevertheless, the Administration promised Butler that they wouldn't harass the compound unless he took action that undermined the government. In that case, Administration officials warned Butler that the compound would be obliterated. As a precaution, Al Rogers, the President's Chief of Staff, dispatched operatives to monitor Butler's annual gathering.

Most of the attendees at Christian Brotherhood were ordinary Christians who believed in the infallibility of scripture and wouldn't tolerate anyone who questioned their beliefs. Butler only permitted white Christian men to attend and declared that, "If any blacks show up, then we'll have us a nigger shoot."

Butler had personally invited Heilbrenner to attend the event, and the Infinity second-in-command had reluctantly agreed. Butler wanted Heilbrenner to allow organizations affiliated with Christian Brotherhood to join the Network, which had the political power he coveted.

Although Heilbrenner didn't like Butler's overt racism and violent rhetoric, he figured he could learn something. He was especially curious about Butler's growing popularity and the methods he employed to convince people to follow him. Butler had a reputation for getting ordinary people to pledge total devotion to the Christian cause and even resort to violence if necessary in the name of their faith.

The crowd of over three thousand white Christian men roared as Butler stepped up to the podium. He smiled, raising his arms in acknowledgment of the applause.

> Thank you. Thank you all for being here. It's my pleasure to welcome everyone here today. I'm happy to tell you that this is the biggest turnout we've ever had. Our Christian army is growing!

Butler paused while the crowd erupted.

> I reckon you've all heard the good news. God has struck down another sinner and brought us one step closer to a society based on moral law. We will not be denied!

A loud whoop and then more exuberant applause filled the meeting hall. Heilbrenner cringed; he knew Butler was referring to the murder of Darren Barnett. Although Heilbrenner didn't care about Barnett, he worried that the violence might go too far and undermine Infinity's use of Christianity. Butler continued:

> Our first speaker today is an old friend of mine. He's a very spiritual man who cares deeply about our cause and is doing everything in his power to help us win this fight. Please welcome our brother in Christ, Reverend Lawrence Pendergraft.

The crowd hollered excitedly as Pendergraft stepped up to speak.

> Thank you. Thank you. Welcome all of you. I want to thank you all for being here. It's more important than ever for us to be true to the Lord in these times of darkness; the Lord is testing our courage and resolve. I'm happy to see so many of you here, willing to sacrifice yourselves to win this war.

You know that we're all committed men of the Lord here, yet people criticize us for what we believe in. They say let gay people sodomize each other and enter into perverted marriages. They say let mothers kill their babies. They say remove God from the schools and allow the neo-pagan, Godless philosophy of secular humanism to poison the minds of our children. We're the ones standing up against that. We're the only ones. God has called us and we have answered. We should stand proud.

You know, I've been called a narrow-minded, intolerant, reactionary, Bible-thumping fundamentalist—a zealot, a fanatic. Well, by God, it's true. I am a narrow-minded fanatic when it comes to living according to God's laws. The reason the United States was once a great nation is because she was blessed by God and founded on truth, justice, and just that kind of narrow-mindedness.

I want you all to concentrate now, close your eyes if you like, and let a wave of hate wash over you. Hate is good. Hate can be powerful. We must summon it against our enemies and take vengeance upon them just as God did in Biblical times. The Almighty calls upon us again to seek vengeance now. Don't you ever forget our mission. Our goal is a Christian nation, and a return to morality. We will destroy what the liberals and the humanists have turned this county into—a modern-day Sodom and Gomorrah.

The crowd's hate bubbled into a chorus of boos and hissing. Heilbrenner questioned whether he should have come. Pendergraft paused until the noise died down and then pumped his fist in the air.

We are the chosen people of God and we've been called by Him to conquer this country using whatever means necessary. This is a war we must win! Fight! Fight! Fight! Thank you!

Heilbrenner had never met Pendergraft before, but he knew of him vaguely. Pendergraft belonged to Christian Reconstruction, a denomination that believed in "reconstructing" society by turning to the Bible for the nation's laws and social order. Reconstructionists held a postmillennial view of history, believing that Christ would only return to earth after a thousand years of religious rule. Therefore, Christians had an obligation to provide the political and social conditions that would make Christ's return possible.

Other Christians adopted a premillennial view, which held that the thousand years of Christendom would only come *after* Christ returned, an event that would occur in a cataclysmic moment of history. This apocalyptic mindset could be traced all the way back to first-century prophets, including Christ and his mentor, John the Baptist, so it held wide appeal and led to the popularity of books about the "End Times."

Both millenial viewpoints were dangerous for different reasons. The postmillennialists justified violence and intolerance because it was necessary to establish the political landscape that would be acceptable to Christ. Believers' own worldly goals were inconsequential so they eagerly sacrificed themselves to the cause in whatever way their leadership deemed appropriate. By contrast, premillennialists encouraged Middle Eastern warfare in the hope of causing Armageddon so that Christ could return.

Other Christian Brotherhood attendees belonged to Christian Identity, which also advocated a society based on Biblical law. However, Identity doctrine focused more on white racial supremacy and anti-Semitism. According to Identity teaching, contemporary social struggles could be traced back to the conflict that occurred upon the creation of the universe. Lucifer, the satanic anti-God of the underworld, became jealous of God's order and tried to seize the world and turn it into a kingdom of evil. Christianity was a major effort by God to counteract Lucifer, but it was plagued at the start by Lucifer's forces. Some of Lucifer's henchmen claimed to be Jews, but they were not; the true Jews were Aryans. Identity scholars believed that those who called themselves Jews were impostors who had descended from an illicit sex act between Eve and Satan.

Christian Identity and Christian Reconstruction represented the majority of the faithful at the gathering, but representatives from other Christian denominations attended as well. Pastor Thomas Monroe, the National Director of the Knights of the Ku Klux Klan arrived with several of his deputies. A devout man of God, Monroe served the Klan in addition to guiding a large congregation in Alabama. Monroe had asked Heilbrenner to allow his church and others with similar beliefs into the Network, but Heilbrenner steadfastly refused. He viewed the Klan as a relic of the past that was losing membership despite its strong Christian credentials. The Klan's mission statement declared:

> We envision an America once again guided by Biblical principles and laws. Whose laws better to follow than those of the creator of our universe. Who has a more perfect knowledge of good and evil, of right and wrong, of pain and pleasure than our creator Jesus Christ. Does it not make sense to then heed his advice and the advice of Biblical scholars inspired by God thousands of years ago?

> We envision a White Christian America just like Washington, Jefferson, Adams, Paine, Lincoln, Webster, Madison, etc.

When Heilbrenner read the Klan's comparison of itself to the Founding Fathers, he immediately thought of the phrase "rolling over in their graves," and concluded that the Klan exhibited a level of arrogance and ignorance that even he couldn't stomach. He also figured that even though Scripture had been used for hundreds of years to justify slavery and racism, the vast majority of Christians would no longer tolerate this.

Other Christian Brotherhood groups that Heilbrenner found distasteful included Aryan Nations, a Christian Identity-affiliated group. Its creed of faith stated:

> We believe there is a battle being fought this day between the children of darkness (today known as Jews) and the children of Light (God), the Aryan race, the true Israel of the Bible.

World Church of the Creator was similar except that it was made up largely of ex-cons. Heilbrenner steered clear of them. *A bunch of wannabe Christian Nazis*, he thought. And nobody likes ex-cons.

In addition to the men of God, representatives from several militia groups came to the meeting as well. Most of them engaged in paramilitary and survivalist training and Butler allowed them to conduct drills on his property. He also helped them locate reliable arms suppliers.

Despite some slight doctrinal differences and goals, all of the groups' views were based on a common conspiracy theory: there was a secret war being waged by evil, satanic forces against moral, God-fearing Americans, and the character of the United States as a religious nation blessed by the Lord hung in the balance. Heilbrenner chuckled at the childishness of the mindset, but he admired their commitment to the cause and their absolute and unquestioning dedication to the Bible. They possessed the intellectual framework that he hoped to sell to the Infinity rank and file—the idea of cosmic warfare.

Heilbrenner's goal was to solidify and expand his power base by strengthening the commitment of the Infinity faithful. He wanted them to adopt three core beliefs: one, there is a cosmic struggle of good versus evil occurring in the world; two, each person must personally identify with the struggle and see it in black and white terms with no room for compromise; and three, each person's efforts are critical to the cause so they must sacrifice themselves.

Although Heilbrenner loved the idea of cosmic warfare, he objected to the extensive use of violence, fearing it would undermine Infinity's position. He reckoned that the faithful welcomed a certain amount of violence because it satisfied their violent impulses and frustrations, and channeled their hate in a concrete way. Violence also made the movement appear serious and its adherents committed, but Heilbrenner knew that the line could be crossed, and the murder of Barnett appeared to cross it.

After the opening speeches, Heilbrenner met with Butler privately.

"Glad you could join our little get-together," Butler drawled amiably.

"You shouldn't have killed Barnett," Heilbrenner said, his voice edgy. "You're jeopardizing our operation."

"I didn't kill anyone," Butler scoffed.

"Who did?"

"That's the beauty of it, John. There's no central leadership or control. Nobody can trace any event that happens any further back than the person who pulls the trigger." Butler knew what he was talking about. He had convinced other Christian leaders and militia groups to act independently and not to consolidate into a central organization. Under this set-up, if there were ever a problem, the worst-case scenario would be the elimination of one local cell, with the rest of the organization still intact. Christian Brotherhood was the only assembly that brought leaders together. Its goal was not to plan any activities, but simply to inspire the Christian soldiers and set the general direction of the cause.

"I don't care how you organize it," Heilbrenner retorted. "The Barnett murder wasn't strategic."

Butler shrugged. "Like I said, I don't make those decisions. I'd rather they kill the actual faggots, but some of these guys have minds of their own." Butler smiled and chuckled lightly at his own joke.

"Well, let's get to it," Heilbrenner pressed impatiently. "What do you want?"

"We want to be part of the same team; all Christian brothers united. Trust me, you don't want us against you." Butler paused to let Heilbrenner process the thinly veiled threat. "Besides, we can bring in a lot of money. We're willing to buy as much political power as you can get us."

"I'll have to talk to Reverend Newhall about this."

"Don't take too long. I don't know how much longer I can control this."

"You better control it," Heilbrenner responded sharply. "And keep me apprised of your operations."

Butler smiled. "We'll talk soon then."

Before he left, Heilbrenner spoke with a few of Butler's lieutenants and several rank-and-file followers who lived at the compound. He concluded that the key to Butler's operation was not only destroying the capacity to reason, but also moral disengagement—extinguishing a follower's ability to empathize with his opponents by dehumanizing them. Indeed, Butler had gotten his followers to base their entire identity on opposition to the group's enemies by preying on several fears—fears of a godless universe, chaos, loneliness, lack of control over their lives, and moral ambiguities. The movement gave them a way to control and simplify their lives. All the follower had to do was sacrifice and obey.

The final thing Heilbrenner learned was that Butler had skillfully marketed his followers' real-world grievances as spiritual issues. Men who had traditionally enjoyed unquestioned societal dominance, but who were now in competition with women, were attracted to the idea that feminism was inspired by Satan and contrary to Biblical law. Similarly, followers who feared homosexuals found solace in condemning them as abominations.

Heilbrenner concluded that it was critical to frame every controversial stance Infinity took in spiritual terms because it gave the position de facto credibility. Even intellectuals horrified by the bald irrational pronouncements made by religious leaders found it difficult to overcome the taboo of attacking religion head on. Heilbrenner left the gathering with a renewed sense of vigor, eager to apply his new understanding to Infinity's operations.

CHAPTER 17

The great trouble is that the preachers get the children from six to seven years of age, and then it is almost impossible to do anything with them...Incurably religious, that is the best way to describe the mental condition of so many people. Incurably religious.

—Thomas Alva Edison

"God is everywhere. God sees you. Are you right with God?"

Chambers read the words carefully and they freshly shocked him even though the Infinity-sponsored slogan had become ubiquitous in newspapers and magazines across the country. The advertising campaign was the most important pillar of Infinity's recruitment strategy, which was designed to scare as many people as possible.

Chambers turned to the next page and read about the murder of Darren Barnett. He paused halfway through the article: "Religious extremists are suspected of the murder." *Suspected?* Chambers reacted. *What other kind of person would commit such a senseless murder? It's got to be a religious fanatic or a lunatic. Why don't people understand the connection between Infinity's message and the increased divisiveness in our country? Hell, most people don't even appreciate the pervasiveness of religious violence throughout human history. God, this is hopeless!*

Chambers was about to throw the paper away when another byline caught his attention: "President Packer Open to Reestablishing Voluntary Prayer in Public Schools." *Can this nightmare get any worse?* Chambers silently fumed. *Why don't they just burn everyone at the stake and call it a day?* He threw the newspaper into the garbage can next to his desk and flopped lazily on the couch.

* * *

"Students, listen carefully please," Chambers' teacher began. "I have an important announcement to make. After the Pledge of Allegiance, we're going to pray together every morning before we begin our work. I'll be the leader, and you can either recite the prayer with me or just bow your heads while I say it." The teacher placed a small stack of prayers on the first desk of each row. "Oh…almost forgot, you're not required to pray and you can wait outside if you wish."

Chambers and the other students in his fifth grade class looked around to gauge each other's reactions. They all feared looking different or being singled out so they silently obeyed.

The new religious regimen was the result of a statute adopted by the Texas legislature:

> Any teacher or professor in any public educational institution within the state of Texas, recognizing that the Lord God is one, may lead willing students in prayer, as follows:

> "Almighty God, You alone are our God. We acknowledge You as the Creator and Supreme Judge of the world. Without you, we are sinners without hope and we pray for your forgiveness. May Your justice, Your truth, and Your peace abound this day in the hearts of our countrymen, in the counsels of our government, in the sanctity of our homes, and in the classrooms of our schools. In the name of our Lord. Amen."

145

Although the First Amendment of the U.S. Constitution required that the government "make no law respecting an establishment of religion," supporters of the new legislation argued that the law was constitutionally permissible because it didn't *require* students to pray; it merely allowed them to pray if they so chose. Two state senators who opposed the bill argued that it was unrealistic to believe that children who didn't want to pray would actually be able to exercise that right freely, given the social pressure they were under. But this didn't sway the law's supporters who were actually relying on this pressure in the indoctrination process. Prayer in school was the first step in gaining tighter control over the childrens' minds and conditioning them to accept God, religion, and obedience above anything else.

Ultimately, opposing the new legislation was virtually impossible because the vast majority of politicians proudly trumpeted that they believed in God and went to church every Sunday. Comparing religion to medieval superstition was political suicide because believers labeled anyone who didn't believe in God as automatically immoral.

Besides the prayer requirement, Chambers had a new classmate named Vijay. Vijay and his parents had recently moved to Texas from India. A boy named James Collins was also in Chambers' class. He was only ten years old, but puberty had already begun to transform him. He was the biggest kid in the class and acne pocked his face. He had long, wiry brown hair and wore scuffed black boots without laces. Although he was a boy of sluggish comprehension, everyone in the class was scared of him and he relished his role as the class bully. He had an abusive father who punished him for the slightest infractions and convinced him that he would never amount to anything. His father also ridiculed and insulted anyone who didn't agree with him. James Collins had inherited this same behavior.

On the second day of school, as the teacher began reciting the prayer, Vijay got up and walked toward the door. He had told his parents the previous evening about the religious routine, and they objected to the public school forcing an unwelcome belief system on their son. They told Vijay to quietly leave the room and stay outside during the prayer.

As Vijay weaved his way toward the door, confused stares shot around the room along with muffled judgments and a collective thought: *He's not one of us.* The teacher recited the prayer with extra sincerity and then went outside to retrieve Vijay. He followed the teacher back in and sat down at his desk, which was directly in front of James Collins.

"Next time we pray, you're gonna stay in here and bow your damn head, sand nigger," Collins sneered, slapping Vijay on the back of the neck.

Vijay didn't look back.

"You understand me!" Collins grabbed him by the shoulder and tried to spin him around, but Vijay resisted and continued to look forward.

Collins and other students harassed Vijay for several weeks, and he was shunned by most of his classmates. None of the other kids wanted to be associated with a boy who didn't pray. Despite the harassment, Vijay always left the room while the teacher led the other students in prayer, and this arrangement seemed to work. There was relative peace until one day after school when Collins and two of his friends cornered Vijay in the bathroom.

"You piece of trash," Collins sneered. "You worship a fuckin' idol. You pray to a cow? Is that what you do?" The three boys grabbed Vijay, pushed him into a stall, and threw him down.

"Hold him a sec," Collins ordered while he peed into the toilet, and then grabbed Vijay by the hair and forced his head into the bowl. Collins dunked his head down as far as it would go and then flushed. Vijay gasped for breath as he choked on the foul water, and then fell to the floor, vomiting.

Chambers was walking down the hall when he saw Collins and his friends coming out of the bathroom laughing.

"That'll teach that Indian!" one of the boys exclaimed.

Chambers went into the bathroom where Vijay was lying on his side, shaking.

"What happened? Are you okay?" Chambers cried as he rushed to Vijay's side.

Vijay looked up with heavy eyes and curled up. Then he began heaving with tears. Chambers had never seen anyone cry like that before. Chambers knelt beside him until Vijay's crying became softer. Then he put his arm around Vijay's shoulder. "Vijay…Vijay…it's okay, it's okay." Chambers ran his hand down Vijay's back like he was petting a newborn puppy until Vijay sat up and put his hand on Chambers' shoulder. Chambers wrapped both his arms around Vijay and pulled him closer. Vijay dropped his head and continued weeping.

That evening, Chambers slumped back into the cushions on the couch, lost in confusion. His grandmother walked in from the kitchen. "What's wrong, David? I've never seen you mope around like this."

Chambers shrugged. "School, I guess. There's some stuff at school."

His grandmother sat next to him. "What's going on?" She put her hand behind his neck and caressed it softly.

"I don't know. There's this new kid at school named Vijay. He's different. He's from India. He wears funny clothes. I don't think he has any friends. We have our prayer at school and he always leaves the room. I guess he doesn't believe in God or something. The other kids make fun of him and sometimes they hit him. I saw him crying in the bathroom. It doesn't seem right, but I don't know, maybe he should pray like everyone else."

"Well, David, I believe that God is about loving each other. Prayer and religion are things that people have to decide for themselves. No one should be forced to pray, and it isn't right to be mean to someone just because they don't believe the same things you do. We have to accept everyone as they are. Do you understand?"

"Yeah, I guess so. I still feel bad for him. He seems sad and I don't want him to feel bad."

"Why don't you talk to him; try to be his friend. You can tell him it's okay if he doesn't want to pray."

"Okay, grandma. But what about these guys who beat him up?"

"Forgive them David, for they know not what they do." Loretta Chambers didn't often quote scripture, but sometimes it came out automatically.

"But they do know, grandma," Chambers insisted. He sighed and lay back on the couch, trying to relax, but a strange thought suddenly entered his mind: *Religion makes the world unreliable.*

"Do you want some ice cream, David?"

"Religion makes the world unreliable."

"What did you say?"

"I said, religion makes the world unreliable."

Loretta Chambers crinkled her forehead. "What do you mean by that?"

"I'm not sure. I just…I just thought it and…and…I don't know…"

The next morning, Chambers' stomach churned and flipped, and his palms broke into a panicked sweat. Terrifying thoughts of rejection littered his mind and panic surged through his veins. He tried as hard as he could not to shake, but he had made up his mind to stand firm.

The teacher walked into the classroom and began the usual morning routine. "Good morning everyone," she said and then motioned for Vijay to leave the room. Vijay walked out and the familiar drone began: "Almighty God…"

Chambers bolted up from his chair, kept his head down tight, and sprang toward the door, hoping frantically that no one would pay attention to him. He wanted to wait with Vijay in the hall and tell him it was okay not to pray. But Chambers hadn't gotten five feet from his desk when everyone stopped reciting the prayer.

"Where are you going, David?" the teacher asked.

Chambers looked up sheepishly. "I'm not going to pray today," he said in a low voice.

"Why? Is everything okay?"

Chambers stood at the doorway and felt twenty-five sets of questioning eyes coalesce into a slicing laser beam of derision. The classroom was silent, but Chambers' face flushed with warm blood and his ears rang in throbbing terror from the silent judgments. He was too frightened to respond so he quickly escaped out the door and waited patiently with Vijay.

A few days later, Collins and his gang cornered Chambers behind the school.

"Well, looky here, we got ourselves a faggot. What's wrong with you boy? Are you a faggot with that Indian?" Collins challenged.

Chambers was silent.

"I'm talking to you, faggot. I said what's wrong with you?"

Chambers looked frantically for an escape route.

"You got a problem, faggot?" Collins stepped forward and pushed Chambers in the chest while another boy tripped him up from behind, causing him to fall awkwardly to the ground. The three boys laughed as he got back up.

"I don't want to fight," Chambers said finally.

Collins moved toward him again. "I don't give a shit. You think I give a shit! I don't give a shit about faggots." Chambers backed up toward the wall, pressing his hands against the cold cement. The boys moved in closer and Chambers' heart raced. His thoughts pounded rapid-fire in his head. *Violence didn't solve anything*, he heard his grandmother telling him. *But grandma, these guys are cowards! I can't let them do this!* Chambers summoned his strength and let the power well up in his body. But there was a boy on either side and in front of him, and he was backed up against the wall. He closed his eyes, and then with one concentrated burst of energy he sprung forward like a slingshot into Collins' torso. The force knocked Collins to the ground and Chambers grabbed his head and slammed it into the pavement, breaking both of Collins' front teeth and tearing his upper lip in half. The other two boys grabbed him from behind, but Chambers whipped around before they could get a firm grip and he swung his eager fists into one of the boy's faces, landing with each fist, bloodying the boy's nose, and then knocking him to the ground. The other boy tried to grab him again and managed to hold his shoulders for a second until Chambers grabbed the boy's throat and squeezed as hard as he could. The boy let go and fell backwards, gasping for air. Chambers flung himself back to Collins, who was bleeding on the pavement, and kicked him in the ribs several times. The two other boys watched from the ground, but didn't do anything to help their friend. Chambers lunged toward them, but they scrambled to their feet and ran away. Chambers went back to Collins one last time and with all the force he could muster, kicked him in the face, shattering his jaw and knocking him unconscious.

Chambers stepped back, shocked at his own power. He waited quietly until a teacher arrived and called an ambulance, which rushed Collins to the hospital where he was treated for a broken jaw and a skull fracture. Doctors concluded that he would need extensive reconstructive surgery to repair the damage to his face.

The next day, the principal summoned Chambers and his grandmother to his office for a meeting with the school's psychologist. Although the psychologist had never met Chambers, she quickly concluded that his actions were the result of pent-up anger. She recommended a psychiatrist. Chambers didn't understand any of the psychological jargon, but he did know that he felt energized standing up to those bullies. And he felt no guilt.

Chambers hadn't thought about the fight with Collins in a long time, but the memory inspired him into action. He rolled off the couch and went back to his desk. He turned on his computer and spent the next two hours writing an op-ed piece for the local newspaper about his experiences with school prayer and why it was a terrible idea. He tried to write a measured argument, but the subject struck a nerve and he couldn't keep the bite out of his prose. He concluded with the final paragraph:

> Forcing our children to talk to an imaginary friend and grovel for forgiveness serves absolutely no useful purpose. While the Packer Administration and its supporters from the Infinity Network think teaching our kids that they are inherently sinful is healthy, let's not fool ourselves. The real sin is subjecting our children to this nonsense. Prayer and ignorance have no place in our public schools.

Because of his popularity and notoriety, newspapers across the country picked up Chambers' letter. When Heilbrenner saw it, he immediately called the President's Chief of Staff, Al Rogers.

"Hi Buzz, John Heilbrenner." The only people who called Rogers by his nickname "Buzz" were a few of his close friends and his inner circle of associates. Rogers got the nickname because he had served as an officer in the Marines and still wore the same short, military-style haircut.

"Morning, John."

"Have you seen that Chambers letter?"

"Yeah."

"We need to do something. We can't let that go unchallenged."

"Maybe."

"What do you mean, maybe?"

"Well, it's a delicate…I haven't decided on a proper response yet," Rogers waffled.

"What's to decide?" Heilbrenner bellowed in exasperation. "Attack!"

Anytime someone had opposed the Infinity Network in the past, Heilbrenner was quick to vilify them as anti-Christian and immoral, and he could always rely on Infinity followers to help him spread the message. All he had to do was turn on the faucet.

"It's not that easy this time," Rogers replied weakly.

"Why not?"

"It's David Chambers for chrissakes. He won a Presidential Medal of Freedom. We need to be careful. I don't want to make a mistake."

"Why? He's nothing. He's an atheist."

"You ever met him?"

"No, and what does that have to do with anything? He's no different than anyone else we've destroyed."

"You're wrong," Rogers reacted, raising his voice. Rogers had met Chambers once before and he vividly remembered the encounter; it was the only time he could recall feeling intimated by another person.

"Well, I don't know what the hell you're thinking," Heilbrenner pressed. "But he's gone too far. My followers are pissed off and they're going to hate the son of a bitch by the time I get through. Come on, this is a golden opportunity. We can channel this hate to support the President's programs."

"Look, I need you to sit tight for now. You understand?"

Heilbrenner didn't respond.

"John? You hear me? I don't want any…"

"I heard you," Heilbrenner interrupted. "Goodbye." *Bullshit!* Heilbrenner raged as he slammed down the phone. Then he quickly picked it up again, dialing one of his deputies. "Pat, I want a full radio and op-ed campaign in response to the Chambers letter. Every city."

CHAPTER 18

The whole thing is so patently infantile, so foreign to reality, that to anyone with a friendly attitude to humanity it is painful to think that the great majority of mortals will never be able to rise above this view of life.

—SIGMUND FREUD, ON RELIGION

Josephine closed the door of the cab and dropped her sunglasses into her purse. She squinted as her eyes adjusted to the sun. She walked across the sidewalk and entered an old, three-story, brick building in the Beacon Hill neighborhood of Boston. She climbed two flights of stairs to Dushane's flat and knocked on the door.

Dushane had returned home from the hospital three days previously and he still felt weak. The knock startled him. He lifted himself slowly off the couch and walked toward the door. He peered through peephole, and then swung the door open excitedly. "Josephine!"

"Hi, Martin. How are you feeling?"

"I'm good, I'm good. Except for this." Dushane held up his arm, which was in a sling.

"Can I come in?"

"Of course. I'm…I'm happy to see you." Dushane looked down at his feet and felt a little embarrassed about the ratty slippers he had on. *I hope she doesn't think I'm a complete slob. Damn! This apartment is a mess, too.*

"Looks like quite a bachelor pad," Josephine said as she scanned the apartment.

Dushane's apartment consisted of one bedroom with a small kitchen, breakfast nook, living room, and a partial view of the city. He didn't have much furniture; a couch and a recliner in the living room, a table and two chairs in the breakfast nook, and a queen-size bed and dresser in the bedroom, all of it purchased at a used furniture store. Dushane didn't care much about any of it. The only possessions he truly valued were his books, which he housed in three large overflowing bookcases.

"Have a seat," Dushane said, motioning to the couch.

"Thanks. You've lost some weight."

"A little. You don't feel like eating much when you're all doped up. I'll be glad to get back to normal. Can I get you anything?"

"No, I just came by to make sure you were all right."

"I'm glad you came." Dushane sat down on the recliner and looked over the full length of Josephine's body. He felt the tingling sensation of sexual arousal. *Don't get carried away. Take a breath and just relax.*

"Are you going back to Harvard?" Josephine asked.

"Yeah, I start next week." The Dean had offered Dushane as much time as he needed to recover, but he had decided to go back as soon as possible.

"Good. Then we'll be seeing a lot of each other." Josephine smiled flirtatiously. "Well, I wish I could stay longer, but I've got an appointment downtown." Josephine got up and moved toward the door.

"Oh." Dushane sprang toward the door and opened it, and then stood silently in the doorway.

Josephine put her hand on Dushane's injured shoulder and caressed it lightly. "Take care of that shoulder."

"I...I will," Dushane stammered, trying to regain his senses.

Josephine leaned in close to Dushane's face. "Come by my office next time you're on campus."

Dushane inhaled a deep whiff of Josephine's perfume and adrenaline shot through his body. "Okay. I'll see you soon. Thanks again for coming over."

* * *

After his Inauguration, President Packer wasted little time reshaping the nation. His first task was to nominate someone to fill a vacancy on the Supreme Court. Infinity recommended Roderick Peabody, an appellate judge from the 5th Circuit and a member in good standing of the Network. Packer agreed that Peabody was a good choice because he shared the President's religious faith as well as his political agenda. Peabody was also black, which was strategic because both Infinity and the Republican Party were trying to convince more blacks to join. But most importantly, Peabody believed in an expanded role for God on the Court. In one of his early writings, Peabody theorized that:

> Because God alone rules human affairs and is the Supreme Legislator, human beings have no right to make up their own laws or take control of their own destiny. God alone is the Sovereign and His Commandments are the law of man.

Peabody's statement alarmed many people because it suggested that he wouldn't enforce the nation's laws—secular laws created to address real human problems. But Peabody defended himself by saying that he simply believed in seeking guidance from God. He scoffed at his critics who accused him of refusing to respect the rule of law, a foundation of Western jurisprudence. "The rule of law is worthless if we don't promote justice and morality," he had proclaimed on several occasions. Shortly after Peabody's nomination, several senators stated that they would vote against him, and it appeared that Packer would have a tough confirmation fight on his hands. But Packer had an able Attorney General to lead the battle for Peabody's nomination.

The new Attorney General, Lamar Wallace, was a former senator from Arkansas. Like many people in his home state, Wallace held deep religious convictions, but he had lost his bid for reelection to the Senate when investigators discovered that he'd been directing large amounts of federal money to members of his church. The people of Arkansas didn't object to their senator bringing federal pork back home, but they were angered that he had singled out his own church for special treatment. Fortunately for Wallace, none of that mattered anymore. He now held the reins of the most powerful law enforcement apparatus in the world.

Before Packer could operate freely, he needed to consolidate his base and ensure that he had broad public support for his programs. He also needed to rally support for the Peabody nomination. That's where Heilbrenner came in. His job was to broker cooperation between all the various Christian organizations, making sure that they enthusiastically supported Packer's programs and attacked his enemies.

Historically, religious groups had united around issues where they shared a common view, such as opposing the Equal Rights Amendment, civil rights, same-sex marriages, and abortion, or supporting religious indoctrination in the public schools. But differing sects also sniped at one another over doctrine, each claiming sole possession of the truth. This bickering always fractured any alliance, which usually only lasted for a single issue. Packer needed support for his entire program.

Heilbrenner implored other Christian leaders to unite because they now had an opportunity to change the country forever. And the climate was ripe for a new coalition. The Catholics had been humbled by the sexual abuse scandal, and were losing members as well as revenue. The Mormons were growing rapidly, but they weren't big enough to be a major political force. Heilbrenner had previously convinced the Mormon Prophet to support Infinity and the two men maintained frequent contact. Infinity already controlled the evangelical Protestant Right. Heilbrenner founded a new political organization called the Christian Action Committee, which included representatives from all three groups.

With the coalition in place, the Packer Administration's first order of business was to propose a new statute explicitly exempting individuals from state "hate" laws if the individual cited sincerely held religious beliefs. The new statute was primarily designed to protect believers who stirred up hatred against homosexuals. Next, the Administration proposed the Religious Freedom Protection Act, which provided:

> Government shall not substantially burden a person's exercise of religion even if the burden results from a law of general applicability, unless it is demonstrated that application of the burden is in furtherance of a compelling government interest, and is the least restrictive means of furthering that compelling governmental interest.

The new law gave religious individuals and organizations the power to challenge all kinds of laws on the ground that the laws "burdened their exercise of religion," and it was difficult for the government to defend any law because there was almost always a less restrictive means of furthering the government's interests. Despite mild protest from law school professors and freethinking groups, the law sailed easily through Congress and quickly resulted in an avalanche of lawsuits.

Infinity already had a battery of attorneys spread across the country to deal with issues that affected its interests, so Heilbrenner directed these lawyers to bring suits under the new law. The Attorney General agreed to assist as well, assigning five full-time attorneys to help Infinity lawyers with their cases, and to scout for opportunities to challenge existing state laws that conflicted with the new federal statute.

The first case involved a Methodist Church in Oklahoma that wanted to tear down its existing building and build a larger one to accommodate its expanding congregation. The Church submitted a building application to the city, but city officials refused to issue a building permit because the existing structure was within a legally designated historical zone. The zone applied to a one square mile area and affected thirty-two buildings, most of which weren't religious in nature. The Church filed suit arguing that the city's zoning ordinance burdened its religious freedom. The city countered that the law was one of general applicability and was not designed to hinder religion; it applied to everyone equally and was designed to preserve a historical district.

The court ruled in the Church's favor, reasoning that the city could have found a less restrictive way to preserve the historical district, and they should have worked with the Church to accommodate its needs. Other building owners, incensed that the Church was given special treatment, filed suit to get relief from the ordinance as well, but all of the lawsuits were dismissed. "The claimants have cited no exercise of religion being threatened," the court concluded.

Another case involved a township zoning board in Maryland that ordered a property owner to dismantle a religious sign in his front yard. The sign was seven feet high and twenty feet wide and said, in large block lettering, "Blessed Be the Lord Who Shall Guide My Life." The township cited a local ordinance prohibiting signs larger than four square feet in communities that were primarily residential. The intent of the law was to prevent eyesores in residential neighborhoods, and the ordinance applied to everyone, and to any type of sign, regardless of the message. But the court agreed with the property owner that the township's ordinance burdened his exercise of religion and was too restrictive. The sign could stay.

More contentious suits involved the Mormon Church, which was sued over two dozen times for failing to report sexual abuse by its members to law enforcement authorities. Church authorities argued that their religious beliefs would be compromised if they were forced to turn members in to secular authorities before they had an opportunity to handle the situation first. The prosecutors argued that no religious beliefs were involved and that Church authorities waited far too long to report abuse, and did little to prevent it.

The court ruled in favor of the Church, stating that while it was important to protect women and children from sexual abuse, the government must accommodate the religious practices of the Church as long as they had a mechanism in place to deal with abuse. Only after that mechanism failed could the government step in. Children's rights advocates and women's groups were furious, but they could do little to stem the religious fervor sweeping the country.

Perhaps the most telling case involved two Native American men who were caught taking peyote, a mild hallucinogenic that was illegal. The men were members of the Native American Church and they used peyote as part of their traditional worship service. After the men were charged, they cited the Religious Freedom Protection Act in their defense. The jury disagreed, returning a guilty verdict. The judge then sentenced each man to fifteen years in prison. On appeal, the appellate court upheld the conviction, reasoning:

> The State has identified a compelling interest in this case—preventing the use of harmful drugs. We cannot permit an individual, by virtue of so-called religious beliefs, to become a law unto himself. This would soon lead to anarchy.

The Packer Administration, consistent with its strong stance against illegal drug use, applauded the decision, despite its logical inconsistency with other decisions under the statute. When Packer's Chief of Staff Al Rogers was asked about this inconsistency, he replied, "It's obvious that drug use isn't part of any legitimate religion."

The upshot of the Religious Freedom Protection Act was the creation of a dual system of justice—one for members of "acceptable" religious denominations, and another for everyone else.

The new law was unquestionably a powerful weapon in the arsenal of religious organizations, but Newhall wasn't satisfied. He knew that schools served a critical role in the indoctrination process and it was unclear whether the statute applied to prayer in public schools. Although the Attorney General assured him that it did, Newhall wanted to make sure that school prayer was explicitly sanctioned so he pressured the Administration to take additional action.

The President responded, asking Congress to propose the following amendment to the Constitution:

To secure the people's right to acknowledge God according to the dictates of their conscience: The people's right to pray and to recognize their religious beliefs, heritage, or traditions on public property, including schools, shall not be infringed.

The House of Representatives and the Senate adopted a joint resolution proposing the amendment, which was then submitted to the states for their consideration. A few members of Congress opposed the amendment, but remained virtually silent, not willing to jeopardize their political careers. Civil rights and freedom advocacy groups argued that prayer in the public schools not only violated the First Amendment's separation of church and state, but more importantly, that it was divisive—separating people along religious lines. One courageous senator argued emphatically that the amendment was wrong because children shouldn't be encouraged to believe in superstition. "At some point, we have to tell our children that there is no Santa Claus." It was a beautiful sound bite for the amendment's supporters and Infinity broadcast it across its media empire for several days. Infinity followers angrily called their own senators and asked how a person so hostile to God, and obviously depraved, was allowed in the Senate.

At first, other senators didn't comment on their outspoken colleague's views, but some of their own constituents began clamoring for a public statement assuring them that their government representatives were God-fearing. Like a rush of lemmings blindly scampering off the side of a cliff, members of Congress, one after another, affirmed that they indeed possessed strong religious faith.

Attorney General Wallace had other priorities besides school prayer, including outlawing pornography and sodomy, and cracking down on recreational drug users. He quietly directed federal authorities to harass adult bookstores and strip clubs, and encouraged judges to loosen their standards for issuing search warrants, giving police more discretion in hunting down "contraband."

Wallace's critics attacked him for wasting law enforcement resources on victimless crimes, instead of dealing with violent criminals. Wallace countered: "Crimes against God are the most important crimes we can prosecute because they affect our entire society. If we don't do everything in our power to stop them, the United States will lose its place as God's chosen country."

Another important item on Wallace's agenda was changing the military. He ordered recruiters from all branches of the armed services to ask about a potential recruit's sexual orientation, and to deny admission to homosexuals. Wallace also proposed changes to the military's religious freedom policies by creating a list of religious practices "consistent with military service." The military's current policy allowed servicemen and women to exercise any religion as long as it didn't adversely their duties or disrupt the military's activities. Most members of the military called themselves Christians or Jews, but the Wicca religion was experiencing a resurgence, and was increasingly popular with military personnel. Consistent with the military policy of religious freedom, commanding officers allowed the peaceful practice of Wicca rituals.

In order to generate enough outrage to support his proposal, Wallace encouraged Heilbrenner to misrepresent to the Infinity masses that the military supported witchcraft and Satanism. Although the Wicca rituals practiced by the vast majority of its adherents had nothing to do with Satanism (a Judeo-Christian concept), linking Wicca with Satanism was a powerful psychological ploy. Heilbrenner directed his professionals in all available Infinity media—radio, television, periodicals, and the Internet—to get the word out. He also directed Infinity members to boycott enlisting in the armed services until the military changed its policy.

Within twenty-four hours of the Infinity media blitz, Infinity members inundated recruiting centers with angry calls demanding that the military prohibit religious protection for those practicing witchcraft, Wicca, paganism, or any form of Satanism.

But the President saved his most devastating salvo in the battle to save America for last. It was the crown jewel of his Administration—the Office of Faith-Based Action. The President proposed the establishment of a new federal agency with the stated purpose of creating partnerships between the government and religious organizations to solve the nation's most pressing social problems such as poverty, drug addiction, and crime. The idea was to allow religious organizations to apply for federal grants, which would be awarded to groups with either established or proposed social service programs. Traditionally, such groups had found it difficult to secure federal money because of First Amendment church-state separation restrictions.

The President's initiative was dramatic in scope. Religious organizations could receive government funding for programs covering child care, adoption, job training and employment, housing, food banks, soup kitchens, health and medical services, literacy and mentoring programs, substance abuse, after-school programs, and anything else that came within the scope of any federal agency. The President also proposed that the government give special tax credits to individuals or corporations that donated money to these groups.

Newhall initially objected to the President's initiative because he feared that his competitors would receive federal funding. The last thing he wanted was for Islamic groups or even Christian sects outside of the Infinity umbrella to receive additional resources. Despite a warning from Heilbrenner that it was a mistake, Newhall released a terse statement.

> While Christians strongly support the idea of a partnership with the government to solve the nation's social problems, we are concerned about the President's proposal. We believe that some organizations, such as those based on Islam, should not be allowed to participate in the program. Based on what I've read about Mohammed, I believe that he was a terrorist, a violent man, a man of war. His religion is based on violence and hatred. If the President expects the support of moral Christians, he must limit the recipients of this new program to religions based on love.

Newhall's statement infuriated the Islamic community, but he knew he could demonize them with little adverse consequence to the Network. Although an increasing number of Muslims lived in the United States, they had virtually no political power.

The Administration reacted coolly to Newhall's statement. Although they shared his views, they saw no reason to stir up the electorate or anger foreign governments with Islamic populations. Officially, the Administration refused to comment on Newhall's statement except to point out that he had a First Amendment right to his views.

Newhall wanted to make sure that unacceptable groups were not funded so he ordered Heilbrenner to take action. Heilbrenner called Warren Bauer, head of the new agency.

"Warren. John Heilbrenner."

"Hi," Bauer replied curtly.

"How are you?"

"Well, I'm a little upset right now," Bauer snapped angrily. "I wish Newhall would keep his mouth shut. I know he's trying to rally the troops, but the last thing we need is to generate more controversy."

"You're right, Warren. We're on the same page here. It's just that we're concerned about inappropriate groups being funded by your agency."

"Well, tell Newhall to keep quiet."

"Look, I share your concern. Robert gets carried away occasionally. I've spoken with him and he's agreed to keep a low profile going forward."

"Good. Because you know as well as I do that we're on shaky political and legal ground here."

"I know, and we're happy to provide any support you need. We all want to see this thing happen."

"We need your unqualified support; no more of this bullshit. Now, as to your concerns about inappropriate groups being funded, you don't need to worry. Under the regulations we're proposing, if we determine that a group is based on hate or un-American values, they won't be eligible to receive any federal money." Bauer paused to let his words his sink in. "Do you understand what I'm saying?"

Heilbrenner chuckled gaily. "Yes. Thanks, Warren. That's all I needed to hear. Call me if I can help."

The President formally announced his vision at a ceremony in the Rose Garden at the White House. "The era of discrimination against religion is coming to an end," he declared.

Newhall and Heilbrenner stood within a few feet of the President as he promised to fund the faith-based initiative with sixty billion dollars. Heilbrenner salivated at the breathtaking amount of pork now available to Infinity. With his well-placed connections in the federal bureaucracy, he reckoned he could double or triple Infinity's revenues. And Bauer was ready to help. He created a guidebook that religious organizations could use to navigate the complicated federal grant process, and he drafted regulations exempting religious organizations from federal and state civil rights laws. This meant that Infinity could openly discriminate by only hiring people who shared their religious faith. No feminists, homosexuals, humanists, or nonbelievers need apply.

CHAPTER 19

Whenever we read the obscene stories, the voluptuous debaucheries, the cruel and tortuous executions, the unrelenting vindictiveness with which more than half the Bible is filled, it would be more consistent that we call it the word of a demon than the word of God. It is a history of wickedness that has served to corrupt and brutalize mankind.

—THOMAS PAINE, *THE AGE OF REASON*

Dushane rolled on top of Josephine and let the full length of his naked body melt into her flesh. He had never felt so alive, intoxicated by the feel of her smooth skin and overpowering feminine scent. Josephine put her arms around his back and gently massaged his shoulders. "I read your article about Peabody," she said.

Dushane sighed. "I know you hate my work; why don't you stop reading it?" Dushane had written a scathing article attacking Roderick Peabody's jurisprudence. Although highly controversial, a Harvard legal periodical had scheduled it for publication in its next edition. The article included a quote from a law review article authored by Peabody while he was in law school. "Death row inmates are lucky they don't get stoned to death, which would certainly be an appropriate penalty according to God," he had said, referring to the sadistic Biblical punishment.

"You know that isn't true," Josephine insisted. She ran her hand across Dushane's buttocks. "I like your work. It just won't get you anywhere."

"Who says I want to get anywhere," Dushane responded testily as he lifted his hips up and slammed his erection into her.

"Ahhh...." Josephine dug her fingernails into his back. "Just don't... ah...get too...wrapped...ah...wrapped up in it," she managed between short gasps.

After a few powerful thrusts, Dushane settled into a comfortable rhythm. "You let me...ah...worry about that," he grunted.

Josephine moved her hips in time to meet him. "You're not...ah... going...ah...to persuade anyone."

Dushane increased the tempo and force of his thrusts. "I disagree," he said angrily as sweat dripped off his face.

"Ahhh...I don't want you to get hurt."

"You let me...ah...worry about that."

"Ahhh...ahhh...be careful."

"Ahhh...ohhhh..." Dushane ejaculated and then rolled quickly onto his back. When he had caught his breath, he swung his legs off the edge of the bed and threw his feet down hard against the creaky hardwood floor.

"Are you okay, Martin?"

Dushane took a few deep breaths, but didn't respond.

"Martin?"

"What?"

"I'm sorry if I upset you."

"You didn't," Dushane responded tersely as he threw his pants on. "But somebody's got to do something. I can't sit on the sidelines and watch this. I don't understand how you can."

Dushane rarely spoke harshly with Josephine, but her conviction that he was wasting his time opposing Peabody aggravated him. He was also frustrated by Josephine's belief that it was pointless to challenge anything that had strong appeal to the masses.

Josephine sat up. "You don't always understand me, Martin."

"And you don't always understand me," Dushane retorted. He felt irritable, although he never forgot how much he loved Josephine. Besides his intense sexual attraction, he admired her impeccable moral standards and found her intellectual vibrancy compelling. She never failed to grasp whatever ideas he offered, even though she didn't always agree.

Although she occasionally chided him for his presumption that he could change people's core beliefs, Josephine also loved Dushane dearly. She saw an honesty in him that she rarely saw in others; although at the same time, she feared his idealism and naiveté would lead to a fall. She knew from her experience growing up in Utah that the mass of people didn't care about rational arguments; they cared about rationalizing the beliefs they already had—beliefs inherited from their parents, teachers, and church leaders. She hoped that Dushane wouldn't spend his whole life struggling against such an indelible enemy.

"Will I see you tonight?" Josephine asked.

Dushane tucked in his shirt and moved hastily toward the door. "Yes," he answered, without looking back.

* * *

"Morning, David. I've got those copies for you." Chambers' administrative assistant placed a stack of papers on the corner of his desk.

"Thanks, Peggy."

Chambers flipped through the stack and shook his head. The documents were letters written by Infinity members that had been published in newspapers across the country. They attacked Chambers for his editorial on school prayer. None of the letters presented rational arguments, instead invoking religious bromides to vilify him.

> Mr. Chambers doesn't know it, but Satan is working through him.
> He's nothing more than a dupe of Satan.

> Any man who rejects God cannot be saved from his wicked nature.
> It's no surprise that such a man wants to keep God out of our schools.

> Is David Chambers the Antichrist?
> Christians need to consider that possibility.

Chambers threw the letters in the trash and picked up the phone. He smiled when he heard a familiar voice on the other end of the line.

"Lassater here."

"Ray. David Chambers."

"Ahhhh…what a nice surprise—though hardly a surprise."

Chambers chuckled. "Well, you know me as well as anyone. Did you see any of the letters about me?"

"Of course. I couldn't have made a better case. Are you convinced yet?"

"I'm convinced there are a lot aimless drifters out there, but I already knew that. I don't think I can draw any other conclusions."

"This is the only the beginning," Lassater said matter-of-factly.

"The beginning of what?"

"You know what's going on in the country—maybe the end."

"I suppose I went too far in my editorial."

"Too far?" Lassater bellowed. "Who the hell is this? David Chambers or some useless impostor?"

Chambers couldn't immediately respond. He wasn't used to being pushed around.

"You still there, David?"

"Yeah, I'm here," Chambers responded weakly. "What would you do?"

"I'm already doing."

"What?"

"You ever hear of a guy named Mike Watson?"

"Infinity?"

"That's right. Second-in-command before Heilbrenner came in. I'm keeping an eye on him; he was forced out of the organization and it's not entirely clear why. He may be the key."

"The key to what?"

"Taking Infinity down. It's a dirty operation and I'm gathering the evidence to prove it."

"Come on. Is that what you're up to? Trying to take Infinity down."

"They're worse than the Catholic Church."

"You mean the ideas?"

"Yeah, and I'm glad I don't have to explain that to you. Christ, nobody understands that. Most people think you can live in an irrational haze without any consequences."

"I'm with you on that; the ideas are horrific. But they can't last. The pendulum always swings back."

"Maybe it does, maybe it doesn't. I'm not going to wait and find out. I'm all in this fight." Lassater paused. "But I can't do it by myself."

Chambers didn't respond.

"You're the man to lead this," Lassater continued firmly. "You're the only man."

"Well…" Chambers started.

"Well what? Why the hell did you call me?"

"I…I just…"

"Do you have any doubt about what I'm saying to you?" Lassater pressed. "Any doubt whatsoever?"

No, none, Chambers thought. *Except…what am I supposed to do?* "Look Ray, I've got a business and a ranch to run. We're going to have a thousand kids running around here in less than a month." Much of Kaleidoscope Ranch had been built and Chambers had already hired over two hundred people to get its research and other programs started. Science and technology camps for children were scheduled to start in three weeks. "Look, I want to help. I will help," Chambers offered.

Lassater sighed heavily. "I need you all in, David. That's the only way; and you're not ready yet."

He's right, Chambers thought. "I'm sorry, Ray. Keep me posted, all right? I'm willing to help where I can."

"Goodbye, David."

Chambers hung up and felt uncharacteristically depressed.

* * *

Dushane was sitting quietly at his desk preparing a lecture for his Constitutional Law class when a call from Dean Richardson's secretary interrupted him. She had called to set up a private meeting with the Dean for the following Monday. Dushane thought the call was odd because the Dean had dropped by his office several times and they had chatted casually. The request for a meeting seemed unusually formal.

On the appointed day, Dushane walked into the Dean's office and greeted the secretary. "Hi, I'm Martin Dushane. I'm here to see the Dean."

"Yes, Professor Dushane, the Dean is expecting you." The secretary smiled. "You know where his office is, right?"

"Sure." Dushane weaved his way past her desk to the Dean's office. His door was open and he looked up as Dushane stepped in. "Hello, Martin. Thanks for coming. Please sit down. Can I get you something to drink?" The Dean motioned to a credenza, which contained a liquor cabinet, a small wine rack, and a mini refrigerator.

"Yeah. How about an orange juice?"

"Sure thing." The Dean poured a glass of juice and handed it to Dushane. "Well, why don't we get right down to business. You know I think you're doing fine work here—great work in fact. And we've already published some of your articles, right?"

"Yeah."

"Well, I'm sorry to say that we've got a little problem."

"Okay."

"It's no secret that your articles opposing affirmative action have stirred some controversy here." The Dean wasn't kidding. Dushane had aggravated the professional civil rights community by accusing them of using racial preferences to increase their power at the expense of those they claimed to represent. His enemies branded him a traitor and accused him of trying to keep his "people" down. Dushane had never understood the tribal mentality, which seemed to be colossally counterproductive in a modern, pluralistic society.

"I don't oppose affirmative action," Dushane responded evenly.

The Dean squinted in confusion.

"I oppose racial preferences; there's a big difference."

"Well, I don't have time to get into a technical debate about that right now," the Dean countered dismissively. "The point is that you've written some controversial scholarship."

"Fair enough."

"But that's not the only reason I've called you here. We've got an even bigger problem."

"Okay."

"I've seen your article about Peabody."

"You've read it?"

"Well, I looked over it."

"All right."

"Martin, I don't know how to say this, but it just seems like you're obsessed with this religious issue. Maybe you need to take a step back and evaluate what you're doing."

"If you're talking about the separation of church and state, that's an issue I'm very interested in. It's an important one, don't you think?"

"Well, regardless, you're pissing people off. And this article will further alienate you." The Dean averted his eyes. "I'm looking out for your best interests here."

Dushane didn't immediately respond. His intuition told him that the Dean was hiding something. Although he didn't know it, officials from the Packer Administration had approached Richardson and other important leaders in academia and asked them to keep the controversy around Peabody's nomination down. Some had been bribed with financial support, political appointments, or in Richardson's case, a federal judgeship. Richardson didn't care much about religion because he didn't hold any strong beliefs, nor did he want to be a judge, but he liked being courted by the White House; it made him feel important and special.

Dushane leaned forward. "What are you suggesting?" he said impatiently.

"I'm suggesting that we don't publish your article right now. It just isn't the right time, or for that matter, the right approach for you."

"I disagree," Dushane countered quickly. "Exposing Peabody is especially critical because he doesn't respect the rule of law."

The Dean sighed heavily like a balloon rapidly losing air. "Well, Peabody isn't the only one with an alternative viewpoint; many on the faculty here reject, to a certain degree, the idea that legal reasoning and the rule of law are appropriate in today's society. Judges shouldn't be restrained by traditional legal analysis if it hinders their ability to foster social change. You'd have to agree that this tradition is fairly well removed from traditional legal thought."

Dushane nodded. "I would agree with that."

"The separation of church and state is fine in theory, but there's just one thing you don't fully appreciate, Martin." The Dean paused for emphasis. "The law is about passion. Emotion. Doing the right thing. It's not just an intellectual enterprise. The average person doesn't care about theories; they want a legal system where judges apply their wisdom and make decisions that move society forward. Harvard must take a leadership position. We have to take into account current societal trends; people are much more spiritually enlightened these days, and Peabody has the potential to move the Court in an exciting new direction."

Dushane tried to hide his disgust, but couldn't. "Peabody's a power-hungry crank. I mean, the guy's a Christian fundamentalist. We can't ignore that. It's...it's wrong."

The Dean forced a smile. "Well, I'm the Dean. I have other considerations. Just because you don't agree with prevailing trends is irrelevant." The Dean paused. "You know, the other thing I just don't get is how you can oppose someone of your own kind."

A burst of heat shot up the back of Dushane's neck. "What the hell are you talking about?" he said angrily.

"Supporting a fellow African-American. I don't understand why you can't just help him; why you don't feel an obligation to help him."

"Because he's an idiot."

"But..."

"And he's not my kind. I don't want anything to do with him. That's why I want my article published."

"Well, I have to look out for the best interests of this university," the Dean said, waving his hand with an air of finality.

"That's fine." Dushane stood up. "You do what you think is right; I'll publish it elsewhere."

"No," the Dean said firmly.

Dushane shot the Dean a hard look. "What do you mean, no? It's my article."

"As an employee of this university you are not allowed to publish that article. Its content will reflect poorly on this institution and I can't allow it."

"That's ridiculous."

"Don't force my hand, Martin."

"What are you saying?"

"I'm saying don't publish that article."

CHAPTER 20

When our leaders speak, the thinking has been done.
When they propose a plan—it is God's Plan.
When they point the way, there is no other which is safe.
When they give directions, it should mark the end of controversy,
God works in no other way.
To think otherwise, without immediate repentance,
may cost one his faith, may destroy his testimony,
and leave him a stranger to the kingdom of God.

—Church of Jesus Christ of Latter-Day Saints

"E-Z Rooter, Mike speaking."

"Hi, this is Steve Staker. I'm the maintenance manager at Salt Lake Public Library. We're having some problems with our water pressure. Can you come out and take a look?"

"Hold on, let me check the schedule. Yeah…I can send a truck out tomorrow."

"What time?"

"Be around ten or so."

"All right, thanks. We'll see you tomorrow."

The next morning, a plumber checked the building's main water pipes for leaks, and then reported back to Staker. "Well, I don't see anything unusual up here, but I still need to check the basement."

"Okay, I'll take you down." Staker led the plumber downstairs where they followed the pipes until they disappeared behind a storage room door.

Staker's hefty set of keys jingled as he pulled them out of his pocket. "I've never been in here," he said as he slid the key in and opened the door. He ran his hand along the wall for a light switch, but couldn't find one so he shined his flashlight around the room. He stopped when he saw a file cabinet.

"It looks like the pipes continue above that cabinet," the plumber said.

"Yeah, let's move it out of the way."

The two men pulled the cabinet forward, revealing another door, which was padlocked.

"Hmmm…I don't have a key for this one," Staker said. "Hold on." Staker radioed one of his maintenance men. "Kevin, can you come down to the basement? We need you to cut a padlock."

After the man cut the lock, Staker and the plumber continued following the pipes down the corridor with their flashlights. Then they came to Katherine McKay's trunks, which were also locked. "Kevin, I need you to cut these, too," Staker directed.

"Yes, sir." The maintenance man cut all of the locks and Staker opened the trunks, revealing Katherine McKay's books and other papers. "What the…?" Staker rifled through the books and instinctively recoiled. He knew that some of the materials were dangerous. They included Church documents, letters signed by Boyd McKay, and a two-hundred-page manuscript with subtitles including "Racism" and "Polygamy."

"What about those pipes?" the plumber interrupted.

"Oh…why don't you and Kevin take care of that? I need to take care of something else." Staker ran upstairs and immediately called the central office of the General Authorities. They sent two agents to the library to investigate. After reviewing the contraband, they notified Boyd McKay, who confronted his wife.

"How could you do this? You betrayed me!" Boyd attacked. "You betrayed your family and your friends in the Church! You let Satan influence you!"

Although Katherine felt afraid, she also felt relieved that she didn't have to live a lie any longer. "This has nothing to do with Satan!" she snapped back at her husband. "We both know the Church isn't based on facts."

"You...you tramp!" Boyd lashed. "What are you saying?"

"Come on, Boyd. Don't lie to yourself. It's sickening—and pathetic. You and the rest of the General Authorities are knowingly promoting lies."

"How dare you speak with me that way!"

"Why? Because I'm your wife!" Katherine erupted, finally losing her temper. "Because it's in the Bible! You expect me to be obedient! We barely have a marriage! We've never had a real marriage!"

"I want you out of this house! Right now! Get out of this house!"

Katherine stormed out and drove away. She spent a few days in a motel and then moved into a small apartment alone. She tried to call her close friends and family, but almost everyone refused to speak with her. Because the scandal involved a wife of one of the most powerful members of the General Authorities, the Church had contacted all of Katherine's friends and family and told them that their loyalty to the Church would be watched carefully. The General Authorities released a terse statement: "Katherine McKay is an apostate who is spreading lies about the Church."

Dutiful followers speculated about what had caused a good Mormon Saint to suddenly turn bad. Some thought Katherine must be possessed by demons; others guessed that Satan had infiltrated her brain. But a few Mormon women knew better—it was the stress of being shut down in a rigid patriarchal social structure that required unquestioning obedience.

After a few weeks of living alone, Katherine began to feel the strain of isolation and she wondered if she'd done the right thing. She hadn't been able to speak with any of her children who were ordered not to talk with her or risk excommunication. Finally, she called Josephine and left a message: "Josephine, it's Katherine. I'm sorry, but I have no one else to turn to. They found the books at the library and the Church has excommunicated me. Most of my family and friends won't speak with me and Boyd has cut me off. I don't know what to do. Please...please call me."

Josephine was out of town and didn't receive the message until three days later, but she called the McKay residence immediately upon her return.

"May I speak with Katherine, please?"

"Katherine's not here," Boyd McKay shot back sharply. "Who's this?"

"This is Josephine Holladay. I'm a friend of your wife's."

"I don't have a wife anymore. She betrayed us and now's she's in the hospital with a nervous breakdown. God has punished her."

"Where is she?"

"I don't want to discuss this any further." Boyd slammed the phone down.

Josephine called every hospital in the Salt Lake area until she found out where Katherine was being treated. The next morning, she caught the first flight to Salt Lake.

* * *

Light snowflakes fell from the steel-gray sky as Josephine's plane touched down at Salt Lake City International Airport. After she retrieved her baggage, she flagged down a cab and headed straight to the hospital. When she arrived, she rushed to the admittance desk.

"I'm looking for Katherine McKay. What room is she in?"

The woman across the desk eyed her timidly. "Are you family?"

"No."

"Well…"

"Look, she called me a few days ago. I need to see her. Please, I've got to see her."

"I'm sorry. Mrs. McKay passed away last night."

"What?" Josephine screamed.

"I'm sorry."

"What…what happened?"

"I don't know all the details. The only thing I know is that it was a suicide."

"Suicide!"

"Yes. I'm sorry."

The energy drained out of Josephine's body and she suddenly felt light-headed. "This happened last night?" she said softly.

"Yes. A nurse discovered her early this morning."

Josephine stumbled backwards and collapsed in a nearby chair. She dropped her head and wept quietly. After a few minutes, the woman from the admittance desk sat down next to her and handed her a tissue. "Is there anything I can do?"

Josephine wiped her eyes. "Thank you. I'm sorry. This is just such a shock."

"If I can help with anything, please let me know."

"Thank you."

Josephine sat quietly for several more minutes and then went back to the admittance desk. "Do you know anything about the funeral arrangements?" she asked.

"No, but you might want to call Judy Marshall; she was here a lot." The woman scribbled a phone number on a small piece of paper and handed it to Josephine.

"Thanks." Josephine walked out of the hospital and caught a cab to her hotel.

In accordance with her written wishes, Katherine McKay was cremated a few days after her death. Judy Marshall, her closest friend since childhood, organized a memorial service. Judy had voluntarily ended her relationship with the Church years earlier, but had remained close friends with Katherine despite objections from Boyd. Judy invited all of Katherine's family and friends to the service, but few attended. Neither Katherine's husband nor any of her friends from the Church showed up, although Judy hadn't expected them. She knew it was a huge risk for anyone in the Church to be associated with a known apostate, even in death, but she was pleased to see three of Katherine's children as well as a few of her co-workers from the library.

After the ceremony, Judy put her hand on Josephine's shoulder. "Mind if I speak with you, Josephine?"

"Of course."

"There's a bench in the garden where we can talk privately." Josephine followed Judy outside and the women sat down.

"Katherine told me a lot about you," Judy said. "She spoke of you as if you were her daughter."

"It's hard to believe she's gone."

"I know. She was a beautiful woman." Judy sighed softly. "She struggled for years over the Church and her life with Boyd."

"She never told me much about her personal life. Every time I asked, she seemed so uncomfortable, so I just stopped asking."

"That's how she was Josephine; she didn't like to burden other people with her problems. But I can tell you that she had a special love for you. Probably because your backgrounds are so similar."

"What do you mean? The Church?"

"No, I guess she really didn't tell you much about herself. Katherine was a gifted child, too."

Josephine's eyes widened.

"It was even less publicized than it was for you, but I knew. She scored higher than anyone else on those IQ tests. Unfortunately, her parents encouraged her to get married and have children. She wanted to go to college, but..."

"God, that makes this hurt worse," Josephine said, her voice cracking.

"I know. It's very difficult to accept, but I thought you should know."

"Yes. Thank you."

Judy held out her hand and Josephine took it. The women sat in silence for a while.

"Do you know what happened at the library?" Josephine asked finally.

"I can tell you what I know. They discovered all of Katherine's books in the basement; most of them were on the Church's suppression list. Katherine was also working on her own book—a book exposing the Church's lies. She had a lot of sensitive Church documents that she must've taken from Boyd. It was obviously all confiscated. It's sad. Her book will never be written."

*　*　*

When Josephine returned to Boston, she felt physically and emotionally exhausted. She wished she could just sleep, but that was impossible. She sat quietly in her apartment for three days, not talking to anyone and not doing anything except taking an inventory of her thoughts, which ranged from grief to despair to murderous anger. At the end of the third day in solitude, she thumbed through the mail that had been piling up. There was a small package from Katherine. Josephine opened it and read the letter inside.

Dear Josephine,

First of all, I'm sorry that I've put you through this. I hope you don't blame yourself in any way for my death. It was time for me to say goodbye, and the recent events were simply a catalyst that set things in motion. It's painful to admit, but I traded my integrity for a comfortable life in the Church. It seemed so easy to just keep quiet and obey the Church and my husband, but it ate away at me every day. It had become increasingly unbearable.

Helping you discover the truth about the Church is one of the few things in my life that I'm proud of, and the only legacy I hope for now.

Take care of yourself.

With love,

Katherine

The rest of the box contained Church-related documents and a computer diskette. Josephine put the disk into her laptop and viewed its sole file, a two hundred and twenty-three page manuscript that chronicled issues the Church didn't like to talk about—racism, polygamy, Adam as God, blood atonement, and several others. Josephine turned off the computer and took the subway over to Dushane's apartment.

"Hey, I wasn't expecting you," Dushane said when he answered the door. "I tried to call you."

"Hi Martin. Do you have time to talk?"

"Of course."

"Let's sit down."

"Okay." They walked into the living room and sat next to each other on the couch.

"I've decided to go back to Utah for a while," Josephine said.

"Why? I thought you hated Utah."

"There's something I need to do."

"What is it?"

"It's about Katherine."

"Did something happen at the funeral?"

"No."

Dushane moved closer and put his hand on Josephine's thigh, but she pushed it away.

"What is it? I want to help."

"I know. I'm just…I need to deal with this…"

"Okay, I'm here…I…"

"Katherine left some materials," Josephine interrupted. "She was working on a book."

"What kind of book?"

"A book about the Church; the truth about the Church."

"Okay."

"She didn't finish it. I need to finish it."

"What?"

"The book. I'm going go back to Utah to finish her book."

"Are you crazy? This sounds…"

"I have to do this."

"Why do you want to waste…I mean, I don't think…"

"I have to do this, Martin. I…"

Dushane looked away and neither of them spoke for a while.

"When are you leaving?" Dushane said finally.

"In two weeks."

"What about your job?"

"I'm quitting."

"Well…what about us?"

"I can't see you anymore," Josephine said quietly.

Dushane had often wondered if and when he would hear those words. To some extent, he had already prepared himself, but the actual articulation struck a raw nerve. It was more painful than he could've imagined. "Why? Why can't we still…?"

"I'm sorry. I need to do this and I can't be with you right now. I can't be with anyone right now."

"Do you love me?"

"Of course."

"I don't understand."

"I know you don't. I'm sorry."

Dushane dropped his head and stared at the floor.

"I want you to publish your article about Peabody," Josephine said.

"Why?"

"Because it's important."

Dushane shook his head.

"I still want to keep in touch, Martin."

Dushane didn't look up. "Yeah, well, that's probably not a good idea," he said softly.

CHAPTER 21

Belief without proof is a virtue for the religious. To the scientist, belief without evidence is gross professional misconduct.

—MARTIN WILLETT

Dushane sat quietly behind his desk and flipped through the legal periodical that had just published his article about Packer's Supreme Court nominee, Roderick Peabody. The article had already generated a buzz in the legal community because the journal's editor noted on page one that the Dean of Harvard Law School had bowed to pressure from the Packer Administration.

Dushane put the article down and waited. His phone had rung several times, but he hadn't picked it up. He finally swiveled his chair around and stared out the window, trying to reflect on what he had done. But he couldn't concentrate.

"What's the meaning of this?" the Dean bellowed as he charged through the open doorway.

Dushane spun back around. The night before, he had thought about all the things he wanted to say, but he abandoned any previous script and said the first thing that popped into his mind. "Get out."

"What?"

"Get out."

The Dean's face contorted as his brain tried to decide which of his emotions held greater sway—fear or anger. The confusion left him temporarily speechless. "You...you can't...you can't talk to me like that," he said finally.

Dushane raised his voice. "I said get out!"

"Well, you're...you're..."

Dushane stood up and held the Dean's eyes as his fight or flight response sprung into action. The Dean backed slowly toward the doorway. "You're...you're fired. Did...did you hear that? You're fired."

"Get out!"

*   *   *

"David, your appointment is here," Chambers' assistant announced over the intercom.

"Thanks, Peggy. Tell him I'll be right down."

Chambers walked to the lobby and shook hands with the young man who stood up to greet him.

"Hello, Mr. Chambers, I'm Paul Vogelson. I'm a reporter from the San Diego Chronicle. Pleasure to meet you."

Vogelson had asked for an interview with Chambers to discuss Kaleidoscope Ranch's charitable programs. Chambers had granted the request because he was eager to bring increased exposure to the problems he was trying to solve. He also hoped to enlist the support of other philanthropists.

As Chambers extended his hand, he met Vogelson's eyes and instinctively reacted. Although the young reporter seemed perfectly normal, Chambers had a feeling of incongruity that he felt often in the presence of other people. Chambers wondered what caused the disjointed feeling, but he quickly decided that Vogelson was probably just nervous. In any case, Chambers had no reason to distrust; he had a long-standing relationship with the paper's staff and they had always dealt with him fairly. Indeed, the paper's business editor, Clark Walbridge, had interviewed Chambers a few times before and the men were friends. Walbridge had tirelessly defended Chambers from attacks by local politicians upset by his refusal to deal with the unions. In several sharply written editorials, Walbridge pointed out that Chambers Aerospace provided high-paying jobs to over two thousand people in the community, and had made substantial contributions to philanthropic projects in the region. Walbridge also argued that politicians, who were more intent on enriching their friends, hadn't achieved a fraction of the same positive impact.

Chambers was excited to present his vision for the Ranch, but what he didn't know was that ownership of the Chronicle was about to change. The Infinity Network had expanded its media empire into newspapers and magazines, and Heilbrenner had his eye on controlling at least one paper in every major city. But Heilbrenner worried that if Infinity openly bought controlling interests in newspapers, it could create a backlash because the mission of any respectable paper was to objectively report the news, not to evangelize religious beliefs. To avoid this problem, Heilbrenner used Infinity's intricate network of holding companies to disguise the real ownership of the purchasing entity. Although the deal with the San Diego Chronicle had not yet closed, Infinity had already begun installing its own people, including Vogelson.

"Nice to meet you, Paul, and welcome to the Ranch," Chambers said amiably as she shook Vogelson's hand. "Let's go back to my office."

Vogelson was quiet as the men walked down the hall. He felt a little apprehensive, but he knew he was prepared. Heilbrenner had personally coached him and provided a list of questions to ask.

"How long have you been with the paper, Paul?"

"Just over a month."

"Good outfit over there. I know some of your colleagues; nice guys. How's Clark getting along?"

"Clark Walbridge?"

"Yeah. Last time I saw him he had his leg in a cast from a ski accident in Tahoe." Chambers chuckled. "I told him he's too old to be skiing double blacks."

Vogelson didn't smile. "Clark's okay."

"Tell him I said hi. I'll be down there in a month or so. We're going to have lunch." Chambers smiled and gently patted Vogelson on the back. "You're welcome to join us if you like."

"Okay." *This guy is nice*, Vogelson thought. *Ahhhh! No, he's not. He's…he's bad. He's bad!*

"Have a seat," Chambers said, motioning to the chair across from his desk.

Vogelson sat down and turned on his tape recorder. "You don't mind the tape recorder, right?"

"No."

"Well, I've read some of your literature and your charitable activities are extensive; I'm not sure where to start."

Chambers shrugged. "Start anywhere."

"Okay, why don't you tell me which of your charitable activities you're most proud of?"

"My company," Chambers replied without hesitation.

"Your company?"

"Yeah. Chambers Aerospace employs over twenty thousand people, ninety percent of which are here in the U.S. Without the company, none of the programs here at the Ranch would be possible. More importantly, the company provides all of us with a way to support ourselves and our families. It also gives us a sense of pride and accomplishment to be part of a team; a united family creating something worthwhile. We demand a lot from each other, but people appreciate being called upon to achieve excellence. I think everyone in the company has grown personally and professionally."

Business as a charity. Ha! Vogelson thought. He tried to maintain a poker face, but he had just drawn his first unexpected ace. He plunged ahead, hoping for additional admissions.

"Why don't you tell me about some of the things you're doing at this ranch."

"Well, we've got our first science and technology camp coming up in a couple weeks. I think I'm probably more excited than the kids. After that, we've got a camp for disabled kids. Preparing for that has been a big challenge. We're trying to create an environment where these kids can do all the same things that other kids do."

"In your promotional literature, you state that part of your mission is to encourage critical thought and freethinking." *Freethinking. That's wrong*, Vogelson thought automatically. *That rejects God.*

"That's right."

"Well, you've been subject to a lot of criticism over your letter about school prayer. Does that fit in with this?"

"They're related, yes. Freethinking people are like everyone else; they may talk to themselves, it's just that they don't expect something magic to happen. They know that things only happen when they take

181

responsibility for their lives and do something."

"Are you an a...a...atheist?" Vogelson stuttered. The word 'atheist' was hard for him to say because it carried a lifetime of negative connotations, first installed into his brain as a toddler.

"Are we talking about my religious beliefs now?"

"I'm interested, if you don't mind discussing them. I think it will give me a little more insight."

"Well, I don't have any interest in creating another pointless controversy. It's a waste of time to discuss religion in rational terms because it's irrational by definition."

Shoot! I'm losing him. Don't panic. "Well, don't worry, Mr. Chambers. This won't be part of the article. I'm just curious." Vogelson forced a smile.

"Okay. I'm happy to talk off the record for a few minutes."

Vogelson pretended to turn off his tape recorder.

"Your question is whether I'm an atheist?"

"Yes."

Chambers shrugged. "The best quote on religion I've ever heard is from an atheist."

"What's that?"

"An atheist knows that a hospital should be built instead of a church."

Vogelson tried to keep his expression as blank as possible. "Why do you like that quote?"

"Because it sums up the difference between people who choose to live in this world—here, now—and people who don't."

Vogelson furrowed his brow. "I'm not sure what you mean by that."

"Well, there's not much else to say. Some people pour money and energy into their superstitions; others focus on helping people or doing something productive."

Superstition? If you're calling me superstitious, you're way off base. We don't believe in superstition. That's in the Bible...I think. No supernatural or witchcraft, that's superstition. You don't know what you're talking about. You...jerk. All right, all right, relax. This guy will get his due. God will give it to him.

"Do you happen to know who said that quote?" Vogelson asked.

"Madalyn Murray O'Hair, although she may have changed her name to just Madalyn O'Hair."

"I'm not familiar with her."

"You should look her up. At one time, she was one of the most popular devils used by religious organizations to channel their hatred and raise money."

"Devils?"

Chambers grinned. "Religious mass movements always have at least one good devil. They don't survive without one."

Vogelson flirted with the idea of considering Chambers' point, but he quickly realized that it was too dangerous. He looked down at his notes. "What are your spiritual beliefs?"

"I believe that questions about a god or a supreme being are unknowable and therefore irrelevant. The only thing that is relevant is our own existence. The work we do here at the Ranch is focused on promoting ideas that improve human existence. My charitable activities are designed with the same purpose in mind."

"Do you think this puts you outside of the mainstream?"

Chambers laughed cheerfully. "I certainly hope so, but think of it this way. People who subscribe to one particular set of religious beliefs are heretics or atheists according to the other ten thousand competing religions. The only difference between those people and me is that I'm a heretic as to ten thousand and one."

"So you believe there is no God?"

"No, I'm not saying that at all. But I certainly don't believe in the violent comic-book god portrayed in the Bible or the Koran."

Vogelson nodded. *I wish I could slap some sense into this guy, but it's okay. I'm going to be a hero.*

"As for some higher power that created the universe, or a first cause, I don't know anything about that. I can't know anything about that."

"Well…" Vogelson started.

"I suspect what's going on is so grand, so spectacular, so beautiful, that humans couldn't fully appreciate or understand it. The only thing we know is that the human brain is the most complex organization of matter in the known universe. To waste that, or to shoehorn it into pointless Biblical limitations would be criminal."

"So you don't believe that the Bible is the word of God?"

"No. I think anyone who believes that has a low opinion of her."

Her? Vogelson reacted. He had never heard God referred to as a woman before. He wondered if that was a sin. "Okay…so you're saying maybe there's a god, maybe there isn't?" Vogelson offered.

"No. What I'm really saying is that I don't care; I don't need a god. I'd rather rely on myself to make decisions to create the life I want. The idea of a supernatural god has no relevance to that. Besides, belief in a god doesn't tell us anything. It creates more questions than it answers. If God created the universe, who created God? If God is all-powerful, why doesn't he alleviate human suffering? If I was all-powerful, I certainly would. Wouldn't you?"

Vogelson nodded noncommittally. *Yeah, that's one of the things I hate about God, too,* he thought automatically. *No, I mean, I don't really mean that. Forgive me, God. Please forgive me God for thinking that.* Then Vogelson remembered what his pastor had told him. *God works in mysterious ways and suffering brings us closer to God. And God's testing us.*

"If God wants us to believe and worship," Chambers continued, "Then why doesn't he just show himself? And if the Bible is God's word, why is he such a terrible writer? Have you ever read the Bible?"

Vogelson had participated in a few Bible study groups, but he hadn't read the text extensively. "No, not much."

"Well, in the end, the existence or nonexistence of a god doesn't answer any ultimate questions or give us any meaning independent of the meaning we create for ourselves."

What is this guy saying? He's making arguments; maybe they sound good, but they go against God. They're just arguments. It's just intellectual... they go against God!

Vogelson glanced at his notes. "Is it fair to say that you discourage religious practices by the children who come to your camps?"

"I don't know if discourage is the right word, but we certainly don't support it. Our primary goal with respect to children is to build their self-esteem. Failure to trust your own mind and relying instead on superstition, or worse, a religious leader to do your thinking for you is contrary to building self-esteem. You have to trust yourself. That's the first and most important rule of self-esteem."

"How do you expect children to become good citizens if they don't have a moral code to follow?"

"Well, it's certainly important for everyone to live by a strong moral code, and we promote that here. The difference is that we encourage kids to think. A moral code is only appropriate if it's based on reality."

"What do you mean by that?"

"Let's take one of the Ten Commandments. 'Thou shalt not steal.' That principle should be part of a moral code not because it's in the Ten Commandments, but because it makes sense in a community of human beings. Can you imagine living in a society that didn't condemn stealing? It obviously wouldn't work."

"So you think people should ignore the Ten Commandments?"

"As the Ten Commandments, yes. To the extent they offer any principles that can be validated intellectually, then maybe they have some value."

"Do you see any value in religion at all?"

"In general, no. Some of the ethical principles are right, but the way they get there—relying on primitive texts and prophets—is colossally misguided. On the other hand, some people successfully use religion as a crutch to overcome challenges. For all his faults, the President is a good example of that. He overcame an alcohol addiction using religion.

Of course, he could've helped himself half a dozen other ways; it's just that using religion is a socially acceptable way to make that type of life change. But when people present religious claims as factual, that's where it takes a wrong turn and really becomes immoral."

"Immoral?"

"Lying—making claims without any evidence. It's the most egregious sin as far as I'm concerned."

Vogelson was beginning to hate David Chambers. *Anybody could start a business or design an airplane*, he thought. *This guy isn't so special. Just because he gives to charity won't get him into heaven. He rejects his own creator!*

"The good news is that people usually only turn to religion when there are gaps in knowledge; like when people used to blame evil spirits for illness. When we began to understand germs and microbiology, that particular religious belief went away. One of the biggest problems we have now is that people like Robert Newhall want to roll everything back and put religion in places where science already gives us better answers. Evolution is the classic example."

What? Come on. You think we came from apes? Maybe you came from an ape, but I was created in God's image. You are hopelessly lost.

"So what do you think of the religious revival Robert Newhall's leading?"

"I think what he's doing is very dangerous."

"Why?"

"We've worked long and hard to escape from thought systems based on superstition. That's an ugly period of history. If you study it, you'll find thousands of Newhalls and more cruelty than I care to discuss."

I've got enough information, Vogelson thought. I can't wait to show this to Mr. Heilbrenner. "I don't want to take up all your time," Vogelson said as he pretended to turn his tape recorder back on. "Let's get back to your charities."

* * *

Josephine walked quietly into Dushane's office. He was kneeling behind his desk, packing his things in a large cardboard box.

"I heard about what happened," Josephine said.

Dushane grunted, but didn't look up.

"Martin?"

"What?" Dushane reacted angrily.

"Do you want to talk?"

Dushane stood up and faced her, but didn't speak.

"What will you do now?"

"Do?" Dushane responded sharply. "What is there to do?"

"I'm proud of you, Martin."

Dushane shrugged. "Whatever."

They looked at each other in silence for several moments.

"I'm going to Utah tomorrow," Josephine said finally.

"Then goodbye." Dushane responded tersely, and then turned back around and continued packing.

"Take care of yourself, Martin. Please take care of yourself. I will see you again. I promise that we'll see each other again." Josephine walked out.

Dushane stood motionless, stung by her presence and an overwhelming feeling of loss. He didn't know if he could live without her.

CHAPTER 22

I contend that we are both atheists. I just believe in one fewer god than you do. When you understand why you dismiss all the other possible gods, you will understand why I dismiss yours.

—STEPHEN ROBERTS

"Thanks for your help with the article," Vogelson stated somberly. Although he was glad to be finished with the piece, he was a little miffed that Heilbrenner had written almost the entire thing.

"You're welcome, Paul. You did a great job; keep it up. God rewards his loyal servants."

The San Diego Chronicle published the following editorial:

The Warped World of David Chambers

Two weeks ago, I had a candid conversation with David Chambers, the billionaire aerospace industrialist, at his sprawling compound in the Northern California wilderness. Mr. Chambers had revealed in a recent letter that he opposes school prayer. I naturally wondered if he housed pent-up hostility to morality in general. What I discovered was disturbing.

Although Mr. Chambers has a reputation as a generous philanthropist, he conceded that his company was his most important "charity." He actually referred to his company as a charity. I found this statement appalling and I think most people would agree that a business enterprise demonstrates few charitable qualities.

Mr. Chambers also admitted that he didn't believe in God. Now, that's his business, but he revealed an additional disturbing fact. He told me that he discourages religious practices by the children who attend his summer camps. I got the sense that Mr. Chambers was trying to create little clones of himself, and I had a nightmare of thousands of little David Chambers running around believing that business was more important than charity. Mr. Chambers expressed no concern for the negative consequences that would result from snuffing out the spiritual lives of the children under his care. Can you imagine what our children would become without proper moral guidance? I certainly wouldn't want to find out.

Chambers also told me that people should ignore the Ten Commandments. Apparently, he believes that we should throw away a moral code that has been followed for two thousand years and replace it with his business ethics—a code of values that has made him a billionaire.

When Chambers read the editorial, he sank into a state of paralyzing disbelief, shocked at the depth of the lie. As he thought about the immensity of the betrayal and how it could affect his reputation, he blazed white-hot. He threw the newspaper off his desk and stomped out in a rage, charging up the steep hill behind his office and thrashing his way through the underbrush, cursing loudly.

A few hours later, after he had cooled down and bandaged several cuts on his arms, Chambers knew he was wrong to be surprised, and he chided himself for the momentary delusion. He reflected that over the years he had met many men and women who weren't quite honest; people who accepted dishonesty as a normal part of life. There were examples of it everywhere. Preachers who didn't really believe the decayed dogma they dealt to their followers. Politicians who would say anything to get elected. People who lied routinely to get what they wanted and then complacently justified themselves by explaining that they had a spouse and family to support, or worse, that they were simply being practical. *What a gruesome disease*, he thought, *always having to be just a little dishonest to make your way in the world.*

Channeling his rage, Chambers ground out a rebuttal to the editorial—a short response, which accused Vogelson of lying and twisting his words. He demanded that the Chronicle print his rebuttal as well as the full transcript of the interview. The paper refused to print the transcript, stating that it was against its policy. They did print the rebuttal, but it had little effect. Hundreds of newspapers across the country reprinted Vogelson's editorial, unleashing a flood of letters. Most of them contained bitter diatribes against Chambers for being a godless and greedy capitalist; unfit to be a role model to children. Many called on their lawmakers to shut down Chambers' camps. Even the President was asked about the story. Did he think David Chambers, previously awarded the Presidential Medal of Freedom, was still a good and patriotic citizen? "I don't know that atheists should be considered citizens, nor should they be considered patriots. This is one nation under God."

Chambers stewed for several days. *What made this groupthink mentality of the population possible? What was the appeal of religious mass movements and mindless superstition? Why did people embrace a thought system based on fear and ignorance?*

Chambers decided to call Ray Lassater.

"Hello."

"Ray, it's David. Did you see that editorial about me?"

"Of course I did. You sound surprised."

"I am surprised. That paper turned on me."

"Cancer spreads quickly."

"I'm pissed off. I won't stand for this."

"Well, do something about it, then," Lassater challenged.

Chambers didn't respond.

"David?"

"I'm all in," Chambers said firmly. "One hundred percent."

"Good, but let me warn you. These guys are sophisticated criminals; more organized and expert than any criminal operation I ever dealt with as a prosecutor."

Lassater had been following the Infinity Network with the help of three private investigators, but they hadn't been able to dig up much useful information. Nevertheless, Lassater knew that Newhall, Heilbrenner, and several other Infinity officials were enriching themselves from the donations of Infinity followers and lucrative government grants.

"I don't care how hard it is," Chambers responded. "We've got to put an end to this."

"Absolutely. Now, let me tell you our biggest challenge; it's been hard to get reliable information. Infinity hides everything and they've got some of the best lawyers in the country on the payroll. I looked into the Chronicle and they've been infiltrated. I'm pretty sure that Infinity-controlled holding companies are about to take over the paper."

"My God."

"It gets worse. They also control politicians at every level. So even if you figure out what's going on, nobody wants to do anything about it. The only way is to get to an inside source to talk."

"Who?"

"Mike Watson. He's our best chance."

"I thought he left Infinity."

"He did, but he was the original architect. He might even be more clever than Heilbrenner; hopefully he has a conscience."

"Have you spoken with him?"

"I tried, but he wouldn't talk; he called me anti-Christian, blah blah blah. Apparently, he's still a believer. You may fare better."

"Okay."

"I have one piece of good news. Do you remember that documentary on the Catholic Church?"

"The one with the Cardinal's trial?"

"Yeah. A guy named Ralph Johansen made that film and he and I have stayed in touch. He wants to make a documentary about you."

"Me? Why?"

"You're the great rags to riches story; the man who achieved the American dream."

Chambers laughed. "I'm boring."

"Come on, people love a good inspirational story—and they still love you."

"I don't know about that."

"Well, Ralph's a big fan of yours. He's already put together the storyline for the film; he wants to call it The American Dreamer."

Chambers smiled.

"He just needs to spend some time with you to fill in the details. He asked me to put a word in."

"Okay, but didn't that Catholic Church film bomb?"

"Yeah, people weren't ready for it. But they're ready for you."

"Okay, tell him to call me."

"By the way, there's someone else you might find interesting. There's a woman in Utah taking on the Mormons. I met her recently and she's quite impressive."

"What's her name?

"Josephine Holladay."

* * *

Dushane slumped on the couch in his apartment and didn't move. He reflected that in a matter of days his life had changed completely. He had lost both his job and the only woman he had ever loved. After several days of restless inactivity, he decided that he needed to make some decisions about his future. He thought about Charlie Geautreuax. A few years earlier, his friend had gone on a long backpacking trip through the Appalachian mountain range. Geautreaux had described the trek as a way to clear your mind, away from dull routine of civilization. Dushane called his mother.

"Hi mom, it's Martin."

"Hey boy, where you been? Don't you ever call your mother no more?"

"I'm sorry, mom. A lot's been going on up here. I can't talk too much about it right now, but I've decided to take a little break."

"Break? What do you mean, like a vacation?"

"Yeah, sort of. I'm going on a backpacking trip. I'll be gone for a few months."

"A few months?"

"Yeah."

"Where?"

"The Appalachian Trail."

"What about your job?"

"Well...the job's over for right now."

"Martin, what the heck is going on?"

"I'm sorry, I can't really talk about it right now. How's Uncle Nat?"

"Martin?"

"Come on, mom, how's Uncle Nat?"

"He's fine, all right, but what about you?"

"I'm fine, too. Say hi to Uncle Nat and I'll give you a call in a few weeks."

"Martin?"

"What?"

"Be careful, okay?"

"I will. I love you."

"I love you, too."

CHAPTER 23

I believe in God, only I spell it Nature.

—FRANK LLOYD WRIGHT

Josephine read the letter a second time and couldn't help laughing out loud.

Dear Ms. Holladay:

Please be advised that we represent the Church of Jesus Christ of Latter-day Saints. Our client has informed us that you have made, and continue to make, false statements about the Church and its leadership, both orally and in writing. You must cease and desist immediately or face very serious consequences.

If you persist in spreading false statements about the Church, be assured that we will pursue our client's legal rights aggressively, including filing a lawsuit against you for libel and slander. We will also seek compensation for the damage you've caused to the Church's reputation, including punitive damages. Finally, we will not hesitate to assist the District Attorney's office if they choose to pursue a criminal investigation.

This matter requires your urgent attention. Please contact the undersigned as soon as possible. If we don't hear from you within three business days, we will take all necessary and appropriate legal action to stop you.

Very truly yours,

J. Chester Hinkman III, Esq.

A classic "fuck you" letter, Josephine thought. *Probably written by an attorney just out of law school. Just what the world needs; another savage produced by America's law firms.* Josephine reclined in her chair and put her feet up on the desk. She thumbed through Katherine McKay's manuscript and wondered what topic she should take on next; there was no shortage of choices.

After Josephine had left Harvard, she had taken all of her money and founded the Utah Enlightenment Project in Salt Lake City. She began the organization by herself with $20,000, but when news of her plans trickled out, she received a few donations from other ex-Mormons, allowing her to hire an assistant and lease a small office.

The Utah Enlightenment Project's first publication was entitled *The Truth About Mormon Racism*, a thirty-page pamphlet that chronicled the history of the Church's racial policies and their scriptural basis. Although Josephine sympathized with followers who had fallen prey to the appeal of shutting off their minds, Josephine penned biting prose, accusing the Church's leadership of preaching hate, and the followers of allowing petty, irrational beliefs to override their basic human decency. Enraged by the criticism, the General Authorities ordered immediate excommunication of any Church member found in possession of the pamphlet or who in any way aided Josephine's organization. Josephine tried to get bookstores and newsstands to carry her work, but most people were afraid to cross the Church so it was scarcely available.

The Project's second publication dealt with academic freedom at BYU. Josephine interviewed several professors who had been terminated for pursuing scholarship that was not in line with official Church doctrine or Scripture. She published their stories as well as the suppressed scholarship.

The most damning pieces of suppressed material included two studies that concluded that the Book of Mormon was not a document translated from ancient America (as the founding Prophet Joseph Smith and other Mormons had claimed), but a work from the nineteenth century. Even more damning was an analysis of the Book of Mormon for historical accuracy. Several professors presented an overwhelming case that no archaeological evidence supported the Prophet Joseph Smith's historical account of early migrants to the hemisphere.

Other embarrassing scholarship included a biography of Joseph Smith that chronicled his money-digging treasure hunting and interest in the occult. Josephine laughed at most of the information she learned about the Mormon founder, but she felt sick when she thought of his forty-plus wives. Smith had justified his appetite for young women (including minors) by claiming that plural marriage was sanctioned by God. Smith's tactic of claiming a divine right to justify his desires was common among cult leaders. Indeed, it was the single most insidious tool of manipulation available to them.

Josephine couldn't help thinking that Mormonism was the largest religion in the world founded by a white-trash prophet. On the other hand, she couldn't help but admire the man's focused ambition. He had started on the fringes of society, yet managed through charisma and a vibrant imagination to attract a large following. Josephine often wondered what it would take to start a religion. What kind of person shunned creative work in favor of pursuing power over others? It was the most pointless act of vanity she could imagine.

Josephine published the work of ex-BYU scholars under several aliases, but the General Authorities determined the true identities of the authors in a few cases. This resulted in immediate excommunication. Josephine always threw a party to memorialize the event and officially welcome the outcast back to reality.

Josephine had become a thorn in the Church's side, but Church leaders generally ignored her; she had few resources and couldn't afford to distribute her literature widely. The General Authorities did, however, explicitly brand her a "disciple of Satan." Although undeniably a playground maneuver, the ploy served as an effective warning to the rank and file; the mere mention of Satan was enough to convince most Saints not to have anything to do with Josephine or the Utah Enlightenment Project.

Josephine put Katherine McKay's manuscript down and picked up the "fuck you" letter. She taped it securely to the bookcase behind her desk so that she would see it often. She was surprised by how much she looked forward to a fight.

* * *

Dushane woke up slowly as the soft light of early morning crept quietly into his tent. He sat up in his sleeping bag and felt the dew that had seeped through the tent's nylon. As he crawled out, he yawned at the red-orange sun, which peeked just over the ridge of the mountains and burst onto his campsite at the top of Stratton Mountain in Vermont. For endless miles in every direction, the trees were so thick that they formed an uninterrupted green wave over the jagged peaks.

Dushane sat on a boulder for several minutes and enjoyed the view. He couldn't feel the rock beneath him, only the thick coat of moss that had exploded in growth around it. He ran his hands back and forth across the side of the rock and let the delicate texture run through his fingers. *This is real happiness*, he thought, *and freedom*. He reflected that he felt like a ghost, or a spirit, freed from earthly cares, with the wilderness speaking to him in a deep and powerful persuasion. It gave a voice to a secret part of his soul that connected powerfully with everything around him.

Dushane took a deep breath and walked back to his campsite. He grabbed his frayed and faded pack, and stuffed his tent and sleeping bag down into the bottom. Then he grabbed his stove, which still reeked of fuel from a spill the night before, and put it in next. The last thing he packed was a small duffel bag of clothes, which also functioned as his pillow. He took a final look at the view and then started down the side of the mountain. The sky was a deep blue, uninterrupted by clouds, and barely visible through the majestic maple trees. The wind blew gently through the leaves and they swayed in a rhythmic dance. It was early fall and the trees had just begun to transform into a palette of color.

As he walked, foliage surrounded him like a warm, green tunnel with the Appalachian Trail meandering gracefully through it. Dushane had been hiking for almost three months and a powerful concept had been growing in his mind since the beginning of the trip. Now, the idea had finally crystallized. *The purpose of living is the appreciation of beauty.* He stopped for a moment, took his journal out and began writing. "The more you appreciate beauty, the closer you move towards God.

God = Beauty. Or maybe God is the ultimate understanding of the concept of beauty." Dushane paused, attempting to clarify his thoughts further. "It's not only the enhanced appreciation of beauty in all things, but also an enhanced concept of what beauty is. At some point, that concept expands and you realize it encompasses everything. Is that the answer?" Dushane's brain blazed with firing neurons and he transformed into an opera singer hitting a high note, the crescendo continuing infinitely outside the bounds of time and space. The feeling was different than love, more intense, encompassing love and everything else life could be. He succumbed to an energy, starting at his fingertips, then rising through his chest and into his face, finally centering on his shoulders like it was going to lift him up and allow him to fly across the countryside, soaking it all in. And then there was a long silence—but it was loud, as if the entire universe was finally responding to his questions.

Dushane tried to attach words to what he felt, but it was impossible to describe because he was so completely in tune with his surroundings and whatever force in nature tied everything together. The act of describing it would have destroyed the moment because it would have injected his cluttered ego, which seemed to have completely disappeared. Dushane reflected that he'd never felt anything similar in a church. Indeed, being in a church had the opposite effect because it created more questions than it answered.

Is this the real church? Dushane thought. *A church without any limitations—where the mind is fully alive. Why doesn't everyone embrace this? Why would anyone try to put limits on the mind?*

The day began to heat up as Dushane neared the bottom of the mountain. There was a pond in the distance between the trees. When he got within a few hundred yards of the water, he galloped happily towards it in anticipation of the cool sensation on his body. As he reached the soft sand of the shoreline, he threw off his pack and stripped down to his shorts. Then he waded in gingerly, testing the temperature of the water. It was warm on the surface, but cool on his feet. He swam out to the middle of the pond and looked up at Stratton Mountain while he floated on his back. *This is the happiest moment of my life.*

* * *

The Chambers Aerospace P-75 jet buzzed over the mountains forty miles east of Salt Lake City International Airport. David Chambers sat quietly at the controls, enjoying the solitude and the clean hum of the plane's propellers. Chambers was on his way to visit one of his factories in Kansas, but he had decided to stop in Salt Lake and drop in on Josephine. Chambers didn't know much about Josephine or the Utah Enlightenment Project, but he had high hopes after Ray Lassater had told him that she was a potential ally in their struggle against the cancer consuming the country. Lassater had also given him a copy of the organization's mission statement.

The mission of the Utah Enlightenment Project is:

To expose the dishonesty of the Church of Jesus of Christ of Latter-Day Saints and to present the truth about the Church.

To support and promote academic freedom at all educational institutions in the State of Utah.

To protect, support, and arrange shelter for individuals desiring to terminate their involvement with the Church.

Chambers smiled every time he read it, and he kept it in his shirt pocket so that he could review it whenever he needed a lift. After he landed, he caught a cab to his hotel.

"Where you in from?" the cabbie asked.

"Northern California."

"Here on business or pleasure?"

"Hopefully both."

The cabbie gingerly fingered a thermos on the passenger's seat. "Are you one of our saved brothers?"

"You mean…a Mormon?"

"Yeah."

"No, I'm not."

The cabbie unscrewed the cap of the thermos and poured a cup of coffee. "It helps me stay alert, driving at night."

The next morning, Chambers caught another cab to Josephine's office.

"Hi, I'd like to see Josephine," Chambers said to a young receptionist as he walked into the unmarked building.

"Is she expecting you?" The receptionist smiled, but didn't recognize him.

"No."

"May I ask what this is regarding?"

"Tell her I'm here to support the Project."

"Can I tell her your name?"

"David Chambers."

"Just a minute, sir."

Chambers scanned the lobby, which was sparsely furnished with a small desk, a leather couch, and a coffee table. There was nothing on the freshly painted white walls except for some small block lettering behind the receptionist's desk that read: The Utah Enlightenment Project.

"Mr. Chambers, her office is down there." The assistant pointed to a narrow hallway.

"Thank you." Chambers walked down the corridor to the only open doorway and waited silently. Josephine was absorbed in a manuscript and didn't look up. Chambers studied her face and watched her movements, which were vibrant and purposeful. He took two steps toward her desk and she glanced up. "What can I do for you?" she said without smiling.

Chambers chuckled lightly, but didn't answer.

Josephine waited a few seconds and then looked up sternly. "Look, I'm a little busy. What do you want?"

"I'm David Chambers."

"Yeah, you look like David Chambers."

"I am David Chambers."

"Okay. You're David Chambers. What does David Chambers want with the Utah Enlightenment Project?"

Chambers closed the door and sat down. He looked firmly into Josephine's eyes. "I'm here to make sure you have all the resources necessary to fulfill your mission."

Josephine smiled casually. "Why?"

"I'm worried."

"So? Wait, let me guess. You're tired of being vilified in the press?"

"No. I mean I am tired of that, but I'm just...worried. I don't know how else to describe it. It's like seeing someone dump trash into the ocean."

"That's a good analogy. What do you think you can do about it?"

"I don't know."

"Well, I'm sorry you came all this way. I don't either."

"Then why are you doing this?"

"I don't have a choice."

"You had to do this?"

"Yes."

"Why? No, wait...let me guess this time. You can't stand the lying?"

"That's right."

"The betrayal of the mind?"

Josephine nodded.

"You hate the prophets, the manipulators."

"Of course, but it's worse than that."

"You hate the followers for closing their minds; for renouncing themselves."

"Yes. I'm surprised you understand that."

Chambers shook his head. "I don't really understand any of it."

"And you won't ever understand it."

"Is that a defect?"

Josephine laughed cheerfully, finally breaking her stoic demeanor. "That's exactly what it is. We're a dying breed."

Chambers chuckled. "Ray was right about you, Josephine. I think you and I are going to be great friends."

"I hope so."

Chambers and Josephine talked for several more hours, sharing their experiences with religion and agreeing that the problem went way beyond religion's mindlessness. The real horror was the self-renunciation that occurred when a person surrendered themselves to any mass movement and allowed a leader to do their thinking for them. When confronted by charges of racism, intolerance, or misogyny, the religious follower could engage in a perverse form of logic. *God is moral. The Bible is God's word. My church leader tells me what the Bible means. I follow what they tell me. Therefore, I am moral.*

Josephine observed that followers of religious mass movements who harbored hate were functionally no different than Nazi officials who argued that they were just following orders when they incinerated Jews. They joined the movement precisely so they wouldn't be burdened with the responsibility of making their own moral decisions, or thinking for themselves.

Chambers was amazed by Josephine's incisive intellect and he became increasingly aroused as they spoke. "I had no idea how much I needed to meet you, Josephine."

"Where are you staying tonight?" Josephine asked, a hint of invitation in her voice.

"I don't know."

"Please stay with me," she said softly as she stepped out from behind her desk. Chambers sprang up from his chair and embraced her.

"I've been waiting so long for you," Josephine whispered.

When they arrived at Josephine's apartment, Chambers undressed her slowly, kissing the length of her body, trying to capture every taste and scent. Josephine surrendered completely as he laid her naked body on the bed and then gently caressed her breasts and nibbled her neck.

"I want you now," Josephine purred softly.

* * *

Chambers rested comfortably in bed with Josephine's head on his chest. He ran his hand over the soft strands of her hair and then down to the small of her back. He had had many intense moments in his life, but the explosive connection he shared with Josephine was by far the most exhilarating. He laughed gently when he thought that what he had just done was considered a sin by many religious traditions—two people expressing their passion and love for each other. *This is one of the most beautiful and empowering acts of life affirmation imaginable. Perhaps that's why so many religions condemned it*, he reflected, *insisting that their subjects remain powerless, needy, and in self-denial. That can't be right. It just can't be right…*

* * *

After Chambers left the next morning, Josephine daydreamed about him while she sipped her coffee. She couldn't get their passionate sexual episode out of her mind and she remained enveloped by his powerful masculine presence. She laid her head back against her office chair and sighed gently. She closed her eyes, but opened them again suddenly when she heard a woman screaming belligerently in the lobby.

"What's going on here?" Josephine yelled as she stepped in front of an angry woman who was berating her receptionist.

"You! You! You're the tramp behind this!" The woman stepped aggressively toward Josephine and bumped her chest.

"What do you want?" Josephine said, not backing away, her face within inches of the woman's.

"I want you to stop! Stop! Stop lying!"

"I'm not going to talk to you until you calm down," Josephine said firmly. "And I want you to apologize to my receptionist. Otherwise, you need to leave—now!"

The woman took a step back and sucked in a deep breath. She turned to the receptionist. "I'm sorry," she said testily. "I didn't mean to hurt you, but I've got issues with your supervisor."

The receptionist nodded politely.

"Do you wish to speak with me?" Josephine asked calmly.

"Yes. You've got a lot of nerve. What possible benefit do you expect to gain from attacking the Church?"

Josephine occasionally had to deal with angry people who showed up at her office, but she always tried to be friendly and sympathetic. She knew from her own experience that years of brainwashing beginning at birth were difficult to overcome, so she never tried to persuade people rationally; rational arguments had no relevance to an irrational belief system. She always offered Mormon visitors the opportunity to explain why the Book of Mormon and the Church were true, but most believers had never thought of why the Church was true—they just "knew," so few people engaged her in a factual conversation.

Josephine concluded that most people didn't care about the lies propagated by the Church. As she heard so often from Church members, "It's a matter of faith, not facts." The General Authorities stated it even more bluntly, proclaiming that facts could be dangerous: "Satan sometimes uses the truth to promote his purposes." To some extent, she felt sorry for the credulous followers, although she chafed at their mental negligence. She directed most of her anger towards Church leaders—the people who knew better. Nevertheless, Josephine remained cordial, surprising her antagonists that a "disciple of Satan" was so friendly and understanding.

"Have a seat," Josephine said, motioning to the couch.

"Okay."

"You want to know why I attack the Church?"

"Yes."

Josephine wanted to say that she attacked the Church because it made bald, irresponsible claims unsupported by any evidence, but she decided on a different approach. "Imagine if you could live your life fully; that you could live the life you dream about; pursue the goals that are important to you; support the charities that you believe in. What would that be like?"

The woman stared at Josephine blankly. "I have a husband and three kids. I have responsibility for a family. That's obviously something you don't know anything about."

"You're right, I don't. But don't you want to give your children the chance to make their own decisions and fulfill their own dreams?"

"You don't understand anything! God has a plan for my kids!" the woman screeched as she jumped off the couch and stormed out in a huff, slamming the door behind her.

"I'm sorry you had to deal with that," Josephine said to her receptionist.

"No, it's okay. It's reaffirming."

Josephine went back to her office and picked up the check for $500,000 that Chambers had given her that morning. The money allowed Josephine to hire additional staff and double the production of literature, addressing subjects where there was strong evidence of false Mormon doctrine—doctrine contradicted by facts or not supported by any evidence other than the say-so of a "prophet." The Enlightenment Project's first full-length book, entitled *Why Didn't God get it Right the First Time?* highlighted 3,900 changes made to the Book of Mormon and other sacred writings after original publication.

In order to counter Josephine's efforts, the Church busily produced its own literature, attempting to prove the factual accuracy of the Book of Mormon and other scripture. Although the Church's efforts were generally lightweight, they produced one book based on a recently discovered collection of documents that provided insight into the early Church. The material appeared to offer some support for Church claims. Unfortunately, the documents were almost entirely forged.

The Church had purchased the documents from a wayward Saint who had been collecting Mormon literature for several years. The documents both supported Church claims and embarrassed the Church. The Church bought all of them, using the supporting documents to bolster its claims, and suppressing the damaging ones. It turned out that the seller was a closet apostate, trying to make a quick buck and embarrass the Church. He had created convincing forgeries, which included a letter revealing that a magic white salamander, not the Angel Moroni, had appeared to Joseph Smith in the prophet's first vision. Another letter in the collection, allegedly written by Joseph Smith, referred to his expertise at money-digging treasure hunting.

Enlightenment Project sympathizers slipped Josephine a few of the "discovered" documents and her expert immediately detected the forgery. She sent her expert's findings to the General Authorities, urging them to listen to reason and avoid making even bigger fools of themselves. As rumors spread about the questionable validity of the documents, the General Authorities hired their own document expert who reluctantly gave them the bad news. Mormon leaders ordered immediate discontinuation of the book's publication and directed all Saints to remove it from their bookshelves. They also issued an official apology to those who had been misled by an "apostate seeking to exploit the faith of loyal Saints."

Josephine laughed cheerfully at the episode. She felt genuinely sorry for the humiliated Church leadership, but she didn't miss an additional opportunity to embarrass them. She took out a full-page ad in the Salt Lake Times.

> While we are concerned about the forgery of documents by a dishonest individual trying to prove or disprove Church claims, we are more concerned that Church leaders didn't recognize the fraud. Since Mormon leaders claim they have prophetic powers, we don't understand how they could've been duped. We are also concerned with Church attempts to paint its historical research and associated literature as a scholarly enterprise. This is an act of breathtaking intellectual dishonesty. We urge the people of Utah to consider the facts carefully.

Officially, the General Authorities refused to comment on the Utah Enlightenment Project, but they did establish the Strengthening Church Members Committee shortly after the publication of the Project's first pamphlet. The purpose of the Committee was to document attacks against the Church and to create a list of all libelous publications. Despite being criticized as McCarthyism, the General Authorities argued that Doctrine & Covenants 123, a revelation received by Joseph Smith from God, justified the new committee.

And perhaps a committee can be appointed to find out these things, and to take statements and affidavits; and also to gather up the libelous publications that are afloat;

And all that are in the magazines, and in the encyclopedias, and all the libelous histories that are published, and are writing, and by whom, and present the whole concatenation of diabolical rascality and nefarious and murderous impositions that have been practiced upon this people.

Privately, the Strengthening Members Committee compiled an "enemies" list that included detailed files on any person who questioned or criticized the Church. Although Josephine had secured a spot near the top of the list, the Church never harassed her directly. Nevertheless, she received large amounts of hate mail and decided to hire a full-time bodyguard.

Although Josephine took pride in the Enlightenment Project's work, she regretted that the General Authorities ordered that access to all Church documents and archival material be restricted to "approved" historians who agreed to give the Church prepublication censorship. This made Josephine's work and the work of other legitimate historians more difficult. The Church also established the Correlation Committee; a group charged with ensuring that all Church publications, from books to periodicals to seminary materials, followed official policy and expressed official interpretations.

Josephine wondered what would happen if an entire society valued submission to authority more than intellectual honesty.

CHAPTER 24

Two hands working can do more than a thousand clasped in prayer.

—Unknown

Ray Lassater walked up behind Chambers on the Kaleidoscope Ranch shooting range. "Newhall's not that tall," he said, pointing to a paper figure that Chambers used for target practice.

"Hey, Ray. Good to see you!" Chambers put down his rifle and embraced his friend. "And that's not Newhall; it's Don Leachman. Don't you recognize that svelte, pear-like figure?"

"Ah, yes…of course. I didn't recognize him without the scowl on his face."

Chambers smiled. "Care to join me; unload a few rounds?"

"Sure. So, how did you get on with Josephine? You look refreshed."

Chambers felt a quick rush of adrenaline as he thought about his explosive connection with Josephine. "Oh, not too bad. She's quite a woman. I'm supporting her efforts."

"Good. I thought you two might like each other."

"Here, try this one." Chambers handed Lassater a rifle. "Put this around your shoulder; this gun's got quite a kick."

Lassater flung the shoulder strap around his neck and peered through the scope. "So, what's the next step for you?"

"I don't know; I've got to keep this place running."

"Josephine's work didn't inspire you?"

Chambers chuckled lightly. "She inspired me all right."

"I heard you were working with Ralph Johansen on his documentary."

"Yeah, Ralph's a good guy. I think he's almost done."

"Excellent."

"You know, it's little unnerving to watch someone chronicle your life, but what he's put together is impressive. He said he wants to put the material in a book, too."

"You should write your own book," Lassater said.

"I think Ralph's book will be plenty."

"No, not about you; about religion."

"I don't have time for that—or the inclination."

Lassater fired a shot, missing the target completely. He lowered his gun. "I'm a little rusty."

"Watch this." Chambers steadied his gun on his shoulder and fired, hitting the target squarely in the Adam's apple.

"I'm impressed. And I'm serious about this book idea. I'll help you with it."

"I don't know, Ray. Haven't you ever heard that saying—discussing theology is like playing tennis without a net."

Lassater chuckled. "No, I hadn't heard that, although I like the analogy."

"Besides, would anybody care?"

"Eliminating a thought system based on ignorance and fear. No, I take that back, a thought system that glorifies ignorance and fear. People sure as hell better care."

"Well, you're right, it is a horrifying thought system, but nobody sees it that way."

"I do. You do."

Chambers raised his gun again and peered down the scope. For most of his life, he had given little thought to religion. As a child, he had attended church regularly with his grandparents, and had believed in God, but by the time he got to high school, he realized that there wasn't much to it. Religion was mostly about a bunch of people who claimed they were "prophets" and had "divine" wisdom. The names changed over the years, but the so-called prophets shared three common characteristics—they claimed to have unique knowledge of the truth not available to other human beings; this truth was based on faith with little or no evidence supporting it; and they declared that other competing prophets and religions were false. Every time Chambers tried to read a book about religion, he yawned. He concluded that religious beliefs were interchangeable—none could be proven truer than any other and there were almost as many different beliefs as there were people on the planet.

Chambers occasionally spoke to believers about religion's violent history, and they typically defended their faith by insisting that it held love as the highest value. He always thought that was a curious response because he didn't know a single person, religious or not, who didn't hold love as the most important value in life. He wondered why people felt that religion somehow gave them unique or original knowledge of this fact.

"I don't know if a book would convince anyone, Ray. You know how religion is; the opiate of the masses, right?"

"No one thought I could convince juries in Boston to convict Catholic priests, either."

"Well…" Chambers hemmed. He hesitated because he knew that people had strong emotional ties to supernatural ideas that they didn't want to be challenged. And since religions weren't based on reason, he knew he wouldn't persuade most believers because religion by its terms was impervious to the light of logical arguments. Chambers knew that believers had powerful emotional needs to satisfy and turned to religion for easy answers. On the other hand, Chambers did feel exhilarated by the prospect of proving another way—a way to connect powerfully with life and with other people that had nothing to do with mystics or charlatans claiming divine knowledge; a thought system that brought out the highest capabilities and aspirations of the human mind.

"I need to think it over, Ray. I've got some concerns."

* * *

"And so man is a fallen creature, unable to save himself. Fortunately, God sent his son Jesus Christ to redeem us. Without a savior of course, man is doomed, no matter what he does."

Chambers sat quietly in the back of the classroom, becoming increasingly upset by the senseless dogma. The lecturer, George Henson, was an ordained minister who had taught Religious Studies at the Stratton Military Academy for over twenty years. The Academy, founded by a prominent Baptist minister in Charlottesville, Virginia, consisted of a middle school for grades six through eight and a high school. While the school had developed a reputation for providing a strong secondary school education, the Academy's administrators trumpeted its focus on strengthening each student's religious faith. The school required all cadets to attend religious services on Sunday and to take the Religious Studies course.

Normally, Chambers participated actively in his classes, but he generally held his tongue in Religious Studies out of respect to his grandparents. He didn't want to get into any trouble and embarrass them because they had sacrificed to provide him with a first-rate education. But the core Christian tenet of original sin, with its depiction of man as a helpless, inherently sinful creature forced to grovel for forgiveness, sickened him. He had no doubt that such a depraved view of humanity was horribly wrong. He raised his hand.

"Yes, David."

"What if a person lives a moral life, is he still guilty?"

"It's impossible for man to live a truly moral life on his own," Henson answered. "As we know, man is sinful by nature."

"So does that mean that a person has no choice? In other words, are you saying that he can't choose to live a moral life?"

"Man can choose to accept the Savior Jesus Christ. God gives us that opportunity."

"But what if a man doesn't believe that Jesus is the son of God, but nonetheless makes a commitment to living a moral life?"

"That's impossible," Henson responded automatically.

"Why?"

"Well, man isn't capable of living a moral life on his own. That's clear from scripture."

"So, if I understand you correctly, what we're talking about here isn't really morality at all because morality implies choice."

Henson thought for a moment. "Uh...well, let's see. I...you know, David, your question is really outside the scope of our discussion, but I'd be happy to discuss it with you later."

After class, Henson scolded Chambers for asking inappropriate questions.

On the way back to his dorm room, Chambers thought carefully about the episode. *What's really going on here? That man is a nice guy; he means well, but there's something...I don't know...ugly about him. Like he's confused. No, not confused, but unreliable or maybe inconsistent. He peddles mindless superstition. That must be part of the reason I get a bad feeling about him, but...No! Wait! He doesn't trust himself! That's it! He doesn't trust himself!* Chambers took a deep breath and let the exhilaration of clarity wash over him. *That's why he seems incongruous and why I don't trust him. He doesn't trust himself.*

At the end of the semester, Chambers wrote a paper for his final project. The topic was comparative religions and Henson had instructed students to compare and contrast the religious beliefs and practices of Christianity, Judaism, and Islam. Chambers wrote a thoughtful, well-researched paper that impressed his teacher until the final footnote.

> The evidence cited in this paper as well as the conclusions drawn must be balanced against the "Imaginary Friend" theory. This theory holds that the common bond among all religious followers is that they worship an imaginary friend that they rely on to make decisions about their life; usually the same imaginary friend as their parents.
>
> There is no evidence that these imaginary friends exist, but there is heated debate about which imaginary friend is the most powerful, moral, true, wise, etc. This disagreement has resulted in centuries of bloodshed.
>
> Since factual evidence and rational arguments cannot be used to determine whose imaginary friend should be followed or worshipped, the only way to resolve the dispute is through violence. If the people of one religion are able to kill all the people from the other religions, then they are entitled to declare themselves and their imaginary friend supreme.

After reading the footnote, Henson immediately called Chambers in to his office.

"Sit down, David," he said stiffly, motioning to a chair on the other side of his desk. "I don't understand this stunt you've pulled. This last footnote...is this some kind of senior prank?"

"No."

"Well, what is it? It's not funny. It's...it's insubordination. And coming from the class valedictorian is especially disappointing."

"I wrote a paper about religion," Chambers responded evenly. "My paper wouldn't have been fully accurate without exploring every avenue of religious thought."

Henson had expected an apology or at least an appropriate display of deference to his authority, but Chambers offered neither. Henson's voice hardened. "This is personal insult to me, and to my faith."

"I'm not trying to insult you; I just tried to express my views honestly."

"Sarcastically."

"Well, I find this whole exercise colossally misguided."

Henson furrowed his brow. "I don't know what you're trying to prove here, but you've gotten yourself into serious trouble. I could flunk you for this. That means you won't graduate."

Chambers sat quietly while blood began to rush into his face. He suddenly feared that he had jeopardized his future.

"If you've decided that you don't believe in God, I don't understand why you felt the need to make a mockery of your schoolwork."

"I never said I didn't believe in God."

"Your paper…"

"Define God," Chambers interrupted.

"I'm not going to discuss this with you."

"You asked me why I did this. Let's define God first."

"God is the supreme being…the divine…"

"Supreme? How? Is he a man?"

"God is…I'm not going to have this conversation. All I know is that you're in serious trouble. Now, let me tell you what you're going to do. First of all, you're going to resubmit your paper without that sarcastic little commentary."

Chambers shrugged. "What's the difference?"

Henson shook his head. "You're digging your own grave, David. I'm trying to help you here. Don't you care about your future?"

Chambers stared blankly at his teacher and wondered what was going on in the man's head. *He's must have some sort of script running; a core program in his psyche that's protecting…no, protecting isn't the right word; it's like a shut-off valve—strangling the honest, rational part of his mind. My God, what a way to live—and not even know it's happening.*

"I don't know what to say, Mr. Henson."

"Well, if you don't care about your future, then this meeting is over."

"Okay." Chambers shuffled out and walked to the courtyard. He had only one place to turn—his faculty advisor, Jack Crawford. Crawford taught physics at the Academy and was an avid pilot who owned a twin-engine Cessna. He flew regularly out of the local airport and invited Chambers to join him almost every weekend.

"Hi, Mr. Crawford," Chambers said quietly as he walked into his mentor's office.

"Hey, David." Crawford greeted enthusiastically. "How are you?"

"Well…I'm not sure. I've got a little problem."

"What is it? Sit down and let's talk."

"I wrote this paper in Religious Studies and I put in a footnote at the end. Mr. Henson didn't like it."

"He didn't like one of your footnotes? So what?"

"I guess he thought it was disrespectful."

"Do you have it with you?"

"Yeah."

"Let me take a look."

Chambers passed the paper across the desk. "It's the last footnote, number 46."

Crawford read the footnote slowly, stroking his chin as he read. "David…my God." He shook his head. "This is something."

Chambers tapped his fingers nervously on his knee. He wondered if he had made a big mistake.

"I don't know how you came up with this, but…" Crawford's face broke into an unexpected smile and he laughed cheerfully. "This is one of the funniest damn things I've ever seen."

"You think it's okay, then?"

"Yeah, it's perfect. I mean you probably pissed him off, but the guy's so tightly wound, somebody needs to shake him up."

Chambers heaved a sigh of relief. "So what should I do?"

"What did Henson say?"

"He said he could flunk me."

"What?" Crawford boomed. "That's bullshit."

"That's what he said."

"Listen, you let me handle this, all right? I won't let you get flunked over this."

"Okay."

Crawford called a meeting with Henson and the Academy's Commandant to resolve the situation. After heated negotiations, including a threat by Henson to resign, Crawford brokered a deal that required Chambers to remove the footnote from his paper and refrain from speaking at the Academy's commencement ceremonies, which was customary for the class valedictorian. The deal also provided that the school would leave Chambers' senior quote out of the yearbook.

I want to maximize the creative force of my mind and harness it to fulfill my dreams. I'll strive to understand everything around me and use that knowledge to benefit myself and others. I won't allow anyone to tell me what to think or do, and I'll answer to no authority other than my own conscience.

"You know it's the right thing to do," Lassater said as he pulled the trigger, hitting the paper Leachman squarely between the eyes.

"Nice shot, Ray."

"What about the book?"

Chambers shrugged.

"It'll be most important thing you've ever done, David—and you've done a lot of important things. You know I'm right. I'm always right."

Chambers swung the gun strap off his shoulder and laid his weapon on the ground. "I know. That's the one thing I hate about you, Ray."

"Good. I know just the person to help us."

CHAPTER 25

[M]ost of our moral intuitions are clear but their origin escapes us, because it lies in mental processing that we cannot consciously access... [W]e know that religious codes and exemplars cannot literally be the origin of people's moral thoughts. These thoughts are remarkably similar in people with different religious concepts or no such concepts. Also, these thoughts come naturally to children, who would never link them to supernatural agency.

Our evolution as a species of cooperators is sufficient to explain the actual psychology of moral reasoning, the way children and adults represent moral dimensions of action. But then this requires no special concept of religious agent, no special code, no models to follow... To some extent religious concepts are parasitic upon moral intuitions.

—PASCAL BOYER, *RELIGION EXPLAINED*

Josephine shut down her computer and switched off the light in her office, exhausted from a long day of work. She grabbed her coat as she walked to the lobby to lock up, but a woman standing outside the window startled her. Josephine couldn't see the woman's face clearly because it was drizzling and a thin layer of condensation covered the window. Josephine waved to the woman and waited for her to reveal her intentions, but she didn't move. Josephine finally cracked the window slightly and called out. "Can I help you?"

The woman walked toward the front door and stood in front of it, but she didn't answer or raise her head.

"Are you okay?" Josephine yelled through the glass door. "Do you need some help?"

The woman put her hand on the door and then looked up.

"Oh my God! Mom!" Josephine cried as she swung the door open. "Mom, what are you doing here?"

"I...I..."

Josephine put her hand on her mother's shoulder. "Come in; come in out of the rain."

Emma Holladay shuffled in slowly. "I...I...had to see you," she said as she slid the hood of her jacket off her head, fully revealing her face. Her eyes were bloodshot; she had been crying.

"Mom..." Josephine put her arms around her mother's back and drew her close. "Mom, I'm so happy to see you." Josephine hadn't seen either of her parents in several years.

"How are you, honey?" Emma whispered.

"I'm okay. I've missed you. I've really missed you. Are you all right?"

"Yes. But...but I've missed you, too. So has your father."

Josephine loosened her grip, instinctively recoiling at the thought of her father.

"Your father doesn't know I'm here," Emma continued. "But I had to see you."

"Let's sit down." Josephine motioned to the couch. "How...how is he?"

"He hasn't changed."

"I'm sorry, I'm sorry I couldn't be what he wanted."

"Please don't say that, honey. I don't want you to feel that way. Your father still loves you; I know that he does. But you challenged his whole identity. Do you understand?"

Josephine nodded.

"Your father believes strongly in his faith. That's always been the most important thing in his life. We married when we were very young. It's been hard, but I don't regret it. He's a good man and I love him."

"I love him, too. It's just...I couldn't..."

"It's okay. I know. I'm so glad you have more choices."

Josephine clasped her mother's hand.

"You were always so confident and sure of yourself; I think your father felt you didn't need him."

"I do need him. I need both of you. I...I...wish I had a family."

Tears began to well up in Emma's eyes and Josephine put her arm around her. "Don't cry, mom. It's going to be okay. I promise it's going to be okay."

"I...I miss you so much, honey. And I love you. God, I love you."

"I know, mom, I know. I love you too." Josephine paused, lightly massaging her mother's back. "But I...I don't want you to come here anymore. You need to go home. I want you to go home."

Josephine briefly thought of telling her mother to abandon the man who was keeping them apart unnecessarily. Indeed, she felt like screaming it. But Josephine loved her mother more than anything else in the world and the thought of making her confront her own life was too scary to fathom. As a matter of practice, Josephine always exercised restraint when she spoke with members of the Church. She had received many visitors who didn't believe the Church's claims. Some of these people asked her if they should leave the Church and risk a break from their families. Josephine almost always said no unless the person was exceptionally strong.

"Maybe we can be a family again someday, Josie," Emma said.

"I hope so, mom. I hope so."

* * *

Chambers sprawled out on a chaise lounge on the back patio of his bungalow at Kaleidoscope Ranch. He squinted at the bright sunshine as he took a pair of sunglasses out of his shirt pocket and then dialed Mike Watson on his cell phone.

"Hello."

"Mike Watson?"

"Yes, who's this?"

"This is David Chambers."

"Okay...do I know you?"

"No, we've never met, but I'd like to interview you."

"What about?"

"Your experiences in the Infinity Network."

"I'm sorry, but I'm not interested in talking about that. Who are you, anyway?"

"David Chambers."

"David Chambers? I don't recall..."

"I'm a concerned citizen."

"What?"

"I'm a concerned citizen—concerned about Infinity's illegal activities. I figured you could tell me something about that."

"What is this? What organization are you with?"

"I'm not with any organization, although you may have read about me in the papers recently. I wrote an article against prayer in the public schools."

"Wait a minute. Is this a joke? Who is this?"

"David Chambers."

"I don't believe this."

"You need proof?" Chambers chuckled.

"What do you want?"

"I have information that you funneled large sums of money from the Infinity Network to the private bank accounts of Infinity leaders. I'd like you to shed some light on that for me."

"I don't know what you're talking about!"

"No? That's interesting. Do you remember talking to Ray Lassater?"

Watson didn't answer.

"Well, anyway, I'm working with Ray. He said you wouldn't cooperate with him so you can talk to me instead."

"I'm not talking to anyone."

"That's not smart, Mike. Trust me."

"I don't where you get off calling me."

"You can make this easy or difficult; it doesn't make much difference to me. If you've heard anything about me, you probably know that I'm relentless. My goal is to get this information—and I will get it. So please don't be foolish."

"Are you threatening me?"

"Yes."

The pace of Watson's breathing quickened, but he didn't speak.

"Mike? You still with me?"

Watson remained silent.

"Well, perhaps I should discuss this with the law enforcement authorities. Sorry to bother you."

"Wait!"

* * *

The next morning, Chambers flew down to Southern California to meet Mike Watson at his small two-bedroom, tract home in Garden Grove, just south of Los Angeles. Watson had sold his mansion and Jaguar, and donated the money to charity. Now, he lived modestly with his wife and two children.

"Hi, I'm David," Chambers greeted as Watson opened the front door of his home.

"Mike Watson. Come on in." The men shook hands and Chambers followed the slightly-built man down a short hallway. They passed the kitchen where Watson's kids sat quietly at the table.

"Your kids; shouldn't they be in school?"

"No," Watson answered gruffly. "I teach them here."

Chambers felt a flash of anger. The thought of a parent projecting their fears and putting their own needs ahead of their children repulsed him, but he kept his thoughts to himself.

"Have a seat." Watson motioned to a leather recliner in the study.

"Thanks. I'm glad you agreed to meet me."

"Well, I can't say I'm happy about it. From what I've read about you and Ray Lassater, I think you're wrong about the Christian faith."

"Maybe."

"We need to reestablish the moral foundation of this country."

"I agree. With the exception of what you did at Infinity, I suspect our moral philosophies are similar."

Watson cocked his head and stared hard at Chambers.

"But that's not important right now," Chambers went on. "You're probably wondering what's motivating me."

"Yeah."

"It's important that you understand because it'll make my job easier. My biggest concern is the increasing spread of fear in the country."

"What do you mean?"

"Well, more and more people are following demagogues like Robert Newhall."

"Demagogue?" Watson reacted. "I don't know about that."

"Why did you resign?"

"Well, I don't agree with everything Newhall does and sometimes we didn't see eye-to-eye. He decided to move Infinity in a different direction, but I have no hard feelings towards him. He's succeeded in bringing Christians together and I think that's important."

"You're certainly entitled to your opinion on that," Chambers nodded conciliatorily. "But that's not what I'm here to talk to you about."

"I've spoken with an attorney," Watson stated firmly.

"That's wise."

"I can't talk to you about any of my responsibilities at Infinity."

Chambers sighed as he casually put his hands behind his head. "That won't quite work, Mike."

Watson leaned forward.

"I'm aware of Infinity's illegal activities. I don't know everything, but I do know that Newhall has enriched himself at the expense of his followers. He's also abused his tax-exempt status and ripped off the government. Of course, he hasn't done it alone. You're equally guilty."

Watson slammed his hand on the arm of the chair. "That's not true!"

"Yeah, how do you figure?"

"I told you that I'm not going to discuss what I did at Infinity."

"We have to start there, Mike."

Watson stood up abruptly. "I'm going to have to ask you to leave."

"I know you don't like hearing that you're responsible for your actions, but I think you need to deal with it," Chambers responded evenly.

"I'm not going to discuss this with you."

"Okay, I thought you might feel that way so we've prepared a summary of the case against Infinity and its leadership—that's leadership past and present." Chambers opened his briefcase and pulled out a five-page document.

"I said I'm not going to discuss this!" Watson angrily grabbed the document and slammed it down on a nearby coffee table.

"Suit yourself. Call me if you change your mind. I need to hear from you soon, though. I'll show myself out."

When Chambers had gone, Watson examined the document. It contained a summary of Infinity's illegal activities including donations to charitable organizations that didn't exist and bogus contracts with corporations controlled by Newhall and other Infinity leaders. There were also records of large monetary transfers from the Network to evangelists' bank accounts. Watson had architected the scheme and been one of its primary beneficiaries.

Watson leaned back and sighed. *This is real. This is bad. I've got to deal with it. But what can I do? If I admit what I've done and ask for forgiveness... I'll pray sincerely and repent. I'll devote myself absolutely to God. I'll obey His commands. I'll always obey His commands. I need strength. Please God, give me strength.*

Two days later, Watson called Chambers and they agreed to meet again, this time at one of Chambers' manufacturing facilities in San Diego.

"Where did you get your information?" Watson asked.

"I can't tell you that."

"Some of it's wrong."

"I know, but a lot of it is right."

"What do you want from me?"

"I want you to help me fill in the gaps."

"Why should I do that?"

"You mean what's in it for you?"

Watson nodded.

"Well, if you don't help me, I'll get the information eventually. And when we take it to a prosecutor..."

"Prosecutor?" Watson gasped. "Now wait just a minute here. I'm..."

"Relax, relax," Chambers interrupted. "I have no intention of going public with this—not yet anyway. But I can guarantee you that Infinity will go down. If you cooperate with me, we can put together an evidentiary package that you can trade for immunity. If you decide not to cooperate, you take your chances."

"This is blackmail, that's what this is."

Chambers chuckled lightly. "Well, let me give you a better reason to help me. You'll be doing the right thing."

Watson tapped his fingers nervously on his thigh. "Well..."

"You call yourself a Christian."

"I am a Christian!"

"What would Jesus do?" Chambers said somberly.

Watson looked away. "I need to talk to my attorney."

Chambers nodded.

"But no matter what my attorney says, no information can be released without my consent—ever."

"Of course."

"And my attorney will be present at any future meetings."

"Okay."

"And you'll pay his fees."

Chambers laughed. "Glad to see you're thinking. Not a problem."

Watson was taking a huge risk, but for reasons he couldn't define, he felt strangely drawn to Chambers. "Well...I don't know where to start."

"Start at the beginning."

CHAPTER 26

Nothing in biology makes sense except in the light of evolution.

—THEODOSIUS DOBZHANSKY

"I think that's it, Mike," Chambers said as he clicked Stop on his tape recorder. "I appreciate your candor. I know this has been difficult for you."

"Yeah, I'm glad I could help."

Chambers had questioned Watson extensively over the course of several meetings, and Watson had detailed Newhall's financial dealings and Infinity's complex legal structure of holding companies and offshore trusts. Watson also provided copies of incriminating documents. Watson's attorney attended the first few meetings, but suddenly stopped coming. Chambers never asked Watson about it, but he could tell that Watson not only trusted him, but liked him. Although their backgrounds and perspectives were totally different, they spoke easily, often discussing personal matters as if they were old friends.

"Well, what now?" Watson asked.

"Now I fly back and talk to Ray."

"So we don't need to meet any more?"

"No, but Ray will be in touch."

Watson sighed. "Okay, I just...I..."

"What?"

Watson thought of telling Chambers that he wanted to see him again, but decided against it. "You're not going to release any of this information, right?"

"It's up to you."

"I'm not comfortable...I don't want..."

"Okay." Chambers respected Watson's decision not to make any of the information public, but he recognized that the man held intense pent-up resentment towards Newhall. "You know, I've been thinking about your situation, Mike."

"Yeah, what about it?"

"Well, just the extent that Newhall betrayed you."

"He betrayed himself," Watson responded automatically.

"He betrayed his followers."

"Well..."

"It's the ultimate betrayal," Chambers added.

"I don't know what you mean by that."

"Deliberate betrayal of trust—in God's name."

Watson looked away.

"Does it get any worse than that?" Chambers went on.

"Like I said, I don't agree with everything..."

"And he used you to do it," Chambers interrupted.

Anger seeped into Watson's face, turning it a light shade of reddish-purple.

"Well, I don't know about you, but I can't let him get away with that," Chambers finished.

Watson clenched his fists and grunted as two thick veins popped out of his neck.

"You okay, Mike?"

"What the hell do you expect me to do?" Watson exploded.

Chambers sat down on the couch and put his arm gently on Watson's shoulder. "Relax, Mike. I have an idea."

Chambers called Sid Copeland, a writer at Enterprise magazine, a widely-read business periodical. Copeland had written a feature story about Chambers two years earlier and the two men had remained friends.

"Sid, David Chambers."

"Hey, David. What's new?"

"I've got an idea for a story."

"Yeah?"

"You remember that article you wrote last year about how people hide their assets?"

"Of course."

"I've got some information about Robert Newhall—shell corporations, offshore accounts, everything."

"Robert Newhall? The religious nut?"

"Yeah."

"I'd like to hear more. When can we meet?"

"How about Thursday around ten? You remember my place in San Francisco?"

"Sure, I'll see you then."

* * *

Jerry Ashworth trotted excitedly into Heilbrenner's office, a broad smile highlighting the creases in his pumpkin-shaped face. "This is the biggest one yet, the biggest one yet," he squealed in delight. "You're not going to believe this."

"What is it, Jerry?"

Ashworth pulled a check out of his shirt pocket and held it in front of Heilbrenner's face. "One…million…dollars…"

"Let me take a look at that." Heilbrenner's face lit up when he confirmed the amount. "You're incredible, Jerry."

"We can really do God's work with this kind of money," Ashworth beamed.

"We certainly can." Heilbrenner stood up to shake his underling's hand. He was grateful for Ashworth's efforts, and didn't want to deflate the simple man's enthusiasm, but Heilbrenner's thoughts came automatically. *I could buy another couple of Ferraris with this kind of money.* "Keep up the good work, Jerry."

* * *

Infinity funded the bulk of its operations through handsome donations from its membership as well as from lucrative government grants. These two cash cows fueled revenue increases at a clip of almost thirty percent a year. But nothing satisfied Heilbrenner. He coveted new sources of cash and his empire-building visions knew no boundaries. He decided to implement an idea he'd had before. He figured that since Infinity had fifty million members, they had the potential to influence companies through their combined buying power. The idea was simple—Infinity would boycott companies that refused to meet its demands.

To help him carry out his vision, Heilbrenner recruited Jerry Ashworth, a believer from a rival Christian organization in South Carolina. Ashworth's specialty was finding immoral messages in the media and the arts, and then bringing pressure to bear on the creating or sponsoring companies to suppress the offending material. Ashworth had been making noise against movie producers and record executives for several years, but his efforts had been largely ineffectual. He had established one important legacy, however. In his crusade against record producers who didn't support Christian music, he frequently attacked the lyrics of their artists as satanic. In cases where the actual lyrics were clearly benign, Ashworth argued that the companies were secretly recording subliminal messages that could cause children to reject God and embrace Satanism. Although Ashworth had no evidence to support his accusations, a wave of fear swept across the country and donations to Ashworth's organization increased dramatically. In order to prevent financial disaster, the recording industry had been forced to prove that Ashworth's claims had no basis in reality. Ashworth's crusade slowly lost steam, but he had shown that mindless scare tactics could be used as a powerful fundraising tool.

In the end, most of the people Ashworth criticized ignored him, and intellectuals had marginalized him as a Bible-thumping crank. But Heilbrenner recognized the man's potential. He convinced Ashworth that Infinity was the only organization big enough to sufficiently employ his talents. He offered Ashworth an opportunity to pursue his mission with Infinity muscle behind him. Ashworth readily agreed, joining Infinity with a renewed evangelical zeal. His first official act was hiring two lieutenants to help him scour the country for immorality and the companies that supported it.

The arts, movies, video games, books, and compact discs were all potential targets of Ashworth's crusade, but he focused his efforts on television because of its one huge practical advantage; it had big corporate sponsors and shakedowns were easier. Ashworth started by establishing the Infinity Rating System, which involved a team of Infinity censors passing judgment on television shows. Ashworth and his lieutenants attacked programs that got Infinity's lowest rating— "Promotes disobedience to God's laws." This included shows that depicted gays, single mothers, or nonbelievers in a favorable light. It also targeted shows that satirized religious violence, bigotry, and ignorance. But Ashworth went even further, criticizing public television programs that promoted science because those shows didn't "adequately take into account the role of God in the universe."

The first successful boycott orchestrated by Ashworth was against the APX television network. APX had aired a program that examined faith healing and exposed it as a sham based on trickery and audience plants. Ashworth had gotten wind of the program before it was scheduled to air and he sent a threatening letter to network executives. APX ignored the threats and broadcasted the program as scheduled. In the next issue of New Hope, Ashworth wrote a scathing article blasting APX executives as "dupes of Satan." He also instructed Infinity members not to watch APX programs and to boycott the show's sponsors. Within three months, sales dropped significantly at each of the sponsor companies and they dispatched representatives to Infinity's bargaining table. After heated negotiations with Heilbrenner and Ashworth, each company agreed to pay three hundred thousand dollars in return for Infinity lifting the boycott. Infinity also agreed not to harass any of the companies again, regardless of the programs they sponsored in the future.

Ashworth objected to giving the companies immunity for future programs, but Heilbrenner insisted. He figured that companies would naturally be more cautious after being shaken down, and in any case, he cared little if the offending material was taken off the air; his only interest was in increasing Infinity's revenues. For their part, company executives didn't like being blackmailed, but they figured that placating Infinity was an unavoidable cost of doing business.

After the first attack against APX, actual boycott was almost never necessary; the mere threat was enough to keep companies in line. But occasionally a company refused to capitulate to Infinity's demands. The first company that stood up to Infinity was Centennial Media, a small company that produced children's cartoons. Most of the cartoons featured talking animals in playful adventure sequences that required cooperation and support to overcome difficult situations. The shows had always received Infinity's highest "Promotes family values" rating, but Ashworth didn't show deference to Infinity's rating system when he felt that censors weren't vigilant enough.

In one of Centennial's cartoons, two talking chipmunks pranced through the forest and stopped to sniff a flower, smiling and "acting high" as they enjoyed the scent. Then the animals (both male) rubbed their cheeks together in a display of affection. Although none of the Infinity censors had objected to the scene, Ashworth insisted that the animals were really sniffing cocaine and that their display of affection promoted perverted homosexual lifestyles. He demanded that Centennial destroy the program and pony up. Centennial refused to pay and demanded to know what type of crack Ashworth was smoking.

Ashworth created a blacklist of companies like Centennial that resisted, and the list was published in New Hope along with a list of the blacklisted companies' sponsors. In Centennial's case, their sponsors demanded to be removed from the blacklist and joined Centennial in a lawsuit when Ashworth refused. The companies argued that their businesses were being irreparably damaged by Infinity's defamatory comments, but the court dismissed the suit.

After suffering substantial losses, Centennial's sponsors finally decided to pull their business in order to get off Infinity's blacklist. Centennial refused to back down even though no one was willing to sponsor or purchase its programs under the dark cloud of an Infinity censure. Eventually, Centennial filed bankruptcy.

Most companies didn't have to go through the ordeal of a boycott, or even respond to one of Ashworth's threats. Company executives quickly figured out that if they made regular donations to Infinity, Heilbrenner and Ashworth would leave them alone. In the first year of the boycott program, corporate donations to Infinity increased by over three hundred percent, and Heilbrenner added another Ferrari to his collection—a 1957 Zagato Berlinetta, purchased at an auction by one of Heilbrenner's attorneys for five hundred thousand dollars.

Infinity boycotts were a huge success, but Heilbrenner worried that Infinity wasn't truly capturing the hearts and minds of its members. He wanted nothing less than total commitment, so he decided to focus on initiatives that hammered home a few key ideas—surrender, sacrifice, guilt, and, most importantly, an overall feeling of insignificance compared to the Almighty. Heilbrenner knew that once these values became firmly entrenched in followers' minds, there would be nothing left to stop them from committing even the most mindless acts on behalf of the cause. Heilbrenner's passion gave birth to the Infinity Spiritual Hotline.

At Infinity Headquarters, Heilbrenner created a four-thousand-square-foot call center that he staffed around the clock with fifty trained evangelists who took calls from around the world via an 800 number. Infinity taped many of the calls, and Heilbrenner often listened to the recordings, both for reasons of quality control and because he found the calls so addictively amusing.

"Infinity Spiritual Hotline."

"Hi. Uh…I've got a problem."

"Who am I speaking with?"

"This is Darren."

"What can the power of the Lord help with you today, Darren?"

"Well, it's my daughter's school. She has this teacher over there who's talking about evolution in science class."

"Okay."

"And my daughter's only eight years old!"

Infinity trained its Spiritual Hotline evangelists to handle callers' problems using a variety of techniques. The first involved referencing a manual that contained a long list of moral and spiritual bromides. For example, if a caller told the Hotline evangelist that they had lied, the evangelist would urge the caller to read the Ten Commandments, repent, and then pray for forgiveness. If a caller faced a difficult moral choice or had a question about what to do in a particular situation, the manual contained answers to questions on an extensive list of subjects: Abortion, Baptism, Being Born Again, Blasphemy, Business and Finances, Choosing a Mate, Demons, Duties of A Christian Wife, Diet, Divorce, End Time Warnings, Evil, Faith, False Prophets, Forgiveness, Fornication, Gambling, Gluttony, God (The True God), Hell, Heresy, Homosexuality, Hunting, Idolatry, Jesus, Judgment, Life After Death, Living Together Before Marriage, Lying, Masturbation, Perverted Sex, Piercing the Body, Pornography, Prayer, Pride, Profanity, Prophecies, Repentance, The Sabbath, Salvation, Satan, Science, Smoking, Spanking Children, Suicide, Tattoos, Temptation, The Ten Commandments, Tithing, UFOs, and Unclean Thoughts. Questions about evolution came up frequently, as did inquiries about the incompatibility between science and religious faith. Infinity provided extensive training on how to answer these questions appropriately.

If a caller's question was beyond the scope of the Infinity manual, Infinity trained evangelists to tell the caller to "read the Bible for strength and inspiration, and pray until the Lord shows you the way." Normally, this advice was harmless enough, except that many people who called in were genuinely depressed or had other mental conditions that cried out for the help of a trained medical professional. But Heilbrenner forbid evangelists from recommending that a caller seek professional help because such advice would imply that human efforts were more effective than prayer.

"Darren, have you spoken with your daughter's teacher about this?" the evangelist asked.

"Yeah, but she wouldn't listen. She said it was important to teach kids about science. I couldn't believe it. My daughter's only eight years old! My wife and I are having a hard enough time teaching her about God. The last thing we need is some teacher corrupting her mind with all this scientific…jargon."

"I understand, Darren."

"And you know what else. My daughter came home the other day and she asked me if God had evolved like humans did. Can you believe that? My wife and I, we…we're…we're worried. We don't know what to do."

The evangelist turned to the section in her manual that dealt with situations where scientific evidence conflicted with scripture, and recited her lines. "Read scripture together, and tell your child that faith is more powerful than scientific facts or reason. Satan sometimes uses reason to carry out his own purposes, so we must be very careful. The Bible is the only true word of God, and the only thing we know for sure is the truth. You must make sure your child understands this."

"All right, well, my wife and I read the Bible together with our daughter all the time, but that doesn't seem to be enough."

After providing a caller with some general advice, Heilbrenner trained Hotline evangelists to move quickly to step two—stoking the flames of fear.

"That's a good start, Darren, but there's one other thing you must do."

"What's that?"

"Let me share some scripture with you. In the Book of Mark, chapter 9, starting with verse 43, Jesus said,

> And if thy hand offend thee, cut it off: it is better for thee to enter into life maimed, than having two hands to go into hell, into the fire that never shall be quenched. And if thy foot offend thee, cut it off: it is better for thee to enter halt into life, than having two feet to be cast into hell, into the fire that never shall be quenched. And if thine eye offend thee, pluck it out: it is better for thee to enter into the kingdom of God with one eye, than having two eyes to be cast into hell fire.

"Yeah."

"And in the Book of Matthew, chapter 13, verse 50," the evangelist continued ominously, "God gives us a description of Hell—a furnace of fire where there shall be wailing and gnashing of teeth."

"Well, I'm familiar with all those verses, but I…I'm not sure how they relate."

"Darren, you need to read these verses to your daughter. You need to make sure she understands that if she turns away from God, the consequence is eternal punishment."

"I know...but...I...I...I...don't want my child to live in...live in... you know, fear...be afraid all the time."

"You have an obligation to make sure that your child is God-fearing," the evangelist responded forcefully. "You must do everything in your power to save your child from the everlasting fire of Hell."

"I know, I know, you're right," the caller replied timidly.

"You need to put your trust in God and our Lord Jesus Christ."

"Yeah."

After the evangelist had put the caller into the appropriate frame of mind, she proceeded to the mandatory finale.

"And there's one other thing that will help you control your own fear," the evangelist offered.

"What?"

"If you know you're doing the right thing."

"Yeah, I suppose that's true."

"It's the only way."

"Yeah. I guess you're right about that, but sometimes it's hard, you know, because I want my daughter to be happy. That's my main concern. I want her to have a better life."

"You want to do the right thing, right Darren? You want to be right with the Lord? Make sure you'll be with your daughter forever in Heaven."

"Of course."

"Then in the name of our Savior, the Lord Jesus Christ, I recommend that you make a generous donation to the Infinity Network so that we can continue to spread the gospel and help people like yourself achieve salvation."

Infinity required its evangelists to end every call with the solicitation of a donation and this paid healthy dividends. Based on the number of calls received and the amount of money that came in, Heilbrenner calculated that each call generated an average of forty bucks, while lasting less than five minutes. Not a bad return, Heilbrenner figured, especially considering that most of the evangelists worked for free.

Some callers asked Hotline evangelists to pray for them. Heilbrenner instructed evangelists to agree to any prayer request as long as it was consistent with Infinity doctrine. This was simple enough; however, a few evangelists suggested that Infinity take down callers' number and check up on them a few weeks later to see if the prayers worked. When Heilbrenner heard about this, he called a special meeting and instructed evangelists that calling people back was strictly forbidden. "Are we going to question whether God is at work answering our prayers?" Heilbrenner thundered to a packed meeting of evangelists. "Of course, we are not! That's an insult to God and I will not tolerate it!"

* * *

Chambers stared at the blank computer screen and yawned. It was eleven-thirty at night after a long day, but he had a meeting with Lassater the following morning to discuss the book project. *Hmmm…where to begin. What's the real essence of this?* He typed a sentence, "Primitive texts such as the Bible and the Koran are the eight-hundred-pound gorillas of human superstition." *No, that's not quite right. What is it? What is this really about? Maybe something about how religion is passed on from one generation to the next. God, that's too depressing.*

Chambers thought about how parents taught their children to accept the absurdities in the Bible on faith, and that it was wrong to doubt. Chambers started typing again. "Since it's natural for any healthy child to think, and to be curious about the world, they will doubt, and doubt often. (This may not manifest itself until young adulthood, but it *will* come out). This doubting leads to guilt because the child feels bad for disappointing his or her parents. But it's much worse than that. A child starts to think that their experience of the world isn't accurate (and therefore something is wrong with them) because they can't see what their parents (and others) insist is really there. The child then concludes that they must be bad (or a fool—Emperor's New Clothes!) because they can't see. More guilt. And then of course the idea of hell is introduced. So not only will the child feel guilty, but now they have to contend with the mental torture of believing that they will go to hell." *What does this say about people who do this to children?* Chambers clenched his jaw in frustration. *Do I really need to write an entire book about this? It's so painfully obvious.*

CHAPTER 27

I am against religion because it teaches us
to be satisfied with not understanding the world.

—RICHARD DAWKINS

"Sweet ginger brown!" Sid Copeland exulted as he typed the last period at the end of his article. Copeland had titled his piece "Stealth Wealth" because it profiled the top ten richest people in the United States whose wealth was hidden from public view. The richest "stealthily wealthy" person was a drug dealer from Miami with an estimated net worth of 1.1 billion dollars. Newhall held the two spot at nine hundred million. Copeland estimated that the value of Infinity's assets ranged from four to five billion, with anywhere from seven to eight hundred million in cash. Newhall's personal net worth was impossible to state with certainty because many of his assets were held in Infinity's name or indirectly controlled by Infinity, but Copeland figured that Newhall controlled at least nine hundred million dollars. Although Copeland's article was pointed, it didn't allege that Infinity or Newhall had engaged in any illegal activities.

Whenever Copeland wrote an article critical of someone, he always called them to get their side of the story. He dialed Infinity Headquarters.

"Infinity Christian Network."

"Robert Newhall, please."

"Uh…" The receptionist hesitated because she had only heard the reverend referred to by his first name one other time. "May I tell him who's calling, please?"

"Sid Copeland from *Enterprise* magazine."

"And what is this regarding?"

"I've written an article about him."

"An article?"

"Yes, an article about him and your organization."

"Just a moment."

Copeland waited patiently until the receptionist came back. "Sir, Reverend Newhall's in a meeting, can I direct you to…"

"No," Copeland interrupted. "I need to talk to him."

"Well, he's…"

"This is very important."

"Just a moment."

"This is Reverend Newhall. "What can I do for you?"

Reverend. That's a great title, Copeland thought. *But it'll garner you no respect here. You're still a conman.* "Robert, this is Sid Copeland. I'm a writer at Enterprise magazine in Los Angeles. I've just finished an article about you and your organization."

"What kind of article?"

"I've written a piece about the richest people in the United States whose wealth is hidden from public view."

"What are you talking about?" Newhall reacted defensively.

"In the article, I profile the ten richest people in the U.S. who have assets that the public isn't aware of."

"What does that have to do with me?"

"Well, I've estimated your net worth to be in the neighborhood of nine hundred million dollars. That puts you in second place on my list. Would you care to comment?"

"I don't know what you're talking about!" Newhall snapped angrily. "What was your name again?"

"Sid Copeland."

Newhall hung up, then picked the phone up again and called Heilbrenner, ordering him to handle the situation. Heilbrenner called Copeland back immediately.

"Mr. Copeland, this is John Heilbrenner."

"Ahhh...the infamous Mr. Heilbrenner."

"We need to talk."

"Well, your boss just hung up on me. That hasn't put me in a very good mood."

"Look, I can assure you that what you're suggesting in your article is incorrect. Reverend Newhall has very few assets. The Infinity Christian Network is a non-profit organization and it owns everything on behalf of its members."

"Okay. Do you or Mr. Newhall have any other comments?"

"You can't publish that article," Heilbrenner responded firmly.

"Oh...I'm publishing it. I'm very comfortable with the accuracy."

"Your information is wrong. You have a responsibility to publish the truth."

Ha! You're right, Copeland thought. *You're absolutely right. You've pinpointed the difference between what I do and what you do.* "Do you have any other comments or not?"

"Listen, if you publish that article, we'll have no other choice but to sue you and your sources for libel."

"That's not a very original threat," Copeland responded flatly. "Surely, you can do better than that."

"Look, let's forget about that," Heilbrenner backtracked. "Why don't you just tell me how got your information and I can tell you why it's wrong."

Copeland laughed. "Well, I certainly can't do that, but I'll pass your threat on to my source."

"You're making a big mistake. Reverend Newhall is a well-respected religious leader; attacking him will destroy your career."

Copeland chuckled again. "I think you've mistaken me for one of your followers. Look for the story in next month's issue. Have a nice day." Copeland hung up.

Heilbrenner knew there was nothing he could do to prevent publication of the article, but he had to come up with something fast. And then the idea hit him. Infinity had fifty million members, many of whom were prominent in the business community. If he could rally them against the magazine... He set up a meeting with Newhall for the next day.

"I have an idea how we can pressure that writer to reveal his source for the article," Heilbrenner said.

"It's Watson! I just know it!"

"Maybe, but we need to be sure. I think we should threaten them with a boycott. We've got thousands of members who subscribe to that magazine and who advertise. If we got even ten percent of the membership to boycott, it'll cost them millions."

"First things first. How damaging do you think this article will be?"

"It could be very damaging. I'm not worried about a government investigation; I think we've got that covered. But you never know how membership might react. Most of them have no idea about the extent of your assets."

"Infinity's assets!" Newhall bellowed.

"Right. Of course." *I can't believe I'm working for this moron,* Heilbrenner cursed himself. *I'm so pathetic. Pathetic!* "The most important thing right now is to find out if Watson's talking."

"Okay."

"I may need to get more aggressive."

Newhall looked straight into Heilbrenner's eyes and met an empty coldness that he had never seen before. A wave of terror rippled through his body.

"Robert?"

"Okay, okay. Do whatever you need to do," Newhall said quietly.

Heilbrenner called Copeland and explained that Infinity was prepared to boycott the magazine, but that he would call it off if Copeland gave him the name of his source. Copeland told Heilbrenner that he didn't respond to threats and hung up. He called Chambers.

"David, it's Sid Copeland. I just had an interesting phone call with John Heilbrenner over at the Infinity asylum."

"Yeah?"

"He threatened the magazine with legal action and a boycott, but I hung up on him. I thought I should give you a call because he was very interested in my source for the article."

"Thanks for calling, Sid. Listen, Heilbrenner may be blowing smoke on this boycott idea, but he's extremely devious. I'd hate to see you guys get hurt by this. If you need to pull the article, I..."

"No!" Copeland interrupted. "Absolutely not! I'll quit before I let some criminal bully me."

Chambers chuckled cheerfully. "Ah…same old Sid. Well, just so you know, I may be contacting them."

"Whatever you want to do."

"How's the article coming?"

"It's done. It'll be in next month."

"Great, I can't wait to read it. Talk to you soon."

Chambers hung up and dictated a short letter to Newhall.

* * *

Dushane swam to shore and then lay on the grass, the warm midday sun drying him off. He briefly fell asleep and then got dressed and hiked out to the road. He felt melancholy as he was finally getting off the trail and returning to civilization. It had been a wonderful three months.

When he got to the road, he put his thumb out and a driver picked him up quickly. An hour later, he arrived at the bus station in Bennington, Vermont where he caught a bus back to Boston. On the ride home, he daydreamed about the possibilities of his future, but he had no idea what he would do next.

CHAPTER 28

What can be asserted without evidence
can also be dismissed without evidence.

—CHRISTOPHER HITCHENS

Alone in his office at Infinity Headquarters, Newhall tore open the envelope from Chambers. A surge of warm blood bubbled slowly up the back of his neck as he read the short letter inside.

Dear Robert:

As much as I enjoyed helping *Enterprise* magazine with its article about you and the Infinity Network, I found the research unnecessarily tedious and time consuming. For next year's article, I hope that we can meet and discuss your finances in person. I would love to come down to Laguna Beach and visit you at the mansion. I've always wanted to see where "God" lives.

Yours truly,

David Chambers

"That...that son of a ..." Newhall cursed under his breath, and then stomped his foot angrily on the floor. He sprang out of his chair and ran down the hall to Heilbrenner's office. "What the hell is this?" he fumed, slamming the letter on his lieutenant's desk.

Heilbrenner studied the letter carefully.

"Now we've got this atheist Chambers to deal with!" Newhall roared as he paced around Heilbrenner's office in an excited frenzy. "I'm tired of all these problems! What are we going to do about this?"

Heilbrenner shrugged.

Newhall had become increasingly agitated over the past few weeks because he had weathered a heavy onslaught of criticism. After the *Enterprise* article had appeared, reporters questioned Newhall about his finances, implying that he had abused the trust of his followers. But Newhall fought back. He disputed the figures in the article and justified his wealth. "I'm helping people make a personal connection to God. I'm giving them hope and spiritual direction."

Although he traveled in style and entertained frequently, Newhall didn't otherwise have extravagant tastes—with one exception. He owned an oceanfront estate in Laguna Beach, complete with two swimming pools, a tennis court, and a helipad. He also employed an estate manager, Sharon Maddox, who took care of everything at the mansion, including scheduling house cleaning, managing contractors, and supervising the gardeners. It was a full-time job because Newhall's wife, Patricia was constantly remodeling the house and she was never quite satisfied, frequently demanding that workers tear things out if they weren't exactly as she wanted them. She also accused Sharon of trying to undermine her.

Newhall explained to reporters that Infinity owned the estate on behalf of its members and that it was used to host religious retreats. To some extent this was true. According to church records, Infinity hosted two church-related gatherings a year at the compound. The remainder of the year, however, the estate was used exclusively by Newhall and his wife, as well as their frequent guests; a who's who of the religious right wing's power elite—televangelists, country music stars, politicians, athletes, and anyone else with enough money or power to attract Newhall's attention.

In the end, the *Enterprise* article had little effect. Infinity's spin doctors portrayed Sid Copeland as a malcontent attempting to discredit Christianity. Fortunately for Newhall, most Infinity followers accepted this interpretation because it fit neatly within the worldview that Infinity had carefully cultivated.

"Well, how are we are going to deal with this problem?" Newhall pressed.

"We do nothing," Heilbrenner replied calmly.

"Nothing! Are you out of your mind? I'm not going to let that pipsqueak pull this! He doesn't know who he's dealing with! I'm the most important moral leader in this country!"

"We do nothing," Heilbrenner said again, emotionless. "He's made a big mistake by showing his hand. We need to keep a closer eye on him, but I don't want anyone in this organization to do anything. Do you understand me?"

"We have to do something!" Newhall bellowed, his face boiling in fury. He wanted to destroy Chambers, and Heilbrenner's stoic reaction made him want to boot his right-hand man in the teeth.

"No, we do nothing," Heilbrenner repeated. "That's it."

"But…"

"No, that's it." Heilbrenner waved his arm dismissively. "I'm not going to argue with you. I've made our decision."

Newhall grunted as he stormed out of Heilbrenner's office.

***

Dushane opened the door to his apartment in Boston and smiled at the familiar surroundings. He felt happy to be home. The apartment had been recently cleaned and he detected a faint scent of flowers. He walked into the kitchen where there was a large bouquet of lilies with a note attached. "Welcome Home, Martin. Your journey is just beginning. Elizabeth." Elizabeth Worthington lived in the apartment next door. She was an elderly, widowed woman with no children of her own. She frequently invited Dushane over to her apartment for dinner. Dushane picked up one of the flowers and held it to his nose.

Dushane called his mother to let her know that he had made it home all right. Then he turned his attention to a large pile of mail stacked neatly on the kitchen table. He sat down and casually flipped through it. The mail consisted mostly of bills and junk mail, but a small envelope caught his attention. It said "David Chambers" in the left-hand corner. *The David Chambers*, he thought. Not possible. He opened the envelope carefully and pulled out a short letter.

Dear Martin,

I hope this letter finds you well. I've been trying to reach you without success. I'd like you to come work for me. Please contact my associate in Boston, Skip Hartley.

I look forward to meeting you in the near future. I'm curious to see what you're like.

Sincerely,

David Chambers

There was an address for Hartley listed at the bottom of the letter, but no phone number. Dushane looked up Hartley in the phone book, but found no listing. The note was written on Kaleidoscope Ranch letterhead so Dushane figured it must be from the famous man, but he still didn't understand the letter. He had never spoken with Chambers before and he had no idea what kind of work Chambers referred to. Dushane went into the kitchen and poured himself a glass of orange juice and then returned to the letter.

Like most other Americans, Dushane had heard much about Chambers over the years. With the exception of the President, Chambers was arguably the most well known person in the country; a modern-day folk hero, and one of the most generous philanthropists in history. Dushane remembered reading an article that had ranked him among the ten most generous Americans.

Dushane went into the bedroom and sat down in front of his computer. He turned it on and then executed a search on Chambers, which returned over a thousand hits. He clicked on one of the links, which led him to a discussion of Chambers by several religious leaders, all connected in some way to the Infinity Network. He read a few passages:

The man has no absolutely regard for human life or any sensitivity to the human condition. He must obviously be a very sick and misguided individual. Christians, and indeed any person of religious faith, should

237

avoid Mr. Chambers and any other godless individual who maliciously slanders our faith.

Another read:

> Mr. Chambers completely misrepresents the views and history of the church and, frankly, isn't the slightest bit qualified to comment on religious matters. The last thing we need in this country is for people to listen to a wealthy businessman whose values are clearly about business and not spirituality. Just because he has a billion dollars doesn't give him a license to mislead people. I can only guess that the man must be a complete egomaniac if he thinks that people care about his religious views.

Dushane read several additional critiques of Chambers, all of which were part of a smear campaign that Heilbrenner had ordered after Chambers had come out publicly against prayer in the public schools. *The guy's got a lot of enemies*, Dushane thought. *But I guess the most successful people always get trashed the most.* Dushane turned off the computer and undressed. After three months on the Trail, he had a new appreciation for the luxury of a bed. He fell asleep immediately, but slept restlessly as his mind drifted over disorderly images, finally settling into a dream.

Dushane could barely see the gaunt figure moving towards him, walking down a worn, cobblestone path lined by tall trees. It was dark, but the light increased as the figure moved closer—slowly, but with easy, graceful movements. The figure came within a few feet of Dushane, extended its hand, and then said softly, "Follow me to the place where there is only love." Dushane looked carefully at the face, but he didn't recognize it. It was a human face, but its features were not well defined. Dushane raised his hand and tried to touch the figure, but it backed away. It moved a few feet down the path, but stopped suddenly when several large gorillas swung down from the trees. The gorillas quickly surrounded the figure and then pounced on it. Dushane tried to scream, but he couldn't speak—or move. Chills ran up and down the length of his body. He tried desperately to get his legs to run, but he remained cemented to the ground until the gorillas suddenly jumped back into the trees and disappeared from sight.

The following morning, Dushane slept late. When he awoke, he loafed to his feet, put on his bathrobe and sauntered into the bathroom where he stopped to study his face in the mirror. He admired a scruffy beard that he had grown on his hike. He gave the beard a few casual strokes and then walked to the small bedroom closet, which was packed with clothes, most of which he never wore. The closet also contained a rack full of ties, but he hated wearing ties. He made a mental note to donate all but two of his ties to charity. He reached for a pair of faded blue jeans and an old long sleeved t-shirt. He dressed quickly.

Dushane went into the kitchen and picked up the letter from Chambers. He stared at it intently for a few seconds and then remembered his dream. He quickly gulped down a glass of orange juice and caught a cab to the address on the letter.

CHAPTER 29

I feel uncomfortable that good Christians all over America, and indeed the world, are using a document [the 1611 King James version of the Bible] commissioned by a homosexual. Anything that has been commissioned by a homosexual has obviously been tainted in some way.

—GARY BAUER, PROMINENT CHRISTIAN AND FORMER PRESIDENTIAL CANDIDATE, *after discovering what several historians had hypothesized— that King James was a homosexual.*

John Heilbrenner pulled a lighter and a small piece of newspaper out of his jacket pocket. He gave the lighter a deft flick, igniting the paper, and then tossed the flame into a ten-foot pyramid built out of wood and books. The pyramid had been doused with gasoline so it burst into flames with a flash, illuminating the sky and delighting the crowd of four hundred faithful. They cheered and clapped, most of them on their knees, celebrating their sacrifice to the Almighty.

It was the first "faith fire" that Heilbrenner had personally attended, although he had pushed the idea on Infinity pastors across the Network for months. They had eagerly heeded his call, staging over twenty fires. Heilbrenner had first become intrigued by book burning after reading about the famous Nazi event of 1933. By burning books that were deemed to have an "un-German" spirit, the Nazis provided ordinary Germans with a strong emotional connection to the movement. Similarly, Heilbrenner advocated burning books that had an "un-Godly spirit," though he cared little about what books were actually burned. It was the act of burning them that interested him because it furthered his idea of pushing people into rabid belief—belief where the rational part of the mind shut off and the emotional floodgates of all-encompassing fear and hatred burst open.

While believers burned hundreds of different books depending on their particular sensibilities, they destroyed the King James Version of the Bible most often. For hundreds of years, the King James had been the preferred edition of the Bible for Christians, but Infinity warned believers that it was tainted because of King James' reputed homosexuality. Infinity urged the faithful to destroy the once-holy book and adopt another "Infinity-approved" version. Believers happily obliged, fearful that reading any book commissioned by a homosexual would cause God to seek retribution with Old Testament-style vengeance.

Other condemned books included the *Koran*, *The Origin of Species* (and any other book on evolution), as well as books authored by, or which humanized homosexuals. Burned books also included those deemed "offensive to God" by the pastor presiding over the festivities. Many parents burned their children's *Harry Potter* and *Lord of the Rings* books because, according to Infinity, the books encouraged "witchcraft, paganism, and a belief in the occult and the supernatural." Infinity warned parents that reading these types of books could ultimately lead their children to Satanism.

Infinity followers consistently derided witchcraft and the supernatural, although they made exceptions for the supernatural claims surrounding Jesus Christ, such as the virgin birth, the bodily resurrection, and walking on water. They made similar exceptions for other supernatural events in the Bible such as the great flood and the parting of the Red Sea by Moses.

Although Heilbrenner had initially worried that book burning might appear too extreme, he soon discovered that his fears had been unwarranted; censorship was nothing new to religious organizations. For hundreds of years, the Catholic Church had practiced the most well known case of censorship, maintaining an Index of Forbidden Books. Church authorities listed thousands of "dangerous" books in the Index and ordered followers not to read them. The list contained individual books (many considered masterpieces by secular intellectuals) such as *The Social Contract* by Jean-Jacques Rousseau, *Principles of Political Economy* by John Stuart Mill, and *Les Miserables* by Victor Hugo. The Church also condemned the complete works of certain authors, including Rene Descartes, Thomas Hobbes, Francois Voltaire, David Hume, and Jean-Paul Sartre. The Church primarily targeted intellectuals and freethinkers because they openly challenged its dogma and threatened its hegemony.

The Catholic Church discontinued the Index in 1966; however, the New Catholic Encyclopedia admonished that, "This does not mean, however, that whatever has been contained on the Index is now automatically permitted reading for all Catholics." Indeed, the Sacred Congregation for the Doctrine of the Faith claimed that the Index still served as a "moral guide in so far as it reminds the conscience of the faithful they must avoid writings which can be dangerous to faith and morals." The Church could also issue an "admonitum," or a warning to the faithful, that a book might be dangerous.

In addition to books, believers also burned videos and compact discs. They targeted rock and roll music in particular because it "promoted illicit lifestyles based on pleasure-seeking, drug abuse, and casual sex, all of which were inspired by Satan."

Occasionally, a bonfire wasn't possible because some cities refused to issue a permit due to safety concerns. In those cases, the faithful resorted to "book cutting," where believers brought freshly sharpened hedge trimmers and sliced books in half. Those without appropriate tools of destruction simply ripped out pages and tore the books apart with their hands.

Heilbrenner watched the fire crackle and burn, enjoying the warmth on his face. Around him, believers held hands and began singing.

Rise up, O men of God!
Have done with lesser things.
Give heart and mind and soul and strength
to serve the King of kings.

Rise up, O men of God!
The kingdom tarries long.
Bring in the day of brotherhood
and end the night of wrong.

Rise up, O men of God!
The church for you doth wait,
her strength unequal to her task;
rise up, and make her great!

Lift high the cross of Christ!
Tread where his feet have trod.
As brothers of the Son of Man,
rise up, O men of God!

* * *

"Afternoon, David," Lassater said as he strolled into Chambers' office.

"Hi Ray."

"The campus is really coming along; everything looks first-rate."

"Thanks."

"How's the book?"

"It's done. It's exactly one sentence long." Chambers motioned to a chair. "Have a seat."

"And…?"

"My god can beat up your god."

Lassater chuckled. "Well, that's a good start."

"Is there anything else to say?"

"I've got a lot more to say."

"Then maybe you can help me."

"Well, first I have some bad news."

"What is it?"

"I spoke with Johansen yesterday. He said he's not going to release the movie."

"Why?"

Lassater shrugged. "He says he's under pressure."

"From who?"

"The FCC; Infinity. I tried to talk some sense into him, but he's scared. He's worried about his career. You should call him."

"I'm not going to call him."

"Why not?"

"He can do whatever he wants. If he's not comfortable, that's his business."

"But…"

243

"No."

"David."

"No. That's it."

"I think you're making a mistake."

"It won't be the first time."

"Well, I've got another problem."

"Do you have any good news?"

"No."

"What is it, then?"

"It's the investigation; it's a little stalled."

"Okay."

"I need to bring in some heavy hitters."

"What does that mean?"

"Well, you probably don't want to know. All I can tell you is that it's going to cost a lot of money."

"I don't care what it costs. I want you to do whatever it takes."

Lassater smiled. "Good, now let's get started with this book."

* * *

Josephine looked down at her watch; it was just after midnight. *One more hour and I'm out of here. I've got to start getting more sleep.* She opened her calendar for the following day and began reviewing her schedule when she suddenly heard the sound of shattering glass. She instinctively jumped back in her chair and tightly grasped the armrests, but quickly regained her composure and rushed out to the hallway to investigate. She stopped when she heard more glass being punched out of the window. Josephine stayed quiet and waited until she saw a masked intruder enter the hallway. "Ahhhhh!" she screamed and darted back into her office, locking the door behind her. She went back to her desk and pulled a small lock box out of the bottom drawer.

Don't panic! Don't panic! Josephine tried to steady her hand while she entered the numeric sequence on the lock box—"90." The intruder began kicking the door, each blow weakening the wood doorjamb. *Damn it! Come on!* Josephine quickly keyed in the last three digits—"125." The lid of the box clicked open and Josephine pulled out a loaded handgun. She disabled the safety latch, but wasn't quite ready to fire when the door flew open and the masked man lunged at her, swinging a tire iron at her head. She tried to get out of the way, but the weapon connected with her shoulder, knocking her to the floor behind her desk. The left side of her body was immobilized by pain, but she clung tightly to the gun and flipped over on her back. The intruder whipped around her desk and lifted the tire iron above his head, preparing to strike again, but Josephine raised her gun and fired twice, hitting the man in the chest both times. He fell backwards and Josephine jumped on top of him, pinning him down with her legs. She punched him in the face several times as hard as she could and then removed his mask. One of the bullets had pierced the man's lung and he labored to breathe as he bled profusely.

Josephine put her hand around the man's neck. "Who are you?" she demanded. "Tell me who you are!"

The man choked and gargled, unable to speak until Josephine loosened her grip.

"We're...we're...we're going...we're going to kill...kill you," the man sputtered between gasps.

Josephine got up and stood over the injured man, pointing the gun at his head. Her fingers trembled as she she clutched the trigger. *No!* She threw the gun against the wall and then grabbed the phone and called 911. She knelt down next to the man and applied pressure to his wound to stop the bleeding. "Keep breathing. Just keep breathing. An ambulance is on the way."

CHAPTER 30

The more intense has been the religion of any period and the more profound has been the dogmatic belief, the greater has been the cruelty and the worse has been the state of affairs. In the so-called ages of faith, when men really did believe the Christian religion in all its completeness, there was the Inquisition, with its tortures; there were millions of unfortunate women burned as witches; and there was every kind of cruelty practiced upon all sorts of people in the name of religion.

—BERTRAND RUSSELL

Dushane waved to the cab driver from the curb in front of his apartment. The car swerved quickly and screeched to a halt.

"Morning," Dushane greeted through the open window.

"Hello, sir," the cabbie responded.

Dushane hopped in the back seat and looked over the driver. The man was stout, probably from India or Pakistan, Dushane guessed, and he wore a light purple turban. He had a thick beard and a long moustache that curled up in a ragged, disheveled mess above the sides of his mouth, as well as a pair of oval sunglasses perched on his nose. Dushane thought the glasses were stylish in contrast to the man's checkered pants and striped shirt, although the shirt did have a hint of lavender, nicely matching the turban.

"Where you need to go, sir?" the cabbie asked.

"144 Dudley Street."

The cabbie looked back and smiled. One of his front teeth was plated in gold and the sunlight reflected off it. "Dudley Street is in bad location, sir. I never go there."

"Well, can we go there, please?" Dushane said impatiently. "It's very important."

The cabbie shook his head. "That's bad neighborhood, sir. I…"

"Look, I'll give you twenty extra bucks."

"Okay sir." The cabbie turned back to the front of the car and flipped on the radio. Soft, rhythmic chanting music filled the cab as they drove. Half an hour later, the cab entered Roxbury, a run-down section of Boston. Several crumbling, abandoned buildings littered the area, which appeared deserted except for a few cars scattered about the street. The cabbie finally turned onto Dudley Street and drove past a large two-story warehouse.

"Here it is. Stop here, please." Dushane motioned to the warehouse. "Can you wait for me here? I'll just be a few minutes."

"You are leaving me some money?"

"Oh, yeah, sure." Dushane passed the cabbie two twenties and got out. He took a quick look around and then walked slowly toward the door, which was iron gray and made of thin metal that was rusted around the edges. The door had no bell so Dushane pushed it forward. It screeched, metal grinding against metal. Dushane stepped in cautiously. Sun shone dimly through the sooted windows onto the cracked cement floor. The inside of the warehouse was cold and empty except for a small staircase in the back. Dushane walked over to the staircase and grabbed the railing, which was dusty and covered with cobwebs. He ascended the steps apprehensively until he came to a door at the top of the staircase where a handwritten sign read: "You've come to the right place. Please knock."

Is this some kind of joke? What am I doing here? Well, I've come this far. Dushane gave the door three firm knocks and waited until it opened to a short, middle-aged gentleman. The man had thinning white hair combed neatly off of his large forehead, and his face was pink and round. Otherwise, his physical presence was nondescript except for a pair of bright, energetic eyes. The man wore a white, collared shirt, a tattered brown jacket, and charcoal-black slacks with matching shoes.

"I'm looking for Skip Hartley," Dushane said.

"Ah, yes…that would be me," the man replied whimsically. "I suppose you'd better come in."

"I'm Martin Dushane. Pleased to meet you." Dushane shook Hartley's hand and then followed him into a large, brightly lit room that contained several bookcases neatly stacked with books. Several colorful Tiffany lamps illuminated and warmed the room, but the floor was covered in the same cold cement.

"I received a strange letter in the mail," Dushane began. "It was from David Chambers; at least that's what it said. He said I should I come here and meet you. Do you know anything about that?"

Hartley paused, took a pair of bifocals out of his jacket pocket, and then looked carefully at Dushane. "Hmmm…" Hartley stroked his chin. "Yes, I know a little something about that."

"Do you know if the letter was really from David Chambers?"

"Yes, it was."

"You work for him?"

"Well, not exactly, but I've known David a while."

"So what's this all about, then?"

"I assume you're not a believer."

"You mean religious?"

Hartley nodded.

"No, I'm not."

"Why not?" Hartley challenged, raising his voice unexpectedly.

"What do you mean, why not?"

"Well, what if you're wrong and you face eternal damnation? Are you willing to risk that?"

Dushane furrowed his brow in confusion. "I don't know what you're talking about."

"Wouldn't it be easier to just believe and not risk hell fire? What if the preachers are right? It's no skin off your nose, is it?"

"If you're asking me whether I'm willing to lie to myself, the answer's no; absolutely not."

Hartley laughed heartily, the loose skin on his cheeks jiggling around the corners of his mouth.

"What's so funny?"

"I'm...I'm sorry. I'm not trying to make fun of you. I just have to be sure that you have the right frame of mind for this. The task we've undertaken is a grave one and we'd like you to join us. But you need to understand that you won't make any friends. You'll make enemies just like you did when you went against the Catholic priests, but on a grander scale."

"What kind of task are you talking about?"

"I'm talking about being part of a book we're working on—David and I and a few others; a book about human superstition."

"And you want me to help you?"

"Yes. David wants to meet you first, of course."

"Tell me more about this book."

"It's called *Church of the Mind: A Citizen's Guide to the Opiate of the Masses*."

Dushane cracked a smile.

"Catchy title, eh?"

"Yeah. Will there be anything in the book about Infinity?"

Hartley raised his eyebrows and smiled slyly. "People are working on that as we speak."

"Good." Dushane didn't have strong feelings against the average person who held religious beliefs, but he loathed the kind of religion packaged and sold by Infinity. Whenever he contemplated Infinity's perversion of the spiritual experience, he thought of someone scrawling graffiti on a work of art.

"You think he, I mean we, can pull this off?" Dushane said.

"With David, anything is possible. That man has no limitations that I know of; this project can only succeed. Despite the attacks you've probably seen in the press, he's still tremendously respected. I think the viciousness of the attacks demonstrates how much people envy his spirit. Some people look for any reason to take a great man down."

Dushane nodded.

"Now, follow me, I've got something for you."

Dushane followed Hartley into his study where Hartley opened the top drawer of his desk and pulled out a large envelope. "In this envelope, there are some notes about *Church of the Mind*. There's also a card you can use to fly from Logan to SFO on a private jet. All you have to do is call the charter company twenty-four hours before you want to go. And there's also a number in here for Kaleidoscope Ranch. Give them a call and let them know when you expect to arrive in San Francisco. They'll pick you up from there."

"This is a little..."

"Strange," Hartley finished.

"Well, sudden."

Hartley put his hand on Dushane's shoulder and patted it gently. "This is how David works, Martin. You'd better get used to it."

"When does he expect me to be there?"

"As soon as possible. Patience is not one of his virtues."

"I probably need a few days to take care of some stuff. I just got back from a long trip."

"I'm sure that'll be fine. I'll show you out."

Dushane tried to smile.

"Relax, young man," Hartley said. "We're going to have fun with this."

* * *

Ray Lassater walked into a spacious, well-appointed office in downtown Providence, Rhode Island, escorted by two burly men, both carrying loaded guns. A man with hard creases across his face sat behind a huge mahogany desk. His name was Leo Salvatore. "Wait outside," he said to the two armed men.

Lassater quivered nervously.

"Well, well, well, Ray Lassater. I'm surprised to see you," Salvatore said. "You're either crazy or stupid."

Lassater looked down, but didn't respond. He had never been afraid of any man before, but Salvatore made him uneasy.

"I could've had you killed," Salvatore said icily.

Lassater nodded. "I know. I'm glad you didn't." He looked up cautiously. Seven years ago, he had prosecuted Salvatore for embezzlement, racketeering, and fraud, putting him in jail for five years. Salvatore had run one of the largest criminal organizations in the Northeast, with expertise in infiltrating legitimate business organizations, hacking into computer systems, and embezzling money. He still controlled the most talented and potentially dangerous team of computer hackers in the country. After his release from prison, Salvatore had quickly put together a highly successful and completely legal business enterprise in computer security services.

"Maybe I should kill you right now."

Lassater's eye twitched. "But...but then you'd miss out on an opportunity."

"You've already wasted too much of my time. What do you want?"

"I need your help."

"I'm a legitimate businessman."

"I know; I'm happy to see that. This is a legitimate opportunity to use your expertise. And in the service of a good cause."

"Sit down."

Lassater took a seat and rubbed his palms across his pants.

"This better be good," Salvatore warned. "If you're fucking with me..."

"Oh, don't worry. This is good. It's very good. I need someone to infiltrate an organization and do some computer work. I naturally thought of you."

"Like I said, I'm a legitimate businessman now. And for you to come in here and ask for a favor…"

"This is a legitimate operation; totally legal."

"If you're lying to me, I will kill you."

"I'm not. And this will be worth your while; that I guarantee."

Although Salvatore might have thought Lassater was trying to set him up, he had no doubt that his former adversary was telling the truth. He put aside his anger; he was no stranger to shifting alliances and cooperating with former enemies when it suited his purposes. "Okay, I'm listening."

Lassater quickly explained that he wanted Salvatore to infiltrate Infinity, hack into its computers, and obtain information about its operations.

"That's an interesting task. What's in it for me?"

"Everything. This will be the biggest payoff of your life. And, like I said, you'll be doing a good deed."

"How much?" Salvatore snapped impatiently.

"Twenty million."

Salvatore's head instinctively shot back at the unexpectedly rich offer. He took a deep breath and tried to conceal his surprise. "And if we get caught?"

"Don't."

"This could jeopardize my other operations."

Lassater shrugged. "There won't be any problem if you do it right. It'll be just like old times." Lassater paused. "But if you don't have the sack…"

Salvatore's face hardened; Lassater had taken a dangerous chance. "What the hell are you saying?" Salvatore challenged. "If you're saying something, you better damn well say it."

"I'm saying that you're the only man for this job," Lassater offered conciliatorily. "The only man skilled enough to pull it off."

"This doesn't add up. Why do you want this?"

"Let's just say I've had a spiritual awakening."

Salvatore frowned. "Where's the money?"

"I can have it wired to a Swiss account tomorrow morning. Ten million up front; the rest when you deliver the information I need."

Salvatore rubbed his chin and fingered a twenty-four carat gold bar on his desk. "Any further communication will be through my associates. I don't want to see your face ever again."

Lassater nodded. "Of course. Thank you. I'll show myself out."

* * *

"And that concludes our tour, ladies and gentleman. I'll be available to answer your questions in the ballroom in ten minutes." Chambers had just finished giving an extensive tour of the Ranch to several journalists. He hoped to gain additional media exposure for the Ranch and enlist the support of other philanthropists with the children's programs that he had developed.

The throng of reporters milled around the courtyard chatting amongst themselves. Chambers could tell that they were favorably impressed by what he had created and he basked in the feeling of pride. He grabbed a quick snack in the cafeteria and then went to the ballroom where he waited behind the podium as his guests filed in.

"I have one announcement to make before I take your questions. As you know, the Ranch has established three annual awards that we'll inaugurate later this year. The first award will go to the person who makes a scientific discovery with the greatest potential to benefit humankind. The second award will go to the person who develops the most innovative new program to provide underprivileged children with increased opportunities in education, athletics, or the arts. The third award is for the most important act of philanthropy. This could be for almost anything and we hope to recognize different areas every year. These awards are tremendously important and we'll provide generous financial support to the recipients so that they can pursue their passion without financial limitation. Now, I also think it's important to recognize the biggest obstacles to our progress—the people and the thought systems that divide us; the cancers that try to limit our understanding of the world around us and pit us against each other. This is without a doubt the most dangerous threat we face, both here and abroad. In light of the bonfires sponsored by the Infinity Network in recent months, we've decided to establish another award, which will be given annually to the worst example of ignorance and intolerance in America. It's called the Witch Burning Award. We won't be having a formal ceremony for this award so let me just announce the first winner since there's no question who deserves it. The inaugural Witch Burning Award goes jointly to Robert Newhall and John Heilbrenner."

A collective gasp swept across the ballroom, followed by the buzz of excitement in anticipation of a good story.

"I'll take your questions now."

A reporter raised her hand.

"Yes, blue blouse in the back."

"Is this witch burning award just another way for you to attack religion? And don't you think it's a little childish?"

"Well, first of all, any person, regardless of his or her religious affiliation, is eligible for the award, so it's not an attack on religion per se. Of course, the award is unlikely to go to a rational person because they simply don't think along the lines recognized by this award. As to your other comment about this being childish, I'm not sure how to respond except to say that children inspire me with their honesty. Adults could learn a lot from children if we'd open our eyes once in a while."

Chambers pointed to another reporter. "Yes, with the red tie."

"What about the charitable work done by the Infinity Network? You're obviously criticizing the leadership there, but don't you think they do some good work?"

"Yes, and I hope they continue to do that. They've got tremendous resources. If they'd stop building churches and put their money to good use, we'd all be a lot better off." Chambers looked down at his watch. "I've got about fifteen more…" Chambers' assistant suddenly appeared in his peripheral vision, walking swiftly up to the podium. She put her hand on his back and whispered in his ear, "David, you've got a call. It sounds urgent."

"Who is it?"

"It's a woman—Josephine Holladay."

Chambers stiffened as his assistant handed him a cell phone. He clutched it firmly and turned to the audience. "I'm sorry everyone, but I'm going to have to cut this get-together a little short. Something's come up that requires my immediate attention. Thank you all for coming."

Chambers trotted out of the room to the courtyard. "Josephine!"

"Hi, David. I needed to hear your voice."

"Where are you?"

"Salt Lake. Somebody tried to kill me."

"What?" Chambers cried.

"A man broke into my office, about a week ago."

"Are you hurt?"

"No, I've got a bruise on my shoulder, but I had a gun."

"You shot him?"

"Twice."

"Is he…?"

"No, he's in the hospital. The doctor says he's going to make it."

"Who was it?"

"I don't know, but the police think he was motivated by my criticism of the Church."

"God damn it!" Chambers erupted. "I want you out of there! Do you understand me? I want you out of there!"

"I don't want to run, David."

"You want to get yourself killed? You want to be a martyr over this? There's no virtue in that. You're damn lucky. Damn lucky. I'm sending a pilot out to pick you up."

"That's not necessary."

"I don't care whether it's necessary or not, I want you here—now!"

CHAPTER 31

Faith in a holy cause is to a considerable extent
a substitute for lost faith in ourselves.

—ERIC HOFFER

The finely sharpened blades of the shredder sliced effortlessly through several hundred pages of documents in John Heilbrenner's office at Infinity Headquarters. Heilbrenner always delighted in the operation because he loved the high-pitched whir of his industrial strength machine, as well as its efficiency—it could process more paper per hour than any other shredder on the market. After all of the incriminating documents had been neutralized, Heilbrenner ran his fingers through the end product—bags of frivolous confetti.

Although Heilbrenner directed his underlings to shred many of Infinity's records, he saved the most damaging documents for himself, especially the ones that incriminated him. Heilbrenner was about to load another stack into the machine when Newhall burst into his office.

"Have you seen this?" Newhall fumed as he slammed the newspaper on Heilbrenner's desk. The paper contained an article about the Witch Burning Award.

"Yeah, I've seen it," Heilbrenner responded softly.

"Well? When are we going to crush this piss ant?"

"There's not much more we can do. We'll continue attacking him, and…"

"No! That's useless! I want real action! I want you take care of this son of a bitch once and for all!"

John Heilbrenner sat back in his chair and sighed. Although he rarely let his emotions surface and never let them stand in the way of his mission, he felt strangely depressed. When he had first heard that Chambers had bestowed the Witch Burning Award on him, he had shrugged it off; but the more he thought about it, the more his thoughts tortured him. He now knew exactly what Chambers thought of him. But what really stung was that Chambers had caused him to focus on what he thought of himself. Heilbrenner had been able to dispatch the thought quickly, but it had nonetheless jolted him. He never went very deep into his psyche, and he still had impeccable control avoiding himself; nevertheless, he recognized the unmistakable breach. He had to concentrate more than usual to control it.

"Well…I…I…" Heilbrenner stammered.

"Call Rogers," Newhall interrupted. "God knows the guy owes us a thousand favors. We got Packer elected for godsakes."

"Okay, I'll call him later this morning."

Newhall stormed out.

Normally, Heilbrenner would have immediately picked up the phone and taken action, but he found himself paralyzed. *Snap out of this! Come on! Snap out!* A knock at the door interrupted his thoughts.

"Come in."

"Hi, Mr. Heilbrenner, I've got the latest numbers for you." Infinity's accountant handed Heilbrenner a ten-page document.

"Thanks, Jake." Heilbrenner quickly turned to the last page of the report, which summarized Infinity's financials for the fiscal year. *Wow! This is incredible! Can this be right?* Infinity's cash position had unexpectedly increased by almost thirty million dollars. Heilbrenner studied the rest of the report carefully and discovered that the huge influx of cash was from the President's faith-based initiative. Infinity had received one hundred million dollars in government grants to build social service centers, but the facilities had only cost seventy million dollars to build. Infinity wasn't required to account for the difference. Heilbrenner suddenly snapped out of his funk.

With the huge influx of taxpayer's money, Infinity had established over two hundred "Infinity Centers," which provided substance abuse counseling, day care, meals, and spiritual support in cities across the country. Although each center varied in the types of services it provided, they all had several aspects in common. Heilbrenner supervised the production of literature designed for the centers, which was similar to the religious tracts Infinity distributed at its church services except that Heilbrenner tailored the rhetoric to appeal to the mostly uneducated audience.

> Are you looking for direction in your life? Do you seek meaning? Do you wonder why life doesn't seem to make any sense? Do you want answers?
>
> God has the answers you're looking for, and He has given us a book with explicit instructions on how to find meaning and purpose in our lives. That book is the Bible, and it's the only true word of God.
>
> God tells us that we must follow His Commandments and accept His son Jesus Christ as our personal savior. Our God is a loving God, but He is also a God of Judgment. If we do not live according to His laws or accept His Son Jesus Christ, then we are destined to spend eternity in Hell. Are you willing to risk eternal punishment in Hell?
>
> Fortunately, God has a plan for our salvation. With belief in Him and acceptance of His Son, you can have everlasting life. God is waiting for you. With obedience, everything is possible.

Each center had a large picture of Newhall prominently displayed on the wall as well as crucifixes, pewter spikes, and pictures of Jesus and his disciples. Infinity Centers required every person who used its services to read its literature, take an oath of faith, and register to vote. They also solicited donations. While most of their patrons lived below the poverty line, they had unemployment and social security checks that could be siphoned, and they were encouraged to make generous sacrifices in the name of their new faith.

Heilbrenner reflected how easy it had been. He had assigned a team of his lieutenants to write grant proposals and work with federal bureaucrats to start the flow of money. Then he had created a few pilot social service centers in order to determine which type was the most effective for recruiting. After a few months, he had determined that centers attracting people living in poverty, or with substance abuse problems, or people trying to turn their lives around were the most promising. These people could be persuaded to "find God" and be reshaped into Infinity converts. The final step involved dispatching teams of local followers to set up franchises. And then the idea had hit him. These new recruitment centers were a perfect cover for a future political operation.

A final benefit of the centers had been further solidifying public opinion against Chambers, who was appalled by the exploitation of society's most vulnerable members. Chambers had written several letters accusing Infinity of using the centers to brainwash and take advantage of frightened people. He argued that what these people really needed was to build their self-esteem instead of relying on Infinity to do their thinking for them.

Infinity responded swiftly and regularly, reminding its followers of Chambers' quote that business was his most important charity, and vilifying him as an atheist and therefore un-American. Most of the public agreed.

Heilbrenner picked up the phone with renewed vigor. When he needed a favor, all he had to do was call the appropriate person in the Packer Administration and they usually granted his request with no questions asked. Administration officials knew that Infinity's support was critical to getting the President's agenda in place as well as ensuring his reelection. But this time, Heilbrenner had a request that couldn't be fulfilled by anyone other than the President's Chief of Staff. Heilbrenner dialed Al Rogers' private number at the White House.

"Al Rogers."

"Hi Buzz, John Heilbrenner here."

"How are you, John?"

"I'm good. Congratulations on your success so far."

"Well, thanks for your help. Infinity's support has been critical. How is everything?"

"Fine, except for one little problem. We're having some trouble with David Chambers."

"We're all having trouble with him," Rogers chuckled.

"I'm serious," Heilbrenner responded coldly.

"All right. What's going on?"

"The guy's been a vocal critic of our social service centers and he's spreading lies about us. I don't know where he gets off, but we can't tolerate it any longer."

"Believe me, the President's not happy either."

"It's time to do something," Heilbrenner said firmly. "Put that troublemaker in his place."

Rogers didn't respond.

"You there, Buzz?"

"Yeah, yeah, I'm here."

"Do you understand what I'm saying?"

"I'm not sure what I can do. The guy's a jerk-off, but he hasn't broken any laws."

"Well…you're a resourceful man. I'm sure you'll figure something out."

Warm blood rushed into Rogers' face as thought about taking Chambers on. He stamped his foot, attempting to suppress the jealousy that threatened to seep out of his pores. Rogers resented Chambers' business success, philanthropy, and charisma, and he desperately wanted to lash out. But he calmed himself and summoned his ego into action. *I'm the Chief of Staff! The guy can't touch me! So what if he won a Presidential Medal of Freedom! Damn right I'll put him in his place!* "Okay, I'll look into it."

* * *

The small passenger jet touched down softly on the Kaleidoscope Ranch airstrip. The pilot hit the brakes and slowed to a comfortable taxi speed, and then turned around and smiled. "Welcome to the Ranch, Ms. Holladay."

"Thank you."

The pilot pulled the plane into the hangar and brought it to a stop. Chambers had been waiting patiently. Josephine disembarked from the aircraft and embraced Chambers at the end of the stairway.

"I had no idea how much I loved you until just now," Chambers whispered.

"I've missed you, David. God, how I've missed you."

* * *

The President sat stoically in the Oval Office and delivered a speech to the nation.

> My fellow Americans, in light of the continuing threat of terrorist attacks against the citizens of our nation, I am proposing today a new cabinet-level department to deal with defending our country against terrorism. Specifically, I am submitting a bill to the Congress that will coordinate

our efforts to deal with terrorist threats and provide our law enforcement authorities with the necessary power to deal with them.

Every American should understand that there is no time to wait. Every minute we delay is another minute that terrorists have to prepare. I therefore urge the Congress to pass this critical legislation as soon as possible so that we can secure the nation's borders and protect our citizens.

The threat of terrorism is a grave one, but make no mistake about it. With our faith in God and our strength as a nation, we will defeat terrorism. God bless you and God bless America.

The Domestic Security Act proposed by the President passed overwhelmingly in both the House and Senate. The legislation provided for the creation of the Department of Domestic Security, a cabinet-level department that consolidated several federal bureaucracies and over 170,000 federal employees into one unified organization. The Department's mission was to coordinate of all the federal government's intelligence gathering and law enforcement activities that protected the nation from internal or external threats.

The new law gave the FBI sweeping new powers to tap telephones, engage in satellite surveillance, seize bank and telephone records, and intercept e-mail messages, with no immediate judicial oversight. It also permitted the FBI to issue "national security" letters, which required businesses to turn over records about its employees' finances, telephone calls, e-mail, and other personal information. These national security letters could be issued independently by FBI field offices and were not subject to review by a judge. The bill gave the Attorney General similar powers, also without any independent judicial oversight.

As part of the new Cabinet department, Rogers established the Office of Homeland Protection, which he controlled directly. The Office's stated mission was to identify and monitor U.S.-based religious groups that might pose a threat to the welfare of America. Rogers now had a powerful weapon in the fight against religious organizations that threatened the new Christian alliance, and the President worked out a deal with Congress to funnel part of the Department of Domestic Security's forty-billion-dollar budget to the new Office. Rogers indicated in a private memorandum to the President that he would focus the office's efforts on "rooting out religious cults," especially those with "un-American" values.

CHAPTER 32

There is no salvation for those outside the [Catholic] Church. I believe it…Put it this way. My wife is a saint. She's a much better person than I am. Honestly. She's, like, Episcopalian, Church of England. She prays, she believes in God, she knows Jesus, she believes in that stuff. And it's just not fair if she doesn't make it; she's better than I am. But that is a pronouncement from the chair. I go with it.

—MEL GIBSON, *explaining why his wife could be going to hell*

When Dushane got back to his apartment, he opened the envelope from Hartley and took out the notes from *Church of the Mind*. He sprawled out on the couch and began reading.

Mind Control

Orwell's parody of the Christian God in *1984* as Big Brother. Discovery of facts is made difficult or impossible and people are brainwashed to believe that factual inquiry is bad. Big Brother uses cameras and other surveillance techniques to control the behavior of the masses. Religious leaders use the person's own mind to do the surveillance work with guilt, shame, threats of eternal punishment, irrational beliefs, etc.

Religious pontifications and dogma, by their nature, cannot be proven or disproven because they're based on faith. The statements and demands of the religious leader cannot be questioned intellectually because religion is superior to the practical application of thought to human problems. Applying thought to "spiritual" issues is deemed crass or immoral.

Religious leaders try to convince their subjects that if they sacrifice their lives to a higher authority, then they will be entitled to eternal life in heaven (or some other utopia depending on the religion), which is portrayed as a much better world than the one in which we live. Conversely, if the religious subject refuses to sacrifice his life to the church and the demands of its leaders, he will burn eternally in hell. Thus, religion promises the greatest reward and threatens the worst possible punishment, although it can't prove the existence of either.

Dushane chuckled. He turned to the next page.

Morality

Religion supplies simple moral codes such as the Ten Commandments and then priests claim the moral high ground as if they've discovered an original idea (i.e. they believe that people need religion in order to know that it's wrong to steal, etc.) It's ironic that the church has consistently taken positions and encouraged practices throughout recorded history which have stifled moral progress and led to unnecessary human suffering.

Example—Racism of the Mormons in excluding Blacks from even the lowest positions in the church until 1978 (fourteen years after the Civil Rights Act of 1964 and decades after the overwhelming majority of Americans believed that racism was wrong). Apparently, Mormon "prophets" were the last people on the planet to receive the "revelation."

Example—Misogyny (still dominates the Abrahamic faiths); cruel and inhumane treatment of women in virtually all aspects of life by Muslims.

Similarly, Mormons and Catholics deny women right to highest positions of authority. Moral equivalent of prohibiting women from being corporate executives or otherwise being leaders in any activity. Not clear why any woman would join such a church? Would any man join a church dominated by women, which excluded them from leadership positions?

Example—Hostility and hatred of the Christians and Muslims toward homosexuals and freethinking "infidels."

Example—Making claims that have no basis in reality. In a rational, secular context, such claims would be considered fraudulent and the liar would be subject to civil liability and/or criminal punishment (i.e. the law requires at least a reasonable belief in the truth). Faith-based claims are exempt from fraud. Why should they be? Or perhaps a better question is: What if we gave people the legal right to lie (that is, make faith-based claims) in other contexts?

Religion's the ultimate exemption from the truth, Dushane thought. *Chambers is right about that.* Dushane turned to the next section.

Psychological Issues in Mass Movements

Mass movements are essentially interchangeable. Ordinary people who followed the Nazis share many of the same characteristics as those who follow religious leaders. A mass movement appeals to people who desire to get rid of their unwanted selves. Their innermost desire is for a new life, a rebirth, where they will have a chance to acquire a sense of purpose that they were unable to acquire on their own. They get their sense of self-worth from the cause and they deride those individuals who would rather rely on their own individual talents and efforts.

Conversely, the secure person doesn't care about the goals of any mass movement unless those goals further the goals of his or her own life. Such a person has a life worth living and their main concern is living it without interference. To both the mass movement follower and their leaders, this person is a threat.

People frequently join religious movements because they're not comfortable thinking for themselves, but they often refuse to take responsibility for policies of their church that cause harm. Example—if the Pope says no condoms and millions of people die from AIDS, is the follower, who donates money to the Church, complicit in the crime? Maybe not, in the sense that a person might support a political party and disagree with some of the party's platform. A person can't be held morally responsible for everything the political party does. But the Church is different in the sense that the Pope's claims (at least according to him and other Church leaders) cannot be challenged because they come from "God." Thus, the religious supporter is supporting the ultimate "sin"—

the idea that people cannot challenge evil/stupid ideas. Thus, followers shouldn't be allowed to escape moral responsibility here, especially since they have the opportunity to support healthier alternatives.

People trade their independence for groupthink and dependency in the body of a mass movement and learn to disregard their own compassionate and decent impulses when they conflict with religious dogma. (But this probably isn't usually conscious; the follower just reacts automatically once he's been appropriately conditioned).

Man, this book is going to be dynamite, Dushane thought. He figured that the book's ideas, while not new, would surely be controversial. Chambers was heaping devastating criticism on a majority of people in the country who embraced irrational, faith-based thought systems. Dushane got up and stretched his legs. He went into the kitchen and grabbed a can of apple juice out of the refrigerator. He sat down in the breakfast nook and turned to the next page.

Most Destructive Ideas

Original sin—Humans are inherently evil creatures that are incapable of living a moral life without belief in the supernatural. Humans must therefore sacrifice their lives to the god, the church, the cause, etc.

Epistemology of faith-based claims—explicitly rejects primacy of perceived reality and the integrity of the human mind. The mental breach could extend to anything; i.e. there's no limit to what a person could make up because faith-based epistemology lacks any standards.

Life on Earth isn't Sacred—In order to persuade a person to give up his or her own aspirations and dreams, the church must convince the person that individual life has little value. The most common tactic employed by religious manipulators is to breed contempt for the present; i.e. this time and this life are merely stepping stones to another place and time. They urge followers to sacrifice this life and obediently follow so that they will be rewarded in the next life.

Misery loves company, Dushane thought. *I think that's what's really going on.*

Why Follow?

1) Fear—not knowing what's going to happen after death.
2) Sense of community. But why couldn't a person be active in a community without the divisiveness inherent in irrational belief?
3) Frees people from having to think. Religion comes nicely packaged and people can feel moral simply by being associated with the group.

4) People typically just adopt the religion of their parents just as they adopt the same language. Perhaps this is the most important reason. But why would they never question it? Or do they somehow rationalize the utter nonsense of it?

Dushane put the notes down and went into his bedroom. He sat behind his computer and did another Internet search for information about Chambers. He scanned the results and clicked on a link to the *Forbes* list of the four hundred richest people in the country. He navigated down the page until he found Chambers at number 181.

David Chambers – 1.3 Billion

Mr. Chambers is perhaps both the most reclusive and the most public person on our list. After studying aerospace engineering at Caltech and working as a flight tester in the Air Force, he founded Chambers Aerospace with Ernesto Sosa, a close friend (see number 267 on this list). Chambers Aerospace is the leading company in the development of unmanned fighter aircraft, advanced weapons systems, small commercial aircraft, and avionics. Mr. Chambers is the largest individual shareholder in the company and his stock holdings constitute the bulk of his wealth.

Two years ago, Chambers purchased 30,000 acres in a remote area of Northern California and established Kaleidoscope Ranch. "The Ranch," as it is commonly known, is not subject to simple description, although it resembles a small university campus. In addition to providing an established curriculum of studies, the Ranch operates a public policy think tank with a team of respected scholars. As of this writing, the Ranch's publishing arm has published seventeen books and over two hundred essays on a variety of topics, usually distributed in pamphlet form. In addition, the Ranch provides extensive housing facilities and programs (mostly camps, including sports camps and science camps) for underprivileged children.

In recognition of his business success, promotion of science, and generous philanthropy, former President Edward Thompson awarded him the Presidential Medal of Freedom, the nation's highest civilian award. Mr. Chambers maintained a close relationship with President Thompson during his Administration, but his relationship with the Packer Administration has been openly hostile. This appears to be largely the result of Chambers' criticism of President Packer's most important supporter, evangelical leader, Reverend Robert Newhall.

I can't believe this guy wants to meet me. Why would someone this successful want to meet me? Dushane called the number on the card that Hartley had given him and scheduled a flight to San Francisco.

* * *

Josephine rested her head on Chambers' chest, which was still heaving after an intense session of lovemaking.

"You're not like anyone I've ever met," Josephine said.

"We're two of a kind, Josie." Chambers paused. "And I've never quite understood that."

"Are you happy, David?"

Chambers chuckled lightly. "Right now I am. But I suppose that's not what you're asking. Happiness is a funny thing. I'm just trying to live—the best that I can."

Neither of them spoke for several minutes. Chambers gently caressed Josephine's back.

"Sometimes, I…" Josephine's voice trailed off.

"What is it?"

"God, this is hard to say, even to you."

Chambers kissed Josephine's forehead. "You're always safe with me."

Josephine sighed. "Sometimes, I…I wake up in the middle of the night and…and I can't get back to sleep. Life…existence…it all seems so random and empty."

Chambers pulled Josephine closer. "I know. I feel it too; not often, but I do feel it. But moments like this, and having you here…"

"I can't stay here, David. I…I need…this is your life…"

Chambers took a deep breath and exhaled heavily.

"It just…it isn't right…not yet. I need to be…"

"I know."

They both stayed silent for a while.

"When are you leaving?" Chambers asked finally.

"Tomorrow."

* * *

"Martin, that's the Chicago skyline off to the right," one of the pilots announced over the aircraft's intercom system.

Dushane was the only passenger on the ten-seat aircraft. He peered out the window and followed the geometric patterns of the skyscrapers. I wonder what the Ranch looks like. *I wonder if it's as majestic as that skyline. And Chambers; I wonder if I'll get to know him.* Dushane pulled the *Church of the Mind* notes out of his backpack.

Heretics

Chronicle the spread of Christianity in Europe, with a detailed account of the Crusades, the Papal Inquisition, the Spanish Inquisition, the Religious Wars, and the Holocaust. Maybe discuss religious conflict/

266

bloodshed currently plaguing the world.

Describe instruments of torture used against heretics—the breast ripper, the head crusher, the heretic's fork, and the wheel: Being broken or "braided" on the wheel was one of the most insidiously painful methods of torture and execution. After hanging, breaking with the wheel was the most common means of execution throughout Europe from the early Middle Ages to the beginning of the eighteenth century.

The victim was stripped naked and then stretched out supine on the execution dock, with his or her limbs spread, and tied to stakes or iron rings. Stout wooden crosspieces were placed under the wrists, elbows, ankles, knees, and hips. The executioner then smashed limb after limb and joint after joint, including the shoulders and hips, with the iron-bound edge of the wheel, but avoiding fatal blows. The victim was transformed, according to the observations of a seventeenth-century German chronicler, "into a sort of huge screaming puppet writhing in rivulets of blood, a puppet with four tentacles, like a sea monster, with raw, slimy and shapeless flesh mixed up with splinters of smashed bones."

Then, the shattered limbs were "braided" into the spokes of the wheel and the victim was hoisted up horizontally to the top of a pole, where crows ripped away the victim's flesh and pecked out the eyes. Death came after what was probably the longest and most atrocious agony imaginable.

Dushane shuddered. *How could any god allow this to happen? Maybe that's the point. Humans have to prevent things like this from happening by standing up against superstition.*

Conflict Between Religion and Science

Galileo story—The idea that the Earth was the center of the universe was so firmly ingrained in European consciousness that it was never seriously questioned until Nicholas Copernicus published a book in 1543 arguing that the Earth revolved around the sun. In the next century, the Italian physicist and mathematician, Galileo, was persuaded by the Copernican theory and began advocating it, even though it conflicted with Vatican dogma. Church officials believed in the Earth-centered universe because it was easier to reconcile with scripture. Consequently, they attacked Galileo for his scientific findings. Galileo defended himself until the matter was submitted to an Inquisition panel, where the Inquisitors made a formal determination that Galileo's views were heretical. They ordered him not to discuss the Copernican theory in writing or in speech, and to cease defending it or believing it. For good measure, they placed Nicholas Copernicus' book on the Church's list of forbidden books until it could be "corrected."

Galileo continued to write and to publish his works, but not without first submitting them to Church censors in Rome. In 1632, Galileo completed Dialogue Concerning the Two Chief World Systems, which advocated the Copernican heliocentric system. The Church initially allowed the book to be printed, then changed its mind and ordered distribution stopped. The book was submitted to the Inquisitors for examination and Galileo was charged with heresy and ordered to stand trial. At the trial, Church officials had no interest in investigating his claims or looking through his telescope because they believed that the devil could make things appear true. (Note that religious zealots have often put this idea forward when confronted by irrefutable evidence.)

Church officials threatened Galileo with torture as well as the standard punishment for heresy—burning at the stake, unless he renounced his belief in the "sun-centered" universe. Galileo capitulated and was sentenced to house arrest for the remainder of his life.

Three and a half centuries later, in 1992, the Roman Catholic Church recanted, acknowledging that Galileo and Copernicus were right after all; the Earth does indeed revolve around the sun.

What a bunch of morons, Dushane thought. *My God, why does anyone follow them?* He turned to the next page.

Why Science Works / Religion Fails

A thought system based on science works because it has built-in error checking. If an idea is proven wrong, it is abandoned. No one clings to ideas that are proven wrong and no one resorts to their "faith" when they can't substantiate a claim. In science, there are no forbidden questions, no matters too delicate to be probed, and no sacred truths. The openness to new ideas, combined with rigorous testing of those ideas, is what science and reason are all about.

A thought system based on pseudoscience, and theology in particular, is based on sacred "truths" that can't be questioned. These "truths" must be accepted without proof or inquiry and skeptical thinking is opposed. Often the claims of pseudoscience are framed in such a way that they can't be proven or disproven and must be taken on faith. At its core, almost all religious doctrine is based on the say-so of a prophet or some other person claiming divine "knowledge."

In some sense, a person who believes something based on somebody else's say-so without any proof has little to fear from science. Science has nothing to say about a thought system based on blind belief except to classify it as fantasy. To that extent, religion and science are compatible because they operate in entirely different spheres. However, with regard to any question that science/reason can speak to (including ethical questions), science and religion are on opposite ends of the spectrum and have no compatibility.

Dushane turned to the final page, which contained a single sentence.

Primary motive of manipulators appears to be power for its own sake.

Ah-ha! That's exactly what I saw at the DA's office. Dushane put the notes away and lay back in his seat.

"Martin, we're flying over the Sierra Nevada mountain range," the pilot broadcast. "Lake Tahoe's off to the left."

Dushane looked out the window, enjoying the view of the lake and the snow-capped mountains. Then he got up and walked to the front of the aircraft. "How far are we from San Francisco?" he asked the co-pilot.

"About two hundred miles. We should have you on the ground in about forty-five minutes."

"Great." As Dushane walked back to his seat, he began to feel more nervous. *What if the guy doesn't think much of me? I'm probably not as smart as he is, and I certainly don't have as much drive. What am I doing?*

After the plane landed, Dushane walked to the end of the jetway where a man was holding up a sign bearing his name.

"Hi, I'm Martin." Dushane said, extending his hand to the stranger.

"Hi Martin, I'm Jim Nielsen. David sent me down to get you." Nielsen was middle-aged with a medium build and salt-and-pepper hair. He was dressed casually in a short-sleeved polo shirt, blue jeans, and a blue baseball cap emblazoned with the words "U.S. Air Force" in gold lettering.

"Yeah, they mentioned that I would be taking another plane up to the Ranch."

"Yeah, my plane. I mean, I'm the pilot." Nielsen adjusted the baseball cap over his eyes.

Dushane looked at Nielsen more carefully now that he was entrusting his life to the man. *Guy seems okay, in his fifties, probably an experienced pilot. He's wearing an Air Force hat. That's good.*

The men walked out of the terminal and caught a cab to a remote section of the airport.

"There she is," Nielsen said, pointing to a small six-seat airplane.

"What kind of plane is it?" Dushane asked, trying to calm the butterflies in his stomach. As a rule, he didn't like to fly, especially in small planes.

"It's a Chambers Windrunner—almost brand new. It's got a twin engine and a turbo prop. Beautiful airplane. David designed it himself."

The men got out of the cab and walked over to the plane against a light wind. A younger man was walking around the plane, carrying a clipboard. He was tall and wiry, with oil-stained overalls hanging loosely on his frame.

"Who's that?" Dushane asked.

"That's Rusty. His real name's Lawrence, but he gets pissed if you call him that. He's doing the preflight check."

"How's it looking Lawr…I mean Rusty?" Nielsen joked.

Rusty shot Nielsen a look of feigned anger and then smiled. "Good. I'm about finished. Give me a couple more minutes. You must be Martin."

"Yeah, nice to meet you."

"You too. I'd shake your hand, but I'm covered with grease."

Dushane waved casually. "Sure."

After Rusty finished the inspection, the men climbed into the plane. Nielsen and Rusty sat in front while Dushane spread out across the two seats behind them. He watched curiously as Nielsen started the engine and adjusted the controls, preparing for takeoff.

"What can you tell me about David Chambers?" Dushane asked, after they were safely in the air.

Rusty turned around. "He's a cool guy; good pilot."

"Well, what's he like? From what I've read, he sounds like a loose cannon."

Nielsen laughed. "He's a cannon; that's for sure."

I wonder what he'll think of me? Dushane couldn't shake the thought. He stayed quiet the rest of the trip and tried to mentally prepare himself to meet Chambers.

It was late afternoon when they reached the Ranch and the sun was setting over the hills, spreading a warm glow over the sprawling complex and surrounding wilderness. From the air, Dushane could see that most of the buildings were tucked into the hillside, surrounded by towering redwood trees.

The plane landed and Nielsen and Dushane walked over to a parking lot with several rows of small electric cars that were used almost exclusively on the Ranch for personal travel.

"Here's your key," Nielsen said, holding up an ATM-sized card.

"Which car?"

"Whichever. Any color you like."

Dushane scanned the lot. "They're all blue…aren't they?"

Nielsen smiled. "Yes."

"Okay…and the key…"

"Works in any car," Nielsen finished.

"Okay, I'll take this one right here, number 73."

Nielsen pulled a small, rectangular device out of his pocket and inserted the card into a narrow slot. He typed a few numbers on the device's keypad and then the card popped back out. "Slip this into the ignition and you'll be good to go."

"Thanks."

"You're staying over at guest housing. Your luggage will be waiting for you when you get there. Take this road down about a half-mile and you'll see a three-story building on your right. You can't miss it; there's a big sign. Marv will be at the front desk. He's expecting you."

"Okay."

"And one other thing. You've got a meeting scheduled with David tomorrow morning at nine. Somebody will come by and pick you up."

"All right. Thanks a lot, Jim."

"My pleasure. Welcome to the Ranch."

Dushane walked to his car and inserted the keycard into the ignition slot, but the car didn't start. Instead, a computer-generated voice responded: "Invalid keycard. Please contact Ranch security." Dushane tried a couple more times with the same result. He crawled out of the car and looked around. At the other end of the parking lot, he saw a person sitting on a motorcycle. Dushane trotted over to him.

"Hi, I can't get my car started," Dushane said to the man, who had already put on his motorcycle helmet. "This keycard doesn't seem to work."

"Need a lift?" the man offered.

Dushane couldn't see much of the man's face, but his blue eyes were so bright that they startled him for a split-second. The man had long hair spiking out of the back of his helmet and was wearing a well-worn brown leather jacket and black boots.

"Yeah, I'm stuck," Dushane said. "I'd really appreciate a ride. I'm staying over at guest housing."

"Sure."

The man started the motorcycle. It had a clean, humming sound and a well-tuned vibration. He unlatched the strap holding the extra helmet stowed on the back of the bike and handed it to Dushane. "Here, put this on."

Dushane squeezed the helmet over his ears and strapped it tightly across his chin.

"Hop on. Keep your feet on the pegs and hold on tight."

Dushane straddled the seat and grabbed the handholds. The man turned around. "I mean hold on really tight. Wrap your arms around my waist."

Dushane hesitated for a second. He felt a little uncomfortable getting so close to another man, especially a man he didn't know, but he figured better to be safe, so he obeyed the man's instructions.

The man wheeled the bike onto the street and pulled back hard on the throttle without warning. Dushane's head shot back and he instinctively dug his fingernails into the man's stomach. They cycle accelerated down a long straightaway, hitting a speed of a hundred and twenty. The wind whipped through the bottom of Dushane's face shield, blasting cold air across his features and making it difficult to breathe. Then the man downshifted suddenly and leaned the bike hard around a turn, almost catching Dushane's pants on the pavement. Dushane thought of screaming "Slow down!" but he checked himself. He didn't want to seem like wimp so he just prayed silently that they wouldn't crash.

The man took another hard corner, but the pavement was wet, causing the back tire to skid. Dushane screamed, certain that he was about to become street pizza, but the man slammed his boot on the pavement in a quick motion, steadying the bike, and then pulled back on the throttle and continued at the feverish pace.

After a few more straightaways and sharp turns, each sending a fresh jolt of terror through Dushane's body, they pulled up to guest housing. Dushane jumped off the bike and ripped off his helmet. "Are you completely insane? You could have killed us! What the hell's wrong with you?"

The man flipped up the visor on his helmet and smiled. "Have a nice evening," he said, and then revved the engine and disappeared.

Dushane stood silently in the grass and wondered whether he should have come.

CHAPTER 33

The study of theology, as it stands in the Christian churches is the study of nothing; it is founded on nothing; it rests on no principles; it proceeds by no authorities; it has no data; it can demonstrate nothing; and it admits no conclusion.

—Thomas Paine, *The Age of Reason*

The next morning, Dushane woke up at eight, refreshed after a comfortable sleep. He loafed to the kitchen in his boxers and opened the refrigerator. He took a quick guzzle of orange juice out of the carton and then walked into the living room, which contained a large bookcase filled with Kaleidoscope Ranch publications. Dushane found a course catalog and casually flipped through it, but stopped suddenly when he saw a course on Marxism. *That's strange. I thought this guy was pro-freedom.* Dushane perused a few more publications until the doorbell interrupted him. He raced into the bedroom, threw on a t-shirt, and then answered the door.

"Morning. I'm Jacob. David sent me here to pick you up."

"Oh…yeah…sorry, I'm not dressed. Can you wait a couple minutes?"

"Sure."

"Come on in, I'll be right back." The driver followed Dushane inside and sat down on the couch. Dushane went into the bedroom and tore into his suitcase. He wasn't sure what a person was supposed to wear to a meeting with David Chambers, but in every picture he had ever seen of the man, Chambers had been dressed casually, so he threw on a pair of jeans and a navy polo shirt. As he got ready to go, he noticed that he wasn't nervous anymore, just excited to finally meet Chambers.

"All right, let's go," Dushane said as he walked back into the living room.

The driver took Dushane to Ranch headquarters, which consisted of five four-story buildings arrayed around a large courtyard. The courtyard took up fifteen acres, with a gazebo and a stage in the middle. Park benches and picnic tables were spread around the large lawn separating the buildings.

"There's the building, right there," the driver said. "Go up to the fourth floor."

"Great. Thanks for the ride."

Dushane climbed the three flights of stairs and walked straight into Chambers office, which took up the entire floor. Chambers stood motionless, staring out the window, the sunlight illuminating his face.

"David Chambers?" Dushane said.

Chambers turned around. "You must be Martin Dushane."

"Yeah."

The men walked towards each other. The first thing Dushane noticed was Chambers' pronounced limp and then the long brown hair that draped down to his shoulders. Then as he got closer, Dushane saw his eyes. *It's the guy from last night!*

"Wait…wait…wait a minute," Dushane stammered.

Chambers extended his hand and laughed cheerfully. "Sorry about last night, Martin. Some people say that I have a vicious sense of humor.

Welcome to Kaleidoscope Ranch!"

"Uh…thanks. I'm sorry I yelled at you."

Chambers shrugged and then shook Dushane's hand firmly. As Dushane released his grip, Chambers pulled him forward and embraced him. *This is a little weird*, Dushane thought as the hug continued for much longer than he expected. With the exception of his Uncle Nat, Dushane rarely hugged other men, especially men he didn't know well. But the hug from Chambers felt comforting.

"I'm happy to see you," Chambers said as he released his hold. "It's a real pleasure to have you here."

"Thanks, I'm glad to be here."

Chambers grinned. "Come over here. The first thing I want to show you is this view." They walked to one of the floor-to-ceiling windows and looked out onto a valley with rolling hills, large redwood trees, and a small lake.

"After I bought this place, I had to decide where to put my office so I surveyed the entire property from almost every possible vantage point. I decided that this spot, where we're standing, has the most magnificent view on the entire property. It's particularly spectacular at sunrise."

"Wow, it's nice," Dushane said. "This is quite a piece of property." Dushane turned and casually scanned Chambers' large, L-shaped desk. It had several piles of paper and books on it, as well as a picture of an elderly couple.

"Before I forget, let me give you my phone number here." Chambers picked up a pencil off his desk and slid it into an electric sharpener. The machine made a loud, grinding sound.

"That thing sounds like a garbage disposal," Dushane said.

"I know; it's the motor. It works great though. Why don't you have a seat?"

Dushane sat down. He stared at Chambers and waited for him to speak, but Chambers just put his hands behind his head and reclined. Dushane tried to think of something interesting to say. "I…uh…was looking through your course catalog this morning. I noticed you offer a class on Marxism."

"Ah, very good." Chambers leaned forward. "We offer a few history courses here and the 20th Century is incomprehensible without a grasp of Marx's impact. That's why it has to be studied very carefully."

Dushane nodded.

"More generally, it's critical to understand how ideas affect people," Chambers continued. "That's where everything starts. Everything." Chambers paused to emphasize the point. "Now, Marxism, and more generally socialism, exemplifies how a few ideas, or even one idea, can completely change the direction of an entire society."

"I guess socialism didn't quite work," Dushane said.

"Of course it didn't. Government bureaucrats couldn't run a business if their lives depended on it, and trying to plan a country's economy is colossally misguided—economic activity is way too dynamic. It's hard enough for experienced businesspeople to make those decisions."

Dushane nodded. "I can see that."

"Theoretical Marxism is an even stranger case because it's based on the idea that people will divide along class lines. Not only did that never happen, it never even came close to happening. Nationalism, on the other hand, is a much stronger unifying force. In any case, because the theoretical basis underlying the Communist state was flawed, it couldn't be exported from the Soviet Union to other countries except by force, or under false pretenses."

"How do you mean?"

"Well, the Soviets exported Communism in three primary ways: direct conquest in the case of Eastern Europe after World War II; reinvention of authoritarian regimes with Marxist window dressing like in China; and a handy form of rhetoric that gave some supposed legitimacy to petty dictators like Fidel Castro. In the end, Marxism produced nothing but misery, tyranny, and mediocrity in every society where it was applied. Today, it has almost no intellectual credibility, but again, it's worthy of study because of its historical impact in the last century."

"What about religion?"

"Ahhh…I don't think you want to get me started on that. We'll be here all day."

"No, go ahead. I read the notes Skip Hartley gave me. You've piqued my curiosity."

"Excellent. Skip's a good mind. He's gotten us off to a good start." Chambers paused. "What do you think about what we're doing?"

"I think you're going to piss a lot of people off."

Chambers shrugged. "Probably."

"So what's worse, communism or religion?"

"Religion," Chambers responded without hesitation.

"Why?"

"Well, religion is somewhat like nationalism. It's a unifying, and then a dividing force that people are willing to kill for; and like communism, one idea can change the entire course of human history. The interesting thing about religion that makes it more dangerous than communism is that, by its terms, it can't be challenged intellectually. That's a big problem because even if belief in mythology were healthy, the idea of not being able to question it is deadly. At least with communism, we can refute it both theoretically and empirically, and we can persuade people.

With religion, believers insist that it's somehow above intellectual discussion even though it's easy to demonstrate that embracing mindless superstition has negative consequences. History is rife with examples of that."

"Is that your mission here—to expose religion?"

"That's part of our mission, certainly. But we also try to expose the real reasons behind things, particularly when there are popular myths that obscure the truth. A perfect example is the Great Depression, which we wrote an essay about recently. I've heard countless times that the Depression was caused by defects in capitalism or free markets, but nothing could be further from the truth." Chambers hesitated. "I don't want to bore you."

"No, please."

"Well, between 1921 and 1929, the U.S. money supply grew more than sixty percent. The Fed kept interest rates low, which encouraged risky loans and excessive borrowing. When the Fed suddenly began raising rates in 1929, this choked off business activity and profits began to fall, precipitating the market crash. To make matters worse, Congress passed the Smoot-Hawley Act in 1930, which raised tariffs and sparked an international trade war, destroying markets for U.S. exports. Two years later, Congress passed what was then the biggest peacetime tax increase in history. Then Congress added an additional burden by establishing Social Security and increasing taxes even more. As thousands of banks failed, the money supply dried up. Wages and prices should have fallen too, and that would've ultimately led to stability and eventual economic improvement, but politicians did all they could to prop up wages. By 1933, unemployment peaked at twenty-five percent and gross national product hit bottom. Roosevelt's New Deal policies only prolonged the agony. By 1939, ten years after the crash, unemployment still stood above fifteen percent, despite huge and costly federal make-work programs. The government made huge mistakes; they made things much worse than they should've been."

"That's interesting," Dushane said. "That's not something I know much about."

"Well, I suppose we should discuss the reason I called you here, but I'd like to give you a personal tour of the Ranch first."

"Sure, as long as it doesn't involve a motorcycle."

Chambers laughed. "Follow me."

As they walked out, Chambers phoned the driver, who met them in front of the building.

"Please take us out to the airstrip, Jacob," Chambers said.

"Airstrip?" Dushane reacted, unable to mask the apprehension in his voice.

"Yeah, I promised you a personal tour."

After a short drive, they pulled into a hangar next to the airstrip.

"There she is," Chambers said, pointing to the smallest plane in the hangar.

"That thing's tiny," Dushane said.

"That's right, and I can land it almost anywhere—short runways, grass, maybe even the side of a mountain. When we get up, you'll see how maneuverable it is."

Dushane tried not to appear nervous. He hoped Chambers wouldn't try to land the plane on the side of any mountain. "Where did you get it?" he asked.

"It's an experimental—built it myself. Actually, Ernesto and I built it. Hopefully, you'll meet Ernesto soon. He's my business partner. He's still down in the Bay Area taking care of some company business."

Chambers opened the hatch of the plane, revealing two seats, one in front of the other, each covered with soft, dark brown leather. The front seat had all of the instrumentation and controls. The second seat just had a stick.

"Here, put these headphones on so we can communicate while we're up," Chambers said.

Dushane slid the headphones over his ears and crawled into the back seat. Chambers climbed into the front, closed the hatch, and started the engine. The propeller sprang to life, slicing through the cool morning air.

After takeoff, Chambers circled around the perimeter of the Ranch, flying close to the ground when he wanted to show Dushane a particular sight. The Ranch's largest buildings were roughly in the center of the property and included a rec center with an indoor and outdoor pool, six tennis courts, two basketball courts, four racquetball courts, a weight room, an aerobics area, and two full-service locker rooms, each complete with sauna, steam room, and hot tub. Another area, where Chambers ran the summer camps, had four dormitories, a large cafeteria, several classrooms, and a recreation area with several sports fields and a gymnasium.

"Are those hiking trails down there?" Dushane asked.

"Yeah, hiking and running."

"Are you a runner?" Dushane blurted out, without thinking.

"No."

God, I'm an idiot, Dushane cursed himself. *Of course the guy isn't a runner. He's got a limp.* Dushane thought of apologizing, but decided against it. "This is spectacular place," he said finally.

"Yeah, it doesn't get any better than this. Hey, you like roller coasters?"

"Well, I…" The last time Dushane had been on a roller coaster, he had puked all over his seat. "Yeah, sure."

Chambers increased power and the plane ascended rapidly. Then he banked sharply to the right, causing the aircraft to stall and flip over into a spin. The plane rotated downward like a corkscrew while Dushane clutched the edges of his seat and tried to find the horizon. After several revolutions, Chambers slammed the opposite rudder and pulled the plane out of its downward spiral, leveling it off. Dushane focused as hard as he could on keeping his breakfast down.

"You okay, Martin?"

"Uh…yeah. I'm okay."

"Would you like to drive?"

"Drive?"

"Yeah, take the stick; try a few turns."

Dushane figured he probably couldn't crash the plane so he grabbed the control and angled it timidly to the right and then to the left, banking the plane slightly in each direction.

"Here, let me show you a couple more tricks," Chambers said. He pulled the stick back sharply and the plane did a full loop. Dushane lost his bearings in a fog of nauseous vertigo. *Don't get sick. Relax. Don't get sick. Don't get sick.*

"You okay back there?" Chambers asked.

"A little queasy," Dushane replied weakly.

"Sorry about that. Let's head on back." Chambers turned the plane back toward the airstrip.

"Okay, thanks for the tour."

After they landed, they drove back to Chamber's office and sat down across from each other in cushy, brown leather couches. Chambers sprawled out and relaxed his body like a cat. Dushane tried to sit up straight.

"So what do you think so far?" Chambers asked, his voice forceful and direct, in contrast to his relaxed posture.

"I was wondering why you decided to contact me."

"I was impressed with the work you did in Boston. And my friend Ray Lassater vouched for you."

"You know Ray?" Dushane reacted excitedly.

"I know him and I love him. Nobody has a keener sense of justice than Ray Lassater, and of course, he's got that irresistible manic charm."

Dushane nodded vigorously. "You're absolutely right about that."

"What interests me about you, Martin—besides Ray's endorsement—is that you've got first-hand experience with the Catholic Church; you've seen up close how destructive the Church can be to people's lives."

"I don't like to think about that," Dushane replied somberly.

"Well, I've always been interested in the use of religion as an instrument of power to control the minds of the masses, as well its role as an obstacle to social and moral progress. The dark, anti-intellectual side of humanity is an interesting subject, although I still cringe at some of the torture employed against non-believers. It's hard to believe what humans with the wrong ideas are capable of."

"I'm certainly familiar with some of that," Dushane said, leaning forward. "I learned more about the dark history of the Church than I cared to, so I'm sympathetic."

"Excellent! I think you and I are going to get along just fine."

Dushane nodded. "I hope so, but I don't think I understand this nearly as well as you do."

Chambers shrugged. "I've spent countless hours thinking about it, but you have practical experience, and you've studied law; so you know how important the separation of church and state is in a free society. It's critically important that the government provide absolutely no aid to religion—or to anything, for that matter, based on pseudoology."

"Pseudo…what?"

"Theology. I call it pseudo-ology because it's really a thought system based on nothing."

Dushane chuckled. "There's got to be something there."

"Nothing more than whims of the leader, priest, prophet, seer, whatever. Theoretically, theology is an attempt to give some order and definition to the supernatural realm, but the problem is, we're not equipped to say anything about the supernatural realm—even assuming that there is a supernatural realm. If you tell me that there's an omniscient god, but that he's only omniscient on Tuesdays, I can argue that your belief has no basis in reality, but your belief is valid as a matter of theology; it's as valid as anyone else's theology."

"I guess that's true."

"Since theology and faith have no real standards, people can and do justify just about anything. But the worst thing is the moral relativism. Believers profess to follow the moral absolutes in the Bible, but they don't even come close to advocating a true Biblical worldview."

"You mean like arguing for slavery?"

"Yeah. And very few believers openly advocate putting homosexuals to death, or stoning women for adultery, or killing people for working on the Sabbath. Most of the time, believers' views are based on what their preacher tells them or what their neighbors think. That's relative."

Dushane nodded.

"But there is another way—a powerful, certain way."

Dushane leaned forward in anticipation.

"The only thing that isn't relative is personal integrity. All that anyone

280

needs to rely on is their own conscience. Sifting through a bunch of primitive and incomprehensible scripture or the competing claims of theologians is a complete waste of time and only clouds the issues. People know how to behave morally; they just need to trust themselves and do it."

Dushane nodded. "So…what do we do?"

"Practically speaking, we've got to eliminate religion and other forms of superstition from society. We need to replace them with reason. Ignorance and intolerance has no place in a human community."

"Didn't the Russians try that?" Dushane countered.

Chambers laughed. "You have a good sense of humor, Martin. Those godless Communists! Actually, communism in Russia had many of the same characteristics as religion."

"How do you mean?"

"Well, the Communist Party claimed sole possession of the truth and punished dissenting viewpoints, just as the Church has historically done. They started with conclusions first and then worked backwards. For example, the requirement in the Soviet Union that scientists accept Lamarckian genetics was one of their greatest disasters. It had many similarities to the creationist and intelligent design movements here. They tried to hijack science and shoehorn it into totally untenable positions. Of course, this makes no sense because science can't be shoehorned into anything. Proper science is an honest attempt to understand reality—just as it is, not as we wish it were."

"Well, the U.S. isn't that bad, right?"

"The United States is a great country. It's produced tremendous innovation and discovery; that's what makes our backslide into superstition so depressing. What's worse is that our leaders just don't get it. They complain that governments in Islamic societies support madrassahs and other dangerous religious brainwashing that fuels the mindset of terrorists, yet we tolerate some of the same ideas here—humans are insignificant compared to God or Allah; we should sacrifice our lives to God; sacred texts trump conflicting scientific discovery. The hypocrisy is breathtaking."

"Yeah, none of those ideas makes much sense to me now, but I guess I believed them for a long time."

"Of course you did. Most of us did. They're so prevalent in the culture."

Dushane nodded. "Well, I'm curious about Robert Newhall. He's obviously not a big fan of yours."

"No, and I'm worried," Chambers said gravely.

"Why?"

"Well, I'm not so concerned about Newhall. He's definitely

charismatic, but he doesn't really get it. He knows he wants power, but he doesn't really understand everything he needs to do to get it. I'm much more worried about his right-hand man, John Heilbrenner. He's a guy who clearly knows what he's doing."

"How so?"

"He understands mass movements and what compels people to join them. He's run successful ad campaigns and successful political campaigns. Now he's running a successful religious campaign. He clearly understands how to get people motivated."

"How does he recruit people?"

"That's easy. He recognizes that mass movements are built by people with a strong urge to renounce themselves—people with little self-esteem who revel in a leader who assures them that the self is unimportant, and that the only thing that matters is the cause. Since the followers have little self-esteem and hate their own lives, the opportunity to disavow themselves and begin anew is very attractive. If the cause preaches selflessness, the person will never have to confront the self that they loathe so much." Chambers lifted his arm and held it up at a forty-five degree angle. "If I were to draw a graph, you'd see a proportional relationship between a person's passion for self-renunciation and their passion for a mindless cause. You know, Martin, it's hard to want something; to really want something and then persevere until you get it. It's a lot easier to just do nothing than to shoulder that responsibility."

"Well, I see the logic in what you're saying, but it seems like the recruits would be ineffectual and nothing would ever get accomplished."

"You're partially right. These people can be ineffectual when it comes to pursuing their own goals, but if a leader finds a way to channel their energy into a cause, they can be a powerful unified force. And they possess an added advantage."

"What's that?"

"Since they don't value themselves and their lives in the present, they generally don't value much of anything in the present that's unrelated to the cause. They're willing to wreck everything, including their own lives, for some glorious future or afterlife sold to them by the leader. Religious mass movements are the classic case. The leaders almost always deprecate the present because they understand the needs of their followers to renounce themselves and their lives in the present. The other thing to remember is that people who join mass movements renounce their freedom as well. The problem with freedom is that if a person is free to make something out of their lives, then there's also the possibility of failure. A lot of people just don't want to face that. And this all leads to the worse situation of all—people joining mass movements to escape individual responsibility. One of the things we've studied in detail here is the Nazi movement because it's so functionally similar to religious movements. When Nazi murderers were brought to trial for their crimes, they defended themselves by saying that they were just following orders, and psychologically they couldn't understand why this wasn't an acceptable defense. They joined the movement for precisely that reason—so they wouldn't have to take responsibility for their actions or make difficult moral choices."

"Sounds like the Catholic priests we prosecuted. But at least they're losing some of their followers now."

"They're losing membership partly because people see weakness."

"What do you mean?"

"Although no one would ever admit it, some believers care less about the sexual abuse than about the fact that the church has shown weakness."

"Come on."

"I'm serious. People want to be part of a strong community, a community where leaders tell them what to think and what to do. If the community revolves around being blessed by a god, or being the chosen people, that doesn't square with a church on the defensive."

"But I still don't understand how they convince people of their beliefs?"

Chambers shook his head and raised his voice. "Martin. The beliefs, the doctrine; that's almost totally irrelevant. All that matters is that the beliefs are strongly held. That's the key. If you don't believe me, look at the Mormons. They've got it down to a science." Chambers chuckled at his own joke. "They're one of the fastest growing mass movements in the world. They absorb drifting people into their community faster than anyone else and give them a sense of belonging very quickly. They've been heavily criticized because most of their doctrine has no factual evidence behind it, but very few people leave the church for that reason. I mean, think about it, Mormon leaders have made thousands of changes to the original scriptures, which supposedly came from an infallible being. People just don't care about that. They don't want to lose their sense of community and their sense of power. All they have to do is adopt a set of beliefs dictated to them by their leaders. For most people, that's a reasonable trade-off."

Dushane nodded respectfully, impressed with Chambers' knowledge and unmistakable charisma. But he couldn't help staring at Chambers' right hand, which seemed strangely artificial.

"You want to know about my hand?" Chambers asked.

"I'm sorry, I didn't mean to stare."

"It's okay." Chambers lifted up his hand and spread his fingers. "This hand is a marvel of modern science." Chambers got up and walked to his desk. "I need to get a tool and I'll show you. The doctors says I'm not supposed to do this, but what the hell, I think you'll find it interesting."

Chambers fiddled under the desk for a couple of minutes and then put his hand in front of Dushane's face. "Check it out." Chambers moved his fingers slowly back and forth. His thumb was original, but his other four fingers were constructed of thin, robotic metal rods.

"Whoa!" Dushane's head instinctively snapped back. He could hear the faint buzz of electricity moving through the circuits.

"Pretty cool, huh?"

"I've never seen anything like that. I can hear the joints move."

"Yeah. Without the covering, there's nothing to buffer the noise. This is the latest and greatest technology. And these fingers can bend a piece of steel."

"Wow."

Chambers went back to his desk and put the covering back on his hand.

"How did you hurt...I mean, if you don't mind me asking."

Chambers' features hardened.

"I'm sorry, it's none of my business," Dushane backtracked.

"I haven't spoken about it in a long time."

"It's okay, forget I asked."

"No, it's okay. It just that the memory throws me off a little."

CHAPTER 34

Withhold not correction from the child: for if thou beatest him with the rod, he shall not die. Thou shalt beat him with the rod, and shalt deliver his soul from hell.

—BIBLE, PROVERBS 23:13-14

David Chambers, age ten, ran through the farmland behind his house with the abandon of a boy on summer vacation. He didn't slow down during the three-mile jog to his friend Matt Gunderson's house, but stopped suddenly when he got there. He couldn't believe his friend lived in such a dilapidated place. The front porch had collapsed from wood rot, two of the windows were boarded up, and trash littered the yard.

Chambers walked gingerly to the door and knocked. Then he took a step back and waited, but no one answered. When he knocked again louder, several loud barks came from the other side of the door. "Who's that out there?" someone yelled from inside.

"I...I'm David. I'm...I'm a friend of Matt's."

The door swung open, the rusty hinges crackling like dry leaves. In the doorway, Matt's father, Terry Gunderson stood holding a beer can in one hand and the collar of a snarling dog with the other. A cigarette dangled from his lips. The dog growled aggressively while Terry Gunderson swayed from side to side, struggling to keep this balance.

"Quiet Blitz! Quiet! Sit boy! Sit!" Gunderson slapped the dog hard on the underside of its belly. The animal yelped and scampered back into the house.

Chambers took another step back and eyed the disheveled man standing before him. Terry Gunderson had greasy, tangled brown hair and his face was severely creased, ravaged by excessive smoking and drinking. His eyes were dark and piercing, but afraid.

"Matt ain't 'round here just now. Go on down to the barn and tell that boy to get his ass up here." Gunderson took a swig of his beer and then leaned against the doorjamb.

Chambers backed up slowly, repulsed by the smell of Gunderson's breath. It reminded him of armadillo roadkill. Terry Gunderson stared blankly into space and then scowled, revealing a set of crooked, light-brown teeth. Chambers turned away and sprinted towards the barn, thirty yards behind the house.

Chambers had known Matt Gunderson for almost a year and they spent most of their spare time together. They usually played at Chambers' house or at the park, and Chambers wondered why his friend never wanted to play at his own house. Gunderson never talked about his parents and Chambers knew little about his friend, except that he had occasional cuts and bruises in addition to the purple scar that cut across his face. Whenever he asked Gunderson about the injuries, his friend told him to mind his own business.

When Chambers reached the barn, Matt was throwing a ball against the wall.

"What are you doing here?" Matt asked.

"I wanted to see where you lived."

Matt shrugged. "Now you know."

"I met your dad at the house. He doesn't seem…well."

"No, I try to avoid him. I usually stay out here."

"I think he was drunk."

"He's always drunk. All he does is drink and watch TV."

"What about your mom?"

"She stays in the house mostly; takes care of Tommy. She brings me food sometimes when my dad's home."

"He said he was looking for you."

"Ahhh…he's not looking for me; he's just being a dick. Don't listen to anything he says."

The boys threw the ball around awhile until they heard the rattling engine of Terry Gunderson's pickup truck. "My dad's leaving," Matt said. "He probably ran out of beer."

"Can we go inside? It's hot out here."

"All right."

The boys went into the house where all of the shades were drawn and no lights were on.

"Matt…is that you?" a timid voice came from the kitchen.

"Yeah, mom. I'm going to my room."

The kitchen door opened and a small, faded woman wearing a threadbare apron appeared. "Who's your friend?" she said softly, instinctively putting her arms behind her back. Normally, she wore a long sleeved blouse to hide the cigarette burns on her forearms.

"This is David, from school."

"Hi, David." Matt's mother flashed a shaky but sweet smile. "You boys better be quiet. Your father'll be home soon."

"Okay, mom."

Matt had his own small bedroom, which was nondescript except for intricately detailed drawings covering the walls.

Gunderson flopped lazily on the bed while Chambers admired the sketches. "These are cool. Did you draw all of these?"

"Yeah."

"You're a good artist. I didn't know you could draw like this. How come you never showed me any of these?"

"They're not that great. My dad hates them. He says I'm wasting my time."

Chambers shot his friend a puzzled look just as the front door of the house slammed shut. "Maggie! Where the fuck did you put my sunglasses? I can't find my goddamn sunglasses!"

Matt jumped off the bed like a frightened animal.

"Hey, what's wrong?"

"We better get out of here. If my father sees you here; sometimes he gets real drunk and…"

Matt's voice trailed off.

"All right." Chambers moved toward the door, but Matt grabbed his shoulder. "No! Let's go out the window."

"Okay."

Matt opened the window and unhooked the screen. The boys crawled out quickly.

Terry Gunderson spread out on the couch, popped a Budweiser, and turned on the TV. He propped his head up with a pillow and flipped the channel to his favorite sport—auto racing. "Maggie! I'm out of chips! I need…" The phone rang, cutting him off.

"Maggie!"

The phone rang again.

"Maggie! Get the phone!"

The phone rang a third time.

"Goddammit!" Gunderson cursed. He rolled off the couch and picked up the receiver. "Hello."

"Hello, this is Richard Legler. I'm the vice-principal at Travis Elementary School. Is this one of Matt's parents?"

"Yeah, I'm Matt's dad."

"I'm sorry for calling you at home on a Saturday, but it's very important that I speak with you about your son. Do you have a few minutes to talk?"

"He in trouble again?" Gunderson grunted.

"No, no, it's nothing like that. We're just a little concerned. I spoke with your wife yesterday, but she said I needed to speak with you."

"Concerned? What are you talkin' about?"

"Well, it's just that Matt's been coming to school with a lot of bruises lately and it appears to be affecting his school work. His grades have been dropping and he seems a little depressed. I spoke with him briefly about it last week and he told me that he keeps falling off his horse."

"Horse? What the hell are you talking about? We don't got no horse."

"Then…the bruises…oh…oh no…I'm sorry. That's what Matt told us. I…I'm sorry…I…I don't know what to say."

"What the hell do you want?"

"I…I don't know. This puts me…well…in an awkward position."

"Mind your own goddamn business!" Gunderson thundered and slammed the phone down. He disciplined his son frequently, usually with a thick wooden paddle. Normally, it didn't leave cuts, but the rough surface of the paddle sometimes left splinters and painful welts.

Gunderson stormed into the kitchen. "Maggie, what the hell did you tell them over at that school?"

"What? I didn't say anything. I told them to talk to you. That's all." Maggie Gunderson backed up against the sink and held her hands in front of her face.

Terry grabbed her by the shoulders and shook her. "They were talkin' about Matt's bruises; the principal over at that school. He said he spoke to you. What the hell did you tell him? It's none of their goddamn business how I discipline my boy! What the hell did you tell them?"

"Nothing! Nothing! I swear!"

* * *

"Hey Gundy, hit me with the long bomb," Chambers shouted as he sprinted across the expansive field behind Matt Gunderson's house. Matt lunged forward, firing a long pass right into Chambers' hands.

"Touchdown!" Chambers celebrated, spiking the ball and throwing his arms into the air.

"It's not a touchdown unless you get past me," Matt yelled back, sprinting towards him.

Chambers picked the ball up and tried to scamper away, but he wasn't quick enough. Matt bowled him over, knocking his wind out. "That hurt," Chambers protested weakly. "I hate playing football with you."

"You need to learn how to play tough." Matt laughed gently and punched Chambers a couple times in the stomach. Chambers pushed him off and the boys sank into the thick grass, looking up at the cottony layer of clouds and enjoying an early-evening breeze. Chambers ran his fingers through the soft blades and tried to stay perfectly still. He felt at peace until a scream came from the house. "What was that?" he gasped, quickly bolting upright.

"I think it's my dad," Matt responded softly.

"Your dad?"

"Yeah." Matt rolled over onto his side, turning away, while a memory from the previous summer started playing in his mental jukebox.

* * *

Just a few finishing touches and this'll be done, Matt thought as he focused on his sketch of a Siamese cat. He lifted his pencil and started to draw, but his father entered his room unexpectedly, holding a gardening trowel and spilling dirt on the carpet. "You didn't pull them weeds like I told you to."

Matt jumped up and backed into the corner of the room while Terry grabbed the sketch. "What the fuck is this? You little pussy." He crumpled the drawing into a ball and threw it at Matt's face. "You punk!" Terry grabbed Matt's neck and slammed him against the wall. "You better listen next time when I tell you to do somethin.'"

"Let me go!"

Terry threw Matt down and pushed his face into the floor, ripping his lip with his bottom teeth. Matt spit out a mouthful of blood as he screamed. "Get out of my room!"

"You obey me, boy!" Terry flipped him over and pinned his shoulders, pulling his head up by the hair. "You cross me again and you're gonna wish you wasn't ever born. You hear me!"

"I hate you!" Matt yelled through tears.

"Shut up! God damn you! You hear me!"

Matt tried to get up with a desperate burst of energy, but his father held him tight. "Stay still, boy."

"Go to hell!" Matt spit into his father's face.

"You…" Terry raised the trowel and slashed it across Matt's face; the sharp edge of the tool tearing Matt's cheek all the way down to the bone. Terry stormed out of the room while Matt jumped on the bed and pressed his face against the pillow. His mother rushed in and helped him stop the bleeding. After she patched him up, she pleaded with her husband to take him to the hospital, but Terry insisted that the boy needed to be reminded of his place.

* * *

"Matt! Hey Matt! What's wrong with you! We need to do something!" Chambers yelled. "Come on, let's do something!"

Matt didn't move.

A louder scream, then a series of screams came from the house.

"Stay here, this might be a bad one." Matt ran toward the house. Chambers followed closely behind. Terry had his wife pinned against the stove, repeatedly slapping her cheeks with his knuckles. "Are you listenin' to me, you stupid bitch? You better fuckin' listen. I'll fry you on this stove." Matt's three-year-old brother Tommy was standing motionless a few feet away.

"Matt, get out of here!" his mother screamed. "Take Tommy with you! Get out of here! Now!"

Matt hesitated for a split-second and then jumped on his father's back, digging his fingernails into his neck, but he couldn't hold his grip. Terry spun around and threw him face first into the floor, and then booted him in the stomach. Matt crawled away, grabbing Tommy's legs. "Let's go Tommy! Let's go!" Matt pulled Tommy out of the kitchen and carried him to his bedroom. Then he flew out the back door where Chambers stood in shock.

"What's going on?"

"He's hitting my mom again! It's really bad this time! Go get help! Run down to the store and call 911! Hurry!" Chambers sprinted as fast as he could toward the store.

Matt ran out to the barn and rifled through his father's toolbox until he found the hatchet they used to chop logs into kindling.

Chambers called the police from a pay phone and then ran back to the house.

"Ahhhhhh…!" Margaret Gunderson shrieked. "You're burning me! Please! Please!"

"Are you listenin' yet, bitch? I ain't through with you." Terry Gunderson pressed her forearm against the stove, sizzling her scarred flesh like a strip of bacon. Tommy had gotten out of his room and was standing a few feet away. Chambers stood frozen next to him.

Matt slammed through the kitchen door and swung the hatchet into his father's shoulder, knocking him down. Matt swung the hatchet again, aiming for his father's chest, but Terry grabbed his arm and slung him into the refrigerator. Matt lost control of the weapon and it slid across the cracked linoleum of the kitchen floor. Terry grabbed it and lunged toward Matt, planting the hatchet into the back of Matt's head, splattering blood and shards of skull.

"Maaaaaaaatttt!" Margaret Gunderson tried to jump on her husband from behind, but he whipped the hatchet around and buried it into her ribcage.

"Momma!" Tommy Gunderson threw himself on top of his mother's body.

Terry brought the hatchet up above his head and then buried it into Tommy's back, rupturing his kidney. Blood bubbled out of his mouth as he tried to seize a last gasp of air.

Chambers sobbed hysterically as he knelt beside his friend, shaking him. "Matt! Matt! Come on! Matt!"

Terry swung the hatchet at Chambers, slicing the back of his right leg, severing the tendons and cutting into the back of his kneecap. Chambers fell forward like a rag doll. Gunderson swung the hatchet a final time and chopped off all the fingers on Chambers' right hand except for his thumb. Chambers lost consciousness.

Sirens blared as a police car and an ambulance barreled onto the driveway and skidded to a halt. The officers jumped out of the car, pistols drawn, and ran into the house. The paramedics tried to revive Matt and Tommy, but they were both dead. The ambulance rushed the survivors to the hospital.

Doctors were unable to reattach Chambers' fingers so he was left with a thumb and four short stumps on his right hand. His knee injury was so severe that doctors weren't sure if he'd ever walk again. After several months of rehab, he could take steps on his own, but with a pronounced limp. His condition slowly improved, but he couldn't walk for more than a half hour at a time before the pain in his leg became too great.

Terry Gunderson was convicted of first-degree murder and sentenced to life in prison. Chambers' memory of the trial was a blur. The only thing he remembered was Terry Gunderson staring down at him from the defendant's table and his overwhelming desire to see the man dead. He didn't care how. He just wanted him dead.

* * *

"Man, that's an incredible story," Dushane said.

"Yeah, I haven't told it in a long time."

"Is the guy still in prison?"

"Yeah, but he's eligible for parole later this year."

"You're kidding."

Chambers shook his head. "No, but I don't want to talk about this anymore."

Both men were quiet until Dushane said finally, "Can I ask you some more questions about your battle against ignorance?"

"Sure."

"You must be making some enemies."

"I get about three hundred letters a week."

"Wow, do you read them all?"

"No, but I have someone who does; he picks out the good ones. My life's been threatened seventeen times, but nobody's burned me at the stake yet." Chambers grinned. "Here, let me show you."

Chambers opened a file cabinet behind his desk and pulled out a handful of letters. "Here's a sampling."

Dushane picked up the first letter.

> You claim that science is superior to Scripture, but have you ever considered that Satan can make things look true that are really false? Scripture was given to us directly from God so we know it's true. Science is based on humanity, which is full of sin and imperfection. People who rely on science are nothing but agents of Satan. You must repent!! Repent or burn in Hell for eternity!!

Dushane handed Chambers the letter. "Take a look at this one."

"Oh yeah, I remember this one. Believe it or not, it's typical."

Dushane shook his head. "I don't see how you can you eliminate this. There's no...no..." Dushane struggled to find the right word.

"Reason," Chambers finished.

"Yeah, there's no way to talk to a person like this."

"Well, it's not easy. You know, the real problem isn't convincing people that there wasn't any hocus-pocus birth of Jesus; I don't think most people really believe that. The problem is that people have their whole identity wrapped up in these belief systems. The only way to fight this is to change people's core ideas about what it means to be human. We have to give them a life-affirming vision of humanity and stress the sacredness of each person's role. That's why you're here."

"What do you want me to do?"

"For starters, I'd like you to help us with the book. In particular, I want you to draw from your experiences with the Catholic Church."

"This sounds like a major battle."

"It is. The religious machines are raising a lot of money and they continue to seduce new members. They're purchasing politicians at every level."

"Sounds like prostitution."

Chambers laughed. "No kidding; although I can't object too much; I had to buy a few whores myself to get this place off the ground."

"Really?"

"Yeah."

"What's that like?"

"What?"

"Buying…bribing a politician."

Chambers didn't immediately answer.

"I don't mean to put you on the spot," Dushane backtracked.

"No, no, that's actually a good question. It's fairly simple to bribe a politician. Normally, it's just a matter of making soft-money contributions to the war chests of the political parties. There's a limit to the amount of money you can give directly to a politician, but there aren't any limits if you donate to the party. They change the law every now and again, but they always leave loopholes."

Chambers never participated in lobbying efforts like other CEOs and he opposed subsidies and other corporate welfare on principle. It made no sense to impose high taxes on companies and then force them to hire lobbyists to get some of their money back. Chambers' favorite description of the government was "a collection of warring tribes that has come together in anticipation of common plunder." Ernesto just called them "ladrones," thieves, in Spanish. Unfortunately, government regulation had become so burdensome that paying somebody off was sometimes the only way to get things done.

Chambers gave frequently to both the major political parties, but he had unique dealings with party officials. Whenever he made a donation, he explained what he wanted and then asked the recipient to acknowledge his bribe. Chambers' payments weren't bribes in the legal sense because they weren't any different than donations made by hundred of companies every day, but he demanded a tacit admission that his contribution and a bribe were functionally indistinguishable.

"Now, buying off bureaucrats is a little more difficult," Chambers went on. "And frankly, not as legal or socially acceptable. You can't bribe them directly like politicians. You have to get creative and that's all I want to say about that." Chambers flashed a Cheshire cat smile.

"You don't feel guilty?"

"Well, in the beginning it felt strange, like it was wrong, but that feeling didn't last long. It's really more of an obligation."

"Obligation?"

"Buying off a government official is just increasing the dose of poison. The host is already sick; you just kill it faster. I don't think there's anything worse than watching some impostor pretend he has integrity. There's certainly no sight more pathetic."

Dushane chuckled. "They can't all be like that."

"Have you ever heard the definition of an honest politician?"

Dushane shook his head.

"Will Rogers said that an honest politician is one who stays bought. You shouldn't be surprised, Martin. Most people have a price for their integrity and it's usually cheap." Chambers looked at his watch and stood up. "You'll have to excuse me, I've got a meeting I need to attend. Why don't you talk to my assistant Peggy; she'll direct you to your new office."

"But…" Dushane started.

"Oh, I know, you haven't agreed to join us yet; talk to Peggy anyway. She can show you around." Chambers paused. "Say, on second thought, why don't you sit in on the meeting? It's our weekly Board meeting. You'll get a better idea of what we're trying to do here."

"All right, sure."

*　*　*

Chambers stood at the head of the long oak table and put his hand on Dushane's shoulder. "Before we begin our business today, I'd like to introduce Martin Dushane. I think everyone here is familiar with Martin's work at the DA's office in Boston."

"Hear! Hear!" the men and women at the table united in cheers and rose in a standing ovation.

Dushane's face lit up and chills ran down his spine. "Wow, I…I…didn't expect…thanks for your kindness. I don't feel like I've done anything special, but thank you."

"Martin, you've helped our cause immeasurably; you and Ray Lassater. Your efforts brought facts to light about the Catholic Church that will have a positive impact for decades. We now have a real opportunity to break the inheritance of religion by the current generation of children in this country. As long as they are consistently told the truth, we have great hope. The powers in the church will have a much more difficult time recruiting and indoctrinating new people."

"Well, thanks again for your appreciation."

During the course of the meeting, Dushane discovered that the Ranch was divided into four main departments: Policy and Curriculum, Charitable Programs, Facilities, and Special Events. Cliff Thornton, the director of Policy and Curriculum, led the policy think tank. He set the direction of the Ranch's scholarship and recruited the appropriate faculty.

Mary Seaver, director of Charitable Programs, coordinated all of the Ranch's charitable activities. This included children's programs, which revolved around the summer camps. The primary goal of the camps was to reinforce personal responsibility and integrity through activities such as starting and running a small business, playing team sports, and participating in projects requiring cooperation and leadership.

The Ranch also offered science and technology camps, which introduced children to the scientific method and critical thinking skills. Chambers personally designed simple science projects and others activities such as nature walks that encouraged young people to appreciate the beauty of the world around them and the virtue of seeking to understand it. Seaver also oversaw educational outreach programs in cities on the West Coast. These programs provided tutoring and mentoring to students living in at-risk neighborhoods.

The Kaleidoscope Foundation funded the Ranch's charitable arm with an initial grant of fifty million dollars, but the endowment quickly became much larger. The Foundation received additional funding of another seventy million dollars from private donors who supported the Ranch's philanthropic mission.

After the meeting, Dushane chatted with Board members, who spoke enthusiastically about their work. Dushane found the excitement contagious.

"I accept your offer to join Kaleidoscope Ranch," Dushane said as he walked with Chambers back to his office.

"Thanks, Martin." Chambers put his arm gently around Dushane's back and squeezed his shoulder. "Here, let me give you your first piece of equipment." Chambers pulled a cell phone out of his pocket.

"Oh, that's okay, I've already got a cell phone," Dushane said.

"Not like this one. I want you to use this whenever you call me. No exceptions."

"Okay."

Chambers had built his own cell tower and he provided his closest employees with special phones. The phones came equipped with encryption technology and operated on a unique frequency, only recognized by other phones using the same tower. It was impossible for anyone to eavesdrop on a conversation.

"You can't call anyone outside the Ranch on this phone, but anytime you call me or anyone else here, I want you to use it."

Dushane nodded and couldn't help grinning from ear to ear. "Thanks, David."

CHAPTER 35

Q: How old is the earth?

A: You know, I was watching a television program recently and some scientist was going on and on about how this or that fossil was a billion years old, and I had to laugh. These scientists; they spend all their time trying to prove things with their machines and their data and their sophisticated techniques, but there's no point to it. We have an infallible record of creation right here in the Bible, and it tells us that this is a young earth indeed.

—QUESTION AND ANSWER SESSION FROM
THE INFINITY BIBLICAL STUDIES COURSE

"There's too much powder on my nose," the President complained to his personal grooming assistant. "I don't want to look like a..." The President's voice trailed off. He had watched a Charles Bronson movie in the Oval Office the night before and kept thinking of Bronson's rugged good looks and tough-guy persona.

"All right, hold still Mr. President." The woman wiped a tissue across the President's nose, removing the excess makeup.

The President admired himself in the mirror. "Thank you, dear. That's much better." He got up and walked backstage, waiting for his introduction.

"Ladies and gentlemen, the President of the United States."

The President adjusted his tie and strode confidently to the podium. He nodded and waved to a few people in the audience. "Good afternoon everyone and welcome. I'd like to announce an important appointment today. I'm pleased to introduce Douglas Cartwright as my choice to lead the new Office of Homeland Protection." The President paused and scanned the audience. There were fewer reporters than usual; most Washington insiders viewed the Office of Homeland Protection as a mostly empty political gesture designed to appease the most hardcore of the Administration's Christian constituency. Few believed that anyone in the Administration would actually start harassing other religious groups.

"This position will report directly to the Attorney General and is extremely important as we fight terrorist organizations within our own borders; organizations that threaten our way of life. Douglas Cartwright is a man who represents the highest ideals of our nation and I'm confident that he'll serve with honor and distinction. Doug, can you come up and join me on the podium?"

Cartwright walked up to the podium and shook the President's hand. He was a gregarious fellow Southerner, who had previously worked as an adviser after the President's election to the Alabama governorship. Like the President, Cartwright was short and stocky and he spoke with a slow Southern twang. He also craved attention, often being photographed at social events wearing a large cowboy hat that rivaled the size of his ego.

Cartwright was considered handsome by most, and as a young man, he had earned a well-deserved reputation as a playboy, often seen in the company of young women attracted to his power and multi-million dollar net worth. Although he had achieved little success in his career and had admitted to being an alcoholic, he claimed at age forty that he had been "born-again."

Despite Cartwright's transformation, he was still a risky appointment, not only because of his previous history, but because he wasn't particularly bright. Unfortunately, the President figured he didn't have much choice because he had a political favor to pay back. Cartwright's father owned a successful oilfield services company and was a huge contributor to the President's cause. Luckily for the President, Cartwright appeared to be moving in the right direction. He was now almost fifty and had married another born-again a few years earlier.

"Thank you, Mr. President," Cartwright began. "I'm grateful for this opportunity and you can be sure that I'll serve to the best of my ability. We face a great challenge in keeping dangerous organizations in check and I'll do everything possible to preserve our American way of life."

* * *

Soft rays of sunshine crept through the open window of Dushane's bedroom, slowly illuminating the framed Picasso reproduction hanging above his bed. The room was silent except for the low hum of a generator that powered the Kaleidoscope Ranch housing complex. The living area spanned fifty acres and consisted of one hundred cottages, ranging in size from one to four bedrooms.

Dushane yawned and stretched his arms above his head. It was early Sunday morning, his first weekend at the Ranch. He got up and sauntered over to the window and looked out across the valley, which glowed under a blanket of sunlight. Dushane had been at the Ranch for less than a week and he hadn't done much other than familiarize himself with the campus and read a few of the Ranch's publications. Chambers had told him to ease into the job and enjoy himself, and Dushane was following orders. He had taken several hikes in the surrounding wilderness and played basketball at the rec center during the day. In the evenings, he had watched a few movies at the media center, which also included a large library.

Dushane rested comfortably on the bed, pondering whether to sleep for another half hour. Then the phone rang. He rolled over and picked it up.

"Hello."

"Hi Martin, did I wake you?"

"David! No, I just got up." Dushane sat up and tried to gather his mental faculties.

"Good. I'd like to meet tomorrow morning to discuss the book project. Can you meet me here at nine?"

"Sure."

"What are you up to today?"

"No plans. I might go over to the media center later."

"If you do, check out Infinity TV; Sunday's always the best day. It'll give you an idea of what we're up against. And make sure you watch the Southern version."

"The Southern version?"

"Yeah. Infinity usually runs three different programming schedules depending on the demographics of its audience. One covers the South; another covers the Northeast and the West Coast; and the third covers everything else in between. The Southern version is by far the most entertaining."

Infinity generally pushed fundamentalist, anti-science views in its programming in the South, although it toned down its message in urban areas such as Atlanta where believers were typically more educated. John Heilbrenner personally oversaw Infinity's programming strategy and he employed a team of demographic analysts whose job was to determine what types of beliefs to advance and the most effective ways to elicit donations. Heilbrenner's analysts also assessed a demographic groups' susceptibility to messages of hate and intolerance. This was important because if the group was open to hate, Infinity would aggressively vilify other groups in order to stoke unconscious fears and resentments. This strategy, properly employed, was by the far most effective for fundraising.

"All right. I'll check it out," Dushane said.

"See you tomorrow, Martin."

"Bye, David."

Dushane swung his legs off the side of the bed and stood up. He yawned as he walked to the closet and pulled out a t-shirt and a pair of jeans. He dressed quickly and then grabbed a banana from the kitchen before heading over to the media center. The center contained a large-screen movie theater as well as ten televisions in private viewing rooms. As Dushane went into one of the rooms and turned the channel to Infinity TV, he still wasn't entirely sure why Chambers disliked Infinity so fervently.

Dushane sat down on a couch as the closing credits from a program scrolled down the screen. A few seconds later, a new program started. It was set inside an elaborately adorned church, with music playing triumphantly in the background.

Joy to the world
The Lord has come
Let earth receive her King
Let every heart prepare Him room
And heaven and nature sing
And heaven and nature sing
And heaven and heaven and nature sing

As the music slowly faded, an unseen narrator announced enthusiastically: "The Infinity Christian Network proudly presents the ultimate Biblical home study course, available for the first time to the general public through this exciting offer." The camera panned to a clean cut, forty-something man neatly outfitted in a conservative navy suit and light-blue tie. The man stood behind an altar with a large choir box behind him. He placed his right hand delicately on top of a Bible.

"Hello friends and welcome," the man drawled in an affected folksy pitch. "My name is Devin Miller and I'm a Senior Evangelist here at the Infinity Christian Network. I'm overjoyed to be here with you today and it's my sincerest pleasure to present one of the greatest opportunities ever offered by the Infinity Network—the Infinity Biblical Studies Course."

Miller paused, stepped down from the altar, and positioned himself in front of a window of exquisitely detailed stained glass. "Our spiritual leader, Reverend Robert Newhall, developed this course with one goal in mind—to provide you with the only authority you'll ever need to understand the Holy Scriptures. That's right. Reverend Newhall personally created this course and it contains the same materials he uses to train evangelists in the Network. Now, for a limited time, we're offering it to the public in an easy-to-use, step-by-step home study course. From Genesis to Revelation, this program has everything you need to know about the Bible. But that's not the best part. The course also prepares you to become Infinity-certified. That's right. After completing the course and passing a short certification exam, you'll be recognized as a certified Infinity evangelist with all the rights and privileges that Infinity evangelists like myself enjoy."

Miller picked up a framed certificate and the camera zoomed in.

Infinity Christian Network Evangelist

The following individual has successfully completed the Infinity Biblical Studies Course and is hereby entitled to be addressed as "Infinity Evangelist," with all of the associated rights and privileges thereto, including the right to evangelize and spread the glory of the gospel on behalf of the Infinity Christian Network.

In the name of the Father, the Son, and the Holy Spirit,

Reverend Robert Newhall

"Imagine how you'll feel when you complete the course and are recognized as an Infinity-certified Biblical expert. Think of the advantages you'll have when you testify at your church or speak with your friends. People will look to you for wisdom and leadership. But that's not all. Course instructors also answer all of your questions about God's law on issues such as abortion, homosexuality, and the role of women. After taking the course, your views on these subjects will be completely compatible with scripture. Think about it. We've done the work for you. You can eliminate those nagging doubts once and for all and fully understand God's plan for salvation. And don't forget the most important benefit. You can share this essential knowledge with your children. There is certainly no greater gift for a young mind."

Dushane grimaced. He thought of turning the program off. He couldn't describe exactly what he felt, but it reminded him of seeing maggots wriggling at the bottom of a trash can.

Miller picked up a brightly colored box. "The program includes six DVDs and a ninety-two page study guide that highlights the most important points, including unique insights from Reverend Newhall himself. And if you order right now, we'll also include a limited edition photograph of Reverend Newhall and the President of the United States conferring in the Oval Office of the White House. At this historic meeting, Reverend Newhall and the President pledged to return the nation to its moral foundation. There's no doubt that this event will be remembered for generations to come as the beginning of a moral reawakening in the nation. Think about it. We all owe our freedom to the courage of Reverend Newhall and the President. And here's the best part. Reverend Newhall has personally autographed this photo and it's ready for you to display proudly at your home or office."

Dushane couldn't believe what he was hearing.

The infomercial shifted suddenly to a sample video from the course; Miller was standing in front of a large whiteboard, giving a lecture to a room full of Infinity evangelists.

"The world of Genesis was very different than the world we live in today. People lived to be nine hundred years old because there was a vapor canopy that enveloped the Earth and kept people from developing cancer. It was a world in which dinosaurs could have survived and people could have grown to an enormous size. Yet that all changed with the flood."

Before Dushane could fully digest what he was hearing, the program shifted to another sample video clip. "The course also includes critical information about Biblical prophecy, explained by some of the nation's most distinguished scholars." The camera zoomed in on an Infinity evangelist dressed up to resemble a university professor, complete with a tweed jacket, beard, and a pair of bifocals perched on his nose. "The return of Christ and the establishment of his kingdom on earth is approaching quickly as Biblical prophecy continues to be fulfilled at a breathtaking rate," the man declared earnestly. "We are rapidly approaching the End Times, which will culminate in the climactic battle of Armageddon." The man held up a Bible and shook it as if he were rattling a saber. "On the day of Judgment, will you be saved or left behind?"

The video clip ended and Newhall came on, sitting behind his desk at Infinity Headquarters. "Hello friends. I'm so excited to be with you today and to have this wonderful opportunity to offer you this life-changing program. I designed it myself and it contains the finest Infinity materials ever offered to the public. I urge you to act now. With four easy payments of only $69.95, you can own the ultimate Biblical studies program and the only opportunity to become Infinity certified. This is truly a once-in-a-lifetime opportunity. Here's how it works. All you have to do is watch the six DVDs and follow along with the study guide. Proceed at your own pace. Course instructors will guide you every step of the way and we provide a toll-free number if you have any questions. Then, simply complete the certification exam and send it back to us. The exam comes with an answer key to eliminate any difficulties whatsoever, so your success is guaranteed. Upon completion of the course, I will personally send you a diploma with my signature certifying you as an Infinity Evangelist. This will attest that you have the unwavering faith and the profound knowledge necessary to spread the gospel—just like the trained evangelists we have here.

"I sincerely hope that I'll have the opportunity to welcome you into the Infinity family." Newhall paused and held out his hands in invitation. "I'm telling you from the heart, if you're going to do just one thing this year, take advantage of this special offer. We've made this program simple enough so that anyone can complete it regardless of their background. It's been designed for people just like you. Isn't it time you served Christ to the best of your ability?"

After a short pause, Newhall's countenance stiffened and his voice became grave and low. "And don't forget the most important reason of all to order this course right now. We are all sinners. We've all broken God's commandments. Our Lord Jesus Christ made the ultimate sacrifice for us, dying on the cross for our sins. Have you done everything in your power to live up to the example set by Christ? Take a moment right now and acknowledge your sinfulness and need for a Savior." Newhall bowed his head earnestly. "I'll pray for you, and I want you to remember that it's not too late; it's never too late to accept Christ into your heart. Please call now and I'll help you achieve salvation with this indispensable program."

Dushane didn't often experience violent urges, but he felt a powerful desire to kick Newhall's face in.

Miller returned to the screen. "Our goal here at Infinity is to spread the word of God and the joy of the gospel to as many people as possible. For the first fifty thousand courses ordered, we're making a special discount offer—just four payments of $49.95. That's a savings of eighty dollars. And remember that the program includes the limited edition, signed photograph of Reverend Newhall at the historic White House meeting with the President. And if you order within the next half hour, we'll also include the Infinity Gospel Music CD. This two-CD collection includes our most cherished faith-inspiring songs. It's the perfect music to share with your family and friends as you worship together.

"Think about it. This is an opportunity to go to Bible College for a fraction of the cost. Just four easy payments. All credit cards accepted. Operators are standing by. Call now!" A toll-free number lit up the screen and then the show ended with the image of a gold cross of light, superimposed over a choir of young children.

> *At the sign of triumph Satan's host doth flee;*
> *On then, Christian soldiers, on to victory!*
> *Hell's foundations quiver at the shout of praise;*
> *Sisters lift your voices, loud your anthems raise.*
>
> *Onward, Christian soldiers, marching as to war,*
> *With the cross of Jesus going on before.*
>
> *Like a mighty army moves the church of God;*
> *Sisters, we are treading where the saints have trod.*
> *We are not divided, all one body we,*
> *One in hope and doctrine, one in charity.*
>
> *Onward, Christian soldiers, marching as to war,*
> *With the cross of Jesus going on before.*
>
> *What the saints established that I hold for true.*
> *What the saints believèd, that I believe too.*
> *Long as earth endureth, we the faith will hold,*
> *Kingdoms, nations, empires, in destruction rolled.*
>
> *Onward, Christian soldiers, marching as to war,*
> *With the cross of Jesus going on before.*

Dushane slumped into the fluffy cushions of the couch. He was thoroughly confused by what he had just seen, but he finally understood why Chambers found Infinity so offensive.

* * *

"Doug, Josephine Holladay's here to see you," Cartwright's secretary announced over the intercom.

"Thank ya, darlin.' Tell her I'll be there shortly."

When Josephine heard about the government's new focus on religious cults, she immediately expressed interest in the position of lead attorney in Cartwright's office. Although she loved the Utah Enlightenment Project and was reluctant to leave, she had hired employees to continue its work without her, so people still had a place to turn if they wanted to learn the truth about the Church's claims.

Cartwright didn't know much about Josephine except that she had done some work critical of the Mormons. That impressed him because, in his opinion, the Mormons behaved like a cult with their secret rituals and unorthodox beliefs. Like many Evangelicals, he didn't think the Mormons were even real Christians, particularly since they believed in false prophets. More importantly, the Mormons simply rubbed him the wrong way. He was sick and tired of their constant refrain that they were the only "true" Christian church.

Cartwright pulled Josephine's file out of his desk drawer and then shuffled out to the lobby. "Hello, Ms. Holladay. I'm awfully pleased to make your acquaintance. Heard a lot a good things about ya." Cartwright extended his hand.

"Nice to meet you," Josephine said as she shook Cartwright's hand politely.

Cartwright held Josephine's hand a second longer than he should have and gave her body a quick once-over. Josephine was wearing a conservative business suit, but her skirt was tailored short, highlighting her long, muscular legs. *Good lord, this woman is gorgeous. Her legs are perfect.* Cartwright smiled. "Let's go back to my office and chat awhile."

Josephine followed Cartwright down the hall to his spacious corner office. She glanced briefly at the walls, which were covered with pictures of Cartwright posing with various VIPs—the President, the Attorney General, several members of Congress, and Robert Newhall and John Heilbrenner. Behind his desk, a large set of deer antlers and a pair of longhorns hung on the wall.

Cartwright motioned to a chair. "Have a seat. Can I git ya somethin' to drink?"

"No, thanks."

Cartwright sat down and stared across his desk at Josephine. He felt the beginning of an erection slowly pushing against the fabric of his boxer shorts. He put his hand under the desk and adjusted his penis with a quick flick of his wrist. Then he returned his attention to the beautiful woman sitting before him. He couldn't take his eyes off her soft, full lips. He sat silently for several moments and imagined bending her over his desk, ripping her skirt off and ramming her from behind, pounding and pounding…

"That's quite a set of antlers," Josephine said, breaking the silence. "Did you kill him?"

"Ahh…well…actually it's a her, and I did."

"You're lucky she didn't have a gun."

"What's that?"

"Nothing. Just admiring your office."

Bitch has an attitude. I like that. "Well, I have to tell ya first off that yer background is impressive."

"Thank you."

"We did a background check; that's standard procedure a' course." Cartwright opened a manila folder on his desk and flipped through it. "It says here you have an IQ over 180."

"183."

"I don't think I've ever met anyone so intelligent."

"It's funny the people who are impressed by that."

What the hell does she mean by that? Cartwright wondered. "Well... lucky in any case."

"Lucky?"

"Yeah, to be blessed as you have."

Josephine shrugged. "I suppose it depends on how you look at it. I find it a bit like solitary confinement."

Cartwright furrowed his brow. *What the...this chick is whacked, but damn sexy.* "Why don't ya start by tellin' me about your interest in the job."

"I'm concerned about religious cults, as you are."

Cartwright nodded. "Yeah, a' course. Well, I suspect that ties in with yer history with those Mormons."

"You might say that."

"They're an odd bunch, aren't they?" Cartwright threw his head back and guffawed, but stopped suddenly when he realized that Josephine didn't share his amusement. "A' course, you understand I don't have nothin' against 'em. And we gotta respect 'em here. They're entitled to their point a' view."

"Of course."

"Well, I have to ask ya about that."

"My history with the Mormons?"

"Yeah, yer antagonistic relationship."

Josephine shrugged. "I have no opinions or feelings toward the Mormons except that many of them are nice, well-meaning people. That chapter in my life is closed."

Cartwright smiled amiably. "That's good cuz there're some members up on the Hill; ya know, the President doesn't wanna antagonize."

"I understand."

"Now, under federal law, I'm not allowed to ask ya about yer religious beliefs, but a..." Cartwright paused expectantly.

"Then I suppose we better not discuss that," Josephine interjected politely.

"Well…I s'pose not." Cartwright frowned. *Shit, this ain't gonna fly.* He didn't think he could get away with hiring someone who wasn't a believer.

Josephine slowly uncrossed her legs and leaned forward. "Of course, I'll believe whatever's required by this office and I expect we'll have a close working relationship," she said, a hint of invitation in her voice.

Cartwright brightened. *That'll work! This woman wants me just like all the others.* "I think that'll do just fine," he said cheerfully. "When can you start?"

"Immediately."

CHAPTER 36

A cult is a religion with no political power.

—Tom Wolfe

Danny Dimarco's well-trained fingers danced across the keyboard as he rapidly entered commands into the computer terminal. He took a quick break and adjusted the volume on his headphones. Another technician offsite was feeding him instructions that helped him analyze the response of Infinity's computers to his probing. Dimarco worked at Infinity as a computer technician, although he had no loyalty to anyone at the religious empire. He answered only to Leo Salvatore.

Before Dimarco had started working at Infinity, he and other technicians from Salvatore's team had tried to hack into Infinity's computers from the outside, but they hadn't succeeded. Fortunately, they had finally been able to plant Dimarco inside, and he had been working for several weeks analyzing potential vulnerabilities in Infinity's network.

Salvatore's operation included an extensive computer lab that his technicians used to simulate hacks against his business clients. Based on information that Dimarco had gathered, Salvatore's technicians had set up a similar mock system of Infinity's computer structure. Then they tried several different strategies to penetrate it. The work was painstaking because they could only use hacking techniques that wouldn't be detected.

"Scan the ports again, Danny," the offsite technician directed. "I need those subnet readings again."

"Okay." Dimarco began executing the keystrokes and then suddenly had an idea. "Hold on a sec, Charlie, I may have something." Dimarco typed as quickly as his fingers would move and he could barely stay seated, he was so excited. A shot of adrenaline surged through his veins as he realized he was getting close. He hit the Return key and waited. Within a few seconds, his monitor displayed the top-level directory structure of Infinity's central server. "Bingo!" he exclaimed.

"You got it?"

"Yessiree—the most beautiful thing I've ever seen!" Dimarco had obtained the highest possible access to Infinity's system. He now had the ability to manipulate any files on Infinity's network.

"What do you think we can get, Danny?"

"Well, I hate to be greedy," Dimarco chuckled. "Actually, I love being greedy. I'm going after everything—every drive on this network. Give me a minute and then we'll start the download sequence. Hang on."

* * *

"How'd ya like yer first day on the job?" Cartwright asked as he plopped himself down in front of Josephine's desk. He'd been thinking about her all day, fantasizing about what she'd be like in bed.

"Fine."

"Well, whaddya say we go out fer a drink to celebrate? I know a nice quiet place where we can be alone."

"Aren't you married?"

"Yeah…" Cartwright drawled matter-of-factly. "Been married now almost three years."

"Don't you think your wife would object?"

Cartwright leaned closer and lowered his voice as if he was talking to a willing co-conspirator. "We don't need to tell my wife, Josie. It'll just be our little secret."

Josephine pushed her chair back and burst out laughing.

Cartwright frowned. "What?"

"I'm…I'm sorry…I'm sorry," Josephine stammered over her laughter. "I'm just…I'm just not interested." Josephine couldn't help but laugh at the pathetic display, but at the same time she felt like ripping Cartwright's balls out for his casual attitude about cheating. She wondered vaguely what type of woman would marry a guy like Cartwright.

"I thought ya…I mean, I got the impression…"

"No, Doug."

Cartwright fidgeted nervously. "Well…I…"

"I'll see you at the staff meeting tomorrow morning. Good night."

Cartwright dropped his head and quickly escaped.

* * *

Heilbrenner wrapped a towel around his naked body and walked into the steam room after a short session on the treadmill. Newhall followed closely behind. Infinity Headquarters was equipped with two recreational facilities, one open to all Infinity staff, and one with access limited to Newhall, Heilbrenner, and the twenty most senior Infinity leaders. The private facility included a weight room, a basketball court, racquetball and squash courts, and a full-service locker room staffed around the clock.

Heilbrenner sat down on the warm tile and leaned back against the wall. He tilted his head up and took several deep breaths. Newhall sat across from him and watched the pectoral muscles in Heilbrenner's chest ripple with each breath. After a few moments, Heilbrenner looked up and made eye contact; Newhall quickly looked away.

"It's time to stop praising the President," Heilbrenner said.

Newhall frowned. "What are you talking about?" He had been regularly extolling the President for his support of morality, fight against Islam, and the faith-based initiative.

"It's time to move the operation to the next phase. We need to take this to the next level."

Newhall chuckled. "Come on. We've got more money than we

can spend. Besides, what does that have to do with supporting the President?"

"I'm not talking about money."

Newhall raised his eyebrows.

"I'm talking about power."

"Power? We've got power. We've got the ear of the Administration on any issue we want to push."

"I don't want the ear. I want the Presidency."

"The Presidency?"

"All the pieces are in place."

"What are you suggesting?"

"First, we start criticizing the Administration; then we challenge the President for the Republican nomination."

Newhall didn't speak, but his eyes widened.

"We need to do it now, Robert. This is our moment."

Newhall watched the tiny beads of sweat trickle from Heilbrenner's shoulders down to his biceps. He took a deep breath and let the familiar intoxication of power wash over him. "Okay, let's do it."

* * *

"Josephine, Mr. Cartwright asked me to deliver this." Cartwright's secretary dropped a memorandum on her desk.

"Thank you." Despite the uncomfortable episode on her first day, Josephine had an amiable and productive working relationship with her boss. He had assigned her the task of making sure the office's intelligence gathering, which included extensive surveillance of groups deemed to be potentially dangerous, was within the bounds of the law. Josephine quickly scanned the memo, which contained a short list of religious cults and cult beliefs. Cartwright had previously created a task force whose job was to define the list so that everyone in the office could properly focus their efforts. The list contained two components: specific religious groups that were deemed unacceptable and beliefs that were potentially dangerous.

Groups

Wicca, Witchcraft, Paganism, or any other earth or nature-based religion

Satanism, or any religion based on the occult

Native American Church, or any religious group that believes in taking peyote or other dangerous substances as part of its worship

Any UFO or alien-based religion

Aum Shinrikyo, or any religion based on radical Buddhism or Hinduism

Islamic Jihad, Hamas, Hezbollah, or any other Islamic group with un-American values

Cult Beliefs

Belief in false prophets, false gods, or idols

Belief in witchcraft, the occult, or the supernatural

Belief in anyone who claims to be a living prophet*

*This provision shall not be construed to include the Pope who claims infallibility when he speaks ex cathedra as Supreme Pastor, and is explaining a doctrine of faith or morals. The Pope is not technically acting as a "prophet" in this case. This provision shall also not be construed to include belief in Biblical scholars who interpret existing prophecies. These scholars do not claim to be independently prophetic, but are merely analyzing the prophecies of previously accepted prophets.

Josephine chuckled at the exception for the Pope. Then she realized that there was no exception for the Mormon Prophet, Seer, and Revelator. Cartwright had specifically decided not to except him. The other exception for Biblical scholars was designed to protect a growing number of Christian authors who were making a small fortune selling books that interpreted Biblical passages and predicted the coming apocalypse.

Josephine went back and reviewed the list of cults; there were no Christian denominations listed. She wasn't very familiar with UFO religions so she did a quick search and stumbled upon the Raelian website.

On the 13th of December 1973, French journalist Rael was contacted by a visitor from another planet, and asked to establish an Embassy to welcome these people back to Earth.

The extra-terrestrial was about three feet in height, had long dark hair, almond shaped eyes, and olive skin. He told Rael that: "We were the ones who made all life on earth. You mistook us for gods and we were at the origin of your main religions. Now that you are mature enough to understand this, we would like to enter official contact through an embassy."

Following the extra-terrestrial's instructions, Rael established the Raelian Movement, an international organization to bring together anyone who wishes to help.

Josephine clicked to the photo section, which displayed "His Holiness" Rael in various poses. She laughed when she saw Rael dressed in an all-white outfit, which looked like a combination of the Pope's garish robe and a space suit. *I guess I shouldn't be so surprised*, Josephine thought. *Followers expected "divine" men to have a certain sense of fashion. If the Pope wore jeans and a t-shirt instead of a ridiculous, medieval costume, would anybody listen?*

Josephine closed the website and sighed gently. She tried to decide whether Raelian beliefs were any worse than the virgin birth, the bodily resurrection, or the parting of the Red Sea. The key, she thought, to the "truth" of religion was the age of the particular belief system. Biblical myths had the advantage of over two thousand years and a primitive historical record, making them much harder to disprove. Josephine knew from her experience that age also hurt the Mormons—their dogma was newer and easier to prove factually inaccurate.

Josephine turned off her computer and lay back in her chair. Although she hadn't thought much about Chambers over the past several weeks, his presence suddenly penetrated her psyche. She indulged herself for a few minutes by daydreaming about him and savoring the memory of their last encounter. Then she noticed that she had picked up the phone involuntarily. She slammed it back down.

CHAPTER 37

Religion does not really support morality,
it is people's moral intuitions that make religion plausible.

— PASCAL BOYER, *RELIGION EXPLAINED*

Al Rogers reviewed Cartwright's list of religious cults and didn't like what he saw. He picked up the phone and quickly dialed.

"Hello."

"Doug, it's Al Rogers."

"Mornin' Al. What can I do for ya?"

"I just reviewed your cult list; I'm concerned."

"Yeah?"

"I don't understand why Kaleidoscope Ranch isn't on the list." Heilbrenner had been breathing down Rogers' neck to do something about Chambers, but Rogers was wary of moving against him directly. He hoped that Cartwright could apply some pressure and then he could take the credit.

"Are you talkin' about David Chambers' outfit in Northern California?"

"Yes."

"They're a strange bunch all right, but they're not a religious group, right?"

"They're a danger. They have dangerous beliefs."

"Well…I…uh…I'm not sure if…"

"Listen to me, Doug. It's important to the President that we root out all dangerous beliefs. It's one of the President's top priorities."

"Well, we're dealing with religious cults over here and…"

"They are a cult!" Rogers snapped.

"I'm not sure what you mean by that, Al."

"They're an atheist cult."

"An atheist cult?" Cartwright had never heard of such a thing.

"Yeah, a radical atheist cult. They reject God. They reject the Ten Commandments and the moral foundation of this country."

"Yeah, I suppose that's true."

"Of course it's true."

"You really think they're a danger?"

"Absolutely. There's no question about it."

"All right then; consider it done."

* * *

In the quiet solitude of his office, Chambers attacked his work; his mind firing on all cylinders. The focused blast of neural activity came together in sublime harmony, but the room was silent except for the ticking of a small desk clock and the slash of Chambers' pen redlining the first draft of *Church of the Mind*. Chambers flipped through the pages quickly, the prose shimmering under a jet stream of light that fell softly from a table lamp.

Throughout history, humans have attempted to explain the world and determine the purpose and meaning of life. Prior to the Enlightenment, which roughly marks the beginning in the West of the reliance on science and reason to explain the world, humans relied on superstition and mythology. This was generally unorganized until the rise of civilization in Europe where it began to formalize, largely in the doctrines of the Catholic Church.

Churches have had a pervasive influence throughout recorded human history; however, the Enlightenment's advancement of science and rational thought threatened the ecclesiastical hegemony, and secular intellectuals and institutions gained footing. This burgeoning threat to religion came in two primary forms: first, Enlightenment thought systems were based on reason, which stood in direct epistemological opposition to thought systems based on superstition; second, Enlightenment thinkers introduced political ideas based on individual rights, including the right of people to govern themselves through democracy. Church leaders bitterly opposed these ideas because they recognized the threat to their status and privilege.

Science and reason have had a profound effect on improving the material conditions of human life and this clearly distinguishes modern civilizations from primitive societies based on superstition. Despite this progress, rational thought has generally been considered inapplicable to questions of morality or the meaning of life. These questions are still largely considered within the domain of religion.

Church leaders have invented various beliefs and championed ancient texts that seemingly provide answers to questions about the origins and meaning and life, but the answers have varied widely depending on the religious leader interpreting the revelations of prophets or the meaning of sacred scriptures. Providing answers to these undoubtedly important questions is not really the main purpose of religion, nor the primary focus of this book. Historically, religion has been used to control people and direct their behavior, to rally them against "enemies," and to justify the leaders' power. Indeed, there has been no more effective means used by would-be leaders to justify their claims to power.

Ahhhh…the seductive intoxication of power, Chambers thought. *The most destructive addiction imaginable.* Chambers looked at his watch—7:25 a.m. He had worked through the night. He paused for a breather when the telephone rang, startling him.

"Hi, it's David."

"David, it's Mel up at the front gate. There's a police officer here; says he needs to speak with you about your grandmother."

"What is it?"

"He wouldn't say. He just said he has news that he needs to deliver personally."

Chambers' heart sank. His grandfather had passed away six years earlier and his grandmother was the only family he had left. She was ninety-three years old, and although she was in good health, Chambers knew that that could change at any time. "All right, send him through. Tell him I'll meet him in front of the building." Chambers turned off his desk lamp and walked down the three flights of stairs.

"Morning, Mr. Chambers; my name's Officer Mendenhall."

"Nice to meet you, officer." Chambers shook the man's hand.

"Unfortunately, I've been dispatched to give you some bad news; your grandmother passed away last night after an automobile accident."

Chambers dropped his head. "Oh, no…"

"I don't know all the details, but I have the number of the local authorities in Texas who can provide you with that information." The officer handed Chambers a small slip of paper. "I'm sorry for your loss, sir."

"Thank you," Chambers replied somberly. He watched the officer drive away and then sat down on a bench, watching the orange glow of the sun rise above the mountains.

*　*　*

Chambers arrived in Houston a day before his grandmother's funeral. He rented a car at the airport and drove to Galveston, fifty miles to the southeast. As he sped across the bridge to the small island town, he rolled down the window and took a deep breath of the ocean air. He thought of all the happy trips he had made to the beach with his grandparents as a child, but he couldn't repress the painful emotions flooding into his consciousness.

Chambers drove along the seawall and turned into a quiet residential neighborhood. He parked on the street in front of a modest but well-maintained bungalow, and then walked up the familiar stone steps. He rapped softly on the door and waited patiently until it opened, revealing a petite, somber woman holding herself upright with a walker. Her face appeared pale and lifeless, but the wrinkled skin around the corners of her mouth quickly formed a smile. "David."

"How are you, Margaret?" Chambers embraced the elderly woman and held her close.

"I'm happy to see you."

"Me, too."

"Come in and sit down."

"Thank you."

Shortly after the murder of her children, Margaret Gunderson had been incapacitated by a nervous breakdown. She was unable to care for herself and the state had institutionalized her. As soon as he was financially able, Chambers had hired a caretaker and bought her a house so that she could live on her own. He visited whenever he was in Houston.

Chambers followed her into a dimly lit living room. The space was sparsely furnished and there were no photos of Matt or Tommy. Chambers had taken them all away at Margaret's request.

"Can I offer you some tea?"

"Sure, let me help you."

"No, no, sit down."

Margaret went into the kitchen and returned with a platter containing two cups of tea and cookies. Her hand shook as she passed a cup to Chambers, so he lightly clasped her arm and held it steady. Margaret put the platter down on a coffee table and sat down across from Chambers.

"David, you…you've been so good to me. You always come to visit."

"I like seeing you."

"Are you here on business?"

"No, I had some personal matters to attend to in Houston."

Margaret smiled. "I'm glad you could come."

Chambers took a sip of tea and then leaned forward, pressing his palms together in a praying motion. "There's something I'd like to talk to you about, Margaret. You know about Terry's parole?"

Margaret looked down and sighed.

"I'm sorry for bringing it up. I just thought…"

"I know about it," she said softly. "They always let me know."

"Then you know he's up again in two weeks."

"Yes. But I can't think about it. I…I can't bear the thought of him… if he gets out…I…"

"The parole board has always done the right thing in the past," Chambers interjected. "Surely they won't let him out after what he did."

"I know you've done everything you can."

"I have. I've written the parole board. I've urged them. They have to do the right thing."

Margaret nodded. "It's been so hard."

Chambers glanced at the synthetic skin covering his fingers. "It's been hard on both of us. You know…" Chambers paused. "I just had to forgive him. As hard as that sounds, I had to let it go."

"I can't do that," Margaret said softly.

"I understand. I wish I could I help more."

They sat in silence for a while, each reflecting on the events that had brought them together.

"David…I…I want to ask you something," Margaret said finally.

"Of course, what is it?"

"Can you…can you make sure he doesn't get out? I can't…I don't think I could bear the thought of him…I just…I just…" Margaret started sobbing.

Chambers got up and sat next to her on the couch, gently caressing her back. "Shhhh…Shhhh… Everything's going to be okay. He's never going to hurt us again. I promise. I promise."

"I hope so," Margaret said, wiping her face with a tissue "I pray to God…"

* * *

Inside the sanctuary of the Cloverton Community Church, Chambers walked up to the altar and pulled some notes out of his jacket pocket. He scanned the congregation, a hundred or so people, many of whom he had met over the years, and some he had known his entire life.

"Good morning, everyone. Thank you for coming. Although I wish the occasion were different, I'm glad to see so many old friends and I thank you all for being so good to Loretta over the years. She was certainly well loved and I thank you sincerely for that." Chambers paused, glanced quickly at his notes, and then put them back into his pocket. "You know, I spent a lot of time here as a kid and I certainly respect everyone that I've met over the years. My life's been enriched tremendously by the relationships I've had with people. But we're here today to honor my grandmother, the kindest and most loving person I've ever known. As many of you know, my parents died when I was very young and Loretta and Hank raised me. I'm sure it was quite a shock for them to become parents again as they were nearing retirement, but I couldn't have asked for better, more loving parents.

"My grandmother spent many wonderful years among you and I know she felt that there is great wisdom in the Bible. As I got older, we disagreed on that occasionally, but I do know that she was infused with a tremendous positive life force. I don't know if that had anything to do with her spiritual beliefs. Maybe it did; I'm not sure it matters. Whatever it was, I'm going to miss it. I'd like to share one of Loretta's favorite inspirational readings, and indeed one of mine.

Be especially careful when you are trying to be good so that you don't make a performance out of it. It might be good theater, but the God who made you won't be applauding. When you do something for someone else, don't call attention to yourself. You've seen them in action, I'm sure—'play actors' I call them—treating prayer meetings and street corner alike as a stage, acting compassionate as long as someone is watching, playing to the crowds. They get applause, true, but that's all they get. When you help someone out, don't think about how it looks. Just do it—quietly and unobtrusively. That is the way your God, who conceived you in love, working behind the scenes, helps you out.

"My grandmother was never a public performer trying to impress an audience. Rather, she spent almost seventy years in this congregation, living according to what Christ called for in his teachings—ministering behind the scenes, with no public fanfare, never saying a word to anyone about what she did. I knew her well, but I've learned a lot more about her loving ways in the last few days from others who've shared their stories; people moved by her compassion. Whenever there was a need, Loretta was there, sharing her time and money, visiting the sick, keeping in touch with people who were going through hard times. She'd probably be embarrassed by my sharing this information with you now, but it's important. She believed that the church should try to unite people by focusing on the here and now, on this earth, in this world.

"Loretta lived humbly, in accordance with her values. I hope we can honor her spirit and affirm that the church should never be about public performance, playacting, or looking good to impress people on Sunday. It's about caring for the world in our own special ways. Thank you all for coming."

Chambers stepped down from the altar. He didn't feel like crying; instead he felt an overwhelming sense of goodness as he reflected on his grandmother's life. After the service, he spoke briefly with a few of his grandmother's closest friends.

"I'm so glad you could be here today, Doris. My grandmother treasured your friendship." Chambers put his arm around the woman's shoulder and kissed her lightly on the cheek.

"Oh…David, your grandmother will be missed." The woman looked up and gestured to the sky. "I'm sure she enjoyed your kind words today."

Chambers nodded. "I hope so."

"Loretta was so proud of you. She was always talking about your achievements."

"Thank you. She always supported me, and that made a big difference. I don't know where I'd be without that. I'm glad she had friends like you supporting her."

"Your grandmother was so loved, David. Her life was a testament to the power of the church."

Chambers forced a smile. "Excuse me, Doris." Chambers shuffled away quickly, not entirely sure why he found the woman's characterization of his grandmother so troubling. *If she and I pursued the same goal, what's the significance of her belief in the church and its supernatural baggage?* Chambers walked outside and sat underneath the shade of a large oak tree. He strained to come up with answers.

Mentally healthy people are inherently moral. When they walk into a church that nominally professes to embrace love as the highest value, it resonates with the person because it's consistent with their own natural inclinations and moral

320

intuitions. Then, they accept the dogma because it gives some sort of specialness to the experience, or perhaps explains what they feel, but don't fully understand. But living morally doesn't need any special theological sanction or supernatural belief. In some sense, that cheapens it because it's as if morality or goodness isn't fully human. Jesus was probably a loving man, but was he more loving than my grandmother? Jesus didn't raise a family. Would my grandmother have been any less loving if she hadn't ever gone to church? What if she didn't believe in a god? Would that change her behavior somehow, or change the essence of who she was?

Chambers got up and walked around the church grounds, oblivious to the other people milling about. He reflected that every time he had been in a church, he'd always felt strangely uncomfortable when preachers put mythology or superstition forward as fact. What made him even more uncomfortable was that he knew it was taboo to question it. He had always loved to explore life and maximize his mind and he hated the feeling of shame that he had occasionally felt for not blindly believing. He simply couldn't accept that it was ever healthy to turn his mind off. But more than anything else, the idea of an invisible, supernatural agent dictating his morality or behavior troubled him. It seemed so divorced from reality and placed his life out of his control.

Chambers drove back to his grandmother's house alone. She had lived by herself since her husband's death, although she had a nurse who came by every other day to look after her. She didn't have any other living relatives, so Chambers was responsible for tying up her affairs. As he walked into her home, he felt her presence and instinctively glanced at the kitchen table to see if a peach cobbler or blueberry pie was waiting for him. He sat down in his favorite recliner and didn't move for several minutes. He just sat, rocking back and forth, his mind a blank, while a deep quiet sank down on the room. *She's still here. I can't see her, but she's…she's here; she's with me. I've never felt her with me this powerfully before. I want to hold on to her. I've got to hold on to her…*

When Chambers finally got up almost an hour later, he went out to the storage closets on the sun porch where his grandmother kept all of her records. He rifled through some manila folders containing official-looking forms, hoping to find her insurance policies and other important papers, but several photo albums and scrapbooks that had his name handwritten down the spine caught his attention. He sat down and began thumbing through them, finding newspaper clippings, photographs, awards, magazine articles, and his diplomas all neatly arranged in chronological order. He saw many things that he had forgotten about, like some of his first aircraft sketches, as well as ten pages containing all of his swim team ribbons. Articles about Chambers Aerospace filled an entire volume.

There were five books in all and Chambers surveyed them meticulously, realizing that she had saved everything. A rising swell of emotion overcame him and he put the books down and rested his face in his hands. He wept uncontrollably, surrendering completely to his feelings and allowing his emotions to twist into whatever shape they chose. He felt both profound joy and deep sorrow as he finally understood that his grandmother had given him the greatest gift. She had truly valued him.

CHAPTER 38

People say "I'm a Christian" the way certain politicians say "I have integrity," like we're all supposed to be impressed and back off and kneel down to that almighty testament to naïveté and hypocrisy.

—BILL MAHER

Terry Gunderson shuffled into the dingy conference room at Huntsville State Prison for his parole hearing. He brushed some lint off the sleeve of his orange prison jumpsuit as the chaplain walked beside him and whispered words of encouragement. Normally, the prison's chaplain didn't attend parole hearings, although he frequently submitted recommendations to the parole board on the "spiritual fitness" of an inmate.

Gunderson tried to smile at the five parole board members who sat stoically in the back of the room, but he felt nervous; he had been denied parole three other times. He hoped that the chaplain would be his ace in the hole this time, and he prayed that the board members couldn't tell what he was thinking.

"Have a seat, Mr. Gunderson," the parole board chairman Gary Winkler directed, and then smiled at the chaplain. "I didn't know you'd be attending this hearing, Pastor."

"Yes, I'd like to say a few words on Mr. Gunderson's behalf, if that's all right."

"Of course, that'll be fine. Have a seat and we'll get started."

The chaplain gently patted Gunderson's back and the two men sat down.

Winkler had reviewed Gunderson's record prior to the hearing and he was sickened both by the man's crime and his behavior in prison. At the same time, he felt intoxicated by the power of his position. He held the fate of another man's life in his hands. "Well, let's get started Mr. Gunderson. You've been here a few other times so I don't think I need to explain our procedures. But I would like to briefly review your previous history at this institution because of its importance to our proceedings today. First of all, you've been denied parole three times before and the reasons for that are pretty clear. You've been involved in six violent altercations during your incarceration here, twice seriously injuring other inmates. We're obviously…"

"Mr. Winkler, sorry to interrupt," the chaplain cut in. "But if I may…"

Winkler instinctively shot the chaplain a hard stare, but quickly softened his demeanor. He didn't like being interrupted, but he always deferred to a man of God. "Sure. Go ahead, Pastor."

"Mr. Gunderson hasn't been involved in any incidents in over two years and I believe he's been genuinely rehabilitated. I'd like to point out some of the positive aspects of his character."

"Okay. Would you like to speak on his behalf?"

"Yes. If that's okay with you, Terry?"

Gunderson nodded.

"In the past two years, Terry has regularly attended services at my chapel and he's shown a genuine commitment to living in accordance with scripture. Indeed, he's been a diligent student of the Bible, memorizing many of its most important verses. I've ministered to him frequently and we've discussed his plans when gets out of prison. He's committed to living a Christian life and I believe he's experienced a spiritual transformation." The chaplain put his arm around Gunderson's shoulder and smiled proudly. "He's truly been born again."

"Is that accurate, Mr. Gunderson?" Winkler asked.

"Yes, sir; that's the truth. The Lord is my shepherd. I answer only to Him now and He guides my life. I know I've sinned in the past, but the Lord, through His mercy, has cleansed me of those sins."

"One of the Lord's most wondrous acts," the chaplain chimed in.

Winkler cringed. Although he was a born-again Christian himself, he couldn't help imagining Gunderson hacking up his children's bodies: *The blood and the bones and the flesh... Ahhhh! What a monster! But the Lord has forgiven him. The Lord has cleansed him. I can't...if the Lord has forgiven him...*

"Thank you for your comments, Pastor," Winkler said gravely. "Now, I'd like to turn the hearing over to my fellow board members who'd like to ask some additional questions."

The other board members questioned Gunderson for twenty more minutes and then dismissed him so that they could confer privately amongst themselves. After a short discussion, Winkler asked each board member to vote. Two members expressed admiration for Gunderson's transformation and commitment to Christ. That, along with the chaplain's recommendation, was enough to convince them that Gunderson deserved parole. Another member, while also persuaded by the genuineness of Gunderson's belief in the Bible, voted against parole because of the brutality of Gunderson's crimes as well as his violent history in prison. He argued that adopting a set of religious beliefs wouldn't necessarily change Gunderson's behavior, and the man had brutally taken the lives of two people. The final board member argued that the violence in the Bible was worse than Gunderson's crimes so he gave no weight to Gunderson's Bible study. He also contended that Gunderson's rote memorization and reliance on Biblical bromides was a negative because it showed that he had yet to develop a healthy moral compass on his own, and therefore wasn't equipped to make difficult moral choices as a member of society.

Since the other four board members were split, Winkler had the deciding vote. He was no stranger to hearing about the religious transformation of an inmate; the prison population was overwhelmingly religious and it was one of the standard tactics inmates used to secure release. Indeed, Winkler rarely heard a prisoner fail to discuss his faith in

God during a hearing because nontheists made up such an infinitesimal percentage of the prison population. And whenever Winkler dealt with an unbeliever or a prisoner who failed to discuss religious faith, Winkler pressed the issue. He expected every inmate to accept God as the creator of all things and the ultimate judge of all men.

Winkler called Gunderson and the chaplain back into the room.

"Mr. Gunderson, I'm impressed by your commitment to Christ. May the Lord provide you with enough strength to live in accordance with His laws. You parole is granted."

* * *

Ernesto Sosa casually sipped his tea at the café next to the Kaleidoscope Ranch airstrip. He had been reading the *Church of the Mind* manuscript for several days and he felt energized as he turned the final page. He walked out to the hangar to share his thoughts with Chambers, who was repairing one of his airplanes.

"I finished the manuscript," Ernesto beamed, patting Chambers on the back. "It's impressive."

"Thanks," Chambers responded flatly, not looking up. He kept his head buried in the intricate machinery of the plane's engine. "Can you hand me that crescent wrench?"

"Sure. And I admire the risk you're taking," Ernesto added as he handed the tool to Chambers.

"Risk?" Chambers laughed tersely.

"You're going to piss some people off with this. I love it."

"Yeah? Does it matter?" Chambers tightened a gasket on the carburetor. "I need to finish this engine."

"What's wrong?"

"Oh…probably nothing. But maybe I'm no different than the characters in the book. Just wired differently."

Ernesto laughed. "Don't put that in your book."

"Maybe I should," Chambers said soberly, wiping the grease from his hands onto the front of his faded blue jeans. "Do you think it would destroy my thesis?"

Ernesto eyed Chambers curiously. "How you define your thesis?"

Chambers shrugged.

"What's wrong?"

"Wrong?" Chambers reacted bitterly. "Let me show you something. Look at this damn thing! No clue how to clean a carburetor!"

Ernesto peeked into the engine. "It's looks fairly clean to me."

"It's not!" Chambers retorted angrily. "Larry!" Chambers yelled across the hangar. "Hey Larry! Get over here!" A young man working on another airplane snapped to attention and trotted over.

"This carburetor is filthy. You cleaned it, right?"

"Yeah."

"Well, it's still dirty. I want you to clean it again."

"You want me to do it now? I'm replacing the fuel line on the Arrow, and...."

"Yeah. Now!"

The kid picked up the wrench and examined the carburetor. Chambers turned to Ernesto. "Let's get some fresh air."

"Okay." Ernesto followed Chambers outside.

"You want to know my thesis? I don't know if I have one anymore."

Ernesto shook his head. "What the hell's wrong with you?"

"I don't know," Chambers replied testily. "I...I just don't know." *I've got nothing to grab on to...no certainty...and it's all so...so fleeting. Damn! It's fleeting.*

"Well, I've never seen you like this. Something must be going on." Ernesto had seen Chambers angry plenty of times, but this was different. Chambers had lost his normally unshakeable confidence. "You need help?" Ernesto offered.

Chambers shook his head.

"Is this about your grandmother?"

"No. Maybe. I don't know."

"Come on. What is it?"

Chambers didn't respond for several seconds. He wiped his forehead with a handkerchief. "Is there..." He tried to sound casual, but quickly abandoned the effort. "Is there any truth to what they say?"

"Who?"

"The...the believers."

Ernesto's face tightened. "Are you talking about religion?"

Chambers nodded.

"Are you crazy?"

Chambers sighed and then said quietly, "Can we...can we...?"

"What?"

"Can anybody say anything with any certainty?"

"Well..."

"I can't say anything with any certainty. I can't see what's going on in people's minds. I can't feel what they feel. I..."

Ernesto stood quietly until Chambers' voice trailed off. "The religious leaders in this book are evil," he seethed. "Evil! Don't you ever forget that. They lie to themselves; they betray their own minds; they understand what they're doing. They understand and they prey on weak people for their own power and ego gratification." A small purple vein popped out of his Ernesto's forehead. "They use religion as a weapon. Don't you ever doubt that! Ever!"

"If there is a God, he doesn't give a damn about this!" Chambers exploded.

"Yeah, but you do! You do! That's all that matters."

Chambers looked away. "Ahhh…" he groaned, and then heaved the wrench against the side of hangar. "It's frustrating. God, it's frustrating. But you're right. Dammit, you're absolutely right."

"Of course I'm right. Now snap yourself out of this sorry state." Ernesto held up the *Church of the Mind* manuscript. "This book is awesome."

"Yeah, I don't know why I feel this way…I just…"

"I know exactly why you feel this way and so do you." Ernesto flipped through the pages of the manuscript. "It's all in here."

"Yeah, it's just hard to get my arms around it sometimes," Chambers said. "The programming…"

"This book is going to be one of your greatest achievements."'

"Thanks, Ernesto." Chambers glanced at his watch. "Oh…I'm late. I'm supposed to meet Martin at my office. I need to run. I'll see you later—and thanks for your…"

Ernesto held up his hand. "Don't worry about it; I'll see you later."

When Chambers arrived at his office, Dushane was already there waiting for him.

"I like your art," Dushane said.

"Thanks. I mean, thank the kids. They did all the work." Chambers had decorated his office exclusively with art created by the children who came to his camps. "So how are you doing? I haven't seen much of you lately."

"I've been reading *Church of the Mind*. It turned out great."

Chambers grinned. "Thanks. So the Ranch is treating you all right?"

"Yeah, I love it here so far. I've met some great people."

"Good, I've got some more for you to meet. And I think it's time we got to know each other a little better. I'm throwing a party on Saturday. Can you make it?"

"Sure, what time?"

"Nineish."

"Okay."

"I'm glad you're here, Martin." Chambers stepped toward Dushane and embraced him.

"You don't have to hug me every time we see each other," Dushane said.

"I know, but one of these times will be the last."

Dushane smiled and nodded in understanding.

The guard's keys hung loosely from his belt, jingling in time with his leisurely gait as he walked down the cellblock. He stopped in front of Terry Gunderson's cell and clanked the metal bars with his billyclub. "Today's the big day, champ." He smirked at Gunderson and then yelled down to Central Command, "Open the Gunderson cell, please!"

The lock on the heavy, steel-barred cell disengaged and the door slid open. The guard stepped into the cell and looked down at Gunderson, who didn't move. "Get up, man!"

Gunderson stood up slowly.

"Hell, I thought you'd be a little happier. You ain't gonna see any more of this." The guard held up his billyclub and smiled. He had used the weapon on Gunderson several times before, knocking two of his teeth out during one particularly violent altercation.

The guard escorted Gunderson to the processing center where he got back his clothes and the possessions he had arrived with—two lighters, a leather bracelet, a wallet with twenty-three dollars in it, and a set of keys. Besides the cash in his wallet, the state gave him a check for one hundred and fifty dollars—enough to get out of Huntsville by bus.

Gunderson walked off the prison grounds into the scorching heat and suffocating humidity of an August day. He wore a heavy cotton shirt and the sweat poured off his ruddy face as he tramped down to the Greyhound station and bought a bus ticket to Dallas. His brother had wired some money to a Western Union there, and Gunderson's plan was to catch another bus to Sacramento, where his brother would help him find a job.

As he waited for the bus to arrive, he thought vaguely about his dead children. He hadn't thought about them much in prison and he hoped to forget completely.

* * *

Dushane straightened his collar in the reflection of the window and then opened the door to a long hallway. He followed the faint sound of disco music until he reached a large room. The room had a dance floor in the middle, surrounded by couches and tables, and a small bar. Dushane scanned the room for Chambers, but didn't see him. He walked up to the bar. "Hey, have you seen David?" he asked the bartender.

"Check the back room." The man pointed to a door.

"Thanks." Dushane walked through the door down a short corridor to another door where he smelled something funny and heard people talking. He knocked softly, but nobody answered. He knocked again, harder, and waited, but still no one answered. He started to reach for the doorknob just as the door swung open and a large man greeted him. The man was bald with a goatee, and he was wearing a sleeveless leather jacket that accentuated his muscular arms.

"Hi. I...I'm Martin Dushane. Is this...?"

"I know who you are. I'm Nick Jablonski. Come on in."

Dushane shook the man's hand and then entered the room cautiously. There were about twenty people milling about. "Nick, have you seen David?"

"He'll be here shortly. Let's go sit down."

"Okay." Dushane followed Jablonski to a couch. "How do you know David?"

"I'm one of his mechanics."

Dushane nodded and tried to smile.

"And we go riding together."

"Motorcycles?"

"Yeah, he's a crazy son of a bitch. He's almost killed me more than once." Jablonski pulled a small cigarette and a lighter out of his jacket pocket. He lit the cigarette and took a long drag, holding the smoke in for several seconds and then blowing a thick cloud towards the ceiling.

"Are you...?"

Jablonski raised his eyebrows. "Smoking pot? Yeah. Want to try some?"

"Uh..."

"Have you ever smoked before?"

"Yeah, of course," Dushane answered quickly. He had smoked pot once before, but the only thing he remembered was inhaling too much and coughing violently. "Is it...does David care?"

"No, this helps him when the pain in his leg flares up. Here." Jablonski handed the joint to Dushane.

Dushane held the delicately wrapped cigarette to his lips and took a small puff. He exhaled quickly.

"You have to inhale," Jablonski admonished. "And hold the smoke in for a few seconds. Watch." Jablonski grabbed the joint and took another hit, demonstrating the technique. Then he passed it back to Dushane.

"Okay." Dushane held the joint up to his mouth again and sucked in the smoke with a deep breath. The potent vapor stung his lungs, but he held it in as long as could, and then exhaled with a heavy cough.

"Good! That'll get you started," Jablonski encouraged.

Dushane continued coughing. "That smoke is....ahhh...it's harsh."

Jablonski picked up a glass on the table. "Here, have some water."

Dushane took a sip. "Thanks."

"Hey, there's David and Ernesto." Jablonski waved them over.

"Evening, Martin," Chambers greeted. "Glad to see you met Nick."

Chambers patted Jablonski on the back. "Martin, you think I'm out of control on a motorcycle; you should see this guy."

Jablonski smiled. "We were just talking about that."

"And he's a bad influence, too," Chambers continued. "Watch out."

Everyone laughed except for Dushane, who was already consumed by the soothing effects of the drug. He sat quietly while the other three men chatted amongst themselves. He tried to focus his thoughts, but after a while, he found himself staring intently at Chambers. He wasn't sure why, but he began to feel increasingly excited as he marveled at the precision with which Chambers moved, as if every cell in his body knew its purpose and was in harmony with everything around it.

"Martin? Martin?" Chambers waved his hand in front of Dushane's face.

"What...what are you saying?"

"You look a little out of it."

"No, no, I'm all right. I was just thinking."

"Ah, excellent. Share your thoughts with us."

"Well...it's...it's not important."

"Come on, we're all friends here."

"It's really nothing. It's..."

"We all want to hear it," Chambers encouraged.

"Uh, I was just thinking about...I'm not sure how to..."

"Just say it."

"Self...self-actualization. Or something like that."

"Self-actualization?"

"Yeah, like, like living your life exactly the way you're supposed to—with a purpose."

Chambers chuckled. "What do you think, Ernesto? Do you know anything about that?"

Ernesto smiled playfully. "It's good; especially for you, Martin."

Chambers gently slapped Dushane's thigh. "I hope you're okay."

"Yeah, I mean I think I'm okay; I feel a little funny, like, like I'm floating off this couch. It's like I'm floating just above this couch and I can't...I can't feel anything. But at the same time everything is so, I don't know, enhanced."

Chambers and Sosa looked at each other and exploded in laughter. Dushane looked around confused.

"This state becomes you, Martin," Ernesto said.

"Maybe I should get some fresh air," Dushane said. He was about to get up, but a man suddenly burst through the door and rushed towards them.

"You've got a call, David; it's important." The man handed Chambers a cell phone.

"Excuse me, gentlemen." Chambers walked outside and held the phone to his ear. "Hello."

"David, it's Ron Fitzgerald. Gunderson's out on parole."

"What? You've got to be...they let that monster out of prison?"

"Yeah, he got out yesterday."

"I can't...I don't believe this. Where is he now?"

"On his way to Sacramento."

"God...this is unbelievable."

"What are you going to do?"

Chambers didn't answer, suddenly lost in a memory.

"David? Are you still there? David?"

* * *

The wind whipped across Chambers' face as he drove angrily towards Huntsville State Prison, pushing the accelerator down and not letting up until the car hit its maximum speed of one twenty five. As he blew past other traffic on the highway, he tried to decide what he wanted to say to the man who had murdered his best childhood friend and left him crippled, but he couldn't focus his thoughts or control his rage.

Chambers, age twenty-four, had just graduated from Caltech and he had flown back to Houston to visit his grandparents before joining his Air Force squadron. He had kept up with Gunderson's status in prison since the day the man had been incarcerated.

Chambers pulled up to the main office of the prison and parked his car. He got out and limped up the walkway toward the front desk and asked to see Gunderson. A heavy-set, balding man eating a sugarcoated jelly donut requested Chambers' driver's license and told him to sign in. Twenty minutes later, he escorted Chambers into a shabby visitor's area. Chambers sat down in a rickety metal chair and looked through the glass panel into the prisoner's holding room.

When Gunderson finally trudged up to the window, Chambers' first thought was that he looked essentially the same—pale and droopy with deep black patches underneath his eyes that shadowed the flesh above his cheekbones. He had a few small bruises on his face and Chambers hoped that someone had beaten him. Gunderson stared blankly at Chambers and then picked up the phone. "What do you want with me?" he sniffed.

Chambers clenched his fists tightly. "I don't want anything from you, you wretched...piece of... Don't you know who I am?" Chambers thundered.

Gunderson squinted and studied Chambers' face. "No."

"I'm David Chambers. I was friend of your son Matt. Do you remember him?"

Gunderson snorted, but didn't speak.

"I said do!…you!…remember!…him!"

"What the hell do you want?"

"You killed your own family! You…murderer!"

"They didn't obey me!"

Chambers punched the glass with his fist. "You better hope you don't get out on parole because I'm going to kill you! I swear I'm going to kill you! You hear that, you son of a bitch, you're dead!"

The guard stomped into the visitor's area. He grabbed Chambers' arm and tried to pulled him away, but Chambers threw him off and bolted towards the door.

"Don't ever come back here, mister," the guard threatened as Chambers slammed through the exit door. "If I ever see you here again…"

Chambers stumbled down the walkway and kicked a trashcan as hard as he could, knocking it over and spilling litter across the sidewalk. "Dammit! Goddammit!"

The guard went back to his desk and filled out an incident report.

A young man named David Chambers (Texas Driver's License #11250193) asked to visit with inmate Terry Gunderson. During the visit, an argument broke out and Mr. Chambers threatened to kill Gunderson. After I heard the threat from Mr. Chambers, I immediately escorted him out of the visitor's area and warned him not to come back.

The guard put the report into Gunderson's file.

* * *

"David? You there, David?"

"Yeah. Sorry Ron. I'm just…shocked."

"Well, what do you want to do?"

Chambers had waited over thirty years for this moment, but he suddenly found himself paralyzed. "I…I don't know. I just…I… I don't know."

CHAPTER 39

Penalties against possession of a drug should not be more damaging to an individual than the use of the drug itself, and where they are they should be changed.

The importation and sale of marijuana is condemned and punished as a serious crime, but we accept as legitimate the manufacture and sale of an infinitely more addictive and deadly drug: the nicotine in cigarettes that cost the lives of 390,000 American citizens last year [1990].

—JIMMY CARTER, 39TH PRESIDENT OF THE UNITED STATES

Donna Hamilton quickly reviewed her notes, underlining the critical points in red ink. She wanted to make sure she covered everything in her most important interview since President Packer had appointed her the nation's Surgeon General.

Hamilton was a former physician and had served in Congress as a Representative from Ohio. The President appointed her to the Surgeon General's post not only because she was a highly qualified health professional, but also because he owed her a favor; she had worked actively on his campaign, helping to secure her home state on his behalf.

So far, Hamilton hadn't proposed anything controversial and she generally kept a low profile, focusing on the prevention and spread of disease. Members of Congress on both sides of the aisle frequently lauded her work.

Although Hamilton rarely gave interviews, she had been working tirelessly on a new public health initiative that she wanted to publicize. She hadn't spoken with the President recently about her proposal, but she felt confident that he would support it because it had the potential to make a dramatic contribution to public health. Hamilton reclined in her chair and tried to relax, but the sudden buzz of her intercom startled her.

"Dr. Hamilton, Steve Markham from the Washington Chronicle is here to see you."

"Great, send him in." Hamilton opened her compact and dabbed a light coat of makeup across her cheeks. Then she glanced at her notes.

Markham tapped on the door with his knuckle.

"Come on in, Steve."

"Thanks, it's a pleasure to finally meet you." Markham extended his hand. "I appreciate your time."

"My pleasure. Can I offer you something to drink?"

"No, thanks."

"Okay, have a seat and we'll get started."

"Thanks." Markham pulled a notepad out of his briefcase and rested it on his knee. Then he clicked his pen and held up a small tape recorder. "Is this okay?"

"Sure."

"Great, I have a few issues I'd like to ask you about today, but you mentioned on the phone that you've been working on a new public health initiative. Why don't we start with that?"

"Okay. I've kept this under wraps for a while, but in a few days this office will be announcing a new nationwide program to combat smoking and nicotine addiction. It'll be the biggest initiative ever proposed on this issue and we'll be working with health professionals, teachers, parents, community leaders, scientists, and anyone else who wants to get involved. Without getting into all the specifics of it, our goal is to reduce the number of smokers in this country by twenty-five percent over the next five years."

"Wow, that's an ambitious goal. Is the President on board with this?"

"Yes, I discussed it with him when I agreed to serve as Surgeon General. Of course, we've been focused on other issues, but he knows that it's my top priority."

"Hmmm…that's interesting." Markham scratched his head. "I'm a little perplexed because it's no secret that the President has accepted millions of dollars from big tobacco. If they lose twenty-five percent of their customers, they certainly won't be happy." Markham chuckled. "I mean, if you propose this, will the President make it out of Washington alive?"

"Well, first of all, big tobacco contributes to many politicians, not just the President; that's an unfortunate fact of life right now. But the President cares, first and foremost, about the health and well-being of Americans. I'm confident that he'll continue to support this. And you have to remember that the President can appeal directly to the people on this. I think most people are tired of tobacco's influence in Washington."

Markham smiled. "Well, I admire your courage. I'm sure you'll face plenty of challenges, but I have no doubt in your resolve. Now, let me ask you about another topic while we're on the subject of courage. Oregon recently passed medical marijuana legislation; the seventh state to take that step. What's your view of this trend, particularly in light of several recent studies showing significant benefits for certain types of patients?"

"I think we need to continue to study that. There's clearly a substantial body of evidence that marijuana helps cancer patients, AIDS patients, and others with things like nausea and increasing their appetites. It's also been shown to give some people relief from pain; for example, by reducing eye pressure in people suffering from glaucoma. So if marijuana provides these benefits, it would be inhumane to deny it."

"Does it concern you that legalizing marijuana for medicinal use will lead to increased use for non-medicinal purposes?"

"Oh, I don't think so. What we're talking about here, in the case of Oregon and the other states that are on the forefront of this issue, is medical clinics that would only dispense marijuana to patients under a doctor's care. I don't see much risk in that. That's not going to have any effect on the illegal users of marijuana anyway; they can easily get it anywhere in the country."

"So, is it fair to say that you support the legalization of marijuana for medicinal use then?"

"Well, that's not my decision to make, but as I said, marijuana has shown great promise for many patients. If it helps people, then I hope the President and the Congress will take a serious look at that."

Markham chuckled lightly. "That's probably easier said than done. As you're well aware, federal law still provides stiff penalties for marijuana users, and both the President and the Attorney General have repeatedly stated that they'll continue to vigorously enforce strict prohibitions, even in states such as Oregon that have enacted conflicting legislation. And of course, it's no secret that all of those states will probably go Democrat in the next election."

Hamilton nodded. "Well, I don't think the President thinks about this issue in terms of politics, but we clearly need some more intelligent and honest thinking on this issue. At a minimum I think we need to change federal law to allow states to care for their citizens in a compassionate way."

"Yeah, but the current Congress is conservative to say the least."

"Well, it's true that the majority in Congress oppose medical marijuana legislation, but they can't be stu...I mean, ignore the facts forever."

* * *

The Chief of Staff and the Attorney General fidgeted nervously as they waited for the President to pick up the phone.

"Hello."

"Good morning, Mr. President. It's Al."

"Good morning, Al."

"I've got you on speakerphone; I'm here with Lamar."

"Morning, Lamar."

"Good morning, Mr. President."

"What can I do for you, gentlemen?"

"Have you seen today's Washington Chronicle, sir?" Rogers asked.

"Yes."

The Surgeon General's interview had made the front page of the paper, and the Chief of Staff's office had already been inundated with calls demanding Hamilton's resignation.

"You need to address the media as soon as possible," Rogers stated emphatically. "We've got to control this."

"Is it that important?"

"Critical, sir. There's been an uproar and..."

"Okay, schedule something for this afternoon," the President interjected calmly. "But let's keep it short. I don't want to waste a lot of time on this." Although the President knew that any compromise on medical marijuana would hurt him politically, he had trouble getting worked up over the issue.

He had smoked several times in college and never found any of the hysterical claims surrounding the drug to be true. But he reminded himself that he had a role to play, and a reelection bid to win.

* * *

The President stood behind the podium and smiled. He waved casually to a few of the reporters in the press corps. "Good afternoon, everyone. Thank you for coming. I'd like to briefly respond to Surgeon General Hamilton's interview in this morning's Washington Chronicle." The President glanced at his notes. "Let me start by saying that the Surgeon General's comments about the legalization of marijuana for medicinal use do not reflect the views of the Administration or federal law. We don't believe that marijuana has been shown to provide any benefits whatsoever to either cancer patients or, for that matter, any other types of patients. I will continue to support the existing federal drug laws and the Attorney General will continue to vigorously prosecute violators of those laws. Our children are too important to allow drug dealers to hook them on these destructive substances and I will do everything in my power to achieve our goal of a drug-free society. I'd also like to reiterate my support for a bill that's currently up on the Hill. It provides for withholding federal highway and law enforcement funds from states that have legalized marijuana for any purpose. I'm confident that this legislation will help us reach our goal." The President pointed to a reporter. "Peter."

"Mr. President, you mentioned the problem of drug dealers. The Surgeon General referred to medical clinics that dispense marijuana to patients under a doctor's care. These doctors are hardly drug dealers. Do you still believe there's cause for concern?"

"Absolutely," Packer responded firmly. "If we adopt a permissive attitude towards marijuana, then we're setting a terrible example for our children; sending a message that marijuana is not a dangerous drug. This makes the job of drug dealers easier."

"Have you asked the Surgeon General to resign?"

"No."

"Have there been any discussions to that effect?"

"No, and I continue to support the Surgeon General. I think she's doing an excellent job and serving her country to the best of her ability. She's aware of our position with respect to marijuana and she knows that the views she expressed yesterday aren't consistent with those of this Administration. But I welcome her opinions. Leslie."

"Mr. President, the Surgeon General stated that people can get marijuana easily regardless of federal policy, suggesting the overall futility of the drug war. How do you respond to that?"

"I disagree with her statement. I think we're making progress and as I've said several times, my goal is a drug-free society. My commitment to that hasn't wavered. We're enlisting every law enforcement agency at our disposal to achieve that goal."

"One follow-up to that, Mr. President."

"Sure."

"We all know that Prohibition was a huge failure in the 1920's and led to a huge increase in organized crime. Isn't the same thing happening now with marijuana and other recreational drugs, but on a much grander scale?"

"No, I disagree with that."

"How do you distinguish…?"

"Marijuana is a dangerous drug," the President interrupted.

"Yes, but so is alcohol. There are thousands of alcohol-related fatalities…"

"I think there's a big difference there," the President interrupted again. "And the Administration's position reflects that difference. Last question. Charlie."

"Have you asked the Surgeon General not to publicly discuss her views regarding medical marijuana?"

"No, we haven't discussed that."

"Are you going to discuss that, sir?"

"No, I don't believe that we will. As I mentioned, although I strongly disagree with the Surgeon General on this issue, I value her opinion. That's all I have time for. Thank you for coming."

After the press conference, the President sat down with his Chief of Staff in the Oval Office. "Everything okay, Al?"

"No, Mr. President. I've got Infinity and the tobacco lobbyists breathing down my neck. I need to calm them down."

The President yawned. He felt like taking a nap.

"I'm serious, Howard."

The President shot Rogers a look of surprise. He rarely heard anyone call him by his first name, but he liked hearing it. "Okay."

"We've got to have their money for your reelection."

"Fine. Tell the lobbyists I'll kill the Surgeon General's nicotine project. It won't see the light of day. As for Infinity, smooth things over with them; invite Newhall to the White House or something. Hire a few more of his cronies if that's what it takes."

Rogers breathed a sigh of relief. "Very good, sir."

"And call Donna," the President snapped. "Tell her to keep her mouth shut. I give her a plum appointment and she pulls this nonsense. We can't have that."

"Yes, Mr. President."

A steady stream of camera flashes illuminated the room as Newhall stepped up to the podium for his own press conference, called to respond to the President's remarks. Heilbrenner stood next to Newhall as the Reverend read a prepared statement.

> The Surgeon General Donna Hamilton should resign her post immediately. Her comments about marijuana were irresponsible, untrue, and show a gross lack of concern for the people of this nation, particularly our youth. If the Surgeon General refuses to step down voluntarily, I urge the President to act swiftly in replacing her with a candidate whose views reflect this country's moral standards.

"I'll take your questions now," Newhall said gravely.

"Reverend, the President indicated his strong disagreement with the Surgeon General's remarks. He also continues to support an absolute ban on marijuana with no exception for medicinal purposes. Are you satisfied by the President's statement?"

"No, I'm not," Newhall responded sharply. "The President should demand Ms. Hamilton's resignation. Period."

"Don't you think that's a little extreme, sir? You've praised the Surgeon General in the past for her work on disease prevention, and she's extremely popular. Isn't there a compromise here somewhere?"

Newhall furrowed his brow. "Absolutely not. The Lord doesn't compromise with His enemies; He takes vengeance upon them. I have no sympathy for that woman."

"What do you mean by that, sir?"

"I mean we can't allow any person in a position of authority, particularly the Surgeon General, who people rely on for guidance on health issues, to maintain such grossly misinformed and immoral views. What's next, will she advocate the legalization of heroin and LSD? Do we want drug dealers on every street corner peddling marijuana cigarettes to our children? I won't stand for it, and I won't stand for a President who tolerates it."

"Are you saying that you no longer support the President?"

"I'm saying that I refuse to support anyone who stands idly by while the moral decay of our society continues. If the President doesn't show some leadership and do the right thing, then no, I can't support him. But I certainly hope it doesn't come down to that." Newhall pointed to another reporter. "Yes, Jim."

"What about the scientific evidence that supports the medicinal use of marijuana for certain patients?"

Newhall waved his hand dismissively. "The scientists, the atheists, the liberals; they're always trying to use science to justify their views. What they're really trying to do is destroy the moral fabric of our country."

"Reverend Newhall..."

"I'm sorry," Newhall interrupted. "I don't have any more comments at this time." Newhall stepped away from the podium; Heilbrenner followed him backstage.

"How'd we do?" Newhall asked.

Heilbrenner smiled and let out a light chuckle. "Perfect."

* * *

Al Rogers snatched up the phone and held it against his reddened face. He angrily dialed Heilbrenner's private number.

"John Heilbrenner here."

"What the hell does Newhall think he's doing?" Rogers blasted. "Is he out of his mind?"

Heilbrenner spoke with Rogers frequently and their conversations were normally friendly, but this time Heilbrenner knew that if he didn't handle Rogers skillfully, their mutually beneficial relationship could be jeopardized. Heilbrenner needed Rogers to think that he was fully behind the President.

"He's standing up for the moral fiber of the nation," Heilbrenner countered.

"Oh! Can that shit! Remember who you're talking to! The President is pissed off! I'm pissed off!"

"Look, calm down. Newhall's a passionate man. He feels strongly about the drug issue."

"So does the President."

"Then he should fire Hamilton; she's a liability. Our people don't support legalizing marijuana. You know that. Newhall has to take a strong stand."

"Well, no more of this questioning the President. We can't afford any controversy right now; we're in for a tough reelection fight. We need to make sure we're on the same page. We need to..."

"Wait a minute," Hcilbrenner interjected. "Wait just a minute. Before we go any further, we need to talk about Chambers."

"What about him?"

"What do you mean, what about him?" Heilbrenner snapped.

"Well, we're planning to monitor that situation."

"Planning! What the hell does that mean?"

"We're working on it. That's all I can say right now."

"We can't have him running around trashing our organization."

"I understand."

"We support the President, but we need some action on that."

"Don't worry."

"This is important."

"I know; so is the President's reelection campaign."

"If you take care of Chambers, you can count on the support of the Network."

"Good. We need to get the President and Newhall together for a meeting on the drug issue. I want everyone to know that they're on the same page. It'll be a good photo-op."

"I'll run it by him," Heilbrenner promised.

"Good, we'll be in touch."

Heilbrenner hung up the phone with a satisfied smile and thought about his next move to undermine the President.

CHAPTER 40

When people are free to do as they please,
they usually imitate each other.

—ERIC HOFFER

Chambers paced nervously across the soft carpet in his office, taking hits off a scotch and soda as he explored the outer reaches of his emotions. Normally he made quick decisions, but he struggled to commit himself to a course of action. "Damn it!" he cursed, kicking over a file cabinet, violently dumping its contents. "Goddammit!"

Chambers sat behind his desk and buried his head in his hands. *I just want this to go away. Ahhhh!* He opened his credenza and pulled out a framed photo of Matt Gunderson taken shortly before his death. Although Matt's face had a sinister scar inflicted by his father, Chambers couldn't see anything but innocence. *It's not fair that he was born into a family with that monster. God…nothing's fair. But does it amount to anything anyway? This random collection of events. There's no order, no…no…justice.*

Chambers stood up and looked out the window over the garden. The moonlight illuminated a row of tulips. He thought of his promise to Margaret, although he hadn't called her since Terry's release. He figured she must be horribly distraught and he didn't know if he could deal with that. His own emotions were spinning out of control.

Chambers guzzled the last of his drink and turned away from the window. *Is there any crime worse than killing a child? How could anyone ever do anything to hurt a child? I can't take this! Ahhhh!* Chambers felt sick at the thought of killing a man, even a man as vile as Terry Gunderson. He felt sick about all killing. Whenever he thought of it, or even heard about it on the news, it immediately brought back the memory of Matt's battered, lifeless body lying in a pool of blood. He found no heroism in his desire to kill, only savagery and hatred. But then he reflected that Margaret had nothing. With Terry out of prison, she would be tortured for the rest of her life. Chambers picked up the phone and dialed Ron Fitzgerald.

"Hello."

"Ron, it's David."

"David. How are you?" Fitzgerald worked for Chambers in an unofficial capacity as a private investigator and a counter surveillance expert. If Chambers needed information, Fitzgerald would get it. But that wasn't his only function. Fitzgerald performed other tasks—tasks typically outside the job description of a P.I.

"I need…you remember that problem we discussed a few weeks ago?"

Fitzgerald gulped. "Are you…are you talking about…?"

"That…that's right," Chambers said, his fingers trembling. "I'd like to…I'd like to move forward on that."

"Have you thought about this? I mean…are you sure?"

"Yes," Chambers responded firmly. "Can you handle it?"

Fitzgerald didn't answer.

"Ron?"

"Yeah."

"Well?"

"Yeah, I'll...I'll take care of it," Fitzgerald said in a low voice.

"Let me know if you have any problems."

"Okay." Fitzgerald hung up the phone and sucked in a deep breath. He slammed his fist into his palm as a shiver ran up his spine.

Chambers dropped the phone and put his hand on his heart, hammering in his chest. He felt a combination of murderous hatred and terrifying dread, and he wondered about the force that had compelled him to act.

*　*　*

Doug Cartwright smiled. *I'm a player in this town*, he thought. He had just spoken with Al Rogers, who had asked for help on an important project. Cartwright instructed his secretary to set up a meeting with Josephine and two FBI agents who were working closely with the Chief of Staff.

The next morning, Cartwright and Josephine waited in the conference room for the FBI agents. They chatted casually over coffee and Josephine had to admit that she enjoyed Cartwright's company. His sophisticated redneck persona and Texas-sized ego consistently amused her, and she never needed to say much around him. He never tired of talking about himself.

There was a soft knock on the door and Cartwright's secretary escorted the agents into the conference room. Cartwright stood up and shook each man's hand.

"Josephine, this is Agent Stottlemeyer and Agent Brady."

Josephine smiled politely. "Pleased to meet you."

Each agent wore a conservative navy suit and appeared to be in his early thirties. They both eyed Josephine carefully, trying to size her up.

"Have a seat, gentlemen," Cartwright directed. "I know you two have been fully briefed, but Josephine isn't up to speed on this yet." Cartwright turned to Josephine. "The reason for this meeting is that a dangerous situation has developed with a cult in Northern California. They're based out of this place called Kaleidoscope Ranch, up in a remote area near the Oregon border."

Josephine's head jerked backward.

"You all right, Josephine?"

"Yes, I'm fine," Josephine replied coldly.

"Okay. Agent Brady, why don't ya start by fillin' us in with the information you have so far."

"Sure. There are two main leadership figures at the Kaleidoscope Ranch. The primary leader is David Chambers, the famous aerospace billionaire. He appears to control the Ranch's doctrine, and like most cult leaders, he's very charismatic. The other man is his business partner, Ernesto Sosa. Sosa serves as Chambers' right-hand man and our sources tell us that they work together closely. So far, we've uncovered two disturbing facts about Sosa. First of all, he grew up on a large farm that his family owns outside of Cuernavaca, Mexico." Brady paused. "The Sosa family has been growing hemp for over forty years."

"Hmmm…interestin'," Cartwright drawled gravely. "I'm not too familiar with that, but I know it's bad a' course."

"I've heard you can get high if you smoke a whole bale of that stuff," Josephine offered.

The two FBI agents remained stone-faced and Cartwright cringed during several moments of uncomfortable silence. Stottlemeyer finally spoke. "The problem with hemp is that it's only a short step from legalizing marijuana, which the Ranch has consistently advocated. That's certainly nothing to joke about."

"I'm sorry," Josephine said casually. "I'm not trying to trivialize what you're saying, but I'm not quite following you. I thought this meeting was about an imminent threat. What does hemp farming have to do with Kaleidoscope Ranch posing a threat?"

"Well, there's one other thing we haven't told you," Stottlemeyer responded. "There's an Indian reservation that borders the Ranch to the east. Chambers employs some of those Indians. We raided that reservation earlier this year and confiscated large stocks of peyote and marijuana. We also arrested several people, some of whom worked at the Ranch."

Josephine shook her head. "You'll have to forgive me, I'm still not getting it."

The FBI agents looked at each other with puzzled stares. "It's self-evident," Stottlemeyer snapped impatiently. "They have radical beliefs at that Ranch."

"Oh…I see." Josephine nodded. "Yes. Now I understand. Thanks for clarifying that."

"But it gets a lot worse," Brady added. "David Chambers believes in witchcraft."

Josephine dropped her pen and stared hard at Brady. She fought the urge to lunge across the table and slap him. "Tell me a little more about that," she said calmly.

"He allows pagan and Wicca rituals at the Ranch," Stottlemeyer said, his voice laced with impending doom. "We interviewed a few people who told us that this is tolerated and even encouraged."

"That's right," Brady seconded. "Not only that, children are exposed to this during Chambers' camps. The man refuses to provide children with normal Christian churches to worship in; all they know is evil."

"We all remember what happened at Waco," Cartwright piped in. "You can't let these things go on for too long."

The FBI agents nodded. "We need to monitor the situation," Brady stated firmly.

"All right, I think we know what we need to do here," Cartwright said. "How long will it take to get surveillance in place?"

"Three months maybe," Brady replied. "Chambers runs a tight organization. It may take a little time to get our people planted."

"Okay, thank y'all for coming." Cartwright turned to Josephine. "Josephine, I need to speak with you privately for a moment."

"Okay." The two FBI agents left the room.

"I need you to draft a legal opinion on this one. We need to git all our bases covered."

"Okay."

Josephine retreated to her office and couldn't help laughing as she prepared the memo:

The Domestic Security Act provides the FBI with authority to engage in all necessary surveillance activities within its discretion if there is a threat to the health, safety, or well being of any citizen. In this case, inhabitants of Kaleidoscope Ranch allow pagan cult rituals as well as witchcraft, and they expose children to these activities. This is clearly detrimental to the well-being of children who need appropriate spiritual guidance in order to become productive and responsible citizens. Since the danger is imminent, the FBI may proceed with surveillance and any other investigative actions without seeking a warrant or any other judicial approval.

Josephine scrawled her signature at the top of the memo and presented it to Cartwright. He read it carefully and smiled. "This'll do just fine."

CHAPTER 41

Does anything take more courage—is anything more challenging and sometimes frightening—than to live by our own mind, judgment and values?

—Nathaniel Branden, *The Six Pillars of Self-Esteem*

"It's too intellectual."

"Your views are highly unorthodox."

"The book and its author lack credibility on the subject matter."

"There's no market for a book questioning religion. Nobody wants to hear that."

"Thomas Paine wrote your book over two hundred years ago and then Sigmund Freud and Bertrand Russell wrote it again. They didn't convince anyone; neither will you."

Chambers quietly thumbed through the stack of *Church of the Mind* rejection letters. He felt disappointed, but not surprised. He knew that the struggle wouldn't be easy. His literary agent had approached all the major publishing houses, but they all rejected the book because they didn't think it would sell and they feared tainting their other books by association.

Without a publisher, Chambers considered self-publishing, but he decided that it would be too difficult to market the book effectively without established distribution channels. He also didn't want the book to be marginalized as an act of vanity. He wanted his intellectual and psychological analysis of religion's core to be represented by a well-known publisher. Chambers finally decided to post parts of the book on the Kaleidoscope Ranch website, hoping to generate some interest. He had hoped to include information about Infinity in the book, but Lassater's investigation wasn't complete. Chambers figured he would only get one shot at exposing the Network, so he withheld the information until he could bulletproof his case.

Chambers posted the first ten chapters. The material was explosive, but none of it mentioned the Infinity Network.

* * *

The alarm buzzed at five a.m. jolting Don Leachman out of a pleasant dream. In the dream, he had been entertaining guests at a lavish party at his five-hundred-acre winery in Napa Valley. The winery produced an award-winning merlot and the guest list included wealthy business associates, respected philanthropists, top-shelf politicians, and Leachman's voluptuous twenty-six-year-old mistress. They all sampled his latest vintage and praised his winemaking acumen.

Leachman had the dream often and he always loved it; but at the same time it was infuriating because it reminded him of Chambers, the reason he didn't own the winery yet. Chambers' abuse of process lawsuit had personally cost Leachman almost five million dollars.

Leachman rolled out of bed and walked out to the front porch to retrieve the morning paper. He ambled into the kitchen and nodded politely to his live-in servant who had coffee and croissants ready for him. He sat down and started to butter his croissant when the newspaper headline jumped out at him. "David Chambers Releases Controversial Book About Religion on the Internet; People of Faith Angered." Leachman scanned the article, which described the book as a critical assault against organized religion and faith-based belief systems.

Leachman tingled with excitement as he rushed to his bedroom. He dressed hurriedly and sped to his office. When he arrived, he immediately checked the morning's stock market action. Chambers Aerospace was down ten percent in early trading. Leachman couldn't believe his good fortune. *I've got that son of that bitch! Yessss! I'm gonna smash that little prick! He thinks he's better than me because he started a company. Fuck him!* Leachman picked up the phone and called Adam Sharf. "Adam, it's Don. Can you come up to my office right away?"

"Sure, I'll be right there."

"Have you heard about David Chambers?" Leachman asked excitedly as Sharf walked in.

"Yeah, it's all over the news."

"I want to get a suit filed against Chambers Aerospace, and Chambers personally by this afternoon. Can you take care of that? I want you to be the lead attorney."

"A suit?"

"Yeah."

"On what basis?"

"The stock's down ten percent. We're going to sock it to that bastard this time."

"Okay…are you thinking securities fraud?"

"Of course," Leachman snapped impatiently.

"Look, I know the stock's down, but has there been any fraud? It just seems like a reaction to the controversy surrounding the book. It doesn't seem like…"

Leachman waved his arm dismissively and raised his voice. "He should've known what would happen by releasing his stupid little book. He's damaged the shareholders."

"Shareholders?" Sharf reacted. Although the firm technically represented shareholders, it was rare for an attorney to discuss a strike suit on those terms.

"Yeah, our job is to represent defrauded shareholders," Leachman replied automatically, as if he had read the statement directly from the firm's marketing literature.

"He wrote about his religious beliefs. He's entitled to his beliefs,"

Sharf countered.

"Not if he communicates them recklessly and damages the shareholders. He has to be held responsible for that. I want to get this suit filed as soon as possible."

Sharf swallowed hard. "Look Don, I don't know if I'm the right person to handle this. I mean I don't like the idea of going after a guy based on his religion." Sharf was Jewish and his great-grandfather had been murdered in the Holocaust.

"What are you talking about? You're the most qualified person to handle the case. You and I are the only people with intimate knowledge of that company. I'd handle the case myself, but I'm in trial right now and this can't wait. I want you on this aggressively. Now, as far as your concern about Chambers' religious beliefs; the guy has no religious beliefs. He's nothing but a filthy little atheist."

"I don't care what he is," Sharf responded firmly. "That's his business. I'd prefer not to be a part of this."

You spineless…fucking…who the hell do you think you are? Leachman instinctively clenched his fists and tightened his jaw. "You work at this firm, Adam. Your job is to handle firm business. This is firm business."

"Yeah, but I'm not comfortable. I'm sorry."

"Are you comfortable with your job here?" Leachman challenged.

Sharf instinctively recoiled, but quickly regained his composure. He had spent many hours working with Leachman and he had gotten used to his boss' disposition. He knew that Leachman wouldn't hesitate to fire him without a second thought. Several other associates had already been summarily terminated for showing weakness. Sharf had learned to be tough because he had a family to support and a huge mortgage. But his conscience screamed that Leachman was wrong, that the law firm was wrong, and that his life was wrong. "I'm in a tough position," he said weakly. "Can't you find another attorney to handle this?"

"No! I want you to do it! What the hell's wrong with you? This is a golden opportunity to handle a high profile case. We're all going to get rich off this one. Besides, this is your job! Do you want it or do I get somebody else?"

Sharf looked down at his shoes and sighed in resignation. "I'll take care of it."

The following afternoon, the firm's senior partner, Mel Grunfeld stomped past the secretary's workstation in front of Leachman's office.

"Mr. Grunfeld, he's in a meeting right now; he doesn't want to be disturbed. Mr. Grunfeld…"

Grunfeld ignored the woman and barreled into Leachman's office. Leachman was having a drink with one of his golfing buddies. "What the hell do you think you're doing?" Grunfeld thundered.

"I'm in a meeting here, Mel."

"Tell your friend to get the hell out of here." Grunfeld glared sharply at Leachman's guest, who quickly scampered out of the room.

"What the fuck is wrong with you?" Leachman snapped.

"What the fuck is wrong with you?" Grunfeld spat back. "What did you think would happen when I found about your latest suit?"

"We've got the son of a bitch this time," Leachman responded matter-of-factly.

"I don't give a flying fuck! You had no authority to file the suit. The last one cost this firm forty-five million dollars. Forty-five million! I don't want anything to do with that man."

Leachman put his feet up on the desk and giggled. "Since when did you become such a pussy?"

"Fuck you."

"No, fuck you. And don't forget who brings in the majority of the big cases here. Hell, if you weren't for me, your wife couldn't buy a new Mercedes every year."

"Leave my wife out of this!" Grunfeld screamed. "I'm going to the executive committee with this. You're fucked!"

Leachman shrugged. "Whatever."

Over the next few days, the controversy threatened to destroy the firm, but Leachman's partners, mindful of his rainmaking prowess, brokered a settlement. If he failed, Leachman agreed to cover the cost of the suit. If he won, he would take seventy-five percent of the winnings.

* * *

Chambers watched the value of his company dwindle almost a billion dollars over the course of a few hours. He wanted to lash out and vent his explosive anger, but he kept his cool. The company faced a crisis and he knew he had to lead it through the storm. He bought as many as shares of the company as he could to help support the stock price, but by the end of the day the company's market cap had fallen seventeen percent. The next day, the stock fell another six percent and Chambers was served with Leachman's nine hundred million dollar strike suit.

CHAPTER 42

If any harm follows, then you shall give life for life, eye for eye, tooth for tooth, hand for hand, foot for foot, burn for burn, wound for wound, stripe for stripe.

—BIBLE, EXODUS 21:23-25

You have heard that it was said, 'An eye for an eye, and a tooth for a tooth.' But I tell you, do not resist an evil person. If someone strikes you on the right cheek, turn to him the other also.

—BIBLE, MATTHEW 5:38-39, *attributed to Jesus*

Terry Gunderson clocked out and walked to the parking lot where his beat-up sedan was parked. The car was a faded, shit-colored brown with a ripped vinyl roof and a rusted hull. When he opened the door, the scent of greasy french fries invaded his nostrils. Empty beer cans and flasks of cheap whiskey littered the passenger side of the car. Gunderson spit out the chewing tobacco from the leathery pouch of his cheek and wiped his mouth on his sleeve. As he plopped his tired frame into the car, a crack in the imitation leather seat jabbed him in the back. "Ouch! Fuckin' piece-a-shit car!"

After his release from prison, Gunderson's brother had helped him find a job with a small construction company in Petaluma, California, thirty miles north of San Francisco. He worked primarily as a laborer on residential housing projects, but one of his additional responsibilities was to make weekly deliveries to the company's other office in Mendocino. He did this every Thursday evening, usually late.

The sky drizzled lightly as Gunderson wheeled the car onto the street. He stopped at a liquor store to grab a six-pack for the drive and then headed toward the freeway.

* * *

"Brrrrrrring… Brrrrrrring…" The pay phone next to the abandoned gas station sprang to life. Jason Keyes picked up the receiver and held it tightly to his ear; an unidentified voice came quietly over the line. "He left five minutes ago."

Keyes smiled coldly. He walked to the back of the station where a large black truck with a heavy, steel crash bumper was parked. Keyes began loading the truck, placing a high-powered assault rifle, a nine-millimeter handgun, and twenty boxes of ammunition on the passenger seat. He had enough firepower to kill a hundred men, but one could never be over-prepared.

Keyes was in his late fifties; a powerfully built man with a set of pecs and biceps that stretched his tight-fitting black t-shirt. He wore a brown leather jacket with an interior pocket that housed an eight-inch, triangular-bladed, Boa knife. Keyes loved the triangular blade because it left a wound that wouldn't close, making the knife a much more effective and deadly weapon. The knife was usually unnecessary and Keyes had actually only used it once, but he carried it out of habit. He wasn't exactly superstitious, but the knife was his pride and joy. He had acquired it from a high-ranking North Vietnamese officer; his first kill in the war and perhaps his most satisfying.

Although Keyes had been initially uninterested in going to Vietnam, military leaders recognized that he had the potential to be an elite fighter. In addition to his physical strength, his psychological profile (based on a battery of tests) suggested that he could be molded. Keyes joined a special conditioning program that had a singular goal—create ruthless killers that could get behind enemy lines and assassinate specific targets.

Rain began coming down harder as Keyes moved the truck out of the garage. Gray clouds moved swiftly across the sky as he waited for Gunderson. When Gunderson's sedan rolled past the station, Keyes followed it onto the freeway. It was almost midnight and there were few cars on the road. Keyes followed about a hundred yards behind.

Gunderson was enjoying the quiet drive and pleasant beer buzz. He didn't notice the black truck until he was eighty-five miles north of San Francisco on Highway 1, which ran along the Pacific Ocean through a stretch of coastal mountains. The winding road had been blasted out of the mountain range with sheets of jagged rock rising over two hundred feet above and below it. The rain had subsided, but a thick blanket of fog hung low, making the road difficult to negotiate.

Keyes moved in closer and flipped on his high beams. The bright light pierced the rear window of Gunderson's sedan, making it even more difficult to see.

"Fuckin' asshole!" Gunderson cursed as he adjusted his rear view mirror to divert the light. Then he glanced quickly over his shoulder—the truck was suddenly within a few feet of his rear bumper. He thrust his foot against the accelerator and sped up, but when he looked back again, the truck was still on his tail. He thought of pulling over and letting the truck pass, but the two-lane road had narrowed and the truck was following so close that he was afraid to slow down. He decided to punch the accelerator again, while behind him Keyes heard a familiar guitar riff on the radio and decided to crank it up.

Keyes tapped his foot in time with the music, while the road shot up several hundred feet above the ocean, then leveled into a straightaway. Keyes hit the accelerator like he was pulling the trigger of a rifle and the truck shot forward like a spring, slamming violently into the back of the sedan. Gunderson's head whipped back and then forward into the steering wheel.

Ahhhhhh…..!" Gunderson cried, his heart jumping into his throat. The sedan lurched forward and skidded uncontrollably over the wet pavement onto the rough gravel shoulder. He fought to control the car and managed to get it back on the road, but he looked back and saw the truck coming at him again like a runaway freight train. He gripped the steering wheel until his knuckles cracked, bracing himself. The black truck hit again, shattering the rear window of the sedan and setting off an explosion of glass throughout the car. Gunderson lost control and the car angled sharply, smashing through the metal guardrail separating the road from the rocks below. The front tires hung dangerously off the edge of the road. Gunderson fell unconscious for a moment and then woke up suddenly with an urgent shudder. When he raised his head, he saw a man coming towards him through the fog. The man moved with the cold precision of a robot, his cheeks hollow, face drawn tight, and eyes focused.

Gunderson's leg had been crushed by the impact and he felt searing pain, but he threw his body against the door with a desperate burst of energy and pried it open. He rolled out of the car and used every available ounce of strength to get to his feet. His injured leg would barely support his weight, but he limped away from the car and looked over the guardrail at the rocks and ocean below. As he staggered down the road he screamed, hoping that another person, anyone, would come, but there was no one in sight.

Keyes ran full stride toward his injured prey. Gunderson looked back and fell to the ground. In a last desperate effort to get away, he tried to throw himself over the guardrail, but it was too late. Keyes slammed him down and pinned him against the muddy ground. He picked up a large rock and lifted it above his head as his eyes narrowed in concentration. Gunderson couldn't scream, but his eyes were wide in terror. A dull thud echoed through the fog as Keyes brought the rock down on Gunderson's temple, splattering blood and soft tissue on Keyes' face and hands.

Keyes picked up the disfigured body and placed it carefully into the driver's seat of Gunderson's sedan. He started the engine of his truck and held the brake while pressing down hard on the accelerator. He released the brake suddenly, propelling the truck like a black bullet into the sedan, blasting it over the edge of the road into the rocks.

The Sonoma County Sheriff's Department investigated the crash. They discovered the empty beer cans in Gunderson's car, and an autopsy revealed that his blood alcohol level was almost twice the legal limit. They wanted to rule it an accident and move on, but there were too many uncomfortable facts, particularly the skid marks from two vehicles and the way the back of Gunderson's sedan was dented. Detectives hypothesized that Gunderson's sedan was hit by another car, but they found no conclusive evidence. One of the detectives obtained the records from Gunderson's stay in prison.

"There's something in here you might want to take a look at, Captain."

"Yeah, what have you got?"

"There's a report here about a confrontation between the deceased and David Chambers."

"Are you talking about David Chambers the aerospace guy?"

"Yeah, Chambers paid this guy a visit in prison several years ago and threatened to kill him."

"Why would Chambers want to kill this guy?"

"I found out that Chambers and Gunderson are from the same town and that Chambers testified against him at his trial."

"Gunderson was in prison for murder, right?"

"Yeah, he killed both his kids and crippled Chambers. According to the trial transcript, Chambers and one of Gunderson's boys were friends. They were at the house playing together on the day of the murders."

"He murdered his kids? My God."

"Yeah, he hacked them up with a hatchet."

"Ooooh...the guy sounds like a real sweetheart."

"What do you think we should do? Should we question Chambers?"

The Captain rubbed his chin. "Yeah...I suppose we should...I mean of course we should, but you know what I really think?" The Captain raised his eyebrows.

"What?"

"I think we need to focus our efforts on the Patterson kidnapping."

"Are you saying...?"

"Yeah. I'm saying that our top priority is Patterson. I don't want to get sidetracked. You okay with that?"

"I don't have a problem."

"Prepare a final report and get it in on my desk by tomorrow morning."

"All right, Captain."

The sheriff's report stated that the incident involved only one car and appeared to be alcohol-related.

*   *   *

"Ouch..." Chambers grimaced as jolts of pain shot through the tendons behind his knee. He sat down and tried to massage away the discomfort, but he found no relief. He lay down on the bed and stretched out his leg, breathing a sigh of relief as the pain gradually subsided, but he couldn't escape the anxiety of another attack. The phone suddenly interrupted his thoughts. He rolled across the bed and picked it up. "Hello."

"David, it's Ron. How are you?"

Chambers hadn't spoken with Ron Fitzgerald in over a month and he was relieved to hear his voice.

"I'm fine, Ron. How did it...is this about...?"

"Yeah, it's over," Fitzgerald replied evenly.

"Over?"

"Yeah, mission accomplished."

"Any…problems?"

"No. And don't worry, it's been officially ruled an accident."

"Does Margaret…?"

"Yes."

"Is she okay?"

"Yes."

"Thank you," Chambers said somberly. He hung up the phone and paced into the bedroom, fighting through the pain in his leg. He pulled an old photo album out of the closet and sat down on the edge of the bed. He hadn't looked at it in a long time and the pages were beginning to yellow with age. After flipping quickly through several pictures, he paused on a photograph of himself and Matt Gunderson at the beach. They were both smiling and had their arms wrapped around each other. "I miss you, buddy," Chambers said aloud as he closed the album and flopped numbly on the bed. He couldn't escape the images of Matt's bloody death and he twitched in feverish spasms until he fell asleep. When he woke up a few hours later, he felt a bleak, all-encompassing despair, but he knew that he would be willing to do it again.

CHAPTER 43

The world is my country, all mankind are my brethren,
and to do good is my religion.

— THOMAS PAINE, *THE AGE OF REASON*

Troy McBride adjusted his headphones and cranked up the volume on his MP3 player when he heard the opening notes of his favorite song. He hummed the words to himself while he typed rapidly, trying to wrap up an important memo. He hadn't quite finished when his boss, Bob Friedlander, walked into his small Pentagon office.

"Hi Troy," Friedlander greeted.

McBride swiveled around and slid the headphones around his neck. "How are you, Bob?"

"Good, good. But I need to talk to you about something." Friedlander shut the door.

"Sure, have a seat."

"Well, let me get right to it. This may come as a bit of a surprise, but I have orders to terminate the J-22 contract."

"What?" McBride gasped. His primary responsibility was overseeing the J-22 contract.

"Yeah, the J-22. I've been directed to terminate it," Friedlander repeated.

The Defense Department had awarded Chambers Aerospace the contract to design and build the J-22, which was a next-generation unmanned aerial vehicle. It was the most sophisticated and expensive military aircraft ever approved by Congress. Chambers Aerospace got the contract because it held a large technological lead over its competitors.

"What happened?"

Friedlander shrugged. "Nothing."

"I don't understand."

"I don't either. Apparently, they want to give the contract to someone else."

"That's crazy," McBride scoffed. "There's no other company with the know-how to build the J-22."

"You may be right about that; I don't know what to tell you. I suspect they'll put the project on hold."

"Who made this decision?"

"Well, I don't know for sure, but I'm told the order came from the Secretary himself."

"This is insane. The J-22 is going to be the greatest feat of aerospace engineering in history. It'll put us miles ahead of everyone."

"Well, I don't make the rules. I just have to make sure this gets done. Can you take care of this as soon as possible?"

McBride shook his head. He had worked with Chambers Aerospace for over nine years and he couldn't terminate their biggest contract without an explanation. "First, I need to know what's going on. I can't do something like this without knowing what's going on."

"I appreciate what you're saying, but I'm in a difficult position."

"Then I can't do it," McBride responded defiantly. "I've got twenty years in this office; I deserve an explanation." McBride had seen contracts terminated before and he usually didn't care, but he felt a special connection to Chambers.

Friedlander frowned. "All right. Let's go grab some lunch then."

"Okay."

The two men got into Friedlander's SUV and drove across the Potomac to Georgetown.

"Where are we going?" McBride asked.

"I know a nice café where we can speak privately."

The men didn't speak again until they arrived at the restaurant. The hostess escorted them to an outside table. "Young lady, can you get us a couple of…vodka martini okay, Troy?"

"Sure."

"A couple of vodka martinis."

The hostess nodded. "Yes, sir."

Friedlander moved his chair a little closer to McBride and leaned in. "Troy, everything we say is confidential, right?"

McBride nodded somberly. "Of course."

"Good. Well, you know that one of the things I've always tried to do is keep politics out of this business as much as possible. That's very important to me. I know you try to do the same thing. But the Department has changed; in some ways for the better, some ways for the worse."

McBride nodded.

"Here you go, gentlemen," the hostess said as she placed the drinks on the table.

"Thanks." Friedlander took a hit off his maritini. "You know, we're getting budgets that are bigger than ever, but the politics have gotten uglier. And Christ, the cronyism now."

McBride nodded again. He knew what Friedlander was talking about. The Defense Department had started to award major contracts to inferior companies based on their connection to officials in the Packer Administration.

"In any case," Friedlander continued, "Chambers Aerospace is not friendly with the Administration."

"Is that what this is about?" McBride reacted, raising his voice. "That's bullshit! Absolute bullshit!"

"I know it is. I'm not happy about it either."

"We've got to have a reason. Hell, for a termination, the contract requires a reason."

"There is a reason, sort of," Friedlander replied weakly. "An official reason at least."

"What is it?"

"Chambers Aerospace isn't capable of building the aircraft."

"Come on; that's dishonest; absolutely not true."

"It is what it is."

"This makes no sense to me; absolutely no sense."

"Well, there's one thing I haven't told you yet. Do you see that TV interview Chambers gave last month?"

"Yeah, I saw it." McBride remembered the interview well. Indeed, he had seen all of Chambers' interviews.

> **Interviewer:** What separates you from other people, David? What's the secret of your success?
>
> **Chambers:** No secret; I probably just have higher self-esteem than most other people.
>
> **Interviewer:** It can't be that simple. There's must be something else you do differently?
>
> **Chambers:** Well, other people pray; they hope; they wish. Then they wonder why nothing changes; why they don't have the lives or the happiness they desire; why their God forsakes them. They look for guidance in ancient texts written by primitive people; people who believed the Earth was flat, disease was caused by sin, and invisible demons caused misfortune. I rely on myself, and I accept full responsibility for all my successes and failures.
>
> **Interviewer:** So you're not religious, then? You don't believe in God?
>
> **Chambers:** Well, I received a prophetic revelation from God once.
>
> **Interviewer:** Really?
>
> **Chambers:** Yes. I've never revealed it before publicly. I hesitate to do so now.
>
> **Interviewer:** You can't leave us hanging like that.
>
> **Chambers:** Okay. He told me that we need to replace the Ten Commandments with only one: Face reality, trust your own mind, and honestly follow the moral intuitions of your own conscience.

"That interview was an insult to…" Friedlander started.

"So what?" McBride interrupted. "So the guy's not religious."

"I heard the Secretary was pissed off; that he really blew a gasket. He didn't appreciate Chambers making fun of his faith."

"Then the guy needs to lighten up. What's he going to do? Take away all of Chambers' contracts? We might as well surrender to the Chinese if he does that."

Friedlander hesitated. "Well…"

"No…they're not going to lose other contracts? Tell me that's not happening."

"Well…there's nothing official, but I've heard a few rumors."

"What rumors?"

"Plans may be in the works to suspend and debar Chambers Aerospace from any future contracts with the Department."

McBride slammed his fist on the table. "I can't believe…this is outrageous!"

"Calm down; let's not jump to any conclusions. Maybe they'll be satisfied getting Chambers off this one contract. Like you said before, Chambers is the only company with the know-how. Even if another company gets the J-22, I don't see how they could keep Chambers from at least subcontracting on some of the more advanced components. In any case, there's nothing we can do."

McBride shook his head back and forth in disbelief.

"Can you do it, Troy?"

"What?" McBride answered angrily.

"Inform Chambers Aerospace of the J-22 termination."

McBride drew in a deep breath and let out a heavy sigh. "What the hell am I supposed to tell those guys? 'You won't lick Packer's boots so you lose a billion dollar contract.'"

Friedlander grimaced. "Don't be foolish, Troy. Believe me, you don't want to jeopardize your own career."

What a bunch of pathetic…but goddammit, I can't quit my job. "Right," McBride replied tersely.

"So you'll do it, then?"

McBride clenched his jaw and grunted.

"Troy?"

"Yes," McBride replied softly. "I'll do it."

* * *

Chambers stood silently over the brightly lit drafting table, carefully studying the drawings laid out in front of him. He could barely control his excitement. "Wow. This is a great design; a truly great design." Whenever Chambers saw a highly creative and disciplined application of thought, it always renewed his faith in humanity. "Man, oh man, I miss this."

"You're the still the best, David." Ernesto patted Chambers on the back. "But he has your potential."

"Where did you find this guy?"

"Your alma mater," Ernesto answered with a satisfied smile. "First in his class. He spent seven years at Boeing and then I recruited him."

"Boeing must've been pissed."

"They were."

"I'd like to meet him."

A knock on the door interrupted the conversation. Chambers' secretary walked in. "David, this just came in. It looks important." She handed him an envelope emblazoned with the Department of Defense logo and labeled "Personal and Confidential." Chambers opened the envelope and pulled out a short letter.

Dear Mr. Chambers:

This letter shall serve as written notice that the United States Department of Defense has decided to terminate Contract Number AC223998 for the design and manufacture of the J-22 unmanned aerial vehicle. The termination shall be effective ninety days from the date of this letter. The foregoing termination is pursuant to section 34.5.6 of the contract and is in accordance with Part 49 of the Federal Acquisition Regulations.

A termination contract officer (TCO) will be contacting you shortly to negotiate the settlement of the contract and to coordinate all necessary matters involved in this termination, including the termination of any subcontracts. Please contact the undersigned if you have any questions regarding this matter.

Sincerely,

Troy McBride
Contract Administrator
United States Department of Defense

Chambers read the letter three times before he looked up in disbelief. He had worked with McBride for several years and they had a friendly relationship. Chambers was also surprised by the formality of the letter and by McBride's failure to give him an advance warning.

"What is it?" Ernesto asked.

"It's…it's…"

"Here, let me take a look at that." Ernesto snatched the letter out of Chambers' hand and read it quickly. "Holy…this is huge. Did Troy call you?"

"No."

"Wow. Did you piss him off?"

"I don't think so. I talked to him a couple of weeks ago and we were

364

kidding around. He didn't mention anything. I...I don't get this. I'm going to call him right now." Chambers picked up the phone and dialed McBride's number, but he got routed to voicemail: "This is Troy McBride, Contract Administrator at the United States Department of Defense. I'll be out of the office until August 23rd. Please leave a message and I'll get back to you then, or press 2 to speak with my administrative assistant."

Chambers hung up. "The guy's out of town for three weeks."

"What should we do?"

"I don't know. Let's get Tom up here."

Chambers picked up the letter again. "This just doesn't make any sense." He turned the letter over, revealing a short message scrawled in pencil: "David, call me at 227-386-4234, 8/12, 21:00, from a pay phone."

* * *

Heavy gray clouds drizzled steadily as Chambers trotted awkwardly from his car to a pay phone outside a local supermarket. He buttoned his coat, trying to stay dry, but water had already seeped through his shirt. He dialed McBride at the appointed time.

"David?"

"Yeah."

"Hey, I'm sorry about all this. You're probably wondering what's going on."

"Yeah."

"Well, since Packer, you never know when they're going to be listening. Everyone's paranoid, myself included. So that's the reason for the pay phone."

"Okay."

"I just wanted to explain what was going on, at least what little I know."

"Okay."

"First of all, the termination of J-22 is pure politics. There's a lot of that going on at the Department these days. To my knowledge, there won't be a finding that you did anything wrong, and I'll do my best to make sure that you get paid for everything you've done. My boss agrees with that, too. You won't lose any money on this deal."

"Okay."

"Unfortunately, I've got worse news."

"Okay."

"It's still a rumor, but I've heard that Department lawyers are talking about suspending and debarring Chambers Aerospace."

"That's outrageous!" Chambers thundered. "I won't stand for this!

Do you understand me, Troy? I won't stand for it!"

"I know, David. I know. I want to help."

"What are grounds for this?"

"I don't know. Like I said, it's just a rumor at this point, but I think you should prepare yourself to the extent you can."

Chambers slammed his hand against the side of the phone booth. "I don't believe what I'm hearing!"

"I know it's hard to understand, but this is Washington. You know what it's like here. Nobody cares about the merits of anything. It's all about paying back favors. I wish I could do something for you."

Chambers felt like ripping the phone off the wall and smashing it on the cement, but he simply slammed it down without saying goodbye. He stomped down the sidewalk with his head down, pacing back and forth, muttering obscenities. Then he stopped and stood quietly, watching the moonlight shimmer off the rain-drenched pavement, his anger replaced by an emotion he had never felt in his life—complete helplessness.

CHAPTER 44

If a man abide not in me, he is cast forth as a branch, and is withered; and men gather them, and cast them into the fire, and they are burned.

—BIBLE, JOHN 15:6. *When popes and other Christian men of God ruled the Western world, believers cited this verse as justification to burn nonbelievers at the stake or torture them to death*

At ten minutes past midnight, Danny Dimarco slipped a thin plastic card into the security console outside Heilbrenner's office suite. Dimarco didn't normally have access to the most exclusive part of the Infinity enclave, but the card he possessed was attached to a sophisticated computer that could dynamically configure the card's magnetic strip to match the code programmed into the lock.

The door clicked open and Dimarco peered in carefully and surveyed the area. It consisted of four offices, a kitchen, and six secretary stations. Several file cabinets lined the back wall. Before beginning his task, Dimarco reached into his jacket pocket and felt for his gun. The sensation of the cold metal on his fingertips always made him feel more secure.

Dimarco moved quietly around the handsomely decorated space until he found Heilbrenner's office. The door was protected by its own lock so Dimarco slipped in his magic card again and waited. It took a little longer, but the door clicked open. Dimarco stepped inside and closed the door softly behind him. He looked around the spacious expanse and couldn't help but admire it. The handcrafted furniture was ultra-modern and exquisitely stylish. Several museum-quality pieces of art graced the walls. Dimarco sat down behind Heilbrenner's desk and quickly looked through the drawers. He didn't see anything important although he was surprised to see several stacks of hundred dollar bills held together by rubber bands. Dimarco swiveled around to Heilbrenner's credenza, and then knelt down and opened it. There were piles of documents inside, which he pulled out and carefully stacked on the floor. He perused them quickly; most of them related to construction projects that Infinity was undertaking. Dimarco was about to put the documents back when he noticed a small circular latch in the back of the credenza. He tried to lift it up, but it was difficult to grasp because of its size. He grabbed a pen out of Heilbrenner's desk and slipped it through the hole. He held both ends of the pen and pulled harder. Finally, the bottom panel of the credenza popped out suddenly, throwing Dimarco backwards. After he steadied himself, he marveled at what he saw. The credenza panel had hidden a storage area in the floor that housed three boxes of files. Dimarco opened all of the boxes and quickly scanned their contents. They contained legal and bank records.

Dimarco pulled the first box out of the hole and placed it on the carpet behind Heilbrenner's desk. He was about to pull the second box out when the door to Heilbrenner's office swung open.

"Who's in here?"

"Oh!" Dimarco's head sprang up from the behind the desk. A security guard stood in the doorway. "You startled me."

"What are you doing in here?"

"Uh…I had to…uh…reconfigure Mr. Heilbrenner's computer system."

The guard glanced at the computer monitor, which wasn't turned on. He put his hand on his gun. "Do you work here?"

"Yeah." Dimarco held up his ID badge.

"Nobody is allowed in here—under any circumstances."

Dimarco thought of reaching for his own gun, but decided against it. "Well, this was an emergency situation. Mr. Heilbrenner needs…"

"I wasn't informed of any emergency," the guard interrupted.

Dimarco shrugged. "Well, I'm sorry you're in the dark, but I've got to get this done."

"I need to call Mr. Heilbrenner," the guard said. "You stay right where you are. What's your name?"

Dimarco slipped his hand into his jacket pocket and pulled out a small cylindrical canister. He held it tightly in his fist. "Look, it's pretty late; I don't think you should wake him up over this. It would probably upset him."

The guard moved toward the phone. "I need your name. Give me your ID badge."

"Okay." Dimarco stood up and then suddenly lunged across Heilbrenner's desk. He pressed the button on the small canister, blasting pepper spray into the guard's eyes. The guard fell backward, but pulled his gun out of its holster and fired a shot. Dimarco instinctively hit the ground, but the bullet lodged harmlessly into the back wall. Dimarco got up and kicked the guard in the face and then jumped on top of him. He wrestled the gun away and then pointed it at the guard's head. "Don't move!"

The guard tried to get up, but Dimarco kicked him in the face again, crushing the bones in his lower jaw. Dimarco threw open Heilbrenner's armoire and took out a large crystal vase. He shattered it across the back of the guard's head, knocking him unconscious.

Dimarco grabbed all of the boxes and escaped down an emergency stairway. He scrambled out to his car and sped through Infinity's gates. When he was safely away, he dialed a number on his cell phone.

"Go ahead," a voice answered.

"It's Dimarco. My cover's blown."

"Get back to Providence as soon as possible."

* * *

Chambers' heart sank as he read the letter.

Dear Mr. Chambers:

Please be advised that the United States Department of Defense has decided to suspend Chambers Aerospace from contracting with the Department for the following reasons:

Noncompliance with obligations under its contracts with the Department.

Under the terms of this suspension, Chambers Aerospace is temporarily disqualified from contracting with the Department until either the suspension becomes final or is removed. You may request a hearing with the Department to contest the suspension. If the outcome of the hearing is to uphold the suspension, the suspension will become permanent and Chambers Aerospace will be debarred for a period of three years. Notwithstanding the foregoing, Chambers Aerospace may be permitted to act as a subcontractor on certain contracts in which the Department is a party, at the discretion of the Department.

The foregoing suspension shall be effective immediately. Please contact the undersigned if you have any questions regarding this matter.

Sincerely,

Robert F. Friedlander
Chief Contract Administrator
United States Department of Defense

Chambers stewed angrily for several minutes and then directed his public relations team to issue a press release stating that the company had received more recognition for outstanding work than any other company in the history of the Defense Department. Chambers also publicly announced that the suspension and debarment was unjustified and that the company would fight it. But the stock price nevertheless tumbled.

The Defense Department refused to comment on the suspension, but others celebrated—Chambers had finally gotten his comeuppance for mocking people of faith. Newhall issued a press release: "A sinner, a man who rejects God's laws and the accepted standards of morality can never succeed. Mr. Chambers must either repent or face the consequences of straying down a wicked path." Several editorial writers picked up the same theme, predicting that the demise of Chambers was finally at hand.

Chambers called an emergency board meeting.

* * *

Heilbrenner was reading the newspaper in the back of his limousine when the ring of the car phone startled him. He hit Speaker on the vehicle's command console. "John Heilbrenner."

"Mr. Heilbrenner, we've got a situation here, sir."

"What is it?"

"There's been a breach of security."

"Where?"

"Your office."

"What...what happened?"

"Somebody broke in. A security guard confronted the intruder, but he assaulted the guard and escaped."

"Do you have any idea who did this?"

"Yes, Danny Dimarco. The guard's in the hospital, but he was able to identify Mr. Dimarco."

"Who's Danny Dimarco?"

"He works in information technology."

"Where is he now?"

"Unknown, sir. We sent someone out to his apartment, but he wasn't there."

"I want a thorough search of his apartment."

"Already in progress, sir."

"Good, I'll be at the office in fifteen minutes. Don't touch anything."

* * *

Nine directors filed into the conference room at Chambers Aerospace headquarters and took their seats around a long walnut table. The board consisted of three inside directors—Chambers, Ernesto, and Tom Jeffries—and six outside directors. The outside directors represented the major institutional shareholders and held majority-voting power as a block.

Normally, Chambers Aerospace board meetings were a lackluster affair. The directors rarely made any decisions of significant import. Since the company had been so successful, the outside directors were content to let Chambers and his management team run it. All of the directors owned stock in the company, and despite the recent downturn, they were rich as a result. But now the company found itself in a tenuous position; another strike suit was pending, the company had lost its biggest contract, and the future of the company's relationship with the government was uncertain.

"All right, let's get started," Chambers began. "The first item on the agenda is the suspension of the company by the Defense Department. The DOD's letter states that the company is suspended pending a hearing, which we plan to pursue aggressively. The grounds for the suspension are shaky and Tom is working with outside counsel who are experts in this area. In their opinion, we should be able to get the suspension overturned. I've also spoken with McBride and Friedlander, our main contacts at Defense. They've assured me that the company will still be allowed to subcontract on the J-22 once a new lead contractor is chosen. We'll also have plenty of opportunities on other contracts. The bottom line is that I don't expect the company's revenues to be affected that much. Of course, the bad publicity could hurt the company on the civil side, but as of right now, I expect that we'll only miss our quarterly target by about five cents a share. That's not bad, considering. Does anyone have any questions?"

None of the directors spoke, pleased with the relatively good news, but the energy in the room remained charged.

"The other item on the agenda is the pending strike suit," Chambers continued. "The status…"

"We've got to settle that suit," one director urged before Chambers could finish his sentence.

"I agree," another piped in. "That ranch of yours is way too controversial."

"Leave the ranch out of this," Chambers retorted.

"Like hell I will. Since you've opened that godforsaken place, the company has been sued twice. Now we've lost a major contract and you've alienated the government. Stock price is at a five-year low. This is totally irresponsible."

Chambers hesitated and then stood up. "We'll make it through this challenge just like all the others," he said calmly. "The last thing we need is your Chicken Little attitude. Do I need to remind everyone that we won the last suit?"

"This suit is different," the director continued angrily. "You should've known that your actions were inappropriate. You risked the welfare of the company in order to gratify your own ego." Everyone waited for Chambers to respond to the insult, but he quietly sat down.

The director spoke up again, "Tom, what's your opinion?"

All eyes turned to Jeffries. Although he almost always supported Chambers, he wasn't a yes man and the outside directors respected his opinion.

Jeffries gently fingered his meeting notes and then glanced quickly at Chambers. "Well, there's a risk here; no doubt about it. A much bigger risk than the last suit. I'm worried because we've struck an emotional nerve. There's almost no chance of getting the case dismissed before trial, and if it does get to a jury, there's no way to predict what might happen. Anytime you bring up religion, the irrational comes out in people. That's a time bomb waiting to explode."

Chambers cringed. He knew Jeffries was right about the irrational aspect of the suit; it was a dangerous wild card that could seriously cripple the company.

"How do you respond to that, David?" another director questioned.

"I think Tom's point is well-taken," Chambers said evenly.

"Well, don't you think it makes sense to settle the suit? We can't risk the future of the company."

Chambers shrugged. "I don't know. I really...I just don't know."

The directors exchanged puzzled looks. Chambers was normally a forceful and decisive leader. They had never seen him so tentative and unsure of himself.

"We need to make a decision," the director pressed.

"I can't settle it," Chambers said softly.

"We'd like to you to reconsider."

Chambers shook his head. "No, that's not possible."

"Well, I'm sorry you feel that way, David. You've put us in an impossible position." The director paused and took a deep breath, gathering the courage to continue. "We've always supported you in the past, but this time we can't. We have a fiduciary responsibility to the shareholders. All of the outside directors met yesterday and we decided that if you refused to settle the case, we would have no other choice but to remove you as President of the company."

Chambers didn't speak, but the color quickly drained from his face. "You went behind my back?"

"We acted in the best interests of the company."

"You went behind my back."

"Call it whatever you like. If you change your mind, we'll reverse our decision. If not, then we'll be forced to vote you out at our next meeting."

Everyone waited for Chambers to respond, but he sat in stunned silence. Ernesto finally jumped in. "We'll have to consider everything that's been said here and make a decision. Your concerns are certainly valid and I think we can resolve this matter to everyone's satisfaction. If there's no other business to discuss, I suggest wc adjourn the meeting."

No one said anything. "Okay, thanks everyone for coming," Ernesto concluded.

As the Board members shuffled out of the room, Chambers didn't move. One of the directors stopped next to him. "David, I hope you understand the position you've put us in. Nobody wanted this, but we've got to be practical. We need you to settle this suit."

Chambers stared at the man, but didn't speak.

That night, Chambers lay restlessly in bed. *They can't oust me! It's my goddamn company!* he silently raged. Later, he felt afraid, like his life was spinning out of control. *Is there any point to fighting? Does it make one ounce of difference? Does anything...anything! make an ounce of difference?* Chambers simmered quietly for several hours until he fell asleep. His mind drifted uneasily until it transported him to a bright red vinyl booth in a diner that he didn't recognize. Behind the counter, there was a sizzling grill with crackling flames and curly wafts of smoke dancing in the air.

Chambers looked around for other people, but he was alone. He started to get up when the front door swung open and a man wearing a long coat walked in. The man wore a gray felt hat with a wide brim that obscured his face. He walked briskly toward Chambers' booth, whistling gaily. When the man got to the table, he looked down at Chambers and tilted his hat up, revealing his face. "Mind if I sit down," he said, smiling.

"You're…you're Robert…Robert Newhall," Chambers stammered.

"Indeed I am." Newhall sat down and let out a loud belly laugh as he placed his hat on the table. "Well, this is a quite a surprise. Quite a surprise indeed. Look at you."

"What about me?"

"I had expected you to be…well…let's just say I never expected to see you here."

"What are you talking about?"

Newhall placed his hands together in a praying motion and nodded solemnly. "I forgive you, my wayward son."

"I don't what you're talking about."

"For your thoughts. I forgive you for your thoughts." Newhall paused. "But it's okay now. We're going to be great friends, you and I." Newhall flashed a cruel smile.

A chill ran down Chambers' spine. "I'm not your friend."

"Oh, but you are. You're finally on the right path. I'd hate to see you end up there." Newhall pointed to the grill where a naked man suddenly appeared amidst the flames, screaming and writhing in agony.

Chambers felt a surge of fear, and then rage. He lunged across the table and grabbed Newhall by the throat, but suddenly found himself clutching a hissing cobra. He recoiled and tried to jump out of the booth, but he couldn't move. The snake threw its head back and struck its fangs deep into his forearm. "Ahhhhhh!" Chambers screamed, jolting himself out of the dream. He grabbed his arm and looked for the snakebite, but then realized he was in his bedroom. *Goddamn it! What's happening to me?* He picked up the phone and called Ernesto.

"Hello," a sleepy voice answered.

"Ernesto, Ernesto, I need…it's David, it's…I need…I need to talk."

"Slow down. Hold on." Ernesto glanced at the clock on his bedside table. "It's four in the morning, what is it?"

"I'm sorry, I had this…this dream…I can't agree to the Board's demands. I can't do it."

"What are you saying? Tell me what you're saying."

"If they want me out, then I'm out."

Several moments of silence passed.

"Ernesto? Ernesto?"

"Relax. Calm down."

Chambers took a deep breath.

"You know I support you, but we need to take some time to think about this. Let's not rush into anything."

"Well, I just know I can't do this. There's no way I can do this."

"What do you want to do?"

"I want to finish the J-22."

"Are you crazy?"

"All I know is that I'm finishing the J-22. If they want to stop me, they'll have to kill me."

"You're serious?"

"Yes. I'm going to finish the J-22. Are you with me?"

"For chrissakes, David."

"Are you with me?"

"Yes."

"Good. I want to unload my shares, too. If they want to take the company, they can have it."

"Come on, David, that's absurd. We built this company and I'm not about to let you throw it away. It's our life's work."

"We built it; that's all that matters."

"It's our…"

"No," Chambers interrupted. "I've made my decision."

Ernesto sighed gently. "I'm not going to change your mind?"

"No."

CHAPTER 45

There is grandeur in this view of life, with its several powers, having been originally breathed into a few forms or into one; and that, whilst this planet has gone cycling on according to the fixed law of gravity, from so simple a beginning endless forms most beautiful and most wonderful have been, and are being, evolved.

—CHARLES DARWIN, *ON THE ORIGIN OF SPECIES (1st edition)*

Josephine strode purposefully across the freshly polished floor at Union Station in Washington. She glanced at her image, glimmering off the long sheets of marble, and hoped she looked exactly as he remembered her. She boarded the 4:45 train to Harper's Ferry, West Virginia.

As the train chugged away from the station into the Virginia countryside, Josephine lay back in her seat and tried to relax. But she couldn't control the rush of thoughts and emotions. She thought of how he looked at her and the charge that electrified her body from his touch. She also reflected on his gentle bearing and the innocent kindness that permeated his soul.

When the train arrived, he was waiting as she stepped onto the platform. She ran toward his outstretched arms and sprang into his chest. "Hi David," she said gaily, fastening her arms tightly around his back.

"Hi Josie," Chambers said softly, rejoicing as he caressed her back. They held each other for several minutes in the middle of the platform, oblivious to the other passengers who stopped to stare at their passionate embrace. Then Chambers suddenly started laughing.

Josephine released her grip. "What is it?"

"I guess I'm just surprised how happy I am. I don't know if I've ever been this happy before. It's like nothing matters."

Josephine smiled and kissed him on the cheek. "Did anything ever matter?"

"What I mean is, it doesn't matter that it doesn't matter."

"Oh, David," Josephine giggled. "You're absolutely perfect."

"Perfect?"

"Perfectly human."

Chambers grinned sheepishly. He never felt as vulnerable as he did when he was around Josephine. Her presence brought out the wide-eyed boy in him, and he was able to completely let go. "Here, let me take your bag," he said.

"Thanks."

"Would you like to take a walk? It's wonderful here this time of year."

"Sure."

Chambers and Josephine exited the station and walked hand in hand to a bridge that crossed the Shenandoah River. They hiked along the bank, enjoying the steady rush of water and lush plant life. Chambers thought back to their first meeting in Salt Lake; it was the strongest connection he had ever felt with another human being, and he reflected that Josephine was the only person who understood him completely.

"It's beautiful here," Chambers said. "You're beautiful. Sometimes it's hard to believe that nature could produce such exquisite art."

Josephine smiled. "It's hard to be away from you."

"I know." Chambers put his arm around her waist and pulled her close, enveloping her in his virile resonance. "I'd forgotten just how much I love you. You know, I tried to convince myself that I didn't need you."

Josephine dropped her head on Chambers' shoulder. "Will we ever be together, David?"

Chambers looked away.

"David?"

"I...I don't know."

They walked in silence for a while though the brisk air. It was early fall and the leaves had just started to turn.

"I have bad news," Josephine said finally.

"What is it?"

"The government—the Office of Homeland Protection—may move against you soon. Infinity's been putting pressure on the Administration. They say you run a cult and that you're a danger. They're going to start watching you."

"Watching me?"

"Yes, surveillance."

"That's ridiculous!"

"I don't want them to hurt you. I want you to give up."

"I can handle them," Chambers said firmly.

"But you can't," Josephine pleaded. "They'll come at you with everything. Nobody can beat them."

Chambers stopped and faced Josephine. "You expect me to give up?" he said, his voice uncharacteristically stern.

"No...I mean...you won't be giving up. You just stop playing their game. Walk away from it. We can go away together."

"You know I can't do that."

Josephine sighed. "I know," she said softly.

"Let's go back," Chambers said. "It's getting cold."

"Okay."

They held their arms around each other as a choppy wind chilled their faces. After a while, Chambers said, "I need your help."

"I know. I'll do whatever I can."

Chambers squeezed Josephine's shoulder. "It's going to be okay, Josie. I promise."

"Okay."

They walked to the hotel and lay quietly next to each other on the bed. Josephine rubbed Chambers' stomach. "I can get anything you need," she said.

"Shhhh...let's not talk right now," Chambers began unbuttoning Josephine's blouse. "I just want your naked body next to mine. I need to hold you."

They removed each other's clothes and made love for several hours. Chambers had planned to be gentle, but when he felt the warmth of Josephine's smooth flesh, his passion ignited. He entered her roughly with a powerful thrust and she bit his shoulder and dug her fingernails into his back in acceptance.

The next morning, they made love again and then took a shower together. Chambers ordered room service and they got dressed and sat down to breakfast.

"You need to take this surveillance seriously, David."

"I don't understand how they can get away with that," Chambers reacted angrily. "That can't be legal."

"They're accusing you of brainwashing kids at your camps."

"Why? Because I promote science. They want me to teach kids that life on the planet is the result of a magic act by that petty tyrant depicted in the Bible. My God, that view of life is so…I don't even have a word for it. Hopeless."

"You're depriving kids of a spiritual life. That means you're a threat to the well-being of Americans. That's all the legal basis they need to come after you."

Chambers' countenance stiffened. "That pisses me off! The dishonesty…"

"They say you're like a cult leader."

"So what does that mean? They're going to crucify me?"

"They can make your life difficult."

Chambers looked away.

"David?"

"I need you to do something for me," he said finally.

"Anything."

"I need two passport-size photos of you."

"David!"

"That's what I need."

"What are you planning?"

"I can't tell you right now; it's best that you don't know. You have to trust me."

"I need you."

"Then trust me."

"Okay."

Chambers glanced at his watch. "We better get you to the station. Your train leaves in half an hour."

On the platform, as they waited for the train, they looked at each other intently, straining to absorb and hold fast the other's image.

"When will I see you again?" Josephine asked, lightly squeezing Chambers' hand.

Chambers hesitated. "I…I don't know."

"David, I…"

"Shhhh…" Chambers interrupted as he hugged her. "Just remember that I love you—always."

"I love you, too."

* * *

Heilbrenner walked into his office and silently surveyed the scene. He stepped over shattered pieces of broken crystal and clenched his jaw. The vase had been willed to him after his mother's passing several years ago. He turned to the head of Infinity security. "I want everyone out of here."

"John, I wanted to brief you on…"

"No," Heilbrenner interrupted coldly. "Get out."

After everyone filed out, Heilbrenner looked behind his desk and saw the bottom panel of his credenza. He kicked it aside and then peered into the now-exposed storage space; it was empty. Heilbrenner sat behind his desk and took a deep breath. He sat motionless until the buzz of his intercom startled him. "Mr. Heilbrenner, you've got a call on line one."

"I don't want to be disturbed."

"It's Reverend Newhall, sir."

"Put him through."

Heilbrenner picked up the receiver. "Robert."

"What happened? I heard there was a break in."

"Yes."

"Was anything taken?"

Heilbrenner didn't answer.

"John?"

"No, just a little money out of my desk."

"Good, I was worried that, you know, I always worry that we might compromise…"

"No, don't worry about that," Heilbrenner interrupted. "Everything's fine. I'm in meeting with security now; I'll call you later."

* * *

As Josephine rode the train back to Washington, she closed her eyes and replayed every moment; every touch, every kiss, every long caress; the warmth and certainty of his being. Josephine reveled in the intoxicating daydream, but something…it was almost imperceptible and she couldn't name it, but something wasn't right.

CHAPTER 46

In any culture, subculture, or family in which belief is valued above thought, and self-surrender is valued above self-expression, and conformity is valued above integrity, those who preserve their self-esteem are likely to be heroic exceptions.

—Nathaniel Branden, *The Six Pillars of Self-Esteem*

The white streaks of the Milky Way lit up the sky and a crescent moon hung easily over the countryside surrounding Kaleidoscope Ranch. The rhythmic chirping of crickets was the only sound until the distant rumbling of a plane interrupted the calm. As the aircraft roared closer, trees began to sway from the windblast of the powerful jet engines, and then a burst of light suddenly ignited the valley. As the plane swooped down and landed softly on the runway, technicians finished downloading the data from its computers and initiated their analysis.

* * *

The grand ballroom of Kaleidoscope Ranch pulsed with excitement at the second anniversary of its founding. It was a proud occasion for everyone who had poured their hearts into the majestic complex in the Northern California wilderness. The room buzzed with a carefree gaiety and a shared feeling of being part of something important. Chambers completely forgot about his troubles and existed in his own perfect universe, floating above the festivities in a state of quiet ecstasy.

Flames crackled in the fireplace and the band played a spirited rendition of *In the Mood* until Chambers took the stage. He raised his arms high above his head, acknowledging the cheers of the crowd, and then brought them down softly. "Let me have your attention for a moment, everyone. I hate to interrupt the party, but I wanted to thank everyone for their contribution to Kaleidoscope Ranch. What we've built here goes way beyond my wildest expectations and this has truly been the greatest two years of my life."

The room erupted in a boisterous cheer while Ernesto waved wildly in the back of the room. Chambers stepped down from the stage and cued the band. The musicians hit Chambers' favorite swing tune and he danced awkwardly through the crowd, embracing his friends as they swirled around him. Ernesto waded through the sea of people and gave Chambers an exuberant bear hug. "I hate to steal your moment, but it's time for our meeting."

Chambers nodded. When they got outside, he sucked in a deep breath of the cool fall air. "Control Room?"

"Yeah. From here on out, I don't think we can take any chances."

Chambers nodded. "Okay."

The men walked to a building on the other side of the courtyard. Chambers slid a keycard into the lock on the back door and it clicked open. Inside, a security console scanned their retinas and beeped twice, accepting each man. Down a short hallway, an elevator door opened, which they boarded for the ride down to the Control Room, a covert space five stories underground, wrapped in cement, and impervious

382

to surveillance. After a short descent, they stepped into a small, dimly lit room with walls forged entirely of steel. The room was furnished with an oak conference table, two high-backed, reclining leather chairs, a liquor cabinet, and a small refrigerator.

"Everything go okay?" Chambers asked.

"Perfect; no problems whatsoever."

"Any evidence of detection?"

"No, we flew below radar and stayed outside of all major flight paths." Ernesto paused. "But I don't think we should ever try this again—way too risky."

"I completely agree; this was a one-time thing," Chambers sat down. "What about the extra weapons systems? Any effect on performance?"

"A slight slowdown, but almost imperceptible. As far as maneuverability, it's hard to tell. That's one thing we'll be simulating in our tests over the next few weeks. But even with extra payload, this plane will outmaneuver anything."

"Well, that's what I like to hear," Chambers said cheerily. "I think that's cause for celebration."

Ernesto grinned. "Okay."

Chambers opened the cabinet and pulled out a bottle of Johnnie Walker Black, a can of club soda, and two glasses. He got some ice out of the freezer and mixed the drinks. "Here you are, my friend."

"Thank you. Here's to your vision of the future." Ernesto raised his glass.

"*Our* vision. And to the J-22." Chambers gently tapped Ernesto's glass.

The men spoke for a while longer until Chambers looked down at his watch. "You ready to get back to the party?"

"No, not me." Ernesto shook his head and yawned. "I think I'll turn in." He downed the last of his sweet amber liquid.

They walked back to the elevator and stood in silence as it lifted them back to the surface.

"Thanks for taking care of this, Ernesto," Chambers said as the doors opened. "I'm glad I can count on you."

"No problem."

Chambers embraced his friend, holding him close and patting him gently on the back. "Good night, buddy. See you tomorrow."

"Night, David."

As Chambers walked back to the party, the huge risk he was about to take suddenly began to sink in. He also began to worry about the surveillance Josephine had warned him about. He knew that he now had powerful enemies and he shuddered when he thought of what he might have to do to protect himself.

"How about two hundred a hole?" George Baker challenged as he pulled a driver out of his golf bag on the first tee.

"Let's make it five." Al Rogers answered.

Baker smiled. "Sure, start us off."

Baker led the President's reelection team. His job was to make sure that the President's speeches and policy proposals were consistent with his team's polling of the electorate. Although the next election was over a year away, Baker's team had been hard at work since the President's first-term victory. They had crisscrossed the country several times, surveying the populace and looking for issues that the President could use as wedges to divide the electorate to his advantage. The polls also gauged the President's level of popularity and identified areas in which he might be vulnerable to attack. Since both Rogers and Baker were avid golfers, they usually conducted their meetings at an exclusive country club in Bethesda, Maryland.

Rogers teed up his ball and took a few practice swings.

"Is that the new Taylormade Bubble Shaft?" Baker asked.

"Yeah, this club's got pop. Watch this drive." Rogers lined up his feet and then swung hard, knocking the ball 230 yards straight down the center of the fairway.

"Nice drive," Baker said admiringly, and then chuckled lightly to himself. He figured that after he delivered his report, Rogers would lose his concentration and his game would fall apart. Although Baker took his job seriously and genuinely hoped that Packer would be reelected, he had a mercenary's mentality. He figured that if the President lost his reelection bid, some other politician would hire him to do the same kind of work at the same considerable salary and expense account.

Baker teed off, driving the ball further than Rogers, but into the right rough.

"Gotta get those hands through, George. Otherwise, you better get out your checkbook."

Baker chuckled. Although he had planned to wait, he decided that if Rogers was going to be cocky, then it was time to retaliate. "Are you ready for my report?"

"Sure, what have you got for me this month?" Rogers pressed the accelerator on the golf cart and drove it down the fairway.

"Well, I've got good news and bad news."

"Don't you always."

"The good news is that people are happy with the President's stand on most of the social issues—especially in the flyover states." Baker's condescending reference to America's heartland wasn't surprising.

Both he and Rogers were prep school products from the Northeast and they related little to the President's core constituency of religious conservatives in rural America.

Rogers nodded. "Good."

"People appreciate that he has a strong moral compass," Baker went on. "Our polls continue to show that he can divide and conquer on the gay marriage issue."

"Okay, that's nothing new. What else you got?"

"The President should stop pretending that he's an environmentalist. Nobody's buying it, and frankly, nobody cares. He should stick to what got him elected."

"Agreed."

Rogers brought the golf cart to a halt next to his ball and grabbed his seven-iron.

"Now, the bad news is bad," Baker said. "Are you sure you want to hear it now?"

"Of course. How bad can it be?"

"We've spoken with church leaders both inside and outside of the Infinity Network. A lot of them think Newhall should run for President."

"Come on. That's ridiculous."

Baker shrugged. "They say that Packer has given their agenda a good start, but Newhall is the man to take it all the way."

"Newhall's never run for office."

"No, but he has the advantage of being a man of God."

Rogers pursed his lips and nodded earnestly, resisting the temptation to tell Baker what he thought of Newhall.

"The President may need to ratchet up his fear, I mean…faith," Baker continued.

"Nobody questions the President's faith."

"Maybe not, but people like Newhall's unequivocal cheerleading for Christianity. Our polls don't always show it, but I'm convinced that people secretly welcome religious intolerance; it bolsters their own beliefs."

"That's too big a risk," Rogers responded gruffly.

"Well, you can ignore my advice; I'm just telling you what I see."

"I'm comfortable with our position on the faith issue."

"Newhall also has the organization," Baker went on. "And Infinity has tremendous political power."

"Yeah, thanks to the President."

"No, thanks to John Heilbrenner," Baker countered.

"Heilbrenner?" Rogers scoffed.

"Don't underestimate him. He's one of the best. And he understands the mindset of his followers."

Slimy snake! Rogers thought automatically. "I know all about Mr. Heilbrenner, believe me." Rogers lived and breathed the suffocating cynicism and hypocrisy of Washington. He had worked in D.C. for over a decade, dealing regularly with politicians and others motivated by power. He trusted no one.

"Then you know that his attack machine makes the GOP look like a bunch of Boy Scouts," Baker continued.

"We'll take him down if we have to; don't you worry about that," Rogers replied testily. "But I won't believe any of this until I see some evidence for myself. Newhall's full of himself, but he's been loyal to our cause. Besides, just between you and me, I don't think he's got the nuts." Rogers stood in front of his ball and lined up his feet. Then he steadied his club and swung forcefully. The club head dug deeply into the soft grass, causing a thick divot to pop out of the ground and land several yards down the fairway. The ball shanked wildly into the woods.

"Damn it!" Rogers cursed.

"That's called a toupee," Baker joked. "Try that on your bald spot."

Rogers' features hardened. "I'm going to go find my ball," he said angrily. "I'll meet you at the green." Rogers grabbed the pitching wedge and nine-iron out of his bag and stormed off.

"You'll need a search party to find that ball," Baker laughed. He took a swig of gin and tonic from his thermos.

As the round progressed, Rogers shot poorly. He wasn't entirely convinced that Newhall would run for President, but the more he thought about it, the more he realized that the idea was not so far-fetched. Since Newhall and Heilbrenner had already convinced Infinity followers to accept absurd, supernatural nonsense, getting people to believe that Newhall could run the country seemed like a small feat in comparison. Rogers wasn't looking forward to discussing the prospect with the President.

By the end of the day, Baker had won sixteen of the eighteen holes and Rogers owed him seven thousand dollars. Fortunately, Rogers had a campaign fund to cover just such an expense.

"Have you spoken with anyone at Infinity about this?" Rogers asked as they walked to the clubhouse.

"No, I figured that was something you'd better handle."

"Yes. Good. Keep me informed on this one. You hear anything; you call me immediately."

"Will do. And thanks for the spending money."

* * *

Chambers bent down and kissed Kitty Collier on the cheek. "Hiya, Kitty."

A tingle of delight raced up her spine. "Hi, David."

Chambers scanned the room at the new employee orientation party. "This looks like a good group." He wanted to meet every Ranch employee so he typically attended the monthly gathering.

"Yeah, we've got twenty-seven new this month." Collier was the Ranch's Human Resources Manager, responsible for hiring all of the support staff. This wasn't an easy task as every prospective employee had to go through a rigorous security screening and background check.

"You want to introduce me now?" Chambers asked.

"Sure."

Collier escorted Chambers around the get-together and he shook hands and chatted casually with the new members of the Kaleidoscope family.

"David, this Juan Vasquez and Emilio Rodriguez," Collier said, referring to two Hispanic men in their early forties. "They're on our building maintenance staff."

Chambers put a hand on each man's shoulder and squeezed it gently. "Good afternoon, gentleman; pleasure to meet you. Is Kitty taking good care of you so far?"

"Buenos días, señor. Inglés no es bueno," Vasquez replied.

"Ah, well…bienvenido a la hacienda. Estoy contento que ustedes están aquí." *Welcome to the ranch. I'm happy you're here.*

Each man nodded. "Gracias, señor."

"Gocen tu tiempo aquí. Espero verle por aquí." *Enjoy your time here. I hope I see you around.* Chambers turned and walked towards another group.

Vasquez and Rodriguez exchanged confounded glances, and then Rodriguez leaned over and whispered into his friend's ear. "Ellos no deben mentir a nosotros. Ese hombre es fuerte." *They shouldn't lie to us. That man is strong.*

* * *

Upon his return to the White House, Rogers tore up his scorecard and tossed it into the trash. Then he called Heilbrenner.

"Hello."

"John, Al Rogers here."

"How are you, Buzz?"

"I'm concerned about what's going on in your organization," Rogers said sharply, abandoning his normal pleasantries.

"Yeah? What's on your mind, my friend?" Heilbrenner's tone was amiable, but lightly condescending.

"I heard a rumor that Newhall's considering challenging the President for the nomination."

"That's preposterous."

"That's what I heard."

"It's just a rumor. You can't believe every rumor."

"No truth to it, then?"

"No."

You'd better not be lying to me, Rogers thought as his blood pressure shot up. He took a deep breath and tried to calm himself. "Well, I'm still concerned. There are pastors out there—pastors that are part of your network—talking about it."

"I haven't heard anything like that."

"They're talking about supporting Newhall for President."

"Well, Newhall has a lot of enthusiastic supporters. Maybe a few of them want him to run for President. That's no surprise; certainly nothing to worry about."

"Well, try to control your own pastors," Rogers said firmly. "I don't want them foaming at the mouth and pumping up Newhall. That's a distraction we don't need."

"I'll see what I can do."

"And for godsakes, we need some public statements from Newhall in support of the President. We've got to keep the base excited."

Heilbrenner hesitated. "I'll speak with him about that," he said flatly. "Anything else?"

"No. Goodbye." Rogers hung up and the felt the anger bubble into his face. *That son of bitch is lying to me! I just know it!*

CHAPTER 47

The creation is the Bible of the Deist. He there reads, in the handwriting of the Creator himself, the certainty of His existence and the immutability of His power, and all other Bibles and Testaments are to him forgeries.

—THOMAS PAINE, *THE AGE OF REASON*

"Here it is," Ernesto announced over the hum of the helicopter's rotors. "Your very own dairy farm."

Chambers gazed admiringly over the rolling hills and gentle meadows. The property encompassed just over two hundred and fifty acres and was located about two miles from Kaleidoscope Ranch. "Boy, this is a nice piece of land. What did they do with all the cows?"

"I don't know; sold them off, I guess. You didn't want to be a dairy farmer, did you?"

Chambers chuckled. "Not in this life. Let's take a look around." Chambers angled the chopper around the outskirts of the farm, enclosed by a jagged barbed-wire fence.

"What's that?" Chambers pointed to another property on the other side of the fence.

"Chicken farm. We tried to buy that one, too, but the guy wouldn't sell—stubborn old man."

"Keep trying; I don't want any neighbors."

Ernesto nodded.

"All right, I've seen enough. Where do I land?"

"There used to be a milk processing area here, but I had all of the equipment removed. It's partially underground. We'll use that as our hangar. It's off to the right, about two o'clock; a hundred and fifty meters further."

Chambers veered to the right and descended. "Down there? On the other side of that power line?"

"Yeah."

Chambers brought the aircraft down gently on a large slab of cement and cut the engine. He slapped his friend's thigh playfully. "Thanks for putting this together."

"Sure."

"You know, I'm looking forward to fulfilling that promise I made you."

Ernesto smiled. He thought of the burning passion that remained from his youth, and he knew that Chambers could help make his dream a reality.

*   *   *

Ernesto Sosa, age thirteen, opened the door to two Catholic priests standing on the doorstep of his family's home outside of Cuernavaca, Mexico. Each priest wore a Roman collar and had a freshly polished silver cross dangling from his neck.

"Hello, young man. I am Father Arguello and this is Father Del Valle. We are here to see your father."

"Is he expecting you?"

"No."

"May I tell him what this is regarding?" Ernesto always questioned unexpected visitors because his father was a busy man who did not like to be disturbed while he was working.

The priests exchanged sideways glances. They weren't used to people, especially children, questioning them, but Ernesto had never been taught to revere priests.

"Young man, we have important spiritual matters to discuss with your father," Father Arguello said impatiently.

Ernesto had never spoken with his father about religion, but the family never attended Mass, nor did they display any religious paraphernalia around the house. Ernesto never gave much thought to his father's beliefs; he just figured his father was consumed by the rigors of farm life and didn't have time. The Sosas owned a large farm and were one of the wealthiest families in Mexico. The farm primarily produced industrial hemp, used to create textiles, paper, rope, and a host of other products. The farm also produced enough food to supply the needs of several nearby villages. Rolando had started with nothing, working in the fields as a common laborer, but he had studied agriculture and had gradually saved enough money to purchase cheap acreage that other farmers had difficulty farming. He developed innovative techniques that allowed him to achieve high yields on land considered inferior.

"Just a moment," Ernesto said. He went back to his father's den and rapped softly on the door.

"Come in."

Ernesto pushed the door open slowly. "Papa, there are two men here to see you."

"Who are they?"

"They look like priests."

Rolando Sosa frowned as he stood up. "Wait here, Ernesto."

Rolando walked to the door. "What can I do for you, gentlemen?" He never addressed any priest as "father," but his manner was amiable.

"We would like to speak with you briefly," Father Arguello said.

"What is this about?"

"It concerns your workers."

"Okay. I don't have much time right now due to the demands of my business, but I can talk for a few minutes. Let's go back to my den."

When the three men arrived in the den, Ernesto moved toward the door. "Papa, I'm going back out to the field."

"No, no, Ernesto; stay here. Have a seat, gentlemen." Rolando motioned to a couch. "Can I offer you something to drink?"

"No, thank you," Father Arguello said.

Rolando Sosa didn't pay much attention to men of the cloth and he had little interest in speaking with them. He didn't ordinarily question their motives, but he believed they were a misguided lot. He didn't understand why they didn't share his passion to create, which for him was as essential as breathing. He also couldn't comprehend why they weren't repulsed at having their beliefs dictated to them by the Vatican. Despite his misgivings though, he recognized that priests held tremendous influence in the community and could improve the lives of his workers.

As a young man, Rolando had tried to persuade Church leaders to promote birth control because he knew that most families couldn't support having a new child every year. He stressed the hardships on the children who often lived without basic necessities. The Catholic Church's promotion of ignorance and irresponsibility sickened him and he urged them to promote education and financial responsibility. He knew many men who gave a significant portion of their income to the Church to the detriment of their families. He argued that if the Church really wanted to help the poor, it would put the welfare of people ahead of religious dogma. Church officials accused him of only being interested in increasing his wealth.

"Señor Sosa, you are one of the wealthiest men in this community," Father Arguello began. "I hope you will consider an opportunity to give back."

Rolando Sosa stared blankly at his visitors. "What do you want?" he said, his voice edgy.

"Several villages in this area, many of which include men who work for you, have very poorly maintained churches. We do not have the money to repair them. Since these churches benefit your employees, we thought you might be interested in making a donation."

Rolando fought back his anger and said calmly, "You mentioned the opportunity to give back. Have I not done that? I provide jobs for three hundred and fifty people. With jobs, they can support their families and live with self-respect. That's a lot more than they will ever get out of a new church."

The priests exchanged puzzled looks, and then Father Del Valle spoke. "You provide them with their material needs, but your workers need spiritual guidance and direction, Señor Sosa."

"Yes, these men and women need to follow their consciences and develop their values; if that is what you are saying, then I agree. But I cannot agree that they need you or the Church. I'm sorry that I cannot respect what you have chosen to do with your lives, but I know the men and women that work for me. They are good people; they don't need someone telling them how or what to think."

"But…" Father Arguello started.

Rolando raised his hand authoritatively. "Please allow me to finish.

The Church has attacked me because I refuse to help them build churches. Instead, I use my money to pay my workers and increase the output of my farm. This farm is a creative enterprise that feeds many people and contributes to the wealth of this community. Also, out of respect for my wife and daughters, I cannot support any organization that treats women as second-class citizens."

"The status of women is God's way," Father Del Valle interjected.

Rolando's features hardened. He was deeply offended by the statement and couldn't help shaking his head at the breathtaking display of arrogance. "I have told the Church before that I will help build additional schools, but the schools cannot be affiliated with any religion. You have always refused my offer. I will help you build schools anywhere in Mexico, but the schools cannot teach ignorance."

"Señor, you do not understand the Church," Father Arguello said. Father Del Valle nodded in agreement.

"I understand what I see in the face of a man who allows another man to do his thinking for him. I'm sorry that I cannot help you." Rolando stood up. "Ernesto, show them to the door, please."

When the priests were gone, Rolando cursed under his breath.

"Papa?"

"They offer nothing. Nothing!"

"Do you believe in God, Papa?"

"I can't believe in a god that would allow helpless people to be taken advantage of. They want us feel guilty for living our lives. I want you to understand, Ernesto. I want you to understand that their view of life is hurtful to our people."

Ernesto was quiet while his father's words registered powerfully in his psyche. "I don't understand why they attack you," he said finally.

"You will."

* * *

"Sheriff Jenkins, you've got a call on line two; sounds urgent."

"Okay, send it through." Jenkins was the sheriff of California's Siskiyou County, which encompassed Kaleidoscope Ranch. "This is Sheriff Jenkins."

"Sheriff, this is Eugene Murray. I've got a major league problem over here."

Uh oh, Jenkins thought. *This guy's trouble.* Murray had a reputation as an eccentric old man who always pushed hard to get what he wanted.

"What can I do for you?" Jenkins asked soberly.

"That old dairy farm, the one next to my place; they've got some sort of helicopter over there and it's scaring my chickens. And when my chickens get scared, they don't lay eggs. I've got a business to run.

I can't have this."

Jenkins didn't know anything about the new owners of the dairy farm. All he knew was that the cows had disappeared and the farm no longer produced milk. "Okay. What do you want me to do?"

"I want you to go over there and tell those people to shut off their damn helicopter," Murray responded angrily. "They'll run me out of business. Otherwise, I'll have to go over there myself. And I'll take my shotgun with me."

"Calm down. Please. Calm down." Jenkins pleaded. "I don't want you going over there. This is a job for the law. You stay on your property and let me handle this."

"What are you going to do?"

"Well...I..."

"I need someone out here right now."

Jenkins hesitated, trying to figure how he could get someone else to handle the problem, but his only available deputy was out on another call. "All right, I'll come out there and take a look. I can be there in half an hour."

"See you in a half hour," Murray replied curtly and hung up.

Damn! I'm gonna miss my skeet shootin' again, Jenkins cursed. He grabbed his keys and went outside to a fenced area behind the station. "Dakota! Here boy!"

A large German shepherd trotted across the grass, stopping at Jenkins' feet. "Let's go, boy." Jenkins led the dog to his patrol car. He opened the back door and the dog jumped in. Jenkins pulled away from the sheriff's station and turned on the radio. He was only able to pick up one station clearly, but luckily it played country music, the only kind he liked.

When he pulled up to the main gate of the dairy farm, Jenkins killed the engine and opened his window. He heard a few crickets chirping, but no helicopter. He got out of his car and looked through the tall barbed-wire fence. There was a heavy padlock on the gate. *Loony old man. This is a waste of time. There's no helicopter out here. But maybe this has something to do with that ranch.* Aircraft frequently flew in and out of the Ranch and the sprawling enclave had always intrigued the sheriff. He didn't pay much attention to intellectuals, but he reckoned that Chambers must be a VIP because the governor had called him twice, asking him to make sure that Chambers and the rest of the Ranch's inhabitants weren't bothered. The governor informed him that the Ranch maintained its own security personnel so they wouldn't need the sheriff's office except to aggressively enforce the "No Trespassing" area surrounding the Ranch.

In return for his cooperation, the governor promised to provide

Jenkins with new "law enforcement" equipment, including SUVs for Jenkins and his deputies, and enough money to build a new station. Jenkins figured that Chambers must be a good friend of the governor's. Actually, the governor was more akin to a whore. Chambers had previously paid him off with several generous campaign contributions.

Jenkins drove back to his office and picked up a message taped to the back of his chair. *Shit! Eugene Murray.* He snatched up the phone and dialed quickly.

"Hello."

"Eugene, it's Harvey Jenkins."

"What the hell's going on?"

"Uh…I went out there. No sign of anybody. Can you hear that helicopter now?"

"No, I haven't heard it again, but my hens are still riled up."

"Tell you what; if you hear it again, call me back. In the meantime, I'll try to get to the bottom of this, okay?"

"If they scare my chickens again, they're gonna pay." Murray snapped.

"Don't worry, Eugene. I'm on top of it. I'll keep you posted on the investigation. Have a nice day." Jenkins hung up and summoned Tony Ferraro, one of his deputies.

"Tony, you got time to run a check for me? I need to find out who owns the old Milford dairy farm."

"Sure thing, sheriff."

An hour later, Ferraro had an answer. "Sheriff, that property is owned by a Thomas Payne. Here, I wrote it down for you." He handed a small sliver of paper to Jenkins. "It's a little strange, though. I ran a search through the public records, but I wasn't able to find anything else about the guy."

"Hmmm…thanks, Tony." *I bet this does have something to do with that ranch*, Jenkins thought. He closed the door to his office and dialed the Ranch's main switchboard.

"Good afternoon, Kaleidoscope Ranch."

"Can I speak with Thomas Payne, please?"

"Who?"

"Thomas Payne."

"Did you say Thomas…Paine…?" the receptionist enunciated slowly.

"Yes."

The receptionist chuckled. "Is this a joke?"

"No, this is Harvey Jenkins from the Siskiyou County Sheriff's office," he said in an authoritative tone. "We're conducting an investigation and we're looking for a Thomas Payne. Is there anyone by that name at the Ranch?"

"Well…uh…" the receptionist stammered.

"Look, it's a simple question. Is there a Thomas Payne there or not?" Jenkins pressed.

"Do you mean a living person? Like a person here now at the Ranch named Thomas Paine?"

"Yes!" Jenkins bellowed in exasperation.

"I'm sorry, sir. There's no one here by that name."

"To your knowledge, has anyone named Thomas Payne ever worked at or visited the Ranch?"

The receptionist paused to consider the word "visited." She thought of the first time she had met Chambers. "Hmmm…well, I guess not."

"What do you mean, you guess? Has anyone named Thomas Payne been there or not?"

"No, no, definitely not," she said, finally concluding that the sheriff didn't know the famous Founding Father and was actually inquiring about a person with the same name.

"Okay." Jenkins hung up and wondered whether he should investigate further. He was a little perplexed by the odd conversation with the receptionist, but then he thought of the equipment the governor had promised him. He knew exactly what he wanted in his new patrol vehicle—leather seats, a GPS, and an eight-speaker sound system. He figured he could use it for hunting when he was off-duty. *Well, if the helicopter does have something to do with the Ranch, it's probably not the worth the risk of pissing off the governor*, Jenkins decided. *Besides, that helicopter is probably in that old man's imagination anyway.* Later that evening, after consuming three beers and two sitcoms, he forgot all about the dairy farm, and its owner—the mysterious Thomas Payne.

CHAPTER 48

[A] mass movement, particularly in its active, revivalist phase, appeals not to those intent on bolstering and advancing a cherished self, but to those who crave to be rid of an unwanted self. A mass movement attracts and holds a following not because it can satisfy the desire for self-advancement, but because it can satisfy the passion for self-renunciation.

People who see their lives as irremediably spoiled cannot find a worthwhile purpose in self-advancement. The prospect of an individual career cannot stir them to a mighty effort, nor can it evoke in them faith and a single-minded dedication. They look on self-interest as something tainted and evil; something unclean and unlucky. Anything undertaken under the auspices of the self seems to them foredoomed. Nothing that has its roots in the self can be good and noble. Their innermost craving is for a new life—a rebirth—or, failing this, a chance to acquire new elements of pride, confidence, hope, a sense of purpose and worth by identification with a holy cause.

—Eric Hoffer, *The True Believer*

"Hey! I've missed you!" Chambers cried happily as he hugged Ray Lassater. "I didn't expect to see you until next month."

"Good to see you, too," Lassater said. "The Ranch is really coming along. One of your associates gave me a tour of the rec center. It's impressive."

"Thanks, I hope you can stay awhile and enjoy it."

"Well, unfortunately I'm not here on pleasure," Lassater said somberly.

"What is it?"

"I need to discuss my investigation."

"Okay."

"I couldn't do it over the phone."

"Okay, let's take a walk."

Chambers and Lassater exited the building and strolled over to a large flower garden across the courtyard. Chambers slipped on his sunglasses and put his hand on Lassater's back. "So, tell me about your investigation. Are you still having problems?"

"No, actually, we've had some breakthroughs."

"That's great. Isn't it?"

"Well, we've come across some information—some troubling information from a reliable source."

"What is it?"

Lassater hesitated. "I...I can't tell you."

"What you mean you can't tell me. You're telling me right now."

"You don't want to be involved in this."

"Involved in what?"

Lassater looked away.

"Come on, Ray." Chambers stopped and put his hands on Lassater's shoulders. "Talk to me."

"I just needed to see you before I..." Lassater's voice trailed off.

"I don't understand. Do you have something to tell me or not?"

Lassater took a deep breath. "I'd like to deviate from the scope of my investigation. Action needs to be taken."

"I don't know if I like the sound of this."

"Action needs to be taken," Lassater repeated. "I just wanted to give you the heads up."

"Can I help? Is there anything...?"

"No, I just needed to see you."

* * *

The Lord has called me and He shows me the way. The Lord has called me and He shows me the way. The Lord has called me and He shows me the way. The mantra had taken over Dale Aiken's consciousness, supplying him with both serene confidence and unbridled hatred. He knew he was doing the right thing; God had chosen him to carry out this task and he would not fail. He would demonstrate his total commitment.

Aiken lit a cigarette and listened for further instructions. He had been hearing voices for as long as he could remember, and he knew that he was special despite what other people said about him. His parents and friends worried that he was psychotic because he frequently experienced paranoid delusions and voiced irrational beliefs about himself and others. But Aiken knew he wasn't crazy; the voices he heard came directly from the Almighty.

Aiken waited outside the Small Miracles Medical Clinic in Jackson, Mississippi. The clinic helped women who couldn't have children on their own get pregnant through in vitro fertilization. This procedure involved uniting the woman's eggs with a man's sperm, thereby creating embryos that could be implanted back in the womb. Hopefully, these embryos would survive and result in a viable, healthy pregnancy.

Since the embryologist almost always fertilized multiple eggs in this procedure, multiple embryos were typically produced. But since not all of these embryos could be implanted in a woman's womb, some of them went unused. These embryos either had to be either frozen or destroyed. If they were frozen, the patient could use them in a future in vitro procedure. The Small Miracles Clinic donated excess embryos to research scientists working towards cures for diseases such as Parkinson's, Alzheimer's, cancer, and diabetes. But there was one problem. When scientists extracted the embryonic stem cells, the embryo itself was destroyed. The Packer Administration had proposed legislation to outlaw embryonic stem cell research and require fertilization clinics to discard all unused embryos. Aiken agreed with the stem cell research ban. God had told him that destroying embryos in the name of scientific progress was tantamount to murder. Indeed, God considered the entire in vitro fertilization procedure to be murder because it so often resulted in discarded embryos—embryos that had already been infused with a soul.

Aiken lit another cigarette and tried to relax. He kept telling himself that his plan was solid. He had been following the doctor's schedule for months and he had rehearsed his plot obsessively; he could picture every detail, including the pride he would feel when he completed his task. He would rejoice in an even more intimate connection with God.

Aiken eyed the red Audi from across the parking lot and waited for the doctor to come out of the building. A thin layer of hazy smoke floated above his head as he took a slow draw off his cigarette and then fingered the pistol underneath his seat. He was about to check his ammunition a final time when another car suddenly pulled up next to him. His heart jumped.

Calm down. Nothin' to worry about, he assured himself. *Keep your cool. Just a few more minutes.*

A stocky, unshaven man wearing sunglasses and a long raincoat got out of the other car. He walked to the driver's side of Aiken's vehicle and tapped gently on the window. *It's ninety degrees outside and there's not a cloud in the sky*, Aiken thought. *Why is this moron wearing a raincoat?* He resisted the temptation to grab his gun. He slowly rolled down the window.

"I was wondering if you could help me?" the man in the raincoat said.

"What…what…what is it?" Aiken stammered.

The man smiled, uncovering a silver-capped front tooth. "I'm looking for a redneck who's planning to murder a doctor." The man slid his jacket open, revealing a holster with a shiny black revolver.

"Son of a…" Aiken reached frantically for his gun while the man in the raincoat pulled the revolver out and took aim at Aiken's temple. He pulled the trigger, splattering the windshield with Aiken's cerebral cortex.

* * *

Bo Shepherd and Billy Joe Bedford pulled their cargo van into the parking lot of the Women's Community Clinic in St. Louis. The clinic counseled women on birth control and the termination of unwanted pregnancies, and performed abortions every other Wednesday.

The two men stepped into the back of the van and loaded their assault rifles. Their plan was to storm the building after all of the doctors and nurses had arrived, and at least two patients were in the building.

"I caint wait to waste those evil bastards," Bobby Ray said as he clicked a fresh magazine into his rifle.

"Me too. We're gonna be famous."

"Pass me a beer, will ya?"

"A'ight. Bud or Coors Light?"

"You know I hate that Coors Light shit. Fuckin' shit's like water."

"I know, but I don't want you to git too drunk."

"That shit's for pussies," Bobby Ray said as he popped the top of a Bud and took a healthy swig. "Nothin' like a brew in the mornin'."

"Hey, you got a smoke on ya?"

"Yeah." Bobby Ray reached into the glove box and pulled out a pack of Marlboros. He tossed the cigarettes to his friend.

"Thanks. Ya know, I've been thinkin' about gittin' that new ATV. Ya know, the one…" Something suddenly crashed onto the roof of the van.

"Fuck! What the hell was that?" Bo reacted, dropping the smokes.

"Sounds like water; like heavy rain."

"Fuck, it ain't rainin'."

"Maybe somebody's throwin' shit on the van. Getcher gun ready. I'm gonna open up the back."

Bobby Ray opened the van's rear door and jumped into the twilight of early morning with his weapon drawn. "Shit…this thing's drippin'; smells like gas."

Bo's eyes lit up. "What are you talkin' about?"

"I don't know. Hold on." Bobby Ray went around to the side of the van. "Holy…what the…fire! Fire! It's…get out of the van! Get out of the van!"

A thin line of fiery gasoline accelerated like a bright orange dragster across the asphalt, coming straight toward the van. Bobby Ray tried to jump into some nearby bushes; Bo never made it out of the van.

* * *

"You idiot!" Heilbrenner yelled. "Don't ever call me on this line!"

"It's…It's an emergency, an emergency!" Butler cried frantically.

"I don't care! Don't ever call me here!"

"You didn't pick up the secure line."

"Call me back." Heilbrenner slammed the phone down. He had agreed to allow several militant Christian sects to join the Network, but he had instructed their leader Marvin Butler not to contact him unless it was an emergency; and in that case, only on a secure line.

Butler immediately called back over the encrypted channel.

"What is it?" Heilbrenner snapped.

"Three of our operatives were killed yesterday."

"Killed? How?"

"One was shot in the head, point blank. The other two were burned alive; someone doused their van with gasoline."

Although Heilbrenner preferred tough talk to actual violence, he did approve of occasional acts of savagery because it made the movement appear serious and committed. If people really believed that life on Earth was merely sacrificial and only mattered as part of a cosmic struggle of good against evil, then surely they would do whatever it took to serve God in the fight against evil. In any case, the compelling theater of a religious killing was dramatic and memorable, and Heilbrenner knew that people were drawn to dramatic events, especially when the actors showed a level of conviction and certainty that followers envied.

"How did this happen?"

"I don't know."

"Who's responsible?"

"I don't know."

401

"What the hell *do* you know?" Heilbrenner barked impatiently.

"Somebody obviously knew our plans."

Chambers! Heilbrenner thought. "What do you expect me to do?"

"I don't know."

"Call off all further operations."

"Already have."

"All right, keep me posted. And don't do anything stupid!" *Damn it! This is the last thing I need! I can't believe people follow that jack-off. Christ, that's not true! Of course it's not true. I know exactly why they follow him.*

CHAPTER 49

The mass of men lead lives of quiet desperation.

—HENRY DAVID THOREAU, *WALDEN*

Juan Vasquez and Emilio Rodriguez wheeled their cart of cleaning supplies across the parquet floor of Chambers' office. It was just after one o'clock in the morning and the two janitors were alone.

Rodriguez began dusting Chambers' desk while Vasquez picked up the electric pencil sharpener and gently popped off its plastic case. He unhinged the small machine's motor and dumped it into the cleaning cart. He picked up a replacement from underneath one of his rags. He fastened the sharpener's case around the new motor and placed it back on the desk. He took a pencil out of his shirt pocket and tested the machine. It whirred softly, producing a perfect point.

The two men continued cleaning around Chambers' desk for a few more minutes and then moved to his sitting area. Vasquez unplugged the table lamp and unscrewed the light bulb. He put the lamp into the cart and carefully replaced it with an identical one. He flipped it on and off to make sure it worked.

Rodriguez slid the couch away from the wall and motioned to Vasquez, who pulled a tiny screwdriver out of his back pocket. Vasquez unscrewed the faceplate of the electrical outlet and attached a transmitter and an antenna to the appropriate wires.

The men went into the conference room next. Rodriguez grabbed the speakerphone from the center of the table while Vasquez unhooked it from its power source. Rodriguez installed a replacement apparatus and then nodded to his partner.

The new items appeared identical to the ones they replaced, but each new piece of equipment contained a small transmitter and an antenna that could capture sound within a fifteen-foot radius. Vasquez and Rodriguez had attached each transmitter to a source of electricity because it allowed them to function indefinitely, without the time constraints of a battery. Each transmitter had also been placed close a window so that repeaters located outside the building could pick up their signals. The repeaters amplified the sound transmitted from the bugs, and then relayed the sound to a remote listening post.

Since each transmitter operated on a different frequency, three repeaters were necessary. The local power company had installed the devices on one of its poles, located on the peak of a small hill five hundred yards from Chambers' office building. The repeaters transmitted the sound to a central listening post that the FBI had set up in an RV parked in the woods about a mile away from the Ranch. The RV was equipped with sophisticated audio technology including four tape recorders manned by three surveillance technicians.

The power company had installed the repeaters on the FBI's order. The Bureau had presented the company with a letter from the Attorney General identifying the Ranch as a threat to national security, and the law required the company to comply with the surveillance requests without any judicial oversight, or any questions. The FBI had presented a similar letter to the phone company, forcing it to let the Bureau listen to any of the Ranch's incoming or outgoing calls.

Vasquez and Rodriguez were two of the FBI's top operatives. Like other g-men, they had sophisticated training in surveillance and counter-surveillance, but they were especially valuable because they played the role of unassuming Mexican laborers so convincingly. No one had ever suspected them of spying and they had completely defeated the Ranch's extensive background check procedure. Both men were born in United States, but the FBI had created new identities for them with the help of Mexican law enforcement authorities. Mexican officials had provided birth certificates, educational records, residence addresses, and employment histories based on the lives of previously deceased men who had no living relatives.

Vasquez pulled a satellite phone from a small pouch in the front of his trousers and entered a four-digit code on the keypad. He waited for the display to light up and then turned to his partner. "Listo." *Ready.* The two men walked within a few feet of each transmitter and had a short conversation. Vasquez entered another code into the phone and held it to his ear until he got the confirmation he needed: "Three posts operational."

* * *

Dushane whistled happily along with the radio as he laced up his hiking boots. He had wanted to explore the outskirts of the Ranch since his arrival, and now he had a whole day to look around. He walked into the kitchen and put an apple and a bottle of water into his backpack. Dushane left his bungalow and started hiking toward the northeast corner of the Ranch, a remote area with no paved roads or footpaths, but with the highest peak on the property.

After an hour of walking, Dushane found himself staring up at a white radio tower perched on the peak of a hill. He continued up, bushwhacking through heavy foliage and scratching his legs. When he reached the top, Dushane sat down on the ground and bit into his apple. Then he took a long gulp of water as he enjoyed the clear sky and a view that went on for miles in every direction. Directly on the other side of the hill, a rugged, tree-filled ravine lay in front of him. He looked across it and didn't immediately notice anything unusual, but as he continued scanning the area, something finally caught his eye. He saw what he thought was the top of a building, although he couldn't be sure because it was shrouded by trees. Dushane descended toward it through more thick brush until he came to a barbed wire fence. He didn't see any

"No Trespassing" signs, so he threw his backpack over the fence, and then tried to find a spot with enough clearance for him to slide under. When he found an ample gap, he lay on his back and carefully slithered to the other side.

* * *

The pager on the guard's belt emitted a series of shrill beeps, startling him. He instinctively reached for his gun, but stopped before pulling it out of its holster. *Probably just a drill.* He went into the control room and scanned the bank of monitors, looking for anything out of the ordinary. When he saw Dushane walking toward the building, he barked at the console. "Zoom in, camera four. Identify person." Within seconds, "Martin Dushane, Employee Number 346835" flashed across the bottom of the screen.

The computer contained a database of images, including all of the Ranch's employees as well as anyone who had ever visited. A sophisticated software program determined identity based on a detailed analysis of the person's facial features.

The guard picked up his cell phone and dialed Ernesto. "Ernesto, una persona viene hacia el garaje." *A person is coming toward the garage.*

"Quién és?" *Who is it?*

"Martin Dushane. Quiere usted mí interceptarlo?" *Do you want me to intercept him?*

"No, esta bien. Permanezca donde usted es. Voy a reunirse con él." *No, it's okay. Stay where you are. I will meet him.*

Ernesto shook his head as he turned away from his computer monitor. The interruption annoyed him because he was engrossed in a critical design problem that plagued the J-22. He was also concerned that someone had gotten near the building, even though it was only Dushane. Ernesto walked from his office into a busy hub of activity where his workers were busily machining aircraft components and conducting simulated tests to determine how the aircraft would hold up in various conditions. As he walked past the J-22, he couldn't help but stop and admire his baby.

Ernesto entered the elevator on the shop floor and entered a six-digit code on the control panel. The elevator responded by lifting him quickly to the surface. As the door opened, Sosa squinted at the bright sunshine, and then pulled a pair of sunglasses out of his shirt pocket. He waved when he saw Dushane.

"Hi, Martin."

"How's it going, Ernesto?"

"Good." Ernesto extended his hand.

"I didn't know anything went on way out here. I…"

406

"What brings you out this way?" Ernesto interrupted.

"I'm just hiking. I felt like exploring the Ranch today."

Ernesto nodded. "It's a beautiful day."

"Sure is. What are you up to?"

"Oh, just tying up some loose ends, helping David with some stuff, my usual routine. How do you like the Ranch so far?"

"I've been enjoying myself."

"I'm sure David will put a stop to that."

Dushane chuckled. "So, what's going on over here?" He pointed to the building.

Ernesto turned his head slightly and averted his eyes. "We train some of our engineers here. It's like a… test lab."

"I'm surprised David never mentioned it to me."

Ernesto shrugged. "It's not that important."

"It sounds interesting. Do you mind if I take a look?"

"Well…" Ernesto hesitated. "Right now isn't the best time. We're… uh…reconfiguring some of the equipment. It's not a good idea to go in right now."

Dushane had never considered himself a great reader of people, but he had no doubt that Ernesto was lying. He thought about pressing the issue, but decided against it. "All right, maybe some other time," he said hopefully.

"You better go back the way you came," Ernesto said, his voice suddenly hard and direct.

Surely there's an easier way to get out of here, Dushane thought. *How does he get out of here?* "Okay."

"I need to get back. Goodbye, Martin." Ernesto turned and started walking back toward the building.

"See you later," Dushane called after him.

Ernesto didn't turn around. When he got back to his office, he called the Ranch's security chief. "I want the fence around the garage fortified. I can't have another intrusion like this."

"But I thought David didn't want…"

"I don't care what David wants," Ernesto interrupted. "I'm in charge of this project."

"Okay, Ernesto. I'll get on it right away."

* * *

Adam Sharf sat quietly at the dinner table across from his wife Marla. He stared blankly at his chicken and mashed potatoes, but made no effort to eat.

"Adam? What's wrong, honey?" Marla asked.

Sharf didn't look up.

"Adam?"

"I'm sorry, what did you say?"

"Is something wrong? You haven't touched your dinner."

"I'm not hungry."

"You seem a little preoccupied. Is everything okay at the office?"

"Yeah."

"How's that big case you're working on?"

"I'm working on it."

"What's wrong?"

"I told you. I'm just not hungry."

Marla took a sip of her chardonnay. "Well, what about that meeting you had today—the meeting with the two partners," she said hopefully. "Weren't they going to start assigning you some bigger cases?"

"We didn't talk about that."

"What did you talk about?"

"I don't remember."

"Adam."

"I honestly don't remember. I just kept thinking the whole meeting, 'What the hell am I doing here? I'm wasting my life on this crap. My God, how can I let myself be reduced to this?' Then I started thinking 'I wonder if these two bozos are thinking the same thing.' And then I realized, 'Hell, they must be.' Then I think that maybe I have a bond with these guys after all. We're all losers who share the same dirty little secret."

Marla frowned. "Adam, I've never seen you this…this negative."

"I'm sorry, I just…I don't know." Sharf picked at his food and then got up abruptly. "I need to review a few things before tomorrow." He walked past his wife without making eye contact. He went into the den and stared at his law books, which were arranged neatly behind his desk in a mahogany bookcase. *Where did I go wrong? What happened to all my dreams of doing something positive, something worthwhile? I'm working for a bunch of little pricks who don't care about anything but their own bank accounts.* Sharf stood motionless in front of his desk. He did need to review some documents before a morning meeting, but he couldn't find the motivation. *Does it matter if I do anything? Does my life…? It's not supposed to be like this.* Sharf sighed in resignation as he collapsed limply into his leather office chair.

Sharf had never spoken with his wife about how much he disliked his career because he knew she wouldn't understand. Her father had been a powerful trial lawyer and she was accustomed to the trappings of wealth and the bragging rights that came with a country-club lifestyle. Sharf wondered if other men had superficial relationships with their wives or if he was the only one whose marital dealings were almost totally without substance. He reflected that it hadn't always been that way. He had met his wife in college and they had fallen in love almost immediately. He still vividly remembered the late night conversations where they had shared their dreams and their deepest emotions. He longed for that powerful connection again, but feared it was too late. He tried to pinpoint exactly when things had gone wrong.

After he had passed the Bar and taken a job with Leachman, the young couple had started to enjoy the good life. They bought a nice house in the suburbs, had three kids, and went to the right cocktail parties. For years, Sharf felt like a lucky man; he was well on his way to having everything he thought he wanted. But as time went on, cracks began to ravage his psyche. He repressed his revulsion towards the lack of meaning in his work and the deterioration of his relationship with his wife. Although he still loved her and always had, she had gotten caught up in the status-driven, suburban lifestyle, which Sharf had never been able to relate to. He had pretended for years that everything was okay, but now he realized that what he longed for was a definite purpose in his life. He thought often of David Chambers.

Marla was washing the dishes when he walked into the kitchen a few minutes later and put his arms around her waist. "I'm sorry, honey. I didn't mean to be short with you."

"I just want to know what's wrong. I want to help; whatever it is."

"Here, let me help you with those dishes." Sharf picked up a plate from the sink.

"Okay. You wash; I'll rinse."

Sharf took a deep breath and exhaled slowly. He grabbed a sponge and squirted it with soap. "You know, I'm just…" Sharf paused as he scrubbed a plate. "I'm just really, really frustrated."

"Frustrated? About what?"

"My job."

"Your job? I thought you liked your job."

"No, I hate my job. Haven't you been listening to me?"

Marla turned off the faucet and squinted in confusion. "You're working with the best attorneys in the business, aren't you? And it's one of the most successful firms."

"Yeah, that's just it. They're the best and I can't stand being around them. Am I going to end up like that?"

"Like what?"

Sharf shrugged. "I don't know—a corpse."

"Adam…come on."

Sharf sighed as he contemplated whether to continue. "Well…I…" He picked up a knife and ran the sponge across the blade. He thought vaguely of slitting his wrist.

"What is it?" his wife prodded. "I want to know what's bothering you."

"I can't stand being around them. They're all dead."

"Who? The other attorneys?"

"Yes!" Sharf snapped impatiently. "I can't stand talking to them. I can't stand listening to them. I can't stand thinking about them. I can't stand anything about them!"

Marla wiped her hands on a dishtowel. "When did this all come about? You're going to be a partner in another year, right?"

Sharf clenched his jaw and grunted, fighting to control his temper.

"Maybe you're just a little burned out," Marla continued hopefully. "We're going on vacation next month. That'll help, don't you think?"

"No!" Sharf exploded angrily. "You're not listening! It's not about that! Didn't you hear a word I just said? It goes way beyond that! I can't stand the work! I can't stand the people! I don't want to be a part of it anymore! I just…I just can't stand it!"

Marla's eyes widened and her faced contorted in confusion. "Adam, it's your career. You can't jeopardize your career."

"That's right! My goddamn career!" Sharf threw the sponge into the sink and stormed out of the kitchen.

That night, he slept restlessly in the guest room. The next day, he called in sick and then phoned Jesse Connors, an old friend from law school. Sharf and Connors had graduated the same year, but Connors had left the law after just two years in practice, going back to school to get his Ph.D. in History. After he graduated, Connors had accepted a teaching position at a local college. He had also started a legal studies curriculum, and had tried to recruit Sharf to join the faculty on several occasions. But Sharf had always declined.

The two men had been friends for many years, but Sharf rarely called Connors anymore because he always felt uneasy when the subject of his career came up. But now adrenaline surged through his body as he dialed Connors' number and quietly fantasized about smashing Leachman's tombstones with a baseball bat.

"Hello."

"Hey, Jesse. It's Adam."

"Adam Sharf. What's up?"

"Not much. Same old."

"It's been a long time. Always nice to hear from one of the big-shot lawyers."

"Sorry I haven't kept in better touch with you. I've been swamped, and a lot has been going on."

"You still with Leachman's outfit?"

"Yeah."

"You must be getting close to partnership by now."

Sharf cringed. "I don't know; maybe. Listen, I've got something I need to talk to you about."

"Okay. Shoot."

"You think you could still get me a teaching job?"

"What the hell are you talking about?"

"I'm thinking about leaving law practice."

"Are you crazy?"

"I can't take it anymore."

Connors laughed. "Man, I never thought I'd hear you say that. I figured you'd be on the dark side forever. What does your wife say?"

"I haven't told her yet."

"You're telling me that you're about to become a partner at a top-notch law firm, and you've gotta be making what, three hundred grand a year. You've got a wife, kids, a house. I know I've been harassing you for a long time, but you better think carefully about this."

"I have—for eight years. Can you help me?"

"Sure I can help you. I'm still trying to expand our legal course offerings, and I'd love to have you here full-time, but I probably couldn't bring you on until next year. You know, budgets and all. Can you wait that long?"

"It'll probably take me that long to explain this to my wife."

"Yeah, that's a tough one. I'm lucky; my wife knew before she married me that I was destined to live in poverty. I feel for you, man, but you're doing the right thing. No doubt in my mind. I'm glad you finally realized it."

"Thanks, Jess. I really appreciate your help."

"No problem. Let me know how it goes with your wife."

"All right. Take care." Sharf hung up and slumped in his chair. *Eight years of my life—wasted!*

* * *

John Heilbrenner picked up his secure phone and dialed a familiar number.

"Afternoon, John." Marvin Butler drawled. "What can I do for you?"

"I know who murdered our brothers in Christ."

"Who?"

"David Chambers."

"Chambers! Are you sure?"

"Positive."

"How do you...?"

"Trust me," Heilbrenner interrupted.

"This is incredible! What...what do we do now?"

"The only thing we can do as soldiers of God." Heilbrenner paused.

"What?" Butler cried expectantly.

"We show him our commitment to winning this war—our total commitment. Do you have anyone who can carry out an operation in Kansas?"

"Of course," Butler boasted. "I can carry out an operation anywhere."

CHAPTER 50

Those who can make you believe absurdities
can make you commit atrocities.

—Voltaire

A harvest moon hung low over the Chambers Aerospace industrial compound in Wichita, Kansas. It was a chilly November evening and the facilities appeared deserted. The only discernible sound was a low hum from three vehicles approaching from the west.

At 12:40 am, two large cargo vans pulled slowly into the parking lot of the complex, which consisted of two large aircraft manufacturing plants and a three-story administrative building. Each van stopped on opposite sides of the administrative building and the drivers got out of their vehicles. Another man driving a sedan picked them up and they drove away quickly. Ten minutes later, each van detonated, blowing the building into the sky.

*   *   *

Ernesto Sosa laid his head on the hotel room pillow, exhausted from a long day of meetings with engineers at the Wichita factory. He slept soundly until someone banged on his door. "Mr. Sosa! Mr. Sosa!" a voice thundered from the hallway.

Ernesto rolled over and squinted at the clock radio next to the bed. *2:16 a.m. What is this?* He rose slowly and stumbled to the door. "Who is it?"

"Sergeant Peterson, Wichita Police. I need to speak with you. It's an emergency, sir."

"Hold on." Ernesto went into the bathroom, threw on his robe, and then opened the door to a short, stocky policeman with a grizzled moustache. "Come in, officer."

"I'm sorry to disturb you at this hour, but there's been a massive explosion at the Chambers Aerospace factory."

"My God. What happened?"

"One of the buildings was blown up."

"Blown up? How?"

"We're not sure yet. We should know more in a few hours. I need you to come with me."

"All right, let me get dressed."

Ernesto rode with the officer to the complex and watched anxiously as emergency crews dug through the rubble and tried to locate survivors. Luckily, only three men had been in the building at the time of the blast—two janitors and a security guard, and they had all been found alive. As an ambulance rushed them to the hospital, Ernesto followed closely behind, calling Chambers en route.

"David, it's Ernesto. The administrative office building in Wichita has been blown up."

"What?"

"This morning, around one a.m., two vans loaded with explosives."

"No!"

"Yeah. The administrative building is gone."

"A deliberate bombing?"

"Yeah."

"I can't...I can't believe it."

"I can't believe it either."

"Was anybody hurt?"

"It looks like there were only three people in the building—two janitors and a night watchman. Two of them have minor burns, but the other guy is in bad shape. The doctor says he may not make it. The next few hours will be critical. He's in intensive care."

"Who?"

"Leon Greenwood."

"Oh, no," Chambers cried softly. He knew Leon Greenwood well. The man had been a janitor with the company for over ten years and Chambers had met his wife and three children on several occasions.

"How did this happen? Who did this?"

"I don't know. The police are investigating."

"How could this happen? I don't see how this could happen."

"You have enemies. But let's not jump to any conclusions."

"Dammit!" Chambers knocked the lamp off his night table with a violent stroke of his arm.

"David?"

"I can't believe this! This is...the...ahhhh!"

"We'll get to the bottom of this. Don't worry."

"I'm coming out there. What hospital?"

"There's nothing you can do here. The police are handling the investigation. The FBI's even here."

"I don't care about the investigation. I can't let that man die. This is my fault."

"It's not your fault," Ernesto countered.

"What hospital?"

"You can't..."

"Ernesto! What hospital?"

"West Memorial."

"I'll meet you there." Chambers dressed hurriedly and drove to the airstrip. He gassed up his airplane and flew alone to Wichita in the twilight of early morning. As he reached the Rocky Mountains with the sun rising in front of him, he tried to relax and focus on something positive. He thought of the many friends he had made at the plant and all the planes he had designed that were still in production there. During one of his most ambitious years, he had lived in his office for three months and slept on a cot behind his desk. The result was a design

415

for the best-selling mid-size passenger jet in history. But none of that mattered now. A man's life was in jeopardy and Chambers couldn't help feeling a combination of blinding anger and paralyzing guilt. He screamed as loudly as he could in the cockpit, releasing a tidal wave of pent-up anguish. He tried to convince himself that he wasn't responsible for the injuries to his employees, but he knew that his outspokenness had put them in jeopardy.

When Chambers arrived at the hospital, he met Ernesto in the waiting room of the ICU. The men embraced. "How is he?" Chambers asked.

"About the same. He's still alive, that's the important thing. The doctor said he's lucky to have made it this far."

"Have you seen him?"

"No, nobody's seen him, not even his family. His wife's staying in a room down the hall. Hopefully, she's getting some rest."

"Where's the doctor?"

"He went in there a few minutes ago." Ernesto pointed to a room at the end of the corridor.

Chambers trotted awkwardly down the hallway and burst in, startling the doctor.

"May I help you? This is a private…"

"Are you taking care of Leon Greenwood?"

"Yes, I'm the doctor on duty in the ICU. I'm monitoring Mr. Greenwood's condition."

"You must save this man!" Chambers pleaded.

"We're doing the best we can."

"I don't want you to spare any expense," Chambers said, the panic rising in his voice. "I want the best possible care. He can't die. Do you understand? He can't die!"

The doctor put his hand on Chambers' shoulder. "Calm down, sir. Please. I promise I'll do the very best I can, but right now, it's up to Mr. Greenwood. He's in a coma and we don't know whether he'll come out of it. There's not much we can do. We just have to wait."

"Can I see him?"

The doctor shook his head. "Nobody can see him right now."

Ernesto entered the room and interrupted the conversation. "David, an FBI agent is here. He'd like to speak with you."

"Okay. Please keep me updated on his condition, doctor. If anything changes…if I can do anything."

"I will."

Chambers went back to the waiting area and met the FBI agent in a handshake. "I'm David Chambers."

"I'm Agent Buranek, FBI. I've been assigned to investigate this incident. I'd like to ask you a few questions." Buranek was based in Washington, but he often worked out of the FBI's Wichita field office. He had no idea that the Bureau was actively involved in a surveillance campaign against Chambers.

Chambers nodded. "Of course."

"Have you received any threats or have any of your employees been threatened?"

"No, not to my knowledge."

"Do you know why anyone might want to harm your company or your employees?"

"I don't know…I've been critical of some Christian groups, but that doesn't seem like a reason…"

"Wait a minute. Does that include Christian Identity?"

"Yes, all of them."

The agent stroked his chin. "Well, there might be a connection here. The explosives and the methods used in this attack are very similar to the bombing of the federal building in Oklahoma City. We've also seen this kind of attack by militia groups associated with Christian Identity and other militant religious groups."

Chambers stared hard at the agent. "You think this was carried out by Christian Identity?"

"It's too early in the investigation to make any firm conclusions, but as I said, the signature is similar to what we've seen before. Are you going to be staying in Wichita for a while?"

"Yeah, a few days at least."

"Where I can reach you?"

"Either here or at the Edwards Hotel downtown."

"Okay."

The agent walked away and Chambers sat down next to Ernesto. "I'm sorry to put you through this."

Ernesto put his hand on top of Chambers' thigh. "We're in this together and we're going to get through it."

"Where are the other two men?"

"They're downstairs. I'll take you down there."

The other two injured men had bruises and minor burns, but both were in good spirits. Chambers chatted with them awhile and waited at the hospital for several more hours, hoping that Greenwood would come out of his coma. He finally went to his hotel room to try and get some rest. He threw his suitcase in a corner of the room and sat quietly on the bed and stared at the TV. He wanted to go to sleep and temporarily escape, but sleep was impossible. Finally, he prayed. He wasn't sure to who or to what, but he didn't know what else to do.

CHAPTER 51

Lawyer: One skilled in circumvention of the law.

—AMBROSE BIERCE

Adam Sharf took a sip of his hazelnut-flavored cappuccino as he read the letter from Tom Jeffries.

Dear Mr. Sharf:

Your recent discovery request for all of the minutes from Kaleidoscope Ranch board meetings is totally inappropriate. Since the Ranch is a totally separate entity from Chambers Aerospace, these records have no relevance whatsoever to this case. Therefore, they will not be provided to you. Furthermore, I will seek sanctions if you continue to press this issue.

Please contact me at your earliest convenience to discuss this matter further.

Very truly yours,

Thomas A. Jeffries, Esq.

That son of a bitch! Sharf picked up the phone and dialed Jeffries. As he waited for an answer, Leachman tapped his knuckles on the door of Sharf's office and walked in. "Hold on a sec, Don," Sharf said, motioning to a chair.

"This is Tom Jeffries."

"Tom, Adam Sharf. I just read your letter."

"Yes?"

"It's crap."

"What?"

"You heard me. It's total crap. You know damn well those records are relevant."

"Can we discuss this in a civilized manner?"

"No! I want the goddamn records. If you want me to haul your ass into court again, I'll do it."

"We're not turning over those records," Jeffries responded firmly.

"Fine. I'll see you in court." Sharf slammed the phone down. "Bastard!"

Leachman smiled. "Who was that?"

"Tom Jeffries from Chambers Aerospace. He's trying to stonewall us on another discovery request." Sharf had already forced the company to produce over 200,000 pages of documents in response to his legal filings. Indeed, during the discovery phase of the case, Sharf had requested every document he could think of, whether or not it was pertinent, and he aggressively challenged every refusal by Jeffries. Although he knew that several of his requests were unjustified, Sharf's strategy was consistent with his firm's policy of beating its opponents into submission.

"You've got to keep hitting them," Leachman encouraged. "You keep hitting until they bleed to death—whatever it takes."

"Yeah, I'll take the motherfucker's head off and shove it up his ass."

Leachman chuckled. "You're going to be a great litigator, Adam."

Although Sharf considered himself intellectually sophisticated and relatively refined, he loved using crude language and blowing off emotional steam in front of Leachman. Since he had decided to leave the legal profession, Sharf had discovered untapped reserves of rage and aggression, and he fed off Leachman's years of pent-up anger and frustration. Each day, coming into the office became increasingly painful and he channeled his hatred of the legal profession into his work. He snapped at other attorneys and verbally abused his secretary. He pursued his cases with evangelical zeal and made bitter enemies of opposing counsel. Leachman heartily approved and took Sharf under his wing, making the young attorney one of his closest confidants. Leachman shared intimate details about the firm's practices, including its strategy to keep at least eighty percent of all settlements, its philosophy of crushing its enemies without mercy, and its ability to get "experts" and other witnesses to say whatever the firm's cases required.

Leachman had assigned Sharf the lead role in the strike suit against Chambers and this made Sharf's boiling emotional cauldron burn even hotter. Sharf still envied the life force he saw in Chambers as well as the standard Chambers set for integrity. Although he idolized Chambers, Sharf simultaneously loathed him because whenever he thought of the man, he couldn't help but confront the truth about himself.

Sharf wondered if a life of inspiration would ever be within his grasp, or if he would continue along a path of piecemeal annihilation. Every day he spent in Leachman's company was like another nail in his self-imposed coffin, and his soul writhed in the agony of a slow death. He hadn't even mustered the courage to tell his wife that he wanted to reclaim his life.

"You're doing a great job on this case, Adam," Leachman said. "Keep up the good work."

"Thanks, I just want to slam that son of a bitch."

Leachman nodded. "We're going to get him this time. You can bet on that."

* * *

The phone rang at 4 a.m., jarring Chambers out of a fitful sleep. He had been in Wichita for three days and hadn't slept much, calling the hospital every few hours to check on Greenwood, who remained in a coma.

"Hello."

"Is this David?"

"Yes."

"This is Dorothy Greenwood. Leon came out of the coma a couple hours ago."

Chambers heaved a sigh of relief. "Is he okay?"

"He has some burns and won't be able to walk for a while, but the doctor says he should be all right except for some scarring on his back."

"I'm sorry, Dorothy. I'm so sorry."

"Don't be sorry. The first thing I told Leon when he woke up was that you flew to Wichita to see him. You should have seen him; his face lit up. You know how much he loves you."

"Thanks, Dorothy. I love him, too. I can't tell you how relieved I am. Can I come over to see him?"

"He's asleep right now. Why don't you come in an hour or so."

"Okay. See you soon."

* * *

Chambers tiptoed into Leon Greenwood's hospital room carrying a large bouquet of fragrant roses. Dorothy Greenwood and her oldest daughter Kimberly were sitting next to the bed while Leon slept.

"Hi Dorothy. Hi Kim," Chambers whispered.

"Hi David," they said in unison and each grasped one of his hands.

"How is he?"

"The doctor says he's probably going to take a while to heal, but he'll recover. He was up a few hours ago, but they've got him on heavy painkillers. He's…"

"What's all that racket over there?" a cranky voice interrupted.

"Leon!" Chambers exclaimed.

"David, I…" Leon coughed violently. Chambers grabbed a glass of water from the night table and handed it to him.

Leon took a quick gulp and smiled. "Ah…thanks. I hope you're here to offer me a long vacation."

Chambers chuckled. "I'm glad to see you're all right. You haven't lost your sense of humor. You had me worried."

"No need to worry. The Lord was looking out for me."

Chambers hesitated and then forced a smile. "I guess somebody was looking out for you." He moved to the side of the bed and clasped Leon's hand. "The doctor says you really put up a fight to stay alive."

"Damn right I did. My number ain't up yet."

Agent Buranek suddenly entered into the room. "Sorry to interrupt, but I'd like to ask Mr. Greenwood a few questions."

"Can you come back in ten minutes?" Chambers said.

"Sure."

"Who was that?" Leon asked.

"That's Agent Buranek from the FBI. He's investigating the bombing."

"Does he know who did it?"

Chambers quickly decided not to tell Leon that a Christian group was suspected. "No, they don't know."

"They're cowards, whoever they are."

Chambers nodded. *I'm so glad this man is alive.*

The next day, Chambers walked to the front of the ballroom at the Edwards Hotel to address his Wichita team. Since the local police had cordoned off the entire Chambers Aerospace facility, Ernesto and the plant managers had called all of the employees the previous day, asking them to come to the hotel.

"Welcome, everyone. Thank you all for being here. I appreciate your strength and support throughout this tragedy. Let me start by telling you that there were three men—Leon Greenwood, Zach Tyler, and Brian Fisher—who were injured in the explosion. I'm happy to report that they are all okay. Brian and Zack have been released from the hospital and I expect Leon to be released shortly. He's over at West Memorial Hospital if anyone would like to visit or send a card. I also want to assure everyone that the plant will open again soon and that all of your jobs are secure. In fact, I'll be counting on you all more than ever to help us recover. We're going to do whatever it takes to get to the bottom of this and we will not be intimidated. We will never be intimidated."

The crowd let out a loud whoop.

"We're working with the FBI and local law enforcement authorities to make sure that everything is safe. We've also hired a full-time security force that will prevent this from ever happening again."

Chambers spoke for a few more minutes and then mingled with his employees. Despite his anger at what had happened, he felt energized as he reconnected with people that he cared so much about. He knew that he owed his success to the great people who helped make his vision a reality and he always felt a tremendous sense of gratitude.

After the meeting, Chambers flew back to the Ranch feeling disoriented as his thoughts and emotions swung wildly. At first, he spiraled into a maddening fit of rage and wanted revenge. *I should kill all of them. They're insects. That's what they are—insects! Dirty, disgusting, filthy little insects!* Later, he felt relieved and grateful that Greenwood and the others were okay. *I can't believe how lucky I am. But I put innocent people at risk! I could've been responsible for the death of an innocent man!*

After he touched down, Chambers retreated to his library and sat in silence for several hours, agonizing over what to do next.

* * *

Agent Buranek tapped on the office door of Elliott Thurmond, head of the FBI, and opened it slowly.

"Come on in, Walter," Thurmond greeted.

"Sorry, I'm a few minutes late."

"Don't worry about it; have a seat. Have you met Agent Stottlemeyer?"

"Yes, I believe we met once." Buranek didn't know Stottlemeyer well, but he had heard that the young agent was arrogant and abrasive.

"That's right," Stottlemeyer said. "We met at the Christmas party." Buranek and Stottlemeyer shook hands.

"Well, the reason I've called this meeting, Walter, is because I wanted you to brief Agent Stottlemeyer on your Wichita investigation."

"Is he going to assist me?"

"Well, we'll get to that in a moment. Why don't you tell us where you are in the investigation."

"Okay. First of all, it's clear that operatives associated with the Christian Identity movement carried out the operation. We also have a pretty good idea of the specific individuals involved, although we haven't made any arrests yet. We should be in a position to do that shortly. Now, in addition to Christian Identity, we have reason to believe that the Infinity Christian Network was also involved." Buranek paused and made eye contact with the other two men. He expected a reaction to his bombshell, but neither man appeared surprised.

"Go on, Walter," Thurmond directed.

"Well, we're still investigating the Infinity connection," Buranek went on, "And we need to gather more evidence, but I think we'll have enough to arrest certain high-level members of the Infinity organization."

Stottlemeyer nodded. "Good, it sounds like you've built a good foundation for me."

Buranek stared hard at Stottlemeyer. "What do you mean?"

"Well, that's one of the things I wanted to talk to you about, Walter," Thurmond interjected. "I've decided to let Agent Stottlemeyer handle the rest of the investigation."

"Why?"

"I need your help elsewhere."

"Look, I've been on this case from the beginning. I'm the only person who can carry it through. I'm very close…"

"I've already made my decision," Thurmond interrupted. "It's in the best interests of the Bureau."

"I don't understand. This is a complex case and I've got twenty-five years experience. With all due respect to Agent Stottlemeyer, I'm the man to see this through. I want to see it through."

"Experience isn't everything," Stottlemeyer piped in.

"It is in this business, son," Buranek shot back angrily.

"Don't call me son."

"I'll call…"

"Gentlemen!" Thurmond snapped. "Bickering has no place in this organization. You are both valuable members of my team and I expect you to show the proper respect for each other."

Buranek and Stottlemeyer both nodded.

"Now, Walter, I want you to work with Brian and get him up to speed on the investigation. From now on, he'll be the point of contact on this case and I want all future correspondence to go through him. Are we clear on this?"

Buranek frowned, but nodded. "Yes."

"One other thing, Walter. As with all matters we handle here, everything is strictly confidential. This is especially important here because the Bureau's under pressure. If any of this leaks, the Attorney General is going to be crawling up my ass. If that happens, heads are going to roll. Do you understand what I'm saying?"

Buranek clenched his jaw and nodded solemnly. He didn't like being threatened.

"Good. That's all."

Buranek and Stottlemeyer got up to leave, but Thurmond motioned to Stottlemeyer. "Brian, can you stay for another minute? I need to speak with about another matter."

"Sure."

Stottlemeyer sat back down while Buranek walked out and shut the door behind him.

"I want you to keep an eye on him—a close eye," Thurmond said. "The White House is worried about this. I've assigned Drummond to help you. If Buranek so much as thinks about the Wichita investigation, I want to know about it."

"Yes, sir."

"Okay, I've got one other matter to brief you on. You're aware that we've set up surveillance at Kaleidoscope Ranch?"

"Yes."

"Good. We've got two operatives on site and they're currently executing our surveillance plan. I want you to take over the management of that operation."

Stottlemeyer nodded. "Okay."

"Now, one final thing. There's a local sheriff there by the name of Harvey Jenkins. He's a bit of a cowboy, but we've advised him that Kaleidoscope Ranch is under your jurisdiction. He's agreed to contact you if anything unusual comes up. He's also agreed not to take any action without your explicit authorization. I suggest you give him a call and introduce yourself."

"Will do. Thank you for this opportunity, sir."

*　*　*

"Good to see you, Ray," Chambers said as he held his friend close.

"You too, David. Are you okay? That was some nasty business in Wichita."

"Yeah, I'm all right. We're lucky that everyone made it out okay. I don't think I could've forgiven myself."

"Have the police made any progress in the investigation?"

"No, but the FBI's on the case."

"The FBI?" Lassater guffawed. "Isn't that like the wolves guarding the hen house?"

"Why do you say that?"

"The FBI's been reduced to one of Packer's political tools."

Chambers shrugged.

"Listen, as long as you're on the Administration's enemy list, I wouldn't trust the FBI."

"Maybe not. Well, then I'm especially glad you're here. We need to get this project finished before they decide to take me out."

"I didn't know you were mortal."

Chambers grinned. "What have you got for me?"

"I've got a manuscript." Lassater laid a thick binder on Chambers' desk. "It needs a little work, but I think you'll like what you see."

"Excellent."

"You have no idea what we went through to get this."

"And I appreciate it."

"We still need to come up with a title."

"That's easy—Fall of the Impostors," Chambers said without hesitation. "That's the only appropriate title."

Lassater chuckled. "Ah...I like that—right to the point."

"In fact, I'm going to scribble that in now." Chambers picked up a pencil off his desk and put it into the electric sharpener. The machine whirred softly. "What the..." Chambers pulled the pencil out and put it in again. The machine repeated the same sound. Chambers frowned. "This is..."

"What's wrong?"

Chambers didn't answer. He popped out of his chair and trotted out to his secretary's desk. "Peggy, did you replace my pencil sharpener?"

The woman shook her head. "No, do you need a new one?"

"No." Chambers went back into his office. "I'll be right back, Ray."

"What is it?"

"I'm not sure. Stay here." Chambers took the elevator down to the lobby and walked out to the courtyard. He dialed Fitzgerald. "Ron, it's David."

"Hi, David."

"I need your help."

"Okay."

"I don't want to talk about it over the phone, but we may have a major league problem. Can you be here first thing tomorrow?"

"Sure."

CHAPTER 52

Faith is such a successful brainwasher in its own favour, especially a brainwasher of children, that it is hard to break its hold. But what, after all, is faith? It is a state of mind that leads people to believe something— it doesn't matter what—in the total absence of supporting evidence.

[I]t is capable of driving people to such dangerous folly that faith seems to me to qualify as a kind of mental illness. It leads people to believe in whatever it is so strongly that in extreme cases they are prepared to kill and die for it without the need for further justification.

Faith is powerful enough to immunize people against all appeals to pity, to forgiveness, to decent human feelings. It even immunizes them against fear, if they honestly believe that a martyr's death will send them straight to heaven. What a weapon! Religious faith deserves a chapter to itself in the annals of war technology, on an even footing with the longbow, the warhorse, the tank, and the hydrogen bomb.

—RICHARD DAWKINS, *THE SELFISH GENE*

Ron Fitzgerald trotted excitedly into Chambers' office with two of his technicians. Of all the jobs he performed for Chambers, counter-surveillance was Fitzgerald's favorite.

"Put it here, guys," Fitzgerald directed. The technicians dropped a large footlocker full of equipment onto the floor.

"Thanks for coming on such short notice, Ron," Chambers whispered as he shook Fitzgerald's hand.

"Good to see you, David."

Chambers pointed to the pencil sharpener. "Why don't you start with this."

Fitzgerald nodded.

"And tell your guys to help themselves to food and drinks in the kitchen."

"Okay."

"Do you need me here?"

"No."

"Okay, I'm going back to my bungalow. I'll be back in a few hours."

"Okay." Fitzgerald motioned to his team, which began unloading the footlockers and laying the equipment on the floor. Fitzgerald picked up a spectrum analyzer and an oscilloscope, and connected them to a handheld computer. He entered the appropriate settings and then put on his headphones. He positioned the analyzer to scan the area around the pencil sharpener, and he ran through the range of frequencies to detect any audio transmissions, but nothing registered. He signaled one of his technicians, who turned on an audio oscillator. The oscillator made continuous white noise that would trigger the activation of a transmitter, but wouldn't tip off anybody listening.

Within minutes, Fitzgerald got the reading he had been waiting for. He gently cracked open the pencil sharpener's case to verify his findings and then motioned to one of his technicians. "Get a shot of this." Fitzgerald pointed to a small transmitter and tiny antenna. The technician snapped a photograph with a digital camera. For the next several hours, Fitzgerald and his team swept the entire floor, finding the other two hidden bugs.

When Chambers came back to his office, Fitzgerald removed his headphones and put his index finger on his lips. He walked over to Chambers' desk and scribbled a note: *Unsafe to talk. Need to go to secure location.* He held up the note to Chambers, who nodded in recognition.

"Follow me," Chambers said.

Fitzgerald grabbed his black leather case and accompanied Chambers to the Control Room. When they reached the elevator, the retina scanner beeped loudly as it analyzed Fitzgerald's eyes. Chambers entered a quick override code and the elevator door opened.

"It's safe to talk now," Chambers said as they descended. "I know this place is clean. I suppose it's about time I showed it you."

Fitzgerald raised his eyebrows. The elevator doors opened and Chambers motioned to a chair. "Have a seat."

"This is quite a place," Fitzgerald said. "Of course, I can't say that I'm surprised. You never surprise me anymore. I just wish I had better news."

"Let's hear it."

"We found three transmitters."

"How did they get there?"

Fitzgerald shrugged. "I don't know. The feds might've planted someone."

"We screen everyone who works here."

"Well, that's hardly a guarantee anymore. The FBI has mastered the art of creating people with new identities. You wouldn't believe some of the stories I've heard from my friends in the business. It's almost impossible to know who to trust."

Chambers shook his head. "This is unbelievable. What about the phones?"

"Probably all tapped. We didn't find anything, but we never find anything anymore when the feds are involved. It's a safe bet that they're intercepting your calls at the phone company's central office. Since the Domestic Security Act was passed, that's how they do it. They get a warrant from the Attorney General's Office and you're basically screwed. But you're not using the those lines much, are you?"

"No, but sometimes we have no choice. What am I supposed to do now?"

"You want my honest recommendation?"

"Of course."

"Be quiet."

"What's that supposed to mean?"

"Don't say anything you need to keep private. It's either that or remove the bugs. But that's a bad idea because then they'll know you're on to them. As long as they think you don't know, you've got an advantage."

"I don't care," Chambers responded emphatically. "I want the bugs removed. All of them."

"I don't recommend…"

"I said I don't care," Chambers interrupted.

Fitzgerald frowned.

"Look Ron, I know you're looking out for my best interests and I appreciate that, but I'm not going to let anyone plant bugs in my office—no way."

"Okay, David. Whatever you want."

"I want to find out who did this."

"Who has access to your office?"

"My secretary. Ernesto. The cleaning crew."

"Anyone else?"

"No."

"We should start with cleaning crew."

"All right, let's head back."

When Chambers and Fitzgerald got back to Chambers' office, his secretary stopped him at the door. "David, there's someone at the front gate to see you. He says he's an FBI agent."

Chambers froze, quickly exchanging a startled glance with Fitzgerald.

"Is he still at the front gate?"

"As far as I know."

"What do you think, Ron?"

Fitzgerald turned to the secretary. "Is the agent by himself?"

"I think so."

"We need to find that out," Fitzgerald said.

Chambers dialed the front gate on his cell phone.

"Entrance gate."

"Hi, it's David. Is the FBI agent still there?"

"Yeah."

"Is he alone?"

"Yeah."

"Did he give you his name?"

"No, I asked him, but he wouldn't tell me. He's threatening to arrest me if I don't let him in."

Chambers looked at Fitzgerald. "What do you think?"

"Let's talk to him."

Chambers nodded and then barked instructions into the phone. "Listen, I'm going to send a car with a couple of security personnel. When they arrive, I want you to check the agent for weapons and then drive him up. If he gives you any trouble, you call me."

"Will do, David."

"Peggy, call security; tell them to send a car and two officers to the front gate."

Chambers turned to Fitzgerald. "This might be interesting."

"Oh yeah. These guys are getting cockier."

"Peggy, we're going to meet our visitor in front of the building. Tell security to page me if anything comes up."

"Okay, David."

"Let's go, Ron."

Chambers and Fitzgerald went outside and waited on a park bench.

"I'd say as little as possible, David," Fitzgerald cautioned. "And don't mention anything about surveillance."

Chambers nodded. "Don't worry."

A security vehicle pulled up next to the curb and a man in a freshly starched black suit got out of the car. Chambers and Fitzgerald walked towards him.

"Buranek!" Chambers reacted. "Agent Buranek, right?"

"Yes."

"What are you doing here?"

"I wanted to update you on the Wichita investigation."

"I thought…why didn't you just call me?"

"This message needed to be delivered personally."

Chambers turned to Fitzgerald. "Ron, this Agent Buranek."

"Pleased to meet you," Fitzgerald said, shaking Buranek's hand.

"Let's sit down over here." Chambers motioned to a picnic table.

Chambers and Fitzgerald sat next to each other across the table from Buranek. "So what do you have to tell us, Agent Buranek?"

"We've concluded that the attack on your facility in Wichita was carried out by members of Christian Identity."

A jolt of anger shot through Chambers body. "Are you absolutely sure?"

"Yes, there's no doubt about it. I'm sorry to give you the bad news."

"Why? Why? Why did they do this?"

Buranek shrugged. "There is no why. They take the Bible very seriously."

Chambers clenched his jaw. "Do you know who was involved, specifically? I want names…I want…"

"There were at least four men directly involved," Buranek interrupted. "But there may be more. The attack was well executed; we're still investigating."

"Have you arrested anyone?"

"No."

"Why not?"

Buranek hesitated. "Uh…well, I think we're awaiting clearance."

"Clearance? What does that mean?"

"We need authorization before we can make any arrests."

"From who?"

"The Attorney General."

"What are you talking about? A crime's been committed—a serious crime."

"I understand, sir."

"When do you expect to get this authorization?"

"Well…that's hard to say, I'm not closely involved with the case anymore, but I think it depends on…"

"Wait a minute," Chambers interrupted, the decibels in his voice rising. "These guys blow up a building and almost kill three of my employees and you're waiting to get clearance. I don't understand this!"

Buranek dropped his head. On his way to the Ranch, he thought it was going to be easy to tell Chambers the truth about the investigation, but he felt increasingly uncomfortable as he thought about destroying the career he had worked over twenty years to build.

"Explain this to me, Buranek!" Chambers demanded.

"These matters can be sensitive," Buranek responded weakly.

"I need a better answer than that. You've got to give me a better answer than that. Why are you even here?"

"Well…I can't…"

"Come on!"

"This isn't easy."

"Neither is having my building blown up!" Chambers erupted.

"Just relax, David," Fitzgerald interjected. "We'll get to the bottom of this." Fitzgerald stared hard at Buranek. "We need whatever information you have, Agent. You owe us that much."

Buranek drew in a deep breath. "All right. Here's the situation. You're not going to like it, but here it is. From a political perspective, the FBI can't actively pursue the arrest of any Christians, at least not until after the election."

"Why?"

"Packer's in a tough reelection fight; they don't want any scandals, especially not one involving Christians."

"What does that have to do with the people who destroyed my building? They're not Christians. I don't care what they call themselves or what they believe in; they're common criminals. They need to be arrested before they kill someone."

"Well, I shouldn't even be bringing this up," Buranek waffled.

"What's that supposed to mean?"

"Well…"

"Don't hold back on us, Agent," Fitzgerald piped in.

"There's one thing I haven't told you. One very sensitive and disturbing fact. We found a connection with the Infinity Christian Network."

"Infinity's involved with the destruction of my building?"

"Yes, indirectly."

"I don't believe this!" Chambers fumed.

"I'm not surprised," Fitzgerald said. "Those people are crazy."

"Now you can see why the Packer Administration is trying to keep a lid on this," Buranek said. "If a scandal hits Infinity, that's a big problem for their reelection chances."

"So now what? If you're not going to arrest anyone, what am I supposed to do?"

Buranek looked squarely into Chambers' eyes. "That's for you to decide."

* * *

"Stottlemeyer here."

"Agent Stottlemeyer, it's Drummond. I'm here with Agent Gustafson. We followed Agent Buranek to the Kaleidoscope Ranch."

"He's at Kaleidoscope Ranch?"

"Yes, he drove in earlier today."

"That's insubordination!" Stottlemeyer raged. "Is he still there?"

"I think so. We lost track of him when he went in, but we have a visual on his car; it's still on Ranch premises."

"Is he by himself?"

"Yes."

"Okay, keep me posted."

"There's one other thing. We contacted Vasquez and Rodriguez and they've been summoned to a meeting scheduled for tomorrow morning."

"What about?"

"Unknown, sir. Did Buranek know anything about the surveillance?"

"He shouldn't have, but we can't discount the possibility of a leak."

"What should we do?"

"Alert our operatives; get them out of there. I can't afford to lose them."

"What about Buranek? Should we apprehend him?"

"No, not yet. I want one of you to go back to Wichita and secure his office. I also want a thorough search of his house first thing tomorrow morning. I'll get you a warrant by this evening."

"Yes, sir."

* * *

"Tres damas," Vasquez announced victoriously. *Three ladies.*

Rodriguez threw his cards down. "Tu es demasiado afortunado." *You are too lucky.*

"Gracias." Vasquez raked in the chips from the center of the table and stacked them neatly by color. He started to calculate how much money he had won when he was interrupted by the buzz of his pager. He pulled it off his belt and scrolled quickly through the text message: "El pollo ha perdido sus plumas." The chicken has lost its feathers.

"Obtenga sus maletas!" Vasquez cried excitedly. "Ahorita! Salimos!" Get your suitcases! Now! We're leaving!

Each man ran to his bedroom and grabbed his belongings, already packed and ready to go. Less than three minutes later, they were driving frantically toward the Ranch's front gate.

CHAPTER 53

If you tell a lie big enough and keep repeating it
people will eventually come to believe it.

—JOSEPH GOEBBELS, NAZI PROPAGANDA MINISTER

"Ohhh…yeah…that's good," Newhall groaned happily. "I really needed this." Newhall swiveled his head toward the other massage table. "God has certainly blessed this woman with strong hands."

"I'm glad you're enjoying it," Heilbrenner said, not looking up. "I get one of these at least once a week. It helps me unwind." Heilbrenner lifted his hips up slightly to take the pressure off his growing erection. He fantasized about grabbing his masseuse, throwing her down on the table, and ripping her dress off. He would do it rough.

The young women were both nineteen and neither spoke much English. Heilbrenner had selected them personally on a trip to Peru. He loved South American women and especially these two. They each had smooth, muscular legs and tight hips—Heilbrenner's favorite attributes. The women regularly serviced senior Network evangelists at the Infinity Headquarters spa.

"Harder, dear; just a little bit harder," Newhall directed. "Yeah, that's it. Oh…yeah…"

"It's about time to move forward with an announcement, Robert," Heilbrenner said.

"God has called me to do this, huh?" Newhall chuckled.

"You're the only man who can do this."

"Okay, what's the next step?"

"I've got everything lined up. In three weeks, we start saturating the media with the announcement of your candidacy. We'll have every preacher in the Network promoting you on Sunday. We've already got the biggest grassroots organization ever assembled. When we get this thing fully cranked up, it's going to blow people away."

"But Packer's an incumbent president. He's got that advantage."

"That's *our* advantage," Heilbrenner countered. "We put him there. Besides, he's vulnerable on moral issues."

"Moral issues? Like what?"

"Well, marijuana for one. There's still some mileage left on that one. But we've got much better ammunition than that. Packer has a drunk driving conviction."

"Really? When?"

"Twenty-five years ago."

"How come I never heard…?"

"The court records were sealed."

"How did you…never mind."

"It's gets better. Packer had sex with another woman while he was married."

"You're joking?"

"No, I met the woman." Heilbrenner chuckled. "It took a little prodding to get her to talk, but…"

"I don't want to know," Newhall interjected.

"It's going to kill him with the evangelicals."

"I agree. I'm impressed. Are you sure she's telling the truth?"

"I don't know."

"What do you mean you don't know?"

"I don't know."

"We need to…we can't…"

"Who are we to say what's true?" Heilbrenner interrupted. "That's for the public to decide."

"Well…"

"Did Moses part the Red Sea?"

"Huh?"

"All we have to do is repeat the woman's story over and over. People will eventually accept the truth of it."

"I don't know," Newhall hemmed.

"Well, get used to it; that's what we're doing," Heilbrenner responded crossly and turned away. "I've already made a decision and I'm not going to argue with you about it." Heilbrenner hated when Newhall waffled or pretended that he didn't know what they were doing. Whenever his boss tried to cop that naïve attitude, Heilbrenner's feathers ruffled.

"What about money?" Newhall asked, changing the subject. "Packer's got the biggest war chest in history."

Heilbrenner smiled. "We're going to make Packer's war chest look like a lemonade stand."

"How?"

"Through our churches."

"But that's…let me guess, you've found a way around the law?"

Heilbrenner sat up and toweled his forehead. "I've found a way for you to win the presidency."

* * *

"Ernesto, it's David."

"What's up?"

"I just met with the FBI agent. They're not going to arrest the criminals that blew up our building! We've got to do something. We can't let them…"

"Hold on. What are you telling me?"

"I met Buranek; you know, the guy investigating this."

"Yeah."

"Christian Identity blew up our building, but he isn't authorized to arrest them."

"Why not?"

"He said he needs clearance from the Attorney General."

"I don't get it."

"I don't either."

"There must be some…"

"He gave me this song and dance about how they can't arrest any Christians until Packer's reelected."

"That's ridiculous."

"It's outrageous! I'm not going to stand for it!"

"So…what are we going to do?"

"What's the status of the J-22?"

"Well, we've still got a few technical issues to work out. I could actually use your help. But what about this FBI thing?"

"I'll give you whatever help you need. When do you think we can fly it?"

"I don't know; a couple of months maybe. Why?"

"Good. Make it your top priority."

* * *

Skip Hartley opened the squeaky metal door to his warehouse where Josephine stood quietly waiting. "Why, you must be Josephine," he greeted.

"Yes, nice to meet you."

"My dear, you're even more beautiful than David described you." Hartley took her hand and kissed it softly.

Josephine smiled and nodded politely. "Thank you. David's told me a lot about you. You're one of the few people he talks about."

Hartley grinned. "David and I have a good relationship."

"He asked me to come see you, but he didn't say why."

"Well, there is a purpose to this visit; that I can assure you." Hartley extended his hand. "Come in. Please. Let's go up to my study and we'll get right down to business." Josephine followed him up the stairs.

"May I take your coat?" Hartley asked as they entered a brightly lit room.

"Yes, thank you."

"Sorry about the mess." Several stacks of books and papers blanketed the floor of the room. "We're on a bit of a deadline." Hartley hung Josephine's jacket on a coat hook. "I have something for you." Hartley pulled a manila envelope out of his desk drawer. "David wanted you to have this."

Josephine reached into the envelope and pulled out a passport. "What is this?"

"It's a passport. In case you decide to leave the country."

"I'm not planning to."

Hartley shrugged. "I know, but in case you change your mind."

Josephine put the passport in her purse.

"I have another surprise," Hartley said. "We have a visitor; someone you've met before."

"Who?"

"Follow me." Hartley led Josephine into the living room where Ray Lassater was slashing through a manuscript with the sharp point of his red pen.

"We have a guest, Ray."

Lassater stood up and walked toward Josephine. "Josephine Holladay. What a pleasure to see you again. It's been a long time."

"Hi, Ray."

Lassater embraced Josephine, his hormones suddenly surging into action. "My proposal of marriage is still open," he whispered.

Josephine chuckled. "Be careful, I may take you up on that."

"Can you stay for dinner, Josephine?" Hartley asked.

"I'd love to, but my train leaves in an hour."

"How about tea, then?"

"Sure."

Hartley bounded into the kitchen while Lassater and Josephine sat next to each other on the couch.

"Have you seen David recently?" Josephine asked.

"Yes, fairly recently."

"How is he?"

"He's David. He'll always be…shall we say…on the edge."

"I worry about him."

"Don't."

Hartley returned with three cups of tea and placed them on the table.

"We were just talking about David," Lassater said. "I told Josephine not to worry about him."

Hartley nodded. "That's good advice. He's going to do what he's going to do."

Josephine took a sip of her tea. "Can you make sure that he doesn't do anything crazy?"

Both men laughed. "Well, crazy's a relative term," Lassater responded cheerfully.

"You really shouldn't worry," Hartley assured. "David's a survivor."

Josephine took another sip of tea and then looked down at her watch. "I wish I could stay longer, but I really should go now."

Lassater stood up. "It's always great to see you, Josephine." He kissed her lightly on the cheek and gave her a long hug.

"You too, Ray."

"Yes, it was wonderful to meet you, Josephine," Hartley said as he escorted her to the door. "I hope our paths will cross again soon."

* * *

Chambers blew his whistle as the basketball flew out of bounds. "Guys, huddle up!"

Ten young boys surrounded Chambers and he barked instructions. "On offense, you've got to move without the ball. Get yourself open for a shot opportunity. Set some screens. And remember that pick and roll play we talked about. Set a high screen and then roll to the basket. And on the defensive end, when the shot goes up, don't run to the basket; find your man and box him out. Okay. Blue team, take it out."

Kaleidoscope Ranch offered multiple sports programs for both boys and girls during its summer camps, and Chambers usually hired coaches, but he took a special interest in basketball because it was his favorite sport. Even though he couldn't play, he enjoyed teaching the fundamentals of the game.

The teams started the scrimmage again and Chambers paced the sidelines until his secretary came up behind him. "David, there's a call for you."

"Oh. We're in the middle of a practice, here. Can you take a message?"

"The caller says it's urgent."

"Who is it?"

"Adam Sharf."

"Adam Sharf?" Chambers blew the whistle again. "Guys, take ten! Transfer the call to the rec office, Peggy."

"Okay."

Chambers walked quickly to the office and picked up the phone. "Adam, this is David Chambers."

"Hi. I need to talk to you."

"What about?"

"The lawsuit."

"Shouldn't you be calling my attorney?"

"No, I need to talk to you."

"What about those ethical rules you guys are so proud of? I'm represented by an attorney. You're not supposed to call me directly."

"I know, but listen, before I change my mind."

"What do you want?"

"Well…I…I…I'm sorry," Sharf stuttered. "This is…uh…more… uh…difficult than I thought it would be."

"What is it?" Chambers pressed impatiently. "I'm in the middle of something. Tell me or call my attorney."

"I'm just…well…I'm uncomfortable with our case."

"Yeah, it's a bullshit case," Chambers snapped angrily.

"I know. It's wrong. I can't do it. I'm not sure what to do. I wanted to talk to you."

Chambers didn't respond.

"David? Mr. Chambers? Are you…are you there?" Sharf stammered, a trace of panic in his voice.

"Yeah, I'm here. But I can't believe what I'm hearing, particularly after all the outrageous discovery requests you've made. Tom tells me that you've been impossible to deal with this entire case, and this suit will cost me thousands, if not millions."

"I know this seems crazy, right?"

"Yeah."

"I'm serious about it."

"Serious about what? I'm still not sure why you called me."

"I'm leaving my firm."

"Okay. So what?"

"But not yet."

"Okay."

"I want to finish this case."

"What are you trying to tell me?"

"I don't want Leachman to win this case."

"I don't either."

"Maybe we can, you know, work together."

"I don't know what you're talking about, Adam. Your firm has a case against me."

"I want to help you win."

"Are you out of your mind?" Chambers boomed, finally losing his patience.

"I don't know; maybe this is crazy. I just want out."

"I can win my case without you pulling some crazy stunt."

"Maybe, but you won't stop Leachman."

"I don't think anyone can stop him. The guy's an incurable cancer."

"I have an idea. I think we can do something."

"Like what?"

"Like destroy Leachman."

Chambers guffawed. "Are you high?"

"I'm serious," Sharf responded firmly. "I'm completely serious."

"Well, I'm still listening then."

CHAPTER 54

Respect for the truth comes close to being the basis for all morality.

—FRANK HERBERT

Skip Hartley heaved a sigh of relief as he made the final edits to the *Fall of the Impostors* manuscript. He had worked tirelessly with Ray Lassater getting the book ready and he smiled as he thought about its explosive content. The book detailed the inner workings of Infinity's fraud and manipulation, and it exposed Infinity's intimate ties with the Packer Administration and militant Christian sects.

Hartley had responsibility for distributing the book so he contacted newspapers in several major cities, buying full-page ads to announce publication. In order to achieve maximum impact, part of Hartley's plan was to allow people to download the book for free. He also lined up several independent bookstores to sell it, although he worried that they might bow to political pressure. To entice bookstores, Hartley agreed to sell them the book for two dollars a copy, guaranteeing a huge profit. He also promised to donate all the proceeds from the book to five children's hospitals and a literacy program operated by the Kaleidoscope Foundation.

Hartley flipped slowly through the manuscript and paused on an occasional paragraph. He laughed gently every so often until he reached the end. He closed the book and rested it on his lap, focusing on the front cover where his name was prominently etched. Hartley blinked his eyes to hold back tears and then held the book tightly to his chest. *This is the most important accomplishment of my life!*

* * *

Tom Jeffries stepped out of the elevator and walked briskly towards his office. His secretary stopped him before he could get to his desk. "Tom, the phone's been ringing off the hook; you've got twelve messages already this morning. They're all about the strike suit."

"Okay, thanks." Jeffries had sent a letter to several of the company's largest shareholders urging them not to opt out of Leachman's class action lawsuit. Jeffries had been expecting a confused response because he knew they wouldn't understand his request. Most of the shareholders were Chambers' friends and business associates, and they shared his disdain for opportunistic shysters that preyed on productive companies. They had all opted out of the previous suit and had spoken out against it. Jeffries wanted every shareholder to be part of the class this time around.

Jeffries flipped through the stack of messages and dialed the first number.

"Mathias Airframe."

"This is Tom Jeffries. Is Stan Mathias available?" Mathias did a large volume of business with Chambers Aerospace and he owned twenty thousand shares in the company.

"One moment."

"Hi Tom. How are you?"

"Good, yourself?"

"Great, but I didn't understand your recent letter. Why on earth would you want me to be a part of the lawsuit against you?"

"Well, we just want everyone to protect their interests on this one. David's insisting."

"That doesn't make any sense to me. I hate these lawsuits with every inch of my body. I'm not about to participate; I've got my own reputation to protect."

"I understand your concerns, and believe me, I share your dislike for strike suits, but you've got to trust David on this one."

"I don't see how it could be in his interest for me to join this suit."

"David knows what's in his interest," Jeffries responded firmly. "Like I said, you need to trust him."

"Oh…wait a minute…is he up to something?"

"Well, you just need to trust him. It's best we leave it at that."

Mathias chuckled. "He is up to something. That old dog. I hope he knows what he's doing. Otherwise, those sharks'll eat him alive."

"We'll be in touch, Stan."

Jeffries called everyone else on his list and they all agreed not to opt out of the suit.

* * *

Heilbrenner focused on the screen as it flickered to life with a car streaking down a rain-soaked road. Raucous, heavy metal music blared in the background. As the car whipped around a sharp corner, the driver threw a beer bottle out of the window, smashing it on the pavement. Seconds later, the screen went blank with the explosive crash of a head-on collision.

The scene shifted to a police officer standing in front of a spinning siren. "I've been a police officer for over twenty years. I've seen hundreds of innocent people killed by drunk drivers."

The next scene showed paramedics trying to save a young girl and then whisking her away in an ambulance. Then a somber narrator delivered the ominous message: "The President has a secret—a dark secret. He has lied to the American people, concealing a drunk driving conviction for almost thirty years."

The policeman came on again. "It's never easy when I have to tell someone that one of their loved ones has been killed by a drunk driver. I know he's our President, but everybody should answer for reckless behavior when life is at stake."

"That's perfect!" Heilbrenner cried enthusiastically. "Absolutely perfect!" Heilbrenner had hired the most ruthless people he knew in the advertising business to create a series of ads vilifying the President. He commissioned them to create the image of a man lacking the moral authority to lead the country.

"Now, what's the schedule with that woman?" Heilbrenner asked excitedly.

"We just finalized her script. We'll start shooting tomorrow."

* * *

Ray Lassater casually sipped his iced tea while he waited for Franklin Tunney at a small outdoor café in Santa Monica. Although he hadn't prosecuted a case in over a year, Lassater felt like he had right before filing the criminal complaints against Catholic Church officials— obsessed by a compelling thirst for justice no matter what the obstacles. Now that he had enough evidence to destroy Infinity, he felt euphoric.

Tunney worked as a federal prosecutor in Los Angeles, and he was one of only a handful of federal prosecutors that had supported Lassater's prosecution of the Catholic Church. Tunney had even risked his own career by publicly defending Lassater and praising his courage in taking on the powerful enemy.

Tunney strolled onto the sunny patio and pulled a pair of stylish sunglasses out of his shirt pocket. He slid them on as he walked over to Lassater's table. "Hi, Ray," he said cordially. "How are you?"

"Great. Nice to see you, Franklin." Lassater stood up and shook Tunney's hand.

"You know, I don't think I've spoken with you since you left Boston. What've you been up to?"

"Oh, just keeping busy."

"Somehow I get the feeling that you've been up to more than that."

Lassater smiled. "What'll you have to drink?"

"How about a lemonade?"

Lassater motioned to the waitress. "One lemonade here, please."

"Thanks. *Fall of the Impostors* is quite a piece of work," Tunney said, pulling the book out of his briefcase. Lassater had sent Tunney an advance copy three days before.

Lassater nodded. "You should be able to take the entire Infinity organization down on at least a hundred counts."

"Ha!" Tunney threw his head back and guffawed. "Is that what this is about? You want me to prosecute Infinity?"

"I've handed you a bulletproof case."

"Maybe."

"Maybe?" Lassater cried incredulously. "What the hell's that supposed to mean? I've reviewed all the evidence myself. Getting convictions will be easier than falling out of bed."

"Well, there are always political considerations," Tunney waffled.

"Pussy considerations," Lassater scoffed as the waitress delivered the lemonade and let out an embarrassed giggle.

"Look, you're not in my shoes. I don't like these con men anymore than you do, but you don't just go after a religious organization. That's not acceptable to the vast majority of people in this country, including the Justice Department." Tunney paused, suddenly remembering that Lassater had prosecuted a religious organization. He quickly backtracked. "I know you got away with it, but I've got other obstacles—the Attorney General for starters."

Lassater shook his head impatiently. "This case will make your career."

"Well…"

"Well, nothing. The way I see it, you've got two choices. You can either take the lead on this and be a superstar or you can wait for the book to be released. But then it'll be too late. Everyone, including the Attorney General, will be on it then. You'll be lucky to pick up crumbs."

"Well, even assuming the Attorney General didn't fire me, a prosecution of this magnitude would require a major shift of my resources."

"You're doing something more important than this?" Lassater challenged.

Tunney shrugged.

"These people prey on human weakness and fear for their own personal gain." Lassater smacked his hand on the table. "And society glorifies them as enlightened men of God! I can think of a few worse crimes, but this has got to be the most insidious. It's certainly the most manipulative."

"Okay, I'll see what I can do—if I don't get fired first. Wallace is keeping a pretty tight rein on us these days. He's obsessed with prosecuting pot smokers and defending the faith-based initiative."

"You won't have any problem with the Attorney General or anyone else at Justice. After *Fall of the Impostors* is released, everyone in the Administration will be running for cover. They'll want Newhall taken down as quickly as possible."

"I hope you're right."

"Of course I'm right."

"What's next, then?"

"Get the case ready for the grand jury and do whatever else you need to do. I'm going to meet with John Heilbrenner."

"Heilbrenner! Why?"

"He's going to cooperate with us."

446

"What are you talking about?"

"He doesn't know it yet, but I'm going to convince him to help us. That's the only way we take down the entire Network and expose everything."

"What about convicting him?"

Lassater shook his head. "No, but that's a trade we should make. Trust me, this will be much worse for him than a jail sentence."

"It seems like a long shot."

Lassater shrugged. "We'll be releasing *Fall of the Impostors* in a couple of weeks. You can get the indictments right after that."

"Okay."

Lassater smiled. "This is going to be good, Franklin. You may not believe it right now, but this will make more of a difference than anything you've ever done."

CHAPTER 55

[G]reatness in every virtue would seem to be characteristic of a proud man…Pride, then, seems to be a sort of crown of virtues; for it makes them greater, and is not found without them. Therefore it is hard to be truly proud; for it is impossible without nobility and goodness of character.

—ARISTOTLE, *NICOMACHEAN ETHICS*

The sides of Ray Lassater's mouth curled into a satisfied smile as he dialed John Heilbrenner's office at Infinity Headquarters.

"Good afternoon, John Heilbrenner's office. This is Tammy."

"Tammy Faye?"

"Huh?"

Lassater chuckled. "Sorry, I'm kidding. This is Ray Lassater. I'd like to speak with John, please."

"May I tell him what this is regarding?"

"Oh…just tell him…let's see…tell him that life as he knows it is over."

"I beg your pardon."

"Put me through, please."

"What was your name again?"

"Ray Lassater."

"Uh…hold on." Heilbrenner's secretary pushed the intercom button. "Mr. Heilbrenner, I've got a call for you on line two. A man named Ray Lassater."

"Ray Lassater? The prosecutor from Boston?"

"I don't know; he didn't say. I asked him what it was regarding, but he said something strange. Do you want me to tell him you're in a meeting?"

"No, no, I'll take it." Heilbrenner pressed line two. "This is John Heilbrenner."

"Hi John, this is Ray Lassater. I don't believe we've ever met, but we need to meet soon."

"Ray Lassater from Boston?"

"That's right. I used to work in Boston. In fact, I used to prosecute men much like yourself in Boston."

There was a long silence while Heilbrenner racked his brain trying to figure out what the call could possibly be about.

"You still there, John?"

"Yeah. What can I do for you?"

"Oh, I just wanted to have a friendly little chat. I think we can help each other."

"What are you talking about?"

"We need to have a meeting."

"About what?"

"We need to discuss the legal proceedings that are about to be launched against the Infinity Network. I like to meet someone in person before I take them down."

Lassater waited for Heilbrenner to respond, but he said nothing.

"Cat got your tongue, John? Well, in that case, let me tell how things'll go down. In the simplest terms, Infinity and its leadership will be destroyed, including you and Newhall." Lassater paused. "But I do have some good news. We've decided to give you the opportunity to save yourself—if you're willing to do the right thing, that is."

"I don't know what you're talking about," Heilbrenner snapped.

"I'm talking about taking you down; bringing you and the rest of the phonies in your organization to justice."

"Are you threatening me?"

"Yes."

Heilbrenner normally dominated everyone he dealt with, but he quickly concluded that Lassater was a formidable adversary. "This is an interesting bluff, but I don't know what you're talking about."

"Oh…I think you do. I assume you remember a gentleman by the name of Mike Watson?"

"Get to the point."

"Or how about Marvin Butler? You know him?"

Heilbrenner didn't answer.

"Well, let's start with Watson. He had some very interesting information about your little network."

"Listen, I don't care whether Mike Watson talked to you or not; what he did or didn't do has nothing to do with me."

"It has everything to do with you."

"I'm hanging up unless there's a point to this call."

"We need to meet. Your office. Tomorrow."

"I don't need to waste my time with you."

"Well, let me be a little more clear, then. I'm offering you a deal. If you fuck with me, I'll make sure you're left with nothing. I suggest you make some time to talk with me."

Lassater waited for a response. "John? You still there? I'm losing my patience with you." Lassater was about to hang up when he heard the line click. "Mr. Lassater, this is Tammy, Mr. Heilbrenner's secretary. How does three o'clock tomorrow sound?"

"That'll be fine."

* * *

"Mr. Wallace, I've got Franklin Tunney holding for you."

"Put him through." Since Tunney was a senior prosecutor in a major jurisdiction, he spoke frequently with the Attorney General and the two men had a good relationship. But they didn't always see eye to eye. Tunney disagreed with the Attorney General's obsessive prosecution of hemp farmers and marijuana users, while the Attorney General had been upset over Tunney's vocal support of Lassater's investigation of the Catholic Church.

"Hi Franklin. How's everything out on the West Coast?"

"Good. Did you get the package I sent you?"

"Yeah, I remember seeing that, but I haven't looked at it yet. Is it important?"

"Yes—very."

"What is it?"

"It's a copy of a book called *Fall of the Impostors.*"

"Okay. Why is this important?"

"When you read the book, you'll understand, but let me give you a synopsis. It chronicles several significant illegal activities by the leadership of the Infinity Network. It also discusses Infinity's ties to the Administration and other Christian groups."

"Who wrote this book?"

"David Chambers, and a few others."

"So David Chambers has crawled out from under his rock again?"

"Well, he's about to publish the book. It'll be released and distributed shortly. I got an advance copy."

"I don't trust a single word from that atheist," Wallace scoffed. "Neither does anyone else. I don't think we need to worry about it."

"The evidence looks pretty solid," Tunney replied evenly. "Chambers put a lot into this."

"I couldn't care less," Wallace snapped. "I'm sure that son of a bitch is real proud of himself. And that's what going to kill him—his pride."

"Well…"

"This whole discussion is irrelevant, Franklin. Everyone knows that Infinity has cut a few corners, but hell, who hasn't? The bottom line is that no criminal case against anyone over there will ever see the light of day—at least not while I'm Attorney General."

"Well, that's actually what I'm calling about."

"What?"

"Pursuing an indictment against Infinity leadership."

"Are you out of your mind?" Wallace boomed. "Didn't you hear what I just said?"

"You need to read the book."

"I don't need to read anything, and you need to forget about pursuing this. It's not going to happen—not on my watch."

Tunney didn't respond.

"Are we clear on this, Franklin?"

"Yeah."

"Good. I don't want to hear any more about it."

Wallace hung up with Tunney and dialed the President's Chief of Staff. "Al, it's Lamar. I just spoke with Franklin Tunney, one of my prosecutors in LA. He's making noise about pursuing an indictment against Infinity based on information in some book written by David Chambers."

"What book?"

"I don't know, I haven't read it. It's called *Fall of the Impostors.*"

"What did you tell your prosecutor?"

"I told him to forget it."

"Do you have the book?"

"Yeah. Tunney sent me a copy."

"I need to take a look at that as soon as possible. Can you meet me tonight at my office, around eight?"

"Sure."

* * *

As Ray Lassater drove through the entrance gate at Infinity Headquarters, he had to admit that he was impressed. The grounds of the seventy-five-acre compound were lush and immaculately maintained. He'd never seen such a diversity of exotic plants anywhere in the world, and he wondered how they did it. He had no idea that Infinity employed three full-time botanists and a twenty-five man gardening crew.

Lassater parked his car and then walked into the lobby of the executive office building, a sleek, modern structure with contemporary decor and furnishings. Although he knew little about high-end furniture or building materials, Lassater had no doubt that no expense had been spared. In addition to imported Italian marble and three original Picassos, the lobby had twenty-foot floor to ceiling windows, situated perfectly to capture the morning light, which illuminated a fifteen-foot sterling silver cross hanging behind the reception desk.

"May I help you, sir?" the receptionist greeted.

"Yes. I'm Ray Lassater. I'm here to see John Heilbrenner."

"Okay. Have a seat while I call someone to escort you upstairs."

Lassater sat down on a white leather couch and admired the artwork. He waited five minutes until a smartly dressed young woman welcomed him. "Hello, Mr. Lassater, I'm Mr. Heilbrenner's assistant. I'll show you to the conference room."

Lassater rode the elevator up to the fifteenth floor and the assistant escorted him to a large conference room where Heilbrenner, his attorney, and two assistants were waiting. Without acknowledging anyone in the room, Lassater walked straight toward the window, which provided a panoramic view of the Pacific Ocean. "Boy, this view is incredible," Lassater said admiringly, before turning to Heilbrenner. "You have a beautiful campus here, John. And this building…I didn't realize God had such extravagant tastes. You've spent your followers' money wisely."

"I don't have time for this nonsense," Heilbrenner responded sternly. "If you have something to discuss with me, let's get to it."

"Okay. But let me give you some advice before we get started. I suggest we meet alone. I don't think you want any of your monkeys to hear what I have to say."

"My attorney will stay with us."

Lassater shrugged. "Then you're not as smart as I thought. The less he knows, the more creative he can be when you're in court."

Heilbrenner turned to the other men. "We'll talk privately, but please wait in the other room. I may need you later."

"I advise against this, John," Heilbrenner's attorney warned.

"It's okay, Phil. I'll call you later."

After all of the men had left the room, Lassater sat down and reclined in a comfortable leather chair. "Man, this is the life, isn't it? I can see how a certain type of man might sell his soul for this."

"What do you have to tell me?" Heilbrenner snapped. "I'm still not sure why I agreed to this. I should call security and have you thrown out."

"I could throw myself out." Lassater sprang up and moved toward the door. "Have a nice day."

"Sit down!" Heilbrenner ordered.

"Oh…I admire the forceful leadership, but the least you could do is offer me something to drink."

"What the hell do you want?" Heilbrenner exploded. Normally, he had no difficulty controlling his emotions, but Lassater was pressing all the right buttons.

Lassater smiled. "I want your cooperation. We've put together enough evidence to bring down the Infinity Network on at least a hundred counts—fraud, tax evasion, conspiracy, racketeering. We also know about your involvement with militant Christian elements. We have the evidence ready to present to federal prosecutors."

"That's outrageous!" Heilbrenner roared.

"It is what it is," Lassater responded casually. "And for chrissakes, lighten up. Remember who you're talking to. I'm not one of your lackeys."

"You…you…" Heilbrenner's cheeks ballooned as blood bubbled into his face.

"Jesus Christ, relax, man. Take a deep breath."

Heilbrenner walked to window and looked out over the ocean. He thought of being alone in the water a hundred miles offshore with no chance of rescue. He wondered if he would face death calmly or wage a desperate struggle to survive. Then he felt a wave of resignation, almost relief. In the basement of his mind, he had always known that someday someone would challenge and defeat him. He also realized for the first time that he had always known that his plan was flawed and that he wanted to be humiliated and destroyed. "How do I know you're telling the truth?" he said quietly.

"You don't."

"Why should I trust you?"

"You have no choice."

"What about Newhall?"

"He's finished. So is Infinity. You're the only one getting this deal."

"What deal?"

"Full immunity from prosecution in exchange for full disclosure. We want everything and everybody."

"Why are you offering me this? This doesn't make any sense."

"Well…I'm…I'm…I'm sorry…I can't…I can't help it," Lassater stuttered over several bursts of laughter. "This is my favorite… my favorite part." Lassater paused, finally regaining his composure. "Our goal is to take the entire Network down. That includes you, but we didn't think we could take you down any further. I suspect the private hell you're living in can't get much worse. On the other hand, if you betray your friends and accept this deal, then you've left no doubt about the nature of your soul."

Heilbrenner cringed, quickly reflecting that he would be betraying the only people on Earth who trusted him. Then he wondered why that thought had entered his mind. *I feel something. Goddammit I feel something! My stomach's on fire! It's burning! No! Control yourself!* He took a deep breath. "What about the money?" he asked calmly.

"What money?"

"The money I made at Infinity, my house."

"You can keep what you've got offshore, but the rest goes." Lassater hated to allow Heilbrenner anything, but he knew that nobody would be able to seize his offshore assets.

"What about my…"

"Oh, and that includes impounding all of your Ferraris," Lassater interrupted.

"I need to speak with my lawyer."

Lassater pulled a book out of his briefcase. "Show your lawyer this," he said, handing Heilbrenner a freshly printed copy of *Fall of the Impostors*. "You're a lucky man, John. This is the first official copy, personally autographed by myself and David Chambers. Probably be worth something someday."

Heilbrenner snapped the book out of Lassater's hand, resisting the urge to throw it back in his face.

"I need an answer by tomorrow at two—no exceptions. I'll show myself out."

Heilbrenner went back to his office and sat alone, quickly calculating all of the possible scenarios. He swiveled around in his chair and eyed a framed photo on his credenza. It was a shot of him and Newhall with their arms around each other, which had been taken at a dinner honoring Heilbrenner for his service to Infinity. Heilbrenner remembered the gathering well because Newhall had praised him effusively and given him credit for Infinity's astounding success. Heilbrenner clenched his jaw and picked up the frame. He turned it over and put it in the bottom of his file cabinet.

CHAPTER 56

Religion is what the common people see as true, the wise people see as false, and the rulers see as useful.

—SENECA

Al Rogers bolted past the desk of the President's secretary.

"You can't go in there right now, sir. He's in a meeting with Secretary Collins. Sir? Sir?"

Rogers ignored the warning and threw open the door to the Oval Office. "Sorry to interrupt, Mr. President, but I need to speak with you. It's urgent."

"I'm in an important meeting, Al. Can't this wait half an hour?"

"No, sir. We need to talk now."

The President forced an uncomfortable smile at the Secretary of State. "I'm sorry, Mark. Can we continue this discussion tomorrow evening before the dinner?"

"Certainly, Mr. President." Secretary Collins stood up and walked to the door, frowning at Rogers as he brushed past him.

"Sit down, Al. What's so important?"

"We've got a problem with David Chambers again."

The President shook his head. "The most undeserving person ever to receive the Presidential Medal of Freedom."

Rogers instinctively reacted with a disgusted glance, but quickly looked away. He didn't like Chambers either, but the President's childish criticism disturbed him. "Well, he's written another book, Mr. President."

"So? Nobody cared about his last book. Besides, everyone hates an atheist."

"Well, this book will be out officially in a few days, but I've already seen it. It includes extensive information about the Infinity Network and how it defrauded its followers, abused its tax-exempt status, and ripped off the government through the federal grant process. They've taken over three hundred million dollars from your faith-based initiative alone."

The President's demeanor stiffened. He knew that Infinity had taken hordes of cash from the faith-based program, but that was the idea. His goal was to strengthen the Christian community and support the election of additional Christians to public office. He also needed the support of the faithful for his own reelection. He felt a little perturbed that anyone would challenge his right to dole out a certain amount of cash to his friends and supporters, particularly since the practice had been an unquestionable prerogative of every modern President. "Where did Chambers get this information?" the President asked.

"I don't know, but it appears that at least one insider was involved."

The President grimaced.

"It gets worse," Rogers continued. "The book also highlights Infinity's close relationship with the Administration. It's not a pretty picture."

"That's nonsense!"

"It is what it is. We need to deal with it."

The President got up and paced behind his desk. "I can't believe we have to deal with people like this," he muttered to himself.

Rogers looked down at his Rolex. *What the hell am I doing here? I'm so much smarter than this guy. But he's the President and I'm not. He had the guts to run; I didn't. Christ, I wish I had some real guts. I'd destroy this guy and the rest of the two-bit poseurs in this town. Hell, I did everything right— all the right schools, all the right contacts, and I have more power than most people ever dream about. No one is closer to the President, but I feel like slapping him. God, snap out of this! Now!* "Mr. President?"

The President pulled a chair next to Rogers and sat down. "How do you think the public will react?"

"Well, people will probably hate Chambers for publishing his book, but I suspect they'll also feel betrayed by Infinity. We've got pollsters out now, all over the country, gauging public opinion."

"This could be damaging," the President offered.

"That's an understatement, sir."

"What's your recommendation?"

"First, we distance ourselves from Infinity ASAP. We should call a press conference and denounce the leadership. Next, we need to clean house—quietly replace every person in the Administration with ties to Infinity."

"That's probably a thousand people," the President countered. "Besides, if we attack Infinity, we'll alienate the public."

"Some of them. But we can't worry about that; we have to act decisively. If we don't take a stand right now, we run the risk of being crucified along with them. Your reelection will be a pipe dream."

The President walked to the window and stared out at the Rose Garden.

"If we separate ourselves from Infinity carefully, you won't lose support of most believers," Rogers assured. "And this could be a great opportunity."

"How?"

"With Newhall out of the way, you can become the undisputed moral leader of the country. That can only strengthen your political position."

The President didn't respond. He thought of his wife, who relied on astrology to make important decisions. She had told him the previous evening to wait two days before making any major decisions so that the stars would be in alignment. The President told himself that he didn't really believe in astrology, but what if his wife was right?

"Is everything okay, sir?"

"Yes," the President replied, not turning around. "It's just…ah… never mind."

"What would like me to do, Mr. President?"

The President turned around slowly. "Do whatever you think is necessary to fix this," he said quietly.

"Yes, Mr. President." Rogers retreated to his office and called the Attorney General.

* * *

Adam Sharf watched the ice cubes dance around his glass as his hand shook uncontrollably. *I've got to control this! Ahhh…! I'm scared. I'm so scared. Ahhh…! I've got to get this done. Focus!* Sharf put the glass down and took several deep breaths. He stared at the empty computer screen and then started typing: "Declaration of Adam Sharf."

Sharf felt a chill run down his spine and he took his hands off the keyboard. He stared at a picture of his wife and three children. Am I really going to do this? I could lose everything. Sharf clenched his jaw. God, I've got to do this. There's no other way. There's just no other way. He put his fingers back on the keyboard and continued working late into the night.

* * *

"Mr. Lassater, this is Phillip Lipton. I'm John Heilbrenner's attorney. My client informs me that you threatened him."

"Yes. I'm waiting for his call. He has just under three and a half hours left to accept my offer."

"Your conduct is highly inappropriate. I'll see that you're disbarred over this."

Lassater chuckled. "Now there's an empty threat. I'm no longer a member of the Bar, but let me give you a piece of legal advice anyway. You have an ethical obligation to pursue your client's best interests. So far, you're not doing a very good job of that."

"Well, we need to meet," Lipton offered. "I want to discuss your evidence."

"No."

"Then we can't agree to anything."

"So Mr. Heilbrenner rejects my offer?"

"No, we just need to discuss this further."

"My terms aren't negotiable, so there's nothing to discuss. I need a final answer, and I need it from Heilbrenner. Take it or leave it."

"But, but, this isn't the way…this isn't the way things are done," Lipton stammered.

"You've got three hours." Lassater hung up and waited. Two and a half hours later, Heilbrenner called.

"Ray, it's John Heilbrenner. We need to talk about this."

"No. Time's up. Do you accept the deal or not?"

"Well…"

"This is a no-brainer, John. It's over. Don't test me."

There was a long silence.

"John?"

"Full immunity, right? And I keep all money offshore?"

"If you give us what we ask for."

"Okay."

"Good. We'll be in touch."

Heilbrenner put the phone down and sat quietly for several minutes. He glanced at his watch as his body retreated into a state of hollow numbness. *Does it matter what time it is? Does anything matter?* He stared blankly at the walls and looked at his watch again. Twenty minutes had passed, but now his hand was shaking. He tried to hold it steady, but couldn't. *Ahhhhhhhhh! Shithead! Goddamn fucking shithead! You pathetic shithead! You're nothing! Nothing! Nothing!*

CHAPTER 57

The Church says the Earth is flat, but I know that it is round, for I have
seen the shadow on the moon, and I have more faith in a shadow than
in the Church.

—FERDINAND MAGELLAN

Franklin Tunney waited nervously in his office at the Los Angeles federal building until it was time to go downstairs and address the media. He had obtained a grand jury indictment against Infinity, defying the orders of the Attorney General, and he jumped every time the phone rang. But the Attorney General hadn't called.

Fall of the Impostors had been released a few days before, creating a stir. Many believers reacted by denouncing the book and the charges leveled against Infinity. Other members of the faithful felt betrayed and demanded an explanation. Most nonbelievers yawned, happy to rid the world of another mystical con, but reasonably certain that another would come along soon.

It was an unusually muggy day in Los Angeles so Tunney walked briskly, fanning himself with his notes. Beads of sweat trickled down his chest. As he trudged down the long hallway, his pace quickened and his heart raced. But then his nervousness was suddenly overcome by exhilaration. He knew his life was about to change. The media room twinkled in a sea of flashbulbs as Tunney stepped to the podium. The room was packed.

"Good afternoon, everyone. As most of you already know, yesterday, a federal grand jury issued a sixty-five-count indictment against Reverend Robert Newhall and eight other top officials in the Infinity Christian Network. Let me start by saying that I've been a federal prosecutor for almost twenty years and I've prosecuted many dangerous criminals, but this is the worst case of organized crime I've ever seen. I can assure everyone here that despite the religious affiliation of the defendants, this prosecution will receive my highest priority and the highest priority of my office. I don't have any other prepared remarks so I'll take your questions. Over here."

"Can you tell us the whereabouts of Reverend Newhall and the rest of the defendants? Have they all been arrested?"

"Well, seven of the defendants have been arrested, including Reverend Newhall. Two men are still at large and it's been rumored that they've fled the country. I can't verify that information at the present time. Right here in front."

"Can you give us some specifics about the operations of Infinity that led to this indictment?"

"Everything is pretty well spelled out in the indictment. The bulk of the charges are based on fraud—fraud against their followers, fraud against the government, and fraud against their franchisees."

"Franchisees?"

Tunney suppressed a smile. "Yes. I use the term franchisees to describe the member churches in the Network because it provides the most accurate definition of the relationship. These are churches that weren't owned by Infinity directly, but became members of the Network. As part of their membership, Infinity Headquarters provided them with the doctrines, the beliefs, the mythology, and the symbols— the entire spiritual package. In exchange, each member church gave Infinity a percentage of its revenues. Legally speaking, this resembles a franchise. Of course, I don't want to disparage legitimate franchises, the vast majority of which don't engage in this kind of deception and fraud."

"Can you go into greater detail about your allegations of fraud?"

"Sure. Infinity agreed to use at least thirty percent of the proceeds from its franchisees to support certain specific charities. What we've found is that almost none of the money was distributed to charity. Instead, it found its way into the bank accounts of Infinity officials, supporting some very lavish lifestyles." Tunney paused. "Let me also point out that many of the churches owned directly by Infinity did the same thing. They promised to support specific charities, and they either didn't support them, or in some cases, the named charities didn't even exist. In the back."

"What about the charges related to the government? Can you comment on those?"

Tunney shook his head in disgust. "By our estimates, Infinity cheated the government out of over three hundred million dollars by abusing the federal grant process through the President's faith-based initiative. I'd add that Infinity abused its tax-exempt status. They conducted campaign rallies and voter registration drives on church property in clear violation of the rules governing tax-exempt entities."

Tunney pointed to another reporter.

"Where did you obtain the information to support this indictment?"

"I have no comment about our sources at this time."

"Is it safe to say that the recently published book *Fall of the Impostors* provided the information in support of the indictment?"

"The indictment was the result of a long investigation by many individuals working together. I have no other comments about that. Yellow blouse in the back."

"Mr. Tunney, several religious leaders unaffiliated with Infinity have called these indictments a witch hunt. How do you respond to that?"

Tunney chuckled. "Well, I personally don't put much faith in anything religious leaders say. If we followed everything guys in robes told us to do, we'd still be living in caves. I have no further comments. Thank you." Tunney stepped away from the podium and darted quickly out a side door. A euphoric shot of adrenaline electrified his body and he punched the sky with his fist. He felt like skipping across the empty hallway, but settled for an exuberant spring in his step and an enthusiastic whistle:

Zip a dee doo-dah...

* * *

The Attorney General straightened his tie as he paced backstage at the National Press Club in Washington. He was scheduled to give a speech about the government's progress in the war on drugs, and his assistant had written a powerful oration boasting that almost twice as many marijuana users were in prison compared to the previous Administration. But the Attorney General didn't get a chance to make the speech. As soon as he stepped to the podium, reporters immediately bombarded him with questions about Tunney's announcement. Fortunately, he had had a long talk with the Chief of Staff about strategy.

"Attorney General Wallace, can you comment on Mr. Tunney's announcement this morning?"

"Yes, I'm happy to comment briefly. As you know, the grand jury handed down indictments against several officials in the Infinity Network. Mr. Tunney and the U.S. Attorney's Office in Los Angeles have been conducting an investigation into the Network's activities for some time and I've been following the investigation closely. I've also kept the President apprised of developments. He shares my belief that we need to move forward swiftly to bring the guilty parties to justice. While the indicted men are innocent until proven guilty, it appears, sadly, that they have abused the public trust in an elaborate fraud. I will continue to provide support for Mr. Tunney and his office as they continue to pursue this important prosecution."

"Do you plan to renounce your membership in Infinity?"

"Yes, I believe that during the investigation it's important that everyone in the Justice Department remain impartial, although I hope Christians will remain united through this crisis."

"Has your faith been shaken, sir?"

"No, not at all," Wallace reacted emphatically. "I firmly believe that God is still in control here. I'm confident that everything will work out according to His plan. I encourage all Christians to remain behind the President as we deal with this crisis."

* * *

"This is it, John—your new home." Lassater opened the door to a spacious bungalow at Kaleidoscope Ranch. Tunney and Lassater had decided that Heilbrenner needed to be sequestered prior to the Infinity prosecutions for his own safety.

Heilbrenner stared blankly across the room as he walked in. He dropped his bag next to the couch and then fingered his new bracelet —a sophisticated GPS tracking device that couldn't be removed.

464

Lassater patted Heilbrenner's back. "Don't worry, John; it'll all be over soon."

CHAPTER 58

I do not believe in the creed professed by the Jewish Church, by the Roman Church, by the Greek Church, by the Turkish Church, by the Protestant Church, nor by any church that I know of. My own mind is my own church.

All national institutions of churches—whether Jewish, Christian, or Turkish—appear to me no other than human inventions set up to terrify and enslave mankind and monopolize power and profit.

I do not mean by this declaration to condemn those who believe otherwise. They have the same right to their belief as I have to mine. But, it is necessary to the happiness of man, that he be mentally faithful to himself. Infidelity does not consist in believing, or in disbelieving; it consists in professing to believe in what he does not believe.

—THOMAS PAINE, *THE AGE OF REASON*

Newhall heaved a sigh of relief as a guard escorted him from a dingy prison cell to the waiting area of the Orange County jail. Several hours earlier, Newhall's attorney, Bob Crutcher, had posted a million dollar bond to get him out. Newhall's driver and bodyguard were waiting for him.

"Are you okay, Reverend?" the driver asked. "We were worried."

"Where's Crutcher?" Newhall snapped.

"Oh, he couldn't make it, sir, but he wants to see you immediately at his office."

"Okay, let's go."

Newhall flopped into the back of the limo and his bodyguard tried to get in next to him. "Sit in front!" Newhall barked. "I don't want you back here!"

Newhall sat alone with his thoughts as the driver sped north up the freeway to Crutcher's office in Santa Ana. Newhall pulled out his cell phone and dialed Heilbrenner again, but there was still no answer. He hadn't been able to get a hold of Heilbrenner since the indictments had been issued and nobody in the organization knew his whereabouts.

Newhall put the cell phone back into his coat pocket, but it rang seconds later.

"Hello."

"Robert?"

"Mom?"

"How…how are you?" she said in a shaky voice.

"I'm okay, but it's a little crazy, everything's crazy. Are you all right?"

"I'm…I'm…on the news, your father and I have been watching the news. They said you were in jail."

"I was only in jail for a few hours. I won't be going back. We're getting this thing all straightened out."

"I was worried, I thought…"

"Don't worry, mom. There are some people out there trying to hurt me, but don't worry."

"Why are they saying these things about you? We…we raised you to be a good Christian. Tell me what they're saying isn't true."

"It's not!" Newhall reacted angrily, the pent-up rage starting to seep into his face. He didn't know what was true anymore and he wasn't sure if he had ever known, despite telling himself for years that he had it all figured out. He had never stopped to consider what he really believed in. It had been so easy to simply believe as everyone else did.

Newhall's mother began weeping softly.

"Mom, don't cry," Newhall begged. "Please don't cry. It's going to be okay."

"I'm sorry, Robert, I…I don't understand, I just don't understand."

The car pulled into the parking lot at Crutcher's office. "I've got to go, mom. I've got a very important meeting right now. I'll call you later."

Newhall jumped out of the car and scurried into Crutcher's office with his bodyguard trailing closely behind.

"Sit down, Robert," Crutcher said somberly, and then turned to the bodyguard. "Please wait outside."

Newhall paced across the plush carpet of Crutcher's office. "What are we going to do? What are we going to do? My God…"

"Sit down, please. Relax. We need to deal with this calmly."

"Okay, okay." Newhall plopped down on the couch, but fidgeted nervously, unable to keep his feet still.

"Now, first things first, Robert. We've got a huge problem. Heilbrenner wasn't indicted. I've got a call in to the prosecutor to find out what's going on, but I think he cut a deal."

"What are you talking about?" Newhall exploded.

"I think that little bastard cut a deal."

"That's impossible. He wouldn't do that."

"Robert, that son of a bitch would sell out his own mother. It's time for you to get real right now and forget about any loyalty. He's going to save his own ass."

"I don't believe it."

"Have you spoken with him?"

"No."

"Why not?"

"I haven't been able to get a hold of him."

Crutcher eyed Newhall incredulously. "And you don't think he cut a deal?"

"No!" Newhall cried defiantly. "That didn't happen!"

Crutcher walked out from behind his desk and stood directly in front of Newhall. "Listen to me, Robert. Listen to me carefully. I'm your attorney and this is a serious situation. I'm giving you some serious advice right now. This is no time for self-delusions. We need to be absolutely real. If you can't get in touch with Heilbrenner ASAP, then we need to plan our next move. Time is a critical element. If that little snake did cut a deal, we're in serious trouble, and we need to deal with it."

"I'm going to find him!" Newhall sprang up defiantly and stormed out of Crutcher's office. He ordered his driver to go to Heilbrenner's mansion. When they arrived, Newhall banged on the door. "John! It's me! Are you in there? Open up!" His bodyguard stood behind him.

A large man in a brown leather jacket finally swung the door open.

Newhall had never seen him before. His name was Jason Keyes. Lassater had hired him and a few others to secure Heilbrenner's estate so that any relevant evidence would be preserved.

"Who are you?" Newhall barked.

"Mr. Heilbrenner isn't here. I'm going to have to ask you to get off the property."

"What? I don't know who think you are, but…"

The man stepped forward and put his face within inches of Newhall's. "I will escort you off the property if I have to. Leave. Now."

Newhall stepped out of the way and his bodyguard lunged forward, trying to tackle Keyes. Keyes grabbed the bodyguard's arm, twisted it around his back, and then put him in a headlock, fastening his bicep tightly around the bodyguard's neck. The bodyguard's face turned crimson as he gasped for air and tried to wriggle free. Keyes kicked him behind the knees and he pushed him onto the stone walkway. As the bodyguard started to get up, Keyes pounced on him, slamming his head against the cement. The bodyguard rolled over onto his stomach, spitting out blood and one of his front teeth. Keyes stood calmly with his hands on his hips, a gun protruding from the leather holster wrapped around his waist. Newhall eyed the gun and stumbled backward, landing in the grass and soiling his designer slacks. He got up quickly and gingerly backed away.

"Get me home!" Newhall snapped at his driver when he reached the car. Newhall's bodyguard jumped into the front seat a few seconds later and the driver peeled off.

When Newhall arrived home, his estate manager Sharon Maddox recoiled from his bloodshot eyes and wildly trembling fingers. After her initial shock, she put her hand on his shoulder. "Are you okay, Reverend?"

"Where's Patricia?"

"Uh…well…it's…"

"I said where's Patricia?"

"She…she left, sir."

"When will she be back?"

Sharon gulped. "She's not…she's not…coming back."

"What are you talking about?"

"She's gone, sir. I'm sorry."

"Where?"

"Back to Florida to stay with her parents."

"She left?"

"Yes, sir."

Newhall smacked his hands together in frustration. "Lord Almighty! Did she take the jet?"

"No, sir. Federal agents seized the jet yesterday."

"They can't do that!" Newhall roared.

"Well…they did. Sir, is God testing us?"

Newhall's countenance stiffened and he stomped into his study, throwing the door closed behind him. He lunged toward his desk and swung his arm across it, knocking a framed picture of his wife to the floor and smashing the glass into tiny pieces.

Sharon ran to the door and knocked several times. "Reverend Newhall? Are you okay? Reverend Newhall?"

Newhall didn't answer.

"Sir? Sir?" Sharon finally opened the door. Newhall stood motionless at the window, the sun illuminating his sallow countenance.

"Sir, I just wanted to make sure you were all right."

Newhall spun around angrily. "Get out of my house!"

Sharon froze. "I…"

"Get out of my house! Now!"

"Sir…I…"

"Aren't you listening? You stupid! Stupid! Get out of here!"

Sharon backed out of the room and ran out the front door.

Newhall grabbed his cell phone and tried to call Heilbrenner again, but there was still no answer. He hurled the phone against the wall. Paint chips and tiny pieces of sheetrock sprayed across his desk. Newhall paced back and forth, muttering to himself, trying desperately to keep his mind together. After almost an hour, he finally collapsed onto the couch in exhaustion and turned on the television. He flipped through the channels until he saw President Packer holding a press conference.

It's a sad day when we discover that our trusted leaders, especially our spiritual leaders, have betrayed us. But make no mistake about it—we will continue our investigation and get to the bottom of what happened. We will prosecute the guilty parties to the fullest extent of the law.

My fellow Americans, the most important thing now is for us to maintain our faith. We must have faith that good will prevail and evil will be punished. Remember that faith is stronger than anything that happens to us; it defines our strength as a nation. God bless you, and God bless America.

Newhall buried his face in his hands and began to wallow in the horror of what was happening. *They've abandoned me. They've all abandoned me.*

CHAPTER 59

For what shall it profit a man,
if he shall gain the whole world,
and lose his own soul?

—BIBLE, MARK 8:36

The phone rang, jolting Adam Sharf out of a bad dream. He rolled over to the edge of the bed and picked up the receiver. "Hello."

"Adam, it's David."

"Hey. What time is it?"

"Four forty-five. Sorry to call so early."

"That's all right. I haven't been sleeping well lately."

"I can understand that."

"Hold on a second, David," Sharf whispered. "Let me go to the other room. I don't want to wake up my wife." Sharf slipped on his bathrobe and walked into the den.

Chambers and Sharf had spoken frequently since Sharf had offered to help him win the strike suit, and the more Chambers got to know Sharf, the more he liked him. Chambers naturally gravitated to people who followed their hearts; especially those who took a courageous stand.

"Okay," Sharf said, as he sat down behind his desk. He propped up his feet and watched a thin layer of mist settle on the rose bushes in his backyard. "What's up?"

"I can't let you go through with this."

"It's too late."

"It's definitely not too late," Chambers insisted.

"For me it is. It's way too late."

"You understand that life as you know it will be over."

"Yes, absolutely."

"It won't be easy."

"I know. I'm terrified."

"You have a wife—and a family."

"I know."

"I don't want you to do this on my account. I don't want this. Believe me, I don't want this."

"Come on, David," Sharf retorted incredulously. "You know damn well this has nothing to do with you."

"Yeah, I suppose not," Chambers backtracked weakly. "But there are other ways; not quite so dramatic ways. You could just quit your job and start over."

"No, too easy," Sharf responded firmly. "This is the only way for me."

Chambers knew that Sharf was finally on the right track and he was excited to see the man's transformation. Nevertheless, he worried. He wanted to make sure that Sharf was totally committed to his chosen course of action. "Is there anything I can say that'll make you change your mind?"

"No, nothing," Sharf replied without hesitation.

"All right. Then I guess it's okay for me to tell you that this will be the most beautiful thing you've ever done in your life."

Sharf chuckled. "I hope so. I've never been this afraid."

"Good luck."

"I'll need it."

"And don't worry. When this is over, I've got a job for you. Welcome to the family."

"Thanks, David."

* * *

Sharon Maddox put the phone down softly after letting it ring for several minutes. She considered calling the police because she hadn't been able to reach Newhall for two days, despite repeated attempts. She prayed for guidance and finally decided to drive over to the estate. When she arrived, she knocked and rang the doorbell, but no one answered. She unlocked the door with her key and quietly walked in. "Reverend Newhall? Reverend Newhall?" She didn't hear anything so she walked to Newhall's study and opened the door, immediately overcome by a foul stench. She covered her nose and mouth as she looked around the room. The floor was littered with debris. Newhall was lying on the couch, intermittently shaking and letting out low moans.

"Reverend Newhall! Reverend Newhall!" Sharon shrieked as she ran over to him. Newhall's eyes were open, but glazed over, and his limp body appeared completely drained.

"Oh my God!" Sharon screamed as she backed out of the room. She ran to the phone and dialed 911.

"What's your emergency?"

"I think this man...this man...my boss...he's had...I think...I don't know...a stroke...or...or some kind of nervous breakdown."

"Can you describe what you're seeing?"

"He's lying on the couch and he's...I don't know...like shaking...and his face...I can't describe it. It's...it's awful."

"Okay. Slow down."

"And I think he pissed himself."

"What's that?"

"Pissed himself! Shit his pants! And he doesn't respond when I scream at him!"

"I'm going to dispatch an ambulance. What's your address?"

"7842 West Oceanfront in Laguna Beach."

"Okay. Try to remain calm. An ambulance will be there shortly."

* * *

Heilbrenner awoke suddenly as the morning sun sliced through the cracks of the window blinds. For most of his life, he had woken up

473

early to the sound of an alarm clock. But as he lay under the covers, he realized that there was absolutely nothing that he needed or wanted to do. He had never felt so immobilized, paralyzed by a dull sense of fear and a bleak hatred of everything around him.

Heilbrenner rolled out of bed and threw on a t-shirt. He shuffled to the door where the morning newspaper was waiting for him. He picked it up and read the lead article on the front page—"Reverend Robert Newhall Suffers Apparent Nervous Breakdown." Heilbrenner stood motionless until his anger boiled into an unbearable crescendo. "Damn it! Ahhhh….!" Heilbrenner screamed, throwing the newspaper across the room. He ran to the door and banged on it with his tightly clenched fist. "Guard! Guard!"

"What is it?" the guard responded from the other side of the door.

"I need to see Ray Lassater! I need to see him right now!"

"Is this something I can help you with?"

"No! I need to see Ray!"

"Okay. Calm down. Let me call him."

The guard called Ray and he agreed to come over to Heilbrenner's bungalow. In the meantime, Heilbrenner tried to satisfy his rage by throwing anything within his reach across the room, and then booting the walls with several awkward karate kicks.

The guard finally burst into the room. "Calm down! Calm yourself down! If you break one more thing, I'm going to restrain you!"

"Where's Ray?"

"He'll be here in fifteen minutes." The guard fingered his gun. "Now, if you don't calm down, I'm calling security."

Heilbrenner continued to pace around the bungalow excitedly, muttering to himself until Lassater walked in.

"What's the problem here?"

"I need to see Newhall."

Lassater stared at him incredulously. "Why?"

"I just…I just…I'm…I just need to see him," Heilbrenner rambled distraughtly. "He's in the hospital. Did you see the paper? The front page of the paper. I need to see him. I've got to see him."

"Relax. Sit down." Lassater motioned to the couch.

Heilbrenner continued pacing.

"I don't know if you've thought of this, John, but under the circumstances, I doubt Newhall has any desire to see you."

"I don't care!" Heilbrenner screamed. "I see him or the deal is off!"

"Come on."

"I see him or the deal is off!" Heilbrenner exploded. "You hear me!"

Lassater shrugged. "All right, man. Relax. Take it easy. I'll see what I can do." Lassater backed out of the room.

"Watch him carefully," Lassater said to the guard. "Make sure he doesn't do anything crazy."

* * *

"Have you heard anything more from the FBI?" Ernesto asked as he walked into Chambers' office.

"No." Chambers got up from behind his desk and embraced his friend.

"I don't get this thing with the FBI," Ernesto said as he sat down on the couch and fingered a wooden abacus on the table.

"I don't either, but it's consistent with our standing in the Packer Administration. And I don't expect action any time soon based on what Buranek said. I just hope we don't get hit again. In any case, I'm not willing to wait for the FBI."

"What we can do?"

"Speed up development of the J-22."

"What does that have to do with the FBI?"

"We need every asset at our disposal."

Ernesto hesitated while he processed what Chambers had just said to him. He still wasn't sure what Chambers was planning to do and he was a little afraid to ask. "We've already got some of our best engineers on it," he said benignly. "They're working their butts off."

"I want you on it full time."

"Well...I don't know if I agree with that. Who's going to run the company?"

"Jamison can take care of day to day operations."

"Jamison?" Ernesto reacted.

"Yeah."

"Don't get me wrong; I like Jamison, but I don't think he's ready for that."

"I think he is," Chambers responded curtly, his tone not inviting discussion.

Ernesto stared hard at Chambers. He knew his friend as a man who always listened to other points of view and rarely made important decisions without soliciting advice, usually his. Now, Chambers appeared to be making a snap decision about appointing someone to run the company—a major decision—and Chambers seemed uninterested in his advice.

"Do you want my advice?" Ernesto asked.

"No."

Ernesto shook his head lightly.

"Look, I'm not trying to shut you out here, but I feel strongly about this decision."

"Okay."

"I'll keep an eye on him. Besides, if we don't give him an opportunity, someone else will."

Ernesto shrugged. "I guess so."

"Can you have the J-22 ready in a month?"

"That's pushing it."

"Then push."

"Should I be asking why you're so anxious?"

"No." Chambers forced a smile. "Not yet."

CHAPTER 60

Now a spark has passed between us now
A momentary recognition
Something lost and something gained
And something shared that feels strange
Something cold that will not go away

There's a heart as cold as ice
In a vault that's made of stone
Over years the walls got higher
Over years the walls have grown

Is there anybody in there in this self-inflicted tomb
If you peel away the layers is there someone in this room
If you peel away the skin, if you peel away the skin

—Danny Elfman, *Skin*

John Heilbrenner trudged slowly down the dull gray hospital corridor. He could smell the reek of scouring powder and disinfectant, but scarcely noticed the swirl of activity as nurses and orderlies moved purposefully around him. Lassater and an armed guard escorted Heilbrenner down the hallway towards Newhall's room, but no one spoke.

Heilbrenner's thoughts raced and he tried to control his emotions. He didn't know what he was going to say and he hesitated when he arrived at the room of his old boss.

"Hold on a sec," Heilbrenner said. He drew in a deep breath and then exhaled heavily. "We need to be alone."

Lassater nodded. "Okay."

Heilbrenner tiptoed gingerly into the room where Newhall lay shapeless on the bed. He was hooked up to an IV and a sophisticated-looking medical device buzzed softly as it monitored his vital functions. Heilbrenner sat down and silently studied Newhall's face. The changes shocked him. Newhall's cheeks had become sallow and sunken, and short, choppy tufts of hair clung to his head like dry, brittle branches of a dying plant. Heilbrenner found it painful to look because he knew that his actions had almost killed the man. He looked away and tried to come to grips with what was happening.

Heilbrenner had betrayed people in the past, but this was different. Newhall had trusted and confided in him—perhaps even liked him. Heilbrenner's inherent sense of self-preservation wouldn't allow him to face the full horror of what he had done, and his conscious mind assured him that he felt bad only because Newhall had been unlucky. He kept telling himself that Newhall's demise wasn't his fault. This left him a little room for rationalizing. *This is a tough business*, he thought. *Only the strong survive. Newhall couldn't hack it. I'm sorry about what happened to him, but that's part of the game.*

For most of his life, Heilbrenner had tightly controlled his thoughts and emotions, but now he found himself uncharacteristically struggling; feelings of guilt and despair began to flood through the gaping holes rapidly springing throughout his psyche.

Newhall finally opened his eyes and gurgled. He tried to smile as he tilted his head toward Heilbrenner and held out his hand. Heilbrenner touched it lightly.

"John…John…John…" Newhall gasped faintly.

"What is it, Robert? Can you hear me?"

"I'm glad you're…here."

"Yeah, I'm here, Robert, I'm here."

"You were my…my friend. Right John. Right? We were…we were friends." Newhall had never found out whether Heilbrenner had cut a deal with the prosecution, although that didn't matter to him now.

He just wanted to know that he had had some connection with Heilbrenner; that the man cared about him.

Another jolt of guilt shot through Heilbrenner's body. "Yes, yes, we were, but...but...listen to me. Please listen to me carefully." Heilbrenner squeezed Newhall's hand firmly. "I'm sorry. I'm so sorry." Heilbrenner's eyes sank; he couldn't bear to look at Newhall any longer. "I betrayed you. I don't know why, but I betrayed you."

Newhall's cheek twitched, but he didn't speak.

"You're going to get better, get out of this hospital, and then we'll start again. We'll win the case against you." Heilbrenner moved his hand to Newhall's shoulder. "What can I do? Can I do anything for you?"

"What we did...I can't..." Newhall's voice trailed off.

"Robert?"

"Don't...don't lose your way," Newhall said, his barely audible voice dry and scratchy.

"What?" Heilbrenner moved in closer. "What is it, Robert?"

"Please...don't lose your way. It's not too late."

"What are you saying, Robert? I don't know what you're saying!" *It is too late! It is too late! God Almighty!*

Newhall coughed and then sucked in a short breath. "You must... you must...do what is right. Follow your heart..." He paused, and then sighed heavily. "I've...I've got nothing. Nothing." Newhall's hand went limp and his head flopped quietly on the pillow.

"Robert? Robert?" Heilbrenner shook his shoulders vigorously. "Robert! Robert! God damn you! Hold on! Hold on!" A wave of terror rushed through Heilbrenner's veins and he collapsed on top of Newhall's dead body and wept, paralyzed by the feelings he had never allowed himself.

Lassater heard Heilbrenner's screams from the waiting area and he ran to Newhall's room and pressed the emergency call button. A doctor tried to revive Newhall for several minutes, but he finally looked at Lassater and shook his head. Lassater put his hand gently on Heilbrenner's back. "It's time to go, John. It's time to go."

* * *

Adam Sharf splashed water on his face and then stared at himself in the mirror. His eyes were bloodshot from lack of sleep. He quickly dried himself off with a paper towel and then made his way down the long hallway. He straightened his tie before he pushed open the thick, solid oak door to the federal courtroom. As he entered, he scanned the room, which was filled with attorneys waiting for their cases to be called. Tom Jeffries was sitting in the front and he looked back as Sharf walked in. The men made eye contact, but both quickly looked away. Jeffries had filed a motion to dismiss the strike suit and Sharf had filed a strongly worded opposition. Now, they were scheduled to argue the motion in front of the judge.

Sharf sat down in the back of the room and waited. He couldn't remember ever feeling so nervous. He folded his hands across his lap and focused all of his mental energy on keeping his body still.

"All rise. The court is now in session," the bailiff announced. "The Honorable Judge Patrick J. Kilgore presiding."

A short, middle-aged man with a neatly trimmed gray beard sat down behind the bench. "Please be seated. The first case on the docket is In re Chambers Aerospace Securities Litigation."

Sharf and Jeffries shuffled to the front of the room and took their positions at the counsels' tables.

"I've reviewed the defendant's motion to dismiss and the plaintiff's opposition, and I'm prepared to hear oral arguments," the judge began.

"Your Honor, before we begin, I'd like to submit some additional papers," Sharf interrupted. He rubbed his palms on the sides of his slacks.

"Counselor, you know it's too late to submit additional papers," the judge scolded.

"Yes, I'm aware of that Your Honor, but I'm sorry…I'm sorry to report that there are some mis…misstatements in our original papers. We obviously don't want to mislead the court so I've prepared some additional papers to correct…to correct the record."

"Are you asking me to review these now, or are you requesting a continuance?"

"A continuance won't be necessary, Your Honor. The document is only…only two pages long." Sharf's mouth was bone-dry.

The judge turned to Jeffries. "Mr. Jeffries, have you seen these additional papers?"

"No, Your Honor, I haven't."

"Do you have any objection to their submission now?"

Jeffries tried to remain poker-faced. "No, Your Honor. I obviously want the record to be accurate, and I'm happy to review the new information now. If it contains any irregularities, then I'll object at that time."

"All right, Mr. Sharf. Do you have an extra copy for defense counsel?"

"Yes, Your Honor."

"Okay, let me see what you've got." The judge motioned to the bailiff to retrieve the documents.

Sharf looked down at his hand; it was trembling. He tried to steady it, but couldn't. Then the shaking spread to his legs. *Come on. Control this. Control this!* The bailiff waited with his hand out, but Sharf couldn't see him.

"Mr. Sharf? Are you going to give the documents to the bailiff so that we can continue?" the judge asked impatiently.

"Oh, yes, yes, I'm sorry, Your Honor." Sharf handed the documents to the bailiff. The bailiff gave one copy to Jeffries and the other copy to the judge.

DECLARATION OF ADAM SHARF
IN OPPOSITION TO DEFENDANT'S MOTION TO DISMISS

I, Adam Sharf, hereby declare as follows:

1. Attorneys at Millard, Grunfeld & Leachman (the "Law Firm"), including myself, made misleading court filings that grossly exaggerated the trading losses of our clients (the plaintiffs herein) in order to secure appointment as lead counsel in this case. In particular, some of the plaintiffs are professional traders who made hundreds of trades in the defendant's stock, including short sales that were not fully disclosed in earlier court filings. Some of these plaintiffs actually made money during the relevant period. Said plaintiffs fully disclosed all of their trades during the class period to the Law Firm; however, attorneys at the Law Firm, including myself, only disclosed selected transactions with the goal of being appointed lead counsel in the case.

2. Some of the plaintiffs in this case are so-called "professional plaintiffs" who own a nominal amount of shares in hundreds of companies, including the defendant. The Law Firm frequently directs said plaintiffs to buy certain companies' shares so they will be eligible parties in the event a suit is filed. Said plaintiffs allow the firm to bring cases in their names without the plaintiffs first evaluating the merits of a case, or being involved in any way with the prosecution of the case. A few of said plaintiffs maintain, or have maintained in the past, business or social relationships with the Law Firm, or with individual members of the Law Firm.

3. The expert witness (the "Expert") retained by the Law Firm to calculate damages in this case has been paid on a contingency basis in previous cases; to wit, the Law Firm commonly paid the Expert more after a successful case, and sometimes did not compensate the Expert after an unsuccessful case. In addition, based on my knowledge and belief, the Expert did not bill the Law Firm after some cases in which there was an unsuccessful outcome. In that event, the Expert recouped its foregone fees from the unsuccessful cases by padding its fees in the successful cases.

I declare under penalty of perjury that the foregoing is true and correct.

Adam Sharf

As the judge read the declaration, his features turned increasingly severe. "What is the meaning of this, Mr. Sharf?" he boomed.

"It has no meaning, Your Honor."

Jeffries tried to act surprised by gesturing excitedly and whispering to his secretary, who was sitting behind him in the gallery.

The judge sprang out of his chair excitedly. "Counselors! In my chambers! Now!"

* * *

Heilbrenner sat behind Lassater in the aircraft on the way back to the Ranch. "What you did was wrong," he said. "Newhall shouldn't be dead."

Lassater turned around. "Your friend was dead a long time ago, although I suppose he did live quite a life under the circumstances."

Newhall's funeral service had been arranged for the upcoming Sunday, but Lassater had decided to fly back to the Ranch immediately after the doctor pronounced Newhall dead. It would have been unsafe for Heilbrenner to appear at the ceremony.

"I still don't understand how a guy like that's possible," Lassater went on. "I'm surprised how long it took him to self-destruct."

"You killed him," Heilbrenner said softly.

Lassater guffawed. "Yeah, that's right. You keep telling yourself that."

Heilbrenner sat quietly for several moments. "You're a murderer," he said finally. "You and Chambers; you're both murderers."

Lassater flipped around and grabbed Heilbrenner's neck. He started choking him until the guard pulled one of Lassater's arms and off. "Get off me!" Lassater boomed as he backhanded the guard, but kept his other hand firmly on Heilbrenner's throat.

"Ray! Let him go!" the pilot yelled. "I'm going to crash this plane if you don't calm down!"

Lassater released his grip while Heilbrenner gasped for air. "If we didn't need your testimony, I would be a murderer."

After they touched down, the guard escorted Heilbrenner back to his bungalow. Lassater dropped in at Chambers' office.

"How'd it go, Ray?"

"Newhall's gone."

"I hope he went quickly."

"He did, but the other guy is suffering."

"What other guy?"

"Heilbrenner."

Chambers chuckled. "Yeah, that's no surprise. How did his visit go?"

"Scary. One of the ugliest things I've ever seen."

"I can imagine. Thanks for taking care of that."

"You know, the guy's suffering. We need to do something."

Chambers shrugged. "What's that saying? You reap what you sow."

"I'm serious, David. I don't like this guy any more than you do, but we need to do something."

"Well, I'm sorry if I seem crass; normally, I'm more sympathetic, but the guy trashed me for months."

"You need to see him."

"Okay, I'll drop by tomorrow morning."

CHAPTER 61

To trust one's mind and to know that one is worthy of happiness
is the essence of self-esteem.

—NATHANIEL BRANDEN, *THE SIX PILLARS OF SELF-ESTEEM*

Dushane awoke suddenly after several loud bangs on the door of his bungalow. He rolled over and glanced at the clock radio on his nightstand—5:17 a.m. "Who is it?" he yelled.

"David."

Dushane sprang out of bed and quickly slid into his bathrobe. He dabbed at the crust around his eyes as he trotted to the door. He tried to look alert when he opened it. "Hi, David."

"Man, I was knocking for five minutes." Chambers grinned.

"I'm a heavy sleeper," Dushane said sheepishly.

"Well, I'm sorry for waking you up so early, but I wanted to see you personally. This was the only time I had available."

"It's okay; I'm glad you came by. Come on in."

"I know you're busy, but I need you to go to Boston to help Skip with some manuscripts," Chambers said.

"Sure. When?"

"As soon as possible."

"Okay."

"Call the hangar when you're ready to go. Someone will fly you down to SFO."

"Okay."

"You should learn one of these days."

"What?"

"To fly. There's nothing like it."

Dushane shook his head. "I'm not like you."

Chambers chuckled. "Oh, you don't want to be like me. Anyway, how's everything going?"

"Great."

"Good." Dushane stood still as Chambers moved to hug him. Dushane still hadn't gotten used to the hugging ritual, although he liked it.

"I'll see you soon, buddy," Chambers said.

"Bye, David."

* * *

Does my life matter? Have I ever created anything? Anything? Is it too late? Is there anything left? Does anything matter? Heilbrenner sat quietly, but he fidgeted restlessly, unable to control his thoughts. He had been sitting in the same spot since the previous evening and hadn't slept.

Chambers greeted the guard at the door of Heilbrenner's bungalow. "Morning, Jared. I came by to see our guest."

"Hi, David." The guard unlocked the deadbolt.

Chambers tapped gently on the door. "John? It's David Chambers. Mind if I come in?" Chambers stepped into the doorway. "John?"

Heilbrenner was sitting in a chair, staring at the television set, which wasn't turned on. "John? You okay?"

Heilbrenner didn't answer.

Chambers sat down in a chair across from him, recoiling when he saw Heilbrenner's face, which was sallow and sunken. "Are you okay? You look a little sick. We've got doctors, here. I can call one."

Heilbrenner shook his head.

"Can I get you anything?"

"No."

"Ray seemed to think you were in some sort of distress. Is everything okay?"

"I…I…I want out," Heilbrenner whispered softly.

"What's that?" Chambers leaned in closer.

"I…I don't know…I…I…" Heilbrenner had never shared his deepest emotions or feelings with anyone before in his life, but he needed to talk.

"What are you trying to tell me?" Chambers pressed.

"I'm just…I don't know…I've never felt this…ah…this helpless. Like…like none of this matters. Everything hurts. I….I can't take it. I just want…I just want out." The deepest layers of Heilbrenner's psyche had cracked, unleashing an avalanche of fear and self-hatred that converged at an excruciatingly unbearable breaking point. Heilbrenner had always hated himself, and at every decision point in his life, he had always betrayed his conscience. He had never created any genuine self-esteem, instead striving for power and domination over others, leaving him with nothing that he could call his own. And now the shell that protected the frightened child was gone.

The depth of Heilbrenner's despair took Chambers aback. He felt revolted and compassionate at the same time. He wanted to reach out and hug the man and tell him that everything was going to be all right, but he couldn't lie. He wished he could change history, but he saw only one solution. "I'm sorry, John. I'm truly sorry."

"Can you help me?" Heilbrenner pleaded. "Please…I need help."

Chambers stood up and patted Heilbrenner gently on the back. "Hang on, John." Chambers left the bungalow and went over to his office. He unlocked the bottom drawer of his desk and pulled out a small case. Fifteen minutes later, he stood quietly in front of Heilbrenner and pulled a small revolver out of his jacket. "Oh, wait a minute, almost forgot." Chambers reached into his shirt pocket and pulled out a single bullet, which he loaded into the chamber of the gun. "This should probably do." He placed the gun on the table next to Heilbrenner's chair. Heilbrenner didn't look up.

Chambers put his arm on the guard's shoulder on his way out. "Keep an eye out, and call me if anything happens."

486

"Sure."

Chambers walked over to the Ranch's central security center. "Turn on the video camera in Bungalow 518," he directed the technician on duty.

Heilbrenner didn't move for several minutes, but he finally turned his head towards the gun and eyed it.

"Zoom in on him," Chambers said.

Chambers rubbed his forehead nervously when Heilbrenner picked up the gun and held it in the palm of his hand. A few moments later, Heilbrenner wrapped his finger around the trigger and lifted the gun up to his mouth.

"Turn it off!" Chambers screamed. "Turn it off!"

The security technician quickly cut the video feed.

"Get somebody over there right away!" Chambers ordered.

A few minutes later, the guard radioed the security center. "I heard a gunshot, a gunshot! I didn't know he had a gun! Where did he get the gun? He shot himself! In the head! Right through the head!"

"Calm down, Jared. Don't worry. Someone will be there soon."

"My God! It's…it's horrible! Horrible! What should I do? I don't know what to do!"

"Call the police," Chambers said calmly.

Two deputies from the sheriff's office arrived half an hour later and a guard escorted them to Heilbrenner's bungalow. Heilbrenner's lifeless body lay on the floor in a pool of blood with a tennis ball-sized hole blown through the back of his head. One of the deputies put the gun in an evidence bag and removed the body. The other deputy questioned the guard.

"What was the victim's name?"

"John Heilbrenner."

"Were you here when this happened?"

"Yeah, I was standing outside and I heard a gunshot, and then I went in and the guy was lying on the floor dead. I didn't know he had a gun."

"Was he by himself?"

"Yeah. My boss was here visiting him a few minutes before it happened, but…"

"Who's your boss?"

"David Chambers."

"Are you sure he left before this happened?"

"Yeah, I was here the whole time guarding the door."

The deputy furrowed his brow. "You were guarding…?"

"Yeah."

"Is there any other way to get into this cottage?"

"No, it's completely sealed off except for this door."

"No windows?"

"They don't open."

The deputy unclipped a small transmitter from his belt and radioed the sheriff. "Sheriff, we've got an apparent suicide here. A guy named John Heilbrenner."

"Heilbrenner!" the sheriff exclaimed.

"Yes, sir. He shot himself in the head, apparently. There was a guard on duty here who says that the victim was alone when it happened."

"Did you find the gun?"

"Yes."

"I want you to run a check on it; find out who it's registered to."

"Okay."

The deputy took the gun back to his car and entered its serial number into a small computer mounted on the dashboard. The name of the registered owner popped up on the screen. The deputy radioed the sheriff again. "Sheriff, the gun used is registered to David Chambers."

"You're joking," Jenkins replied skeptically.

"No."

"Are you absolutely sure?"

"Yes, sir."

"Okay, good work."

"Should we question Mr. Chambers about this?"

Jenkins hesitated. "No…not yet. I want you to come back to the station. This may be a delicate situation. But tell Henry to stay there and secure the location. I don't anyone touching anything."

"Okay."

Jenkins hung up and dialed Stottlemeyer.

"Stottlemeyer here."

"It's Harvey Jenkins. John Heilbrenner is dead."

"What?"

"It looks like he shot himself."

"A suicide?"

"Seems to be; we're still investigating."

"Where did this happen?"

"Kaleidoscope Ranch. The gun that killed him is registered to Chambers."

Stottlemeyer gasped. "This is unbelievable."

"What do you want me to do?"

Stottlemeyer didn't answer.

"It seems like the next step would be to question Chambers," Jenkins went on. "We can…"

"No," Stottlemeyer interrupted. "Arrest him."

* * *

An overcast sky drizzled lightly over the Ranch, which was almost completely deserted two days before Christmas. On Jenkins' orders, two sheriff's deputies drove back to the Ranch and demanded to see Chambers. He agreed to meet them alone in his office.

"Good evening, gentlemen," Chambers began amiably as the deputies tromped in with their heavy boots and rain jackets

"Good evening. I'm Deputy Wood and this is Deputy Ferraro. We have a few questions we need to ask you about the death of John Heilbrenner."

Chambers nodded politely. "Certainly. Can I get you guys something to drink? I've got…"

"No. No, thank you," Deputy Wood interrupted. "We'd like to focus on our investigation."

"Whatever you like."

"Now, the gun used to kill Mr. Heilbrenner was registered in your name."

"Yes."

"Why did he have your gun?"

"Are you sure I can't get you guys something? I've got some sparkling apple cider or some hot chocolate if you're cold."

"No, sir," Wood responded impatiently. "We're here to investigate the death of John Heilbrenner. Now, why did Mr. Heilbrenner have your gun?"

"I gave it to him."

"You gave it to him? Why?"

"So that he could take care of himself."

"Commit suicide?"

"Yes."

"Let me understand this. You gave this man a gun so that he could kill himself?"

"Yes."

"Why?"

"He was suffering."

"That's no justification for helping a man take his own life," Deputy Ferraro jumped in.

"You didn't see him," Chambers retorted.

"What's that supposed to mean?"

"He was in pain. There was no other way to help him. The only compassionate thing to do was let him go."

"You're responsible for the death of another human being!" Deputy Ferraro erupted.

Chambers shrugged.

"I can't believe what I'm hearing. We should arrest…"

"Hold on, Tony," Deputy Wood interjected, putting his hand on his partner's shoulder. "Let's focus on the facts here. The guard said he heard the gunshot right after you left Mr. Heilbrenner's room. Is that right?"

"Yes."

"Are you sure no one else could have entered the room after you left and shot him?"

"Yes, I'm sure. Would you like to see the video recording?"

The deputies looked at each other quizzically. "You have a recording?"

Chambers nodded. "Yes."

"Of course we'd like to see it."

Chambers walked over to the DVD player and inserted the disk. "Before I start this, I have to warn you; it isn't pretty. You guys should sit down." Chambers motioned to the couch.

The deputies remained standing.

Chambers sat down on the couch while the disk played, but he jumped up quickly and stopped the tape right after Heilbrenner pulled the trigger.

"Oh my God!" Ferraro cried. "How could you…how could you let this happen? That's disgusting!"

Chambers ejected the disk. "You can have this copy. I've got another." He handed the disk to Deputy Wood. "If I can be of any further assistance, let me know."

"I can't believe what I just saw," Ferraro whined.

"Relax, Tony." Deputy Wood turned to Chambers. "We need to take your fingerprints to match them against the prints we took off the gun."

"I just told you that I gave him the gun, so my fingerprints are obviously on it."

"It's standard procedure."

Chambers shook his head. "You don't need my fingerprints." He took a step forward and stared hard at each man.

The deputies looked at each other, each hoping the other would challenge Chambers, but neither of them did. Deputy Wood didn't know what to do next. Sheriff Jenkins had ordered him to arrest Chambers, but he wasn't sure if Chambers had committed a crime. In any case, Chambers' manner made him feel strangely afraid, like his life was in danger. Wood just wanted to get off the Ranch as soon as possible.

"We should get back to the station," Wood said to his partner.

Ferraro made eye contact with Chambers and then quickly looked away. "All right," he agreed.

"We may need you to come down to the station at some point," Wood said as he backed out of the room. "We'll be in touch."

Chambers nodded. "I'm happy to help in any way I can."

When the deputies arrived back at the station, Sheriff Jenkins confronted them. "Where is he?"

"He supplied the gun, Sheriff, but it was a clearly a suicide. I don't think he committed a crime."

"You idiots! Your job is not to question your orders, but to do as you're told."

"I'm sorry, Sheriff, but…"

"But, but, nothing! Get the hell out of here! I'll handle this!"

Wood held up the DVD. "Well, you should watch this, sir."

"What is it?"

"The suicide."

"What are you talking about?"

"Chambers recorded it."

"That's sick."

"I know."

"All right, let me have it." Jenkins snatched the disk out of Wood's hand and retreated to his office. He plopped down in his chair and ran his hand over his scalp. *Christ, I got no frickin' hair left. Now I'm gonna have to go out to that damn ranch and arrest that crazy son of a bitch myself.* Jenkins fingered the disk. *Well, let's have a look at this.* He walked into the interrogation room and put the disk into the DVD player. *Holy mother of…* He went back to his office and called Stottlemeyer.

"Stottlemeyer here."

"Jenkins."

"Did you get him?"

"No, we didn't. I don't think we have enough to arrest him. Heilbrenner's death was a suicide. Even if we did arrest him for assisting the suicide, we couldn't hold him on that charge."

Stottlemeyer thought quickly. "I think we can get him on a federal charge."

"What's that?"

"Don't worry about it," Stottlemeyer said, not bothering to mask the condescension in his voice. "This is a matter for the FBI now. I'll be there tomorrow with an arrest warrant. Keep me posted if anything happens in the meantime, but don't do anything until I get there."

"Okay."

When Stottlemeyer arrived the next day, he and Jenkins drove over to the Ranch in the sheriff's patrol car. The guard at the front gate peered into the open window of the police vehicle. "What can I do for you, gentlemen?"

491

"We need to see David Chambers," Stottlemeyer said from the passenger seat.

"Okay. May I tell him your name, sir?"

"I'm Agent Stottlemeyer. I'm from the FBI." Stottlemeyer flashed his badge.

"Just a moment." The guard went back to his station and dialed Chambers.

"This is David."

"David, there's an Agent Stottlemeyer here from the FBI. He says he needs to see you."

"Is he here about the Wichita investigation?"

"I don't know. Let me ask him."

The guard walked back to the patrol car. "Is this about the Wichita investigation?"

"No," Stottlemeyer replied curtly.

The guard eyed Stottlemeyer, waiting for an additional explanation, but then realized none was forthcoming. "What is it about, then?"

"I have a warrant for Mr. Chambers' arrest." Stottlemeyer handed a one-page document to the guard. "We need to see him now."

The guard went back to the phone. "David, he's got an arrest warrant—for your arrest."

"Let me talk to him." The guard handed the phone to Stottlemeyer.

"Mr. Chambers, this is Agent Stottlemeyer from the FBI."

"What's this about an arrest warrant?"

"Yes, I have an arrest warrant. You're wanted for obstructing a federal prosecution."

"That's ridiculous."

"John Heilbrenner was scheduled to be a witness in several important federal cases. Your actions have wiped out his ability to testify. You're lucky I'm not arresting you for murder."

"You've got a lot of nerve threatening me. Do you know who I am?"

"I don't care who you are; you can either surrender yourself at the gate or tell your guard to let us in."

"What about the criminals who blew up my building?"

"I don't know anything about that, sir."

"Well, I don't know what kind of two-bit operation you're part of, but I need some action on that before I agree to any cooperation with the FBI—any cooperation whatsoever."

"This isn't about cooperation!" Stottlemeyer snapped, finally abandoning his dispassionate FBI-trained demeanor. "I have a warrant for your arrest! You've got five minutes to come out!"

"No."

"We'll take you by force if necessary."

Chambers hesitated for a moment. "Let me speak with my security guard."

Stottlemeyer gave the phone back to the guard.

"David?"

"Don't let them in under any circumstances. Understand?"

"Yeah."

Chambers hung up the phone and called the Ranch's security office. "I need every available man at the front gate immediately. We have an intruder."

"You want a fully armed response?"

"Yes, but I don't want any shots fired except on my orders. No exceptions."

"Yes, sir."

The guard handed the warrant back to Stottlemeyer. "I'm sorry, sir. I'm not authorized to let you in."

Sheriff Jenkins had agreed to let Stottlemeyer handle the arrest and do all the talking, but he suddenly erupted. He threw his door open, clipping the guard's leg and knocking him down. Jenkins jumped out of the car and drew his gun, standing over the stunned guard and pointing the weapon at his head. "You open that gate or I'll blow your head off!"

The guard got up gingerly and raised his arms in surrender.

"What are you doing, Jenkins?" Stottlemeyer cried.

"I'm not going to let these people push us around!" Jenkins cocked the trigger of his gun. "Open the goddamn gate!"

"Okay, okay, take it easy." The guard backed up to his station while Jenkins followed, keeping the gun aimed at his head. The guard flipped a switch and the gate swung open. Jenkins and Stottlemeyer got back into the car and drove slowly down the entrance road, but the blinding headlights of four large trucks greeted them. Jenkins threw the car into Park and was about to get out when several rifle-toting men jumped out of the trucks. They took positions surrounding Jenkins' car. One of them had a bullhorn. "You are trespassing on private property. I repeat. You are trespassing on private property. Turn your car around and leave the premises immediately."

"Shit!" Jenkins cussed. "I better call for backup."

"Are you crazy?" Stottlemeyer shrieked. "Turn this car around!"

"But..."

"Turn this car around or I'll have you arrested! That's a federal government order! Now!"

CHAPTER 62

Great spirits have always encountered violent opposition
from mediocre minds.

—ALBERT EINSTEIN

Jenkins and Stottlemeyer sped away from the Ranch and skidded to a halt in front of the sheriff's station. Stottlemeyer jumped out of the car and ran inside, picking up the telephone at the reception desk. He called Al Rogers at home.

"Sir, I'm sorry to call so late, especially on Christmas Eve, but we've got a situation here."

"Where are you?"

"I'm at the sheriff's station, just outside Kaleidoscope Ranch."

"What's going on?"

"John Heilbrenner shot himself yesterday in an apparent suicide."

"Heilbrenner's dead?"

"Yes."

"And it was a suicide?"

"Yes, although the gun he used to kill himself is registered to David Chambers."

"This is incredible. I can't believe Heilbrenner's dead."

"It surprised me too, sir."

"So what are you doing there?"

"When the sheriff called and told me what had happened, I thought I should investigate."

"Yes, good work."

"I also wanted to assist the sheriff with Chambers' arrest."

"Did you get him?" Rogers asked excitedly.

"No. We went to the Ranch with an arrest warrant, but Chambers refused to come out."

"Why didn't you go in and get him?"

"We did, but he sent several armed guards out to stop us; they forced us to leave at gunpoint."

"Unbelievable. So he resisted arrest?"

"Yes, sir. And he could've killed us. What should we do now?"

Rogers couldn't believe his good fortune. "This is the opportunity we've been waiting for. My God, I'll brief the President first thing tomorrow morning."

"Should I do anything, sir—in the meantime?"

"No, no, sit tight. Don't do anything until you hear from me."

"Yes, sir."

* * *

Chambers got on the phone with the head of Ranch security and barked instructions: "I want all possible entry points to the Ranch sealed off and patrolled. And all security personnel to remain on high alert until further notice."

"What about weapons?"

495

"All personnel fully armed, but I don't want any weapons used except in self-defense. Is that clear?"

"Yes."

Chambers wasn't worried about the sheriff coming back because he figured the man didn't have either the resources or the resolve to risk the lives of his men. On the other hand, Chambers knew that the FBI would use whatever force necessary to apprehend him. He hoped he would have enough time before they mobilized. He called Ernesto, who was away on a business trip in Southern California.

"Hello," a sleepy voice answered.

"Ernesto."

"David. You always seem to call me when I'm in bed."

"Things are starting to happen. Not exactly as I'd expected, but I need you up here."

"What's going on?"

"I'll explain when you get here."

"Can this wait until tomorrow night? I've got an important…"

"No, I need you here now. We don't have much time."

* * *

The Boeing 737 touched down at Boston's Logan Airport and rumbled to a stop. Dushane pulled his backpack out of the overhead bin and walked casually down the jetway, unaware of what was happening at the Ranch.

"Welcome, Martin. Nice to see you again," Hartley greeted.

"Nice to see you, too, Skip."

The men shook hands and rode the escalator down to retrieve Dushane's baggage. Dushane was expecting to stay in Boston for three weeks so he had packed two large suitcases. Each man grabbed a bag and they exited the terminal. Hartley was normally talkative, but he said little as they drove back to his warehouse.

"So how are things?" Dushane asked, trying to stimulate a conversation.

"Busy," Hartley replied.

"Yeah, what's going on?"

Hartley didn't answer.

"Skip?"

"I'm sorry, Martin. Did you say something?"

"Yeah, I was just wondering what was going on with you."

"Oh, you'll have to forgive me for being so preoccupied. I've got a lot on my mind."

"Don't worry about it," Dushane said. "We can talk later."

Hartley smiled. "I'm glad you're here."

When they arrived at the warehouse, they walked up the stairs and Dushane grinned as he recalled the first time he had visited. He reflected that his life had taken quite a turn since then.

"Here, let me take your suitcase." Hartley said, as they stepped into the living space. He grabbed the handle of Dushane's bag and wheeled it into a back bedroom; Dushane followed closely behind.

"I wouldn't recommend that you unpack; you're only going to be here a couple nights," Hartley said.

"I thought I was going to be here for three weeks."

"No, change of plans."

"David said he wanted me to help you with some work."

"Well, something's come up; he needs you elsewhere."

"Where?"

"He wants you to fly to Mexico City the day after tomorrow."

"Mexico City?"

"Yes."

"What's in Mexico City?"

"That's all I can tell you, Martin."

"What did he say?"

"That's all he said."

"Okay, I need to call him. Can I use your phone?"

"You won't be able to do that right now."

"Why not?"

"Martin, you're going to have to trust me. Believe me, the less you know the better."

Dushane stared hard at Hartley. "What are you talking about?"

"In case something happens, you don't want to know anything."

"In case what happens?"

Hartley shrugged.

"Look, I don't know what he said to you, but you need to clue me in."

"Do you trust David?"

"Of course."

"Well, you need to trust him now. He'll explain everything later."

Dushane stared blankly into space and shook his head.

"Follow me, Martin. There are a couple of things I need to show you."

Hartley sat down at his desk and pulled a plane ticket and a passport from the drawer. He handed them to Dushane. "You'll need these."

Dushane glanced at the ticket and put it in his pocket. Then he thumbed through the passport, stopping to look at his photograph. It was a recent picture of him, but the name underneath the photo read "Arnold Jackson."

"What the hell is this?" Dushane erupted.

"You need that passport for your own protection."

"Look man, I need to know what's going on. You tell me to use a fake passport to sneak out of the country and go to Mexico for some unknown reason. I'm not okay with this."

"I'm sorry, Martin. I know this a little odd, but it's for your own protection."

"You keep saying that, but I have no idea what that means."

"I'm sorry I can't tell you. You've got to trust David."

Dushane cursed under his breath. He didn't like what he was hearing, but he did completely trust Chambers.

"What am I supposed to do for the next two days?"

"If you like, you can help me with some things I'm working on. In fact, I'd like to bounce some ideas off you."

Dushane sighed. "All right."

* * *

Don Leachman simmered quietly in his office after receiving news of Sharf's courtroom bombshell. He still couldn't believe what had happened and he had tried to reach Sharf several times without success. He felt like driving over to Sharf's house and strangling him, but he knew that he needed to focus all of his energy on damage control.

Leachman thumbed through the stack of messages on his desk. He stopped when he came to a message from the court. The judge wanted to schedule a meeting with Leachman and Jeffries so that he could decide how to proceed in light of Sharf's revelations. Leachman dialed the court's number and waited for someone to answer, but the law firm's senior partner, Mel Grunfeld, suddenly burst into his office.

"Get off the phone, Don," Grunfeld ordered.

Leachman swiveled around, turning his back to Grunfeld.

"I said get off the goddamn phone!" Grunfeld screamed.

Leachman spun back around and put the phone down. "Calm down! Christ! Can't you see that I'm busy here? I don't have time for any of your bullshit right now!"

"I just got a call from the State Bar. They're launching an ethical investigation of this firm. You know what that means. It means we're fucked! And you fucked us!"

"Well, I'm trying to deal with this if you'll let me. So stop whining. The last thing we need is a fucking crybaby. Those ethics guys are bureaucratic pussies, anyway; you know that."

"This firm will deal with this, but without you. You're out."

"Get the fuck out of my office."

"We had a meeting this morning. The executive committee has voted you out of the firm."

Leachman sprang out of his chair. "You little prick. I built this firm and it's nothing without me. You can't vote on anything."

"You're a reckless, vindictive son of a bitch, and you're out."

"Like hell I am. Get the hell out of my office." Leachman grabbed one of the alabaster tombstones from the table behind his desk and launched it at Grunfeld, who quickly jumped out of the way. The tombstone bounced off of the window behind him, causing it to shake, but not breaking it. Grunfeld stared at the window, surprised that it didn't shatter. Leachman chuckled. The window had previously been fitted with bulletproof plastic at his insistence.

"You're finished," Grunfeld said as he walked out. "You can clean out your desk and walk out of here, or I'll have you thrown out. And take those goddamn tombstones with you!"

Leachman sat down and took a deep breath. He wasn't surprised by the heated confrontation with Grunfeld. In fact, the two men had had many spirited arguments over the years, and Grunfeld had threatened to kick him out of the firm several times. Although they had been friends for over two decades and frequently socialized outside of the office, whenever they disagreed about money or something threatened the firm's bottom line, each man's venom came out. Fortunately, in the past, they had always been able to compromise. Though neither man trusted the other, they each trusted the certainty of the other man's greed. In the end, they both recognized the insanity of putting their multimillion-dollar salaries at risk and an uneasy truce had always existed between them; Leachman was the flamboyant rainmaker who took credit for the firm's success, and Grunfeld kept the firm running smoothly, stroking the egos of the other partners who chafed at Leachman's petty vindictiveness and grandstanding.

Leachman dialed the court a second time and connected with the judge's clerk, but Grunfeld interrupted again. This time, he was accompanied by four other people—two other partners from the firm's executive committee and two security guards.

"Last chance, Don," Grunfeld warned. "I'm serious this time."

"You're insane."

Grunfeld turned to the security guards. "Please escort Mr. Leachman out of the building."

"You bastards better not come near me," Leachman challenged.

The security guards hadn't expected a violent confrontation so they stood frozen. They looked at Grunfeld for guidance.

"I want this man out of the building!" Grunfeld thundered.

The security guards came at Leachman from each side of his desk. One of them tried to grab Leachman's arm, but Leachman backhanded him across the face. The other guard wrapped his arm around Leachman's neck and wrestled him to the ground. While Leachman squirmed on the carpet trying to break free, the other guard punched him squarely in the nose, breaking it in three places. Leachman shrieked wildly, frightening the guard, who released him from the headlock. Leachman writhed on the floor, his face covered in blood, and his nose now disfigured and starting to swell.

The two partners scurried quickly out of the room. They disliked Leachman, but they couldn't bear the sight of any man being so humiliated.

"What do we do now?" one of the guards yelled.

"Get him out of here!" Grunfeld cried.

"How?"

"I don't know—carry him!"

One guard hooked his arms underneath Leachman's armpits while the other guard grabbed his legs. They carried him down the hall to the elevator, leaving a trail of blood drops down the corridor. Leachman moaned softly and twitched every so often from the pain. The guards took him outside the building and threw him into a taxicab.

CHAPTER 63

Deus vult!

Latin for "God Wills It!" The battle cry of Christian pilgrims in response to Pope Urban's appeal in 1095 to liberate the Holy Lands from the Muslims, setting off a two-hundred-year killing spree of Muslims and Jews.

Al Rogers pounded his fist on the President's desk in the Oval Office. "Mr. President, this is the opportunity we've been waiting for. He resisted arrest. He pulled a gun on an FBI agent. We'll never get a better opportunity."

"I don't want another Waco, Al. The American people don't want another Waco. I won't let that happen."

"Trust me, sir. This won't be another Waco. We've got a team of well-trained National Guardsmen; they're experts in these types of operations. I'm fully confident that we can send them in and just take Chambers and his inner circle. No one else will get hurt."

"I'm not so sure about that, and even if I was, I can't just take someone out."

Rogers shrugged. "Why not? You're the President."

The President stared at Rogers harshly. "He hasn't done anything!"

"He hasn't done anything?" Rogers shot back incredulously. "Mr. President, may I remind you that he obstructed a federal prosecution. He resisted arrest. He threatened the life of…."

"Save that for the spin doctors," the President snapped. "If I'm going to order a murder—and that's what this is—I want to make damn sure I'm doing the right thing."

"Look, I know you're concerned, but the people elected you to protect them from evil. You're the nation's shepherd. We're talking about sacrificing one man—a lone wolf who threatens our most basic values—for the benefit of a nation."

Packer's features hardened.

"Don't forget the story of Abraham and Isaac, Mr. President."

"I know that story, but I don't see what it has to do with this."

"God was testing Abraham just as he's testing you now. You must rise to the test."

"But God told Abraham not to sacrifice his son," the President protested. "That tells me that…"

"Well, what about Jesus then," Rogers interrupted. "God sacrificed his only son for the benefit of mankind, for all eternity. All He's asking you to do now is sacrifice the life of one nonbeliever."

The President shook his head and swiveled his chair around, turning his back to his Chief of Staff. He stared at a portrait of Thomas Jefferson while he thought about what to do.

"You know it's the right decision, Mr. President."

Packer spun back around. "I don't know…this just feels…"

Rogers put his hands together in a praying motion. "God is on our side, sir," he said somberly. "He's chosen you to carry out His will."

Packer instinctively dropped his head, remembering how small he was compared to the Almighty.

"Trust me, sir. This is the right thing to do."

The President sighed. "All right. But I only want Chambers targeted. If more than twenty-five innocent people are killed, I'm going to be really pissed."

"Yes, sir."

* * *

Ernesto began his final descent in preparation for landing at the Ranch, but the faint sounds of sirens interrupted his concentration. As he got closer, the volume of the blare increased. Several patrol cars were lined up next to each other, blocking the road a quarter mile outside the Ranch. Ernesto entered the traffic pattern and then landed his plane softly on the airstrip. Chambers greeted him as climbed out of the aircraft. "Feliz Navidad."

"What's going on? There's like six police cars out there blocking the road. Not far outside the gate."

"Ah…sounds like a roadblock. We probably don't have much time. I reckon they'll be trying to get in here soon enough."

"What's going on?"

"Let's discuss this in private."

Chambers and Ernesto drove to the Control Room and descended. When they were comfortably seated, Chamber explained the situation.

"You dissed the FBI?" Ernesto exploded. "Are you out of your mind?"

"Probably," Chambers replied casually.

"This is…crazy! Totally insane! Even for you."

"It is what it is."

"How do we…how do we…how do we get out of this?" Ernesto rambled nervously.

Chambers shook his head. "We don't."

"Then what the hell do we do now?"

Chambers grabbed a long cylindrical tube from the corner of the room and pulled out a large map. He spread it across the table.

Ernesto stood up and peered over the map. "What is this?"

"It's a map of the Christian Identity compound in Clarksville, Idaho," Chambers answered.

"Where did you…? Never mind. What are you…you're not going after them, are you?"

Chambers stared hard into Ernesto's eyes. "The FBI won't do anything and I'm not going let those thugs get away with it."

Sosa lifted his hands up and backed away. "Look, this is too much, way too much. I don't want to be responsible for the death…"

"Don't worry."

"I am worried," Ernesto shot back sharply. "Of course I'm worried."

"You know me and I'm telling you not to worry."

"Then tell me what's going on."

"I can't." Chambers trusted Ernesto completely and wanted to tell him about his plan, but he didn't want to put his friend in a potentially compromising position in the event something went wrong.

Ernesto shook his head. "I can't believe the situation we're in!"

Chambers put his arm around his friend and chuckled lightly. "You remember that promise I made to you; about what we're going to do in retirement together?"

"Yeah."

"Well, retirement's coming early."

"Not if we're dead."

* * *

Dushane emerged from the jetway in Mexico City and looked around hopefully for someone or something to indicate where he should go, but he didn't see any familiar faces. He continued walking toward baggage claim until he heard a friendly voice behind him. "Bienvenidos á Mexico, Señor Jackson."

"Rusty!" Dushane exclaimed.

"That's me."

"What are you doing down here?"

"Jim told me to come down here and pick you up."

"Nielsen?"

"Yep."

"Is he here?"

"Nope. Just me. I flew up from Costa Rica yesterday."

"Costa Rica?"

"Yeah, that's where we're headed."

"What's in Costa Rica?"

"Everything, man. It's paradise. The most perfect place on Earth."

"Well, I don't know what's going on."

Rusty shrugged, and then smiled. "Me neither. But don't sweat it. It's all good."

Although Dushane still worried, Rusty's enthusiasm assuaged some of his apprehension. "All right. How do we get down to Costa Rica?"

"I'm flying us. You remember that twin Jim and I picked you up in when you first came to San Francisco?"

"Yeah."

"Jim's letting me fly that one now."

"Okay. What's down in Costa Rica? Where are we staying? Who's down there?"

"Don't worry, man. Everything's taken care of. We've got a sweet setup down there. You're gonna love it."

"Are we supposed to do something down there?"

Rusty laughed gently. "No. That's the beauty of it, man."

"Oh." Dushane forced a smile.

As they flew south towards Costa Rica, Dushane's emotions bounced between a vague fear of the unknown and wild exhilaration; it reminded him of being on the Appalachian Trail—living in the moment and not knowing what to expect next.

The plane flew low, skirting the coastline as Rusty occasionally pointed out a landmark. "Over there, about ten o'clock, that's the biggest rain forest in Costa Rica," Rusty said.

"Wow."

"Jim and I went a long hiking trip through there. That's divinity, man. Incredibly beautiful."

"You heard anything from David?"

"No. Nothing."

"What's going on?"

"Like I said, I don't know."

Dushane stayed quiet the rest of the trip, lost in his thoughts until the plane began to descend. As they got closer to their destination, Rusty announced his position over the radio and then pointed to the makeshift runway. "Hold on," he said. "This runway can be a little rough."

Dushane eyed the rudimentary airstrip and his heart began to race. "Is that dirt? Hey…wait a minute, that runway is too short. You can't…"

Rusty smiled. "Don't worry. I've done this once before. Just gotta hit it right."

Rusty brought the plane in a little high and then tried to compensate at the last second by diving at a steep angle. "Hold on, Martin."

Dushane slid his damp palms across the front of his jeans, checked his shoulder strap, and then wrapped his hands tightly around the sides of his seat. The plane hit the dirt with a hard thud and bounced back up into the air, angling sharply to the left, away from the runway. "Rusty! What are you doing?" Dushane cried.

"Hang on!" Rusty leveled the aircraft's wings and gave it a little thrust as he brought it down again. This time, the plane landed without a bounce, but off the runway. It shook and bucked as it rolled across the uneven surface. "Got it down just right that time," Rusty congratulated himself.

Dushane sucked in a few deep breaths and tried to calm himself. "I'm not cut out for this."

"Don't worry, you'll get used to it."

Dushane shook his head. "Where are we, anyway?"

"Tamarindo. One of the most beautiful towns in all of Costa Rica."

"So what are we supposed to do now?"

"Do? We're in Costa Rica, man. We're gonna go surfing, scuba diving, hang at the beach, drink some cold cervezas." Rusty put his arm around Dushane's shoulders. "Relax, buddy. You're free."

Free. Dushane struggled to understand exactly what that meant.

CHAPTER 64

The Lord is a man of war.

—BIBLE, EXODUS 15:3

Chambers rolled up the map of the Christian Identity compound and put it back in its cylindrical container. He tried to make eye contact with Ernesto, but his friend refused to meet his gaze. "I directed one of the technicians to make the final preparations," Chambers said. "The flight plan has been programmed and the plane is in the hangar, fully armed and ready to go."

Ernesto clenched his jaw. "Okay."

"It won't be long now."

Ernesto turned away.

Chambers put his hand on Ernesto's shoulder. "Don't worry," he said with a few gentle pats. "It's going to be great."

"All right, let's go then," Ernesto replied stiffly.

Chambers pulled a small lever on the Control Room wall, causing one of the steel panels to pop loose. He held the panel steady with his hands until Ernesto helped him move it aside. Behind the wall, there was a narrow concrete corridor that extended about twenty feet to another door.

"You got everything?" Chambers asked. "We're not coming back here."

"Yeah," Ernesto nodded.

Chambers walked to the end of the corridor and entered a four-digit code on the keypad next to the door. The door clicked open and Chambers pushed it forward, entering a small, dark space. Chambers flipped a light switch, revealing what looked like a miniature version of an air traffic control tower. The room contained all of the equipment necessary to monitor the J-22's progress and, if necessary, modify its mission parameters.

"It's show time," Chambers said as he walked into the room.

"Yeah, it'll be a miracle if all this stuff works." Ernesto sat down in front of the main control console. "We really could've used more time."

"Well, you know how I love miracles," Chambers chuckled.

Both men were confident in the technology they had developed; the problem lay in the lack of testing in real-world conditions. The J-22 was an extremely complicated aircraft and there were an almost unlimited number of things that could go wrong. Besides an extremely sophisticated design and an intricate set of jet engines and hydrogen fuel cells, the plane had highly sensitive sensors, GPS systems, avionics components, and several tiny cameras mounted on its nose and tail. The plane also had an additional infrared camera specifically designed for low light and night flying, as well as a radar system for seeing through smoke, clouds, or haze. All of the systems were designed to work together to give the controlling technician as much data as possible about the status of the plane's mission—position, weather conditions, speed, terrain, and other aircraft.

The J-22 had a level of sophistication and refinement unmatched by any other UAV ever built and it didn't require any human input after its mission parameters had been entered. Once a technician had programmed a flight plan into its memory, the plane could make adjustments to its course, speed, trajectory, and any other parameters based on the conditions it encountered. The plane also featured an automated collision avoidance system, giving it the ability to avoid enemy aircraft and incoming missiles.

The J-22's offensive capability was equally impressive. It was equipped with twelve laser-guided missiles and a multi-spectral targeting system. Although untested in combat, Chambers figured that the J-22 would have little trouble destroying any conventional, manned fighter aircraft in a head-to-head dogfight because it could maneuver in ways that would kill a human pilot, and its special steel alloy frame could withstand the extreme stress of high-speed, radical maneuvers.

The J-22 had been designed with an experienced pilot working in a simulator so that engineers could estimate the parameter ranges of its controls, especially defensive maneuvers in heavy enemy fire. Since Chambers and Ernesto hadn't been able to test the aircraft in real conditions, they had relied on sophisticated computer modeling technology.

Once the plane was airborne, navigation decisions could be made by a technician communicating with the aircraft from the ground—either by directly observing the plane, or by watching video feeds from the on-board cameras. The plane could be controlled through a graphical user interface, which simulated being in a traditional cockpit with familiar controls. Alternatively, an experienced technician could simply enter parameters into the computer and the aircraft would respond.

Satellite communications were the last important piece in the J-22's operation. A ground station transmitted coded radio signals to a satellite, which were then transmitted to the aircraft. The aircraft then decoded the transmission and executed the instructions.

"Let's make the final calculations and get ready to roll," Chambers said.

"I'm on it," Ernesto replied, already busily working the controls.

* * *

Alone in Sheriff Jenkins' office, Stottlemeyer fidgeted restlessly, swiveling back and forth in the sheriff's buckskin chair. Earlier in the day, Stottlemeyer had exercised his federal government authority and ordered the sheriff to vacate the building. Jenkins briefly objected until Stottlemeyer threatened to have him arrested. Jenkins had no interest in tangling with the feds, who he knew could make his life miserable.

Despite the concession, however, Jenkins had expected to be part of the operation to apprehend Chambers. After all, no one knew the county better than he did and he had a loyal team of men. But Stottlemeyer warned him and his men to stay out of the way.

Stottlemeyer had been waiting for several hours to receive instructions from Washington and he had already scanned the walls of the office and rifled through the sheriff's desk looking for something to hold his interest. But he couldn't keep his boredom at bay. He kept himself occupied by reading the sheriff's hunting and fishing magazines, but he wondered how anyone could be interested in those activities. *Well, at least hunters get to shoot things*, he thought. When the phone finally rang, it startled him.

"Agent Stottlemeyer."

"It's Rogers."

"Yes, sir."

"We've alerted the California National Guard; they've agreed to work with you as the Administration's representative."

"Okay. What's the next step?"

"Well, first of all, understand that this is a delicate operation; it's very important to the President. I'm sending out Frank Liotta, one of our top negotiators to assist you. If possible, we'd like to avoid any violence, but..." Rogers paused, and then added icily, "The President is prepared to take Chambers and his lieutenants out if necessary."

"Okay. Thank you, sir," Stottlemeyer replied enthusiastically. "I look forward to completing this mission." Stottlemeyer's blood began to pump. *Finally a chance to make a name for myself!*

"Stand by until you're contacted by the Guard," Rogers concluded.

"Will do, sir."

Later in the day, Stottlemeyer received a call from Major General Randall Pearson, the ranking officer in command of the California National Guard. The two men agreed to establish a command post at the sheriff's station in order to formulate strategy and to coordinate the deployment of troops and equipment. Pearson designated Lieutenant Stephen Briggs to act in his stead as the officer in command of the ground troops, and he dispatched Briggs to rendezvous with Stottlemeyer at the station, along with two hundred and fifty soldiers, tanks, artillery, and other assorted combat weaponry.

Frank Liotta, the Administration's negotiator, was one of the government's most experienced operatives as well as a close friend of President Packer. He had been surprised when the Chief of Staff called him about Chambers because, like many others, he had been inspired by Chambers' story. Liotta had even held Chambers out to his kids as a positive role model. Now, Liotta wondered what had

510

gone wrong; why a man who had everything would suddenly throw it all away in a no-win standoff with the government. At the same time, he wondered vaguely if the Chief of Staff had given him the full story. Liotta remained fiercely loyal to the Administration, but he knew what the Administration's men—and Rogers in particular—were made of. They didn't possess the character traits he wanted his children exposed to, although he recognized that he sometimes exhibited some of the same characteristics. He tried to conceal them as much as possible.

While being shuttled from the airport to the sheriff's station, Liotta consciously decided that neither the respect he had for Chambers, nor his distrust of the Administration would affect his commitment to the mission. He was a seasoned pro who couldn't let his emotions get in the way of doing his job. I'm taking on David Chambers, he thought. *This is the chance of a lifetime. I've got to be at the top of my game.* He pumped himself up with a few of his favorite mantras. *The guy's mine. He's nothing. I'm the man. The guy can't touch me. Can't touch me. I've got him! He's all mine! All mine! All mine!*

When Liotta arrived, he joined Stottlemeyer and Briggs in the sheriff's office and they discussed strategy. Briggs proposed deploying a contingent of two hundred men and three tanks on the Ranch's borders in a show of force. The two other men agreed, although Stottlemeyer stressed the Chief of Staff's directive to negotiate for Chambers' surrender before they came down on him. Briggs nodded slightly in acknowledgement, but all he could think about was the excitement of battle and the brilliant military moves he would make to ensure victory. Liotta felt apprehensive, but at the same time exhilarated. Soon he would be talking with, and if he were lucky, perhaps even meeting David Chambers.

As the National Guard troops and tanks took their positions around the perimeter of the Ranch, one of Briggs' adjutants drove the commanding triumvirate to the Ranch's entrance gate. When they arrived, the two military men drew their guns and exited cautiously, while Stottlemeyer and Liotta waited in the jeep.

Chambers had directed his front-gate guard to give any law enforcement authorities a phone number where he could be reached. With the exception of the guard, Chambers, Ernesto, and a few technical personnel, everyone at the Ranch had already evacuated.

The guard walked gingerly out of his shack with his hands up.

"Put your hands on top of your head and get down on your knees," Briggs ordered, pointing with the barrel of his gun.

The guard threw his hands up and the two soldiers rushed him. They aggressively spun him around and threw him to his knees.

"David gave me a phone number for you to call!" the guard yelled as Briggs' adjutant cuffed him.

"Okay, let's go." Briggs lifted the guard up by the collar of his jacket and dragged him to the jeep. "Frank, the guard says he has a phone number to reach Chambers."

Liotta turned to the guard. "Give it to me."

The guard recited the number and Liotta tried to dial it on his cell phone, but he suddenly went blank. He tried to remember, but couldn't. *What's wrong with me? Why can't I remember? I can't focus. I can't focus!* "What's that number again?" he asked finally.

The guard stared at Liotta quizzically, but recited the number again, pausing on every digit so that the scatter-brained g-man would be sure to get it. Liotta entered all of the numbers and carefully clicked the call button; Chambers answered on the first ring. "This is David."

"Uh…Mr. Chambers, uh…this is Frank Liotta. I'm here with Agent Stottlemeyer from the FBI and Lieutenant Briggs from the California National Guard."

"Who are you?" Chambers demanded.

"Liotta. Frank Liotta, sir. President Packer sent me here personally to talk to you. I'm one of his closest personal advisers."

Chambers chuckled. "Well, I admire your willingness to admit that, but it certainly doesn't inspire much confidence."

Liotta realized that he had already made a mistake, so he tried to quickly backpedal. "Well, regardless of your opinion of the President, understand that this is an important matter to the United States government and we need to resolve this."

"What do you want?" Chambers replied tersely.

"I want to put an end to this situation. This isn't doing anyone any good."

"I agree. What do you propose?"

"Why don't come out so we can talk about this?"

"So you can arrest me?"

"I'm not here to arrest you. I'm here to make sure nobody gets hurt."

"Are you saying that I won't be arrested if I come out?"

"I'm saying that I don't want to see anyone get hurt."

"I don't either."

"Are you coming out, then?"

"No."

"Well…"

"Hold on, Frank," Chambers interrupted. He put his hand over the mouthpiece of the phone and turned to Ernesto. "Takeoff," he said softly.

Ernesto nodded.

"What were you saying, Frank?"

"I don't want to see anyone get hurt. The only way to avoid that is for you to come out peacefully."

"Hold on again, Frank. I need to discuss this with my associate."

"Who's in there with you?"

"Ernesto. Give us a few minutes." Chambers put the phone down and waited for five minutes until the J-22 was airborne. Meanwhile, Briggs' adjutant had established a GPS lock on Chambers' position based on the signal from his cell phone. Briggs radioed his troops and ordered them to surround Chambers' location and close in.

Chambers picked up the phone again. "Frank?"

"Yeah."

"What were we talking about?"

"The Ranch is surrounded by National Guard troops and armory. The only way to end this peacefully is for you and Mr. Sosa to give yourselves up. If you don't come out now, I can't guarantee your safety."

"I don't think that'll be necessary."

"Look..." The roar of the J-22's jet engines suddenly blasted over Liotta's head. "What the..." Liotta turned to the Lieutenant. "Was that one of our planes?"

"No, I've never seen anything like that before. It doesn't even look like U.S. military."

"Do you know anything about that plane that just took off?" Liotta barked into the phone.

"That's mine."

"Yours? Who's in it?"

"No one."

"What do you mean no one?"

"Unmanned. You ever hear of the J-22?"

"No," Liotta replied.

"I know the J-22," Stottlemeyer piped in. "It's the UAV you were hired by the Defense Department to build. But your contract was terminated."

"Well, I'm glad somebody does their homework," Chambers responded.

"What's the meaning of this?" Liotta snapped, angry and embarrassed at being shown up by both Chambers and the young FBI agent.

"You don't need to worry about it, Frank. That's plane flying to Idaho—Clarksville to be precise. I've got some unfinished business there."

"What are you talking about?"

"You know damn well what I'm talking about!" Chambers blasted.

"Christian Identity," Stottlemeyer interjected.

"They blew up one of my buildings and almost killed one of my friends. I waited for you jack-offs to do something—it's too late for that now."

Briggs trotted back to the jeep and radioed Major General Pearson. "General, David Chambers has an aircraft at his disposal; some sort of UAV. He says he's flying it to the Christian Identity compound in Clarksville, Idaho."

"What? What the hell is he doing?" Pearson bellowed.

"I don't know, sir, but I believe his intentions are hostile."

"How long ago did the plane take off?"

"Three to four minutes."

"Okay, we'll scramble some fighters. Are you still in contact with him?"

"Yes, sir."

"Good, keep me updated."

"Yes, sir. Briggs out." Briggs trotted back to Liotta, who was still trying to negotiate with Chambers.

"Let's work something out," Liotta offered. "I'm sure we can work something out."

"I said it's too late for that."

"Look, I promise you I'll do my best to get you what you want. Just tell me what you want."

Chambers didn't respond.

"Mr. Chambers? Mr. Chambers? Can you hear me? Are you still there? Mr. Chambers?"

"I'm here, but call me David for chrissakes."

"Okay, sure, sure," Liotta stammered nervously. He hadn't been consciously aware of the display of deference. "Now, what is it that you want? You must want something."

Chambers chuckled. "Ahhh...now I think we're finally getting somewhere. The truth is that I don't want anything. I guess that's the real beauty of this situation."

"Come on, let's be reasonable here. You have an opportunity to get out of this; to save yourself and your ranch. Otherwise, you have no chance."

"Is the lieutenant still there?" Chambers asked.

"Yeah, I'm here," Lieutenant Briggs spoke up.

"Lieutenant, I want you to make sure that none of your men come within a half-mile of the Control Room."

"What control room?"

"The room where Ernesto and I are right now."

"Why?"

"You're going to have to trust me," Chambers said firmly. "Otherwise, I can't guarantee the safety of your men."

"What are your intentions?" Liotta interjected.

"To stay right here."

"You're making a big mistake, Mr…uh…David."

"Maybe. But it'll all be over soon." Chambers hung up.

"Chambers? Chambers? Chambers! Goddammit! He hung up." Liotta dialed again, but no one answered.

Briggs radioed his troops. "Retreat back to the perimeters of the ranch, to your original positions. I repeat, retreat back to the perimeters of the ranch, back to your original positions."

"What are you doing?" Stottlemeyer challenged. "You're going to let him get away. This is no time to be a coward."

Briggs whipped around quickly and jumped into Stottlemeyer's face. "What did you say?" he roared through seething teeth.

"You're letting him get away."

Briggs grabbed the front of Stottlemeyer's shirt and pulled him forward. "You shut your goddamn mouth! These are my troops! I'm not going to the risk the lives of my men for this psychopath!" He pushed Stottlemeyer away with his fist.

Stottlemeyer stumbled backward. "The President wants us to take this guy out," he said timidly.

"Then you take him out yourself!" Briggs boomed as he stomped back to the jeep.

* * *

On Major General Pearson's orders, two bombers from the California Air Guard cut through the sky and draped the Kaleidoscope Ranch airstrip with bombs, rendering it unusable for any additional takeoffs or landings. The Air Guard also scrambled four F-16's from a base in Northern California to pursue the J-22, but military commanders quickly realized that the J-22 was too fast to be caught from behind. Pearson radioed another base in Montana, which scrambled four additional planes to intercept the J-22 before it reached Clarksville.

* * *

"Uh oh. We've got company," Ernesto said.

"What?"

"I've got three…no wait…four incoming, on a course to intercept."

"How far away are they?"

"A hundred and twenty kilometers."

"What do you think? Take it low, make it more difficult for them to maneuver?"

"Yeah." Ernesto entered the new parameters into the computer and the plane went into a steep descent.

Chambers patted Ernesto on the back. "I guess this is where the rubber meets the road as they say."

"Should I...should I activate the weapons systems?" Ernesto asked quietly.

"Not yet," Chambers responded without hesitation. "That shouldn't be necessary. I'm expecting to see some pilots' jocks on the floor."

"I'll try."

The F-16's only had one good chance to take the J-22 down, which was a coordinated attack from the front. Despite the firepower and maneuverability of the F-16's, they would be completely neutralized once the J-22 got in front of them. When they got within striking distance, the four F-16's fired their missiles simultaneously from different vantage points hoping that it would be impossible for the J-22 to dodge them all. But the J-22 made a few sharp maneuvers and continued on its course.

"That's impossible!" the commander of the Air Guard exclaimed as he watched the radar screen and received the reports from his pilots. He radioed Pearson. "We can't touch it, General."

"It's one lousy plane!" Pearson barked.

"It's got capabilities I've never seen before. Short of a nuclear blast, I don't think we can take it down."

"Damn it! All right, stand by. Pearson out."

Pearson radioed the command center closest to Clarksville and told them to order an immediate evacuation of the Christian Identity compound.

* * *

"I don't think the F-16's are a threat any longer," Ernesto said.

"Good. What's our position?"

"We're just across the Oregon-Washington border."

"What's the ETA for Clarksville?"

"Forty minutes."

CHAPTER 65

The religion-versus-science debate took a special turn in the West because of the existence not only of doctrinal religion but of monopolistic doctrinal religion that made the crucial mistake of meddling in empirical statements of fact, providing us with a long list of particularly precise, official and officially compelling statements about the cosmos and biology, supposedly guaranteed by Revelation, that we now know to be false. In every instance where the Church has tried to offer its own description of what happens in the world and there was some scientific alternative on the very same topic, the latter has proved better. Every battle has been lost and conclusively so. This is of course inconvenient. Obviously, a few people manage blithely to ignore what happened and to live in a fantasy world where Biblical sources are a good instrument of geological knowledge and paleobiology. But this requires a lot of effort.

—PASCAL BOYER, *RELIGION EXPLAINED*

A thin layer of steam wafted gently above the water as Marvin Butler and his female assistant eased slowly into the hot tub. The woman pressed her thigh against Butler's and he sighed happily as she began gently stroking his leg. Butler took a swig of his beer and then slid his arm around the woman's back. He gently cupped her breast as she snuggled closer.

The hot tub was situated on the edge of a small lake, surrounded by pine trees, two hundred yards behind Butler's mansion. It was Butler's favorite part of the Christian Identity compound, and a place that he came often to relax. Behind the hot tub, there was a two-room bungalow that included a kitchen and a bedroom with a queen-size bed.

"How ya doin,' darlin'?" Butler leaned over and kissed the woman on the cheek.

The woman smiled. "I'm feeling good now, Reverend."

Butler was married with four children, but he spent long hours with his assistant. Although his wife occasionally complained, Butler was proud of himself for exercising restraint. By his count, he had only had sex with the woman twenty-seven times and he usually wore a condom.

Butler told his wife that his assistant needed close and regular access to him because she was helping him write his autobiography. Butler knew he'd never write a real autobiography because he had no illusions about the value of his life, but he did like hearing himself talk. The young assistant didn't mind listening because Butler took good care of her, and she had actually written two chapters—one about Butler's vision of the End Times, and the other about his leadership philosophy.

Butler didn't actually believe in evangelical accounts of the End Times, but at the same time, he had no doubt that humanity would destroy itself. He reckoned that if the people who lived under his rule exemplified the level people could sink to, the species simply wouldn't survive long term. As for his leadership style, Butler's philosophy was simple—he led by the force of his will. That was only way to lead a group of believers. He didn't allow anyone to question his prophetic visions and his views could never be attacked as irrational or insane because they had the force of God behind them.

Butler slid deeper into the water and let his chin float on the surface as the tub's powerful jets massaged his back. He felt relaxed until his cell phone rang, startling him. "Grab that, will ya dear?"

The woman popped out of the water and Butler admired her muscular legs and perfectly-shaped buttocks, which were accentuated by a skimpy two-piece bathing suit. The pace of his breathing quickened, but he tried to calm himself as the woman handed him the phone.

"Butler."

"Reverend, it's Ken Barlow from the command center."

The Christian Identity compound had a central command center staffed by ex-military men. They had several important duties including monitoring the activities and whereabouts of all the people on the compound, keeping track of the weapons inventory, and maintaining the high voltage fence that surrounded the compound's borders.

"What is it?" Butler barked. "You know I don't like to be disturbed."

"It's an emergency, sir. We just received a call from the Idaho National Guard. They've ordered us to evacuate; we're about to be attacked."

"Attacked? By who?"

"I don't know, sir; they didn't say."

"This is crazy. Get them on the phone again. I want to speak to somebody over there."

"Uh, I don't have their number, sir."

"Well, get it!"

"Hold on, sir."

Butler turned his back to the woman and angrily slapped the water.

"Are you there, Reverend?"

"Yeah. Go 'head."

"I haven't been able to reach the Guard, but another call just came in. A man named David Chambers says he needs to speak with you."

"Did you say David Chambers?" Butler drawled slowly.

"Yes, sir."

"Hold on." Butler turned back around to his assistant. "Grab my jacket."

The woman picked up Butler's coat from a nearby chair and held it in front of him. He reached into the interior pocket and pulled out a loaded handgun. Butler always carried a gun with him because it helped ease his paranoia. A few years earlier, one of his rivals in the Christian Identity movement had been assassinated in a power struggle.

"Get back in the water," Butler ordered.

"Are you there, Reverend?" Barlow asked.

"Yeah, put the caller through."

"Yes, sir."

Butler waited until the line clicked over. "Who is this?" he snapped.

"Is that you, Marv?" Chambers replied breezily.

"Who the hell is this?"

"David Chambers. You know, the guy whose building you blew up."

"I don't know what you're talking about."

Chambers chuckled. "Whatever you say, Marv."

"What's the meaning of this? My man said somebody's trying to attack us."

"Yes, I'm sorry to have to do this, Marv. It's nothing personal, just payback. You tried to kill some of my guys; now I come after you. It's a fairly straightforward deal."

"I'll kill you if you come anywhere near me."

"Well, I'll keep that in mind, Marv. And I'll see you soon." Chambers hung up and Butler's line automatically clicked back to Barlow at the command center.

"You little puke! I'm gonna kick your teeth in! I'm gonna destroy you!"

"Reverend? Sir?" Barlow interjected timidly. "I think Mr. Chambers hung up. You sound upset, is there anything…?"

"No!"

"Well, the authorities said we need to evacuate as soon as possible, sir. What should we do?"

Butler didn't answer.

"Sir?"

"Uh, let me think about this for a second…"

Butler's assistant inched her fingers underneath his swim trunks and began gently massaging his penis.

"Get your hands off me!" Butler boomed. "Are you stupid?" He pushed the woman away forcefully.

"Sir?" Barlow interrupted. "We need to…"

"Okay, okay. Here's what I want you to do. Wait fifteen minutes and then initiate the evacuation procedure. You got that. But make sure you wait fifteen minutes."

"Yes, sir."

Butler jumped out of the water and grabbed his towel. He wrapped it around his torso as he sprinted towards his house.

"Reverend? Where are you…?"

Butler turned his head, but didn't stop. "Get the hell out of here! Get in your car and get the hell out of here!"

* * *

The deafening blare of sirens blasted across the Christian Identity compound as the command center initiated the evacuation procedure, jolting believers from their evening prayers. The men, women, and children who lived at the religious enclave had heard these sirens before; they had drilled frequently in anticipation of a strike by the government or some other satanic force. But this was no drill. Loudspeakers announced that the Idaho National Guard had ordered everyone to evacuate immediately—an attack was imminent.

The evacuation command confused most Identity members because they deeply distrusted the government and were skeptical of any government order. Besides, few of the compound's faithful had ever considered running from a fight or abandoning the cause, especially since they were certain of victory with God on their side.

Butler's followers hadn't thought much about the actual details of a battle either; they simply assumed that the promised end had finally arrived and they would be reunited with their Savior. Many rejoiced and thanked the Lord in prayer. Others prepared themselves for an all-out war, figuring that the Almighty expected courageous sacrifice against evil.

The men ran to the weapons storage facility to get high-powered automatic weapons, hand grenades, and artillery cannons. A few even grabbed bayonets. The anti-aircraft hardware that Butler had purchased on the black market was already positioned on rooftops.

Most of the women and children gathered in the central courtyard around a statue of Christ's lifeless body nailed to the cross. They knelt in submission and prayed to God to either save them or accept them into Heaven. "Don't be afraid. The Lord will protect us," they assured each other. Others cried, "This is the final battle against Satan. The Second Coming is nigh! Rejoice!"

When Butler got back to his house, he gathered his most cherished belongings—his favorite Hawaiian shirt, a couple of bowling trophies, a set of mounted moose antlers, and a photograph taken with President Packer at a fundraising dinner. Then he ran downstairs to the basement and entered the combination to a wall safe. When it clicked open, he grabbed a nylon satchel stuffed with eight hundred thousand dollars in cash.

Butler loaded his SUV and instructed his wife and four kids to lie down in the back of the vehicle and stay out of sight. Before he got behind the wheel, he ran back into the house and strapped on a bulletproof vest. Butler figured that some of his followers might react violently to his desertion because he had always preached that abandoning the cause was the most unforgivable sin. But the fact that he had equipped his vehicle with bulletproof windows comforted him. He also kept a loaded sawed-off shotgun underneath the seat just in case.

Butler pulled out of his driveway and drove past hundreds of his faithful servants milling around the compound. Many of them recognized his SUV and tried to flag him down; some even stood in the street blocking his path, expecting him to stop. Butler quickly veered off-road and accelerated. But he didn't make a clean getaway. The steel grill of his vehicle clipped a teenage boy, knocking him underneath the tires and killing him instantly. Butler didn't stop. He sailed through the exit gates and drove west. He had friends in Spokane who could help him disappear, out of the country if necessary.

News of Butler's desertion spread quickly and his second-in-command, Billy Cochran, took charge. He addressed the men gathered at the weapons repository. "Our moment of triumph is here! We've waited our entire lives for this!"

"What about Reverend Butler!" a man in the crowd yelled.

"The Reverend is a coward," Cochran answered without hesitation. "He abandoned us. But we don't need him. All we need is the Lord!"

The men agitated restlessly and Cochran calculated that he had to make a bold move to establish his leadership. "God has spoken to me and revealed that Butler was a false prophet," Cochran proclaimed. Cochran had never claimed that he had prophetic powers or received direct revelations from the Almighty, but his strategy worked. Although shocked by Butler's betrayal, the men accepted Cochran's pronouncements, which filled their mental vacuum of psychological needs.

"God doesn't tolerate cowards," Cochran continued. "He doesn't allow doubters and two-faced Judases to enter the Heavenly kingdom. Brother Butler deceived us, but now we are stronger in the eyes of the Lord because we've demonstrated our faith and commitment." The men cheered enthusiastically.

Since nobody at the compound knew what to expect, they prepared for a full-scale conflict. They took positions in bunkers around the perimeters of the grounds, and the men trained to operate the anti-aircraft missile launchers waited on rooftops. They had no idea that their weaponry was totally irrelevant.

* * *

"We're ninety kilometers out," Ernesto reported. "What do you want to do?"

"Increase altitude to ten thousand feet," Chambers answered.

"Okay." Ernesto inched the stick back and the plane ascended rapidly before leveling off. "All right, we're there."

"Let's try one of these missiles," Chambers said.

Ernesto whipped around and shot Chambers a look of disbelief.

Chambers smiled. "Don't worry. Detonate it directly above the compound, but high enough so that nobody gets hurt. These people are probably expecting a show—something of supernatural proportions. The least I can do is put a little more fear of God in them."

Ernesto nodded and swiveled back around. "Okay." He activated the firing sequence as Chambers watched the video feed from one of the plane's cameras. Within a few seconds, the missile launched and exploded directly above the main courtyard, lighting up the sky with a thunderous crack.

"God clapped His hands," Chambers joked.

"Wow! Those missiles pack quite a punch."

"Let's try one more. There's a wooded area on the northwest border of the compound. It's near Butler's mansion, but not too close. Let's drive one into the ground and shake things up a bit."

"All right, let me get those coordinates." Ernesto quickly reviewed the map and then initiated the second firing sequence. The missile exploded as it hit the ground, causing a series of tremors and a mushroom cloud of dust. Some believers on the ground ran for cover; others opened their arms in surrender and waited to be lifted up to Heaven. Most continued to pray.

"Now what, David?

"Turn it around."

"Back to the Ranch?"

"Yeah, and let's stay with the return flight plan. I don't see any reason to deviate from that—operator error and all."

Ernesto turned around.

"I know you're good, but not even you..."

"Agreed." Ernesto activated the return flight sequence, which called for flying as low as possible between the troughs of the mountain peaks in order to avoid radar detection. By relying entirely on the computer's execution of the flight plan, there was no risk of getting too close to mountaintops or miscalculating any maneuver. The computer already had a record of all the oncoming terrain in its database, and it was downloading the most current weather conditions. It could precisely calculate the best route back.

* * *

"They fired two missiles, sir, but they both missed," the air commander said over the radio to Pearson. "Now they've reversed course."

"How in the world did they miss?"

"I don't know, sir. They must've missed on purpose. One missile exploded above the compound; the other missed completely. There doesn't appear to be any damage to the buildings, or any injuries."

"Where are they now?"

"Unknown, sir. We lost them shortly after they left the airspace above Clarksville."

"Let me know when you get a lock on their position. Pearson out."

Pearson radioed the commander of the Idaho Guard ground forces.

"Lieutenant Skerritt here."

"Lieutenant, this is Major General Pearson. I assume you've been briefed on the air attack at the Christian Identity compound."

"Yes, I understand that they were fired upon, but no targets were hit."

"That's correct."

"Well, there's some chaos on the ground. We're preparing to move in and restore order."

"Are you crazy?" Pearson thundered. "That's the absolute last thing you should do!"

"Why? We're…"

"No! Those people are lunatics! They probably think this is Armageddon!"

"My men are trained…"

"No! No! Listen to me!" Pearson interrupted. "Absolutely not! They're liable to fight anybody they don't recognize. Do you want your men killed? Keep your forces on standby, but don't move in without my explicit orders. I repeat. Do not move in!"

"Yes, sir."

* * *

"David, we're within seventy kilometers of the Ranch."

"Good. Is there anybody within a quarter-mile radius of this control room?"

Ernesto checked the sensor readings. "No."

"Manually enter the final coordinates of the flight plan."

Ernesto carefully typed the instructions into the computer. "Okay, it's set."

"Good work." Chambers stood behind Ernesto and patted his shoulder. "The J-22 is a success—a crowning achievement to your career. You've proven once again that you're the best."

"Thanks." Ernesto smiled, but his mood turned somber. "It's a shame it'll never go into production," he said quietly.

"Come on," Chambers reacted. "That doesn't matter at all. We created it."

Ernesto brightened. "Yeah, you're right. What now?"

"I guess that's it. Do you mind if I monitor the controls for the last stretch?"

Ernesto pushed his chair away from the console. "It's all yours."

CHAPTER 66

Of all the modes of evidence that ever were invented to obtain belief for any system, or opinion to which the name of religion has been given, that of miracles is the most inconsistent. For, in the first place, whenever recourse is had to miracles, for the purpose of procuring belief, it implies a lameness or weakness in the doctrine that is preached. And, in the second place, it is degrading the Almighty into the character of a showman, playing tricks to amuse and make the people stare and wonder. It is also the most equivocal sort of evidence that can be set up; for the belief is not to depend upon the thing called a miracle, but upon the credit of the reporter who says that he saw it.

—THOMAS PAINE, *THE AGE OF REASON*

"I can't stand all this waiting around," Stottlemeyer whined as he paced restlessly in front of the entrance gate to the Ranch. "I'm tired of doing nothing. We need to do something."

"Waiting's part of the job," Liotta responded impatiently. "Don't worry; Chambers can't stay in there forever."

"Yeah, is that what you think?" Stottlemeyer shot Liotta a hard look. "Chambers is probably going to escape…or…or…he's going to kill us. We're giving him all this time."

"Why don't you just relax? Get in the car and listen to the radio or something. I'm tired of listening to you."

"Relax? I can't relax. We're sitting ducks here. We need to attack."

Stottlemeyer and Liotta had been waiting for several hours, but with the exception of a little petty bickering they hadn't spoken to each other much. The uncertainty of the situation and the desire of each man to be chief had created tension. Stottlemeyer thought that he should be in charge because he had been appointed by the Chief of Staff to oversee the operation. Liotta, on the other hand, was an old friend of the President and had many more years of experience than the young FBI agent. There was also the issue of credit to consider. If and when the National Guard captured Chambers, each man wanted his share of the glory. They both feared that the other man would try to steal the spotlight.

Despite Stottlemeyer and Liotta's imaginary power struggle, the real man in charge was Lieutenant Briggs—he controlled the troops. Briggs thought that Stottlemeyer and Liotta were useless civilian poseurs so he stayed in his jeep and didn't talk to either man. He spoke occasionally with Major General Pearson and with his troops, but there wasn't much to say. Pearson had ordered him to hold the troops' positions until further notice. The only thing Briggs could do was direct his men to prepare their anti-aircraft weaponry in case the J-22 came back.

Stottlemeyer finally sat down on the hood of the car and contemplated all the possible scenarios. He wondered whether Chambers would fire on them. They were completely unprotected from an air attack. *I could die without any warning*, he thought. *But I'm too young to die!* Stottlemeyer took a deep breath and tried to relax. He wished that Briggs would order the troops into battle and flush Chambers out. *So what if a few of them got killed. That's the risk they assumed when they signed up for duty.* Stottlemeyer finally decided to sit in the car and listen to the radio, but there was only one station and it played country music. *Ahhhh…!*

* * *

"How far away are we?" Gary Hammond asked anxiously from the back seat of the helicopter.

"About ten miles," the pilot shouted over the whir of the chopper's rotating blades.

Hammond was a reporter from a television station in Redding, a city one hundred miles south of the Ranch. News of the confrontation at the Ranch had spread quickly and the TV station had dispatched Hammond to cover the story.

Hammond turned to the other man in the helicopter. "Pete, get your camera ready. I want to tape an intro before we get down there. How does my face look?"

"You look a little tired. You've got some black patches under your eyes."

Hammond pulled a compact out of his satchel and dabbed some makeup on.

"All right, we're getting close," the pilot advised. "I'm going to take her down."

"Good, let's start on the southeast side," Hammond said. "That's where the entrance is."

The pilot nodded.

"All right, you ready, Pete?"

"Yeah, but why don't you open the window? It'll blow your hair around a little bit—make you look a little more adventurous."

"Yeah, good idea." Hammond flung the window open and the wind swirled around the cockpit.

"Whenever you're ready, Gary."

Hammond hardened his features and took his voice down an octave. "Good evening, this is Gary Hammond, Action 5 News. I'm flying above the Kaleidoscope Ranch near the Oregon border where we're monitoring a very tense situation. During the last twenty-four hours, a mysterious suicide occurred here and the FBI is on the scene investigating. Earlier this evening, the FBI tried to question David Chambers, the billionaire aerospace magnate, but he has refused to come out. Now, there's a standoff as government negotiators try to get Chambers to cooperate. National Guard troops are amassed on the ground below us, awaiting orders to move in and capture Chambers and his partner, Ernesto Sosa. We'll stay airborne above the ranch and continue to provide you exclusive coverage as this dramatic situation unfolds. All right, cut it there, Pete. Let's get some shots on the ground."

"There's a lot of armory down there, but it looks pretty quiet," the pilot said. "No one seems to be moving."

"Okay, let's get some quick footage and then fly over the middle and see what we find."

"Will do."

* * *

The J-22 came in low and fast as it neared the outskirts of the Ranch. Chambers sat behind the console and quietly manipulated the controls.

"You shouldn't have to do too much," Ernesto said. "The flight plan should get us home."

"I know, but since this my last chance to do this, I…" A series of loud beeps suddenly interrupted the conversation; Ernesto rushed to the console.

"It looks like surface to air missiles," Ernesto said. "They're firing surface to air missiles."

"Do we need to worry?"

"I don't think so, but we'll know in a second." Ernesto scanned the data, which streamed rapidly down one of the monitors. The J-22 tracked the path of anything fired at it within a hundred-mile range. "Looks okay, David. So far, none of the missiles have come close, but the plane had to increase altitude a bit."

Chambers smiled. "Okay, I'm going to circle around before I bring her in." He entered the coordinates and the J-22 skimmed over the mountaintops surrounding the Ranch.

"Let's go down to the basement," Chambers said.

"What basement?" Ernesto looked at Chambers curiously.

"Follow me. We don't have much time."

* * *

The J-22 swooped into the valley, steep and fast. The sharp angle of the descent caused the plane to oscillate, slightly at first, then increasing as it continued to accelerate downwards. As it neared the ground, it flipped over and spun out of control. Part of its tail sheared off just before it took a nosedive less than a hundred yards from the Control Room. The plane's two remaining missiles detonated on impact and a series of explosions violently shook the ground. The sky lit up with a huge fireball, followed by a billowy cloud of smoke that could be seen thirty miles away.

The TV helicopter had been hovering at five hundred feet, but the explosion blasted it sideways. Hammond slammed into the video equipment, pinning the cameraman against the window. The aircraft lost three hundred feet of altitude in a few seconds and the pilot struggled to regain control. He managed to level off less than a hundred feet from the ground.

"Is everyone all right?" Hammond screamed.

"Yeah, what the hell was that?" the pilot yelled back.

528

"I don't know, some sort of explosion. You all right, Pete? Did you get any footage of that?"

"Ahhh...my shoulder, it hurts...I think I'm okay."

"Did you get any footage?" Hammond repeated.

"Yeah, I think so—as long as the camera wasn't damaged. That was a plane that just crashed."

"A plane?"

"Gary, I'm worried that the chopper may have sustained some damage," the pilot interjected. "I suggest we get back. I may even have to take it down."

"All right, let's get out of here."

* * *

The following afternoon at a press conference in the White House, the President fidgeted uncomfortably in front of the podium. He thought he should be happy about Chambers' demise, but he felt nauseous.

"Mr. President, can you tell us your reaction to all this?" a reporter asked.

"Well, the brave men and women of the National Guard served their country well," the President offered diplomatically. "They prevented the deaths of innocent people and this nation should be grateful."

"There have been reports, Mr. President, that David Chambers and Ernesto Sosa were killed last night. Can you verify this?"

"Yes, it appears that they committed suicide by firing missiles from their own airplane into the control room where they were hiding. Investigators on the scene have reported that there is nothing left of the building, and that there are no survivors."

"Chambers and Sosa were vocal critics of your Administration, sir. Any reaction to their deaths?"

"No, except when I watched the video last night, I couldn't help thinking that it was like Hell had swallowed them up. We should thank the Almighty that no one else was killed."

News stations across the world began broadcasting footage of the explosions at the Ranch along with the President's remarks. Al Rogers initially thought that the President shouldn't have couched the conflict with Chambers in religious terms because it made him appear simple-minded. On the other hand, the majority of the rank-and-file who supported the President believed in the Administration's oft-stated refrain that a cosmic war between good and evil was occurring in the world and that the United States had God on its side. As it turned out, the President's statement powerfully satisfied the desire of the faithful masses to see the conflict with Chambers as a religious struggle. Believers were relieved to see any event happening in the real world in religious terms because they had been taught their entire lives that God cared about what transpired on the planet. Although none of them had ever seen any actual, concrete evidence other than their own wishful thinking, now, they thought, maybe God did step in and maybe He did really care. The people who needed to believe finally found support for their deepest hopes.

Religious leaders went further than the President, claiming that not only had Chambers and Ernesto gone to Hell, but that a miracle had occurred. God had intervened to cause the J-22's missiles to miss the Christian Identity compound and then He had rerouted the plane back to the Ranch to destroy the satanic forces incarnate in the form of David Chambers and Ernesto Sosa. It was great triumph they said, and a clear indication that God would bring about the End Times soon—destroying unbelievers and saving the faithful. Chambers and Ernesto were the first infidels destroyed by God.

* * *

Al Rogers sat comfortably in a leather chair in the Oval Office and waited for the President. He took a sip of his morning coffee and smiled. The President's secretary fixed it just how he liked it—strong, but with two cubes of sugar and a teaspoon of half and half. "I really think I should go out there," Rogers said to the President as soon as he walked in.

"Where?"

"Kaleidoscope Ranch."

"Why? Can't you handle the investigation from here?"

"No, I don't think that's possible, sir." Behind the scenes, Rogers and his staff had worked to make sure that Rogers controlled the investigation. Although he couldn't explain why, Rogers felt that being intimately involved in the investigation would bring him closer to Chambers, the man he passionately hated and secretly admired.

"Well, I need you here," the President replied nervously. "The press is all over us. I can't handle this alone."

"I just want to make sure everything is…uh…taken care of."

"Taken care of? What needs to be taken care of? We've got our best investigators out there, right?"

"Yes, but I'm concerned. I…"

"You don't think Chambers is dead," the President interjected.

Rogers fumbled the saucer underneath his coffee cup and had to quickly steady it with his other hand. The President had startled him by reading his thoughts and catching him in an unspoken lie. Rogers had planned to say that he was concerned about evidence not being handled properly. "No. I mean I think he probably is…of course he is, but…"

530

"But what?" the President pressed.

Rogers couldn't put his finger on it, but he did worry that Chambers was still alive. Although he knew Chambers was no longer a factor regardless of his fate, Chambers still posed the worst sort of threat—a threat to Rogers' identity. Rogers tried not to face the issue directly and every time it popped into his mind, he tried to distract himself. But now he couldn't avoid it. He couldn't fully describe his emotions, but he felt horrified and guilty, with spasms of hopelessness and momentary jolts of terror. Rogers knew that Chambers could expose him, and in the most frightening way imaginable—not to the public, but to his own soul. Although he hated to acknowledge his respect for Chambers, Rogers saw his own highest aspirations in the man, although he had always managed to repress them.

Rogers had never really faced himself and he didn't have the courage to do it now. The weight of it, he thought, had the potential to crush him, or worse, to send him spiraling into the depths of conscious self-loathing. He wondered if the President shared his fear, although he quickly concluded that the President had probably never even thought about it.

Now, in the midst of dealing with some of his own demons, Rogers hoped and prayed that Chambers was dead. Somehow the fact that of Chambers' demise was comforting because it made him seem less real, making it easier for Rogers to justify his own life. "I just want to be sure," Rogers said finally. "That's all."

* * *

Ray Lassater sat quietly in his library and rested his head in his hands. He stared across several bookshelves and wondered bleakly if knowledge made any difference. *Is it even worth standing up for? Or should I just accept the orgy of faith claims and deny my own mind?* Lassater shivered at the thought and quickly erased it from his consciousness.

Lassater had wept off and on for several days and he had never felt more despair in his life. He reflected that Chambers was only person who really understood him, and the man with whom he had shared his most powerful human connection. He wished he could see Chambers one last time and hold him close, sharing all of his innermost thoughts and feelings.

Lassater hadn't answered his phone or spoken with anyone for several days, but he knew that he needed to snap out of his depression. He got up and walked into kitchen where the red light on his answering machine was flashing. He pressed the Play button: "Ray, it's…it's Ralph Johansen, please call me. I need…I need to speak with you as soon as possible. Please, it's very important."

"Ahhhh…!" Lassater screamed, pulling the answering machine out of the wall and heaving it into the hallway. *That weasel! That pathetic little weasel!* Lassater snatched up the phone and dialed Johansen.

"Hello."

"What the hell do you want?" Lassater thundered.

"Ray? Is that you?"

"Of course it's me, you spineless little twirp!"

"Calm down, Ray. Please…calm down."

"What the hell do you want?"

"I called because I…I want to release *The American Dreamer.*"

"You're a week late, you idiot! Do you get that? Do you?"

"Yeah, I mean I…"

"You could've done some good! But now it's…it's over!"

"Look, Ray, I know you're upset. I made a mistake. God knows, I made a mistake. I'm sorry. Please…listen…I need your help."

"Are you out of your mind?"

"I've got to make this right," Johansen pleaded. "I need your help to make this right."

"You make it right! You screwed up! You make it right!"

"I will Ray. I promise that I will. I'm going to promote this movie. I'm going to do everything I can to make sure people…"

"You're damn right you're going to do that! You're going to use every penny you have! And you'll make no compromises! Do you understand me? You will make no compromises!"

"Okay, Ray. I'll do it. You're right. I promise you that I'll do it. Can you help me?"

Lassater booted the breakfast table with a quick karate kick and sent a glass smashing to the floor. "Goddammit!"

"Ray? Ray? Is everything okay?"

"Chambers is dead!"

"I know, but his movie…can you…will you…help me?"

"Of course I'll help you. But I want this done now. Right now!"

"Okay. I'm starting today. Don't worry. I promise you. We're going to do this. It's going to be great. Okay, Ray? Okay?"

Lassater didn't answer.

"Ray? You still there? Ray?"

"I want you to listen to me very carefully because I'm only going to say this once. If you fuck this up…if you fuck this up even one iota, I'm coming after you. You understand? I'm coming after you and I'll rip you're fucking head off with my teeth. You got that?"

"Uh…okay, don't worry, I…"

"Call me first thing tomorrow morning," Lassater interrupted, and then abruptly hung up.

* * *

Thirty thousand feet above the cornfields of Iowa on his way to the Ranch, Rogers downed a gin and tonic and then called the head of the FBI, ordering him to put a five million dollar dead-or-alive bounty on both Chambers and Sosa. Rogers dialed Stottlemeyer next. He had put Stottlemeyer in charge of the cleanup, providing him with over one hundred federal employees. Stottlemeyer and his team were responsible for clearing the debris and analyzing any potential evidence, but their most important task was to find evidence that Chambers and Ernesto were dead.

"What's the status, Brian?"

"Well, we finished digging out the control room and the area around it…"

"And?"

"There's not much here—just a big crater and a lot of destroyed equipment. That's about it."

"Did you find the bodies?"

"Bodies?"

"Yes. Did you find the bodies?"

"They must be dead, sir."

"That's not what I asked," Rogers fumed. "I said did you find the bodies?"

"No, sir."

"I need bodies."

"I'm sorry, sir. I don't think we're going to find any bodies here. The whole place was incinerated."

"I don't want excuses! Your job is to find conclusive evidence that Chambers and Sosa are dead. If you can't find bodies, I want teeth, or bones, or…anything."

"Well, we've scoured the entire area; there's nothing left. I don't see how anyone could've escaped. And my team has searched every corner of this ranch."

"Keep looking!" Rogers thundered. "I want dead bodies! Two dead bodies!"

CHAPTER 67

Just trust yourself. Then you will know how to live.

—JOHANN WOLFGANG VON GOETHE

Dushane wandered barefoot down the beach, basking in the soft orange glow of late afternoon. His toes sank into the warm sand with each step, slowing his progress, but he was in no hurry; late afternoon was his favorite time of day and he didn't want the moment to end. Watery mist breezed across his face and the ocean radiated a stillness that drew him close. He ambled a few miles down the coast, away from any sign of civilization. He felt wonderfully alone.

A flock of seagulls soared gracefully above him as he came to a jagged outcropping. He moved in among the rocks until he found a smooth place to sit. The sun dipped slowly below the horizon and the sky's canvas changed from dark orange to a light shade of crimson as the daylight sank into the ocean. It was quiet except for the sound of small waves lapping against the rocks.

Dushane had been in Costa Rica for almost two months and he took distant walks down the beach almost every day. It reminded him of being on the Appalachian Trail; he had long stretches of time to explore his thoughts, and he was getting to know himself better. He loved the solitary time, but he also liked spending time with Rusty, who had taught him how to surf and scuba dive. Dushane enjoyed both activities, but what he loved most was not having any plans or worrying about the future—just living in the moment. For most of his life, he had worried about the future, or worse, how other people would react to his life choices. He was finally learning to let go, and he felt that his life was now completely his own.

Dushane stretched out his legs and his toes met the ocean. He let the water cool his feet and then dug his toes into the soft sand, feeling completely relaxed. *I wish Chambers could be here with me. I miss him so much.* Dushane didn't have any particular belief in the afterlife, but he couldn't help thinking that Chambers wasn't really gone. *How does a life force like that just disappear? Or does it disappear? I feel it. It seems so real.*

Dushane put his hands behind his head and laid back against the rock, reflecting on recent events. A month ago, Jim Nielsen had explained what had happened at the Ranch, and that he didn't know whether Chambers and Ernesto had survived. Dushane closed his eyes and prayed that his friends were alive and that he would see them again. He sat up after awhile and threw a shell into the ocean. He thought that despite the uncertainty surrounding Chambers and Ernesto, he felt more alive than he had ever felt in his life. But it was more than just a feeling of being alive that resonated so powerfully in his psyche; he no longer felt any guilt.

Throughout his lifetime, Dushane had felt guilty about many things— being more intelligent than other people, having greater opportunities, being loved by a supportive family. He had also felt guilty for his opposition to racial preferences, which seemed only to perpetuate racial stereotypes and divide people along racial and ethnic lines. A few had accused him of betraying his "people." But racial tribalism was no different than religion, he thought. Both thought systems divided people unnaturally along lines that had no relationship to a person's character. Dushane had never felt any group identity except to humanity as a whole, and he had always believed that every person and everything else in nature was connected. He wondered how any thought system that betrayed this fundamental truth survived.

After spending so much time around Chambers, Dushane's guilt had gradually melted away, and he finally figured out what Chambers had been trying to teach him. All he had to do was trust himself.

* * *

Alone in her hotel room, Josephine lounged comfortably on the couch, reviewing her testimony for the Senate hearing in the morning. She had been called to testify regarding her role in authorizing the surveillance of Kaleidoscope Ranch. Josephine was staying at a hotel in downtown Washington because she had been unable to get any privacy at her house in Alexandria. Reporters had harassed her for several days, trying to get her to make a statement.

Josephine started to doze off because she hadn't slept much in the past few days, but a knock at the door startled her. She wasn't expecting any visitors. "Who is it?" she called out.

A barely audible voice came from the other side of the door. "Josie?"

The voice sounded familiar, but Josephine didn't think it was possible. She walked to the door. "Who is it?" she asked again.

"Josie. Josephine. It's…it's your dad."

Josephine hadn't seen or talked to her father in almost twenty years.

"Josie, can I come in? I'd like to see you. Please…let's talk."

Josephine opened the door slowly and met her father's eyes. Gordon Holladay was now in his sixties and his thinning hair was mostly gray. Josephine thought that he still had handsome features, but years of repressing his emotions weighed in his face. They stood in the doorway and remained silent for several moments, each one struggling to absorb the other's image and figure out the right thing to say.

"Come in, dad," Josephine said quietly. "This is….this is a surprise."

"I know. I'm sorry to just show up like this, but I didn't know if you'd see me."

"How did you find me?"

"I read about the hearing in the paper. Your mother had your address from the last card you sent so we flew to Washington yesterday. We drove over to your house and your housekeeper told us where you were."

"Let's sit down." Josephine motioned to the couch and they sat down next to each other.

"I don't know what to say, dad. It's been such a long time. You never responded to any of my letters. I thought I'd never see you again."

"I know, honey. I came to apologize. I know I hurt you and I'm sorry. I…I just didn't know any other way to love you. I loved you so much and I tried my best. All I ever wanted was for you to be happy. I did what I thought was right. Do you understand that? You've got to believe that."

"I do. I believe you."

Gordon Holladay looked down sheepishly. "Can you forgive me?"

Josephine put her hand on top of her father's. "Of course I forgive you," she whispered. "I'm just happy to see you again."

"Thanks, Josie. I hope we can start again. I want to start again."

"We can." Josephine wrapped her arm around her father's back and pulled him close. "I love you, dad."

"I love you too, honey. Your mother's downstairs. She was afraid to come up because she thought you must hate her."

"No, no, I never stopped loving either of you. I just had to live my own way. It was hard because I knew it hurt you, but I just couldn't lie to myself."

"I know that now, honey. I know that now. I'll go down and get your mother."

* * *

Chambers carefully placed two 45-caliber handguns on his lap and loaded them with ammunition. He whistled happily as he twirled one of the powerful firearms around his finger and then tossed it to Ernesto. "I'll be glad to get out of this place," Chambers said as he stroked his thick, gray-streaked beard.

"Me too," Ernesto agreed. "What's it been, three months?"

"Yeah. Three months as of yesterday."

"Should we take anything beside these?" Ernesto held up the gun and a pair of two-way radios.

"Yeah, grab a few granola bars. I don't know when we'll get our next meal. I've got the binoculars. And don't forget your flashlight." Chambers walked to the corner of the room and began unscrewing the bolts that attached one of the metal floor panels to the wood sub-floor. When all of the bolts were off, Chambers wedged a crowbar underneath the panel and pried it up. Ernesto grabbed one of the edges and helped him slide it away. Below them, a steel ladder descended fifteen feet down into a dark hole. "I wonder if there are rats down there," Chambers said.

Ernesto took a step back. "You better go first."

Chambers clicked on his flashlight and descended. The air had a strange chemical smell. "Man, I hope there's nothing toxic down here."

Ernesto shined his flashlight on Chambers' face. "I'll let you know if your face turns green."

After both men had made it down, they walked two miles to the end of the corridor where there was another ladder bolted to the wall. It extended eighty feet up. Chambers pointed his light up the long, cramped shaft as a cool draft blew softly over his face. He climbed up the ladder until he reached a round steel cover that looked like a manhole. A few rays of light pierced through the holes in the metal so Chambers turned off his flashlight. Then he tried to push the cover open, but couldn't force it all the way up. "Need your help, buddy," he called down to Ernesto.

Ernesto climbed up a little further and squeezed next to Chambers. "Ready. One…two…three…" They pushed the steel lid up and flipped it over on top of some pinecones.

"Damn, that's bright," Chambers moaned, squinting at the sunlight flooding the hole. "We should've brought sunglasses."

"Shhhh…keep it down, David."

Chambers waited for his eyes to adjust and then climbed out, kneeling in the surrounding brush. Ernesto came up behind him and they listened carefully for any sounds. They were on a remote edge of the Ranch and it was quiet except for the shrill chirps of a few birds.

"I'm going up on the ridge to take a look," Chambers whispered. "Why don't you go get the chopper ready?"

Ernesto nodded. "Radio me if you see anything."

"Okay."

Ernesto put his hand on Chambers' shoulder. "Be careful."

"I will. You too." Chambers took a small pair of binoculars out of his pocket and walked quietly up the hill. Ernesto moved slowly from tree to tree, careful to make as little noise as possible as he made his way to the helicopter, which he hoped was still there.

When Chambers reached the top of the hill, he scanned the valley and the rolling hills below him. He could see the entire expanse of the Ranch, or at least what was left of it. He shook his head as he reflected on the breathtaking beauty of the land and the tremendous community of people he had assembled. *What a waste. My God, what a waste.* He tried to convince himself that he wasn't upset, but a wave of sadness overcame any attempt at emotional denial. He sighed and stood quietly without moving, forgetting where he was. After almost thirty minutes, he felt his radio vibrate. He took it out of his pocket and placed it against his ear. "Ernesto?"

"Where are you?"

"I'm still up on the hilltop above the Ranch."

"We need to get moving. What's going on?"

"Nothing. Everything's okay. No signs of life down there. I'm leaving now. How does everything look there?"

"Great. I've got the roof open and the bird is gassed up. I just started the engine and it's purring like a kitten."

"Good. Keep it humming and do all the routine checks. I'll be there soon. Over and out." Chambers took a long final look and then hiked back down the hill.

* * *

Sheriff Jenkins swung the sledgehammer down forcefully, driving a four-by-four wood post into the ground on his property line. Beads of sweat cascaded down his brow and he wiped them off with the shoulder of his t-shirt. He took a swig of his beer and was about to swing the hammer again when he heard his telephone ring. He went inside to answer it. "Sheriff Jenkins here."

"Sheriff, it's Eugene Murray. My chickens are going crazy. It's that damn helicopter next door again."

"What helicopter?"

"The same helicopter as last time. Remember? Six months ago. I can hear it right now, out at the old dairy farm next to my property. We need to put a stop to this right now."

Jenkins suddenly remembered. *Oh no, not this crazy story again.* He figured there probably wasn't any helicopter except in the old man's imagination. "Well, this is a bad time, I'm kinda busy…"

"Come on, sheriff. We're gonna miss him again. I'm a taxpaying citizen and I want action on this! Hurry! You're gonna miss him!"

"Can't this wait? I'm right in the middle…"

"No! Come on! Otherwise, I'm gettin' my shotgun out."

"All right, all right, keep your pants on. I'm leaving now." Jenkins threw on his holster and cowboy hat and drove out to investigate.

CHAPTER 68

Believe nothing, no matter where you read it or who has said it, not even if I have said it, unless it agrees with your own reason and your own common sense.

—BUDDHA

The patrol car screeched to a halt, grinding over the gravel in front of the dairy farm. Jenkins jumped out of the car and tried to open the gate, but it was locked. He momentarily considered barreling through it with his vehicle, but he could hear the chopper and didn't want to give himself away. He grabbed a couple extra rounds of ammunition and slithered through a gap in the barbed wire fence. He ran down the dirt road toward the sound of the helicopter, his heart pounding in anticipation of a confrontation.

Ernesto sat comfortably in the cockpit of the helicopter, methodically checking the instrumentation and controls. He whistled happily as he contemplated the possibilities of his future, including Chambers' promise to help him realize his lifelong dream.

Jenkins tiptoed through the bushes behind the chopper and then snuck in behind it. He drew his gun and sprung into the cockpit, pointing the gun directly at Ernesto's head. "Cut the engine!"

Ernesto jumped back in surprise.

"Cut the engine! Cut the engine now!"

Ernesto turned the key, shutting it down.

"Now, step down. Slowly."

Ernesto swung his legs toward the door, but Jenkins grabbed his shoulder. "Get out on this side!" Jenkins ordered. "And put your hands up where I can see 'em!"

Ernesto crawled across the seat and stepped down, keeping his eyes locked on the barrel of the sheriff's gun.

"Get your hands up!" Jenkins yelled.

Ernesto lifted his arms up and Jenkins took a good look at him. "Well, I'll be damned. You're the Mexican; that wanted Mexican. You got a five million dollar bounty on your head. They gave up looking for you, but I figured maybe you wasn't dead. And now I got you." Jenkins paused and let out a light self-congratulatory chuckle. "Where's your friend?"

Ernesto blinked, but didn't answer.

"You better answer me. You're worth five million whether I take you in dead or alive." Jenkins cocked the gun. "Now, answer me! Where's your friend?"

"Who?"

"Chambers!" Jenkins boomed.

"He's dead."

"I don't believe you." Jenkins stepped aggressively towards Ernesto, waving the gun within two feet of his face.

"Believe whatever you like." Ernesto said as he took a small step backwards. "David didn't make it out alive."

"You're a liar!" Jenkins snapped angrily. *And you're a greasy wetback!* Jenkins didn't like being lied to, especially by a Mexican, but he had learned from years as a public official to suppress any racial slurs that sprung automatically into his mind. "I'm gonna take a look around, and if I find out you was lyin'…" Jenkins took another step forward and held the gun against Ernesto's cheek. "Lie face down on the ground and put your arms behind your back. And don't try anything—I will shoot."

Ernesto flopped onto his stomach and the sheriff pinned him to the ground and cuffed him. Then he tied a rope tightly around Ernesto's ankles and frisked him. "Ah ha! What do we have here? A little radio. Now, who you gonna talk to with this?" Jenkins got up and paced around, fantasizing about how famous he'd be if he brought in David Chambers. He figured he'd get his own made-for-TV movie at least. "I'm gonna to get him," Jenkins muttered to himself. "Damn right I'm gonna to get him."

I hope David can hear us, Ernesto thought. "What are you doing out here?" he asked loudly.

"Shut up. I'm not answering any questions."

"I just thought everyone left the area; that's why I came out."

Jenkins jammed his knee into Ernesto's back, pushing his face into the dirt. "I told you to shut up!" Jenkins continued his search for Chambers, but he kept one eye on Ernesto, who didn't move.

"Where were you hiding all this time?" Jenkins asked after he'd satisfied himself that Chambers wasn't in the vicinity.

"I don't talk to Podunk rednecks!" Ernesto yelled as loud as he could.

Jenkins stomped excitedly over to Ernesto and kicked him in the face. "You keep your mouth shut!"

Ernesto grimaced as he spit out a mouthful of blood.

Chambers emerged from the woods and saw the sheriff's patrol car. His leg had stiffened from the long walk, but he hobbled as fast as he could and entered the farm along its heavily wooded, westernmost boundary. Chambers figured his only chance was to sneak up on whoever was there and ambush them. He only had six bullets in his gun and wasn't carrying any additional rounds. He hoped it would be enough.

Chambers bushwhacked through the heavy foliage, stopping about thirty yards away from the helicopter. He could see Jenkins and Ernesto through the trees. *Thank God he's still alive. And it looks like only one police officer.* Chambers drew his gun and took aim, but he didn't have a clear shot. He couldn't risk firing because if he missed the sheriff might shoot Ernesto.

"Get up!" Jenkins ordered.

"I can't! Untie my ankles!"

Jenkins knelt down and loosened the knot. "I'm going to find your friend. I'll git my dogs out here if I have to."

Ernesto stood up.

"All right, let's go. Now if you try to run, I'll kill you," Jenkins warned.

The two men started toward the patrol car, with the sheriff walking a few feet behind Ernesto. When they were safely out of earshot, Chambers hobbled through the brush towards the road as fast as he could, but the pain in his leg increased with every step. He found a tree branch to help support himself, but adrenaline was the only thing that prevented him from collapsing. When he got to the edge of the road, he bent over and rested his hands on his knees, trying to catch his breath.

Jenkins shoved Ernesto into the back of the patrol car and then pulled onto the road. He started driving towards Chambers, who was waiting in the brush eighty yards away. Chambers readied his gun. When the car got close enough, he jumped in front of it and fired several shots, smashing the windshield. Jenkins instinctively swerved out of the way, his car careening off the road and crashing into a small tree. Chambers rushed to the front of the car and lunged through what was left of the windshield. He grabbed Jenkins by the throat and squeezed with his robotic hand. He used his other hand to pummel Jenkins' face. The sheriff gasped, but couldn't scream, finally sinking into unconsciousness as the blood flow to his brain had been temporarily cut. Chambers rolled down the hood of the car and opened the door to the back seat. "You okay?"

"Yeah." Ernesto held up his cuffed hands. "Check his pockets for the key."

Chambers rifled through Jenkins' clothing until he found the right key and then uncuffed Ernesto.

"Did he radio anybody?" Chambers asked.

"No, not while I was with him." Ernesto put his head next to Jenkins' mouth and then placed two fingers on his throat.

"Is he dead?" Chambers asked nervously.

"No, no, he's got a pulse, and he's breathing—barely."

"Good."

"Man, you did a number on the guy's face."

Chambers shrugged. "He'll be okay. We need to get rid of the car."

"How?"

"Let's find a clearing and drive it into the woods. I don't think we have time to cover it, but let's get it off the road."

"Okay. What about the sheriff?"

"We can't leave him here."

"You want to take him with us?"

"I don't think we have any other choice. You take the car. I'll tie up the sheriff before he wakes up."

Chambers pulled Jenkins out of the car and put the handcuffs on him. Ernesto drove the patrol car a short distance down the gravel shoulder and then fifty feet into the woods so that it wasn't visible from the road.

"Well, let's haul this sack of potatoes to the chopper," Chambers said. "I'll help the best I can, but my leg's acting up."

When they got to the helicopter, Ernesto finished prepping it for takeoff while Chambers tied the still-unconscious Jenkins to a heavy steel storage rack in the back of the aircraft. The rear of the chopper was tiny, so Chambers had to pull off the sheriff's boots and cowboy hat and compress him into the fetal position.

"You ready to rock n' roll?" Chambers said.

"Yeah, but that's disgusting. I've got to wipe off his face." Ernesto gently dabbed the sheriff's face with a rag.

Chambers put on his headphones and started the engine. The rotors sprang to life, blowing leaves and debris around as the chopper got airborne. Chambers angled the aircraft toward the ocean, on a course heading south.

"What a day," Chambers remarked.

"Yeah," Ernesto replied softly.

Neither Chambers nor Ernesto said much during the flight, so the cockpit was quiet until Jenkins regained consciousness.

"Ahhh…" Jenkins moaned. "Ahhh…what the…where…what's…?"

"Sleeping beauty awakes," Chambers joked.

"I think the guy needs a little more beauty sleep."

"What happened? What's going on? Ahhh…my face…my face hurts," Jenkins whined, still trying to bring the memory into his conscious awareness.

Ernesto turned around and flashed a playful smile. "Welcome to heaven."

"Hey! Untie me! Untie me!" Jenkins struggled to escape.

"Ignore him," Chambers said. "He's not going anywhere."

"I said untie me!" Jenkins bellowed. "You're under arrest!"

"Quiet back there!" Chambers ordered.

"You won't get away with this," Jenkins warned. "They'll find you. And this is kidnapping."

Ernesto turned around. "Who's going to find us? You're the only person who knows we're alive. And you won't be talking."

"If anything happens to me…" Jenkins' voice trailed off.

"Look, buddy, I'm in no mood to listen to you," Chambers said. "I've had a long day and I'm tired. You either shut up or it's a gag in your mouth. Your choice."

Jenkins lay quiet for a moment until he realized that the bones in his nose were moving around like pebbles in a bowl of oatmeal. "You bastards broke my nose! You broke my goddamn nose! You won't get away with this!"

"Shut up!" Ernesto snapped as he pulled a handkerchief out of his pocket and held it to Jenkins' face. "Or I'll shut you up! For good!"

Jenkins didn't say another word.

Just before nightfall, Chambers brought the chopper down in the desert forty-five miles east of San Diego. He cut the engine and he and Ernesto rolled Jenkins out. Chambers drew his gun. "Lie face down on the ground, sheriff." Chambers pointed the gun at Jenkins' head.

"You're not going to kill me? Please don't kill me. Please...Please..." Jenkins begged.

"Flat on your stomach! Now!"

"Please! I'm begging you! I won't tell anyone about this. I promise you! I'm begging you! Please!"

"Ernesto, show this gentleman how to lie on his stomach."

Ernesto grabbed the sheriff's collar and threw him down. "Flip over on your stomach!"

Jenkins didn't move.

"On your stomach!" Ernesto kicked him in the ribs.

Jenkins rolled over, finally breaking down into uncontrollable sobs. "Please! Please!"

Chambers reached into his pocket and tossed the handcuff key to Ernesto. "Uncuff him."

Ernesto unlocked the handcuffs and untied Jenkins' legs. "You stay down, sheriff," Ernesto warned. He kept a gun on Jenkins until they took off. As the chopper ascended, Jenkins heaved a sigh of relief, but continued sobbing softly as he flipped over onto his back and watched the helicopter disappear.

CHAPTER 69

The government of the United States is not in any sense founded on the Christian religion.

—FROM THE TREATY OF TRIPOLI, RATIFIED UNANIMOUSLY BY THE U.S. SENATE IN 1797 AND SIGNED BY PRESIDENT JOHN ADAMAS

Ray Lassater sat quietly in a packed theater in San Francisco for the premiere of *The American Dreamer.* He watched Chambers' struggles and triumphs unfold onscreen and he remembered why he loved the man so much. Johansen had created a beautiful film that elegantly captured Chambers' spirit.

When the movie ended and the credits began scrolling down the screen, Lassater didn't move; he didn't want the moment to end. He thought of the mutual love and respect that had run deep between him and the man who had provided so much inspiration. His only regret was that he hadn't told Chambers how much he loved him the last time they had been together. He silently wished that they could laugh together one last time.

As the theater emptied, Lassater felt wonderfully at peace, delighting in a well-deserved sense of pride. He had had a major role in supporting the movie and ensuring its success. After Johansen had decided to release the film, Lassater had called everyone he knew and asked them to donate money to help promote it. Lassater had worked tirelessly, raising fifteen million dollars, all of which had been used in a nationwide marketing campaign to increase exposure for the film.

After several minutes of reflection in the empty theater, Lassater walked to the lobby where other guests surrounded Johansen, complimenting him on the power of his film. Johansen beamed. He knew that he had created something great and loved being recognized for his efforts. Lassater put his hand on the filmmaker's shoulder. "Ralph."

"Hi Ray. I'm glad you could fly out for this."

"Of course. This is your crowning achievement. I wanted to see you bask in the glory. You've earned it."

"Thanks, Ray. Thanks for sticking with me through this."

The men embraced.

Over the next few months, *The American Dreamer* achieved huge box-office success as people couldn't resist the story of a man who had lived his life to the fullest without compromising his own conscience or values. But the film did more than just entertain and inspire people; it began a societal shift as people realized that Chambers wasn't the evil person he had been labeled by religious authorities. Indeed, many people were drawn to him and no longer felt threatened by his approach to life.

But Johansen's documentary wasn't the only thing that contributed to a shift in people's attitudes. As people from the Ranch filtered back into society, they shared their stories about Chambers—his gentle bearing, his inclusiveness, his contagious life force, and the way he cared. People also began to discover Chambers' record of philanthropy. Even those who didn't like his freethinking couldn't ignore his works, which exemplified a deep commitment to humanity's welfare.

Lassater chatted with a few other people and then exited the theater. The evening was foggy and brisk. He buttoned his coat and took a deep breath as the cool air whistled across his face. He was glad to be alive.

* * *

The mood was solemn with seven senators enthroned atop the committee room ready to begin their questioning under the white-hot spotlight of the national media. Josephine strode gracefully to the witness table with her attorney, Mitchell Sutherland, a high-powered Washington lawyer who Josephine had known since law school. Sutherland had represented her twice before, after the Mormons had sued her for libel. He had succeeded in getting the cases dismissed.

Josephine was dressed casually compared to the senators, who were tightly packaged in their designer suits, starched shirts, and burnished shoes. She wore a clean white blouse and a dark gray skirt, with her long hair pulled back taut in a ponytail. She looked as radiantly beautiful as ever and seemed unaffected by the prospect of testifying before the world.

The atmosphere in the room was tense because nobody knew what Josephine was going to say. Many of her colleagues in the Justice Department expected her to remain loyal because she had always followed orders in the past and had never caused any trouble. But some members of the Packer Administration worried that her testimony could unleash a major scandal and seriously cripple the Packer presidency. Al Rogers had contacted Josephine personally, offering her any job in the Administration, or a high-paying consulting position in the private sector. Josephine gracefully declined the bribe.

The Senate committee included four Republicans, all of whom remained fiercely loyal to the President. But on the other side of the aisle, the three Democrats recognized the opportunity for political gain. Since the documentary on Chambers had aired, the public's attitudes had begun to shift and many felt that the government had gone too far in provoking the confrontation with Chambers. Packer's supporters thought these people could be brought back into the fold, but some of them had begun to question whether they really believed in the dogmatic mythology and superstition promoted by the Administration and the institutional churches. Did they really need to believe in order to live a moral, purposeful life? Others began to question whether they needed an authority telling them how to exercise their spirituality. The betrayal by Infinity had convinced some believers that it was time to seek a connection with the universe on their own.

Trent Cheetham, a Republican senator from Arkansas, opened the proceedings. Cheetham had a close relationship with the President and they went on frequent hunting trips together. In fact, Cheetham had

548

recently mounted the stuffed head of a large buck above his fireplace. He had killed the animal on his last outing with the President.

"Good morning, Ms. Holladay and Mr. Sutherland," Cheetham began stoically. "If you're ready, we'd like to begin."

Josephine nodded.

"Raise your right hand, please. Do you swear to testify to the truth, the whole truth, and nothing but the truth, so help you God?"

"Yes," Josephine responded.

"The reason you've been subpoenaed to testify here today is to assist our investigation of the incident at Kaleidoscope Ranch. The Department of Domestic Security was involved in that operation, and as an attorney in that office, we hope that your testimony can shed some light both on what happened and why it happened. I'd like to begin by asking you to explain your role at the Justice Department."

"I was the lead attorney in the Office of Homeland Protection, which as you know is a small office within the Department of Domestic Security. I was primarily responsible for supporting the intelligence gathering of the office, and in particular, I oversaw surveillance. One of my jobs was to determine whether specific government surveillance activities were legal. I advised various members of the Office of Homeland Protection and the Department of Domestic Security, as well as other members of the Justice Department's law enforcement apparatus."

"So, you operated primarily as an attorney in the Office of Homeland Protection and you provided opinions to your superiors as to the legality of surveillance and other related issues. Is that right?"

"Yes."

"And who did you normally report to?"

"Doug Cartwright."

"Mr. Cartwright was your direct supervisor?"

"Yes."

"Can you describe your relationship with Mr. Cartwright?"

"There's not much to describe. He was my boss. He assigned me various tasks and I carried out those tasks."

"Well, as I'm sure you're aware, Ms. Holladay, Mr. Cartwright testified before this committee last week. He stated that he was concerned about the legality of the surveillance at Kaleidoscope Ranch, but he relied on your legal opinions for the actions he approved. He said he wouldn't have acted without your explicit authorization."

Josephine shrugged. "I wasn't aware of Mr. Cartwright's testimony."

Cheetham squinted and then raised his voice. "Not aware? Aren't you concerned with these proceedings, Ms. Holladay? You're potentially subject to criminal prosecution. You'd be well-advised to pay attention to what's going on."

"I'm concerned with these proceedings, Senator, but …" Josephine paused with a light chuckle. "You've met Cartwright."

An audible gasp rose from the audience. Cheetham hesitated momentarily until the buzz subsided. He considered chastising Josephine for the politically incorrect comment, but he had spoken with Cartwright socially at a fundraising dinner. Cheetham didn't want to jeopardize his own credibility by defending the man, so he quickly moved on. "Well, is his description accurate? Did he in fact rely on your legal opinion for the surveillance he ordered?"

"Yes, I believe his description is entirely accurate," Josephine stated evenly.

Cheetham flashed a self-satisfied smile. He got the admission he hadn't expected to get and it had come easily. "Well…"

"I'd like to speak with my client for a minute," Sutherland interjected.

"Okay, we'll take a five minute recess," Cheetham said.

Sutherland leaned over and whispered in Josephine's ear. "You're the most beautiful and the most ridiculous woman I've ever met in my entire life, but you're a naughty girl. Can I take you outside and give you a spanking?"

Josephine suppressed a smile. "How am I doing?" she whispered.

"Great. Now I'm going to pretend to chew you out for incriminating yourself." Sutherland scowled and gestured excitedly for several moments while Josephine tried to look concerned.

After the recess, Cheetham resumed the proceedings. "That's all the questions I have at this time. Senator Porkmire will continue the questioning."

Porkmire hailed from Missouri and he also avidly supported the President. He stared down on Josephine with pop-eyes through his large, horn-rimmed glasses. He spoke with an affected fervor and a nasally drone. "Ms. Holladay, you mentioned that you were the lead attorney for the Office of Homeland Protection. Can you tell us specifically what your role was with respect to Kaleidoscope Ranch?"

"We monitored the Ranch closely. As you know, their leader David Chambers was a vocal critic of the Packer government, so we took a special interest."

"You took a special interest because of the dangerous cult activity at the Ranch. Wouldn't that be a more accurate statement?"

"Yes, that's correct. The people at Kaleidoscope Ranch and Mr. Chambers in particular were advocating a very different view of the world than most of us here are comfortable with—a view that rejects myth and superstition. This was clearly at odds with most Americans, and certainly inconsistent with the views of the Administration."

"You determined that Kaleidoscope Ranch posed a danger. Isn't that right, Ms. Holladay?"

Josephine laughed gently. "A danger? Well, I suppose they did. They pursued knowledge. Knowledge and ignorance have never peacefully coexisted."

"In fact, you recommended taking action against Kaleidoscope Ranch specifically because of the danger it posed. Isn't that right?"

"I approved the legal basis for the phone taps and the audio surveillance. As you know Senator, the Domestic Security Act allows the government to monitor organizations that pose a threat to the welfare of Americans. The people at Kaleidoscope Ranch were clearly a threat. They advocated that people think for themselves. Surely, that posed a danger. Instead of a docile, unthinking mass, the Ranch infused life and gave a voice to a group of independent thinkers that the government would never be able to control easily. I think we were fully justified in exercising our authority under the law."

Porkmire scowled. Although Josephine provided all of the answers he wanted, he found himself getting increasingly infuriated. He felt as if Josephine was mocking him, even though she spoke respectfully.

"The people from that ranch were advocating complete disrespect for the government, Ms. Holladay!"

"The Packer government, yes."

"And complete disrespect for the Judeo-Christian tradition of this country!"

"The irrational tradition."

"Irrational? The nuts at the ranch were irrational!" Porkmire snapped.

Josephine shrugged. "Then I suppose their views are protected by the First Amendment. Freedom of religion has always protected irrational beliefs."

"Well, we all know about freedom of religion here, the First Amendment and all that, but that doesn't change the fact that this country was founded by Christians who recognized God as the supreme authority."

"That's an interesting viewpoint," Josephine replied evenly.

"It's the truth!" Porkmire boomed.

"I object to this discussion, Senator," Sutherland jumped in. "If you have a question for my client, ask it. We don't need a lecture on the First Amendment or the history of the country's founding."

"What I'm trying to get to the bottom of, Mr. Sutherland, is exactly what happened at that ranch. So far, we know that those people were involved in a cult and that they had no respect for government authority or the morality of decent Americans. Then, like many other crazy cult groups, they committed suicide. That's all clear from the testimony this committee has heard so far. Now, my next question…"

"Did anyone ever find any bodies?" Josephine interrupted.

"Bodies?"

"You said they committed suicide."

"They blew themselves up. Haven't you watched the news lately?"

"Yes, but I'm curious if anyone ever found any dead bodies."

"There were no bodies to be found. The whole area was completely destroyed. There were no survivors."

"Have you ever met David Chambers, Senator?"

"No, but I heard everything I needed to about him."

"Interesting."

"Are you trying to tell me something? Do you know something I don't?"

"Probably not."

"If you know something about this incident, I suggest you share it with this committee. I remind you that you're under oath."

"I don't know anything specific about the current whereabouts of David Chambers or Ernesto Sosa."

"That's because they're dead, Ms. Holladay. Case closed."

"Okay. That's the beauty of belief, I suppose."

Sutherland started to chuckle and quickly put his hand over his mouth.

"I don't know what kind of game you're trying to play, but if you have any information, you'd be well advised to share it with us now. I will hold you in contempt," Porkmire threatened.

Sutherland leaned over and whispered in Josephine's ear. "I'm serious this time. Take the fifth."

Josephine nodded. "I refuse to provide any additional information pursuant to my right against self-incrimination under the Fifth Amendment."

"Do you have information, Ms. Holladay?" Porkmire pressed.

"Senator!" Sutherland snapped. "Ms. Holladay has exercised her Constitutional rights. Back off."

"I'm going to get to the bottom of this!" Porkmire fumed. "This isn't over!"

"We need to be on the Senate floor for a vote in half an hour," Cheetham interjected. "I suggest we recess until tomorrow."

Porkmire simmered angrily, but nodded.

"Okay. We'll reconvene at nine a.m. tomorrow morning," Cheetham concluded.

* * *

The dispatcher at the FBI office in Washington picked up the ringing phone. "FBI."

"David Chambers kidnapped me! David Chambers and Ernesto Sosa! They're alive! They're alive!"

"Slow down, sir. Please, slow down. Who am I speaking with?"

"This is, this is, Harvey Jenkins. I'm, I'm a sheriff in California."

"You say you saw David Chambers and Ernesto Sosa?"

"Yes! Near their ranch in Northern California. I had Sosa in custody, but he escaped and then they kidnapped me and put me on their helicopter. They tied me up. They let me off near San Diego. Get me Stottlemeyer! I need to talk to Stottlemeyer!"

"Hold on a moment, sir. Let me see if Agent Stottlemeyer is available."

The phone clicked over. "This is Agent Stottlemeyer."

"It's Jenkins. Harvey Jenkins."

"You saw Chambers and Sosa?"

"Yeah, I saw them near their ranch, and then they kidnapped me and we flew in a helicopter. They let me off near San Diego."

"Are you sure it was Chambers and Sosa?"

"Of course I'm sure! I know what they look like!"

"Where are you now?"

"El Cajon, I think. This town is called El Cajon."

"Where's that?"

"Near San Diego—east."

"Okay. Where exactly?"

"I'm in a restaurant."

"What restaurant?"

"Uh…Hooters."

"What?"

"Hooters."

"Hooters?"

"Yes! The restaurant, they have the waitresses with the big…uh… breasts, you know, big tits."

"Is this is a joke?"

"No."

"What's the street address?"

"Hold on." Jenkins asked the hostess and then came back to the phone.

"1280 Fletcher Boulevard."

"Okay, stay there. I'm going to dispatch a field agent to meet you."

* * *

Adam Sharf carefully opened the glass case and admired the three medals inside—two Congressional Medals of Honor earned by Hank Chambers and Fred Carson, and the Presidential Medal of Freedom awarded to David Chambers. Chambers had given Sharf the medals and asked him to find a place where other people could find inspiration in them.

Sharf lifted one of the medals out of the case and fingered it gently. *Man, these guys really did something. They did something important. I'm finally doing something important, too.* Sharf now worked for the Kaleidoscope Foundation and was responsible for the Foundation's support of children's hospitals and medical research.

In addition to the new job, Sharf's life had changed radically since he had left the legal profession. After his dramatic final court appearance, he had immediately resigned from the bar. The state bar association formally disbarred him anyway, but Sharf didn't plan on resuming a legal career. He moved to another state across the country with his family and hoped to start over. His marriage had been seriously strained and his wife had almost divorced him. But she still loved him and decided to stay with him. The couple did have to adjust to a scaled-back lifestyle in light of Sharf's less financially motivated new career, but the change had brought them closer together.

Sharf put the medal back into its case and reflected on his previous life. He didn't think about whether he had done the right thing by leaving the legal profession. His identity and the possibilities he now visualized for himself had completely changed. Doing something he didn't believe in wasn't even possible anymore, and he never had any of the thoughts that had enslaved him in the past. He never thought of money or status or how other people measured success. His present life was so rich with opportunities to make a difference that he thanked everyone who came into his new life

CHAPTER 70

The further the spiritual evolution of mankind advances, the more certain it seems to me that the path to genuine religiosity does not lie through the fear of life, and the fear of death, and blind faith, but through striving after rational knowledge.

—ALBERT EINSTEIN

Stottlemeyer had just finished pouring himself a cup of coffee in the kitchen when he heard the phone ring in his office. He trotted to his desk and picked it up. "Agent Stottlemeyer."

"Morning, Agent. This is Agent Porter."

"How'd it go last night?"

"Fine. I think Jenkins is credible."

"Really?"

"Yeah, it was a wild story, but I pressed him and he stayed consistent. My gut tells me that he's telling the truth."

"Wow, this is incredible. I've got to get over to the Hill ASAP. E-mail me your report."

"Will do."

Stottlemeyer grabbed his jacket and jogged out to his car. He sped over to the Capitol Building and arrived at the committee room fifteen minutes before the Kaleidoscope Ranch hearing was scheduled to begin. A few of the senators, including Cheetham and Porkmire, had already taken their seats. Stottlemeyer came in behind them and delivered the news.

Porkmire slammed his fist on the table. "That woman knows something about this and I don't give a damn about her Fifth Amendment rights. I'm going to get to the bottom of this!"

Senator Cheetham nodded. "Don't worry. We'll be able to question her shortly."

Nine o'clock arrived, but Josephine hadn't. The senators waited until 9:15, but still no Josephine. At 9:30, Cheetham called a recess and summoned Stottlemeyer to his office.

"Something's going on. I want you to find her."

"Okay."

Stottlemeyer drove to Josephine's house in Alexandria and banged loudly on the door. "Ms. Holladay, this is the FBI! Open up!" He waited for thirty seconds and briefly considered knocking the door down, but Josephine's attorney, Mitchell Sutherland, finally opened it.

"Where's Ms. Holladay?" Stottlemeyer demanded.

"Beautiful morning, isn't it?" Sutherland greeted breezily.

"Wait, you're...you're the attorney."

"That's right."

"How come you're not at the hearing? You and Ms. Holladay."

"I left a message with Porkmire's office this morning. Josephine won't be attending any future hearings. She had other business to attend to."

"What?"

"Josephine won't be attending any future hearings."

"That's...you can't do that!"

Sutherland shrugged.

"Where is she?" Stottlemeyer demanded.

"She's gone—long gone."

"Where?"

"I have no idea."

"This…this is an obstruction of justice. If you know where she is, you better tell me. I'll arrest you right now."

Sutherland held out his hands. "Okay."

"I want to know where she is!"

"Do you think Josephine would be stupid enough to tell me or anyone else where she was going?"

"I want you to tell me everything you know."

"I only know one thing for certain—don't waste your time trying to find her."

* * *

The cab driver whistled happily as he sped up the narrow cobblestone street and whipped around a sharp corner. Cool air whizzed through the open back-seat window and whisked across Chambers' face as he held onto the seat in front of him and enjoyed the scenery.

Chambers was happy to be in Lausanne, one of Switzerland's most beautiful cities, and one of his favorite places in Europe. The large but quaint municipality was characterized by steep hills and breathtaking vistas, with tree-lined, lakefront promenades that spilled over with vibrantly colored flowers.

Chambers took a deep breath and watched the sun set over the snow-capped Alps, which peeked through the gaps between buildings and at the tops of the steeply dropping streets. The cabbie pulled up to a curb in front of a young man wearing a neatly pressed white shirt and a black bowtie. He opened the passenger door of the cab and bowed politely. "Bonsoir, monsieur. Bienvenu au Christophe."

"Bonsoir. Merci." Chambers always dined at Christophe whenever the occasion called for an intimate, romantic setting. The restaurant offered exquisite candlelight dinners, private rooms, and an impeccably trained staff.

Chambers walked into the restaurant and turned left into the bar. Josephine was sitting on a stool, sipping a cocktail. She spun around when she saw Chambers' image reflecting off the glass behind the bar. "David!"

"Josie."

"I've missed you." Josephine wrapped her arms tightly around Chambers' back.

"I've missed you, too." Chambers held her close and kissed her neck.

After a while, they each loosened their grip, but remained holding each other's shoulders.

"How is everything?" Josephine asked. "You're okay?"

"Yes. How about you?"

"I'm glad to be away."

The maitre d' walked into the bar and placed his hand lightly on Chambers' back. "Pardon me, monsieur; your table is ready."

"Excellent. Thank you."

During dinner, Chambers and Josephine exchanged glances, but they spoke little.

"You're as beautiful as ever," Chambers said after a long silence.

"Thanks, David," Josephine responded quietly without making eye contact.

"What's wrong?"

"I…" Josephine dropped her head. "God, this is so much harder than I thought it was going to be."

"It's me, Josie," Chambers said softly. "You never have to worry with me."

Josephine took a deep breath. "I know…it's just…I…I've been thinking about us…I…I…just…"

"You don't want to be with me."

Josephine's head shot up and she held Chambers' gaze. "I…how did you know?"

Chambers chuckled. "You're easy. I was waiting for you to say it. And I'm happy that I didn't have to."

"You're not upset?"

"No."

"You feel the same way?"

"Yes. I love you more than you can imagine, but…I'm not sure how to put this…"

"We're not right together."

"No."

"You have to be on your own?"

"You understand that?"

"Yes."

"And you need to follow you own path without me getting in your way. Unfortunately, we're cut from the same cloth."

"When we first met, I thought we'd end up together," Josephine said. "I had no doubt about that."

Chambers reached across the table and clasped Josephine's hand. "We'll always share a bond. That will never go away."

Josephine sighed. "It's so easy with you, but it's so hard with other people."

"I know. It's easy for us because we don't try."

Josephine laughed, finally breaking her stoic demeanor. "You're right.

I've never thought about it that way, but that's exactly what it is."

Chambers smiled. "I'm glad we've come to this understanding. I'm relieved."

"Me too. What will you do next?"

"I'm going away for awhile." Chambers paused. "I want you to take one last trip with me."

"When?"

"We leave tomorrow night."

"Okay."

"Are you ready to go?"

"Yes."

"I'll walk you back to your hotel."

On the short walk to Josephine's hotel, Chambers thought about what made his relationship with Josephine work. He concluded that they connected so powerfully because they didn't have to break through any layers to get to each other. They each presented themselves, naked, to the other person without any fear.

"I'll send a driver to pick you up tomorrow evening at six," Chambers said.

"Okay. Good night, David."

Chambers kissed Josephine on the cheek and hopped into a cab. The next morning, he directed the driver to a location on the outskirts of town.

"There it is," Chambers said. "On the other side of that lamppost."

The cabbie screeched to a halt in front of a nondescript three-story building that had no windows and only one door, which was forged out of dull gray steel. A small sign above the entrance read "Authorized Personnel Only" in English, French, and German.

"Probably take me a few hours," Chambers said to the driver. "I'll call you when I'm done."

"Oui, monsieur."

Chambers stepped out of the car and turned the handle of the building's door, which swung open easily. Behind the door, there was a small anteroom, which was empty except for a tiny camera and a scanner that hung from the ceiling. There was also an intercom built into one of the walls.

Chambers had been to this place before so he knew the drill. He looked up at the scanner and it whirred softly as it analyzed his retinas. Seconds later, the overhead monitor in the bank's security office lit up and an alarm chimed in the background. The screen displayed the name of the banker assigned to handle the account of the visitor at the door. The security officer on duty pressed a button on his control panel, which rang the extension of Claude Van Berkum, the firm's most senior banker. When Van Berkum picked up phone, he received an automated message: "Your client is waiting in the lobby. Please enter your security code." Van Berkum quickly typed the code into his computer and "David Chambers" popped up on the screen. *David Chambers! My God, it can't be. Or could it?*

Van Berkum picked up the phone and called security. "I'd like a secondary confirmation, please." Van Berkum had only requested a secondary confirmation one other time. Retina scanning was considered almost one hundred percent foolproof, but Van Berkum wasn't about to take any chances with his most important client.

"Please stand by, Mr. Van Berkum."

In the anteroom, Chambers waited patiently until a palm scanner dropped out of the wall, accompanied by a voice over the intercom. "Sir, if you please, place your left hand, palm down, into the tray."

Chambers laid his hand on the scanner and a bright yellow laser moved back and forth across it.

"Thank you, sir." The wall slid open to a small waiting room furnished with a sofa, a small table, and a cut-glass pitcher of water and two glasses.

The security guard buzzed Van Berkum. "Mr. Van Berkum, secondary confirmation is affirmative."

"Thank you, thank you," Van Berkum responded excitedly. "I'll be right down."

Claude Van Berkum was ethnic Dutch, but he was born in Geneva. His family had emigrated to Switzerland at the outbreak of the Second World War and Van Berkum had lived his entire life there. He had been a banker since graduating from college and had established his own bank at the age of thirty-three. The bank catered exclusively to people with at least fifty million U.S. on deposit and its privacy and security were unparalleled. Van Berkum personally managed the accounts of the bank's biggest clients.

Swiss bankers were obligated by law to keep all information about their clients strictly confidential and any banker revealing such information could be prosecuted and sentenced to prison. The privacy rules also applied to foreign governments, which were unable to obtain any information on Swiss banking clients except by order of a Swiss Federal Judge in the case of a serious crime punishable under Swiss law. Even if the client authorized the bank to give information to a foreign government, by law, the bank could not do so.

Chambers had a Swiss numbered account, which meant that his name was separated from his account number. Van Berkum and his two assistants knew Chambers' identity, but after the account had been opened, Van Berkum placed all the documents containing Chambers' name and address in a safe. The bank did not maintain a database connecting any client's name with their corresponding account number. The only method of accessing this information was by verifying the contents of the safe. Generally, only a handful of people had access to these documents according to a strict procedure, including a requirement that a safe could not be opened without Van Berkum present.

Van Berkum strode gaily into the waiting room. "Ahhh…David, I'm so thrilled you are still alive. I was terribly worried." Van Berkum hugged Chambers and then kissed him lightly on each cheek.

Chambers smiled. "Always great to see you, Claude."

"And Ernesto?" Van Berkum asked delicately.

"He's here. In Lausanne, that is."

"Excellent. My mind is finally at ease. It's always so difficult to lose clients. I've made so many wonderful friends over the years."

Chambers loved Van Berkum not only for his banking skills, but because unlike most bankers who were tightly wound and unemotional, Van Berkum always revealed a sentimental side.

"Ernesto is planning to come by tomorrow morning. He would've come with me, but under the circumstances…"

Van Berkum nodded. "No need to explain; I certainly understand. Please, let's retire to a more comfortable room where we can discuss your business."

Van Berkum escorted Chambers down the hall and they took an elevator to the basement. The elevator opened into a room that looked like a salon from a Renaissance chateau. It contained a stone fireplace, vaulted ceilings, intricately crafted wood furniture, and hand-woven tapestries. The room was also equipped with modern amenities including a full bar and two computer terminals.

"Make yourself at home, David. Can I pour you a drink?"

"Yes, thank you."

"Scotch and soda, yes?"

"That's right."

Van Berkum opened a small bucket of ice and dropped several cubes into two glasses.

"You know, I've spent the last fifteen years managing your money," Van Berkum said as he poured the well-aged alcohol. "If you had met your demise…well, I wasn't sure what I would do. You are certainly the bank's most interesting client."

Chambers nodded politely. "I'm sure you'd continue on without me."

"Perhaps. I suppose you are right. It is in my blood. By the way, your government has shown an active interest in locating your account in Switzerland."

Chambers raised his eyebrows.

"Of course, their efforts will be for naught; they should know better." Van Berkum handed Chambers the drink.

"Thanks."

"To your continued survival," Van Berkum toasted.

"To life," Chambers responded, lifting his glass.

Each man took a sip of his drink. "You always have the finest scotch, Claude. Maybe that's why I like coming here so much."

"Only the best for my friends," Van Berkum said. "And to celebrate your resurrection."

Chambers grinned.

"You know, I was worried when I saw the news reports," Van Berkum continued. "I couldn't bear to watch. Of course, your government still believes that you are dead."

"Then I must be dead, then. Belief is the same as truth according to my government."

Van Berkum chuckled. "I'm glad to see you haven't lost your sense of humor."

"And I am dead—in the United States anyway."

"Of course. Well, I suppose you'd like to get down to business. How may I assist you?"

"I need to set up a few trust accounts."

Chambers explained his plan to divide over a billion dollars between the Kaleidoscope Foundation and several other charities, including a large donation to Mexico Libre, a social service organization in Mexico. The men spent the next three hours going over the details.

"Thanks so much for your help, Claude," Chambers said as they finalized the last of the documents. "I hope our paths cross again soon."

"I certainly hope so. I take great pleasure in working with you. Please look after yourself."

The men hugged and then Chambers called his driver. The cabbie met him outside and drove him back to his hotel.

"How did it go with Claude?" Ernesto asked as Chambers entered the room.

"Fine."

"And Josephine?"

"She's as wonderful as ever."

"What now?"

Chambers smiled. "It's time to fulfill that promise I made to you."

Ernesto's face lit up. "You mean it?"

"I do. But let's take a little vacation first."

CHAPTER 71

[T]raditional dogmatic or authoritarian religions that place revelation, God, ritual, or creed above human needs and experience do a disservice to the human species. Any account of nature should pass the tests of scientific evidence…the dogmas and myths of traditional religions do not…We find insufficient evidence for belief in the existence of a supernatural; it is either meaningless or irrelevant to the question of survival and fulfillment of the human race. As nontheists, we begin with humans not God, nature not deity.

We appreciate the need to preserve the best ethical teachings in the religious traditions of humankind, many of which we share in common. But we reject those features of traditional religious morality that deny humans a full appreciation of their own potentialities and responsibilities…Too often traditional faiths encourage dependence rather than independence, obedience rather than affirmation, fear rather than courage.

Promises of immortal salvation or fear of eternal damnation are both illusory and harmful. They distract humans from present concerns, from self-actualization, and from rectifying social injustices…[S]cience affirms that the human species is an emergence from natural evolutionary forces…There is no credible evidence that life survives the death of the body. We continue to exist in our progeny and in the way that our lives have influenced others.

We affirm that moral values derive their source from human experience. Ethics is autonomous and situational needing no theological or ideological sanction. Ethics stems from human need and interest. To deny this distorts the whole basis of life. Human life has meaning because we create and develop our futures.

Reason and intelligence are the most effective instruments that humankind possesses… But reason must be tempered by humility, since no group has a monopoly of wisdom or virtue…[C]ritical intelligence, infused by a sense of human caring, is the best method that humanity has for resolving problems.

The preciousness and dignity of the individual person is a central humanist value. Individuals should be encouraged to realize their own creative talents and desires… We believe in maximum individual autonomy consonant with social responsibility.

—FROM THE HUMANIST MANIFESTO II

The warm midday sun beat down on Dushane's back as he watched the water rise slowly out of the ocean and build into a five-foot swell. He flipped around on his surfboard and started paddling as the cresting surge rushed towards him, finally catching his board and thrusting him down the face of the wave. Dushane held on tightly to the sides of the board and then popped up in a quick motion. He stayed in a low crouch and rode the wave for five seconds before falling down sideways into the whitewater. When he resurfaced, Rusty yelled over to him. "Nice ride! That's was your longest ever!"

Dushane spit the saltwater out of his mouth and grinned. "Yeah!"

"You're getting the hang of it!"

"Yeah! I'm just happy if I can stay out of the washing machine!" Dushane was referring to something every surfer experienced—getting crushed by a wave and then being held under while the water swirled and churned around you.

"Hey! You ready to head in?" Rusty called.

"Sure!"

They men paddled in to shore together and jogged to their towels, quickly drying themselves off.

"Good session, buddy." Rusty held out his hand.

"Yeah." Dushane smacked it in agreement.

"Hey, let's go grab a drink. I want to take you to a new place."

"Okay."

Dushane and Rusty trotted a quarter mile down the beach until Rusty stopped and laid his board down on the sand in front of an expensive hotel. "Here we are."

"What is this place?"

"El Capitan Suizo. It's the best hotel in town and they've got a killer bar. I think you're going to like it."

"Can we go in like this?" Dushane put his hand on his bare chest.

"Sure, why not? Come on."

Dushane followed Rusty past a large swimming pool and then into the bar area where they sat down on stools.

"Buenos tardes," Rusty greeted the bartender. "Dos Coronas, una margarita, y…vamos a ver…how 'bout a scotch and soda."

Dushane shot Rusty an odd glance. "Why did you…?" *Scotch and soda.* "Wait a minute…"

Rusty grinned. "Look behind you."

Dushane spun around on his barstool. "Hey!" Chambers and Ernesto were walking towards the bar. Dushane jumped off the stool and ran towards them. He lunged into Chambers' arms and hugged him as tight as he could.

"Ahhh…Martin, Martin, I can't breathe."

"Oh, sorry," Dushane loosened his grip. "I just can't believe it! This is incredible! I thought I'd never see you again!"

"Well, I had to make sure you didn't squander your opportunity down here."

"I'm so happy you're alive. Gosh, I missed you guys." Dushane hugged Chambers again and then hugged Ernesto.

"Look at you," Chambers said. "You're learning. Can you believe this, Ernesto? It's all over his face."

"Quite a transformation," Ernesto agreed.

Rusty walked up with a tray of drinks and placed them on a nearby table. Then he put his arms around Chambers and Ernesto. "Afternoon, gentlemen."

Dushane turned to Rusty. "You knew these guys were alive?"

"Yeah."

"The whole time?"

"Not the whole time."

"I can't believe you didn't tell me."

"I only found out a couple days ago. Believe me, I wanted to tell you; I was about to bust. But I wanted you to have a good surprise."

"God, I've got so many questions."

"Well, they'll have to wait, Martin," Chambers said. "As much as I'd love to hang around here and have a few drinks, we need to get back to the boat before it gets dark."

"Boat?"

"Yeah, Ernesto and I have a little sailboat. Why don't you guys grab your stuff and meet us in an hour on the beach."

* * *

"Man, I still can't believe this," Dushane gushed excitedly as he packed his duffel bag.

"Yeah. Shit happens, I guess." Rusty flipped on the stereo.

"Hey, how long do you think we'll be on this boat?"

Rusty shrugged. "I don't know. Probably a long time. I don't think we're coming back here."

"Really?"

"Yeah."

Dushane stopped packing and scanned the room, quickly chronicling its contents—a stereo, a television set, two couches, a coffee table, a few plants, three overflowing bookshelves, two computers, a large oak desk, and two swiveling office chairs. "What are we supposed to do with all this stuff?"

"What do you mean?"

"If we're not coming back…"

"Pack your favorite books."

"Yeah, but what about everything else?"

"Leave it here. We don't need it."

"Yeah, but we can't just leave it here."

"Don't worry. I told a few of the guys down at the surf shop that they could have it."

"But…" Dushane started.

"Come on, Martin. This is all a bunch of junk. If we come back, we'll get some replacement junk."

Dushane looked around the room again; he knew Rusty was right. He didn't really need any of the stuff, and he was surprised how good it felt not to worry about any of it. "Yeah, that sounds good."

Rusty chuckled. "You're going to wonder why you ever cared about any of your possessions."

After they had both finished packing their duffel bags, they met Chambers and Ernesto on the beach next to a small dinghy. Each man grabbed a corner of the boat, carried it into the surf, and then jumped in. Chambers cranked the motor and then navigated the boat a quarter mile offshore towards a seventy-two-foot sailboat. As they got closer, Dushane squinted to block the sunlight, and then read the name of the boat, painted prominently in red block letters on the stern— "Common Sense." *I knew it!* Dushane thought. *I just knew it!*

As the dinghy got close to the side of the sailboat, two young Costa Rican men helped everyone on to the deck.

"This is our crew," Chambers said to Dushane. "The tall one's Jorge. The other guy is Pablito. They're helping us navigate through the area."

"Where should I put my stuff?"

"Leave it on deck for now; you can take it down later. I'll show you your quarters in a minute."

Ernesto and Rusty disappeared below deck while Chambers and Dushane stood next to each other on the bow.

"So, how are you feeling, Martin?" Chambers asked as he put his arm around Dushane's back.

"I'm good; a little shell-shocked, but good."

"This all must seem a little strange."

"Yeah."

"I suppose you're wondering what's going on?"

Dushane glanced away for a moment, and then turned back and looked squarely into Chambers' eyes. "Why did you…?" Dushane's voice trailed off.

"What is it?"

"I don't know, I mean…why did you do it?"

"Do what?"

"You had everything a man could want, but you…"

"Threw it away," Chambers finished.

"No, no, I didn't mean it like that," Dushane backtracked.

"It's okay. That's a fair question. I'm just not sure I can answer it."
Dushane cocked his head and narrowed his eyes in concentration.
"You know, I've just never really thought about it, Martin."

Chambers was one of the most intelligent people Dushane had ever met, so he had trouble believing that Chambers had never thought about it. *But what if he hasn't? God, maybe that's exactly the point. I need to understand him. I've got to understand him.* "Well…" Dushane began.

"I don't know, Martin," Chambers interrupted. "I've always felt the need to keep myself interested."

"There's got to be more to it than that."

Chambers let out a gentle sigh and then his demeanor turned melancholy. "Yeah, I suppose. I guess I just wanted to make a difference in my lifetime. But that's nothing special; it's probably built into our genes."

Both men were quiet for a while. Dushane watched the gentle blue-green swells lap up against the hull of the boat.

"But I'm not sure whether I've made a difference or not," Chambers said finally.

"Of course you have," Dushane responded emphatically. "You've helped thousands of people."

Chambers shrugged. "Maybe, but moving people into new ways of thinking is a slow process that usually takes centuries. Did we make a difference? I hope so. In the end, it doesn't really matter. We stood up for what we believe in. That's all we can do. That's all anyone can do."

Dushane nodded. "You don't find that difficult sometimes?"

"No. In fact, just the opposite. I mean I've never seen any reason to compromise my core values. That's a hard thing to do, isn't it?"

Dushane looked at Chambers intently, but didn't speak.

"It's always struck me as odd how little it takes for people to betray their most important possession, Martin—their own soul."

Dushane suddenly began to feel the familiar thrill of realization. *That's it*, he thought. *That's the only real difference between Chambers and most other people. His success, his passion, his humanity, all comes down to that.*

"History will judge our ideas and our actions," Chambers went on. "That's our legacy; our contribution." He smiled. "But that doesn't matter at all right now. What's important to me now is being here with you. There's nothing more important than my relationships with the people I love." Chambers squeezed Dushane's shoulder and pulled him close. "I'm so glad you're here."

"Thanks, David. For everything."

They stayed silent while the sun set gently below the horizon. A pink glow radiated over the water and the boat rocked gently in the current.

"Hey, you hungry?" Chambers asked.

"Yeah, sure."

"We've got a cook on board. Let's go down; I'll introduce you."

Dushane followed Chambers down the steps to the galley. There was a woman standing in front of the sink facing away from them, but Dushane recognized her immediately. "Josephine!" he cried.

Josephine spun around. "Hi, Martin."

"How did you…why are you…?"

"Shhhh…how about a hug?" They hadn't seen each other since Dushane had left to hike the Appalachian Trail.

"I don't understand. What's…do you know David?"

"David and I were lovers."

Dushane turned to Chambers and then back to Josephine. "What? When?"

"When I was in Utah before we met and then after we broke up."

"This is…I don't know what to say."

"I've missed you," Josephine said.

"God, I've missed you, too. You look…you look as beautiful as ever."

Josephine smiled and then kissed Dushane lightly on the cheek. "How about some dinner? I've got a big bowl of pasta here and some hot garlic bread."

"Sounds good to me," Chambers said. "Let me go tell the crew to get under way." Chambers climbed the stairs up to the deck and Dushane followed closely behind.

"Why didn't you ever tell me about Josephine?" Dushane said as they walked to the stern.

"I didn't want it to affect our relationship. Does it?"

"No…I guess not. I guess there's no reason it should."

"Good. She still loves you, you know."

Dushane froze. "What?"

"She still loves you."

The revelation brought back a rush of feelings that Dushane hadn't experienced in many years. He had always tried not to think about Josephine because the thought that he would probably never love any other woman as much was hard to bear. "I…I still love her, too," Dushane said, his too low for anyone to hear.

"Jorge, pull up the anchor, please," Chambers directed. "Let's get underway."

"Where we headed, David?" Dushane asked.

"I don't know. Away. As far away…" Chambers' voice trailed off. "Let's head back down and eat. We'll think about a destination tomorrow."

CHAPTER 72

For century after century after century, the Christian church had designated the people to be despised: the religious believers called Jews, the "Christ killers," the "enemies of God." All the religious massacres... by Crusaders pursuing infidels, by inquisitors hunting backsliders, by superstitious mobs fearing tales of well-poisoning—branded Jews as accursed. When popes ordered Jews to wear badges and live in ghettos—or when they were expelled entirely—it told the populace that these pariahs were unfit to live among decent folk. Passion plays depicting Jews as cruel mockers of Christ, and cathedral paintings of the evil non-Christians, fanned hatred of those the church called "the perfidious Jews." Thus, when Adolf Hitler needed a scapegoat group to rally the discontented majority to his cause and catapult himself to power, natural victims clearly marked by the church were at his disposal. The Christian public, not only in Germany but also throughout Europe, was predisposed to receive the Nazi message of Jew-hatred.

—James A. Haught, *Holy Horrors*

Soft rays of morning sunlight reflected off Dushane's sunglasses as he wheeled his car, top down, into the Westside High School parking lot in New Orleans. The air was already heavy with humidity and Dushane wiped his brow with a tissue as he pulled into a parking space. He cut the engine and picked up a small red balloon from the passenger seat, placing it on the floor behind him. The balloon was left over from his birthday party the previous week; he had just turned fifty-eight years old.

Dushane had been teaching World History and Civics at Westside High for the past four years and he had worked in various capacities in the Louisiana public school system for the past twenty. After he had returned from Costa Rica, he had decided to devote his life to improving educational opportunities and remedying the inequities of Louisiana's dual school system—neglected public schools for poor kids and top-notch private schools for wealthy ones. Over the years, he had earned a reputation as a tireless fighter who produced results, including a steady rise in the quality of Louisiana's public schools and a significant increase in the percentage of public high school students who went on to college.

Dushane smiled as he walked into his first period World History class. He loved his students—twenty-six kids, including his seventeen-year old son Spencer. Many of his students came from families living barely above the poverty line in some of New Orleans' worst neighborhoods, not unlike his own childhood background. He knew that the difference for him had been his commitment to education and the love and support of his family. He felt lucky that he had a chance to give his students at least some of the same opportunities, and he tried to get them hooked on learning as a lifestyle choice. He knew that a lifelong commitment to education was the one thing that would change their destiny, and the only sure way to escape ignorance and poverty.

Dushane's spacious classroom had recently been equipped with the latest digital technology. Even compared to the most expensive private schools, it was arguably the most technologically advanced classroom in the state of Louisiana. Each desk was outfitted with a laptop computer and a high-speed, wireless connection to the Internet. Students also had access to a tablet PC, allowing them to take notes directly on the screen. In the front of the room, there was a six-foot high by twenty-foot wide monitor that could display each student's work in an individual quadrant of the screen.

Dushane's classroom was the only one of its kind in the Louisiana public school system and he had spearheaded the project. Neither the state nor the local school boards had the funds to equip classrooms with much computer technology, but they had agreed to try a pilot program in one classroom if Dushane led the effort to get it into place.

Dushane had several million dollars at his disposal from a Kaleidoscope Foundation grant and from other philanthropists committed to increasing educational opportunity.

"Good morning," Dushane said as he stepped in front of his class. "I hope everyone had a good weekend. Please open your computers and we'll continue our discussion of World War II. The war will be our focus for the rest of the week. Last class we began discussing the period prior to the outbreak of war; specifically Adolph Hitler's rise to power in Germany. As we saw from Hitler's speeches as well as from his book *Mein Kampf*, he had a deep-seated hatred of Jews, blaming them for, among other things, Germany's defeat in World War I. What we'll discuss today is that Hitler wasn't alone in his beliefs; he tapped into strong anti-Semitism across Germany and throughout Europe. The first question we'll explore is why Hitler was able to vilify and scapegoat the Jews so effectively, and why so many Europeans welcomed his message of hatred. After that, we'll talk about the Holocaust itself."

Dushane had one Jewish student in his class and he glanced over at her. She made eye contact with him and smiled, assuring him that she was okay. Although he was concerned about describing the horrifying amount of hatred aimed at Jews, he had spoken with the girl's parents before class and they had urged him to tell the story of the Holocaust in as much detail as possible.

"Why did you think the German people, and indeed much of Europe, embraced Hitler's message of hatred?" Dushane asked. "Does anyone have any ideas?"

Dushane waited expectantly for someone to raise their hand, but no one did. "Come on. What did we talk about last week? What's generally true about every religious or nationalist mass movement?"

A girl in the front row raised her hand.

"Yes, Natalie."

"They use a devil to stir up their followers' emotions; to unify them against the enemy."

"Yes! That's right!" Dushane responded enthusiastically. "Natalie's point about the use of a devil to rally support for a cause is important because it's been used so effectively over the last two thousand years. We're going to come back to this topic a little bit later because it's closely related to the Holocaust; but right now, let's focus specifically on the question of anti-Semitism in Europe prior to the Holocaust. A moment ago, I mentioned Hitler's extreme hatred of the Jews as well as the widespread hatred of Jews across Europe. We discussed Hitler a little bit last week, but I don't think we should spend any more time on him; the more interesting question is why ordinary, otherwise well-meaning people embraced anti-Semitism. These were people who generally obeyed the laws, provided for their families, and went to churches that ostensibly preached love for their fellow man. Does anybody know why so many of these people were anti-Semitic?" Dushane paused. "Jason."

"Wasn't there like religious tension? There was an Inquisition."

"Yes, there was definitely religious tension. The Inquisition was earlier, but the same sort of animosity clouded the outlook of Christians towards Jews in the twentieth century. Vast numbers of people were products of anti-Semitism propagated by their churches." Dushane pulled a Bible out of his desk drawer and held it up. "We have to go back seventeen hundred years to the fourth century when the Christian Bible was formally constructed and Christianity became the official religion of the Roman Empire. At that time, and for hundreds of years after that, people widely believed that the Bible was the literal word of God, transcribed on God's behalf by people known as prophets. According to believers, God singled out these prophets to receive his instructions and to spread them to the rest of the population."

A student raised her hand.

"Yes, Maya?"

"How many prophets were there?"

"That's a good question. Nobody knows for sure, but it certainly wasn't a small group. There were thousands of people claiming to have prophetic powers, and some people believed that certain prophets were true and had a direct connection to God. On the other hand, these same believers accused other prophets of being liars or conmen. You may wonder how a believer decided whether a certain prophet was true or false." Dushane shrugged. "That's something we just don't know. It was probably the same thing that makes one politician more popular than another; they said things that appealed to the masses, or perhaps they made better promises or had more charisma. In any case, the spiritual views of the gospel writers and certain prophets were taken very seriously and it was very dangerous to question them. In fact, when religious institutions controlled the machinery of the state, millions of people were tortured and executed for challenging the prevailing orthodoxy."

Dushane placed the Bible on the edge of his desk and felt a twinge of shame. *God, after all of these years, still feeling some guilt.* He reflected that the weight of his childhood programming would probably never fully leave him. The only consolation was that he now understood how ideas such as guilt and fear of eternal punishment got passed from generation to generation. Such ideas survived because they had a powerful psychological effect and their grip was especially tight when they were installed in early childhood. Dushane hoped that none of his students would have to deal with the same issues. He wanted them to know—indeed, he wanted everyone to know—that it was okay not to believe and no boogeyman would come after them for freely exploring the power of their minds.

"Now, let's get right to the original source of anti-Semitism by taking a look at some of the most important verses in the Bible, starting with Chapter 27 of the Book of Matthew. In this scene, we have Jesus Christ under arrest and the Roman official Pontius Pilate asking the Jewish mob what he should do with him. Let me quote the relevant verses." Dushane pressed a button on his desk console and the text popped up on each student's computer. Then he read it aloud.

> [22] Pilate saith unto them, What shall I do then with Jesus which is called Christ? They all say unto him, Let him be crucified. [23] And the governor said, Why, what evil hath he done? But they cried out the more, saying, Let him be crucified. [24] When Pilate saw that he could prevail nothing, but that rather a tumult was made, he took water, and washed his hands before the multitude, saying, I am innocent of the blood of this just person: see ye to it. [25] Then answered all the people, and said, His blood be on us, and on our children.

"Now, what's happening here is pretty clear. Pilate says he doesn't know why he's condemning Jesus to death and he refuses to take responsibility for it by washing his hands. I don't think there's any doubt that the author of these verses puts the blame for Christ's death squarely on the shoulders of the Jews. And note the last sentence where the Jewish mob says 'His blood be on us, and on our children.' The writer places the blame not only on the Jews at the scene of Christ's crucifixion, but also on the Jewish people as a whole, including future generations. Keep that in mind; that's a very important point. Jeff, you have a question?"

"Yeah. Why did they blame people who weren't even there?"

"That's a good question. I should point out that many Christian apologists argue that despite this Biblical verse, the gospel authors didn't really intend to blame the Jews for all eternity for Christ's death. I think that's a plausible argument. Biblical writers probably didn't think that far ahead; their immediate concern was to separate themselves from Jews who didn't believe that Christ was the Messiah. So, to answer your question, maybe they didn't want to blame future generations. But even if the apologists are correct and the gospel writers only intended to blame the Jews on the scene, the fact remains that Jews were killed and persecuted for hundreds of years because of religious leaders and their interpretation of the Scriptures.

"First and foremost, believers thought that the Bible was the word of God, so it became acceptable, even compelling, to dispense with their own individual morality to follow what they thought was an absolute truth—that the Jews were evil for killing the Messiah. The point is that these believers allowed something outside of themselves, and something with no rational basis, to override their basic human decency. It allowed them to commit acts that to us are unfathomable."

Dushane studied the faces of his students; some appeared puzzled. "Don't worry if you don't understand exactly what I'm talking about; it will become clearer as we move on. The next thing I'd like to discuss is the historical accuracy of the gospels. Were the Jews really to blame for Christ's death?" Dushane shook his head. "Most scholars don't think so. Although there's no doubt that some Jews wanted Jesus killed, it appears that the Romans executed him on the grounds of sedition, a common charge at the time. Apparently, the Romans viewed Jesus as a disruptive force who could potentially ignite opposition to Roman authority. The gospel account of Christ's crucifixion is particularly suspect because Pilate's ambivalent, almost sympathetic behavior towards Jesus is inconsistent with every other historical account of the man as a brutal Roman law enforcement authority. So why did the gospel writers blame the Jews? There are a few plausible theories. First of all, the writers wanted to validate their own spiritual views and to establish group identity and unity in the beginnings of the Christian movement. For example, as the New Testament progresses, the gospel writers increasingly vilify and demonize their Jewish rivals. Remember, the early Christians were almost all Jews, and before Christianity became a separate religion with its own unique set of beliefs, the rivalry between the Jews who believed in Christ and the majority of Jews who rejected him as the Messiah was intense. So, the vilification of their Jewish rivals helped unite Christians against a common enemy. The Christians also needed to deflect the blame for Christ's death away from the Roman Empire; remember, they had to live under the Roman authorities and the Romans didn't look upon the new religion favorably. In fact, the first New Testament gospels appear to have been written at the end of an unsuccessful Jewish war against Rome, some thirty-five years after Christ's death. The Jews, including Christian converts, had to deal with the Romans delicately.

"Let's look at one more important scene from the New Testament, which illustrates how the Bible demonizes the Jews. In Chapter 8 of John, we find Jesus accusing the Jews of plotting his murder."

[37] "I know that you are descendants of Abraham; yet you seek to kill me, because my word finds no place in you. [38] I speak of what I have seen with my Father, and you do what you have heard from your father." [39] They answered him, "Abraham is our father." Jesus said to them,

575

"If you were Abraham's children, you would do what Abraham did, [40] but now you seek to kill me, a man who has told you the truth which I heard from God; this is not what Abraham did. [41] You do what your father did." They said to him, "We were not born of fornication; we have one Father, even God." [42] Jesus said to them, "If God were your Father, you would love me, for I proceeded and came forth from God; I came not of my own accord, but he sent me. [43] Why do you not understand what I say? It is because you cannot bear to hear my word. [44] You are of your father the devil, and your will is to do your father's desires. He was a murderer from the beginning, and has nothing to do with the truth, because there is no truth in him."

"You are of your father, the devil," Dushane repeated. "That's the most important line. Biblical scholars almost all interpret this passage the same way: the Jews' unbelief in Jesus stems from being children of the devil. This is one of many places in the New Testament where Jews are demonized and equated with Satan. In fact, Jesus' crucifixion is depicted as the culmination of the struggle between good and evil, with Christ's Jewish enemies firmly aligned with evil.

"Now, how does all this relate to the Holocaust and hundreds of years of violence against Jews? Over the years, Christian leaders and their followers exploited the Biblical verses we've discussed, using them as an excuse to treat Jews as enemies in a cosmic war between God and Satan. But the situation in Germany had an additional toxic element— the influence of Martin Luther. As we discussed a few weeks ago, Luther was the father of Protestantism, leading the break from the hopelessly corrupt and hypocritical Catholic Church. Luther was regarded as a great hero, becoming tremendously influential in German history from the 16th Century onward. I have a short description of him, which I've downloaded to your workstations."

In addition to instigating the Protestant break from Catholicism, Luther is also known for his ferocious anti-Semitism. In 1543, he published *On the Jews and Their Lies*, where he described the Jews as a "base, whoring people…full of the devil's feces…which they wallow in like swine." He described the synagogue as a "defiled bride, an incorrigible whore and an evil slut." He wanted Germany rid of the Jews and he urged that they be deprived of "all their cash and jewels and silver and gold" and "that their synagogues or schools be set on fire, that their houses be broken up and destroyed…and they be put under a roof or stable, like the gypsies…in misery and captivity." He also seemed to advocate their murder when he wrote that "we are at fault in not slaying them."

Luther was a towering figure in German history and his powerful influence extended down the generations, especially among the Protestants. When the Nazi regime came to power, almost all of its anti-

Jewish literature contained references to quotations from Luther and the Nazis proudly displayed *On the Jews and Their Lies* at the Nuremberg rallies.

Although to some extent Luther merely carried on the anti-Semitism of Catholicism, he arguably took it a step further by hardening German culture against them; completely demonizing and dehumanizing them with the hysterical hatred of his writings. Without Luther's influence, it's harder to imagine Germans adopting the murderous hatred against Jews that ultimately resulted in the Holocaust.

"Now, let me be clear on one point. I'm not saying that the Nazis weren't to blame for murdering Jews; what I am saying is that the Holocaust could not have happened, at least nowhere close to the extent that it did, without both the Nazis and religious anti-Semitism. Before the Nazi party even existed, the intellectual groundwork for the Holocaust was already in place from centuries of Christian doctrine and hatred. All the Nazis had to do was light the match."

Dushane glanced across the sea of young faces and none appeared upset by his comments. The argument that Christian anti-Semitism had played a major role in the Holocaust had become well accepted, although there was still a significant population of Christians who knew nothing about the underlying causes of the Holocaust.

"Now, let's stop for a minute and see if we can draw some conclusions. I think the key here is that leaders not only taught people to hate the Jews, but to demonize and dehumanize them on a cosmic level by linking them to Satan. As a result, people associated Jews with the ultimate evil. This made it much easier to ignore the atrocities against them.

"The situation was particularly bad in Germany and Eastern Europe because after World War I some of the countries established—Poland, Hungary, and Croatia, in particular—had strong Catholic identities and Jews were considered outsiders. Prior to the Holocaust, murders occurred in these countries, but the killing of Jews entered a new phase when the Nazis decided to implement their 'Final Solution.' This meant the complete extermination of all the Jews in Europe.

"The Nazis carried out the most systematic extermination in the death camps, which were scattered across Eastern Europe and Russia. The most infamous camp was Auschwitz in Poland, where an estimated one million people were slaughtered. I have a video that provides an account of the gas chambers at Auschwitz, although I have to warn you that it's somewhat graphic. It's probably like nothing you've ever seen before, but I think it's important you see it."

Dushane turned to a thimble-sized computer on the corner of his desk that could process over three hundred trillion instructions per second.

"Good morning, Miles," Dushane said in the direction of the tiny machine.

"Good morning, Mr. Dushane," Miles responded in a crisp metallic voice through a set of speakers mounted on the ceiling.

"Play the Auschwitz video, please."

The large monitor in the front of the room lit up and the video began. It contained simulated footage based on survivors' accounts.

> The gas chambers at Auschwitz did not appear to be foreboding places at all. They were covered by manicured lawns and the entrance signs merely said "Baths." When the men, women, and children were led into the chambers, they were told to undress in order to take a shower. After large numbers of prisoners were packed in, the massive door was shut and sealed. The executioners then released the cyanide crystals that would emit toxic gas through the vents.

> It took a little while for the gas to take effect, but when prisoners became aware of what was happening, they usually panicked, hysterically stampeding away from the poison toward the huge metal door where they mauled and trampled each other, desperately trying to escape.

> Once all of the prisoners were dead, pumps sucked out the poisonous air and the door was opened. Then other Jewish prisoners took over. These were prisoners whose lives were spared for performing the most horrifying task imaginable. Their job was to remove the dead bodies so that it could be taken to the furnaces for incineration, the final step in the procedure.

The video ended, but the room remained charged with a collective hum of disbelief. "I debated whether to show you that, but I think it's the only way to get any kind of appreciation of what it was like. Of course, there's no way we can really appreciate what it was like."

Dushane took a deep breath.

"The worst of the Holocaust occurred perhaps in the middle of 1944, when an estimated four hundred thousand Jews were slaughtered at Auschwitz in a two-month period. To dispose of so many corpses, the crematoria had to burn day and night. I..." Dushane stopped when he heard a girl in the back of the room crying. "Michelle, are you okay? Michelle?"

The girl jumped out of her chair, covering her mouth and then bursting into hysterical sobs. Dushane followed her out to the hallway. "Michelle, Michelle, I'm so sorry."

"That's so...so gross. I don't...I don't...I don't understand...I don't understand...how...how... people...could...could do that."

Dushane figured that at some level he did understand what made

Nazism and religious bigotry possible, but the realization that the Holocaust had actually occurred still shocked him. Dushane hugged his student and whispered softly in her ear. "It's okay, Michelle. I don't understand it, either. Nobody understands it." He held her silently and softly caressed her back until she stopped crying. "If you'd like to go home…"

"No, no, I'm okay now," she said, wiping the tears from her cheeks. "I want to go back to class."

"Okay." They walked back into class and Dushane continued. "These are emotional issues and no one should be embarrassed about being upset or reacting emotionally. It certainly upsets me. The only thing we can do is make sure that it never happens again. I have just a few more things to say about this and we'll wrap up this discussion. So far, we've discussed how the Bible, the government, and religious leaders demonized the Jews. The next topic we'll address is the response of the Catholic Church, and the response of the Pope specifically, upon learning that Jews were being systematically slaughtered. The Pope's actions are important to consider because Catholicism dominated Europe. Had the Pope made stopping genocide a priority, there was at least a possibility that the killing could've been significantly reduced. Unfortunately, with a few minor exceptions, the Pope did virtually nothing.

"Now, did it really matter what the Pope did? He was just one man, right?" Dushane paused. "Actually, it mattered a great deal because the Church was extremely authoritarian. People generally followed what the Pope said or did, or in this case, what he didn't do. But then why did people blindly follow this man? One reason is that at the First Vatican Council in 1870, the Church had declared that the Pope was infallible on questions of faith and morals. In addition, Catholic officials, as well as the Church's followers, had been accustomed to a dominant papacy and centralized church authority. Followers were conditioned not to question the Pope or the Church hierarchy—ever. Since the Pope didn't speak out against the murder of Jews, people figured that it wasn't that important. This mindset of ignoring the crisis filtered down to the bishops, then to the priests, and finally to the followers. Since the Church, as I said, was extremely hierarchical and authoritarian, people generally followed the example of the authority figure above them. On the other hand, a small percentage of Church members did engage in rescue efforts, but the failure of central Church authorities to speak out crippled the overall rescue effort. In addition, what little aid the Vatican did provide was often contingent on whether or not the Jews in question were baptized into the Christian Church. But most importantly, had the Pope shown greater concern for Holocaust victims, there surely would have been far greater numbers of rescuers and far fewer numbers of Jews murdered.

"By this point in the semester, you may not remember our discussion of the American Revolution. I hope you do, but let me refresh your memory. One of the great achievements of the Founding Fathers is that they rejected the idea of the divine right of monarchs to rule. Instead, they embraced the idea of allowing people to govern themselves through a democracy. But the Catholic Church didn't accept this doctrine and retained its rigid, authoritarian power structure. Followers were expected to keep quiet and obey, with no voice in Church policy.

"After the war, the Vatican's record wasn't much better. They sought clemency for convicted war criminals; they were uncooperative in extraditing potential German war criminals; they abetted the escape of fugitives by appointing Nazi sympathizers to key positions; they allowed fugitives from justice to hide on Vatican properties; they refused to extend diplomatic recognition to Israel; and it took decades for the Church to repudiate its 'Christ-killer' accusation. Nicholas, you have a question?"

"Why did they do that?"

"That's a great question. How could they have so little sense of justice after all that had happened? Many historians argue that the Pope cared more about a strong Germany than either the genocidal slaughter of Jews or bringing the Nazis to justice. And his primary reason for wanting a powerful German state was so that it would serve as a bulwark against communism, which theoretically championed atheism. As we'll see when we discuss communism later this term, what communists tried to do was replace religious dogma with another set of dogma that was equally rigid, authoritarian, and anti-intellectual.

"One other interesting point sometimes made by Christian apologists is that it's unfair to associate the Christian churches with the Nazis because the Nazis eventually wanted to destroy Christianity. There's certainly some evidence to support this contention, although Hitler made religious references often when it suited his purposes. In a speech to the German Reichstag, he said:

> I believe that I am acting in the sense of the Almighty Creator.
> By warding off the Jews I am fighting for the Lord's work.

He also admired religious methods, stating for example:

> The Catholic Church is a model above all in its uncommonly clever tactics and its knowledge of human nature, and its wise policy of taking account of human weaknesses in its guidance of the faithful. I have followed it in giving our party program the character of unalterable finality, like the Creed. The Church has never allowed the Creed to be interfered with. It is fifteen hundred years since it was formulated,

but every suggestion for its amendment, every logical criticism or attack on it, has been rejected. The Church has realized that anything and everything can be built up on a document of that sort, no matter how contradictory or irreconcilable with it. The faithful will swallow it whole, so long as logical reasoning is never allowed to be brought to bear on it.

"This quote sums up my final point. Everything I've said about the Nazis and the Christian churches during the Holocaust was powered by a destructive and dangerous mindset. In order to kill Jews, or do nothing while they were being slaughtered, people had to associate them with evil. In this case, they associated Jews with the ultimate evil, Satan, in a cosmic struggle against God. People were able to dehumanize Jews by linking them to the most despicable and unforgivable crime imaginable—killing the Messiah. But note that both of these beliefs are supernatural in nature; that is, they have no connection to reality. Both the concept of Satan and the concept of a Messiah are superstitious beliefs based on religious faith. Once compassion is rejected in favor of faith, any and every kind of hateful action is possible. Bringing this back specifically to the Holocaust, Church dogma created moral ambiguity; people naturally felt that murder was wrong, but irrational religious beliefs conflicted with, and ultimately overrode, these impulses."

Dushane couldn't help reflecting on his experience hiking the Appalachian Trail. The memories and the realizations from that trip, now almost thirty years old, remained fresh and vivid in his mind. *After all the layers of nonsense we're bombarded with in popular culture are stripped off, there's only one thing left that feels completely real— the appreciation of nature, including humanity, in all its variations. Nature never lies to us, perhaps that's why it's so compelling. It just works perfectly according to definite and predictable laws that humans can understand. And the act of trying to honestly understand and appreciate nature has to be one of the most ennobling human pursuits. Why do people still fight that? Nature doesn't lie to us; why do we still lie to ourselves?*

Dushane suddenly realized that he had paused for several moments, momentarily forgetting that he was in the middle of a lecture. He smiled sheepishly at his students. "I'd like to end this discussion on a positive note because I am optimistic about the future. The idea of sacred texts or prophets that can't be questioned is a relic of the past, at least in this country. Today, any person who claimed to be a prophet or wrote a book claiming indisputable knowledge of God would immediately be marginalized as delusional. The Bible and other primitive religious texts had the advantage of age and a credulous population of believers who had no concept of scientific inquiry. All right, let's move on. Miles, let's visit the D-Day museum, please."

The computer responded by projecting a three-dimensional image of the National D-Day Museum in New Orleans, the largest museum in the country devoted exclusively to World War II.

"First of all, I'd like to encourage all of you to go over to the D-Day Museum," Dushane said. "I've purchased tickets for everyone, which are up here in front. It's a wonderful museum and you'll get a much better sense of the war than from hearing me talk about it. As I've said before, I believe that World War II represents one of humanity's darkest periods, but it also demonstrates how people can band together and fight for an important cause. We owe a tremendous debt of gratitude to the men and women who won that war. I think the museum will also help you come up with an idea for your term paper if you don't have a topic yet. The museum is celebrating the eightieth anniversary of the Allied victory in the war with several new exhibits. I would especially recommend the Kaleidoscope exhibit in the Pacific theater section of the museum. It's very beautiful. That's all for today. Don't forget that we have a test on Friday."

Dushane watched his students file out of the classroom and he reflected how much he loved teaching. It was his favorite part of being involved in education, although for all the joy he felt, he still remembered many painful confrontations with religious believers over the soul of the system. There had been bitter disputes at school board meetings between believers who wanted to inject religion into the public schools, and educators who argued that it would be disruptive and inconsistent with an educational mission. Dushane had fought especially hard to rid the curriculum of creationism, intelligent design, and any other theological claims made under the guise of science. Dushane especially loathed intelligent design advocates because they tried to prop up a dishonest thought system while simultaneously trying to hijack an honest one.

Although believers conceded that the murderous violence and savage brutality glorified in the Old Testament were inappropriate for children, what they wanted to establish was simple—the idea that humans were sinful, fallen creatures that couldn't make moral decisions on their own. Believers also argued vehemently that the public schools had adopted the "religion" of secular humanism, which they claimed shouldn't get special treatment over Christianity. They contended that humanism was, like Christianity, based on a specific set of tenets about humanity's relationship with the universe, therefore making it a religion. Humanists argued that their philosophy was not about a set of dogmatic beliefs, but just the opposite—an open and rational approach to solving real human problems in a modern, inclusive society.

But public attitudes gradually changed. Since its apogee during the Packer Administration, the cycle of religious fervor began losing force as more and more people began to appreciate religion's divisive consequences. They also finally understood that superstitious belief simply wasn't necessary to live a moral, productive, and happy life.

Dushane was influential in the debate over the future of Louisiana's public school system and he argued that humanists should concede that schools really did favor humanism over Christianity. He wanted public schools to specifically reject Christian epistemology—the idea that something is a fact because a religious authority says it is, or worse, that knowledge can be acquired by resorting to faith or wishful thinking. He ultimately persuaded members of his local school board to adopt a resolution explicitly recognizing the tenets of humanism as the foundation of the educational system.

> Our mission is to provide the best education possible to the children in our public schools, and to give them the greatest chance to succeed in life. Therefore, we adopt the following tenets to guide us:
>
> Dogmas, ideologies and traditions, whether religious, political or social, must be weighed and tested by each individual and not simply accepted on faith;
>
> Reason, factual evidence, and scientific methods of inquiry, rather than faith and superstition, should be used to find solutions to human problems and to answer important human questions;
>
> The fulfillment, growth, and creativity of both the individual and humankind in general is a paramount value;
>
> A constant search for objective truth, with the understanding that new knowledge and experience will constantly alter our perception of it, is fundamental to the long-term survival and success of the human species;
>
> We must concern ourselves with this life and commit to making it meaningful through a better understanding of ourselves, our history, our intellectual and artistic achievements, and the outlooks of those who differ from us;
>
> We must search for viable individual, social, and political principles of ethical conduct, judging them on their ability to enhance human well-being and individual responsibility;
>
> With reason, an open marketplace of ideas, goodwill, and tolerance, progress can be made in building a better world.

Every time Dushane read the statement he felt the warmth of genuine pride. He knew that his efforts would make a positive difference for years to come.

CHAPTER 73

Religion's monopoly in the field of ethics has made it extremely difficult to communicate the emotional meaning and connotations of a rational view of life. Just as religion has pre-empted the field of ethics, turning morality against man, so it has usurped the highest moral concepts of our language, placing them outside this earth and beyond man's reach.

The man-worshippers, in my sense of the term, are those who see man's highest potential and strive to actualize it. The man-haters are those who regard man as a helpless, depraved, contemptible creature—and struggle never to let him discover otherwise…The essential division between these two camps is: those dedicated to the exaltation of man's self-esteem and the sacredness of his happiness on earth—and those determined not to allow either to become possible.

It does not matter that only a few in each generation will grasp and achieve the full reality of man's proper stature—and that the rest will betray it. It is those few who move the world and give life its meaning.

—Ayn Rand, Introduction to the 25th Anniversary Edition of
The Fountainhead

The mid-morning sun peeked through the clouds after a short rain, glistening across the lightly soaked pavement. Spencer Dushane and his friend Kevin ambled down the red brick walkway to the National D-Day Museum. Every brick contained the name of a United States serviceperson who had died in the war. Across the street, a full-length mural memorialized the raising of the United States flag at Iwo Jima.

"Your dad sure likes this place," Kevin said. "It seems like every time I see him, he talks about it."

"I know. He kept bugging me to come over here."

"Maybe it'll be cool."

Spencer shrugged. "I hope so."

Neither boy had been to the museum before, but the elder Dushane had visited many times and never tired of it. He felt deeply grateful for the sacrifices made by the men and women in the war, and he hoped that his own sacrifices, especially his fight against ignorance in the public school system would leave a similar legacy.

Spencer opened the door to the museum's lobby. Inside, there was a tank and a PT boat on display, as well as fighter aircraft hanging from the ceiling. As the boys walked in, Spencer pulled out his ticket and read the mission statement printed on the back aloud:

> The National D-Day Museum celebrates the American spirit, the teamwork, optimism, courage, and sacrifice of the men and women who won World War II and promotes the exploration and expression of these values by future generations.

"That sounds just like your dad," Kevin said.

"Yeah, he says we're lucky."

"My dad says that, too."

"You want to check out the upstairs first?"

"Sure."

The museum had extensive exhibits, which told the story of both the European and the Pacific theaters of the war, including a large section devoted completely to D-Day. After touring the European theater, the boys drifted into the Pacific section. Spencer scanned the main display area. "Hey, there's the exhibit my dad was talking about," he said, pointing to the back wall.

The Kaleidoscope exhibit contained the actual kaleidoscope that Fred Carson had given to Hank Chambers as well as a large photograph of the two men on the deck of their PT boat shortly before a Japanese battleship destroyed it. The exhibit also displayed their Congressional Medals of Honor and included a brief description of their careers.

Fred Carson and Hank Chambers were on the PT boat shown here during the Allied invasion of the Philippines in 1944. They fought with courage and resolve in service of their country. With the cooperation and bravery of many others, they took back control of the island from the Japanese Imperial Army. During the battle, however, a Japanese warship destroyed the PT boat, throwing Carson, Chambers, and the rest of their crew into the water with the burning wreckage. Chambers suffered burns in the attack, but managed to rescue Carson, who was also severely injured. Unfortunately, despite being picked up quickly by a U.S. cruiser, doctors were unable to save Carson's life because of his extensive internal injuries. Congress awarded Congressional Medals of Honor to both men for their service.

Another part of the exhibit recounted the story of Carson giving the kaleidoscope to Hank Chambers, and then how Hank Chambers had given it to his grandson. There was also a short history of Kaleidoscope Ranch along with a picture of David Chambers sitting behind his desk, looking through the kaleidoscope. His Presidential Medal of Freedom was displayed next to the picture, along with a short narrative:

> This exhibit was sponsored by the Kaleidoscope Foundation, which was established by David Chambers. In addition to providing generous financial assistance to the National D-Day Museum, this foundation is devoted to medical research, education, and various other philanthropic activities. It is one of the largest charitable foundations in the United States.

> In a letter delivered to the museum, David Chambers described his grandfather and the spirit that moved them both: "My grandfather was an ordinary man. He raised a family, he worked, he gardened, he loved to read. But, most importantly, he believed in freedom. That's why I would characterize him as ordinary. I believe that most human beings share that unquenchable thirst for freedom, and that it is a truly an essential and compelling need of our species. My grandfather and I had that in common—a burning desire for the freedom to live the life we desire, to think and believe within the dictates of our own consciences, and the freedom to love people without limitation in our own ways."

Adam Sharf had delivered the medals and the letter to the museum, and he had helped the museum create the exhibit. Sharf had been working as the managing director of the Kaleidoscope Foundation for the last twenty years and was widely recognized as one of the most effective philanthropists in the country, particularly with respect to helping at-risk children and funding important medical research.

"Cool exhibit," Kevin said. "Your dad knew David Chambers, right?"

"Yeah, they were friends for a long time."

"What was the guy like?"

Spencer shrugged. "I don't know."

"What do you mean you don't know? What did your dad say about him?"

"He told me I have to get to know him myself."

Kevin looked at his friend quizzically. "I don't get it."

"I know; I don't know what he means by that either."

* * *

Martin Dushane plopped down on a rocking chair on the front porch of his house and turned the radio to his favorite jazz station. Dushane lived in the Garden District of New Orleans and his house was situated one street off St. Charles Avenue; close enough to hear the light rumble of the streetcars and within walking distance of a large park. The house was painted white with dark blue shutters and had a wrought iron fence that enclosed a small rose garden. From the street, a stone walkway led to the front of the house where a United States flag waved proudly.

Dushane eased the chair back and stretched his legs across an ottoman.

"Martin?" his wife called from inside the house. "Would you like a glass of lemonade?"

"Sure! Thanks!"

Josephine walked out with a drink tray and sat down next to her husband. "Charlie called."

"What did he say?"

"He wanted to know when you're going to get some bachelor time. He wants to plan another fly fishing trip."

"Great. Tell him that Spence and I are in. You have a meeting with him tomorrow morning, right?"

"Yeah." Josephine had been working with Charlie Geautreaux for several years. Like her husband, she worked in the Louisiana public school system, but she and Charlie had established a separate foundation that worked exclusively with parents. Although the idea of focusing on parents had never been tried extensively before, Josephine and Charlie decided that a parent-centric approach was critical because no matter how good a school was, if the parents didn't support their child, the child had little chance.

The foundation offered several counseling and educational programs designed to convince parents of the value of education and give them practical ways to support their children's intellectual and social development. The foundation also offered literacy, math, and other educational assistance to parents so that they could also enjoy the benefits of increased opportunity and self-esteem.

Josephine put the lemonade on the table and placed her hand gently on top of her husband's. "I also got an e-video from David," she said casually, masking the intense emotion she felt.

Dushane sat up. He was always excited to receive correspondence from Chambers, especially since it was so rare. They usually only heard from him once or twice a year, and they hadn't seen him in almost fifteen. After sailing along the coast of Central America with him for almost a year, Dushane and Josephine had settled in Belize, where they had lived for another three years. During this time, they had developed a deep connection and love for each other, and they had both decided to devote their lives to improving education.

Dushane had always hoped that Chambers would move back to the United States, or at least visit, but he had always refused despite the fact that all of the charges against him had been dropped many years earlier. Dushane had no doubt that if Chambers did return, he would surely receive a hero's welcome. But Chambers had no interest in that. Although he loved the United States and still believed it was the greatest place in the world, he had nothing else he wanted to accomplish in the U.S. He had forged a new life in Mexico, focusing on new goals.

Josephine flipped open a handheld computer. "Start Chambers," she said.

The video began with Chambers sitting in a large, sunny courtyard. "Greetings from Mexico; I hope you're both well. I miss you. I don't have much to report except that the work Ernesto and I are doing down here is helping. We continue to increase the number of kids finally getting an education. I've never seen Ernesto more excited and I have to admit that I've never felt more hopeful about anything in my life."

Dushane and Josephine exchanged quick glances.

"Last month we converted the largest cathedral in Oaxaca into a school and God hasn't struck me down yet." Chambers laughed. "We've converted seven churches so far and we have plans to convert two more this month. As for our other efforts, I've attached an article from yesterday's New York Times." Chambers' face broke into a broad smile. "The historical tides are turning. I'll talk to you again soon. I love you both."

Josephine clicked on the link to the article.

Mexico Severs Diplomatic Relations with the Vatican

Benito Ortega, the new President of Mexico, announced today that his government would sever diplomatic relations with the Vatican, ending years of cooperation and support. In his announcement of the new policy, President Ortega cited serious differences in the mission of his country and the mission of the Catholic Church on several issues including birth control, in vitro fertilization, the spread of AIDS, education, medical research, women's rights, discrimination against homosexuals, and the solicitation of donations. In a sharply worded statement, the President accused the Church of promoting ignorance and contributing to the spread of poverty by taking money from people that could barely afford to feed their own families.

When asked if he was anti-Catholic, President Ortega reiterated his commitment to respecting people of all beliefs, but he said he couldn't in good conscience lend any support to the Church at the expense of the Mexican people. The President was questioned specifically about whether he held any religious beliefs, and he stated that his only personal religion was "serving the people of Mexico to the best of my ability."

Mexico has approximately eighty million Catholics and Catholicism is by far the dominant religion in the country. Many Mexicans expressed shock at the President's statement and small demonstrations were reported in Mexico City, Guadalajara, and León. In addition, several religious leaders across Latin America, as well as the Pope and other high-ranking officials at the Vatican, called for the President's resignation. At the same time, several prominent intellectuals in the country praised the decision, including Marta Zavala, president of Mexico Libre, one of the largest independent social service organizations in the country. She hailed the government's decision and the President's new policy statement as "the most important act taken by a President in the history of Mexico." She also stated that, "We finally have a real chance to break the cycle of poverty and ignorance in our country."

Although Mexico Libre is universally praised in Mexico for its work with poor families, religious leaders have been vocal critics of Ms. Zavala because she has accused the Church of being more concerned with its own power than with the welfare of the people. Ms. Zavala's critics have also chafed at her financial support for President Ortega, estimated to be in the tens of millions of U.S. dollars. When asked about this, Ms. Zavala did not deny her financial support for President Ortega, but stated, "I will fight until the last breath in my body for a better future for the Mexican people."

"That guy is unbelievable!" Dushane exclaimed, leaning over and kissing his wife enthusiastically on the lips.

Josephine smiled, but her demeanor quickly turned serious. "How do you think he is?" she said.

Dushane wondered often about Chambers and he wasn't sure whether he knew everything about the man or nothing at all. He thought of telling his wife how much he loved Chambers, but it wasn't necessary. She felt the same way and there were no words that could match the feeling of shared experience. "I don't know," he said, and then took a sip of his lemonade. "He seems happy."

"I hope so," Josephine said softly, lightly squeezing her husband's hand.

Dushane lay back and let his head rest comfortably against the back of the chair. He chuckled gently as he ran his fingers across the small circular scar, just above his heart.

THE END

AFTERWORD

The genesis for this book occurred during a two-and-a-half-month hiking trip on the Northern half of the Appalachian Trail several years ago. On that trip, after freeing my mind from the concerns of a busy, urban existence, I drew some conclusions I thought I could build a good novel around. I began writing shortly after I returned.

Over the ensuing months, four important events occurred, changing the original focus of the book. The first was the child molestation scandal that disgraced the Catholic Church. Not only had Catholic priests molested thousands of children over several decades, but the Church hierarchy had either looked the other way, shuffled abusive priests around, or tried to cover it up. Then, when law enforcement authorities finally confronted them, they showed little remorse and failed to adequately help the victims. They also fought the ensuing investigation, clearly demonstrating the vestiges of a medieval attitude that the clergy is above secular law. The episode spoke volumes about the underlying nature of the Church's power elite.

Perhaps even more surprising though, was the reaction of the public. Although everyone, believer and nonbeliever alike, was repulsed by the behavior, the degree of surprise seemed substantially less than what might've been expected. Secular intellectuals I spoke with weren't terribly surprised for the reasons I highlight in this novel. The muted reaction of believers, on the other hand, is more complex. I think that believers, at some level (though probably not conscious), weren't that surprised either. The Church's behavior was consistent with their deep-rooted subconscious perceptions of the institution. The history of the Church's past transgressions is, after all, fairly common knowledge.

The second event was the U.S. response to the 9/11 World Trade Center attack by Islamic believers. After the attack, the most curious thing was that people in the U.S. (including many leaders) began ratcheting up their own faith; apparently hoping that God would bless America and presumably curse (and destroy) our enemies. To put it mildly, this attitude is an unqualified recipe for disaster. Trying to combat mindless Islamic faith with mindless Christian faith is counterproductive and harmful, and this becomes ever more dangerous as religious warriors acquire increasingly powerful weapons. We need to try another approach; an approach where we refuse to accept the current underlying premise of the disagreement. That is, we shouldn't accept the validity of Islamic (or any other) faith claims. Faith doesn't solve problems—*any* problems. If Muslims want to fight us, then we certainly must defend ourselves, but let's not stoop to their level by trumpeting our faith in the Judeo-Christian deity as some sort of counterargument. That's way beneath the ideals of the United States.

The third event was the proposal by President George W. Bush for a Constitutional amendment limiting the recognition of marriage to a man and a woman. This unleashed a torrent of venom from people opposed to equal marriage rights that had been simmering for a long time. In San Francisco, where I live, the true colors of believers came out when our mayor Gavin Newsom began allowing homosexual couples to obtain marriage licenses. San Francisco has a well-deserved reputation as one of the most tolerant and inclusive cities on the planet, so it was a bit shocking to residents here when Bible-wielding fanatics descended upon our city chanting slogans of hate.

As I followed the story closely, I realized that the views of religious believers were based primarily on a combination of ignorance (for example, that sexual preference is a choice, gay couples aren't as committed or loving as heterosexual couples, or that they can't be good role models, etc.), and a belief that the Bible overrides basic human decency. Since the Bible unequivocally contemplates death for homosexual behavior, it was clear why religious believers supported the amendment proposal and vilified the homosexual community. For me personally, it was the worst display of hatemongering and blind faith I'd ever witnessed.

The fourth and final event was a happier one. My wife gave birth to a baby boy. As any parent can attest, the joy of a new baby is indescribable. At the same time, the sense of responsibility is truly awesome. As my wife and I raise our child, we'll naturally insist on the same high moral standards for him as we do for ourselves, although I suspect he will be bombarded with many bad ideas, particularly in a culture so laden with negative religious messages—guilt, intolerance, disrespect for reality, and exclusion to name a few.

While all of these ideas are bad, what strikes me most profoundly is that millions of people are teaching their children that they are inherently guilty and sinful. Indeed, this is still core doctrine in most Christian churches. When I look at my child, I see nothing but beauty and innocence, and I'm horrified that anybody would label such a glorious creature anything less than perfect, much less sinful.

This raises one of the most critical issues every generation faces—developing our children's self-esteem. There's no doubt that telling children that they're inherently guilty and sinful does not support this. Indeed, I wholeheartedly agree with Nathaniel Branden, one of the pioneers in the self-esteem field, who had this to say:

> The idea of Original Sin—of guilt where there is no possibility of innocence, no freedom of choice, no alternatives available—is anti-self-esteem by its very nature. The very notion of guilt without volition or responsibility is an assault on reason as well as on morality.

Every child deserves to be nurtured and given the best chance to succeed, and every parent has a moral obligation to provide a loving, supportive environment. The religious doctrine of Original Sin is surely one of the most toxic ideas in recorded human history. It should be unequivocally rejected.

I've always believed that education is the best cure for hatred, racism, and other conditions that plague us a species. I'm also convinced that religious and other irrational belief systems, while often well meaning, are ultimately divisive and unhealthy. History confirms this in bloody detail. For those who don't read the history books, they can see stark, immediate evidence of violence in the name of religion as the United States and other countries battle the worldwide Islamic community.

I've heard it stated several times by well-meaning people that Islam is a religion of peace. That proposition is totally untenable. A cursory reading of the Koran or an examination of Islamic culture (particularly their attitudes toward women and infidels) is anything but peaceful. But let me be clear. It's not that Islam or Christianity (notwithstanding the Old Testament) are inherently violent religions (i.e. most people worship their chosen god peacefully); the point is that a person who embraces irrational religious beliefs is orders of magnitude more likely to engage in bigoted behavior or rationalize violent acts in the name of a senseless cause.

Religion will continue to divide us. It always has. By its very nature, it is a not a thought system that unites us because it glorifies absurdities, guaranteeing division. By contrast, rational philosophies such as humanism recognize that we are one human community. Humanism shares many of the same moral values professed by religion (although recognizing that the roots of moral values are not found in the supernatural, but in millions of years of biological evolution and thousands of years of cultural evolution), but unlike religion, it's designed to unite us under the common banner of our humanity, without the nonsense of religious belief.

Unfortunately, in the case of religious beliefs, we face a unique challenge—both because these beliefs are embraced without question in our society and because children are indoctrinated from birth not to question them. But the biggest problem seems to be the misunderstanding that religion is a necessary condition for morality. This view is simply not correct.

Fortunately, science has a lot to say about human morality and behavior, although on a much sounder epistemological foundation to say the least. There have been many books written on the scientific, evolutionary basis for morality, so I won't belabor the point here. But it is a critical one. I urge readers to explore it.

One final issue I'll mention is the underlying esthetics of this debate. We live in a world where a significant percentage of the population values men of God more than they value people who apply rational thought (scientists, engineers, teachers, businesspeople, etc.) This has always struck me as monstrously upside down. We have spectacular creations of the human mind all around us (airplanes, skyscrapers, vaccinations, computers). All of these wonders were created by the disciplined application of human thought, not by faith or any other mystical process. Whenever I see these products of the mind, or when I've had the privilege to work with creators, I always feel a tremendous sense of awe and gratitude. To me, there is nothing more beautiful than humans exercising their minds to create better conditions on the planet.

By contrast, whenever I see a preacher on TV babbling about the virgin birth of Jesus and groveling for money, I feel an overwhelming sense of repulsion. The work of these manipulators requires no disciplined application of thought and no creative ability. With a little charisma, some incontrovertible dogma, and a few hollow promises, they have everything they need to take advantage of others. It doesn't matter whether it's a Christian televangelist or a Muslim recruiting suicide bombers. Both of these impostors offer nothing but empty promises, totally devoid of any connection to reality. The fact that we allow these people to operate freely and prey on the weakest members of our society is truly an abomination.

So where do we start? I doubt that fundamentalists of either the Christian or Islamic persuasion can be reasoned with. They simply don't value reason very highly. Fortunately, fundamentalists are not the majority of religious believers. Which brings me to religious moderates. And let me say this first so that there is no misunderstanding. I am a man of tremendous faith (in the positive sense of that term) —faith in my family, faith in nature, faith in humanity, and most importantly, faith in the integrity of my own mind. I also believe that given what we know about the universe, something undoubtedly quite spectacular is going on. It's awe-inspiring to ponder. I'm sure that most religious moderates feel the same way. Unfortunately, although virtually all moderates are productive and responsible citizens and they behave ethically the vast majority of the time, they clear the path for fundamentalists. They do this by *accepting* (indeed championing) the fundamentalists' primary claim—that reality is negotiable and faith supersedes reason. With that hurdle out of the way, the rest is easy. Once faith trumps reason, anything is possible.

To be fair, most religious moderates wholeheartedly embrace science, especially when it suits their purposes. When they get sick, they ask for the best medical science available. When they fly, they expect that the engineers who designed the plane understood aviation physics. In a court of law, they demand evidence. In none of these cases, do they care one whit about faith (indeed, they would surely get nervous if the surgeon who's about to operate on them says that he's going to rely on his faith for guidance). Now, before I'm accused of creating a straw man, let me state my point: Not only do religious moderates support fundamentalism, but they undermine the epistemological foundation of science whenever they make statements that have no evidentiary basis or which defy common sense. In other words, whenever they cite their "faith" for any factual assertion.

Reason and science have been spectacularly beneficial in improving living conditions on the planet as well as improving our social relations. It's much easier to deal with one another if we can agree on a common language and reject irrational nonsense that has no benefit to anyone. Thus, we shouldn't tolerate any superstition in our debate. If we're talking about using embryonic stem cells to cure disease and alleviate suffering, any person who starts his sentence with "God says this" or "Allah says that" shouldn't be taken seriously. Injecting gods into the debate is not only meaningless and irrelevant, but hopelessly divisive.

Ultimately, I'm optimistic that a rational view of the world will prevail because it's so much more consistent with our survival and our uniqueness as a species. In fact, unless humanity destroys itself, I think people will eventually realize that we must remove superstition from our discourse in order to build a truly harmonious global community.

ACKNOWLEDGEMENTS

I'd like to thank the following people for their valuable insights, ideas, love, and support. Without them, this project would not have been possible.

My wife for her love, support, and tolerance of the long hours required to complete the manuscript.

My three children, who inspire me every day and constantly remind me of the power of love. When they are old enough to read this book, I hope they take its message to heart: trust your own mind and conscience, despite what others insist you must believe. Your self-esteem and intellectual integrity is infinitely more powerful than any hollow judgments directed against your independent spirit.

My parents, for their love and support. I hope I can pay this forward to my own children.

Russell Rowland, a novelist who commented on an early draft and led a writing workshop where I came away with many good ideas and improved my writing.

Thomas Bright, Sean Hamilton, Matt Schmuecker, and M.L. Shannon, for providing assistance with technical details.

All of the people I interviewed for the book: Kathleen Bennett, Ward Connerly, Thorn Coyle, Eileen Donahue, Joan Fausett, Erik Gage, Julie Garagliano, Elizabeth Maynard, Paula Mochel, Annette Oliveira, Paul Rivers, T.J. Rodgers, Sandra Tanner, and Marlene Zeigler. I gained critical insights and enjoyed our stimulating conversations.

Elizabeth Ludington, a dear friend who passed away just before this book went to print. She was easily the biggest fan of the book in its early stages and she harassed me for three years to publish it. She was a wonderful, loving, freethinking, artistic, creative spirit who had an enormous impact on my thinking.

Anila Manning, who is not only an outstanding editor, but also a person with an incredible passion for ideas and conveying them through the written word. Her loving and nonjudgmental attitude made her a joy to work with, and the best adjective I can use to describe her is true. She engaged me intellectually like few people do and always made sure that I told the truth (as I saw it) without compromise. This book is far better as a result of her efforts.

Kevin Barnard, the graphic artist who designed the cover and interior layout. He read the entire manuscript before beginning his work and clearly understood the spirit of the book. He also brought strong positive energy to the project, particularly at the end when I really needed a boost to finish up the final details.

Finally, I have to recognize Thomas Paine, one of my heroes, and a man who provided much of the inspiration for this book. Although Paine usually only gets a few paragraphs in the history books and is frequently maligned by religious leaders, he was truly a great American, and certainly one of the most underrated Founding Fathers. He was such an influential American that I describe his background briefly here for readers unfamiliar with his contributions to the cause of freedom.

Like most other American Revolutionaries, Paine's worldview was largely shaped by the Enlightenment, a period characterized by the development of science, the rejection of superstition and religious dogma, and the rise of individual rights. Paine fervently championed all of these causes.

Paine was born in England, but arrived in America in 1774 on the brink of the Revolutionary War. He found work as an editor of *Pennsylvania Magazine* where he wrote about social issues such as slavery, women's rights, animal cruelty, and U.S. independence from England.

Paine is probably most famous for writing *Common Sense*, a pamphlet that called on the American colonies to completely separate from England. It sold over 500,000 copies by the beginning of the war and more than one-fifth of the colonists read it, or had it read to them. Paine's work brought much of the intellectual foundation for the American Revolution to the common people in simple, understandable language, and many citizens found inspiration in his words. He certainly moved a large segment of the population, including other Founding Fathers, to support his call to freedom. Five months after its release, the principles Paine espoused in *Common Sense* were enshrined in the Declaration of Independence.

Despite the success of *Common Sense*, Paine did not profit from it. Instead, he donated his share of the proceeds to the American cause. Later in the war, when the prospect of defeating the British looked bleak, Paine donated five hundred dollars, nearly all of his savings, to the war effort. Paine's donation stimulated additional contributions, leading to the accumulation of more than three hundred thousand pounds (over twenty-five million 1991 U.S. dollars) for the army. This sum was the impetus for the creation of the Bank of North America, the institution that successfully funded the war effort to the end.

Paine also helped the war effort by writing a series of pamphlets called *The American Crisis*. These writings were designed to instill confidence and resolve in the troops, and they undoubtedly achieved their purpose. Military leaders, including George Washington, read Paine's words aloud to soldiers under his command. In "Crisis Two," Paine coined the term "the United States of America," the first time that name had ever been used. It quickly gained popularity.

Paine also took strong stands on moral issues. While others cited Scripture (with much persuasive force) for the proposition that God condoned slavery, Paine was one of the few prominent Americans of his day who vehemently opposed the institution. He also argued for the rights of women, generations before it became politically acceptable to do so, and in clear contravention of Biblical mandates. Like many other influential Founding Fathers, Paine was a Deist, and he attacked formal religion because of its harm to humanity.

People on both sides of the Atlantic revered Paine as a great thinker. After the United States had achieved independence, he went to France where he received an enthusiastic welcome. He was elected to the National Convention where he worked to replace the French monarchy with a republican government.

While in France, Paine wrote *The Rights of Man*, which called for the British people to overthrow the monarchy. The book also attacked hereditary government and argued for equal political rights. As a result, British authorities convicted Paine of seditious libel in absentia, and he could not return to England. Even though the English monarchy banned *The Rights of Man*, it was widely read, helping lay the foundation for eventual democratic reforms throughout Europe.

Paine's next book, *The Age of Reason*, questioned the truth of Christianity and criticized the Bible as immoral and ridiculous. Although Paine recognized Jesus as a great moral teacher, he argued that the Bible couldn't possibly be the word of God because it was full of cruelty and absurdities. Paine's friend, Thomas Jefferson, took a similar view.

Although the masses and many U.S. leaders condemned Paine for the views expressed in *The Age of Reason*, many others felt it was long overdue. Despite the controversy, *The Age of Reason* has inspired several generations of thinkers, including Thomas Edison, the great twentieth-century inventor, who recognized the "flash of enlightenment that shone from its pages."

Paine is considered one of the fathers of the Freethought movement, which finally made it possible for people to reject blind faith and superstition without the risk of persecution. The men and women who refused to accept the Church's unsubstantiated claims became known as "freethinkers," and Paine was one of the most uncompromising. Ultimately, after a long struggle, Enlightenment intellectuals and freethinkers achieved their most lasting legacy—the separation of church and state, one of the greatest achievements in human history, and arguably the most important principle embraced by the U.S. Constitution.

Unfortunately, Paine's life took a turn for the worse while he was in France. He wound up in a French jail awaiting his own execution because he had argued against sending the former French aristocrats and the king to the guillotine. U.S. officials did little to help him, and he was extremely lucky that he wasn't executed. After the Reign of Terror ended in France, he was released from prison, a sick and bitter man. He felt betrayed that the United States didn't do more to secure his release.

Upon his return to the United States in 1802, Paine might have expected a hero's welcome for everything he had done for the country. Instead, his detractors branded him a monster for challenging the prevailing religious orthodoxy. He was generally shunned and died in obscurity in New Rochelle, New York.

Jack Fruchtman, Jr., in his excellent biography of Paine (*Thomas Paine: Apostle of Freedom*), summarizes the spirit of the man eloquently:

> His passion for his fellow human beings, for humanity, was his abiding, consuming concern. He only wanted to help the voiceless, the hopeless, the physically and spiritually impoverished, all those who were dominated not only by a tyrant who ruled their bodies, but also enslaved by the tyranny of superstition and falsehoods...Paine's goal was to do all he could to work for human autonomy, universal independence.

Paine's writings, his heroic spirit, and his courage have inspired countless freethinkers, humanists, intellectuals, and ordinary citizens. I hope this work captures his spirit.

A NOTE ON SOURCES

While I've read hundreds of books over the past several years in order to build the framework for this novel, I'd like to give special mention to a few that I found particularly helpful.

Thomas Paine: Apostle of Freedom by Jack Fruchtman, Jr.
The Age of Reason by Thomas Paine
Freethinkers: A History of American Secularism by Susan Jacoby
Why I Am Not a Christian by Bertrand Russell
Creating Equal by Ward Connerly
The Greatest Generation Speaks by Tom Brokaw
Mormon America by Richard N. Ostling and Joan K. Ostling
The True Believer by Eric Hoffer
Culture of Complaint by Robert Hughes
Shakedown by Kenneth Timmerman
The Demon-Haunted World by Carl Sagan
The Science of Good & Evil by Michael Shermer
The Battle for God by Karen Armstrong
Terror in the Mind of God by Mark Juergensmeyer
A Pilgrim's Digress by John Spalding
Gospel Truth by Russell Shorto
100 Banned Books by Nicholas J. Karolides, Margaret Bald, and Dawn B. Sova
The Fundamentals of Extremism, edited by Kimberly Blaker
Religion Explained by Pascal Boyer
Terror in the Name of God by Jessica Stern
The Six Pillars of Self-Esteem by Nathaniel Branden
The Gnostic Gospels by Elaine Pagels
The Origin of Satan by Elaine Pagels
The Popes Against the Jews by David I. Kertzer
The Catholic Church and the Holocaust, 1930-1965 by Michael Phayer
The Rise and Fall of the Third Reich by William Shirer
Betrayal: The Crisis in the Catholic Church by the Investigative Staff of The Boston Globe
The End of Faith by Sam Harris
Letter to a Christian Nation by Sam Harris
The God Delusion by Richard Dawkins

ABOUT THE AUTHOR

Paul Gehrman lives with his wife and three children in
Northern California. In addition to pursuing a writing career,
he has worked as an attorney, a software developer,
and a research scientist. This is his first novel.